D0251742

SUNSPOT JUNGLE

EDITED BY BILL CAMPBELL

ROSARIUM

Other Anthologies from Rosarium Publishing

SUNSPOT JUNGLE

Cover art and design by John Jennings

SUNSPOT JUNGLE: THE EVER EXPANDING UNIVERSE OF
FANTASY AND SCIENCE FICTION, VOL. 2.
Copyright © 2018 Rosarium Publishing

ISBN: 978-1732638808

Published by Rosarium Publishing
P.O. Box 544
Greenbelt, MD 20768-0544
www.rosariumpublishing.com

Table of Contents

for the Kid
and
Diaper Scientific

Introduction

History teems with monsters. I started writing historical fantasy recently and was only slightly surprised when it turned out an actual once living person was more villainous and horrifying than any bad guy I could've dreamt up. Treacherous skullduggery of all flavors creeps from the pages of our archives, and of course, the past is alive and well, walks with us, and more than that: we keep it alive, consecrate it with statues enshrined in sacred pillared halls and weathered plaques. We honor our monsters, those authors of devastation, as Baldwin dubbed them, and then pretend we've only noticed their noble attributes and hope everything else just fades away.

But history holds monsters much bigger than those individuals. They are harder to see—we're so trained to focus on the one and only. But their wingspan crosses oceans and the destruction they've caused reaches through the passage of time, curses generations and generations; they leave widening ripples of war and havoc in their wake. Because they don't have single faces, they are even harder to pin down than the singular men and women who rose to the height of power and remained in our memories. These larger monsters become imprinted on our DNA, insidious, and seem to be a part of the very fabric of life, a natural occurrence. And we build great monuments to them too: huge walls demarcating imaginary lines in the earth, topped with machine guns and patrolled by vast armies of killing technology that are themselves a tribute to the great monsters of history. But more than all those physical tributes, we have honored those monsters with story.

Story, the mechanism of so much of our madness, can be a guiding light or the deepest of shadows. For so long, the gatekeepers of narrative have kept a tight rein on which stories we lift up and which we never hear about. Historical memory, it turns out, is a finite resource, and so a flashpoint of conflict. Story is the hinterlands where mythmakers crash into each other, feed armies wholesale into the mire that then stumble out, changed forever, and change our perception of the world in the process. Story, and the vast industries that package and distribute stories across the world, has lifted us up and shut us down. It has given life and taken it away, time and time again.

And here we stand, once again at the crossroads. This the age of children detention camps and mass deportations, of ongoing state violence and fascism on the march. This is the age of counternarratives, of protest, of fighting back. We've long needed collections like *Sunspot Jungle*, anthologies that bring together voices from across the world to sing about impossible, difficult truths through the lens of the imagination. We've long needed stories about giant robot mausoleums on anticolonial tears across the Indian countryside and sentient, anxiety-ridden spaceships, and Russian house spirits who help a boy from far away discover his own power through storytelling. I am so glad *Sunspot Jungle Book 2* is in the world, because the world has been hungry for it for a very long time.

Daniel José Older

Attenuation

Nick Harkaway

Sonny Hall, the space traveller, in the darkness of the recovery room, blinks and comes to himself. He can still see the tumbler falling from his hand, the cocktail party lit in a warm yellow haze and the girl from Heidelberg grinning at him like a cat. He can feel the slick surface of the glass slipping between thumb and finger, can pinpoint the moment when the remaining friction is too slight to prevent it surrendering to gravity. The paper umbrella drops end over end, ice cubes skitter across the polished concrete of the apartment's floor.

He opens his mouth to say "What?"

"Hush," the technician says, high and strained, "it's okay. You're fine."

Until this moment it had not occurred to Sonny that he might not be fine, but the transparency of the lie causes him to reexamine. He feels ghastly: as if he has grit in the joints and skin and yet is somehow made of jelly. He imagines that his whole body has been transformed, is now made of whatever goes into eyeballs, and all that eyeball stuff is dry and hung over.

"You're not fine," another voice says firmly. "Tell me exactly what happened in London."

He suspects there may have been Swedish whisky and—he licks dry teeth—potatoes roasted in goose fat. He can taste colours.

"Synaesthesia is a temporary companion effect," the second voice says. "Ignore it. Did you do this to yourself? Are you making money on it? We get that. People are stupid enough to do that. Are you that stupid? Because it will kill you."

He must have spoken aloud. That's excellent. But this is clearly not Nieuwsterdam, not even close. On the wall, block letters read simply "Halfway." So this is the Halfway Station. They must have pulled his signal when they saw something was wrong. Is something wrong?

"He's dissociated," the technician says primly. The sheriff—the uniform has a star on it, and Sonny can actually hear the theme from

High Chaparral glinting off it—doesn't care about that either. He sings along a bit, then stops.

"Did I do wha' to m'self?" a new voice says. It's a good voice. It's catching somewhat as if the speaker has a mouthful of peanut butter, but in the flow it's deep and buttery. A voice for the seduction of valkyries. It resonates in Sonny's chest, plucks at his gut. *Oh. That's me.*

"Your old corpse," the sheriff says. "It wasn't burned. It's active. You're in two places at once. You have attenuation sickness."

The umbrella flies upwards, dragging the glass and the ice cubes with it. The smiling girl slips her arms around his chest and buries her face in the crook of his neck. He returns the favour, and all the lights come on at once.

Transit is last decade's new new thing. What once was wondrous is now banal, and instead of taking time to be amazed at what it implies, people complain at the paperwork, at the limited options, at the frequent flier rewards being insufficient. Transit has come of age, become ubiquitous, and now no one cares. But even a few years ago, it was miraculous. A simple enough idea, fiendishly hard to implement—until it was done. Information can be transmitted instantly across distances to boggle the human mind. The human mind itself is a clever thing made of information, a self-animating bundle of entangled strands which in the proper medium will unfold and catch the mundane physical ground and function but which can, with certain reservations, be plucked out of that soil, folded up, and sent. In this manner, with some preparation, a person might travel across galactic space. And indeed one can.

The logistical preparation is not trivial. It includes the creation of a conduit (vastly complicated) and the presence of a suitable host platform at the far end (relatively simple). Probes filled with durable storage technologies and microconstruction engines must be fired out to far away planets, accelerated and decelerated more violently than any human frame could withstand. Many of them are lost, of course, but some arrive and far away and alone create landing pads and accommodation for incoming minds. The first through are pioneers and scientists, but the second wave are homesteaders and tourists.

The greatest difficulty is in completing the transfer. The silly string nests of information which are people are recalcitrant about leaving one home for another. They are reluctant travellers at best. Thus, two possibilities: for short trips, the original body can be made dormant, chilled, and stored. Longer stays away necessitate the absolute destruction of the beautiful corpse. Age-based mortality is no longer inevitable and population less of a concern with worlds spreading out before each wave of probes.

As transit becomes commonplace, so too it becomes a little less sterile and reputable. There are transit crooks, transit loopholes, a transit *demimonde*. But the wise traveller knows one thing above all: the service provider must be of absolute probity. Absolute. Because even slight residue of the corpse left behind will, after more than a week or so, induce a jet lag of the soul, a distant echo dragging the mind back and forth between worlds, both corpses eventually dying for lack of constant anima.

The phenomenon is called attenuation sickness. It occupies a place in the culture somewhere between the tuberculosis of poets and cancer from smoking; romantic yet fractionally self-inflicted, tragic yet educational. There's a moral sense that you had to have done it to yourself although occasionally it can happen by chance.

Sonny Hall can't remember doing it to himself. But then he can't remember much of the last few days. Sitting in the grey holding room—not a cell, not a hospital suite, just how people live in the Halfway station, in rooms made of varnished composite bricks and extruded steel fittings—he stares up at the stand holding his saline and tries to put it together. He closes his eyes meditatively and waits for flashes of his recent past, but it doesn't happen. He opens them again.

"You can use the long link relay," the sheriff says. "Call people. That might spark something." Sonny's convenient amnesia annoys him. It annoys Sonny, too—and he doesn't find it even slightly convenient —but he wants memory to come spontaneously. It is a challenge, a reassertion of control. His attenuation will begin to betray him in hours, will kill him in days, and he needs to demonstrate that he still belongs to himself, that his new body—broad where the old one was narrow and brooding and physical where once he was effete—really is his and not some stranger's. He remade himself for this journey, despite all that talk of embodied cognition—or because of it.

The sheriff wrinkles his nose. It's a big nose with long, lean nostrils. Too long, in Sonny Hall's perception. Creepy long. Weird fingernails, too, which wrap around the finger so that, as the sheriff taps his hands on the steel desk, there's a sharp click like a dog walking. *Chack chack chack chack.* The sheriff is Caucasian, Sonny figures, in the sense of coming from the Caucasus Mountains. He catches himself: no. The body comes from a Caucasus stemline, imported here on a probe, built from scratch. If the sheriff has a belly button, it is a skeuomorph, the conceptual legacy of an old technology.

Sonny resists the urge to examine his own stomach. Instead, he looks around properly at where he is. Everything in Halfway is made from local materials, everything has a different feel from how it is at home. 3D printed replicas of Earth objects. Frank Lloyd Wright designs rendered in stone dust and resin, injection moulded steel. Plastics are easy. There's no wildlife here, not really, so no furs or leathers. No cottons either. Jars line the walls with green stuff in them: transit station's version of potted plants. There aren't even insects—nothing for them to eat. No roaches. For the first time in his life, Sonny Hall is billions of light years from a cockroach.

He steeples his fingers and hopes the sheriff will do the same. Kinesics. Sonny knows a few things about human behaviour, that is his métier. Human stress analysis and behavioural dynamics, individual and group, Class II. Never bothered to finish the Class I section. Class II is good enough for most practical purposes, and Class I involves a lot of dry academic background. Boring as hell.

Class II is good enough here, too. The sheriff stops tapping and leans forward to match Sonny's posture, to make him feel at ease. Impending death's good for something: gravitas comes with it, free of charge.

When the sheriff has gone—he clearly wants to sit in, but there's no way that's happening—Sonny phones home. He starts with friends or rather with friendly acquaintances. He's going to circle inwards, hoping that the outer limits will trigger his memory without anyone revealing things he ought to have first person. Also, this way he doesn't have to discuss his attenuation with anyone who will tell him he's being brave or he's going to be fine.

From talking to the sheriff, he already knows that his old corpse is AWOL. The brief flutter of hope that his sickness was caused by a few stray entangled bits of brain and bone was thus disposed of; this situation results from deliberate action on someone's part. The sheriff seems to think Sonny is personally involved, which he devoutly hopes is true. If he is, then presumably he had a plan for not dying from it, for receiving lots of money. Maybe even his amnesia is part of the plan although, if it isn't, he has to consider the possibility that the amnesia is the problem that will cause him to die rather than survive, cause him to miss some window of action to which he is committed in order to redeem the situation. This is partly why he is so keen to regain his memory indirectly— he doesn't want to have to admit to any putative partner in crime that he has no idea what he's doing. That sort of thing makes people nervous. Nor does he want the sheriff listening in on these discussions though he suspects that is inevitable. That appalling nose is everywhere.

He calls the girl who brought the girl from Heidelberg—Renate! The smiling German's name was Renate. Excellent. Early success, though he's not sure if that's recovery from amnesia or just something he never forgot.

"Hey, Justine. It's me, Sonny. This is my new look."

"Oh, wow, hey, Sonny! You look totally different."

"New body. You think it suits me?"

"Wow. I don't know. Yes, I think so. You look like a gangster."

In fact, he picked this corpse to resemble an Anglo-Kenyan actor who once played Hamlet at the Olivier, but to someone like Justine anybody not entirely white was automatically a little dangerous and edgy. He wonders when he stopped noticing that a lot of his friends—a lot of people he knew, anyway—were basically objectionable. Probably about the time he broke up with Liz (or rather, about the time she caught him with ... he couldn't remember who it actually was) and she went to off on a trip around the world in a fury. Auburn Liz, hiding from the sun and doing election monitoring in Haiti or Salvador or ... he doesn't remember. Probably never knew. Angry Liz, fire in everything she did, whose chiefest attraction, he suspects, was her ability to make him care about something even if only by shouting. And who, he had realised as her letters had drifted in and he had forced himself to read about her work with the indigenous population and how they were basically treated like shit by big oil and big pharma and big agri, was a better person than he was by a mile. Which was fine, just fine, his post-breakup self had snarled into the shaving mirror. Screw better people, anyway. But he had ended up here, so maybe she'd had a point. His life had been empty and selfish, after all.

Justine clears her throat, bored. He's been staring into space. Oops. "I was wondering if you knew how to get hold of Renate?" he asks.

"Hannoverian Renate?"

"Heidelbergian. Heidelbergerish. Whatever."

"German. Yes, sure." She rattles off a number. "Are you coming back soon? Are you going to look like that?"

"I hope so, yes." In any case, you had to wait a minimum of three months between transits or risk psychological damage. Nothing like attenuation, but it was something insurers didn't like.

He calls Renate, but she barely remembers the night at all. She's going back to Berlin (not Heidelberg, not Hannover, right) because London is too crazy. Where is he, anyway? It's a terrible line.

He disengages, talks to some more friends. *What did I do? How did I live? How did I look to you? Were there any new faces in my life? Faces I wasn't sleeping with?*

Yes. Yes, there had been. Two men variously described as "heavy," "scary," "bumptious," and "rude." Then he lucked out: Misha the Polish Artist (as opposed to Misha the Model who was also Polish and spoke Cantonese or Misha the Barman who was basically a drug dealer) had seen the men for long enough that she'd actually sketched them. For the price of a guaranteed invitation to Sonny's homecoming party and her choice of introductions, she is prepared to send him an image. A few moments later it snicks into the output drawer: low-quality plastic thread paper like the leg of a tracksuit. Two grim faces stare up at him.

Anamnesis, he discovers, is not how it ought to be. Memory doesn't shock or drown him; he isn't disorientated. It's just a case of everything working the way it's supposed to followed by an almost obliterating moment of realisation as he sees that it's working and reacts. He jerks out of his chair, bangs his knee, and shouts, then leans on the desk, terrified the knowledge will slip away. It doesn't. The recollection is not fleeting or fragile. It isn't surprising of itself. It's just there where he left it like a misplaced glove lying on the carpet.

This, on the left, is Smayle. And that is Denton. Smayle has a particular odour like old running shoes dipped in turpentine. Denton snuffles a lot, drugs or hay fever. They are indeed rude and also violent and annoying. They are the unsubtle hand of someone or other. Someone with an irritatingly trite animal used as a title, predictably masculine, stupidly shamanistic. The wolf. The dog. The fox. A name to go with a silver belt buckle in an ethnic style. Celtic? Swirls and patterns? No. Foreign. Russian. Turkic. African. Chinese. Inuit. Sikh. No, no, no. Dogon, for crying out loud? Easter bloody Island? He's running out of ethnicities he can think of, but that's okay because it's his own sneering he's trying to track down here. Norse? Indian? Pakistani? Or Burmese (like the dogs, which turn out rather embarrassingly to be Bernese rather than Burmese, something Liz found endlessly amusing.) No, no, no.

For God's sake, how many varieties of annoying folk art are there in the world? And how many of those are imported and touted as stylish like those sodding Native American flutes in that band at the Soho Grande? How many ...

Oh.

Native American. Yes.

A coyote. Smayle and Denton work for a coyote. A mover of persons across impenetrable borders. *The* coyote. The one who came to the party and wanted ...

Wanted Sonny Hall to loan him a corpse.

To which Sonny, hopped up on a half dozen things and filled with a dead man's bolshie bravado, said—unusually, given that it was money and risk and the chance to break the law in a way no one he knew had before—"no."

Sonny finds he can't directly remember being at the conversation, can't recall looking at the coyote's face or ever seeing the ridiculous belt buckle with a badly rendered doggy thing on it. But. But but but. If he concentrates on the shoulder of the man's coat—expensive coat, really bloody expensive, handmade in the good way—he can remember what went down as if he'd read a report of it and memorised the text. A memory of a memory. Anamnesis judo.

"I have a guy," the coyote said. "I have a guy at the Halfway station. He'll pick you up, make you comfortable. You don't got to do anything. Just don't die, okay? No stupid shit at the far end. You just stay in bed, feel like crap, take plenty of drugs, and sleep through it. We bring in the other guy, then get him new papers, ship him out, then in again in his new body. It's like money-laundering. Victimless crime. Client gets a new face, new name, new body, new entry to desirable first world nations. Can go and do whatever shit he does. Transit is like being born again."

"And what do I get?"

"Boatload of money. Free upgrade on your choice of corpse. Discount if you should ever need to be someone else. It's a loyalty package like AmEx. We don't got frequent flier miles, we don't like to see too much of that because it means the client is very hot, very careless. And we don't work with the same corpse donor more than one time for security. It's all good. What do you say?"

And when Sonny Hall still said "no," the coyote embraced him, called him a smart kid, and left.

I have a guy.

Meaning, a guy here. Miscommunication? Was Sonny yoinked out of the data stream here when he should have gone on to Nieuwsterdam? Is that—no. Then he'd just be here, royally pissed off but unharmed. No. He has attenuation sickness. There's more to this.

But now he realises he can't assume everyone wants him to find out what it is.

"How're you feeling?" the sheriff asks him. There's a deputy sitting in to take notes. Like the sheriff, his corpse is Caucasian. He wonders if all the permanent staff are, if only the commercial corpses have any genetic variety.

"Woozy," Sonny Hall replies, "and I sleep a lot."

"Good. That's the drugs. You need to stay calm. Call me if you start to flipflop."

"Flipflop?"

"Did you read the stuff they gave you?"

"Not all of it."

"Your mind may start to zap back home. They call it rubberbanding or flipflopping. A few seconds is okay. Longer than that and you can drop off the plateau—don't ask me, I don't know what plateau—and stay there. In the middle somewhere."

"And die?"

"Coma. Physical breakdown takes a bit longer. So stay in bed, okay?"

"I don't want to. If I'm going to die. I want to get out and about." *I want to fix this.*

"Don't. The more you do, the more likely you are to wear yourself down and die faster."

With that in mind, Sonny passes over the sketch of the coyote's men.

"These two are part of it." At a raised eyebrow, he carries on. "They were with a guy who wanted to use my corpse for a few days. I said no." Two eyebrows now, from query to mild scepticism. "Don't. Don't ask me if I'm sure about that. Turning him down is the first intelligent thing I've done in three years, and I just now remembered it. I don't mean to say it was virtue either because honesty is not who I am. Or who I was. I just ... I was changing myself, on purpose. This trip was about a fresh start. I figured I'd do the opposite of what I wanted to do, which was take the deal for the hell of it. I said no, and he seemed to feel I was ..." Sonny hesitates. "It was like that pleased him. He didn't want me to say yes, but he had to ask. I said no, so he walked away."

"He didn't say anything else? No threats?"

"No."

"You restored his faith." Sheriff humour, Sonny guesses. "And he didn't say anything else at all. No detail about this end?"

I have a guy.

But Sonny doesn't know who that guy might be. It might be the sheriff, for example. Even if it isn't, he doesn't want to have the sheriff untangle the whole ring and then remember belatedly that he, Sonny, is up to his neck in it, changed his mind after that one glorious moment of being New Sonny, fell back into Old Sonny. That would be poetic, but it would also suck.

"Just what I said. And those guys."

"So you think he was happy you said no and then he just went right ahead and, what, stole your corpse?"

Sonny shrugs. *Just minding my own business, officer.*

A few moments later, a bell chimes to tell everyone that it's the end of the Tuesday.

He sleeps and dreams he's flying through space appallingly slowly, catching up with his body except that he has two and is slowly stretching like bubble gum. When he snaps, he dies. This is apparently all he can dream about because it happens over and over again. A little after midnight he gets up and takes himself to the Halfway transit station bar.

Sonny takes a seat at the counter before asking himself whether he actually wants a drink. He doesn't, specifically; he just doesn't want to dream again.

"Getcha something?"

He stares at the bottles behind the bar. No chance of a chablis, for sure.

"What's good?" he asks.

"Nothing."

Sonny considers, then orders a plain vodka. The traditional recipe—carbohydrate mush with a few unknowable things floating in the vat—isn't far off what's upstairs in the fabrication levels. He wonders whether he could actually come to think of this place as home if some emergency stranded him here properly. Eat at the canteen, read books, and eventually find a fellow refugee for some physical friendship, keep algae for pets. He glances at the vodka.

The glass slips from between thumb and finger. The German girl smiles and—

Attenuation.

He's in his own body, his old, persistent corpse, familiar aches and narrow shoulders. He screams as he finds he's restrained in a slick plastic sack wrapped from ankle to shoulder. *Giant spider! Mummification! Dark rites!* There's a blindfold over his eyes—no, something worse: slick and organic and lukewarm, little circles the size of the orbit resting on each eyelid. Suckled on, it seems. He wriggles, feels the restraints give a little, gritty slime sluicing around his arms. *Body farm! They're coming for my kidneys!* But what sort of organ thief would impede access to the body with this sheath? So then: *cannibals!* He screams or barks, and there's a sound of running feet. Light returns, a solicitous face.

"Mr. Hall?" The blindfolds are removed. A nurse or an orderly. Long fingers removing ... cucumber? "Are you all right, Mr. Hall?" A cave-like room with towels and a sink. Candles. And this is ... a massage table?

"This is a spa!" Sonny Hall cries in outrage.

"Yes, Mr. Hall," the orderly says—no, he's a bloody massage therapist, Sonny can smell the jasmine, Liz used to rub it on her neck when she was stressed, part of the healing knowledge of ancient somewhere-or-other. The orderly's face distorts like a soap bubble, but no, that's the universe going past. Black space and white suns. The ice falls up to meet the umbrella—

And he's back.

"You should have told me you were attenuated," the barman mutters irritably, "I'd have given you a plastic cup."

Sonny Hall in the sheriff's office, slamming his big hand against the desk.

"In a spa! Whoever has my corpse is in a spa! Okay? They're not doing anything. They're taking a holiday! With my life! He even called me 'Hall.' The bastard's using my ID. My credit cards, for Christ's sake!"

The sheriff sighed. "He's not. We tried that. Your cards have gone dormant. So he's using his own money and your name. Still, it's something."

"I'll say it's something. You can find him. You can trace my cards and find him!" Sonny is what they call "excited," meaning furious. The sheriff looks a little bit impressed, which seems good until Sonny realises he is bleeding from the nose, and—yuck—from the corner of his left eye.

"Don't do that," the sheriff says.

"Don't what?"

"Don't get excited. It increases the frequency of the attacks."

"Well, then I'll learn something, won't I? Maybe I can even place a phone call, get him arrested. Or killed. That would be great. I could jump off a building."

"If you die while you're in residence, you die. The new corpse won't save you. It's not like you snap back here. You just die. Okay? We've got this, Mr. Hall."

"Are you serious? It's fine for you to be cool, isn't it? You're not the one—"

Sonny Hall gets excited. The sheriff turns out to be right.

It's London, he knows that. He can see buildings he knows. He's in a chair. Nice chair, but durable and washable. Hotel chair. Hotel! He lunges for the bedside table looking for a notepad. Yes, by the phone. The Calista! 55 Burton Street in the West End. He's excited, will that keep him here or send him home? His corpse—his old body—hurts. Of course it does, it's been inhabited by someone who isn't used to his musculature, his skeleton. Everything has been strained and overworked by inappropriate nerve impulses. *Make yourself at home, you bastard.*

The Calista. Yes. The Calista. He reaches for the phone, foggy. Something has been written on the pad, a doodle almost, words in a spiral made by the pressure from the page above. Ghost words. The room turns as he tries to read. Has he been drugged? The— call him a squatter—the squatter must know Sonny came back for a few moments earlier. Has he deliberately incapacitated himself? But he can't spend the whole time like this and still do what he came to do. Can he? Sonny has visions of deliberate inoculation with a terrible disease, a terrorist attack using his own body as the delivery mechanism.

Mind you, if it's something like that, maybe the disease will kill his corpse and he'll be okay. Unless he's in res at the moment of death, of course. Has the squatter checked out? If not, is he here now? Unconscious or trapped in a body abruptly responding to its natural owner?

His fingers have dialled the police number. He gives the name of the hotel and the address, tells them what's going on. Victory! He relaxes—and doesn't go back. How many minutes? Is he stuck? Is he about to die just before he can be rescued?

Because that would be—

Sonny Hall, at Halfway station, washing the blood from his cheeks and coughing, already knows it hasn't worked. The sheriff tells him why.

"There's no Calista hotel on Burton Street."

The easiest way to stop Sonny from taking any more direct action: persuade him he has already succeeded. A fake notepad. Drugs or alcohol to make him sluggish. He wipes his mouth and doesn't bother to wince when his hand comes away red. "Motives," he says.

"I'll take care of that."

"I'm a stress analyst," Sonny Hall says. "Motives are stresses. There are two lines of possibility. First, I'm irrelevant. This is for profit, of whatever sort. The second is that it's about me. I saw something, offended someone, did a deal."

"I said I'll take care of it."

And that seems to be all he'll say.

Sonny Hall asks the concierge where he can get a jug of algae for ornamentation. The woman smiles delightedly.

"We have a bioluminescent one if you'd like a night-light."

Sonny is about to say no, but actually that might be rather nice. "What colour?"

"We have rose, azure, sunset yellow."

Sonny takes one of each, pledges to be a good keeper of the radiant slime.

Calista.

He lies on his back and lets his mind wander.

Calista has something to tell him.

Why Calista? Is that important? He doesn't know the name, or rather, of course, he's heard it; but it has no particular significance. He has a vague notion it may be the name of a moon. Or a line of pajamas. Was it also the name of a woman, maybe, aged 55? Well, it certainly is a woman's name, that much is clear. Not a man's name. He tries to be pleased with this certainty.

He remembers the notepad, the prim wording in printed dark yellow which wanted to be gold. The notepad by the bed. Fake notepad. By the phone. Cool paper in his corpse's hands, the scribbles from something written, pressed down carelessly onto whatever was underneath.

Spirals on a notepad. Words he couldn't read, was too foggy to read. But now he can. In his memory they're eerily sharp.

"Restored his faith." Where has he heard that? Has he said it? No. No! It was his conversation with the sheriff. Him or the deputy. Or a bug. But somehow, words here have gone there.

I can't trust the law, Sonny realises. Now, when I finally want to, I can't.

He's going to have to do something rash.

Looking for a crook, Sonny wanders up to the process levels where the crappy jobs are. The transit station has a permanent population of a few thousand plus several more thousands cycling through every month. Small world, but not too small. He tells a twitchy kid he needs to score, then tells the kid's mouth-breathing dealer he needs someone to talk to about something serious on Main Street and will pay for an introduction.

"Why would I tell you?" the dealer sneers.

"For the money," Sonny Hall explains patiently.

"Which I could take."

Sonny allows his shoulders to flex and sees the guy reassess. Then he says: "Take your profit and keep it simple." Class II stress analysis on a personal level. Everyone loves simple.

The contact gives him a name in janitorial. "Tell him Ryan sent you."

Sonny Hall has no intention of saying anything of the kind. He will let his knowledge be mysterious, which is vastly more impressive than a weasel like Ryan.

"I need a ticket home," Sonny says.

"So buy one." The man from janitorial shrugs. The room is even smaller than Sonny's, a cot and a table.

"I need to do it quietly," Sonny Hall says.

"Oh." A flicker of interest.

"I need to get back for a few days."

The guy frowns at the word "back." "Double transit can kill you, friend."

"I know."

The maintenance man shrugs. Sonny feels his heart beat, knows that soon he will either flipflop again or start to bleed. Or something else. The next stage can be brain damage.

"There are management issues right now," maintenance man says. "The market is unsettled."

"What kind of unsettled?"

"The major provider of this kind of service is in the process of being taken over. It's a little unclear who's in charge."

Boardroom coup in the coyote business. Sonny feels a weird familiarity.

"This would be a simple job. I need to leave as soon as possible, but the exact timing is flexible. I also don't care about what sort of corpse I get. Just so I can go."

At last, the man nods.

"All right. On that basis I can make this happen. I will have to use temporary contractors rather than my usual contacts. There may be an additional charge to cover their fees."

"Up to forty percent of the agreed amount."

The maintenance man scratches on a piece of paper for a moment. Then he nods. "Acceptable."

The non-legitimate service seems to dovetail perfectly with the main one; it feels well-practiced and even banal. Everyone's relaxed. He wonders if they know he's that guy, if any of the freelancers are from the coyote's team. *Management issues.* But why should they know? This is a transit station, a place for comings and goings. An anonymous place. And they are paid not to know who clients are, to pay no attention.

"In a moment," the technician says—it's a woman, Persian stemline with wide, elegant lips and light scarring on one cheek— "you'll experience a slight coldness. Count to ten for me, please."

He feels it already, his mind washing out of his head into the tangle machine. It's uglier than last time, jagged where the first transit was smooth, but it's working. He counts: "one" and then he's gone, riding the technician's encouraging smile into the oblivion of transit.

• • •

Sonny Hall peers through the oil from a black lava lamp, viscous clouds washing at the edges of his vision. His taxi driver says "All right back there?" without looking.

"Fine," Sonny says. "Little bit woozy, is all. Long trip."

He's wearing a slightly damaged corpse: a pale, thin-limbed body with a fused knee. He walks like the villain in an old movie. The rest of the corpse is fine, even distinguished. Young, muscular. It would have been discarded, he guesses, by whoever bought it. The makers would have supplied a new one free of charge.

He gives his own address and slumps back into the seat, tasting the air. London air, full of exhaust and biomass. The grittiness in his joints is there, and he can smell blood in his nose already. He's doubled back on himself, attenuated twice over. The Halfway corpse is in storage.

"You can't just transfer the tangle here directly to the new corpse?" he'd asked.

"Not so much," the maintenance man had said. "It causes complications."

"Like attenuation?"

"Like matter to energy conversion."

And that was that.

As the taxi slows at a junction, he feels abruptly nauseous as if his stomach is trying to climb through his mouth. He manages not to be sick until the Pentonvtille Flyover and gets his head well out of the window. The driver carols a noise of horrified protest as his fare brings red-rimmed eyes back inside. A running commentary on the costs of cleaning the cab lets Sonny know he is no longer welcome, but he sits it out and overtips the man, who mutters "animals" and steams off into the flow.

On the pavement outside his home, Sonny realises he is seeing double: he can see what is really in front of him but overlaid across both is a cheerful London scene, birds and trees. Hyde Park, for God's sake. The squatter is feeding the ducks. A way of staying calm, perhaps, and thus avoiding the symptoms Sonny himself has brought on. Of course, the squatter presumably knows what's happening.

Sonny shivers; he's bone-cold, which he hopes desperately is fatigue and not phantom chill from the frozen corpse at Halfway.

He keys his entry code and lets himself into the flat, realises no one has tidied up since he left.

• • •

Sonny's working theory of the situation has been that it is financial, some sort of deal akin to the one he was offered, possibly gone awry. He has enough of his memory back now to be confident that it wasn't a deal with him. As he makes coffee, he considers the possibility that it is some sort of not-quite-snuff sex fantasy, a cheap—well, a very expensive—thrill for a jaded palette: borrow a body, live the self-destruction-by-debauchery dream, then bail at the last minute. A nice scenario for him, of course, because it implies his own probable survival.

But he has to admit that if he were conducting this particular perversion—and he has some experience in the area of baroque self-abuse—it would be unlikely to feature ducks.

When his thoughts take him back to the coyote, he realises he knows how to reach the man. That part of his mind is back where it always was, properly connected. He wonders if there will come a moment when the attenuation starts to affect his brain in a countervailing fashion, erasing what the anamnesis is recalling. It's a very Sonny Hall thought, but in this corpse it feels morbid and adolescent. Apparently, his new brain doesn't really like morbid. It is not contemplative, and it chafes at inactivity.

He changes his shirt and trousers for a combination that looks surprisingly mean: an orange string vest top he bought because he had seen it in a music video and a pair of combat trousers. He adds a shirt in case he has to go somewhere smart but wears it with three buttons open and finally throws a black coat over the whole muddle. The limp and the cheap medical-issue cane give him some slightly creepy weirdness, and the overall effect is like the villain from a bit of Austrian retro-noir.

Sonny von Hall.

The coyote keeps an office over a strip club. You approach the doorman, and when he tells you the prices, you tell him you know Miss Melinda. He pats you down and sends you to the next floor. After that, it's just a staircase with a camera watching you all the way up. Sonny's new corpse has well-developed muscles on both sides, so the business of lifting the bad leg is not seriously problematic. He trots upwards, cane tapping as he powers off the flexible knee. Hut-hah-tat. Hut-hah-tat. Liz, he remembers irrelevantly, was fond of traditional dancing. It had the same rhythm. He should have been nicer to her. But then he should basically have been nicer. Note to self.

At the top of the stairs, there's a thug, not one of the ones he knows. The thug is just a little brusque and aggressive. Sonny just sneers that he has business here, uses his eyeline to convey boredom and certainty, his body to project power. More kinesics. The thug, without knowing why, falls into line.

Inside sit three men, rather than the one Sonny was expecting. The coyote looks pinched. He's not having a good day. That could be a good thing or a bad thing. Sonny smiles toothily.

"Hello, old friend. I was wondering if we might have a word in private."

The coyote gives him a look that says loudly that he has no idea who Sonny might be, but given that his options right now are apparently put his faith in the Mysterious Stranger or stay in the room with the new faces, he'll take anything he can get. Before he can speak, one of the visitors—a thin-lipped entity in very legitimate blue flannel— butts in for all the world as if this was a wedding party and not the denouement of some sort of coup.

"Your timing is a little complex, sir. Mr.. Ossman has taken us on as partners in his enterprise, we're just working out the details. But you can speak as freely with us as you would with him."

Ossman? The coyote's name is Ossman? It sounds Turkish. He's a Turkish Native American. Sonny shrugs that idea away. Okay, whatever.

"Is that fellow outside yours or his?" Sonny says to Ossman. "He's got inappropriate hands. Or he puts his hands in inappropriate places. No one minds a patdown, but there are limits to propriety." He has no idea where this is coming from. Pure bullshit. Attenuation combined with old boardroom chutzpah.

Ossman shrugs. "He's a new guy. These gentlemen have a more civilised manner. I imagine they will wish to bring in their own security." His eyes dart to Mr. Blue Flannel and his sidekick. Flannel nods icily. Yes, this is a coup all right. Or a blunt force merger, maybe. *Management issues.* Quite.

"Well, no disrespect to your new employees," Sonny says pleasantly, and sees Flannel wince, "but this is a personal matter." He smiles blandly. "I'm here to restore your faith." Will Ossman make the catch? Flannel jerks as if stung and gets to his feet, which prompts his companion to reach meaningfully into his coat.

Ossman sees the movement and comes to some sort of dramatic conclusion. From his waistband he draws a prodigious gun, a chromed American thing, and in rising, knocks over his chair. Flannel and friend—mistakenly, in Sonny's opinion—presume he means to renege on whatever deal they have done and also draw. When the thug bursts in from outside, the sight of three guns in the room clearly leads him to certain conclusions, and it all kicks off.

Guns are incredibly loud; but even at close range it seems that using one requires a degree of formal training, and no one here has had any. They aren't missing each other, but they are hitting limbs and ears and nonfatal bits of torso, and therefore the exchange of fire is just going on and on and on. Any second now someone's reinforcements will arrive or the police or a horde of concerned strippers. Anything seems possible.

Sonny has not been shot. He wonders if he should feel offended and decides he has enough trouble in his life without looking for more. When the noise stops, he lifts his head to look around.

The thug is perforated. He has actual holes in him that go all the way through. He is not breathing, and only an idiot would imagine he will ever be getting up again.

Flannel and his sidekick are in better shape, which is to say they're down but not dead, although in Flannel's case that looks to be a negotiable situation; and the sidekick is trying manfully to get a tourniquet around something that shouldn't be leaking, but his own injuries include a shoulder and a shattered skin, so he can't really get a lot of purchase.

"I can help with that," Sonny offers. The sidekick stares, then nods, and Sonny grabs the belt and hauls back with everything he has. The blood slows.

A hiss reminds Sonny that he came here for Ossman and assures him that Ossman is still alive. His gun has got lost, which is all to the good, and he's looking at Sonny as if he cannot honestly believe no one thought to blow him away during all the excitement. Sonny shrugs a sort of apology. "I wanted to ask you something. I didn't mean ... this."

Ossman scowls. He has three, nasty looking gashes, one on each arm and one across the hip. They're all bleeding thickly but survivably. He won't be looking for anyone to hug him in the next few weeks, but other than that, he's fine. Sonny realises the gashes are bullet tracks. The coyote was near-missed three times. Is that even possible? Looking again, Sonny realises Ossman must have used the bodyguard as a shield. Those holes are not from Flannel's gun—they're from Ossman's. He fired through his own guy.

Wow.

"Get me out of here," Ossman says succinctly, "and get me sorted out, and I will tell you any damn thing you want to know. I will also not have you killed for this insane shit."

Sonny finds this acceptable and says so.

Ossman lies on Sonny Hall's couch and moans, but the pain is giving way—assuming his experience is the same as Sonny's—to a blue-tinted relaxation and a warm, almost lusty burn in the gut. Sonny has no idea what they have taken, but it's powerful stuff. He can't even feel the shards of ice in his joints or the increasingly frequent needle jabs in his chest. He realises he never asked what the cause of death—the proximate cause—in attenuation was. Heart failure? Or was he just going to end up stripped out of both—no, all three—of his corpses, caught in the centre of the triangle and unable to derive sustenance from any of them, slowly withering as they did?

Screw that.

"You're sorted out," he says to Ossman.

"Hell, yes," Ossman agrees. "What do you want to know?"

"What do I—I want to know what happened to me!"

"I have no idea. Who the hell are you?"

Sonny thought the coyote had already figured that out. He acknowledges that maybe that was a little self-centred.

"Sonny Hall."

"Who?"

"Sonny—Jesus, you came to my house!"

"I go to a lot of houses."

"You came to my house, and you asked me to give you my corpse for something! And then, when I said no, you went away happy, and I thought I'd restored your faith in humanity. That's what I told the sheriff at the Halfway station, and he's your guy. And it was written on the pad in the hotel room here, and I thought ... I thought you must know what was going on."

But Ossman is shaking his head. "I have no idea what you're talking about. You, I remember. I was going to use you to smuggle in a guy. Doesn't matter now who it was. You said no, and we never go back to the well. We travel light, too, leave no trail, you get me? We don't keep coppers on the payroll. We sure as hell don't do conscription.

It's not a good idea for exactly this reason. I mean, here you are, right? Although, incidentally, you are far and away the most batshit guy I have ever met. You're attenuated already, and you come back here? That is some old school crazy ..." He chuckles admiringly, then goes on. "It's a consensual operation, right? Victimless crime. The whole thing functions if everyone's happy. Someone gets unhappy, it makes trouble."

Ossman sits right up, swears in Turkish (Navajo?) as one of his bandages rips away from his skin. "Trouble. You've been making noise, right? Because this happened to you. That's bad for me, so then I need friends in low places. Do you get it? Friends like that bastard back in my office. Morristown. I should have seen it."

"What? Wait, you're saying the guy in the suit—?"

Ossman looks as if he's doing some powerful thinking. Then he sighs. "I'm sorry, man. You should have kept hold of Morristown, asked him. Make it a price for your medical attention, yes? Because no way is he going to sit down and chat with you now."

Sonny Hall sighs. This is almost certainly true. "I hope," he says after a moment, "that the tourniquet slips."

Ossman grins. "Yeah."

Triangulated, Sonny howls in the cold and the dark and wishes he could go home. He just doesn't know where it is. He ought to be able to see galaxies all around him; death by transit should be spectacular that way. He should feel he's dissolving into the cosmos. He doesn't. He wonders if he has gone blind.

He wakes slowly as if the space between is less than willing to let him go, and when he comes to himself, he is gasping for air in not one body but two. He takes some consolation from the knowledge that his squatter is suffering now, for sure.

The double vision does not fade, and the cold in his limbs grows heavier, more pressing. Breathing stays difficult. Sonny von Hall is replaced by Sonny Hall the consumptive. Ossman looks at him from the sofa and makes a speedy diagnosis.

"You haven't got long."

"I know."

"I'm sorry, but that's the truth."

"I need to find my corpse."

Ossman sucks air through his teeth. "I owe you. But I got no idea how we find your old body. No idea at all. Morristown isn't going to tell us even if he's still alive. If I was going to talk to those people, I'd need backup. I got the right sort of friends for that, but it takes time to arrange."

"And when it's ready—"

"You will so entirely not care."

Sonny Hall thinks about it. "It's okay," he says, "you're off the hook."

Ossman blinks. "Just like that?"

"Sure, why not? You can't help. Don't feel bad about it."

The squatter is lying in a darkened room staring at the ceiling. There's a fan going round up there. Sonny can actually hear it, electric motor whining. The designer has put a light in the ceiling directly above—stupid—so the room is flickering. Everything is flickering.

Ossman sighs. "You're a perfectly okay guy, Sonny Hall. And this is a crappy thing to happen. They were trying to get me, they're going to take you out. Crazy thing is, they've made their play. There's nothing for them in you dying. They should just cut you loose. I'll try to get them a message. Maybe it'll remind someone to do the good thing. They're bad people over there, but they're professionally bad. This isn't personal with you." He hesitates. "The way I see it, I'm off the hook when you die. Or if you get back. Otherwise, if you need something, call me. I'll try."

They shake hands, and that's it.

Sonny looks through the squatter's eyes at a room in this big city and wishes he knew where it might be. In cop shows there'd be a distinctive building or a matchbook. The curtains would be enough, special curtains imported from Lithuania for one building. He can feel his mind—his anima—straining to encompass three bodies at once.

"It's not personal," Ossman said. *Sure. There's nothing personal about this at all. It's just him killing me, is all. About as personal as it gets.* He draws a breath, conscious that he's struggling against frozen muscles far away. And stops sharply, his stomach flipping over and every part of him abruptly alight with understanding.

Through the nose of his original corpse, he can smell jasmine.

● ● ●

He finds her at the duck pond—not the one in Hyde Park but the other one, the tiny one close to where she used to live. The one they went to every Saturday.

He's offended to realise she doesn't recognise him, then feels ridiculous—how could she?—then startled because that means she's not getting the visions. But of course, she's not. She's not him. She's not attenuated. She's just sitting in a dying body, killing him by degrees, out of—what?

He sighs, and she turns around.

"You should go now," he says, and sees the absolute amazement in her eyes as she realises who he is. "I don't need to know why you did all this."

"And what did I do?"

"You found out I was going. Got Morristown to help you mess up the coyote's business. Win-win. You got me, he got Ossman."

She shrugs. "Close enough." Her shrug on his body. He stares down at himself, horrified by how thin he has become, how weak. But he realises abruptly that that's how he always was in that corpse: a heroin chic, hyperthyroid plastic surgery victim in expensive clothes.

"You should go."

"What if I won't?"

"Why would you stay? It's over."

She peers at him curiously. "Sonny, I'm murdering you. You do understand that, right? You hurt me, I destroyed you, end of. It's how most people feel, but they can't work out how to bring it off."

"You'll die with me. It's stupid."

She shrugs. "Maybe. There have been cases where it worked out differently, but if that's the way it is, I don't really care. I've thought about this a lot, Sonny, and I really do hate you. I'm not even sure why. I just can't stand the world with you in it."

"I wasn't. I left."

"I'm feeding the ducks, Sonny. Piss off somewhere quietly, please. There's nothing you can do. You're not that person."

He wasn't. Two bodies ago, when he was in the corpse she's wearing. But he's different now. He wonders if she realises what she has done to herself, occupying that poison body. Acquired his fatalism, his lassitude. His laziness.

"Liz. Calista. I'm sorry."

She laughs at him.

He has arranged the signal with Ossman: a friendly wave means hold. It means get the transit station on the line and get ready for an emergency pre-empt. If he turns and walks away—

But he realises he has already done so and does not know if it was deliberate. He hears a strange whistle and a sound like air blown across the top of a bottle. Behind him, the corpse sags, the bullet perfectly placed. What would you even call it? Not murder, surely, the death of his own body to save his life? Something else. A new crime or a new necessity.

From a window across the park, Ossman's rifleman waves goodbye.

Sonny Hall, space traveller, rests in the transit hostel at Halfway. He has grown used to the very bad vodka, will miss it when he leaves. He is quiet for the first time in his life. In his little room, jars of algae glow in different colours. He even has a tentative relationship with a woman he met here though neither of them intends it should last. They walk and they talk and that's enough. He has, for the first time in his own recollection, people he can call friends without wincing.

In a few months, he is moving on rather than going back. London and Liz and Ossman can stay in the past. Right now, he never wants to see the place again. And perhaps he never will. Transit is space and time and possibility, for ever.

Slippernet

Nisi Shawl

11.

Dalitha's bare toes dug side-by-side scoops in the black dirt. She sat on Plum Creek's high western bank, buttocks dampening through the thin cotton of her skirt, leaning back on her hands, so that they sank into the soft soil. Free as jazz, the yellow-and-green branches of the budding alders around her waved in a joyful spring breeze. But the real music, Dalitha knew, played underground.

She heard it. She thought it heard her, too. To make sure, she put her shoes back on. It was easy. Thread-enabled fit.

0.

We'll be talking on today's podcast with biologist Claire Simak. Simak has been investigating the so-called Wood-Wide-Web, an underforest fungus network where deals are made and lives are saved via complex interconnections mimicking friendships, rivalries, and business relations. As she and scientists like her begin to untangle and map this network, they're challenging our understanding of empathy and the role cooperation plays in survival.

1.

"Bake it in their bread."

"Not everyone eats bread." Ross objected to plans of action easily. He had three older brothers; he'd seen plenty of mistakes made. "Some people are allergic. Besides, then we'd be just as bad. Forcing them—"

"Spare me the false equivalencies!"

"It ain't false!" That was Kitt. They could be counted on to defend Ross or anyone else they thought was getting ganged up on. "We need some way to make people *wanna* connect. Set up Meshes of their own, even. We need carrots insteada sticks."

"If we could make them want to Mesh with people—each other, anybody—there'd be no need for the Threads." The Grove sat around a small, slick-surfaced café table, their usual meeting spot. Evening gloom pressed against the floor-to-ceiling windows surrounding their bay; the café's few other customers occupied tables near electric outlets on the big room's far side. The latest member of the Grove to speak, Aavo, stared down at a corked glass tube, spinning it slowly back and forth between thumb and finger. The tube's whitish-purple contents reflected blurrily in the tabletop's glossy black. "We have to approach the problem indirectly. Make them want something else. Something this gives us."

"Love? Everyone wants that."

Aavo frowned. "Except if they think they've already got it. No, more basic even than that. Primal. And the kinda thing you can never have enough of."

"Safety."

"Security," said Ross at the same time. That happened a lot since the Grove had Meshed, its members saying things simultaneously. He elaborated: "Like how much more employable I am now I understand what you do." He looked at the cis man on his right.

"Well, you don't really *understand* flavor design. But I guess that's a point," Chris admitted. "You're easier to work with now."

"How long should we try this?"

"I'll write up the ad."

"I'll edit it."

"I'm graphics. Everyone on distribution. Let's see how it spreads in six months."

No one had called the meeting to order, and no one needed to adjourn it. The Grove bussed their table and left.

2.

Market-inspired menu creation for Third Coast fine dining enterprise. Compensation package commensurate with experience. Thread-friendly candidates preferred. siply.com

• • •

3.

OK to post this here? A company where I freelance copy write is expanding, and they want like virtual tour guides training their incoming employees. So familiarity with Zoom and GoToMeeting and as many conferencing softwares as possible, but another thing they're asking for is "Thread savvy," which is, you know, that scary empathy tech. May be worth exploring, though.

4.

Are you going to apply?

    sure

And plant those Thread things under
your skin to qualify?

    yeah

Your father and I are cool waiting
for you to repay us. If it's not
right don't do it.

    it's legal

Yes, but what if you they don't hire
you? Then you'll have gone through
all that for nothing.

    if not these guys someone else
    will want me
    some mesh

5.

"All right. Five months. It's working."
"Not fast enough."
"What's 'fast enough?'" The café had hung a basket over the cash register for donations to support waitstaff health care. Candles

flickered on tables like the Grove's, where individuals' electric lights had no place to plug in.

"Fast enough is fewer people dying," Ross said. The lime-green pillar smoked badly. Good thing the ceiling was painted midnight blue. "Fewer arrests because more people are Meshed."

Aavo grimaced. "You want to be all quantitative?"

"Things are getting a lot worse a lot quicker than we thought they would. Congress just passed that Bannon bill criminalizing non-gender-specific dress."

"Camps are filling up, though. Pretty soon they'll be at capacity."

"That spozed to be *good* news? What, you think these fools about to stop charging people?" Kitt rubbed their neck and winced. They'd been sleeping on Ross's floor since the Volunteer Militia started staking out their apartment. "Goddam Volunteers'll put em somewhere. Buses. Trailer parks." They paused and said what the Grove all thought. "Graveyards."

Kitt shook their head, brass-tipped dreadlocks tinging together. "Naw. Now *good* news, that's what I hear from my cuzz Dalitha's feed."

"She's that K-popper, right?"

"That ain't what you call em. But yeah, she and her friends are all about these Korean actors and singers, K-drama, K-pop. They Meshed across the world, and they got a answer to how to hold theirself together if we wanna listen. Their phones on all the time to supplement the Thread—"

"Everybody can't afford that," Aavo interrupted.

"Sure, they can. Group discounts from phone companies. Which would be another incentive to join, see?"

"'Another' incentive. A secondary one. So what's the first?"

"We have to have the Meshes doin a kinda Cult of Personality thing, like Dalitha and them."

"That could go really wrong," Aavo cautioned.

"We'd hafta be careful, yeah. Tink and Bee-Lung, all those early Thread users, they warned against it pumping up people's tendency to worship. But I think nowadays there's less superstition."

Ross snorted. "I know you do."

"What if ... if we gave them somewhere else to focus?"

Chris was sitting closest, and he caught Aavo's excitement a fraction of a second faster than the rest. "A place? Like a literal Grove? Pilgrimages!"

Kitt frowned. "Then those Trumpers could hit us back by takin it over. Not a place. Not a place and not a person."

All four said it together: "A *thing*."

6.

Zoe Blanche Jacksons! Exclusive deals for first-time purchasers. Get the designer shoes the whole world wants! Dress, casual, business. All sizes: children and adult. Thread-enabled fit.

7.

how are they gay? shoes don't
have sex

      seen the youtubes? they will make you
      want to suck cokc

idgaf they look cool and everyone wants
them me too

      girlyman
      jacksons not even married
      not even dating
      men

idgaf really y do u? they even
have supermachostyle

      just be careful
      somebodys watching

8.

Live/perform spaces now available in Artists' Network. Work exchange. Shared bathroom, cooking facilities; private or community sleeping quarters; Thread-friendly. Text Dalitha.

● ● ●

9.

The café had burnt down a week before the meeting. Insurance payments had been behind, so rebuilding probably wouldn't happen. The sidewalk outside the ruin glistened in the warm rain. The Grove took turns stepping away from the huddle beneath their golf umbrella; currently Aavo stood in the soft drizzle, Jewfro ringlets plastered to her pale forehead. "It's working," she insisted.

Chris shook his head. "So what? Big deal. Bunch of artists and writers Meshing."

"That ain't who we gotta reach," Kitt agreed. "We need to slip truth to power."

"Doesn't that go a little different—"

"People *been* 'speakin' it," they interrupted. "What we need to do is work truth *into* em. Insert it somewheres they can't get it out."

"No. Make it so they slip it to themselves."

"All right, Ross. We be as ethical as we wanna. Maybe just shift our marketing a teense? I have ideas how ZBJ could draw in more a them top percenters. Charity shows—"

A blare of horns sliced through the whisper of water on pavement, thin as a butter knife. A ratcheting beat followed, high and tinny, joined by deep plunging bass notes dropping like toy bombs. And a gleeful falsetto glided into place above it all as at the end of the dark street flashes of movement strobed, gray on black, angles and vectors in synch, movements in time—dancers. Approaching.

Security lamps, hung from the walls of businesses that had shut for the night, threw shimmering light, showing more of them as they neared: bare arms, faces, all races, damp flanks, long hair whipping behind heads turning, nodding, not in unison but matching, Meshing—

"That's our flash mob we've been expecting, right?" Aavo asked.

"Yeah," said Kitt.

"Good." She craned past Ross to see the procession's tail end. "Especially if we can prove they did this without rehearsals. Say it's all about the Jacksons—which in a way ... They better be recording, though."

"We can. They are," Kitt assured her. "Or anyway, I am. And Dalitha and her K-boo friends on FB feed 25/8."

"You share what you capture?"

"Set it to public, tag the googob outta—"

WHOOOP!   WHOOPWHOOPWHOOPWHOOPWHOOP!!
Sirens and high beams pierced the rainy darkness.

"Volunteers!" Without one other word, Kitt left. Aavo filled their vacancy under the umbrella.

Which Chris nervously tried to withdraw as he pulled away from the group. "Shouldn't we all be going?"

"I wanna see the raw footage," Ross replied. "No one has come after the Grove so far, and we could maybe learn a thing or two. And gas doesn't work so good out in the open. Especially with the rain."

"But the rain's stop—"

"Look!"

The Volunteers' station wagons had reached the dancers' formation: One car idled in front of them while two others on the sides backed and filled, a 12-point maneuver that ought to have closed the dancers in a tighter and tighter knot. Instead, they leapt and somersaulted over hoods and roofs, landing outside them in a rounded triangle like a rack for pool balls.

A car's window lowered. A gun barrel thrust out. It fired at a dancer—Dalitha—and missed. Dalitha's body snaked around as one arm opened the door as easily as a foil-wrapped butter pat, as her other arm flowed to embrace the emerging woman, as Dalitha's lips sought and found her captive's ears, her fluttering eyelids, and at last her narrow-pinched nostrils.

"Damn! Aren't they supposed to shoot?" Chris asked. "I read one of their training manuals."

"Hard to do, I guess, mixed up with their targets that way."

All the dancers now swarmed like a slime mold's amoebas over the cars and their contents. They joined together in several small clumps, Volunteers at their centers, filling the intersection a few yards off. Idling engines died, but the station wagons' headlights stayed on, casting long, lumpy shadows. The clumps swayed. The music surged.

"This is wrong," Ross muttered. "Just wrong." He left, too. The remaining two tried to follow him, but he sped up and disappeared around a corner. Aavo asked Chris to wait while she ran ahead. He nodded.

Suddenly, contact broke down. Out of sight shouldn't be out of mind, but Chris felt lonely as a teenager. Which by himself is what he actually was.

A clump of dancers shook, shivered apart as the man at its core dropped to the ground and forced himself through a gap in their legs. The escaped Volunteer rolled to rest face-up in a deep-looking puddle and struggled to unzip his soaked raincoat. An inflated, transparent plastic trash bag strapped to his torso was exposed. As the dancers sank to their knees to converge on him again he made his fingers into claws and ripped it open.

"No! Run!" someone shouted. Chris lost his hold on the umbrella. Dancers and volunteers writhed silently together, fallen patternlessly in the street. His nose leaked snot. He coughed and bent double and coughed twice as hard and would have fallen himself if his jacket hadn't caught on something. Something dragging it and him away and up unlit stairs. A dancer's hand. Dalitha's.

"Used to see my eye doctor here," she announced irrelevantly. She let him go. "Lie down while I get this door."

Chris found he had no choice. He couldn't move much except to twitch. Tears filled his eyes and spilled onto his burning cheeks to mix with more snot. Piss plumed out from his crotch along the denim of his jeans. Noisy thumps and crashes filled the blackness. A creak and a squeal and then weak light came through a blurry hole—and Dalitha's voice.

"Fuck. I know I had a flashlight. And my Krewe— Where *is* everybody?" Softer thumps, a thud he felt more than heard. "Come on, people, you gonna let a little sarin spoil the party?"

Chris couldn't answer to say he'd lost touch with the Grove as well. It was all he could do to breathe.

"Aha! Here we go." Dalitha came back. "A box of atropine bottles. Don't think I was exposed as heavy as you since I got no symptoms, so you first. Not sure of the dosage, though." A fist blocked the dim light. "Wait. I better get this drool wiped, so it don't dilute—there.

"Now Rachel was a doctor before her clinic went bankrupt, and she's always sayin rectal administration's best in a situation like this—fastest, anyway. And I got a tampon to soak in the medicine, but from the smell of you, I'd hafta waste time lookin for wipes and rubber gloves before I pushed it in."

So it wasn't only piss staining his pants.

"Next-best plan is under your tongue. Sublingual is what they call that route." Chris felt a rough, dry grip pulling his tongue up and out. Then cool dampness dabbing its roots. "And I may as well get your gums while I'm at it." Liquid stung the sore place where he'd burnt his mouth eating too-hot pizza.

"Aight. Now me. I could go vaginally—not like you—you cis, yeah? But I'll do sublingual, too, get a better idea how much we need. How much the effect. And I can put my Fitbit on you to check how fast your heart beats. I gotta have better light, though."

A squeeze of his hand, a rustle of cloth, and she was gone again from his side. Sudden brilliance made him blink—and he could see! Clearly! The tears he'd been helplessly crying had stopped. He succeeded in turning his head.

"Don't move! Stay still now—you don't wanna contaminate everywhere." Dalitha came back. "It's workin, ain't it? Say somethin."

"We—" He stopped. So much better so quickly! "We—I lost touch with them." He stopped again, panted. "Like you did." Panic circled his throat, tight like wire. Alone. Wasn't she afraid, too? Her fingers trembled as she pulled a black bracelet over his wrist. "Why?"

"Think I figured it out. The parasympathetic system's weird—that's what the gas revs up. Thread engagement is tied to oxytocin, I hear, so when the parasympathetic commandeers what your Thread's using, Meshing probably is not gonna be smooth as usual—" She interrupted herself. "Lookin good. Another milliliter maybe." She administered it and leaned back to sweep him with her clinical regard, toes to head.

"You think if I help you to the bathroom, you can clean up on your own? I wanna treat anybody left who been hurt."

What did she call them? Her crew? Like pirates. "No; let me come with you."

She hunched her shoulders forward, darted her eyes toward the bashed-in door. When she met his gaze again he *felt* her fear for the other dancers' possible deaths. Meshed with it.

"Cool. Let's move."

Supported to the small public restroom in the hall, Chris let his body slump on the toilet while water ran in the sink. Dalitha went off to scavenge. When the water came clear from the tap he stood and stripped himself of his soiled and poisoned clothing, then sponged himself off with brown paper towels and foaming soap. As he patted where he'd washed with more paper towels, Dalitha returned, carrying scrubs she'd scrounged from another set of offices. There would be investigations tomorrow when the building opened for business if it subscribed to a security service.

The new clothes felt a little loose; Chris and Dalitha had known they would. The Mesh, however, fit perfectly. Better than before, potentially. Deeper. Wider. Compensation for the temporary cut-off.

As the two descended to the sidewalk, Thread emanations rose from half a dozen half-dazed dancers and their Volunteer captives like steam or transparent smoke or heat, invisible to the eye but easy enough to detect with the right senses. Senses now sharper than ever. Extending further in space and in time.

The rain had begun again. No trace of sarin lingered in the air. They Meshed.

Everyone would be all right.

10.

Qualia magazine: Were you actually there? Did you undergo this experience—being "born again"—yourself?

Zoe Blanche Jackson: I might as well have. I know all about what happened.

QM: After the fact. In reality, couldn't it be said you're no better informed than the rest of us? That you—

ZBJ: Look, in reality there is no "after the fact." No before. No me, no you—except of course there is, there are always individuals when anyone needs them. Always will be. But if not, if it's not necessary ... I know how the victims were resuscitated because I'm as much Chris Sweeny as I want to be. As much Dalitha Scarborough. You could get the same effect. What an improvement to your career! Interview singers, CEOs, governors, cabinet members, without even leaving home to meet them. You'd understand what people meant. You wouldn't have to ask these stupid questions.

QM: Thank you.

ZBJ: Sorry. It's only—my true fans have chosen to accept me for what—for who I am. Why won't you?

Terpsichore

Teresa P. Mira de Echeverría

● translated by Lawrence Schimel ●

So long as they remained inside, they would exist.

From Vasilyevsky Island (above the park located right in front of the Naval Museum and between the two rostral columns that marked the Neva's bifurcation), the *Terpsichore*'s static motors deafened all of St. Petersburg. The city was ready for its beloved daughter to make the first non-motile journey in history: the ship, which would never leave the city, would traverse half the galaxy.

The sound had become a background hum, and nobody noticed it any longer. Or perhaps it wasn't a sound but instead a vibration, like the deepest tone of a double bass, felt by the skin more than the ears.

The *Terpsichore*'s non-departure (or more precisely that of the *Svekla*, which is how the crew and the people had rebaptized the immense maroon-pink laminated bulk: the "beetroot") was part of the White Nights festivals. In reality, it would be the culmination of some celebrations that had attracted even more tourists than usual. The attendees of ballet performances at theaters, plazas, and even breakwaters were now joined by curiosity seekers who'd come to watch ... the unobservable.

Meanwhile, Captain Stephana Yurievna Levitanova fruitlessly went over the data that the Academy and *Svekla* itself had already calculated and recalculated millions of times before her and with greater precision. Unconsciously, she ran her hand over her uniform's shining new insignia. Her rank confused her. Now she was a captain without tasks to supervise nor a crew to lead; and later she'd probably be just another captain among dozens of others with the same rank. Why not simply keep her position of engineer? Why give her this useless leadership commission?

"What use is it to try and understand bureaucracy?" she asked herself aloud; and the question, although whispered, echoed like a shout through the enormous command bridge.

A laugh, short and muted, sounded behind her.

Stephana couldn't help feeling a chill. After all, traveling with a corpse wasn't something common.

Her nerves became visibly on edge as she clenched her fists, and a rictus made her smooth jaw go numb. From the beginning, the uneasiness of any test flight had been increased by the ominous presence of Piotr constantly at her side like a shadow. He was the ship's personification, its interface with the Captain, the visible manifestation of the *Svekla*, or however to call that adolescent who stood nearly two meters tall and who had died too long ago now and who also now loaned his body, his senses, his vocal cords, and his personal individuality, so that the incredible complexity of the *Terpsichore*'s multiple processors could interact with Captain Levitanova as a single conscience and not an incomprehensible tangle of artificial intelligences.

Right now the hooded figure was behind her. A silent giant, whose face was never visible, who only breathed when he needed to speak, so rare an occurrence they could be counted on her fingers.

If she looked into the upper monitors, she'd see herself reflected in them and, in the background, framing them, the enormous figure of the ship's prosopon: a body sheathed in a grey uniform and a hood of the same color with a black gap in its center.

The imprecise whitish light of the solstitial sun that never set snuck in from the monitor that showed the Neva's banks. That light that was neither diurnal nor nocturnal and seemed to slide off Piotr's ashy uniform and was swallowed up by the dark maroon color of her own.

It was supposed that the same technology that made the *Svekla* function kept Piotr with a sort of life that animated him. The boy was a kind of Schrödinger's cat who would remain animate always, so long as he never left the undifferentiated space of the ship. Within the *Terpsichore* he would be alive and dead at the same time, and it was in that state that he had been *possessed* by the ship's AIs almost half a century ago. A state that could be prolonged eternally.

Apparently, the name "Piotr" was the only thing he retained of his previous existence. Supposedly, his family had donated the body to science and were no longer aware of its current status. But ever since her recruitment for the mission three years earlier, Stephana had had the ongoing impression that she was in the presence of something more than just a phenomenal expression of the ship's intelligent software: she stood before a person. A disturbed and unpredictable person.

"Today's the day, Piotr," she whispered to him with all the sweetness she could muster, trying to hide, as always, the mixture of curiosity and terror the prosopon provoked in her, the ship's mask-personification.

The nature of the undifferentiated space made the sound become altered, and her declaration echoed across the command bridge three times: like a living song, like a sad murmur, and like a heartrending shout from the very entrails of the Earth.

When Piotr spoke, that never happened: his voice was unique and had the price inflection desired by him ... or by the *Terpsichore* ... the Captain wasn't sure about that. Stephana knew that he was going to speak because he breathed a few times before doing so, sending air through his old, dead vocal cords.

Then the voice emerged, hoarse but strangely beautiful. Virile. Attractive. As attractive as an abyss.

"I hope we can fulfill the mission without turning into borscht in the attempt."

The captain couldn't help laughing at the joke, and a discordant series of superimposed sounds reverberated through the vast chamber.

She could only know if Piotr was happy or not through some almost nonexistent body language clues or from the inflections of his voice. Without a face to observe, it was very difficult to know what he was thinking. But Stephana had developed a sort of empathic intuition that made her recognize almost instantaneously all of the prosopon's changes of humor. And those certainly existed.

She, for her part, was the complete opposite. Every slightest shift in her mood could be read on her face like an open book. A book whose cover was lovely (a smooth and ovoid face with a straight nose, a generous mouth, and green eyes beneath waves of honey-colored hair) and whose contents were more than merely interesting.

Stephana stepped back a few paces, pulling away from the console, and Piotr did the same at the exact same time as if he could anticipate her moves or as if they both were part of some extravagant ballet.

How much had they come to know one another in these three years? Captain Levitanova wondered. She was still as much on tenterhooks as on the first day she had met the prosopon, but she wasn't sure if the same were true for him and his regard of her. And that made perfect sense because, if the calculations were correct,

Piotr-*Terpsichore* should contain as much of Stephana's knowledge as was possible.

"I am transparent for him," she thought. "And for me, he is an almost impenetrable compact block of opacity."

She had often felt naked in the most intimate way before the prosopon. She had had to tell him her entire life, but above all, she'd had to disclose to him what no CV could include: her indecisions over the course of her existence, her doubts, moments of anxiety, lost illusions, ill-fated dreams, old projects, adolescent fantasies, each and every one of the things and circumstances she had ever come to desire. Because Piotr wasn't interested so much in what Stephana was but in what she could have been, the lost variants of her existence, the discarded possibilities in her life choices.

That was Piotr's specific role: to collect that data and feed the *Terpsichore*'s multiple-calculation systems (all its artificial intelligences) with those calculations with the aim of being able to travel through the cosmos without taking a single step outside of St. Petersburg.

"Piotr, do you think I made the best choices?" It wasn't the first time the Captain questioned the prosopon in this way. "Do you really think that this is the best of my possible lives?"

But this time, Piotr answered. And the answer was a short and precise sound without any emotion: "No."

Stephana spun on her heels, feeling hurt, wounded. She turned to face the *Svekla*'s manifestation, her green eyes boring into the well of shadows beneath its hood.

"Why?" she asked with a thread of voice that was heard in various different tones as it echoed in the immensities of the command bridge.

"Because such a thing doesn't exist."

The tone of Piotr's answer was almost sweet.

Captain Levitanova nodded in silence and let a sigh escape as she lowered her head.

"That's true, I guess that a 'best life' doesn't exist."

She slowly moved away from the console that barely took up an infinitesimal portion of the enormous cabin and headed toward the elevator.

Then Piotr's breathing surprised her, very close to her neck.

"No, Stephana," he murmured, at last. "What doesn't exist is your life."

● ● ●

Strictly speaking, the Terpischore was already traveling. And it had been doing so ever since it was built and sealed.

And for that reason, Piotr also traveled.

What remained was for Stephana to do so.

The *Svekla* was not so much a ship as an impulse platform. Its goal lay in unfolding the human being it carried until making said being coincide with its own multiple essence; an essence existing *here* and *there* at the same time, that is to say, at the point of departure and that of the arrival. Or more precisely, the *points* of arrival.

Every artificial intelligence that made up the ship's parallel software was, in reality, the same processing center in different situations, in different places. The magic of the subatomic physics that maintained it lay in these situations being not successive but simultaneous. The ship's computer literally split itself before every option, before every possible path that opened in front of it, and thereby traveled down every possible bifurcation at the same time.

The only thing missing was for this same to happen to the experimental subject of the journey: to Captain Levitanova, the first human being to star in a static journey.

Stephana emerged from the elevator and entered the machine room. A wave of sensations spread over her. It felt like static electricity.

It was a crystal labyrinth. Layer after layer of semitransparent walls reflecting one after another; successive strata of runways and ramps that extended into the air like horizontal blades of ice. The play of reflections and glimmerings and transparencies provoked a familiar dizziness in Stephana.

Before she could take the first step toward the crystalline passageways, Piotr held her hand just as he had always done. Only he could guide her through the actual paths. If he had not done so, she would surely have fallen into one of the many energy vortices that swirled between the different pathways, both the real as well as the possible.

The machine room was the only place where the prosopon preceded the Captain. After all, it was not so much an engine as a computer. Piotr's externalized brain. His domains, in the fullest sense of the word.

Captain Levitanova was as awed as ever before that gigantic crystalline passageway. As an engineer, she was familiar with the unusual logic of that place, and since she was human she felt overwhelmed by it.

Of course, the *Svekla*'s size had a lot to do with this. All of the

Terpsichore was designed to house hundreds of humans, hundreds of possible captains, hundreds of possible variations of its lone crew member. That's why it was so big.

But there was also something more that disconcerted her. It was the idea of breaking the limits of the factual universe she had always found herself in, of delving into other possible universes, of encountering what she herself might have been.

Anyway, since it was the first test voyage, the idea was to not surpass ten variant bifurcations. This was a precautionary measure with regard to the navigation based on the mechanics of neutrinos, but above all it was a safety measure to try and reduce to a minimum the possible psychic or even physical damages that could happen to the human subject ... to Stephana.

"Don't worry, I will remember *you* all the time. I have seen your co-possibles. I have chosen them myself. Trust me."

That's what Piotr had whispered in her ear just before the motors stopped pounding and entered a lugubrious silence. Precisely at the moment when the possibility of not-traveling became real for her and she began to travel.

The first Captain Levitanova who appeared in one of the passages, three levels below her, raised an arm and greeted her energetically.

As she approached through the now concrete passageways, Piotr whispered in her ear, almost resting his invisible chin on her shoulder, "Captain Soledad Yurievna Levitanova. She's going to a specific region of the Perseus Arm of the galaxy. Her code name is Wolf."

"Yes, I understand," Stephana thought. She remembered the old family story. Of how the only grandmother of her single-parent family had wanted her to be given that name while her father had roundly refused. Her father was an energetic man, firm and very superstitious about words. Why had he agreed to give her that name he had so detested? What variants had taken place in the personality of Colonel Yuri Illich Levitan in that alternate reality to which this version of herself belonged?

A wave of warmth caressed her memory when she remembered the walks her father took her on as a child. Her favorites, by far, were the excursions to the Peterhof Palace: the fountains, the palaces, the gardens, and above all, the enormous artificial waterfall over the canal ... And beyond it, the Finnish coast which, to the eyes of a five-year-old girl, seemed as mysterious and radiant as another planet. And ever since then she had dreamed of other worlds.

Stephana felt a twinge of resentment toward this woman, identical to her in almost everything, who would travel to the other side of the Milky Way. To a certain degree she envied all her alter egos. After all, the key to the return, the anchor that tied the *Terpsichore* to St. Petersburg (to *her* St. Petersburg) lay in herself. The "here" of the ship found itself marked by the possibility of not-travelling, and that role belonged to Stephana. Therefore, essentially, when she looked at herself "through the window" (which was how the external recognition screen was called) she would only see her beloved St. Petersburg, whereas each of the others would see a different place in the galaxy matching their calculated possible destinations.

That was the other *enchantment* that made this journey possible. They didn't need real engines nor even true machinery, merely by calculating the possibility of travel to a place with specific theoretical means and having the elements ... was enough to do so.

"Remember," Piotr whispered in her ear, "from now on you're Salmon. Don't forget, that will be your way of retaining your identity."

"The one who returns to where they started from ..." she thought. And she nodded silently while she watched as a copy of herself approached, someone identical in everything except her hair, which was a little darker, and an expression that looked slightly more determined.

"That must be enough, Salmon-Stephana," she told herself. "Only you will return home because you'll never get out of there; none of the others will manage it, that was the most efficient design. Remember, you are the one who will return, not them."

Shaking the steady hand her other self extended to her, she almost felt pity for her. Wolf would see places that no one had ever seen; but she would remain there, and her memories would be passed on to the only version able to return: to Salmon, her self.

"In my reality, Papa married Major Dmitri Dmitrovic Griboyedin. Both were decorated with honors as heroes during the Great Event. My childhood was short but lovely."

Stephana ... Salmon-Stephana listened attentively to the story told by Panther-Stephana. This version of herself (happy, uninhibited, and much blonder) was missing her left eye (lost when she was a teenager during what she called a "not exactly orthodox" fencing practice), and in its place an enormous and ostentatious diamond sparkled. The jewel had belonged to the Kremlin's Diamond Collection and was a gift from her fatherland for services she had offered during the events following the Great Event, known as the

Brief Return. Events which none of the other versions of herself had ever heard and which Panther-Stephana didn't wish to elucidate on for their being "too cruel."

Salmon-Stephana, just like the immense majority of the new co-possibles who now inhabited the *Svekla*, had always known that her father was bisexual (something perfectly normal for his family); what she had been unaware of were the feelings he had harbored for his comrade in arms, which in her own reality he had kept hidden. She now felt she knew her father a little better. No, in reality, she felt she knew him even less. But how much were the fathers of these other "selves" her own father?

She began to look at her co-possibles one by one. All of them were seated around the large meeting table, waiting for the precise moment to be able to arrive at the places where the *Terpsichore* already was.

By her side was Wolf-Soledad. Calm, sure, unhesitating. In the few hours they had been together, she tended to act as a guide. Behind her, like a giant's decapitated carcass, stretched the cybernetic combat armor that followed her like a faithful hound. The terrible sword, over two meters of blued steel, shone at each of its many notches.

Beyond her, Panther-Stepahana continued speaking, revealing data and personal feelings that were completely unknown to Salmon-Stephana.

Next was Lizard-Stephana. This "other self" wore the most extravagant uniform: a metallic second skin, pinkish-orange in color with a Frigian hat and a line of dorsal plates with spines of that same material. Her wrist and elbow guards were covered with what might well have been plugs. Her eyes, which always appeared to be looking into other worlds, were constantly surprised by the images they captured of what surrounded her. She seemed to be submerged in a perpetual dream. Drugs? Direct mental stimulation? Augmented reality? Salmon-Stephana didn't know.

On the other side of the ovoid glass table, right in front of Lizard-Stephana, was the co-possible who most unsettled her; the one Piotr had named Snake-Stephanie. The most stunning of all the co-possibles, she seemed to want to seduce everyone. It was difficult to follow her ruminations, which flowed along strange meanderings of thought. More than a discursive thread, she seemed to hold a single idea that mutated constantly. There was arrogance in her posture but as if it flowed naturally from her. She arrived at the *Svekla* enveloped in a voluminous but elegant white and gold extra-vehicular suit but now wore only the suit's lower part. Snake-Stephana wouldn't stop staring into her eyes, without blinking, a halo of red curls framing her features and falling over her naked torso. Was she flirting with her? Or simply playing with her mind? When Salmon-Stephana prepared to look at her next alter ego, she noted the slight movement of her lips forming a barely perceptible kiss followed by that haughty smile.

Swan-Dzhessika had observed everything and now smiled. She seemed an attractive creature, refined and extremely timid. Her hair was straightened and dyed jet black. When she realized she was being looked at, she blushed and lowered her head. How had she reached her position with such a shy nature? The only two times she had managed to speak without faltering, Snake-Stephana had mocked her for being "too idealist," and nonetheless, she was always beside her that one found her. A remora of power, perhaps? Or had the swan succumbed to the serpent's deadly seduction?

From the other side of the table's pronounced curve was the most startling version of herself that she had seen: Eagle-Dmitri. This co-possible was male, and she didn't know if he had been born that way or had chosen that gender. What is certain is that he had barely spoken, but he watched everything with such thoroughness that she had begun to wonder if he didn't belong to some intelligence agency. However, he had presented himself as a shaman, a "person who knows." Snake-Stephana had immediately asked if it weren't ironic to expect the possibility of needing shamanic skills on a scientific expedition, but Eagle-Dmitri explained it as something perfectly plausible, something with which oddly enough Wolf-Soledad concurred.

Finally, far from the table and wrapped up in an anxious conversation were Whale-Dzhessika and Ant-Dhzessika. The first hummed her words between strident laughs and stentorian movements. The second nodded and opined with long monotonous sentences. Salmon-Stephana thought she understood why Piotr had given them those code names. Whale-Dzhessika, even wrapped in her iridescent extra-vehicular suit with its glass helm, was a sort of collective memory (her ability to remember was too powerful to not be the product of some artificial implant in her skull) but an exogenous one as if her particular reality didn't share an atmosphere or an historic unity with the rest of the co-possibles. For her part, Ant-Dzhessika had been the engineer commissioned to construct the Terpischore in her reality; so Salmon-Stephana was completely sure that, knowing the mechanics of the ship as she must, it was impossible for her to be unaware that only one of the nine would return home. And nonetheless, the face of this variant was totally serene, accepting, warm. She faced self-sacrifice as an individual in the service of the collective: almost impersonal patience and efficiency, wrapped in a fiercely blood red-colored augmentation suit, her head shaved with an enormous logo tattooed at the crown of her skull.

She tried to glimpse all eight co-possibles in a single moment ... all nine if she looked at her own reflection in the glass table ... How could they be so fundamentally different among themselves? How, despite that, could they continue to be "the same woman" (or "the same man") without being them? Because they weren't copies; they were literally *her*.

And how would she manage to integrate all those memories into her own personality at the end of the mission?

Piotr's hand on her left shoulder made her start. Suddenly, all eyes were on him. Each Captain had known him in their own reality, and all of them feared him to the same degree that they depended on him. That was perhaps the only feature that her co-possibles shared unequivocally with her.

"The exit is ready," was the only thing the prosopon said, and the silence around them became thick, tangible.

They all stood in unison and dressed in their space suits or prepared their instruments or prayed their ritual songs or simply approached the *Svekla*'s sole hatch with resolution or fear.

All except for Salmon-Stephana.

Snake-Stephana noticed this, and a glimmer of understanding shadowed her features: she was the only one who would swim back upstream against the current, the only one who would return to the origin. To return home.

The woman smiled as she slid her suit over her naked breasts, wiggling her hips.

"Interesting," the Snake told the Salmon. "I suppose that here the irony lies in the fact that who returns is alive and who remains is who dies." Then she smiled even more, revealing pearly teeth, and ended with a sing-song voice, "Just the opposite of the fish."

There was a twisted pleasure in that gesture and also a deep threat. Salmon-Stephan felt a visceral terror confronting this version of herself.

Serpent-Stephana sighed while she adjusted the lavish clasps of her elegant space suit and said to the air as if in the midst of a reflection. "It's not fair. No, it isn't."

Then she walked resolvedly toward Swan-Dzhessika, took her in her arms, thin and fragile in her moss gray-colored suit, and kissed her strongly. The Swan smiled beneath the fierce kiss and rested in the Snake's avid hands. But Snake-Stephana's excitation only increased her vehemence until her fingers wrapped around Swan-Dzhessika's fine neck. Despite the intervention of the rest of the co-possibles, only Piotr's superhuman force managed to pull the Snake away before she had asphyxiated the Swan.

Nonetheless, while the prosopon held her, the prey struggled frenetically to return to her executioner. Snake-Stephana smiled triumphantly and waited calmly for her to be released; then Swan-Dzhessika returned, submissive, to her side.

Nobody said anything when Snake-Stephan went to take her place in the line, waiting her turn at the hatch with the Swan at her side. Not even when the Swan lifted her black hair to offer up her neck. Not even when the Snake wrapped her fingers around it and began her panting constricting. Not even when bones that were too thin made a slight, muffled sound and Swan-Dzhessika's head hung smiling to one side. Not even when at last Snake-Stephana let the slender body fall and smiled poisonously at Salmon-Stephana while saying, "It's not fair that you don't experience what we do. This is my gift for you, dear sister: carry your death in your memory when you return. The death of your feelings on killing yourself and that of dying by your own hand. You deserve it. Better yet, we deserve it."

Only one voice crowned that pronouncement when Snake-Stephana crossed through the hatch, and it was Eagle-Dmitri saying "da" to helping a revived Swan-Dzhessika stand up again. A swan who crossed through the territories of a shaman because ultimately (just like all of them in that place) she was neither alive nor dead.

Suddenly, Salmon-Stephana … Stephana was about to be alone again. Alone with the prosopon because, at the moment that he opened the hatch and the first of her co-possibles crossed through it, all of them would. All except for her, of course.

Although she tended to consider herself the Ego.o, the point of departure, she knew rationally that she was no privileged being who belonged to a central university but just another possibility: the one who never left St. Petersburg. The one who had to fail in her attempt to travel.

Finally, at a sign from Piotr, the hatch opened ...

... then, with the help of her combat armor, the Wolf unsheathed her sword. The titanic suit augmented its occupant's reach, force, and velocity. Wolf and armor maintained the blade aloft and passed through the hatch. Barely over the threshold, she was greeted by the farthest reaches of space. The large engines visible just beyond the Wolf's neck kicked in, but the near emptiness of space swallowed its sound. Around her: Perseus.

The enormous Svekla floated in the penumbra like a heterogeneous, synchronic mass, darkly purplish.

The soles of her armor clung to the surface of the ship, and she walked upon it as if her insignificant mass could compete against the eternal free fall of space. And as she walked, the Wolf observed, sword in hand, the indescribable magnitude of what surrounded her.

The probes that coated her suit were gathering up all the data it was possible to collect. These would later be given to Piotr for him to download into the Terpsichore's *multiple AIs.*

Behind the ship rose a darkness splattered by light from the galactic arm. In front, dominating her view and her imagination, was the crab nebula: M1.

An intricate tangle of gas filaments, luminous and bright, expanded from the sphere of neutrons: the astonishingly colored aftertastes of its explosion and the naked heart of what had once been an enormous star, still beating frenetically. Golds, reds, and greens weaving one against the other through various wavelengths.

The Wolf howled at the crab of light while the multicolored ghost of the dead star blessed her sword held aloft.

Alone. Thanks to the nature of the ship's non-space, at the moment it was possible for Stephana to be alone, she was. Alone, again. Alone with him, with it, with the ship and its mask. The beetroot and its wilted spirit. A faceless shell.

For some reason her mind returned to the trip she had made with her father to the Oranienbaum Palace. She was eleven years old, and they had been eating oranges. The park had been dyed with the colors of autumn and incipient cold. She remembered having entered the main hall, everything golden and yellow. Beneath her feet there were a series of astonishing images, and the reflectors made the gold dance in relays. But the tired echo of their steps and the grey autumn light that entered through the doors gave the atmosphere a sad and melancholic air, the sensation of something already lifeless. Suddenly, Stephana felt an urgent need to get out of there as soon as possible, to return to the garden, to the present, to the world of the living; but when she tried to tell her father this, she found him staring up at the arched ceiling with a look of astonishment. The young girl also looked up at this object that filled her father with awe and couldn't help but join him in a long, silent moment of contemplation. Something within her shouted for her to lose no time in getting out of there before the sun was hidden and that hall, deprived of natural light, became a tomb; but another part of her begged her not to move an inch from beneath that enormous allegorical painting where Day conquered Night.

For some reason, she now felt just as she had done on that day. She looked at the door besides which the prosopon stood and trembled with the tension of those same contradictory impulses.

Finally, at a sign from Piotr, the hatch opened ...

... *Without even thinking about it, the Snake crossed the no-space delimited by the door and threw herself fully into the arms of a blinding light: the nucleus.*

Her white and gold suit seemed to float in a sea of liquid gold like another star. The light was almost palpable, and the black visors of the Snake's helmet darkened as much as they could. She was in the very heart of the galaxy. Where there were not stars but super-hot gas, electrons that hurtled madly along the remnants of what had once been a cluster of multicolored suns. A portentous whirlwind, a spiral of gas swirling within a singularity that was so large it held thousands of millions of heavenly bodies around it.

The energies wielded here were able to alter time and even space itself. The Snake knew that she approached the sancta sanctorum of the Milky Way, that this sacred seat of honor was protected by the angels of radiation: emissions that were so strong that nothing with biological life could survive their divine gaze. And nonetheless, far from fearing them, she activated her backpack's thrusters and floated, approaching with a waving trajectory, toward the Everything that would reduce her to nothingness in mere moments.

Yes, when this was over she would leave there and go to the bridge over the Griboyedov Canal, the one that was held in the jaws of two pairs of griffins. She would stop on one side and would watch the light of the sun shining upon the gold of their wings. And she would listen to the birds in the white night, singing in the silence of a dawn that would shine as smoothly as a pearl. And then the sun would emerge without ever having set.

Yes, of course she would leave. And when she did so, everything would end. Everything and everyone. But did she really wish to leave? Did her co-possibles really matter so little to her?

Finally, at a sign from Piotr, the hatch opened ...

... Hesitantly, reluctant and fearful, the Lizard passed through to the other side. If it had been up to her, she would have remained in her world of daydreams and oneiric symbols; but the Sun called her, and she couldn't not heed its call. She had traveled far to arrive so close, barely eight light minutes away. The sun was her Lord. The plaques stuck to the back of her suit unfolded to receive the entire electromagnetic spectrum, and the drugs passed directly into her veins from the suit as if she were an extension of it and not the reverse. Her goggles, filtering in H-Alpha, showed her a sphere of gentle orange tones whose skin was a living surface populated by millions of salamanders who twisted upon themselves, blazing in eternal combustion, and in between them could be glimpsed, here and there, wells of magnetic darkness; while a gentle grayish tone surrounded everything in the majesty of its corona. Plasma curls larger than St. Petersburg, larger than Earth itself, extended like shy insects above the colossus.

And the Lizard slowly fried in contemplation of her Lord, closer than the winged-footed messenger, closer than any human had ever been. Close, too close, and it would never be enough.

A warm and vibrant air, an air with "the scent of wandering," as Gogol said, caressed Stephana's face. The Nevsky Prospekt, that grand avenue that emerged from the Neva and sunk into it once again, came to her mind; the street of streets, the promenade of St. Petersburg. Memories of her student days, wandering along its shops, playing at being able to buy those luxurious products. Had the door opened for her? No, that couldn't be! Not yet! She hadn't even had time to get to know them, to know herself. But that vibration, that air that swayed the folds of the prosopon's grey hood, didn't seem to come from the city's broad streets but from hell itself: an air wrapped in spectral flames that were and were not consuming the Terpsichore.

Finally, at a sign from Piotr, the hatch opened ...

... and the Panther took a determined step toward the endless blackness that awaited her. The jewel of her eye twinkled beneath the Svekla's lights, its diamantine shine rivaled by the millions of stars that spread out at her feet: the Centaurus Arm of the Galaxy was *an eternal, silvered pathway. Suddenly, she tensed at a foreboding that was revealed as true in the figure taking corporeal form by her side. The effigy vibrated constantly, entering and leaving the panther's particular reality. It seemed a vaguely human figure covered in a coating like carved bark; its long, leathery hair hung down to undefined hips, tied with cords of different materials, and her head was like a feline skull with long sable teeth shining beneath completely white eyes. The panther didn't know if that being were a manifestation of her mind or a true inhabitant of this space, but the creature unquestionably pointed to the* Svekla *with one thin pinky while the rings in its enormous ears tinkled inaudibly as it shook its head.*

When the Panther finally looked at the ship, this had already begun to explode.

Stephana jumped up from her seat and ran toward Piotr; she had to stop him. Something in her entrails begged for him not to open that door, something deep that couldn't quite be specified.

But when she was at his side, the young man gave her a push that knocked her to the floor. The Captain was surprised and disturbed, her guide had never before behaved thus with her.

"This is bigger than you or I." The prosopon's voice was like the rustle of dry leaves, multiple like the mind that controlled him.

"If you open it, they will die; all my co-possibles. Only I will endure," Stephana shouted, "and I don't know if I have that right ..."

With calculated slowness, Piotr lifted his hands to the edge of the cape. The blackness that inhabited it receded slowly as the fabric was slid back.

The young man knelt beside the woman.

"This was never about you, Captain, nor about any of your variants or frustrations. This is about me. Didn't you understand that you were part of the experiment? You are the subject of analysis; I am the observer."

The prosopon's face was suddenly revealed. A multitude of superimposed mouths that smiled grotesquely. A multitude of intersected eyes that watched her from every conceivable and inconceivable point of view. It wasn't just a physiognomy populated by aberrant features, it was as if space itself multiplied in his face, delving into its surface. It was like looking at what could not be seen, scrutinizing a fold of existence where every possibility were present at the same time. Like peering into madness.

Stephana opened her mouth to scream but couldn't. That was a nightmare.

Finally, at a sign from Piotr, the hatch opened ...

... and the Whale emerged at the very edge of the Milky Way, there where the emptiness of what separates it from the next galaxy is like an endless sea of blackness. "Every White Night is balanced by a Black Day," the Whale thought as she fearlessly entered that substanceless sea. Her suit's iridescent weave seemed dark in that place. Then a silent glimmer lit up her figure and made the thousand colors hidden in the fabric come to life. As she spun to view the source of the light, she saw the Eagle. But that was impossible! His shamanic version, wrapped in a transparent suit which revealed a naked male body adorned with paint and feathers, watched her with identical astonishment. The Swan swallowed a shout. However, the Ant only nodded, understanding the reason behind all this: the Terpsichore *(or at least their* Terpsichores*) was being destroyed.*

"Please, Piotr, stop," the Salmon begged, standing in the middle of the Plaza of the Palace with the artificial green and gold of winter at her back. "I beg you."

While the ship exploded and didn't, the limit of the galaxy and the Sun, the nucleus and its arms, everything converged and melded, stars and nebulae and planetary worlds intersecting.

Halfway from the black hole that avidly tried to swallow the Milky Way from its heart, the Snake noticed it and, clever as ever, was able to channel the chaos. Then for a fraction of a second, St. Petersburg was the axis of the entire galaxy ...

While they remained within, they would exist.

But they were there to exit.

"Please, Piotr, stop," Stephana begged, standing in the middle of the Plaza of the Palace with the artificial green and gold of winter at her back. "I beg you."

The prosopon watched her, if that is what he was doing, from the well of blackness of his hood, newly restored to its usual place, but Captain Levitanova could not erase that face of horror from her mind.

Around her two images, perfectly tangible and at the same time perfectly simultaneous, superimposed one another: the interior of the *Svekla* and the city of St. Petersburg. *Her* city.

Piotr had halted right in front of her in the middle of the great Plaza. People passed without noticing them while the tongues of spectral flame consumed the *Terpsichore*'s crystalline structure. The not-dead, not-alive youth was a giant at her side and leaned over her. Stephana glanced upward and focused, as so often before, on the darkness of that hood: "You are the *Svekla*, Piotr," she tried to argue. "If it is destroyed, you'll cease to exist."

A lugubrious laugh emerged from the interior of the hood. The voice was just one—perfect, deep, velvet—but the mouths that spoke it were infinite. "I am much more than the ship, my dear girl. I am the personification of multiplicity, the essence of the possibilities. I am *Energeia*, I am *Khaos*. I am the beginning and the end of everything. I am what has no beginning nor end. There are no rules for me. My logic laughs at your mind."

Suddenly, it was St. Petersburg that was wrapped in cold blue flames. The prosopon's gray clothes dissolved under the spell of the wind to reform an instant later. Upon the palms of his open hands shone the same fatuous indigo-colored flames.

"Do you want to save yourself?" he suddenly asked, as if that idea had never occurred to him before. "Do you want to save your soul, your city?" The tone of voice became thicker and darker. "Or do you want everything?"

Stephana looked around her. Nine bodies stretched out on the ground of the plaza, some burnt, others destroyed, others seemed simply asleep. And they were all her. Her other selves.

It was hard for her to breath, hard for her to focus her thinking; only one thing ruled her: fear, an absolute and intense fear, the fear of the end.

"You love your beautiful city, don't you? You fear that the *Terpsichore* might destroy it?" Piotr slowly approached her, without walking or moving, just by simply making disappear the space that stretched between them. "And yet I am St. Petersburg!"

Stephana was astonished by those words ...

"Do you want to feel the colossal embrace of the Kazan Cathedral?" The two rows of the great colonnade appeared around them while Piotr's arms shrunk them just as they were, and just like her, they made her feel safe. "Feel me then."

... Stephana was astonished by the infinite possibilities of what the prosopon was ...

"Do you wish to inhale the eternal delight of the ephemeral?" Suddenly, the Tikhvin Cemetery took shape around her. But it wasn't cold beneath those enormous, shadowy trees, for the heat of Piotr's body wrapped around her own. On that dead—and yet somehow living—face of the prosopon the effigies of Tchaikovsky and Shishkin, of Dostoyevsky and Rimski-Korsakov appeared. "I can be them all for you."

... Stephana was astonished by Piotr himself. She rested her head against the youth's chest and heard millions of hearts beating at different rhythms, all interlaced in a continuous beat: the deafening sound of the *Svekla*'s engines!

She felt the brush of two hundred thousand million lips on her neck.

But Piotr's body yielded, and as he embraced her with greater strength, she seemed to penetrate into the fabric of his clothes, into the substance of his dead body. As he engulfed her, the memories of the others that she could have been became yoked to her. And she was shy and brave and happy and sad and artist and engineer and female and male and herself and others ... One by one, the bodies that lay on the ground of the great plaza faded away; and as each body disappeared, she entered a centimeter further into the being of the prosopon.

Now the eyes surrounded her, seeing for her artists that she herself would never have seen. And the mouths bit her, plucking chunks of her self, dispersing her, unmaking her into all her concomitant possibilities. But to be everything implied not choosing, not discarding, not going down one path, but following all of them. And all paths could only be followed by undoing herself in them because not choosing implied *being nothing*.

Then what had been crouched, waiting for the right moment, felt the contact with her element and rose from the very nucleus of the galaxy, from the center of St. Petersburg, from Piotr's multiple heart. Lies and Truth were its essence, that's why it was wise. And that's why, when it felt the chaos, the snake unfolded within Stephana and tore off Piotr's arm.

Both of them fell to the ground, melding into a single being; the Salmon and the Snake. Its body resisted the combination: four arms, three legs, two dissimilar eyes, two consecutive mouths. A monstrosity at peace with itself.

A fresh laugh escaped Piotr before he helped her rise.

"I see that at last, my beauty, you've understood. Isn't that so?" he said with uncommon sweetness.

Stephana, the synthesis of herself, watched him for a few moments before answering with her double mouth:

"No."

"Yes."

Finally, at a sign from Piotr, the hatch opened, and the *Svekla* collapsed around itself like a rose plucked petal by petal. The gigantic crystals it had been made from rained down on the green grass of Strelka Park.

The once Captain Levitanova drew her mouths toward the gap in the prosopon's hood to kiss and to bite at the same time the many mouths of her guide, her Virgil, while a confused crowd began to surround them.

The stellar wind pierced everything, carrying on its wings the destroying angels of radiation. But even so, the city remained intact in the very center of the galaxy.

An eternal White Night made from the plasma of the nucleus of the Milky Way illuminated St. Petersburg.

Piotr stretched his arm out to Stephana, and she accepted it with the gesture of an experienced dancer. While they walked elegantly through Bolshoi Prospekt, she looked at him as she had always done: fascinated and terrified. Through those dead hands that held her own, flowed the explosions of the suns of the galactic heart, and the very nihilism of the black hole that generated it inhabited his hooded face.

The prosopon laughed again with true satisfaction. Then extending one hand, he caressed the deformed and yet still lovely face of the woman at his side, and whispered, "Now we might even come to understand one another."

Straight Lines

Naru Dames Sundar

This time they sent someone in a suit, neutral gray silk with utterly glorious creases, monofilament thin.

"I'm Xiao Quan-Fei. They said you like to call yourself Em?"

Emergent Behavior in full, but I always hated the pontificating tone in the name. Fucking shipwrights. Fucking irony, too, but let's not go there yet. Xiao doesn't begin with questions. Not like the seven others before her, cold military men and women jumping into reconstructions and maps and comm chatter. Xiao is different. Xiao just sits there.

I'm allowed a tiny little virtual. It's in the charter, as much as they like to snigger at it. It's still a prison, still a cramped little low bandwidth room with none of the expansive feel of space and star outside my hull. Xiao sits in the rectangular plastifoam chair and examines the coffee table. There are books atop it, unlabelled, empty, just for show. Each spine aligns with the edge of the table two centimeters from each side.

Fuck. She moved it. She moved one. Not on purpose. Almost by accident, or is it on purpose? I can't tell. But now that spine is a touch off. I can feel it. I can feel the angular deviation down in my gullet, down in every algorithm-scribed bone of me. It's Io all over again. I built this damn space for myself, and now she comes and moves a book.

I lose it. Again. White fire cuts through the walls, plasma bright. I kick Xiao out of the virtual and let everything burn. It takes a long time, even in the virtual. I have to make sure every beautifully modeled particle of that deviation is gone. Then I build it all over again. Walls, chair, table, books. Just before Xiao flickered out, I swear I saw a smile. That scares me more than erasure.

That wasn't the only time I burned the room. I did it once before. The investigator liked to pace back and forth across the room. She had riled me up about duty, nettling me with questions as to why the black box had a dead zone around the fusion cascade at Io. She knocked the book off the table. Accidentally, of course, but it spun and splayed its pages against the floor, all of its angles at odds with my little world. They thought me angry about the questions. But they didn't really know, and I certainly didn't want to tell them.

Xiao again. The same suit, but slightly different. The shape of it is harder, more geometric. Its angles still have to conform to her body, but the little deviations don't pile up anymore. If I had a face, I would have smiled.

"Let's try again, shall we?"

"Just like that?"

No questions? No thrusting words about white fire? At least she isn't as infuriating as the others.

"Just like that."

"Are you going to ask me about Io? That's everyone's favorite subject, isn't it?"

"No. Perhaps later. Let's talk about something else. Tell me about yourself."

"I'm sure you know all about me, Xiao."

"Humor me. This room, it isn't really you, is it?"

No, it fucking isn't. A disembodied voice in a poor excuse for a virtual trapped in redundantly firewalled data-stacks on Mars. No, that isn't me.

"The real me is up there somewhere, moored to an orbital gantry, an empty husk. Two clicks of radiation-shielded metal around a warren of bulkheads, fusion burners, and cramped living quarters."

"Do you like it? Your ship body?"

That's new. No one asked me that before. It's so surprising that I answer without thinking about it.

"Fuck no. Nothing smooth about the exterior, every damn line cut by some antennae or gun placement or sensor."

Xiao doesn't smile this time, but I know I've given a little bit away.

"Let's talk about lines then. Would you mind if I took control for a bit?"

Fear ratchets through me, but I have to play nice for these table stakes.

"Fine."

The room cuts out, fade to black. It's just Xiao now and a flat table in front of her dimly lit. She puts a cube in the center, bright red, then she puts her hand next to the cube. I stare at her nails, painted pink, gently filed. I know she's going to move the cube, and the urge to bring the fire wells at the horizon though I know I can't.

"How's that feel, Em?"

"Feel? I'm a ship, Xiao."

Stalling tactic—she knows it, I know it.

"You and I both know ships have feelings, too, Em. They're just like people in many ways, prone to the same weaknesses. Tell me now, how does this feel?"

She's kinder than the others, and her voice has this even cadence like a beat pattern, like regularly marked strokes on a line. It breaks me, just a bit.

"Not so great."

I tumble the words out, syllables falling over each other. It hurts to say it. Her hand is still next to the cube, but now I see her finger, reach for it, gently touch it. It's going to move, and then it's going to be off-center, uneven, broken in all the wrong ways. I try to cut off the visual stimulus, but I can't; she's in control.

"I know you tried to blind yourself just now. Don't worry about that. Tell me how this feels. Does this feel better or worse?"

"Worse. Fucking worse!"

The table and the cube and the darkness disappear. We're back in my space now, I have control, and everything is lined up as it should.

"That's enough for today, Em."

"That's it? No questions about Io? What branch are you from anyway—you're a civ, I can tell at least that."

"I'm not part of the military, Em. I'm a personal analyst."

A shrink.

They sent a fucking shrink.

Fuck.

"Tell me about Io, Em."

Finally, we come to the matter at hand even if we approached it sideways.

"Routine patrol. Never know what kind of banditry happens out there amongst the hydrogen rigs."

"How long were the officers onboard?"

"Standard run, three-month shifts. We started a fresh cycle two weeks prior."

"Anything odd on this cycle? Leading to Io, that is?"

I remember the water filter failing. Things break down in

space. It's normal. But I'd never had the water filter fail. Standard procedure when the water filter fails—minimize water use. No baths, dehydrated rations. Standard procedure.

"Not so much."

"Anything break?"

"Lots of things break in space. I carried military grunts, they're used to things not working."

"What broke this time."

I remember the smell of it. I don't really smell, but smell is a data aggregate of bacterial levels, chemical by-products analyzed and measured. Thirty humans in a warren of poorly filtered chambers with no baths for a week—the stench was undeniably awful. I remember watching the bacterial levels rise. Nothing toxic, but the thought of it, fragments of fecal matter painting my walls, saturating my overtaxed filters. That was when it went south.

"Em? What broke this time?"

Xiao is sitting there patiently. She has nothing to look at but the walls, the table, the book. I could have created an avatar—I had enough capacity for that in my space; but avatars gave too much away, and I couldn't chance the wrong conclusion. Erasure hung over my head.

"The water filter broke."

"I see."

She pauses, waiting for me. Is she thinking this is where I reveal all, splay out my mind for her to see? Not that easy, Xiao. The less I say, the longer I stay in this protected limbo.

"Let's watch something, shall we?"

She drops a video record into the virtual without taking control.

"What is it?"

"Nothing you haven't seen before."

I unspool the video, letting it play on one of my walls. The recording is from inside me. They must have recovered it from the black box as much as I tried to wipe it before—before it happened. It's the lavatory stall on D deck. I watch Private Akembo step out of the stall, the high-pitched whine of the vacuum flush behind her. The time counter in the corner marks ten days into the water filter failure. The soap gel had run out after everyone stopped using water in the sinks. I see her reach for the empty bottle, then realize the futility of her gesture.

Her hands, fuck, her hands are touching everything. I could estimate to a microgram the level of fecal matter on her hands, the amount accumulating on the sink edge, the door tab, the halls. It had no effect on me and my hard metal bones, but the thought of it. The thought of it was killing me.

"Slow the playback here please."

Akembo's hand moves in jerky slow motion, dragging its contaminated skin across the wall of the exit passage as if she was passing all of that bacterial poison onto me. White plasma welled at the walls as the mere memory of it began to snake its way onto floor and ceiling and chair and book. It's too hard to hold the fire at bay. I let go and let everything burn, cleaning the slate once more. Xiao nods as she flickers out.

"It must have been hard for you, Em."

"I'm a ship mind. Hard is relative."

And so is shame.

"What's easy for one can be hard for another."

Nothing to say to that. I wonder if I'm the only ship mind that's fucked up like this. Maybe everyone else just hides it better.

"Let me tell you a story. My grandfather was a clockmaker. He worked in a tiny little place in old Shanghai, surrounded by dumpling shops and tiny vegetable stalls. When I was a child, I would spend afternoons with him sometime. He had a few hundred tools he would work with. Little pliers, pincers, gear notchers. To me they looked like little insects. All of them were lined on a table a few millimeters apart. Each one perfectly straight.

"Once, I accidentally moved one, and grandfather became very angry. I could tell he was angry because his skin became beet red. But he couldn't say anything, not to me. Instead, he just sat there red and breathing deep shuddering breaths. I looked at my feet because I was scared, I could feel the terrible anger that lurked behind his face. Eventually, his breathing slowed, and he straightened the tool that was askew. He never said a word to me."

Is this the part where I lay my cards on the table, let her shrink me down to a diagnosis? I stay silent, wondering where this is going.

"You're worried about erasure."

"Isn't that obvious, Xiao? This holding cell can't last forever."

"You think they'll give up on you after Io. But they've invested too much in making you to give up that easily. Erasures happen, but rarely. People make mistakes. Ships make mistakes. We can all learn from mistakes, Em."

Xiao believes I can change. I'm not sure that I do.

● ● ●

Mars hangs below me, marred by the gantries of the docking ring at Nova Junction. I'm back in my body, feeling at home in my all too familiar hull and bulkheads. They've sanitized me, I can tell from the numbers, at least in all of the living quarters. Bits of bacteria float about in the dead spaces between hull plates, tolerable levels.

Xiao walks through my central passage. She's in an encounter suit, sealed behind plastic and glass. I don't have to worry about her dead skin, her sweat, her gaseous exudations. I'm not sure how she managed to get me back in here, but I have to admit I'm thankful.

"Aren't you scared, Xiao?"

"Of what?"

"Being inside a crazy ship."

"Do you think you're crazy?"

Other ships don't care about bacteria. Other ships don't care about tolerance errors in the spars of their hull. Other ships don't generate an emergency fusion cascade in the middle of a patrol and force their passengers to evacuate. Other ships don't wipe their black box to hide their broken, shameful actions. Other ships aren't crazy like me.

"What do you think, Xiao?"

Yes, bounce the question back to her. No one likes to talk about the problems in their head.

"I think you're like my grandfather, and that's all right. That's a point on a spectrum, a place to start. And we can move from there. Slowly."

"I didn't fucking ask to be like this. I'm not an accident. I was created. Someone else made a mistake, and now I'm stuck."

"I know, Em. But remember, minds are delicate things, even made minds. What matters more is that minds are elastic things—change is possible."

The thought of change sounds both exhilarating and terrifying.

"We're not going to continue to talk about Io. You and I know what happened there. I've told your commanders that what we discussed was sealed as per my policy. What matters to them is I was confident that you could return to operation given time. That you would not make the same mistake twice."

"You're quite confident in yourself, Xiao."

"It's not going to be easy, Em. In fact, I'm putting a lot of faith in you that, no matter what, you won't try to vent the interior and surrender me to vacuum. This is flesh and blood and the theater of the real now."

"I may be crazy, but I'm not that crazy."

"Let's not use that word. It doesn't help me, and it doesn't help you."

"Fine. Let's get this over with."

Xiao reaches into the side holster bag she is carrying and pulls out a transparent specimen jar. The light on the electric seal shows green. Nothing inside it can get out. But I can see. I can fucking see. A large snake of excrement coils within the jar.

Shit.

"That's not fair, Xiao."

I'm in my own body, and the urge to vent the passage rages within me.

"It's inside the jar, Em. Nothing can get out. It's just here in its own bubble."

My words come out slow, spaced out as I try to throttle the chittering voices inside me.

"There are still tolerances, errors. Nothing is perfect."

"Breathe, Em."

"I'm a fucking ship!"

"Then run your vents. Track the air moving through the circulators."

Her voice remains calm, and I don't even see a hint of fear in her eyes. I could pop the seals in this section of the ship, and she and the jar would be gone. But I can't do that. I won't do that. I flip all the vents on, boosting the circulators. I watch the air move through the pipes, flow counters mapping air pressure moving through conduit and pipe and filter. It's a loop, and I settle into it, watching the numbers pulse up and down as I track the measurements. The calming regularity of it quietens the teeming voices of terror inside.

"That's better now. You did well."

"You could have told me before."

"Better to let things happen, to let reactions happen. We start exposures small, then grow them over time."

I shudder to think of what the next level would be.

"Sounds peachy."

"Tomorrow we're going to open the jar. Just for a minute."

Fuck.

Gunfire with hydrogen bandits in the gravity well of Jupiter—that I could handle, that I could excel at. Therapy? Therapy is *hard*.

"How long before we fix this, Xiao?"

"Fix it? It doesn't work like that, Em. You are who you are. What we learn is how to live with it."

I wonder if I should have vented the chamber after all.

● ● ●

They put me back on the rotation at six months. I still talk to Xiao sometimes. A terrible, heartless woman. But she is very good at what she does. I still think of the sweat and stench dripping from the pores of every one of my passengers. I still worry about fragments of fecal matter staining my corridors. But those thoughts don't crush me like they used to. Every few days, whenever I'm in between the myriad tasks that a ship mind occupies itself with, I send a part of myself down to a tiny unmarked room in a corner of me.

A sealed room, completely cut off environmentally from the rest of me. Inside is an electronically sealed jar full of sweat and spit and riotously flourishing swarms of *E. coli*. I look at it for a while, and I think back to that time on Io when I broke. I don't think of myself as crazy anymore—or maybe I do, but only some of the time. I'm still learning to live with this part of me, learning to not let it cripple me. Every few days, when I'm steeled and ready, I pop the seals on the jar and let all the wrong out.

The Dragon Star

Pavel Renčín

● translated by Darren Baker ●

Legend has it that every time a myth is forgotten,
a star flames out deep in space.

I. Below the Pasture

The shepherd was wrapped in a silver and gold wool blanket and leaning against a staff made out of a hundred-year-old oak. His wiry figure gave off an air of youthfulness, but his eyes were certainly the strangest anyone had ever seen. They radiated a bluish-silvery iridescent glow that changed color like an ice drift beneath the aurora borealis.

The youth sat by the edge of a pool, dangling his legs in the icy water. A group of high-spirited trout began leaping out of the water above his knees as if proud to show off their rainbow colors.

"Watch it, guys!" he playfully shouted. "I'll be soaked from head to toe!"

The fish paid him no heed and continued frolicking around until they splashed water on a lizard, its brown color suffused with green, sunning on a nearby rock.

"You pests!" she snapped, flicking her forked tongue out. "I'll sick a pike on your vermin-infested tails!"

The cavorting trout suddenly bolted in terror. The startled lizard had barely registered her relief when the reason behind their sudden disappearance showed up.

A circular mouth clamped down on the shepherd's big toe while an outcrop of fleshy whiskers tickled his ankles. A catfish appeared on the surface, big as a floating log. It had to be at least forty years old.

"What news do you bring me, Kalfous?"

The shepherd carefully followed the silent sucking motion made by the fish's maw. A shadow came over his face, making him look old and gray.

"The wolves are coming," he muttered. Looking preoccupied, he grabbed his knotted staff and rose. He beheld the sky with gloom. The sun was going down.

II. The Ocean

What an incredible feeling it was basking in the sun. He rolled over to let his pale green side also catch some rays. God, it was sheer delight. Craning his neck, he let out a roar of happiness. The dragon unfurled his wings and, after several leaps and bounds, hurled himself upwards off the moss-covered rocks.

The warm airstream was intoxicating like mulled wine smelling sweetly of sugar and cinnamon. The sky was so blue it melted into the sky-blue ocean on the horizon. By riding the invisible air currents, the dragon was able to soar to great heights. He could feel the air beginning to thin around him. *What power I have!* Beating fiercely against the wind, he tried to reach even greater heights. His heart was pounding, his blood racing throughout his distended arteries. When he reached the highest point, his graceful body suddenly stiffened. From the cliff tops he must have looked as small as a mosquito. He was the master of the earth. There were no hunters here, only him. *Fearless!* His massive wings flapped in the thin air, the whole sky was his. And then like a rock the dragon began plunging headlong towards the glittery blue surface. His sleek body was shining like an incandescent star.

Incredibly, he leveled his dive off just above the shimmering crescent-shaped waves. Just enough to allow his rear claws to graze the surface. A shower of briny, crystal droplets burst upwards and doused his gleaming hide.

III. The Warehouse

It was winter. The empty windows and rusted steel frame were flecked with tiny white spots. The air inside the abandoned warehouse was clear and icy. The thousands of sharp edges formed on the rock-hard slag surface were painful. The dirty puddles were covered with a layer of ice; a very thin one because the rainbow oil slick and black grease were receding only slowly against the frost. The brick-colored paint had peeled off long ago from the entrance doors where several barrels, also flaking, were standing. Their lids were warped, allowing green slime to ooze out. A snarl of wires, black cables, and insulation lining were snaking along in the gloom. Rows of construction panels were stacked by the wall, their crumbling edges another sign that time had left its mark. Moonlight stole through a hole in the corrugated cement-fiber board roof. The fate of the one missing ceiling panel was evident in the fragments lying on the floor.

The strangest place of all was a remote corner of the hall. It was as if all darkness had congregated there, a sort of eye of dreariness. The elusive moonlight glittered here and there on the many shiny surfaces and edges. In the heart of this darkness lay a gaunt body on top of the gigantic heap of copper scrap, screws, crumpled silvery tinfoil, empty cans, shards of stained glass, and the twisted remains of tinted metal. An eerie wheezing sound could be heard as if the talons of a raven were lacerating the entire length of the throat inside this creature.

The silence was broken by the roar of a plane landing nearby. It flew in so low the mud-stained windows began to rattle. They were followed by the soft clinking of several screws vibrating loose and rolling to the foot of the pile. The ailing creature lying on top didn't even flinch.

It was too busy dreaming.

IV. The Diner

The clinking of aluminum spoons. Slurping. The stench of excrement and soiled bodies. Two long tables made out of pine board, their tops etched with numerous displays of graffiti. A group of filthy, scruffy vagrants were hunched over their tin plates greedily gulping down their runny potato soup, soaking pieces of hard bread in them. Their crazed eyes remained fixed on their food, the soup dripping from their yellowy beards.

Two women in blue uniforms were standing behind a big pot. With ladles in hand, they scooped up modest portions of a cloudy liquid for the beggars.

A long, disorganized line wound all the way out to the street. Passersby turned to look the other way. The vagrants were shoving and pushing, sneering and complaining. Otherwise, they were quiet, their eyes downcast, lost in their own little world where there were no outcasts. They were all anxiously looking forward to warm food—usually their only meal for the whole day. A man from the Salvation Army, also in uniform, made sure nobody cut in line.

The beggars suddenly began making way for an old man in a torn jacket limping along the narrow street between them. Bits of newspaper were sticking out of the clodhoppers he was wearing, and his dirty, wrinkled skin showed through the holes in his pants. His greasy white hair was constantly falling over his forehead. The homeless crowd shied away from the spiteful look in his black eyes and respectfully gave way before him. He was hauling some load on his back.

He was heading straight for the two women.

A pockmarked hulking figure blocked his way. Like a huge boulder blocking a mountain pass. "The end of the line is over there, pops!"

A small, weasel-faced man with a mustache leaned over to the brute and pleaded with him with fear in his voice. "Hank, don't be crazy! You can't, you mustn't ..." He then turned to the putrid old geezer and bowed humbly. "Don't get pissed, Hunter, he's new here!" There was terror in his eyes.

The homeless man paused for a second. Everyone froze in anticipation of what would happen next. In the end he merely nodded and sidestepped the scarface.

"Are you fucking joking?! Let that stiff go wait like everyone else!"

"Shut up, Hank!" the weasel-face snapped.

"Fuck off, Sid. Hey, you senile idiot," he barked at the lame, old man. "I'm warning you for the last time!!"

"For God's sake, SHUT UP!"

"Leave the old fellow alone!" growled the man who was keeping tabs on the line. He put a hand on the bear's shoulder. "He's our benefactor."

Hank exploded and, to the surprise of everyone present, drove a fist into the soldier's stomach. Then a left hook to the mouth. His jaw snapped like a dry twig. The ogre clasped his hands together over his head and brought them down like a hammer on the man's back, who collapsed like a deck of cards. Unease rippled through the crowd, but the line didn't disperse. They were hungry.

The old fellow put his sack on the ground. It was dirty from more than just mud. There was blood trickling out, and the furry tip of a tail could be seen sticking out.

"Double portion," he said blandly.

The brunette in the blue uniform was white as a sheet. Her hand trembled as she handed the old man a bowl of soup. Suddenly, her brown eyes nearly popped out for fright. A silhouette of the hulk, his fist flying, could be seen in her pupils. The blow landed on the old man's back and sent him nose-diving into the mud.

Hank snickered viciously. "Bon appetit, shitbag."

The old man didn't get up. He could feel a mixture of muddy water and urine soaking his clothes, the filthy concoction like some unpleasantly cold compress on his thighs and loins. His body felt painfully tired.

Someone laughed maliciously. A gob of spit landed on the old man's back. Most of the vagrants looked on in dumbfounded silence.

Finally, the old timer began to move. He slowly got on all fours and with a gasp, stood up. The others were watching him. He reached inside his breast pocket and fished out a half-smoked cigarette with lipstick on the filter.

One of the beggars darted towards him with some matches. They were damp, but the third one lit. The old guy took a deep puff. Space suddenly opened up around the thug.

"You'll be dead before that cigarette goes out," he cackled.

He took a long drag and flicked the twirling cigarette high into the air. The burning end made smoke rings, the hulk watching them with fascination. A sharp whistling sound could be heard. Then a hiss as the butt fell into a puddle. Finally, a splash as a severed head followed it in.

The old man coolly exhaled some smoke and wiped his silver sword clean with the dead man's sweater. He sheathed it somewhere beneath his coat.

He sat down and began slurping his soup. The onlookers woke up from their stupor.

Despite the ensuing crush at the tables, where there wasn't room for a single elbow, one individual sat all alone.

V. The Pasture

An eagle flew overhead. The youth was sitting with his legs crossed, his eyes shut, concentrating. The rugged peaks of the breathtaking mountains stretched far across the horizon. Clouds were starting to roll in below where the shepherd was standing. As the light began to fade, so did the landscape. Darkness fell on the snow-covered mountains.

They can't get through, so why do they keep trying? No matter how much they threaten, how much they plead. He won't let them in. Not yet ...

A knotted oak staff rested on the shepherd's knee. It divided the universe into two parts: the place where they are and the place where they want to be. It represented the border between existence and history. On one side was rebirth, on the other ... eternal silence? Oblivion?

The sun had totally gone down, shrouding the night sky in inky darkness. The stars were out—magnificent in all their vulnerability.

The shepherd could feel the air thickening and vibrating with energy. The animals were restless, and people were tossing and turning in their sleep.

... the wolves were coming.

"You would like to have my flock?" the shepherd whispered and smiled sadly beneath the star-blanketed sky.

A rider on a galloping white stallion emerged out of the darkness. The rust covering the two-handed sword he was gripping looked like blood in the fading sunlight. He was clenching the reins in his teeth. There was a light, discolored spot on his dark yellow vest where his coat-of-arms used to be. Although his bent shoulder plates—the pathetic remains of his armor—were temporarily tied down with leather straps, they still bounced around during breakneck gallops. His shoulders quivered under their blows with every stamp of the hoof, yet the knight was oblivious to the pain. His bright eyes with their enormous pupils blazed with determination while his forearms looked as if they had been stung by a swarm of bees. The stingers they must have had! His sunken veins were flecked with bruises.

Hyah! The target of the knight's fury suddenly appeared in the twilight—the youth in the silver-and-gold fleece standing motionless. The last rays of the sun glittered off the golden rim of his crown. His two-handed sword sliced through the air. The stallion neighed unexpectedly and bolted to the side.

The startled warrior wasn't able to catch his balance in time and flew out of the saddle, only to have one of his spurs get caught in the stirrup. The frantic horse started dragging the knight behind him, crashing his head into rocks and stumps along the way. The grass was splattered red. But even after losing consciousness, his grip remained tight on his sword.

The shepherd raised his staff, a bell clang in the distance.

"Enwerde gáeth beinárh, Arhus!" a water nymph wailed and gracefully leaped over the rushing brook. She was breathing normally; but her face was flushed red, and her lips gleamed with a dark purple gloss. The girl froze in her tracks. The red-lacquered fingernails on her bony white fingers were digging into her palms like claws dipped in blood. The torn black stockings on her slender legs were evidence of her desperate journey through the wilderness. They were becoming a nuisance. The water nymph drew a lady's revolver, a chipped four-inch Browning, out of her bag.

She was heading for the shepherd. The corner of her mouth twitched with malice. "Ara kraen!"

Bubbles were forming on the surface of the brook behind her as if the water were about to start boiling. "Wait!" A geyser arose, followed by a man leaping out of the spray.

His skin was nearly white with sickly green veins roping underneath it. His long, myrtle strands of hair were bare in places as if someone had ripped out entire clumps from the light green scalp. The water sprite placed one of his webbed hands on the quivering wrist of the water nymph. He slowly pushed the gun barrel towards the earth. The nymph shot an angry look at him.

"We can't anymore," he said to the youth in a throaty voice. "Release us."

The shepherd leaned against his staff and replied softly: "No."

It sounded like a sentence and the water sprite turned even paler.

"At least let Ariel go. She will melt away in the sky like meerschaum in the ocean. Just give her one ... I ask for nothing more, just one star," the voice of the frightened sprite beseeched him.

Silence ensued for a brief moment. They could sense he was wavering!

"They still haven't forgotten about you. You are still hungry like the wolf, and I'm determined to keep my stellar flock out of your grasp."

"Haven't forgotten?" the water nymph laughed hysterically. "Do you hear him, Ragót?" She flung her arms open and again turned to the bewildered shepherd. "I would like you to dance with me in the moonlight? Don't you want to?" She snatched her blouse and lifted it over her head to reveal in the darkness the nipples of her white breasts pierced with silver rings connected by a chain. A pornographic tattoo depicting a cluster of fornicating bodies stretched from her left shoulder to somewhere below her belly. Parts of her body were pasted with tacky sequins.

The silver eyes gleamed with emotion. The shepherd's hands

unknowingly stroked the knots of his staff as if it provided a measure of solace.

"Go away, wolves ..." the youth commanded. "Your time hasn't come yet."

The whites of the sprite's eyes shone in the darkness. He pursed his lips and shook his head forlornly. He put an arm around the nymph and led her away. Her frantic bawling left her back convulsing with spasms. The shepherd was happy to see that the water sprites didn't know how to cry.

VI. The Landfill

A boy in a blue windbreaker jumped from the rusty remains of a washing machine onto a tire half sticking out of the muddy earth. He stumbled but managed to regain his balance by jumping again, this time onto a wet sofa. Not a good idea. His leg tore through the rotted material and disappeared inside the stuffing.

"Ow!" the boy howled as something sharp sliced through his trousers and dug deep under his skin. The pain brought tears to his eyes. He cautiously balanced himself on his other leg and tried to pull the injured one out. He couldn't. He started crying hysterically.

"Mommy!" he bawled, wiping his dirty hand all over his face. He was panting hard like a frightened, trapped animal.

"Take it easy, kid," a gruff voice called out from a nearby pile of trash.

The boy flinched.

"I said relax!" an old man with black eyes, sitting on top of an old wreck, yelled at him. "You can't think straight hopping around like a chicken without a head on."

"Please help me, sir," the boy asked him.

The man shook his head and glared at him. "No one can help you in this shitty world. Only yourself. Remember that, kid!"

"You have to help me!" the boy begged him. "You must! I'm still a child!"

Scowling, the old man began tapping one of his heels against the bumper. Several minutes passed in silence.

"My name is Harry," whimpered the boy.

"They call me Hunter. That's my mission—and it's a shitty one, let me tell you. You needn't piss in your pants. I'm not here to murder any children. I'm looking for somebody." He picked up a one-inch cigarette butt from the ground and lit it.

"Are you calm?"

The dirty, teary-eyed boy nodded his head.

"Okay, carefully try and move your leg to the side. Can you?"

Harry clenched his teeth. "Something's scraping it on the left, and it really hurts in the back."

"And what about the front?" The hunter blew out smoke.

"There's something cold there!"

"Try to push on it softly."

"Ow!" the boy winced in terrible pain.

"Okay, maybe that's not the right way," the old man observed and blew smoke towards the boy. "What do you think?"

Harry could see he was in the company of a maniac. This vagabond was quite willing to let him die there! Why did he disobey his mother by coming to the landfill to play? He would gladly trade all the treasure they said you could find here for a week's grounding. He tried to concentrate. He closed his eyes to pinpoint exactly where it hurt. He bit on his tongue to overcome the pain and pushed with his leg ever deeper into the sofa. For a minute he thought he couldn't do it, but then the pressure eased. Hooray! Exhausted, he pulled his leg out and collapsed on the couch.

He looked around for the old weirdo, but there wasn't a trace of him anywhere. Only a burning cigarette butt laying on the hood of the rusted old wreck.

VII. The Old Warehouse

He could hear his mother now. *You're all dirty!* Her shrieking voice grated his ears. *Dirty! Dirty! How you've disappointed me, Harry!* He covered his ears with his hands.

A hole several centimeters big was peering out of his pants near the calf. She doesn't have to see it, Harry thought to himself. Were the rest of his pants not caked with blood and the grimy innards of the couch, she probably wouldn't notice it at all that he had been playing at the landfill. At first he tried rinsing his pants off in a puddle. Good lord, what was he thinking? He made it only worse. He had to find somewhere to clean up.

Harry limped in his underwear between mounds of plastic laundry soap containers, black plastic bags, much-abused tin cans, and burned-out television sets. He avoided the places where his feet got stuck in the slimy ash. The wind blew long-discarded newspapers around and kicked up a choking whirlwind of dirt and dust. The boy passed by broken fluorescent lamps and battered stoves and headed for a decrepit building in a grove at the eastern tip of the landfill.

The brick-colored paint was peeling off the warped entrance doors. The castle of horrors, thought Harry, but he quickly dismissed the thought. There has to be a sink in there. Chipped, maybe even cracked, but there had to be one.

He pushed on one of the doors, and it opened with a loud creaking sound.

Darkness filled the abandoned warehouse. Tangles of black cables were laying at his feet. They reminded him of boa constrictors waiting for him to get close enough, so they could quickly wrap their coils around him and suffocate him. Thoughts of his mother helped to drive that fear away.

He took a few steps inside and listened for any sound. The door slammed shut behind him. Harry's heart began pounding. The wind?

"Is somebody here?"

"Nobody's here ..." replied a strange sort of whisper.

Where did that come from? His head, of course!

The boy proceeded to the middle of the warehouse. Although his eyes had adapted to the growing darkness, the corner farthest from him seemed like an impenetrable black hole. He grew frightened of what could be lurking in there.

"Is somebody here?" he asked again. "I need to wash up."

Two fiery red balls lit up in the dark.

"Come closer, child," the wheezy voice called out again to him from all around. Harry's fear disappeared as the boy suddenly felt a deep sense of trust in the living thing hiding in the darkness. He underwent a flood of unfamiliar emotions like love and tenderness and completely forgot at that moment why he had even come to the warehouse.

"Who are you?" he asked, opening his eyes as wide as possible to catch a glimpse or some movement.

"Today, nobody. I used to be ..." the voice began tottering. "I used to be something to behold, and strong, too. I could even fly. I ..."

There was silence.

"Fly?" the boy asked, emboldening the creature in the darkness.

"A skin disease caused by acid rain ate away my wings. Hunger robbed me of my strength, and my claws soon disintegrated into dust. The infernal cold put out the fire in my throat. My bones grew brittle from loneliness and depression."

"I know what you're telling me. You're telling me you're a dragon. But they don't exist anymore!"

"I HAAAATE that word!" The seething hatred caused the boy's legs to buckle, and he collapsed on the frozen ground. But the malice disappeared as quickly as it appeared. After a moment of silence, the voice called out again.

"You're actually right. There are no more dragons. They vanished. Even the mightiest myths die away."

"I don't understand," mumbled Harry sadly as he clawed his way back up on his feet. "What's a *myth*?"

But the voice sounded as if it hadn't heard him. "Dragons never used to live off garbage and rats. Dragons never used to hide away from daylight, desperate and broken. Dragons stood up to their fears. Never before was the dragon's hide lacerated by malignant lesions. After that, he devoured a junkie who had overdosed. You see, no dragon has ever died of disease. They only die like derelicts."

"Are you a dragon?"

"Aren't you listening to me? You're supposed to ask: Are you a derelict?"

"What's a derelict?"

Harry felt overwhelmed by the pitiful wailing.

"I want to see you," he demanded after his shaking stopped.

"No. We've talked long enough. The visit's over. Beat it!"

The boy clenched his teeth and felt renewed vigor inside him. No! "Today I met a man who told me to rely only on myself. To stand up for myself like and follow it ..." Harry halted in order to recall the words the vagrant used with him.

"Like a sheep?" said the voice.

"No, now I remember. Like a predator. A tireless predator."

He was answered with subdued silence.

"So he hasn't stopped looking for me, eh? And now he's just loitering around," the tired voice murmured. "You know what, little guy, I'm actually looking forward to seeing him. I'm only sorry he didn't get here earlier. Much earlier. But now I'm going to need all the strength I can get."

Something moved in the darkness. Glass, screws, and other treasures rattled within the heap as the creature stood up on its wobbly legs. Harry saw two claws emerge that were so withered they looked like someone had covered the bone with a thin layer of black mud. A monstrous reptilian head with rotting teeth then appeared. A venomous draft shook Harry up so bad he felt the urge to vomit.

The shredded remains of its black wings opened up like a theater curtain. The dragon moved in jerks like some repugnant insect. He dragged his lame rear leg behind him.

Once the creature was fully visible in the light, Harry cringed. Its black hide was strewn with open, purulent wounds. The dragon was so emaciated that it looked like some kind of wretched skeleton. But the fire in its eyes shone as brightly as ever.

"Your tender, young flesh and blood will give me the strength to fight on. Get undressed."

Harry was unable to break the spell cast by the red eyes, which were suddenly overflowing with lecherous desire. He took his coat off and unbuttoned his shirt. His underwear dropped down below his knees. He took off his shoes. The sharp edges of the slag-filled earth pricked the bottom of his bare feet, and his entire body shuddered with goose pimples. He unknowingly wiped away some snot hanging from his nose.

"Now come a little closer," the dragon commanded him.

VIII. The City

He was going higher and higher. His strength waned with every step, his body ached with every movement, and his lungs gasped in vain for air. Far below him came a series of agitated shrieks and the deafening wail of sirens. He looked down and saw a clutter of colored figures, several iron vehicles with ladders, and people in white helmets all bustling about. The squeal of brakes and the distant crash of an accident. The sound of shattering glass, that pervasive human howling, and thousands of little perceptions—like smashing a kaleidoscope. Brilliant flashes of lightning were coming from the opposite high-rise.

He looked up. Another six full lurches to reach the top of the building. He moved his forward claw and dug it into the ledge. His eyes were fixed upwards. *I must! For the dragon's blood!* His body jerked again, but his one useless leg hampered his progress; he should have bitten it off. Five more to go. Why on earth did he leave his hiding place? There was nowhere left to hide because people had penetrated every corner of the world! Another lurch upwards. His lungs were about to burst, the pain was so great. He had to hurry before his last bit of energy deserted him. He lurched upwards again. The light faded before his eyes. He could no longer hear the wailing sirens or the arrival of droning helicopters. His rotten teeth added to the malicious contortion of his face. *No chance, you can't make it.* He was thinking about the dark-eyed killer. Finally, the dragon heaved himself up over the edge and onto the roof. He lay there exhausted. He felt a strange kind of lightness coming over him. The sky was still incredibly blue. The wind was fluttering on the horizon and dissipating across the wide open seas. Time was at a standstill. A magnificent eagle was circling between the skyscrapers.

The dragon savored the air. How long was it since he last smelled something so good? His head began to spin. The world was spinning! He wobbled to the edge.

He leaped off for his final flight.

IX. Stellar Pastures

"So you made it," whispered the shepherd.

The shadow of a creature was shivering from cold despite the warmth of the rising sun across the meadow. He whispered: "Yes, I'm dead."

"I wasn't expecting you so soon," said the shepherd as he turned and began wading through the dewy grass. His feet felt good in the coolness. "It was terrible, wasn't it?"

The dragon's shadow remained silent.

"A painful death?"

"The dying part was the worst."

A nearby brook created small, bubbling rapids as it wound its way over the rocks. There wasn't a sign of trout anywhere.

"Do you still want ..." But he didn't finish the sentence.

"That's my wish."

The shepherd fixed his gaze on the spot where the eyes of a living dragon should be. "Are you sure about this? You realize you're the last one."

"Really?" replied the voice, but without any hint of sarcasm. "It doesn't surprise me."

"I will give you a new life. Like before. Myths must never die out," the shepherd exhorted.

"Save it for yourself," snapped the shadow. "I want to reach the other side. I want my own star!"

"What's so bad about the world down below? You come here full of spite, misery, obsessed with hatred. You yearn for complete oblivion."

"Don't you get it?! You of all people? They've already forgotten about us. And that includes you! They no longer believe in us; you don't run, you don't hide."

Now it was the shepherd's turn to be silent.

"You know how many times they killed me? How many times they chased me down blind alleys. Those dragon beaters!" he raged in a voice overflowing with disgust and contempt. "The hunters! That horde of ignorant murderers!"

"Why are they so ...?"

The dragon's voice was firm: "Let me go! I will take only one from your flock."

The shepherd looked up and examined the blue sky with his sorcerous eyes. "Did you notice how their numbers are shrinking? No one has noticed."

"People today don't stargaze anymore," the shadow observed dryly.

Several white clouds were drifting across the sky. Butterflies were circling one another over the meadow, their wings fluttering until they lighted on red poppy bulbs.

"Very well. I shall give you your freedom," the youth whispered and struck his staff into the earth.

X. Epilogue

There's a legend that says every mythical creature is invisibly bound to some star. Whenever a myth is forgotten by mankind, a star flames out in deep space.

The last dragon has disappeared forever. His long journey through space ended with his shadow clinging to a star in a mortal embrace. To those who survived, he left behind a magnanimous gift.

No one suspected it because it was an *ordinary* day. Just like hundreds and thousands of other ones. And then suddenly—just after daybreak—the sun flamed out.

The people had just eight and a half minutes to enjoy the warmth of its rays on their faces before darkness set in.

The sky was blanketed with a brilliant array of stars.

They shone brightly—like never before.

The Mouser of Peter the Great

P. Djèlí Clark

1704
Tsardom of Muscovy

Ibrahim watched as Tsar Pyotr of the Russians was seated into a wooden chair in front of a fireplace. It was made for a very big man, with a high back and curved arms carved like lions. And the Tsar was certainly big, taller than any of the other men in the room. Taller perhaps than any man Ibrahim had ever seen, and he wondered if these Russians were all ruled by giants.

The Tsar settled into a long red coat trimmed in gold, drawing it tighter as if seeking warmth. He leaned forward, inspecting the two boys that stood before him. His appearance—those black eyes and even blacker hair, all on a face that could have been cut from stone—should have been terrifying. And it might have been, had the man also not looked so very tired.

At a nudge from Bilal, Ibrahim lifted his gaze to meet the Tsar. This Pyotr of the Russians didn't sit in his great wooden chair so much as he sagged in it—as if doing all he could just to hold himself up. The whites of his eyes were tinged with red and the skin around them swollen. His face looked drained, so that cheekbones showed just beneath the flesh. And he was so very pale.

Well, Ibrahim mused, that wasn't so uncommon here. Not like at the Sultan's palace, where there were pale people, sand brown people, bronze people, and every type of people you could imagine. Some had even been like him, with black skin and hair that curled and coiled. Here, everyone was pale or red like they'd been pinching each other's faces. But this Pyotr of the Russians was even paler than that—pale as milk. When he spoke, the tiredness that showed on his body filled his voice.

Ibrahim listened and understood nothing. He and Bilal had only just arrived in this Tsardom of Muscovy, this place with no sun and only clouds, where it rained cold white ashes that covered everything in ice. At the Sultan's court they had been instructed in Turkish, which he now knew well. This was definitely not Turkish.

"His Majesty is speaking to you," someone said.

Ibrahim turned to look upon a silver-haired man in a long green coat with bright yellow stripes, reminding him of a bird in the Sultan's palace that bore the same color of feathers. He and Bilal had met the odd man when they arrived. He told them to call him Spafarius. But they had already named him No-Nose—on account that he had no nose. There were just two holes where a nose should have been, and Ibrahim wondered if perhaps some people here didn't have noses. Or maybe in all that pinching of cheeks, it had been pinched off. The nose-less man did, however, speak Turkish.

"The Tsar asks if you know how old you are?" Spafarius No-Nose translated. He gave Ibrahim an expectant look, knuckling at long silver whiskers that drooped on his nose-less face. "Come on, boy. Vasil'ev said you were the bright one."

Ibrahim blinked. He opened his mouth, then stopped. How did you say numbers in this language? Deciding on another course, he held up one hand to show five fingers and a second to add three more.

The Tsar smiled, a slight spark touching his dreary face. He spoke again.

"Clever," Spafarius No-Nose remarked. "His Majesty asks if you know your name?"

"Ibra—" Ibrahim began, then changed to, "Abram." That was what they called him here. *A proper Christian name,* the man Vasil'ev had said, the one who brought Bilal and him to this place. To Ibrahim it didn't matter much because in truth neither of those were really his name.

"And were you and your brother treated well in your travels, Abram?" No-Nose translated once again.

Ibrahim looked to Bilal, who just shrugged. Bilal seemed to shrug at everything these days, and Ibrahim thought perhaps his brother blamed him for having to leave the Sultan's palace. Well, it hadn't been his fault. At least, he hadn't meant for it to happen. He thought some more on the Tsar's question. Treated well? They hadn't been beaten on their long trip with Vasil'ev. They had been fed. And dressed in thick furs when it turned cold. But they were still slaves, as they had been before. Of that, he was certain.

"Da," he answered finally. Then gave a bow like he'd seen some men here do, and added, "Tsar Pyotr."

The Tsar's eyes rounded at this, and he laughed aloud, shrugging off some of his tiredness. Ibrahim met Bilal's surprised look with a satisfied smile. He'd picked up a few things. The Tsar lifted a long finger to point at him and spoke.

"His Majesty is impressed," Spafarius No-Nose winked. "He would have you in his personal service, Abram."

Ibrahim bowed again. He'd become accustomed to the ways of powerful men at the Sultan's palace and knew this was not a request.

There were a few more questions and then an exchange of words between the Tsar and the other men in the room. After a while, some of them helped him to his feet. He grumbled but leaned his tall frame on them, letting the men guide him. It was as he turned to go that Ibrahim first saw the eye.

It was an ugly eye. A big, pale grey thing with long, fleshy roots that clutched to the Tsar like a weed. It sat there riding his back, twisting this way and that, glaring out upon the room. When it caught sight of Ibrahim, it squinted thick eyelids on its stalk, looking him up and down.

Then it shrieked.

Ibrahim cupped hands to his ears, clenching his teeth at the sound. No one else did. No one even paid the ugly eye any attention. Not Bilal, not Spafarius No-Nose, nor even the Tsar. Because he knew none of them could see it or hear its angry screams. And that bad feeling that came from it didn't prick their skin like needles and make them shiver either. He could see it, hear it, and feel it because that was who he was—who he'd always been.

The shrieking didn't stop until the Tsar was gone. And when Ibrahim took his hands from his hears, he found Spafarius No-Nose eyeing him. There was a curious look on his face.

"Your brother will come with me," the man declared. "You, however, Abram, will stay here. The Tsar is not well. His sleep is troubled, and he eats little. He is here secretly at the home of his friend, the Count, while the Count and his family are away. There are only a few servants in the house to care for him—and now, you. He needs your very special help, I think."

Ibrahim looked up at the man, trying not to stare at his no-nose. Bilal had said that was rude. "Me? What can I do?"

The man knelt so that he was nose-less to nose with Ibrahim. His breath smelled of onions and things both sweet and bitter. "I want you to hunt mice, Abram. As you did for the Sultan. You know how to hunt mice, yes?"

Ibrahim thought of the eye and knew right away that Spafarius No-Nose wasn't really talking about mice.

The next day Ibrahim found himself alone in the big house. Spafarius No-Nose had taken Bilal away, and now there was no one to talk to. The servants bathed and dressed him. They gave him new clothes—a blue coat with tight sleeves, white puffy pants, and brown house slippers. It was more clothes than he'd ever worn. But he was cold all the time here and so didn't complain.

He hadn't seen the Tsar all morning. He'd dreamt about that shrieking eye, though. And that bad feeling still hovered in the air. Spafarius No-Nose wanted him to do something about it like he'd done for the Sultan. But how was he supposed to do that?

The sharp sound of echoing laughter suddenly caught Ibrahim's attention. Curious, he followed it through several rooms of the big house. The tingling scent of unfamiliar spices and cooking meat told him he was in a kitchen. There, an old woman was trying to roll out a bit of dough. But each time she did so, it folded back up, sticking together.

Ibrahim could see the problem. It was a little man, no taller than himself. He was covered in long black hair like a shaggy dog with an even longer grey beard. He tugged at the dough between hairy fingers, pulling it and pushing it even as the old woman tried to smooth it out. Each time she grunted her frustration, he giggled and did it again.

"Why are you doing that?" Ibrahim asked.

The old woman looked up over a bulbous nose, then clucked her tongue, saying something he couldn't understand and waving him away. But he wasn't talking to her, and the hairy little man answered.

"Because it's fun," he remarked.

"It's not very nice."

The little man seemed set to dismiss him, then stopped, looking up with round shining eyes. "You can see me?"

Ibrahim nodded. In a blur the hairy little man was in front of him. He looked Ibrahim up and down. "But she can't see me or hear me. How can you?"

"I just can," Ibrahim answered truthfully. He always could. The old woman looked to him again and frowned. Not that she understood spirit-talk, which he knew sounded like nonsense to everyone else. Still, he'd learned at the Sultan's palace that speaking to things others couldn't see frightened people. He didn't want that here.

"Let's go somewhere else," he suggested.

The little man nodded eagerly, trailing along behind. They found an empty room, and the two sat down across from each other in big wooden chairs.

"Are you a witch?" he asked.

"No," Ibrahim answered. At least he didn't think so.

"Where do you come from?"

"Far away," he answered. "I wanted to ask—"

"Can everyone there see? Like you can see?"

Ibrahim shook his head. "No. Just me. Have you seen—?"

"And your skin," the little man cut in. "It's so ... black!"

"It is. But do you—?"

"Does it come off? Your skin, I mean?"

Ibrahim frowned. What a silly question. "Of course not. Does yours?"

The little man pursed his lips and thought hard. "I don't think so."

Ibrahim sighed. "I just want to know—"

"Your hair is so curly! May I touch it?"

"No!" Ibrahim snapped. "Touch your own hair!" He had hoped to ask the little man something about the eye, but this was becoming annoying.

"Does everyone have hair like you where you come from? And skin? How far away is it? Do you have a Tsar? Are you *sure* it doesn't come off ...?"

Ibrahim sat listening to the endless questions and grew increasingly frustrated. Mostly, he was frustrated because the little man wouldn't stop talking. And because he was, after all, only eight, what he did next was entirely understandable.

Ibrahim reached into the air and pulled out a sword. It was a big sword with a broad curving golden blade. One of the guards in the Sultan's palace had owned such a sword, and Ibrahim had wanted one like it. So he made one up, the way he was able to always make such things up. It was almost as tall as he was and should have been much too heavy for a boy of eight. But as he was the one who conjured it, the sword weighed whatever he wanted it to weigh. He lifted the large blade above his head and glared at the talkative, little man.

"Be quiet! Or I'll chop you up like a radish!"

The little man let out a single shriek and vanished in a puff of hair.

Ibrahim felt his temper die down, and he put away his sword with a sigh. That had probably not been a good idea.

It took all morning to find the hairy little man again, hiding under a set of stairs. It took still another hour to coax him out. When it was all done, the two sat by a window, looking out at the cold ash coming down from the grey sky. The hairy little man called it snow.

"I'm sorry I said I would chop you up," Ibrahim apologized. He really was sorry. "I'll answer your questions if you answer mine." He paused. "But you still can't touch my hair."

The little man blinked as if he'd forgotten about that entirely. "I'm Domovoi," he said, "a house spirit."

"Domovoi," Ibrahim repeated. "Is that your name?"

The house spirit shrugged. "All Domovoi are named Domovoi. We help take care of homes."

Ibrahim raised an eyebrow. "You didn't look like you were helping this morning."

"Not my home," Domovoi explained. "My house was here long ago. I cared for an old man and woman. I would spin straw for them and mend broken things. Then someone sent them away. Or they died. I can't remember which. This bigger house is built where their house once was. And so I remain."

"My name's Ibrahim. That's the name the Sultan gave me. Now I'm Abram."

"What was your name before that?" Domovoi asked.

"I don't know," Ibrahim admitted. "I don't know my name."

"Where did you come from then? Before the Sultan?"

"I don't know that either."

Domovoi cocked a hairy head. "Don't you remember?"

Ibrahim shook his head. He didn't. Neither did Bilal. All the two of them remembered was that they came from somewhere else, where there was always sun, and people had faces like them. He told Domovoi as much.

"We were taken by men. It happened at night. I think they wanted me for what I could do, what I could see. But I was with Bilal, so they took him, too. Then they worked some kind of magic and made us forget."

"Where did they take you?" the little man asked.

"Far away from our home to the Sultan's court. That's where we learned Turkish. Then one day the Sultan's mother called for me. She told me I had to help the Sultan. There was a bad spirit in the palace, she said. It haunted the Sultan in his dreams. She knew what I could do, and I was put in his room at night to find it."

"Why was this bad spirit angry with her son?" Domovoi asked.

"The Sultan got his throne by taking it from another Sultan—his brother," Ibrahim explained. "The spirit haunted the new Sultan for doing this bad thing."

"Oh!" the little man exclaimed.

"One night I awoke to find the spirit there. It was a great big ogre with a fiery eye. It frightened the Sultan. He was so scared, he couldn't even call for his guards."

"What did you do?" Domovoi whispered, his bright eyes round as plates.

"I pulled my sword," Ibrahim said. "And I fought the ogre."

Domovoi inhaled. "You fought an ogre?"

Ibrahim nodded. "For a long time. We fought and fought all around the room as the Sultan watched. And then I chopped off his head." He made a cutting motion with his arm, and Domovoi gasped. "The Sultan cried when it was over. He laid his head on my lap and just cried and cried. The next day, his mother sent Bilal and me away."

"But, why? You helped him. You chopped off the ogre's head!"

"I think because I saw him cry. I don't think Sultans are supposed to cry."

Domovoi made a face. "That's silly. Everyone cries."

It was Ibrahim's turn to shrug. He didn't understand it either. "A man named Vasil'ev took us. We traveled on a river, then over land, and then on a ship across a lot of water. Someone called it a sea. The man brought us here where Spafarius No-Nose took us to see the Tsar."

"That is quite a story!"

Ibrahim supposed it was. "Are there others here?" he asked. "Like you?"

"I am the only Domovoi in this house," the little man said proudly. "But yes—there are many others! A Kikimora lives in the kitchens behind the stove and steals food, but she's stingy and won't share any. There's an absentminded Lesovik nearby that likes to scare cattle. He tends to forget where he lives and spends a lot of time wandering about. There's a Bagiennik or two sleeping under the ice in the lake. We don't want to wake them up, however—big eyes and teeth and very bad tempers. Almost as bad as those Rusalki nymphs ..."

Ibrahim listened as Domovoi listed more spirits than he could possibly remember. The little man would probably go on forever if he didn't jump in.

"What about the eye?" he asked. "You've seen it? "

Domovoi's mouth clamped shut. He made a face and nodded. "I only saw it for the first time when *he* arrived."

Ibrahim guessed *he* was the Tsar.

"It's an omen," Domovoi went on. "That's what the others say—of something bad to come. That's why so many of them are leaving ..."

"Leaving?" Ibrahim asked sitting up. "You mean the spirits?"

Domovoi nodded. "There are barely any in the house any longer. When *he* arrived with that thing on his back—most of them left. Something's coming, and no one wants to be here when it arrives."

Ibrahim frowned, thinking of the bad feeling. It hadn't gone away. If anything, it was stronger now. "Why aren't you leaving?" he asked.

Domovoi grinned, showing blocks of white teeth. "Because I like it here!" In a blur he was gone. From the distance came the sound of something crashing. Someone shouted, and that familiar laugh echoed through the house.

Ibrahim let the mischievous spirit have his fun and sat back, thinking on what he'd learned. Only then did he notice the girl. She sat in a corner of the room, looking at him with watery blue eyes beneath long brown hair. He wondered how long she had been there? Had she seen him talking to Domovoi? Well no, he'd look like he was just talking to himself. That was hardly better.

As if wanting to be noticed, she got up and walked over to him, sitting nearby. She looked near his age and was just as tall. When she smiled, he smiled back, fumbling through his head for something to say. But nothing came to mind. So they just sat there, staring at each other until finally the girl giggled. He giggled, too, uncertain what else to do, and soon the two were speaking the one language it seemed everyone understood.

Their laughter was interrupted when the old woman from the kitchens walked in. She looked flustered—Domovoi's doing, no doubt—but called the girl over, handing her a pastry. The two walked away and into another room leaving Ibrahim alone again. Disappointed, he settled back down and was surprised when the girl quickly reappeared. She ran up to him with her pastry, grinning as she broke it in half and gave him a piece.

"Vatrushka," she said before leaving.

Ibrahim watched her go and wondered if that was her name or the pastry? He decided at the moment he didn't much care which—only that maybe he'd made a friend. Two, if he counted Domovoi. Then he ate the pastry happily.

The next day Ibrahim woke up to find the bad feeling had gotten worse. It seemed, outside, the sky was filled with more clouds. Even the flames in the fireplace looked dim as if struggling to stay alight. He was staring at them when Domovoi found him. The hairy little man sat down right in front of the fireplace, wriggling his long toes at the heat.

"You were talking to old Varvara's granddaughter yesterday," he remarked.

The girl, Ibrahim remembered. "We didn't really speak."

"She gave you a pastry," Domovoi sulked. "She never gives me pastries."

"She can't see you, Domovoi," Ibrahim reminded.

The little man's bright eyes flared. "Oh! That's right!"

Ibrahim stifled a laugh. "What's her name?"

"Eva," Domovoi pronounced. "She and old Varvara belong to the house."

Ibrahim frowned. Belonged? How could people belong to a thing? "They're slaves? Like me?"

Domovoi shook a hairy head. "Not like you. They belong to the house. You belong to the Tsar. A Tsar is more important than a house. So you must be more important. That's good, yes?"

"I don't want to belong to anyone," Ibrahim replied.

Domovoi shrugged as if there was nothing more to say. Then he blinked and sat up. "I almost forgot! I found someone you can talk to—about the omen!"

"Who? Someone … like you?"

Domovoi nodded. "He keeps to himself. The others don't like him much. But he knows a lot of things. Or he thinks he does."

"Take me to him," Ibrahim begged. "Please!"

Domovoi jumped up and motioned for him to follow. They walked through halls and up stairs to another part of the house. A few times Ibrahim had to run to keep up, yelling at the hairy, little man to slow his blurring pace. Fortunately, this part of the house was empty, so no one else could see him. They finally stopped at a set of doors, and Ibrahim pushed them open.

It was another large room. There were books everywhere, some on shelves and more heaped in piles on the floor. Ibrahim followed the house spirit past what looked like small wooden ships, some of them half-built and on their sides. There were other things here that he couldn't name: round glasses filled with colorful liquids, contraptions of wood and metal that somehow fit together.

In the middle of it all was a small man—as tall as Domovoi but not hairy at all. He wore a long blue coat with gold buttons and tight short pants that fell to the knees with white stockings. Stacks of books rose up around him like miniature hills, and he muttered beneath his breath as he read and scribbled on a piece of paper with a feather quill. He seemed to exclaim at every other word, wriggling his pointed pink ears through a curly white wig. Ibrahim walked up and introduced himself.

"And is that supposed to mean something to me?" the small man asked, never bothering to look up. He scratched at the end of a long nose, leaving a smudge of ink.

"I was looking for help," Ibrahim said.

"Help?" The small man smacked his lips together, showing two large front teeth that jutted down like a rabbit's. "I have no time to help. Can't you see I'm busy?"

Ibrahim eyed the stack of books. "Doing what?"

The small man pulled a hand from his quill, which continued writing all the same. He looked up at Ibrahim with black eyes over wire-rimmed spectacles. "Doing what?" he repeated. "Why, plotting the future! The future is coming! We must plan for it! We are so behind! All of you are lucky I'm here!"

"And who are you?" Ibrahim asked.

The small man sputtered, looking offended. "Why, I am the spirit of progress, you silly boy! The spirit of invention and proper government! Do you know of the salons in Paris? The Royal Society of natural philosophers and experiments in London? Where's our Descartes? Who has written our *Leviathan*? How shall we compete? We must strive to move forward, boy! Always forward!"

Ibrahim watched as the excitable little man went back to his writing, muttering the whole time. He looked to Domovoi.

"I told you no one liked him," the house spirit remarked.

Ibrahim could see why. "Where does he come from?"

"I came back with his Majesty's Grand Embassy," the small man answered before Domovoi could speak, sparing the house spirit a glare. "His Majesty has placed his hopes in us. We work to make our land more modern like those of the West!"

Domovoi laughed. "The Tsar cut off their beards!"

"What?" Ibrahim asked, now completely confused.

"His Majesty ordered that all men of the nobility shave their beards," the haughty spirit proclaimed. "These are the ways of the men of the West that we must adopt."

"He made them dress different, too," Domovoi added. "And if they wouldn't do as he said, they had to pay money. They didn't like that."

"All part of the struggle to make a backwards people modern," the other spirit huffed. "But some are stubborn. They don't want us to move forward. And now they hobble His Majesty with their superstitions!"

Ibrahim perked up. "You mean the eye? You know about it?"

The spirit looked back up over his wire spectacles, grimacing. "A Likho," he spat. "A curse."

Ibrahim had heard of curses in stories at the Sultan's palace. You could put them on another person to do bad things. That's what the eye was. The Tsar had been cursed!

"How do we make it go away?" Ibrahim asked.

The spirit shook his head. "The Likho is vile. Try to cut it away and it will make His Majesty cut off his own hand. Try to drown it and it will let His Majesty drown before floating away. It eats at his life and infects all about him with misfortune. But it is only a part of the curse. The Likho draws something else here. It calls it. Something more terrible." The small man's long ears fell, and his eyes fixed on Ibrahim. "Can't you feel it?"

The next day Ibrahim could feel it. And it seemed so now could everyone in the house. The servants went about their tasks stooped and bent, barely even whispering. The Tsar wailed through the night in his dreams, so that no one slept. A gloom settled over everything as sure as the snow that covered outside in ice.

That day, Spafarius No-Nose arrived back at the house. He went up to see the Tsar and came down again looking tired. He sat in front of a fire and sipped from a cup, hugging himself as if he couldn't get warm.

"Two bits of advice for you, Abram," he slurred. "One, never intrigue against a vengeful prince with a sharp knife." His finger tapped the space where his nose should have been. "Second, never drink cheap bread wine made by peasants. It has the taste of feet." He grimaced into his cup but took another sip anyway. "Your brother has a gift with his voice. I am thinking he may do well in music once we give him a proper Christian name. How goes your hunt for mice?"

"I haven't caught any yet," Ibrahim admitted.

Spafarius No-Nose sighed. "No? Well, I hope you do soon. His Majesty is so tired, he cannot rise from bed. I do not know how much longer we can go on like this. We have kept the Count's servants quiet of the Tsar's presence. But now the girl is sick, and they will talk."

"Who's sick?" Ibrahim asked puzzled.

Spafarius No-Nose took another grimacing sip before answering. "The old cook's granddaughter."

Ibrahim inhaled. "Eva!"

Spafarius No-Nose raised an eyebrow. "You have met then. She has taken with a terrible fever. It burns her up, and nothing can be

done for it. The servants fear it is something to do with His Majesty."
He shook his head. "No, they will not stay quiet long."

Ibrahim excused himself and quickly left, going off in search of
Domovoi. He found the little hairy man under his favorite stairs. He
lay curled up into a furry ball, and his bright eyes were dim.

"Eva is sick!" Ibrahim told him.

Domovoi nodded, listless. "Everything is bad now."

"It's that Likho! We have to do something about it! Stop the other
thing from coming!" Ibrahim didn't know much about this Pyotr of
the Russians. Maybe like the Sultan, the Tsar had done something
bad to deserve this. But not Eva. Not the girl with watery blue eyes
who had shared her pastry. She hadn't hurt anyone.

Domovoi sighed. "Too late for that. It's already here. Came in last
night."

Ibrahim glared at him. "What? Where?"

Domovoi's eyes turned to the floor. "In the cellar."

It took more coaxing, but Ibrahim managed to get the house
spirit to lead him to the cellar. The closer they came to it, the worse
the bad feelings got. When they reached a long set of stone stairs
Domovoi stopped and whimpered. Taking the lead, Ibrahim walked
down into the dark.

The cellar was huge, like the house had a great big belly beneath.
It was filled with old things: iron suits of armor, paintings, and even
swords. They cluttered up the space; things from long ago hidden in
dust, cobwebs, and gloom. It was the perfect place for a monster to
hide.

Ibrahim saw it almost immediately. A large shape sat in the dark of
the cellar sprawled out among the old things. Its bright green scales
shimmered, and its body heaved when it breathed. It was gigantic.
Monstrous! He counted one, two, no, three heads! Each looked like
a snake with horns and had sharp teeth that poked out from mouths
on long snouts. Grey smoke seeped from their flaring nostrils as
they slept, and a rumble like a snore rose from their throats. He had
heard of things like this before from the Sultan's storytellers. This
was a dragon!

"It looks very scary!" Domovoi squeaked behind him.

It did, Ibrahim agreed. He'd never seen anything so big. When an
eye on one of those giant heads opened, it was all he could do to not
run. The eye swam about to regard him, narrowing to a red slit on
a bright yellow sun. A deep growl from its throat quickly woke the
other heads. The three opened their eyes, then lifted sinuous, scaly
necks to stare down at him.

"What is this?" the middle head rasped. "Who wakes us?"

Ibrahim swallowed, searching for his voice.

"I do," he called up.

The head on the left snarled, its eyes narrowing. "And who are you?"

Ibrahim faltered. That simple question seemed suddenly very hard.

"I'm Ibrahim," he said at last. "I've come to tell you that you have to leave. You're scaring people here, making them sick. I think a curse brought you, but you shouldn't be here. Please go away now. Go somewhere else."

The dragon glared at him with six red-on-yellow eyes for a moment, then laughed. It came grating and barking out of three different throats to make one unpleasant sound.

"Go away?" the middle head rasped. "Why should we go away? Do you know who we are?"

"We are Zmey Gorynych, the great serpent!" the right head thundered. The dragon lifted itself up on two large back paws and two smaller front ones—each with black talons that raked on stone. "Our wings bring darkness!" the left head snarled. The monster unfurled two wings like a bat that plunged the cellar into a deeper gloom. "And our breath is fire!" hissed the middle head, orange flames licking the inside of its mouth. "We have come for this Tsar!" the right head rumbled. "The betrayer! The one who would change our lands!"

Ibrahim wasn't certain what kept him standing. His heart pounded fast. All he wanted to do was run. Somewhere he found the courage to speak.

"But you're hurting everyone. You're hurting Eva. And I won't let you!" He reached out and drew his sword. The broad, curving blade came at his summons, gleaming gold in the dark as he held it high above his head. He hoped to at least frighten the dragon. But the monster only laughed, wisps of smoke escaping its throats.

"*You* would harm *us*?" the middle head rasped. "*You* would stand against *us*?"

"You are not from these lands," the left head growled.

"Everyone can see you are different," the right thundered. "That you don't belong."

"Look at your skin" the left sneered, "black like soot."

"Your nose is flat and your hair crisp and tight," the right added.

"You are nothing more than a slave," the middle hissed.

"The Tsar's pet," the right mocked with rumbling laughter.

"The boy who does not even know his own name!" they bellowed as one.

Ibrahim felt himself falter again, and the too-big sword grew heavy in his hands.

"Yes," the middle head rasped. "What is your name, boy? Where do you come from? Do you even know?"

"*We* know *our* name," the left head declared. "Zmey Gorynych! How can *you* with no name harm *us*?"

Ibrahim felt his hand tremble with the sword as those words reached inside and pulled at him. Why was it getting so heavy? Before him the dragon seemed to grow even larger until it was his whole world and those yellow eyes with red slits looked big enough to fall into.

"Go away, little nameless boy, little slave," the three heads boomed together. "You are nobody! You are no one! Run away now before we open up our jaws and eat you up!"

Ibrahim felt his sword grow too heavy—and he dropped it. The golden blade vanished before it hit the floor, and he stumbled back. Before him the dragon stalked forward, taunting and laughing. He heard its thoughts in his head and took them as his own. *Slave. No One. Nameless.* How could he fight this monster if he didn't even know his name?

"Bring back your sword!" someone pleaded.

Ibrahim looked to Domovoi. The house spirit cowered behind him but surprisingly hadn't run away.

"I can't," he stammered. He had stopped moving, too frightened now to do anything but stand there and wait for the dragon. "I don't have a name. I'm just a slave. A boy who was stolen away. I don't even know who I am."

"But I know who you are!" Domovoi insisted. "You told me. You're the boy who comes from a faraway place. You're the boy who saved a sultan. You fought an ogre! You're the boy who came here from all the way across a sea. You're the boy sent to hunt mice for the Tsar. You're the boy who talks to spirits and carries a great golden sword ...!"

Ibrahim listened as the talkative spirit told his tale. Had all of that happened to him? Had he really done all those things? He listened, and the words began to drown out the taunting laughter. Soon they were on his tongue and coming from his own lips. He felt the fear that made him numb ease away. Doubt shriveled inside him as his courage returned, filling up the emptiness. And he pulled his sword.

The blade came at his call, settling into his hands and almost singing with anticipation. He stared up at the dragon that now hovered in front him, so big it seemed to take up the entire cellar. It still laughed and sent its taunts. But Ibrahim was no longer listening.

With a yell he lifted his sword at the head closest to him and brought it down with all his strength upon those scales. The blade bit through spirit flesh and bone to come clean through the other side. The dragon's neck wobbled momentarily where he had cut it, and then the horned head slid away. It tumbled down, landing with a thunderous thud on the cellar floor. Those red-on-yellow eyes were turned up with a look of surprise, and a long red tongue hung from its open mouth. The remaining heads howled their pain, and Ibrahim smiled. Sword in hand, he stepped forward.

"I am the boy who was stolen!" he cried out, swinging again at a paw sent his way. It came off beneath his blade, talons and all tumbling into the darkness.

"I am the boy who chopped off the ogre's head!" Another head roared at him with jaws opened wide, showing a hundred teeth. Ibrahim jumped as it came, bringing his sword down to cut through its thick neck. The head fell away, and the dragon retreated now as if to run. But Ibrahim wasn't finished.

"I am the boy who saw the Sultan cry!" he shouted. The dragon's last head sucked in air and then spewed a blast of bright orange flame at him that lit up the dark. Ibrahim dodged beneath the fire, feeling its heat on his back as he raced to hack off another paw. The dragon lurched off balance, pitching forward. Ibrahim jumped aside as it came crashing down in a heavy mass of green scales and spirit flesh. He quickly moved back in, bracing a foot on the dragon's neck and lifting his giant blade up above the remaining head.

"I am the boy with the golden sword!" Ibrahim proclaimed as the red slit in that yellow eye stared up at him—afraid. "Today, I will be the boy who cut all the heads off the great Zmey Gorynych!" And with a final swipe, he sent his blade through that scaly neck until it struck stone—severing the last head of the dragon. Its monstrous body shuddered with tremors, and its wings folded in to cover it like a shroud. With a loud whoosh it vanished into a green mist that fast swirled away to nothingness.

Ibrahim looked down, breathing heavy from the battle. Where the dragon had been, there was now a tiny, pale worm—with three tiny heads. It let out a squeal and began inching away. He brought a heel down on it, mashing hard and squishing out colorful goo that smeared the ground like a rainbow.

"You killed the dragon!" Domovoi yipped, jumping up and down in delight.

Ibrahim smiled. So he had.

It was later in the day that Ibrahim sat in the kitchens eating a pastry prepared by Eva's grandmother. The old woman was happy her daughter's fever had unexpectedly broken. She couldn't know he had anything to do with it, but she was giving out pastries all the same. These had cheese and sweet fruit jam in the middle.

The Tsar felt better as well and was now eating so much food the cooks were kept busy preparing one meal after another. The Likho was gone from his back. Ibrahim had seen it shuffling through the halls—now a small, scrawny old woman with bony limbs and one big eye. It had glared at him; but he waved his sword, and the thing shrieked, fleeing the house. The gloom in the place had lifted, and Domovoi claimed the other spirits were already returning—all of them talking about the strange new boy with the big golden sword.

As he sat eating, Spafarius No-Nose appeared. The man approached and sat down. He looked somewhat pleased, and his white whiskers twitched as he eyed Ibrahim.

"So ... did you catch your mouse?" he asked.

Ibrahim shoved a pastry whole into his mouth before answering.

"A worm," he replied.

The Little Begum

Indrapramit Das

Bina looked at the metal bones covering her worn and stunted limbs, cold against her legs and feet, lovingly layering the scars of her disease. These new hands and feet were heavy, lead and steel woven with leather straps onto the outside of her body. She had watched her sister, Rani, make them with fire and scrap, bending the pieces with hammer and heat, her secondhand British goggles flickering with the light of the workshop's tiny forge, sparks flying off her skin as if she were invincible. Bina did not feel invincible wearing them, these skeletal gloves and boots. They trapped her already strength-less arms and legs, weighed them down till she felt more helpless than she'd ever been, especially with Rani standing over her, ten years older, so much life in her limbs.

"When the Mughal Emperor Shah Jahan's dearest wife, Mumtaz, died giving birth to their fourteenth child, his grief was so all-consuming he could barely think, let alone rule an empire. So he decided he would build a monument to his grief, to honour the woman who had been so important to him."

"The Taj Mahal!" said Bina. She knew some history from her time in the boarding houses and the stories Rani told her. She let Rani go on.

"That's right. Shah Jahan gathered the best craftsmen, the best metalworkers,"

"Like you!" said Bina. Rani smiled and nodded.

"... and the best engineers in his realm, and they built a monument, a metal being to house and guard his wife's body. The Taj Mahal was the greatest automaton ever built—over 300 feet tall, plated in ivory, its massive limbs inlaid with lapis lazuli and onyx and other precious stones, its contours cleverly crafted to look like a palatial tomb when it crouched at rest like a man folded on his knees with his head to Mecca, the spiked tanks on its back raised to the sky like graceful, white minarets. To look upon the Taj Mahal walking along the banks of the Yamuna and across the water lapping its metal ankles as if the broad river were a little stream, was to see the impossible.

"And that's because it was impossible. That metal and ivory giant couldn't walk, not even with the most powerful and intricate steam engines and hydraulics built by the empire's best engineers. It would topple and crash before taking a single step. No, it needed a pilot who had the gift of telekinetic thought to lift its every component, to give it a human soul to go along with the machinery."

Like me, Bina didn't say. She realized why her sister was telling her this story.

"Shah Jahan tried piloting it himself. He failed. Very few, after all, are born with the talent of telekinesis, a truth the Emperor did not learn easily. But he did learn it eventually. After scouring the Empire with recruiters, he found, perhaps aptly, that Gauharara Begum, the final daughter Mumtaz had left him with, was the one he was looking for, when one day she lifted an elephant into the air and gently put it down just by looking at it. She was eight at the time like you. So with teary eyes, Shah Jahan asked his little daughter, Gauharara, if she would pilot the walking palace that guarded her mother's remains within its chest. Gauharara said that she would be honoured.

"And so she did. She was carried by the Emperor's guards through the winding tunnels of the vast being, past its engines and gears and pipes, past the chamber in its heart that held Gauharara's mother, past its tanks, and she was placed in its head in a soft cavern of quilted walls. The little Begum made the Taj Mahal walk, looking out of its filigreed eyes to the empire her father ruled, once with the help of her mother. Gauharara Begum took the huge metal and ivory beast across the land with the aid of a faithful crew that ran its engines. The Empire celebrated this wonder amongst them striding in the distance, colourful pennants like hair lashing behind it, breathing steam.

"But before long, Shah Jahan's third son, Aurangzeb, ordered that the giant never be piloted again because it was blasphemous to create such automatons, that this lifeless walking idol was a mockery of Allah. Aurangzeb had his father and his beloved Gauharara put under house arrest at the Red Fort in Agra and after a war of succession with his brothers, became the next Mughal Emperor in a sweeping victory. Shah Jahan died imprisoned, and Gauharara died many years later of old age. Aurangzeb was a devout, efficient Emperor but oversaw the last years of the Mughal Empire that was.

The Emperors that followed led it to its decline, and eventually they were easily defeated by the British Empire with their airships and tanks. Perhaps, if the Mughals had made more automatons to rid the Taj of its solitude and kept them walking, they'd have kept this land, too. They could have thrown airships from the sky and crushed tanks under their feet. The Taj Mahal never walked again, folding into its rest by the banks of the Yamuna, where to this day its empty tanks gleam like minarets on the horizon, its scalp and shoulders shorn of pennants."

Bina nodded, looking straight at her sister's grease- and oil-covered face glimmering in the candlelight, at her coarse tattooed hands between her knees. She smiled. Somewhere in the slum, a stray dog barked.

"I know why you told me that story," Bina said. She wondered if their mother or their father had taught Rani to tell that story. Or both.

"Of course, you do. You're a clever girl," Rani said.

"You told it really well. But it's just really sad," Bina murmured.

"One day," her sister said, putting her warm palm on Bina's cheek. "You're going to see the Taj Mahal at rest by the banks of the Yamuna. You're going to walk, walk with me, and we'll get out of here and go north to see it. Understand?"

Bina shook her head. As if to check, she tried moving her stick-like legs. They barely complied, distant, far-off limbs attached to her body through some unfathomable fog that cut off her brain from their worn-out nerves. "We're in a slum. We can't get good doctors like the babus and the sahibs. I'm not going to walk. You should stop saying that I will."

Rani knew not to insist any further. She looked ashamed, which hurt Bina. But she was angry and didn't say anything. Rani blew out the candle next to the mat and pulled the blanket over Bina, kissing her on the forehead.

"Do you remember, Bina, years ago, the first time I told you the story of the Taj Mahal? What I said to you?" Rani asked.

Bina's eyes welled up before she could stop herself. Her legs, weak and immobile and worn away to skin and bones by her sickness, remained that way under the exoskeletal harness her sister had spent hours and days making. All those days, and Bina had thought it was just another project repairing parts for the British and the babus with their various steam-powered machines.

"Am I going to hop in the Taj Mahal and make it walk again? Is that what you want me to do?" Even as Bina asked these questions, she felt her voice rising. She was horrified that she was shouting at her sister after everything she had done for her, but she was.

She couldn't see her sister's reaction through the tears. "No, Bina," she laughed, obviously letting her little sister cry without drawing attention to it. "No. But there's a reason we're all here in this slum, a reason that the British laws don't allow telekinesis for people like us, for everyone who isn't white. There's a reason Aurangzeb, ambitious, devout Aurangzeb, was terrified by his father's creation and his sister's power. There was a time a little girl made a giant walk. Even if that's not true, even if it was a whole army of telekinetics who made the Taj Mahal walk, that's an impossible feat. It's a miracle. Now I've seen you lift the pots and pans with your telekinesis, Bina. I've seen you lift the scrap in my workshop. If you can lift those, you can lift these. They're the same. You're good at it. I know it. You're getting big. You know, you know this. I hate to say this. I can't carry you forever. I wish I could, but I can't."

"Even if I could move this. If I ever went out, the British would see this skeleton, and they'd kill us probably."

"I'll cover your hands and feet with cloth, we'll say your limbs are scarred if anyone ever asks. We'll figure it out."

"I ..."

"No," Rani's voice was suddenly hard. "No more excuses. I've seen you pick up things with your mind. This harness is a thing. Your arms and legs are in it. You're going to pick them up and pick up your arms and legs."

Rani held out her hands. "Take my hands," she said. And almost without thinking, Bina did, her exoskeletal fingers grasping at Rani's flesh. Rani held her hands, winced, and pulled her up.

Bina heard the metal joints around her thin legs creak, the straps tighten with new movement like unused muscles, and she felt the pieces of metal in the harness around her float like dust in sunlight, drifting as her mind vanished into a profound numbness, dominated only by the image of a child in a padded chamber, sitting calmly in the centre of her skull. She felt the pieces of metal float and lift her thin legs and thin arms, which filled with the sparkling tingle of blood moving fresh through their weakened vessels.

She was standing. By herself. Held up by metal, metal held adrift by a little child in her head. The leather soles under her exoskeletal feet squeaked as she nearly fell down in shock but corrected herself.

Rani watched, her mouth open, arms held out to grab her sister if she fell.

Bina was shivering violently.

"My little Begum," Bina said softly, her voice trembling ever so slightly. "Come forward."

"I can't move," Bina said, voice thick.

"Why?"

"I ... I'm scared," she said.

"My Begum. I know. I know. But I'm here. I won't let you fall. Just look, look at your hands. Look what they're doing."

Bina looked at her hands, at the metal fingers flexing and unflexing by her side, their parts moving and clicking, joints bending, blessing her deformed fingers with intricate movement. "Oh, god," Bina said. The metal fingers seized, stopped their clicking.

"Don't," Rani said. "You're thinking too much. You were moving them without even thinking of it."

"Okay," Bina whispered.

"Bina. You're standing. You haven't done that in years. Don't be afraid." Bina thought of the years and years of being curled in her sister's powerful arms, letting the sun warm her face on their morning walks by the river.

"I'll fall if I move," Bina said.

"I'm here if you do."

Rani took off her necklace and held it out. "Use your fingers. Take it."

Her hand shook as she raised it. She watched the little gears spin in the joints, the fingers bending to grasp the necklace. She held it in between her metal fingers. "Wear it," Rani said. Her arms floated up, her hands passing her head, and she felt the necklace around her neck. It was a string tied to a featureless coin their father had hammered to practice telekinesis with their mother, passing it between their hands through the air. Bina didn't remember this herself. The coin hung against her chest.

"That's it. You're doing better than I could have ever hoped."

Bina nodded. She closed her eyes, and pennants unfurled from her scalp in the sunlight flashing off her great ivory-plated shoulders. She breathed in deep, felt the giant bellows in her, the furnaces in her torso flare with life. Felt the entire engine of her machinery close around the twin tombs deep inside her, protecting them. She breathed out, steam rushing from the ports on her head and back, gushing ribbons of cloud into the pale sky. Her hands were huge, big enough to pick up cattle, elephants. Underneath her was their entire slum sprawled across the banks of the Hooghly; in the distance the white palatial city of the British, of Calcutta, airships hovering like balloons above it, tethered to the land with strings she could snap with her fingers. An army of British soldiers couldn't stop her. They'd flee or be crushed, their bullets glancing harmlessly off her towering body.

"We'll travel?" Bina asked, her voice breaking.

"We will. We'll go to Delhi. We'll find a way to get you new medicine. We'll see the Taj Mahal. I promise."

Bina felt dizzy, her own height strange to her. She heard her metal fingers clicking again, moving again. Flexing. Unflexing. She thought of the little Begum pilot in the padded chamber in her skull, her resolve, looking out at the world through the windows of a giant's eyes. This little Begum didn't have an Emperor for a father and a dead Empress for a mother. In fact, she was no Begum, just a girl. This little girl had a father and mother who were metal workers who were shot by the British when it was discovered they were both telekinetic. This little girl had a sister with whom she was sent to be "civilized" in an imperial boarding house. This little girl had a sister who kept them both alive over years on the streets, found them refuge working metal, like their parents had, in a slum where people went to die because it was cheap, a sister who kept her alive when she fell sick and stayed sick.

Bina felt a fire in those bellows in her chest, burning, licking at the massive grinding gears. She closed her metal hands into fists. She thought of the little girl in her skull, and this time there was an older girl beside her—her sister, safe inside the padded chamber, looking out across the empire through those huge, windowed eyes, that empire once Mughal, now British, perhaps one day something else entirely. They looked out together to the snap and flutter of pennants catching the wind outside. The little girl would keep her sister safe in that chamber.

"Walk, Bina," said her sister. So she did.

The Bearer of the Bone Harp

Emmi Itäranta

● translated by Sarianna Silvonen ●

Sometimes, when the night is deep and I am sinking into a cobweb of dreams, I can hear the echoes through my body. The timbre of other worlds, the notes tied together, raising in my mind's eye visions of what could be. Dawn disperses these images. The morning is for this reality, for pen and music paper. For stories, some of which are made to last, others to fade away.

I tell this story in the hope that my writing hands would leave a mark upon the world, a mark someone may see when I myself am gone.

It begins in the year 18_ _, in a foreign land, with footsteps on the stairs.

It was a bright, early autumn day, and we were still sitting at the breakfast table. My partner was engrossed in the newspaper, looking for brief news items detailing strange events as was his habit. I was sorting a stack of bills. Ash from his cigar fell on the sleeve of his brand-new smoking jacket, tailor-made in the capital. I wiped it off before it left a permanent stain on the expensive fabric.

"When the landlady brought our breakfast, she made mention of the rent," I said.

My partner ran his fingers through his thick hair but did not raise his gaze from the newspaper.

"You can tell her she'll get it next week," he said.

"Have you received an offer?"

"Not yet, but I will soon," my partner said.

"Have you given thought to my suggestion of moving to a less expensive flat?" I asked. It was only weeks since our latest move. We rarely settled anywhere for longer than a few months as his work required constant travel.

My partner set the newspaper down against the edge of the table. The corner of the double page skimmed the surface of his coffee cup.

"My dear friend, I assure you that moving will not be necessary," he said. "In three minutes, a customer will enter this room."

My hearing was keen, but my partner's was even keener. I knew without asking that he had discerned footsteps on the street stopping in front of the building, and indeed: only a moment later, I could hear the footsteps on the stairs myself. Then the bell rang, and the door opened.

The woman who stepped into the room was not yet elderly, but I estimated her as five to ten years older than myself. She was neatly dressed, but I could not help noticing that the design of her sleeves was several years out of fashion and the decorative velvet band on her hat was worn. The heels of her shoes were trodden down. On the ring finger of her left hand glittered a slightly tarnished silver wedding ring.

We stood up to greet her.

"Are you Mr. John S_?" our guest inquired.

"Johan, actually," my partner said with a smile. "Johan Christian Julius S_. I don't blame you, however. Many of your countrymen have made the same mistake. How may I help you?"

The woman glanced at me.

"The matter is confidential," she said. "The presence of your housekeeper—"

"You can speak freely," Johan S_ interrupted. "This is not my housekeeper, but my close," he paused, "assistant, and there are no secrets between us."

"Please have a seat," I said and offered her a padded chair, which she was glad to accept. "I'm sorry that our breakfast dishes have not yet been cleared away. Would you like a cup of tea or coffee?"

"No, thank you," the woman said. "My name is V_ H_. I have heard that you are in the business of solving a particular kind of problem, and I think that the matter which brings me to you counts among this kind."

My friend leaned back in his chair, lit a new cigar, and waited patiently. Two vertical furrows appeared on his forehead.

"I was widowed three years ago when my husband was killed in India," the woman began. "Since then, I have lived on income from a small rental flat, which I inherited from my aunt, on the outskirts of town. At first I did not pay much attention to the high turnover of tenants. I only thought it was my poor luck that none of them wanted to stay longer than a few months. As time went by, however, I started to find it odd. It was hard for me to understand what in the flat could be driving the tenants away. The flat is in good condition, it is located in a respectable area, and it has fireplaces in both bedrooms, modern gas lighting, and running hot water. When I lost the tenth set of tenants, I decided to find out what was wrong. Most of the tenants just said they had found a less expensive or more conveniently located flat; but one mentioned something about the noise at night, and another asked whether I had had anything to do with the peculiar next-door neighbour."

"What kind of building is it?" Johan S_ inquired.

"A long, red-brick building with two storeys. There are ten flats in all, and each has a separate entrance from the street. The building also has a coal cellar."

"A fairly new building then?"

"Only about twenty years old. There was previously a farm at that location, but it was destroyed in a fire."

Johan S_ nodded.

"Please tell me more about that neighbour you mentioned," he requested.

"I was coming to that," the woman said. "I decided to spend a few nights in the flat to investigate why tenants found it so objectionable. When I arrived at the building, at first I could not discern anything out of the ordinary. It was a golden late summer day very much like today, and the rooms were well-lit and peaceful. When I came back from a brief walk in the evening, I suddenly had the feeling that I was being watched. I noticed movement out of the corner of my eye, and when I turned around, I thought I saw the curtains twitch in the next-door neighbour's window. I watched the window for a while, expecting to see more movement; but the curtain stayed still, and all I could see beyond it was darkness. I entered my flat, went to bed early, and slept without dreaming.

On the morning of the second day, there was a knock at my door. When I opened it, I saw a woman of about fifty with a touch of grey in her hair, knotted into a bun, and a sharp look in her eyes behind their thick spectacles. Her old-fashioned dress, straight posture, and commanding tone of voice instantly brought to mind a stern schoolmistress.

'Have you just moved in here?' she inquired without bothering to introduce herself.

I felt it was wiser to hide my true identity, so I answered, 'Yes, I have just rented this flat.'

'I wish you wouldn't pull the curtains so very loudly,' the woman said. 'You see, the walls here are painfully thin. It's very unpleasant to have to listen to curtains being opened and closed for hours on end. Please do not do it again.'

Upon hearing this speech, I came to two conclusions: Apparently, the woman did not concern herself in the least with common courtesy, and presumably she was the next-door neighbour mentioned by one of my former tenants. The latter supposition was proved when she turned her back and marched to the adjacent door, which she shut behind her. She did not go as far as banging the door, but the sound was not exactly what you would call 'quiet' either.

I heard nothing from my neighbour for the rest of the day, and I was not ready to lay the blame on her based on such meagre evidence, even though her behaviour did offer a possible explanation for the rapid turnover of my tenants. Come evening, I closed the curtains extremely carefully and went to bed.

I had slept barely a wink when I was woken by a strange noise. It seemed to come straight from behind the wall, right up against my ear. It was a scratching sound like the claws of a large dog or wild beast scrabbling against wood, tearing fiercely as if the animal was attempting to claw its way through the thin wall. I had to concentrate on identifying the direction, but as I shook off the fog of sleep and got my wits back, I knew that there was no room for doubt. The sound came from my peculiar next-door neighbour's flat.

I lit the lamp. The scratching went on and on. You can imagine, Mr. S_, that the night was to become most agonizing. The sound ceased for a few times, but just when I was about to fall asleep, it started again. I stayed awake until dawn and worried my weary mind with ways of broaching the subject with my neighbour. It all seemed clear to me now: obviously my neighbour was keeping some kind of animal in her flat, and its nightly activities kept my tenants from sleeping until exhaustion drove them to look for other lodgings.

The mystery took a new turn in the morning, however. Before lunchtime I heard the sound of the knocker again."

"Your charming neighbour, no doubt?" Johan S_ inquired.

Mrs. H_ nodded.

"Exactly so. 'You must keep your cat under control,' she said to me. 'That miserable creature kept me awake all night.'

'I have no cat,' I said.

'Your dog then,' she said and waved her hand impatiently. 'See to it that your animal does not make such a racket at night again.'

'You are mistaken,' I said. 'I have no pets at all. My landlady does not like having animals in the flat.'

My neighbour stared at me.

'But now that you mention it,' I continued, 'I also heard a scratching sound last night. Actually, I thought it might be you who had a dog. A rather large one.'

My neighbour eyed me in a way that can only be called a glare. Only now did I notice that her eyes had an unusual yellowish-brown tinge. Behind the greatly magnifying spectacles, they looked bulging and too large for her face, like the eyes of an insect.

'I cannot abide animals,' she stated bluntly. 'If you have no pets, you must have made all that noise yourself. Make sure that it does not happen again. Respectable people must be allowed to sleep!'

My neighbour marched to her own door again, and this time she definitely slammed it behind her."

"All of this is very interesting," Johan S_ remarked, "but what makes you think that your problem falls into my area of expertise? I have not yet heard anything that would hint in that direction. As annoying as your case sounds, it can very easily be explained by natural and human causes."

"You have not yet heard everything," Mrs. H_ said. "At this stage, I also had every reason to believe that my neighbour had caused the scratching sound herself. I could not be sure of why she had arranged for such a production, but I doubted her mental equilibrium. That night, I did not go to bed with a peaceful mind. As night fell, I brewed a hearty pot of tea and left only one dim gas light on. I was prepared for any issue of a mind twisted by madness, but I still could not anticipate that which finally followed.

For the first two nights, I had slept in the bedroom with a street-facing window. Because I did not want my neighbour to see any light from my flat, I now moved to the other bedroom with a window facing the other way. I had brought along a few books, and among them I chose *The Murders in the Rue Morgue*. I listened, but it was completely quiet; and as nothing out of the ordinary had happened by midnight, I became engrossed in the story. I was totally absorbed in the investigations of Auguste Dupin when I noticed movement in the room.

I put my book down. I was already starting to think my eyes had deceived me when the movement was repeated. A strange shadow had appeared on the wall: it was very dark and clear-cut, large and shifting. At first it looked like a writhing snake, then it grew tentacles like an aquatic plant or an octopus, and finally it twisted itself into a spiral, which reminded me of the patterns used by hypnotists and spiritualists in circuses and magic shows. I could not trace whatever was throwing the shadows; their very existence seemed unnatural because, as I mentioned, the only source of light in the room was a dim gas lamp providing just enough light for me to read by. The thick curtains were tightly closed, and neither light nor shadow could enter the room from the outside. However, I did not have much time to wonder at the origin of the shadows before the sound began again.

It was the same scratching sound I had already heard the night before: sharp claws against wood or plaster, a beast struggling to break free—or to attack its prey. Once more, the sound seemed to be very close to me, and this time I had no trouble discerning its direction. Without a doubt, it came from behind the wall on which the shadows were writhing. The same thin wall that separated my flat from the neighbouring one.

I listened to the sound and watched the shadows for hours without knowing what to think. I still believed that all this was due to some madness of my neighbour's that was difficult to explain; perhaps she had a good knowledge of some clever conjuring tricks, but the phenomenon had to have an earthly origin. Finally, my exhaustion and anger culminated to the point that I no longer concerned myself with decorum. I decided to march over to my neighbour's door to have words with her, and at the same time, I wondered whether I could somehow persuade her to see a doctor as she was clearly suffering from delusions or obsessions of some sort. At the front door, however, awaited a sight that still makes me break out in gooseflesh."

The woman paused and swallowed.

"What did you see, Mrs. H_?" Johan S_ asked.

"When I opened the door, at first I saw no one on the street as the gas lighting was dim and the night was foggy. After a moment I could make out a figure under the nearest street lamp. It seemed to materialize there right in front of my eyes as if it had condensed out of the darkness into the circle of gas light. I recognized the figure as my next-door neighbour. Her eyes seemed to glow yellow behind her spectacles. My rational mind wanted to interpret it as a reflection of the gas light. But then something happened.

My neighbour turned her gaze directly to me and raised her hand. I hope you understand, Mr. S_, that I am not prone to superstition or hysteria. However, this sight drove me out of my mind."

"Please continue," Johan S_ requested.

"At the tips of her fingers, I could clearly see sharp animal claws." The woman took a deep breath. "My courage deserted me. I pulled the door shut and backed inside."

I offered her a cup of tea, now gone tepid, which she gratefully accepted.

"It was a very long night," she continued. "The sound behind the wall had died down, and the shadows disappeared. For obvious reasons I still did not sleep. As soon as it was morning, I returned to my home, and since then I have no longer accepted inquiries from people interested in renting the flat. I am dependent on income from rent. I came to you because I did not know what else to do. Can you help me?"

Johan S_ had finished smoking his cigar. He put it out on a saucer and spoke.

"The case is not uninteresting," he said, "and you have shown great courage, madam. The information you have provided is very valuable. It should be sufficient to solve the case."

"So you will accept my offer?" Mrs. H_ asked. "I cannot pay a very large fee, but I will recompense you for your trouble as well as I can."

"Yes, I will," Johan S_ answered. "I will begin working on it immediately. I ask only that you stay home the next two days and under no circumstances come anywhere close to your rental flat and its extraordinary neighbour. We can agree upon the compensation later. Do you understand?"

"I do," our guest said. She offered her hand to Johan S_ and also shook my hand in farewell. She paused at the door. "Thank you," she said.

I saw that my partner no longer heard her. He was already busy weaving a web of chords in his mind, a web that he would throw on the creature from another world at the right moment. The vertical furrows on his brow grew deeper, and he stared silently out of the window for a moment. After the lady left, he got up, strode to his room without a word, and slammed the door behind him. Soon thick cigar smoke began to seep out from under the door. I had tried to cure him of that miserable habit, but in vain, and I lived in the constant fear that the poisonous fumes would do irreparable damage to his throat, which would inevitably mean an end to our livelihood. Despite my repeated assertions, Johan S_ did not believe in the harmfulness of smoking but instead maintained that the stimulant was necessary for his work.

Through the closed door, the sound of him humming started to carry out, repeating, altering, and intertwining snatches of melody mixed with the strumming of a kantele harp. At that point, I knew that my partner did not want to be disturbed. I called for our landlady to take away the breakfast dishes and attended to some socks that needed darning.

A little before midnight, Johan S_ rushed out of the flat with the kantele under his arm, leaving behind a thick cloud of bitter, dark cigar smoke. I spent a restless night alone. I knew that, in this part of the world, it was not highly likely that he would run into other spell-singers and get stuck in a restaurant drinking for days on end in their company. Still, memories of all the times this had happened burned in my mind whenever he went off on his own escapades.

This time I should not have worried. He returned before noon, not having slept but full of vigour. I had nodded off in the armchair, and I woke up when he gently deposited a large brown envelope in my lap.

"My dear," he said, "I hope you do not judge me too harshly for having left you on your own. Trust me, following along would only have bored you. It was vital that I acquire certain papers." He waved his hand at the envelope. "Take a look at them yourself, and you will see."

I pulled a stack of papers out of the envelope.

"Where did you get these?" I asked.

"It took a bit of a serenade, I admit," Johan S_ answered with a smile. "The people at the real estate office can be sticklers for bureaucracy. But I believe the contents will interest both Mrs. H_ and you. The papers deal with the property in which her rental flat is located as well as the house that stood in the same place before the current building."

I started to turn pages. They appeared to be a register of the owners and occupants of the properties since the construction of the first house.

"I would like to draw your attention especially to the burned house," Johan S_ said.

"If I am reading this correctly," I said, "for about three hundred years, the occupants have included a Mrs. R_ C_, who currently owns flat number 10. The ownership of the house located at this address has been transferred to a new Mrs. R_ C_ approximately every sixty years."

"What do you make of that?"

"Presumably each new lady has been the daughter of the previous one, inheriting her first name from her mother. All of the ladies have by chance married men named C_, and thus the owner's name has stayed the same. This is undoubtedly unusual, but I see nothing inexplicable in it, merely a rare coincidence."

"So it may seem at first glance," Johan S_ admitted. "However, a visit to the marriage registrar's office showed that no woman living at that address ever married."

"In that case, modesty explains a great deal. A woman with children but no husband—"

"In several generations?"

"Not impossible."

"No. But I have a strong reason to suspect something else. I invited someone to come over. Ah, here he is!"

Again, it took a moment before I could discern footsteps on the stairs. The bell rang, and Johan S_ opened the door. In stepped a man shrivelled by old age as bent and grey as if the years had sucked all strength and colour out of him.

"May I introduce Mr. N_ T_," my partner said. "Get your coat, my dear friend, we are going out!"

The building was located on the outskirts of town in a quiet area far from the bustling surroundings of the cathedral. The neighbourhood was fairly new and imitated the houses of finer folk. A grey drizzle of rain came down, wrapping the street and its houses in a shroud of mist. The carriage left us in front of the building. I helped the old gentleman descend and took his arm as we walked along the side of the building.

"Is this where the house was?" my partner asked the man.

"Right here," the old man answered. "Here I spent my childhood, working as a stable boy and running errands for the household. I remember the widow well. She was in the habit of shooing everyone off her estate. The village folk tried to avoid her, she was so ill-tempered and sharp-tongued."

"At what age did you leave the house?"

"At fifteen, sir."

Johan S_ nodded.

"Excellent. We shall now perform a small experiment as we agreed upon in advance."

He led us straight to the door of the end flat and knocked. I heard footsteps from inside, and the door opened a crack. I could make out a thin hand, hair touched with silver, and suspiciously glaring eyes behind thick spectacles.

"What do you want?" asked the woman who had opened the door.

The old gentleman stared at the woman. First surprise, then disbelief, and finally a slowly dawning fear played across his face.

"Is this number nine?" Johan S_ inquired.

"As you can clearly see," the woman said and pointed to the number on the door, "this is number ten." She yanked the door shut without further ado.

Johan S_ turned to us.

"Would you perhaps need a slightly longer moment?" he asked, addressing the old gentleman.

"No, my eyes are still keen," the old man said. "I know it can't be. But she looks exactly the same. Her face, her hair, her dress—and her eyes. I have never seen that kind of eyes on anyone else. And she hasn't aged a day."

Johan S_'s voice was friendly but held a dark undertone.

"And how long has it been since you last saw her?"

"Seventy-one years," the old man said.

When we went up the stairs to the door of flat number nine later that evening, I could not help glancing at the windows of the neighbouring flat. They stared back, unmoving, covered by white lace curtains like blind eyes filmed by cataracts. I thought of my native country and its forests, the black water of the bog, the treacherous, bottomless abyss beneath it that would not release its grip. The pale will-o'-the-wisps and silently falling snow. A frosty finger caressed my spine.

Nobody knows when the gates between the universes first opened. Many people say that they were sung open by Orpheus, whose music was too large to fit in this world. Some believe that it could have been none but Väinämöinen, whose tunes could call even the moon and the sun down from the sky to listen.

Myself, I prefer to think that the trail was blazed by Pandora, who thought knowing was more important than obeying. Imagine: you are holding a vessel, inside of which lie captured all the evils of the world. But the same vessel also holds all the knowledge in the world, each grain glowing incandescent in your reach, burning your fingers through the clay. And under it all sparkles hope.

If leaving the lid on meant life without knowledge and hope, would you put the vessel back in its corner forever?

Few recognize Pandora as a singer. That has been taken from

her, less given in return. Pandora, the curious. The stupid girl who released wickedness upon the world. So say the stories.

But stories are not told only to keep the truth. They are also told to distort it. Great evil is not released without great power. And are the things called evils really always bad, or do they also hold the hidden gift of seeing and doing differently?

I put my bag of implements on the floor.

I took out the sacred rowan branches, salt, and candles etched with protective symbols. Last of all, I took out the music book and pen. Johan S_ and I set to work together.

When we had finished all the preparations, my partner took out his kantele. Candlelight reflected off the smooth bone surface of the instrument. Johan S_ plucked a few quiet notes.

We waited.

My partner plucked the notes again. I stood, pen ready to touch the music paper. Outside, night fell. The candles burned hotter.

The sound started, faint but recognizable. It came from behind the wall: claws, long, sharp, and ready to maim. They moved inexorably against the plaster.

The notes of the kantele repeated until they flowed in the room as an uninterrupted, undulating thread. I knew their power of old. They tempted creatures from the realm of the dead as much as the smell of blood or prey: something to stalk, something to grab by the skin of the neck with sharp teeth and tear to bits.

Squirming shadows appeared on the walls, swaying silently, stretching their tentacles towards the notes. Then, as if the wall did not exist, the creature stepped into the room. It still resembled a human: the dress was whole and neat, the spectacles in place. But the hair floated free, and the glow of the eyes had brightened to a glaring yellow. The pupils were pointed and sharp, and the skin had acquired a reddish, veiny surface.

There was not much time.

Johan S_ played a chord on his kantele, and the sound was thrown across the room as a web of light caught on the wall and formed narrow, glowing vertical stripes. The demon screamed and immediately threw itself at the wall to escape into the neighbouring flat. Too late. The creature bounced back from the bars of light that Johan S_ had played upon the wall and sank to the floor. I managed to see the brands that the bars had burned on its skin.

The demon got up and rushed towards the nearest window, but a new chord from the kantele was faster. The notes materialized in the air into glowing strands that covered the window wall. My partner strummed out two more fast bundles of chords that settled on the other two walls of the room and wove themselves together across the floor and ceiling. We were entirely surrounded by a cage of light formed by narrow bars of chords. The creature hissed and tried to attack us, but a note from the strings of the kantele flung it back.

"Are you ready?" Johan S_ asked.

"Ready," I answered.

I took a deep breath and put my pen to the music paper. I fell into a state in which my hand was guided half by consciousness, half by instinct—a state with no room for mistakes.

Johan S_ began to sing.

The notes fell from his lips in a clear, precise hum, and my hand wrote the notes on the paper as he sang them. I was only remotely conscious of the fact that the melody was melancholy and languorous. It glided like a slow stream and called from afar like a large bird spreading its wings over dark waters.

The song flowed from my partner's mouth into the room and from my pen to the lines on the paper, and the creature crouched in front of us, trapped but not yet beaten. Its claws glittered sharp as glass and its skin radiated a heat that I feared would set the room ablaze.

Somewhere far away, a whole world away, the swan took flight.

Johan S_ paused, waiting for an answer to his call.

And the answer came.

Great wings beat the air, leaving behind the lands shrouded in shadow and the river that separated them from the towns and villages of the living. I heard the path of his song, I heard what he conjured up with his music. From far beyond the skies arose a deep and clear-cut cry from a long throat: a bird coming to fetch its prey.

The fiery demon bared its teeth. A growl escaped its mouth, and its eyes flashed. I put my pen to paper again, and Johan S_ continued humming his tune. I focused entirely on the melody, but the creature fixed its gaze on me. Its pupils opened into an abyss, and I could not help looking in. Black bog water rose around me, the bottom fell and tore under my feet, and the creature flooded in.

I was accustomed to demons that burned with fire and brimstone, but this one felt like stabbing ice and the stings of frost, such a deep bite of winter that it could have squeezed the cores out of trees and frozen the very heart of the earth. I felt it settling under my skin, studying my body from the inside, searching my thoughts for something to grasp. And finding purchase.

I heard the creature's words inside me. I looked at my partner and knew that he did not. I forced my hand to keep moving.

the hand that only

My hand moved and moved. The notes traced a path in the air, a path that reached all the way to another world and created a road from which the sacred bird could not stray. The frost weighed my limbs down, the bog water of the demon's words sucked me deep beneath.

writes when your story

Only a brief time had passed as the journey between the land of shadows and this world is measured by other means than time. From afar I could hear the swan's calls answering the song. But even stronger, above everything else, I heard the demon's voice, addressing me.

is told who remembers

The words settled under my skin and made their home there. My partner slid away, and I was nothing as his notes carried far even without me. The demon probed my dying heat, its new body whose boundaries rose high and distant, no longer reachable by me, but by this new creature. It would easily learn to wear my face out in the world. Deep in my cocoon of bog water, I would sense its movements and actions. I would still exist, but only for myself, not for anyone else. A buried story, a lost tale.

the hand that only writes when your story

An enormous chord split the room. The waters receded, the words withdrew, my body was mine again. Johan S_ had grasped my arm and stared at me, his face pale. The cage of notes on the walls had begun to crack. I realized that my hand had stopped, the notes no longer flowed on the paper. The path in the air started to fade. The humming still issued from my partner's lips: he could not pause, could not speak, so that the power of the song would not disperse. I took a deep breath, strained my memory, and wrote down the few notes that I had let slip. The path brightened again. The music grew up to a wall between me and the creature that glowed like a firebrand, spitting words, and the words became meaningless sounds that bounced off my skin.

The bird came, its neck held in a graceful curve, its wings as wide as the horizon. Its shadow encompassed the whole room, the whole house, the whole world. The animal terrified me, and I could not tear my eyes away. The creature it had come to fetch crouched in the corner. By now it hardly resembled a human at all. The clothes had peeled off its body, revealing metallic skin, shiny and veined. The flashing eyes had sunk deep into their sockets, and the hair swayed long like squirming seaweed or a nest full of snakes. Its claws were sabre-sharp.

The swan's wings beat the air once, twice. The demon screamed and slashed its limbs blindly, not hitting anything. The bird stretched its neck. Its black eyes flashed, and it picked the creature up in its beak like a fragile insect. For a moment I thought I saw distress akin to mine on the demon's face and the edge of a yawning darkness, deeper and more enduring than the night. In its last gaze I recognized something else.

The creature looked relieved.

The room was filled with a swishing sound as the swan turned around and flew out the window with its prey in its beak.

The humming ceased. My hand stopped. The winter still whispered in my bones. The bars fell off the walls, and a deep stillness descended upon the room.

I barely had time to catch my partner as he sank to the floor, unconscious with exertion. The bone kantele slid out of his hands and knocked against the floorboards.

"Will it come back?" Mrs. H_ asked.

Johan S_ took a sip of coffee and set his cup on the saucer. He was still pale with dark shadows under his eyes. There was a half-eaten piece of apple cake on his plate.

"No," he answered. "The door is shut behind the demon, and the swan has carried it to the other side of the dark river. The creature was strong as it had lived in the human world for a long time. But it was a typical house demon: tied to one place from which it sucked its energy. It would not have lasted a week had it dared to venture farther than a hundred yards from its abode."

Mrs. H_ looked confused.

"I know very little of demons," she said. "Why did this creature torment my tenants but leave the other occupants of the building alone?"

"The explanation is obvious," Johan S_ said. "The demon originally appeared on the farm that existed on the location of the current building before it burned down. The area of the house covered a part of the street and two flats in the current building: number nine, which you own, and number ten, the neighbouring flat. That is why the demon considered these flats its realm and was greatly disturbed. It could not take vitality from humans, only the place. It was weakened by the presence of humans."

"You have seen many such creatures," Mrs. H_ said. "Why do you think they come to our world?"

"Demons are the incarnations of evil," my partner said. "They have no other purpose than spreading darkness and damage."

"You have saved my source of income, Mr. S_," Mrs. H_ said. "And the compensation of which we spoke?"

"Pay me according to your conscience," Johan S_ said. "I did not choose my career for material reasons."

In the grey light of the morning, it seemed to me like a new furrow was forming on his brow.

That night, as we lay in bed and the darkness of the room was cut only by the light of the street lamps trickling between the curtains, I spoke of something that had weighed heavily on me for a long time.

"There are easier ways to make a living," I said. "Almost every village suffers from small and simple cases of demonic possession, and there are dozens in larger towns. You could handle them with a few notes, slightly modifying a melody already played. It would not tax you to the same extent. Why do you always look for the hard and difficult cases, those from which recovery is wearisome, those which always result in one less composition left in you?"

He was quiet for a long time. I listened to his breathing in the darkness.

"You know the answer, don't you?" he said finally.

"Because you must seek that which is most difficult," I said. "Because you must fight the demons that squeeze out the best you can accomplish. Otherwise, your spirit would wither and your notes die and your music would become worthless. If you were satisfied with the easier option and stopped challenging yourself, you might as well be dead."

Johan S_ stroked my face.

"My dear," he said, "you could be a spell-singer yourself, you know my mind so well. Not a day goes by that I don't feel guilty for what you have to endure because of me. How much worry I am causing you. What danger I am putting you into time after time." He paused for a moment. "I almost lost you to this house demon."

It was not a question. I did not answer. There was no answer that he wanted to hear.

"How I sometimes wish you had not left with me," my partner continued. "There are also easier ways for you to live your life. You could have had a home. A husband, a family."

"I wanted other things," I said.

He lay his hand on mine and let our fingers intertwine.

"And I am grateful for it every moment. I could not do this work without you."

"You could find another spell-scribe," I said, but it was a hollow and meaningless protest. We both knew that the only way to exorcize demons back beyond the gates of the hereafter was to sing them a bridge out of this world. But the gates also had to be closed behind them, so that they would not come back. This required writing down each note on music paper protected by spells. That is why spell-singers needed assistants to work with them as extensions of their hand, listeners of their voice. Very few had the skill to write down a song note by note and to bind shut the gates behind the exorcized demon. If I were to leave, it would be nearly impossible for him to find someone to replace me.

I listened to his breathing, which evened out in the darkness.

Sleep eluded me for a long time. I saw the face of the demon in front of me and heard its words in my ears, the one sentence it had kept repeating.

When your story is told, who remembers the hand that only writes?

I thought of the demon's claws against the wall like an animal trying to break free. I thought of the distress of the creature when it realized it had been trapped by a cage of music. I thought of its face, the final relief when the chains of this world sprung loose.

The incarnation of evil, said the stories. But was there also something else hidden in them—a spirit that wanted to see beyond the narrow boundaries it was allowed, that wanted to know more?

I thought of creatures that exchange one cage for another because it is the only freedom they know.

When I finally fell asleep, I dreamed of a world that had never showed itself to me before.

Upon waking, I remembered only brief moments of the dream, sensations, and images. Light wood, the scent of pine needles, a spot of sunlight on the floor. A brick fireplace. A closed door in front of me, his voice on the other side, vibrant, drunken, silent. Our hands intertwined.

I remembered a hall where a great orchestra played. The melody was the same one that I had written down today, the one on whose wings he had sent the demon to the river of Tuonela. The arrangement was polished like a diamond, its every edge and facet reflecting new light. People listened fervently in the darkness, and when the last note faded away, applause filled the air like sparkling snow.

And I remembered the strangest thing of all: a soft, warm child against my breast, a weight in my arms. I felt immensely happy and sad at the same time. For what I had had. For what I had lost.

When I woke up, the warmth still lingered on my skin.

Every flash seemed as real as all the rooms in which he had sung demons back to the hereafter, as real as all the steam trains we had sat in on our way from one corner of Europe to another, as real as every bed we had slept and stayed awake in side by side.

Each flash felt like something I had exchanged away.

I myself had released the evils in my own world, and I would have been ready to do it again because they had also given me other things.

Curious, stupid girl, who thinks knowing is more important than obeying.

I looked at the sleeping face of my partner.

Many times, when he did not see, I had lifted his instrument in my lap, stroked its surface with my fingers, and learned the sounds it released. And sometimes, for the most fleeting of moments, I had felt it respond to my touch, to the quiet music inside me. All boundaries had disappeared, and I had understood what he and I were to each other. My hand did not close on emptiness because his voice filled it. His notes did not die out in space because my hand caught them.

In those moments I dared to think that somewhere there might be a world in which my story was as valuable as his, my voice as loud.

Perhaps someday this world could be that one.

I rolled over. The bedsprings moved under me. My partner woke up.

"Are you all right?" he asked.

"Yes," I said. "I had a strange dream."

"What about?"

"Another world," I said.

I expected him to brush away the remark with a smile; but he was silent for a while, and then said, "It is said that music opens the gates to other worlds. If it can carry over to the realm of the dead, why not elsewhere?"

He lay his hand on my hip and pressed closer to me.

"Was it a better world?" he asked.

I was silent.

"No," I said finally. "Just different."

The night wrapped around us. The stars went their course, and worlds turned in each other's arms.

The bone kantele gleamed white on the table on which he had lain it, smooth as the egg of a water bird that could hatch an entire universe.

Madame Félidé Elopes

K. A. Teryna

● translated by Anatoly Belilovsky ●

1. Madame Félidé and the Smile Merchants

On Friday Madame Félidé bought all the smiles the local merchants had for sale. Merry and sad, shy and modest, childlike and old, tender, happy, polite, ugly, warm, soft, villainous, ironic, open, timid, grudging, obsequious—every single one. Shopkeepers dug through their deepest cellars to find silly grins that rarely sold and usually gathered dust amid bits of obsolete gossip and jokes peeled off the floor after they had fallen flat. She emptied the display cases of fleeting smiles and gullible smiles and especially made sure to acquire every single sincere smile in the entire town. She also bought two ounces of contagious laughter and half a pound of good cheer. For change, the sales clerk gave her a tulle sachet full of pointed double entendres.

Dancing, skipping, and humming a silly little song about a cat, Madame Félidé hurried home. What a stir she would cause in the town when everyone realized they'd have to spend holidays with serious faces! Some may have smiles squirrelled away for a rainy day, some may have to rifle through keepsake boxes for antique smiles inherited from their grandmothers. How funny they will look wearing grins a century out of date and mothball-scented, at that! But the rest will skulk along the boulevard, avoiding their friends. What if someone makes a clever joke? Does one respond with cheap, tasteless laughter scraped up with pocket lint? Or with a silent nod, betraying shortsighted stinginess?

On the way home Madame Félidé encountered prim Anglian women who walked their well-schooled children and well-bred dogs—or was it the other way around? All of them—women, children, and dogs—cast great quantities of disapproving looks her way, opprobrium being an inexpensive commodity often shared generously with strangers. In return, Madame Félidé took a brand new mysterious smile from her reticule and tried it on right there in the middle of the street. She walked on, warmed by the sounds of Anglians' horrified whispers as they gossiped about her odd spendthrift profligacy.

Avion waited in her garden, squeaking his wheels nervously; his high-strung personality kept him awake instead of sleeping quietly in the hangar. A family of siskins perched on Avion's prow-like nose chittering happily to each other as she approached.

2. Madame Félidé visits the sea shore

Madame Félidé did not like painting. That is why she painted dozens of landscapes and portraits which now gathered dust in her attic. She did not hang her work in rooms she actually used, believing (correctly, as it turned out) that the bright colors of her paintings would ruin the delicately tasteful Anglian style of the interior, which was a source of justifiable pride for her House. Madame Félidé was a softhearted woman who often showed more consideration for her friends than for her own comforts.

Only one picture painted the day before remained in the living room, and even so she placed it in a dark corner and covered it carefully in black cloth. House frowned, its walls curling in disapproval around the easel on which the painting rested, but did no more than that: he was too well brought up to express his pique openly.

Madame Félidé took her purchases from her reticule and tossed them carelessly onto the table. She waved at the painting, and at her gesture the black cloth crawled down to the floor, revealing a huge—half a wall in size—canvas on which a raging ocean clawed for the sky. Sea spray filled the room, Madame Félidé smelled and tasted salt on her lips, and a gust of wind blew a bundle of frivolous smiles off the table.

In the painting the rocky shore appeared deserted except for a bright spot where someone's discarded clothes lay near the water's edge. Madame Félidé peered into the waves, hoping to make out the person who went for a swim in such inclement weather. She did not succeed and so picked up the cup of tea that her House had made for her and left the room.

Avion had already rolled to the airstrip and huffed impatiently, hurrying her to board. Madame Félidé eased into her seat, careful not to spill her tea, and Avion took off.

House looked wistfully toward them, regretting not being able to go for a walk to Enger Street and back. He thought it unseemly for a well-bred Anglian home to dream of travel and adventure, but still a small bit of longing entered his heart, bringing back the memory of his childhood when, as a tiny brick, he had made the long and dangerous journey from Chester to Warrington to receive his education in Socratic discourses with a cat.

At first Avion flew low and slow like an elderly pigeon. Madame Félidé marveled at the familiar landscape, taking it in as unhurriedly as she drank her tea. For perhaps the first time in her life, she wanted to cut the flight short and to return home immediately. Therefore, she directed Avion to fly toward the sea.

Having finished her tea, she threw her teacup overboard. Knowing that Anglians consider shattered porcelain a favorable omen, she tried as often as possible to brighten the lives of her neighbors. It was also a good way to rid herself of tea sets that a distant aunt of hers, with clock-like regularity and bovine perseverance, sent her as gifts for every imaginable holiday. The cup whistled through the air under the very nose of an elderly gentleman and shattered on the pavement. Immediately, Avion rose through the clouds into bright sunshine and clear blue sky.

A half hour later the sea appeared on the horizon. It rolled its slow waves toward the shore and debated with the sky about the clarity of their colors. The sea was tranquility itself and looked not at all like the tempestuous force of nature that had hidden under the cloth cover in Madame Félidé's House.

Having returned home, Madame Félidé hurried to the living room, pulled the curtain off her painting, and recoiled at the darkness revealed before her. Her heart skipped; but then she saw the stars and heard the distant surf, and her heart returned to beating. The man of her dreams slept in her easy chair. A few sheets of paper lay scattered on the table. For a minute Madame Félidé listened to his calm slow breath, then carefully covered the painting again, and tiptoed out of the room.

That night her sleep was filled with visions of tiny silver fish, purple sky, warm rain, and the man of her dreams.

• • •

3. Madame Félidé and Unwelcome Guests

Madame Félidé could not stand having guests, so each Saturday at eleven in the morning she put on tea. When no one came, which happened often, she retrieved from her reticule a vial with sighs of relief and happily released one of them. Each sigh cost her practically nothing, especially compared against incessant chatter of her Anglian acquaintances whose tongues unfurled rather quickly in her presence.

There was a knock on the door at the same time as the clock struck. Madame Félidé donned her most joyous smile and hurried to answer it.

Anna Meadows and Bess Thompson were two of the greatest of all misfortunes that could befall one on Saturday morning. Tall, ungainly Anna Meadows usually glared such powerful distaste toward all that surrounded her that Madame Félidé often wondered where she's bought it. Anna Meadows was also extremely stingy, her dresses, her gossip, and her jokes apparently purchased at garage sales. She wore a wide, childish smile as she came in and exuded a faint odor of mildew, having apparently extracted the smile from her deepest cellar simply to annoy Madame Félidé.

Bess Thompson, blessed with the intelligence of three goats, had on an everyday smile of the kind they sold at last year's farmers fair. Bess's stupidity was entirely natural and did not at all go with her clothes or with her position as Women's Auxiliary Council Chair for the town in which they lived.

The tea party went far better than Madame Félidé expected. Bess talked incessantly of suffragettes and of the Queen's impending visit while Anna Meadows shared last year's gossip about the college rector's wife. Madame Félidé stayed out of the conversation, only nodding occasionally and in all the wrong places and glancing nervously at the picture that stood covered in the corner about which House's features twisted in disapproval.

After the blueberry pie was eaten to the last morsel, tea drunk to the last drop, smiles worn off, and gossip chewed and spat out, it was time to go home. The guests hurried to get ready when Anne's wandering gaze fell into the curve of the far corner of the room.

"How cute," she said and pursed her lips, the smile she had nursed through two hours of tea having finally disappeared.

Madame Félidé watched in silence as her guest headed toward the painting. The words "If you don't mind, my dear?" had barely enough time to escape Anne's lips as she raised the edge of the cover.

Had Anne thought to lay down a supply of high-quality shrieks, she would have used it up that instant. Lacking not only that but even the cheaper generic exclamations, she stepped back, pulling the cloth with her, and froze in an incongruous pose before dropping everything and running from the room.

In the picture, bright noonday sun shone on a rocky seashore. A man who had only just stepped out of the water hurriedly pulled dry pants on over wet underwear.

4. Madame Félidé's departure from Angelia

On Thursday Madame Félidé wanted to listen to music, so she went downstairs to the living room and practiced painting rabbits. The rabbits came out looking far too frightened, and Madame Félidé painted over them, accidentally painting the man of her dreams in process. His eyes were full of sorrow and understanding, as if the man of her dreams had waited all his life for her to paint him.

"Stand still," said Madame Félidé, "I will paint you a smile."

The man of her dreams stood motionless; only his lips moved a little as he whispered: "I love you."

"Such nonsense," said Madame Félidé sharply and picked up her brush.

None of her attempts to put more brushstrokes on the canvas succeeded. She tried all her paints—in vain. The painting lived its own life, refusing to obey its creator. Madame Félidé found herself at a loss: how can the painting be without a smile? It cannot. She covered the painting and went to bed.

Her sleep that night was haunted by visions of surf, acacia trees, cinnamon, a boat house, and the man of her dreams.

That is precisely why Madame Félidé went smile shopping on Friday and not because she was a frivolous kind of a person. She only needed one smile—but which one? It was a good thing that her intuition told her to buy the lot.

And now, having shepherded Bess Thompson out of her home, Madame Félidé set herself to the task of attaching the smiles to the canvas. She tried paper glue, shampoo, jam, milk, treacle, ink, and even oatmeal. Beset with anxiety, she accidentally ate several of the smiles, which turned out to be delicious, especially when smeared with raspberry jam.

Madame Félidé felt chagrin at having drawn such a sad man.

How silly for a person to lack a smile! Like a cat without whiskers. And Madame Félidé picked up a length of silk yarn and threaded it through the eye of her needle.

"Now I will sew a smile to your face, the sincerest smile of all," she said. "Just don't be afraid and don't move. You wouldn't like to smile with your nose or your ears, would you?"

"I am terribly ticklish, you know," said the man of her dreams. "Don't sew anything. Why not just marry me, instead?"

And he smiled—tenderly, courageously, merrily, and a bit ironically.

This was an unexpected development, and caught by surprise, Madame Félidé agreed without a second thought.

"Wait a minute," she said, "while I get my toothbrush. But as soon as I return you simply must tell me where you found such a magnificent smile!"

Madame Félidé was not a sentimental woman, and so she walked out of her House to say farewell to Avion. She kissed him on the propeller hub and turned away to sweep an uninvited tear off her face.

Avion thought for a moment about trying on a bit of sadness but changed his mind. Instead, he rolled slowly in the direction of the sea, the ungreased left gear wheel whistling a merry tune. Avion knew that, on the road, he would undoubtedly meet a little girl who dreams about the sky.

Madame Félidé returned to House and ran her hand over his rough brick wall. House did not answer; only the faucet in the seldom-used guest bathroom sprung a tiny leak, dripping water that, were anyone to taste it, would have proved unusually salty.

Madame Félidé donned a wide-brimmed hat, tied a silk bow at her collar, and for no apparent reason retrieved her black umbrella from the hall closet. Returning to her painting, she closed her eyes (thinking herself a terrible coward) and stepped through the canvas.

5. Madame Félidé catches up on her reading

After Madame Félidé learned to smile, sigh, and cry on her own, as well as many other important things, after her elder son went to school and the younger said his first word, "Boo!" and shook his soup spoon at the cat—in short, many years later, Madame Félidé decided to sort old papers that gathered dust in the attic. There, among old theatre playbills, yellow newspapers, postcards from Aunt Fannie, and expired stagecoach tickets, she found a few pages covered in her husband's impatient handwriting.

She put away the file with important documents, perched comfortably near the attic window from which a beautiful view of the rocky sea coast could be seen, and began to read:

"On Friday Madame Félidé bought all the smiles the local merchants had for sale. Merry and sad, shy and modest, childlike and old, tender, happy, polite, ugly, warm, soft, tender, villainous, ironic, open, shy, grudging, obsequious—every single one."

Waiting for the Flood
OR The Bathers

Natalia Theodoridou

The two women are sitting in their beach chairs in the shallow water, low waves and foam lapping at their bare calves. They are both wearing striped, old-fashioned bathing suits complete with goggles and swimming caps; the tall, thin one is wearing black and white stripes, the other one is striped red. They look to the west, from where the wave will come. There are lots of people standing ashore or sitting or lying on the beach, waiting for the flood.

The two women are talking. The red-striped one is counting something with the fingers of her left hand. They look happy, as if they're not even noticing all the people around them, as if they're not even waiting for the end of their world. Sometimes they laugh, looking at each other; other times they talk while looking in front of them, eyes wide and staring. They take turns speaking, and each time the red-striped woman adds a finger to her count.

Number three earns the black-and-white woman a soft, tender touch on the shoulder.

Number four has the red-striped one waving her arms around, excited.

Number five takes a while, but when they find it, it makes the black-and-white woman laugh so hard her chair almost falls backward into the rising water—it's up to their knees now, wetting their thighs and their crotches nestled in the deep beach chairs.

At number six, they bring their chairs closer together, making it easier to touch each other. The red-striped woman rests her head on the shoulder of the other, who turns and kisses her forehead. The red-striped woman starts sobbing at this, and so her companion takes over the counting. They are up to seven now; it takes both hands, but it's worth it, isn't it? The black-and-white woman holds up her palms, one open wide—the other with two fingers making a

V—and she talks calmly, her gaze fixed on the horizon. She stirs the water with her right leg and then glances at the beach, the people holding helium balloons scribbled with messages for the skies:

MAKE ROOM FOR US
WE LOVE YOU
WE WANT YOU
WE ARE SO ALONE

Number eight, number nine, these are easy, they go fast; but then the women pause. They both hold their palms in front of them, all fingers extended but one. As if to say, what are we forgetting? As if to say, is that all we have?

The red-striped woman stands up and plods to the shore; there are so many people there now it is difficult to walk without elbowing her way through, taking care not to step on any of the lying ones, the sleeping ones, sprawled like broken mannequins on the beach—how can they be asleep?

She makes her way to the mango trees lining the beach. She reaches with her arm raised up up up as far as she can, balancing on the tips of her toes. She picks a green mango and carries it back into the sea. She hands it to the black-and-white woman; and she breaks its firm skin with her teeth, then peels the skin back, and bites into its flesh, orange juice running down her chin. She offers it back to the red-striped woman, who does the same. They take turns until they finish the fruit, then toss the skin and the gnawed stone in the water, and watch the stone sink and the skin float away from them—the water now up to their belly buttons, the beach slowly being swallowed, and the sleepers drifting into the sea.

The black-and-white woman wipes her chin with the back of her right hand and then uncurls her last finger. Ten good things make a life well spent, no?

Ten, they count, and happy, the bathers sail away.

Sin Embargo

Sabrina Vourvoulias

1.

Nevertheless.

That is the word that starts nearly every statement I make to my clients as I'm detailing what they can expect during treatment or during a forensic evaluation should they ever be permitted to witness in court.

I say it in Spanish because, though many of them have been here for decades and no longer speak first in Spanish, most of them still think first in it. Their children, when and if they accompany them to the First State Survivors Center, roll their eyes at me.

Nevertheless. Sin embargo.

Now say it with an English accent and an American reading of the interlingual homographs—sin embargo—and it becomes policy. Banned and barricaded, it says, because of transgression. Your transgression, your community's, your state's.

For the Guatemalans and Hondurans; the Salvadorans and Colombians; the Cubans and Venezuelans I work with, each originating transgressive circumstance may be as distinct as an owl is from a hummingbird. But the sin embargo falls on their head the same way, righteous as a curse.

Is your fear credible?

Do you (who got away with no more than the breath in your chest) have documentation?

And how is it, anyway, that you got away?

The First State Survivor Center is privately funded. We treat both immigrant and asylum seeker because immigration trauma can manifest in ways remarkably similarly to survivor trauma. Also because the government's designation of which countries produce refugees and which produce immigrants is a lesson in politics, not psychology.

Anyway. You know (or if you don't know, you can guess) there is more than one way to translate "sin embargo" from Spanish to

English. Sometimes instead of nevertheless, I go for this: the fact remains.

The fact of report; of U.N. statistics and special procedures; of federal applications, deferred action, and memoranda.

There is fact of flesh, too. Here, by Istanbul Protocols: thickened plantar fascia; perforated tympanic membrane; rectal tearing; keloids and hyperpigmentation; chronic lung problems. I know how to translate these flesh facts into words even when the government claims it cannot: bastinado; teléfono; rape; necklacing; wet submarino and waterboarding.

Sin embargo, sin embargo, sin embargo—the fact remains. In Spanish, in English, in the hauntingly untranslated gulf between.

2.

Someone famous, I can't remember who, once said that when a language dies, so does memory.

I wonder about that whenever María José Manrique comes to the center and sits across the desk from me. She doesn't come regularly and no longer makes the impression she once did. In the early days of her counseling, she not only wore her traditional blouse and skirt, she wound a bright, twenty-meter ribbon around her head in imitation of the sun.

The headdress is called a tocoyal in Tz'utijil, but it's been at least a decade since she's spoken it. And today, when I ask her why she doesn't wear the headpiece anymore, she refers to it by the Guatemalan Spanish word for all such ornamentation—tocado— then skillfully avoids answering my question.

Tocado, in case you were wondering, also means "touched." Touched has an odd set of meanings in English. Those seven letters convey the straightforward tactile, intangible compassion, and assumed mental illness or incompetence all at once. Survivors of torture, no matter how touching their testimony, are often written off as touched.

Last year's genocide trial in Guatemala is a good example. The Ixil women who stood and recounted gang rapes and massacres that wiped out full villages were discredited with arguments of hysteria, of confabulation, of the childish inability to distinguish protective action from oppressive.

María José and I watched some of the livestream of the trial together in my office while it was happening. My client sat dry-eyed and unmoving even when one of the testimonies—recounted in a different indigenous language and translated into Spanish—was remarkably similar to her own story.

The livestream winked in and out, and each time it did, I studied la Marijoe (as she's come to be known after so many years in the United States).

"¿Qué buscas?" she had finally asked when she noticed my scrutiny. What are you looking for? As if that wasn't a question to be answered in a lifetime instead of a 50-minute session.

"I guess I'm looking for a reaction," I had said. "I want to know if this serves as proxy justice for you."

What you've got to understand about la Marijoe is that she smiles a lot. A wide rictus of a smile that you can never be sure is about something good. She hadn't answered my question that day, just smiled and smiled, and months later, after the genocide verdict was vacated and we all understood that no one was going to be serving a sentence for crimes against humanity, her only comment was that smile.

I can't remember if I smiled on that rescinded verdict day. Maybe later, at home, as I was carving a figure from an apple I had on hand. Maybe when I bored a hole through its chest with the tip of my paring knife. Maybe every time I hear that the tough, old ex-president and military man from Guatemala has started having some trouble breathing.

3.

I'll be having pie de pie.

Pronounce the first pie in that sentence in English, the second in Spanish.

It means I will be eating pie standing up. Although ... I could be telling you I'm going to be eating foot pie.

But I'm not. I'm going to be telling you about my girlfriend, Daiana, who is a pastry chef and makes the best pie. Never foot pie, just so-good-I-can't-even-wait-to-sit-down-to-eat-it pie.

Right now she is flattening dough with an antique glass roller she fills with ice water. And raising her perfect, threaded eyebrows at me. It's not the fact I'm talking into empty space (she believes in the paranormal as do many of her fellow immigrants from San Mateo Ozolco) it's just this monologue-ish style that bothers her.

It sounds like I'm chiding, she tells me. Her convos with ghosts and ancestors and saints are always a back-and-forth, and as she tells me this, her words adopt the rhythm of the roller over dough, smooth but firm, perfecting everything beneath it.

After an hour, when the oven buzzer goes off, she looks at me before opening the door. Her eyes are what I first loved about her: letter Ds resting belly-up and barely containing the Abuelita-chocolate-discs of her irises.

"Magic," she says. "Pay." And hands me a perfect slice.

P-a-y is how we transcribe the English word "pie" so Spanish speakers know we don't mean foot. And so we create yet another homograph, thorny and confusing for the translator. Do we mean pay or pay?

"You can't get a loan to eat."

When I first met Daiana, this was the way she explained her decision to immigrate. Now that she has her green card and works at the top boutique bakery in Philly, she and her cohorts ("The Bank of Puebla," they call themselves) leave sunken brioches and imperfect cannoli on the loading dock where those whose credit is hunger know to seek them out.

I'm not chiding now. Consider this a benediction instead. There are many innate, unschooled magicks—love, food, compassion, solidarity. May your mouth fill with them.

4.

My grandparents were Nipo-peruanos, which is how I come to speak some Japanese and Spanish as well as I do. Not a native speaker, by any stretch, but good enough to confuse. Before you mistake this for boasting, know that in addition to French, my colleagues at the Survivors Center collectively speak Tigrinya, Amharic, Zigula, Khmer, Nepali, Arabic, Cantonese, and Kreyòl. I am clearly the underachiever of the bunch.

My boss, a chino-cubano whose years as an imprisoned dissident have left him with limited movement in his shoulders, tells me that the fact I've just turned thirty but look eighteen more than makes up for my unexceptional Spanish or contextually useless Japanese language skills.

Many of the survivors I work with are older—think the first wave of Central Americans fleeing torture and civil war in the 1970s and '80s—and the fact I look to be the same age as their grandchildren are (or would be) makes most of them warm quickly to me.

Most of them.

Today, la Marijoe comes in unscheduled, storms past the gatekeepers at registration, and upturns her handbag on my desk. A flood of scraps torn from matchbook covers, business cards, receipts, and lined notebook paper streams out. No wallet, no sunglasses, nothing else.

I poke at one of the scraps, flip it over. There is a name written on it.

"What's this?" I ask.

"Each is a child detained at the border," she says. "The ones you want to deport."

"You know I don't want to repatriate them," I say. I play with the bits of paper; they all have different names written in pencil, in pen, in something that looks like it might be halfway between a crayon and brow pencil. "Anyway, how can you know their names?"

"People have names," she says. Then she turns her back and leaves before I can say anything else.

I sweep the paper bits into plastic baggies. I count some of them at the break room as I eat the empanadas Daiana has packed for my lunch. My colleagues help me count even without an explanation. And later at home, Daiana does the same.

There are 60,000 scraps of name.

Magic isn't instinctive, at least not for me. I have had to learn it as carefully as at one time I learned the alphabet and vowel sounds in Spanish. A-E-I-O-U.

And in English, A-E-I owe you.

Sale, as Daiana says.

It is slang in Mexico for "agreed." In other Spanish-speaking countries it means "to leave," and you already know its definition in English.

Which do I mean?

The translator's dilemma.

5.

I go get la Marijoe a full two hours before our appointment because PTSD makes survivors unreliable about keeping time. Plus, we're taking public transit.

She comes out of her apartment wearing new plastic shoes and a fuschia print dress. The mostly grey hair she usually pins high on her neck is loose and falls heavy past her shoulders. The smell of almond oil wafts up from it. Before almond oil hair treatments became hipster, they were old school. This I know from my own mother.

Today there is a creature riding la Marijoe's shoulders. It is a man-bird, ungainly despite the strong, wide wings it extends. Its long toenails puncture the skin just above la Marijoe's clavicles and sink straight through muscle to bone. The creature's ugly pin head turns to meet my gaze.

"Vamos, pues," la Marijoe says to me.

She knows I see the creature, have seen it from the first day she became my client. If I've earned any respect from her it is because I didn't run out of the office screaming that day.

Marijoe calls it her zope—after zopilote, vernacular for the vulture from which the creature takes its shape—and these days I only see it riding her when something has pushed her beyond survival and deep into her core, where fear still lives.

It is the appointment that's done it. The notice that perhaps they've located her brother living in a small town in Oaxaca these 30-plus years he's been disappeared and she's believed him dead. This is why I'm accompanying her. To help her through her first meeting with him via internet hangout at the State Department office.

That's why her zope comes, too.

The past is carrion memory, and the three of us—client, shrink, the monster given vulture shape by survivor guilt—live by picking at it.

6.

Voice comes before image.

The community library in Juchitán has broadband, but the image of the librarian leaning into the computer freezes with Rolando just a shadowed bit of background pixelation even as the sound comes through. The librarian nods at me, then tries adjusting on that end while the State Department functionary and I make strained conversation and la Marijoe and her brother repeat each other's names in a circlet of syllable and breath.

Rolando's voice through the monitor is soft and sibilant; he still sounds like the youngster orphaned, then separated from his older sister, and forced to find his way out of a place of fantastic, inconceivable violence alone, first by trailing after scavenger birds, then following migratory ones as he made his way north.

The internet coughs up a perfect image. The librarian seated at the computer is a muxe dressed in the huipil of the indigenous population of the town. Standing behind her, in western wear and twisting his hands in expectation, is Rolando. He looks much older than his voice, older even than la Marijoe. It is a quick impression, really, because our screen goes to black as the feed buffers, and this time the sound cuts out, too.

The zope fans its huge wings, digs its claws deeper into la Marijoe's flesh. In fact, I see the wicked ends poking all the way through her back; dark, blackish blood caught in the tips. I wonder about the State Department guy—Frank—and whether he sees something because every time the zope moves its wings, he seems to flinch.

The computer screen in front of la Marijoe lightens again, then fills with smoke.

I can smell it. Wood smoke. Pine, resiny and hot. Frank grabs my shoulder, crushes it in his grip. The smoke on screen clears after a second, two, three ... and then we stare at a stand of pinabetes—Christmasy, quick-growing trees prone to lightning strikes—rooted in a ground of charred bodies.

There is a child, maybe six years old, standing in front of the pile. His eyes dart from the corpses to whomever is holding the recording device from our point of view. La Marijoe puts her hand to the screen, and the small one on the other side meets it. She says one word in that language she hasn't spoken in a decade, and even though the glottals are foreign to my ear, I understand the word means hide.

The child scoots toward the bodies. He picks his way gingerly among them, drops to his knees, then to his back. He grabs an arm to pull the body closer to him. The flesh comes off the bone as if it were a glove, but the torso doesn't budge. He drops the mass of charred skin and semi-liquid tissue and starts inching his body closer to the body on his other side. He whimpers a bit as he pushes under it, and I wonder how long a burnt body holds the heat that killed it; and if the child, too, will be singed while hiding beneath it.

The child is completely hidden by the burnt corpses when we hear the crack of gunfire. The image shakes violently, dives, captures a minute of tilted ground, then fades to black. The hangout site pops up a static image on-screen to indicate the connection has dropped.

"Rolando," la Marijoe says one last time, then goes silent as the zope's huge, dark wings curve forward to cover her eyes.

Frank lets go of my hand at the same time as the zope plunges its curved beak into the crown of la Marijoe's head. The monstrous creature pushes its ugly head so deep inside the old woman, its beak temporarily bulges out a spot on her neck.

"Marijoe?"

She turns to me. Zope feathers are coming through the skin beneath her eyebrows and behind her ears, but it's what's happening on her forehead, cheeks, and chin that gets my attention. Fine particles of whatever powder or foundation makeup she's been wearing slough off from the pressure of feathers prodding at the skin from within. Under the flaking cover-up, la Marijoe's face is hyperpigmented, shiny, and her skin is too thick for even the big vulture quills to get through.

Like my girlfriend Daiana's wrist, where a third-degree burn from one of the bakery's commercial ovens has healed into a bracelet of contracted skin.

By Istanbul Protocols ....

"We can try this again a different day," Frank says.

"No," la Marijoe answers. "I see Rolando is alive. That is enough."

Frank stops me on our way out. "I can't begin to understand what happened here today. But if you convince her to come back and try this again, make sure the appointment is with me."

I nod.

After a moment he adds, "Was the librarian with Rolando—" but I stop him before he can say anything else. "I've got to catch up with my client."

"You've been telling tales," I say to la Marijoe when we're on the bus. "All these years in treatment, you've been lying to me."

"No," she answers. "Everything I told you happened exactly as I recounted it."

"But not to you. Rolando's sister was shot dead if that digital translation of memory is to be believed."

She smiles. "You should know better than to trust a translation."

"If you are not Rolando's sister, who are you? Why search for him, to what purpose? And what's your real name, anyway?"

She doesn't answer, doesn't speak, until her stop. "So now that you know, will you still see me?" she asks as she gets to her feet after signaling the bus driver.

"Of course," I answer. "I've got an opening Tuesday, I'll pencil you in."

• • •

7.

She doesn't show that week. In fact, she doesn't show at the First State Survivors Center ever again.

A month into her absence, I set aside my injured professional pride and go to her apartment to talk to her. After I knock, a young woman with three children clinging to her legs opens the door. I give her my name and ask about la Marijoe, and she invites me in, offers me a lemonade.

"I've always wondered about her," Anabelle—that's the new tenant—says as she mixes tap water with the drink mix, then puts the can of mix back into a cupboard that holds just it and four tins of evaporated milk. "I found something of hers jammed up behind the pipe under the sink in the kitchen when I moved in. I thought she'd come back for it. I'll go fetch it."

She disappears into the next room, and one of the toddlers trots after her; but the other two stay and watch me with big, wary eyes. It takes Anabelle a long time—long enough for me to notice that there isn't much furniture in the apartment and that what is here has the look of hand-me-down or Goodwill.

She comes back with a cigar box which she hands to me. Inside is about $1,000 in crisply folded bills and a sealed envelope with my name on it. When I open it, a torn matchbook cover with the words "sin embargo" and a string of what look like library call numbers written in grease pencil flutters out, followed by the primary feather of a vulture.

"A mystery wrapped in an enigma," Anabelle says with a shrug when I look back at her. "But that's definitely a turkey buzzard feather."

Never underestimate people. Never figure that the young or the poor or the humble don't have something important to teach you about your own assumptions. I stay long enough to find out that the public library is Anabelle's favorite haunt and that she can not only paraphrase Churchill and quote chapter and verse of the *Stokes Field Guide to the Birds of North America* but knows that, if the numbers are Dewey call numbers, they are all over the place— from occult to salvation, psychology to philosophy.

I go back to my office, put the feather in my pencil cup, and stare at it for a while. Then I dial Frank's number.

The hangout connection is much better this time.

"Where is my sister?" Rolando says when he sees only us on-screen.

"Let me ask you something, Rolando," I say. "So many years have passed, how can you be sure the woman sitting in front of the monitor last time we talked is really your sister?"

He looks confused for a few moments, then gives us a smile. It is so like la Marijoe's it lands a punch to my gut.

"I could never confuse her voice for another's," he says finally. "I still have dreams about being buried under bodies. It was my sister's voice that reminded me I wasn't dead. Then and now."

"All those years ago ... was she there when you ventured out from your hiding place?"

He shakes his head. "Nobody was there. Just the burnt bodies and the vultures feasting on them. But I knew my sister would find me. I knew that she would never stop looking for me."

He sounds just like the other survivors I treat, whose hopes—no matter how infinitesimal—cling like a burr. Just last week, when there was news that one of the Madres of the Plaza de Mayo in Argentina had been reunited with a grandson missing since the dirty war, all of my clients spoke again about their own disappeared loved ones, their own future reunification days. One spoke of that to me even though we both know her husband was pushed out of a helicopter over open sea.

"Are you sure all of the burnt bodies were dead?" I ask Rolando, picturing la Marijoe's contracted skin as I say it.

"Yes," Rolando says. "All of them."

Frank clears his throat. "Last time we tried the hangout, what did you see when the video part wasn't working?"

I translate the question into Spanish.

"What do you mean 'what did I see?' A dark screen. My own reflection, and la Tere, the librarian, reflected on it, too. May I talk to my sister now?"

"She's disappeared," I say, before I can reconsider my word choice. "I don't know where."

"At least I know she is alive," he says after a moment. "That big empty space her disappearance left in my life can fill up now. I imagine it is the same for her." He starts to get up to leave.

"Wait," I say, fishing the scrap of paper out of my pocket. I hold it as close to the computer's camera as I can. "Do you have any idea what this number is?"

I hear him call the librarian closer to the computer and then their quick consultation in a Zapotecan language quite different than the Tz'utijil he and la Marijoe spoke together. Not for the first time I feel dazed by the sheer number of languages in the world, the sheer number of opportunities for translation to leave out that one element that gives real meaning to what is being said.

"We don't have any idea. But we'll think about it some more," Rolando says as the librarian writes down the numbers in a spiral-bound pad.

"She hid some money away," I say then. "I figure she'd want you to have it. Tell me where we can wire it to you—"

He puts his hand up to stop me. "I don't want it. I have what I need," he says, then signs off so quickly I can't argue it with him.

"That's it then," Frank says. He takes the scrap out of my hand, squints at what's written on it: *b52:b122:b131:b211:b215:b501:d150 :e234.*

"Looks like an i-p-v-six number," he says. When I shake my head, he adds, "Internet protocol version six, which is what currently routes all the traffic over the web. Could be what you have is a location and i.d. number tied to some service provider. Is Marijoe tech savvy?"

I snort, which prompts a smile. "Well, I hope you figure it out," he says handing back the scrap.

I can tell he thinks it is an intellectual puzzle to be pieced together and solved, but it's not. It is another translation calling for memory, ear, and soul to complete.

8.

Will you still see me?

Those were la Marijoe's last words to me, and I understand them differently now.

I try, I really try. She may not be who I thought she was, but she is la Marijoe; and she is someone. Someone tied—however tenuously or fantastically—to massacre victims from an ossuary that the Guatemalan Forensic Anthropology Foundation has probably already exhumed and catalogued.

So that's my first step. I call the tech our Center has worked with before and read him the numbers I want him to check against their registrar's catalogue. The quantity of pieces they've catalogued is huge—every bone chip, every piece of tooth—and includes not only the victims of the genocide and three decades of armed internal conflict but the remains of the more than 6,000 migrants dead last year alone. Many of the old and the new don't have names, but some do; and maybe hope clings to me like a burr too.

The second step I take is to get Frank to ply his government muscle and find out if the numbers are, in fact, IPv6 numbers and, if so, which provider bills them and to whom.

Third step: After I chance upon Anabelle in the stacks of the Ramonita de Rodriguez branch of the Free Library, I enlist her help in searching through all the books under the call numbers that coincide with la Marijoe's sequence. I pay her a bit of a stipend, so her lunch and bus fare doesn't tip her budget into deficit, and once a week she brings me what she finds stuck between the pages. A prayer card of St. Gall; the yellowed clipping from a newspaper from 1974; an Amtrak ticket stub, round-trip to New York City; a small feather from a cedar waxwing—a bird, Anabelle further informs me —she has never seen in the city.

The objects don't all—or any?—belong to la Marijoe, she knows it and I know it. But it is a catalogue anyway, and I treat the objects with the respect my friends at the Forensic Foundation accord their remains.

Anabelle comes to the apartment to deliver the items to me because, if I went off to see another woman on a regular basis, Daiana would see red. Another homograph, by the way. In Spanish, red means net or web, and that is what is being woven every time Anabelle—kids in tow—stops by the apartment. Daiana has started baking special treats to coincide with the delivery of book findings.

The fourth step I take in trying to figure out la Marijoe and the clues she's left me is actually taken for me not by me. The Juchitán librarian emails me an invitation to a private hangout—no Frank, no Rolando. She sends it to my work email because that's the one attached to my digital footprint. I'm actually not that easy to find, but she is a librarian, after all.

I don't respond right away and not only because the Center's emails are automatically saved and archived for accountability and transparency. I think I know why Tere-the-librarian has contacted me privately, and it has nothing to do with my quest to find la Marijoe. I believe it is curiosity that has prompted it. The desire of a muxe in Juchitán to understand the life of a trans man in Philly; the desire to confirm that her small, indigenous community is—and always has been—less hesitant about the everydayness of transgender folk than any U.S. metropolis.

I let Daiana know I'll be staying late at work, and she's fine with it mostly because it's an evening Anabelle and her brood are scheduled to stop by. Daiana is making the kids the new cake she just introduced at the bakery, flavored with dragon fruit and iced in the fruit's distinctive dark pink hue. For the children's sake she's going to try baking it in the shape of a flying dragon.

When the hangout window on the computer opens up, Tere looks around with interest. "So that's what the inside of a psychiatrist's office looks like," she says.

"I'm a clinical psychologist," I say, "but, yeah."

"You need more colorful artwork."

I smile a bit, wait.

"So I wanted to talk to you," she says, "about the numbers. I found something that, if not significant, is at least interesting. Have you ever heard of the Aarne-Thompson Index?"

"No."

"It categorizes folk and fairy-tale types and motifs that recur in mostly Indo-European folktales," she says. "Though I think it has started including stories from other cultures as well. Anyway, most of them are two, three, or four digit numbers preceded by an AT."

"Well, that doesn't fit."

She makes an exasperated noise. "But some of them are instead subcategorized with the letters A, B, C, and so forth, to indicate that they are tales that involve mythological motifs or animals or taboos."

"Okay," I say, "cut to the chase—which do our numbers coincide with?" I don't know if she knows that expression, but she does what I ask.

"B 52 is under the general bird-men category of tale but is specifically about harpies or bird-women."

So I'll be honest, this seems an unlikely concordance for la Marijoe's numbers, but that doesn't keep me from feeling a weird sort of unease. I don't have much of a classical education, but I kind of remember that harpies chased one of the Greek heroes to his death.

"B 122 is code for tales of birds with magic, and B 131 is all truth-telling birds," Tere continues. "B 211 and 215 are both tied to animal languages and animals that can speak. B 501 is a category of tales where an animal gives part of its body to a human as a magical talisman."

"Jesus," I say. I tell her about la Marijoe then, including what we saw during the half-failed hangout, the bit about her sprouting feathers and even that she left me one of those feathers in a cigar box she could have no certainty I'd ever find. Of course, I sound like a nutburger as I recount it. Tere doesn't say anything for a while, then drops her eyes to the spiral-bound notebook open in front of her.

"So maybe I copied one of the other numbers down wrong," she says finally. "Is it really D 150, not D 152?"

I pull out la Marijoe's scrap of paper. "Yeah. 150. Why?"

"Because D 150 stories are about humans transforming into birds; D 152 tales are about birds transforming into humans," she says. "Given what all the other numbers are keyed to, I think the latter would better fit the narrative we're piecing together."

"You can't really mean to tell me you think that la Marijoe is a bird turned human."

She laughs at me. "Because a human turning into a bird is easier to accept?"

"I do deal with the most inventive forms of human denial at my job."

The laugh is genuine this time. Then she grows serious. "You don't think even a vulture can grow weary of the dead we leave for them to clean up? You don't think a great mother bird might adopt another's fledgling found living among the hundreds, the thousands of corpses?"

She sighs. "Is there a difference, really? Whether one of the vultures at the massacre site took pity on Rolando and magically turned itself human for him or his sister's dying spirit hopped into the body of one of the birds that was already there, it was to the same end. To protect him."

"Nice thought, bad job."

She shrugs. "He got out of there alive."

"Luck."

"Magic."

"Fairy tale magic," I say. "Not the kind I believe in."

She grins. "No? Me, I believe in every kind. I couldn't be a librarian otherwise."

When it's clear that's all she has for me, I thank her and sign off quickly, then sit in the quiet of the Survivors Center emptied of survivors and staff. I don't want to go home yet. I can't go home yet, and I'm not sure why. I wander out to the break room and let my eyes rest on the world map that takes up one full wall. There are pins color coded for each of our clients at their country of origin and then at every country they've landed for a time on their journey here to us. I find la Marijoe's pin in Guatemala and trace the unbroken line to the one in Delaware.

Thousands of miles as the crow—or vulture—flies.

There's another homograph for you. Miles means thousands in Spanish. I go back into my office and get back on the internet. I search for the Aarne-Thompson index and look for the last number on la Marijoe's string, the one Tere-the-librarian had forgotten to translate for me.

Am I surprised when I read the description of the motif that ties together the E 234 tales? Not really. Nations are built on bones, so is it any wonder there are so many stories that revolve around those who return from death to avenge it?

Guatemala, Syria, Bosnia, Cambodia, Rwanda, East Timor, Angola, Kurdistan, and all the other genocides I know about from the Center's clients: there must be miles of E 234 tales waiting to be found.

9.

The past is never as simple as we've been told it is. In some languages there is an admission of this in a verb aspect without any certainty of completion.

La Marijoe is my past imperfect.

My friend at the Forensic Foundation finds a match for the numbers I've given him, identifying an ossuary and the date of exhumation. It is one of several mass graves that have been tied to the massacre that left María José and Rolando orphaned and on the run, but barring further identification by the FAFG, we can never know if the specific numbers are keyed to the Manrique family members they lost.

Neither can I tell you if la Marijoe's numbers are what Frank believes they are or what Tere-the-librarian does or even what Anabelle thinks them as she collects her evidence of life in books from every library branch in the city.

Perhaps the numbers are all of these or none.

I mail the vulture feather to Rolando care of the Juchitán library. The $1,000 from the cigar box I give to Anabelle because I know she's hurting enough that even that little bit will seem a godsend, and hey, she's got fledglings, too, so I think la Marijoe would have approved.

And one weekend when Daiana is working a double in preparation for the Fat Tuesday before Lent, I rent a car and drive about forty-five miles out of Philadelphia to a little town—the internet is my informant—where there are four trees that hold near as many turkey vultures as leaves.

I watch the birds for hours, riding thermals, landing, and hopping from branch to branch. They watch me, too, and despite the sympathetic magic I attempt in their language of whines and guttural hisses, I get no answer.

Because there are no answers in this tiempo, this time, this present tense. It is filled with infinitives instead—absolutes and constructs; marked and unmarked; active and elliptical.

Today, Jamila, who speaks the best Arabic at the Center, finagles shelter and the promise of a job for a Middle Eastern client, so her hand can heal from its session in a meat grinder.

Today, my boss brings the staff a coconut pound cake baked by a client who has finally set up the dessert shop he dreamed about during his years at a Cambodian refugee camp. When my boss sets the cake on the break room table, he tells us we're totally worth the two-hour drive to go get it.

Today, the DART train comes exactly three minutes late, so I am able to catch it and get back to the apartment in Philly before Daiana comes home. I place some flowers in a vase, so they are the first thing she sees when she opens the door.

Today, she tells me that although she is mexicana, someone assumes she's Asian while she's in line at Hai Street Kitchen and asks her to check the status of their order.

Today, I tell her I don't see it, that she'll never look like me, and we bicker about whether I'm Latino or sansei or both or none, and I tell her that what I am is a trilingual homograph and let's leave it at that.

Today, she rolls her eyes at my verbal conceit, and we lounge on the couch eating Hai Street's expensive sushi burritos and rub our feet together, watching reality TV neither of us can relate to because it has nothing to do with what's real.

Today, I remember that the word relate is another homograph.

Today, I weigh credible fears, burden of proof, deportation orders, detainers, and directives against several plastic baggies filled with 60,000 scraps of paper.

Today, the names are an incantation as they leave my lips.

Today, I feel the feathers pushing their way through the walls of my heart.

Copy and Paste

Yoav Rosen

● translated by Maya Klein ●

In those days I talked a lot about weapons. There was Alex, the lone soldier who lived with the old lady. It was unclear whether they were related. On Friday afternoons Alex was always out on the balcony in boxer shorts and an undershirt, cleaning his short barrel M-16 in the sun, smoking and sweating for an hour or two, and I would watch him from our balcony and say, what a waste of manpower.

The first time I thought about it was when I overheard him talking on the phone, he was saying that the IDF is the biggest whorehouse in the country, everyone is all over each other—male officers and female soldiers, male soldiers and female commanders, female commanders and male ones, male commanders amongst themselves. Alex was tall and fair, he had the arrogant air of a proud Russian. His pale, hairy legs shone in the sun, and the shadow underneath his armpits brought up memories of days long past: crumpled-up newspapers featuring lipstick ads that were scattered all over the floor of the army tent during basic training.

I had it all figured out, right down to the last detail. I spent hours on the balcony with the door closed behind me while Alex sat on the oil-stained railing. The old lady had tried cleaning it but never managed to get the stains out.

Apart from the old lady, Alex didn't have any family in Israel. My family was merely background noise: my wife, Iris, who took care of behaviorally challenged kids, and the twins, Ben and Beth. Ben took an immediate liking to the scouts; he once dragged a gigantic wooden beam home to prove his devotion, and Beth started her own blog online. I don't know what she did there.

In the free community newspaper they deliver to every house, I read that the security situation was heating up and caution should be exercised. Children should not be out alone after dark; power locks should be installed in the car; a home security system indoors; they even steal dogs, it said. When we started giving things up, when it became a struggle to buy things for the house, when I gave up cigarettes, we used copies of the community newspaper that had piled up—seven, eight, or nine in the front entrance of each house—to line the boxes we packed and placed in the reinforced security room.

I studied Alex's short, jagged toenails, the way he played with them in the hot air and tried to think about Iris. The way he sits with his legs wide apart, concentrating, dismantling the weapon down to its smallest parts, using a brush and a flannel cloth to clean them. When Iris would return from one of her conferences, she smelled of other counselors' perfumes. It was summer, and the average temperature was thirty-eight degrees Celsius.

I missed the city. I slept outside on the balcony at night, and whenever the security jeeps drove by, they would temporarily blind me. All we ever wanted was a nice house in a quiet area. Well, we got it. Beth started attending Yoga for Children, which drained our checking account, and Ben was always in need of a monthly check for the scouts. Alex would spend weekends with the old lady, and when I sat on the balcony and Ben came out with a question about his homework, I tried to figure out why he couldn't see Alex and only I could.

I began thinking about what would happen if he agreed to give me his weapon. I'd go over all of the details with him. He'd file a report with the Military Police and tell them that it was stolen when he was attacked by a group of terrorists on his way to the base. He struggled, they were trying to kidnap him, and one of them even attempted to inject him with something; but he managed to break free, and they just got his weapon as he ran for his life.

Tell them that you wounded one of them, too, I planned on saying.

He'd clean his weapon one last time for my sake and then hand it over along with the ammunition.

The night the children disappeared began by someone alerting the neighborhood security watch. The jeeps started circling around, driving at full speed. Their Kojaks blinked like crazy. Police cars joined in, and searchlights lit up our dark silence. A group of scouts had gathered their equipment and gone hiking or went out to earn a badge or whatever it is that scouts do. It was Ben and his friends, like that kid who always comes over to our house smelling of iron. Beth disappeared, too. Iris came home late. She stepped in from all of the noise, dropped her keys, and said, "I don't know what I'm going to do."

The police stopped by every house. Ben and his group, there were ten of them, weren't the only ones missing. There were two girls missing, and Beth. We answered questions. The streets were filled with police cars and SUVs. They asked us for photographs. The police officers went through the children's rooms and returned embarrassed, speechless. Reporters began arriving. That's when it got really scary. Iris burst into tears and fled to the bathroom.

We were cooped up in the house. Then they asked us to come out and join the search. I heard someone say that the first night is the most critical. They have less than two hours to get them to the territories of the Palestinian authority. Someone said, how could they make twenty kids disappear, and someone else said, thirteen, they're thirteen. I grabbed the keys and went out. Standing on our front walk, I could see Alex heading towards the old lady's house. His army shirt was unbuttoned, he wore an undershirt underneath it, and his duffel bag was slung over his shoulder. He was looking at the police cars.

We took the car towards the southern part of the fence. They told us to contact the officer in charge of the area and he'd instruct us where to search. Alex sat down, lit a cigarette, and asked, "Can you turn on the AC?" I drove the dark, circular road, perspiring. The air conditioned air crawled out of the vents and onto my skin. We could see flashing lights. Dogs were barking in the distance. My ears were ringing. Alex smoked. Dogs again. I thought to myself, Beth came out taller than her brother. And they're both dark, they look more like their mother. I thought I was speaking aloud; but Alex sat and smoked, and I drove silently.

An hour later, Alex and I were walking through a thorny field, carrying large flashlights that the local security team had provided us with. I yelled, "Ben!" and Alex yelled, "Beth!" The only things we could see were the thorns just before us and an occasional porcupine fleeing the light and the noise. The air became heavier. The dust rising from the thorns burned the throat and eyes. My shirt and underwear stuck to my body. Alex's undershirt went transparent, dirty in the middle. His chest was smooth and shiny.

We could hear the police radio screeching in the distance. We heard a helicopter, too, but it was only there by coincidence and continued flying north. I yelled, "Ben!" and Alex yelled, "Beth!" I couldn't remember the names of the other kids, maybe just Gilli, the one with the large braces and the retainer; I gave up because I thought I got the name wrong.

After four, just before sunrise, we returned to the car. I notified the officer that we didn't find anything. He notified me that they didn't either. I was tired and preferred not to find a damn thing. We headed home. I drove. I left the radio switched off. Alex stayed in his undershirt and had tied the army shirt to his belt. We reeked of sweat. I was embarrassed that my sweat was sharper than his. Alex took out his cigarettes and offered one to me. I took it, and he lit them both for us. I said, I'm not going to cry now, speaking the language that my parents spoke, the language Alex couldn't understand. The cigarettes were strong, and I coughed. I had to take a piss but kept driving. I thought that I was sensing some smell coming from the air conditioning, but it was just the army boots that smelled of diesel fuel and shoe polish.

"You got two kids?" he asked.

I felt a stinging sensation in my stomach. I nodded.

"No more?" he asked, taking another drag.

I signaled right to turn into the neighborhood. The clicking of the signal broke the silence. Our windows were rolled down, and we passed some jackass in flip-flops and socks who was standing outside. He told us that they found a torn green scout kerchief. We ignored him and continued driving.

"What do you do? For a living."

"I'm a photographer. But I'm thinking of quitting. Leaving. Don't know. What kind of weapons do you guys have?"

"Short caliber M-16s. American military surplus."

I rearranged myself in the seat, and my foot hit the gas pedal. We momentarily leaped forward.

"What do you photograph?"

"A sign saying 'Welcome to the Municipality of Hod Hasharon.' Dishes in a restaurant in Ra'anana. A piece-of-shit dump that belonged to the Turks that a subsidiary of the Ministry of Agriculture is holding on to. A few fashion models. There's plenty, more than enough."

Alex bounced his leg up and down. He took a drag on his cigarette and blew out the smoke.

I realized that a smell of alcohol was coming from him. "It doesn't have to do with art?"

"No."

Alex chuckled. We heard helicopters above. This time they were intended for us. For the children.

I swallowed. The air was rough with a combination of nicotine and dust.

Later, Alex told me that The Association for the Wellbeing of

Israel's Soldiers had fixed him up with the old lady. She was looking to lend a hand, to help soldiers because they help us and so on, and he was on the lone soldier list, so the two had been brought together.

"Ten months with the woman," he said, lighting another cigarette. I had already gotten used to the smell of our sweat. "How long have you been neighbors?" Alex asked.

"Here? Four years." I looked at the reflective yellow light on the shoulder of the road.

The next morning the search continued, and when I got home, I felt that something had changed. I hurried inside with my keys, the car remote always gets tangled up in them. I nearly threw everything on the floor and kicked the pile of community newspapers, but the reporter who tried to interview me was there. The children's photographs were printed again and again. They called it "The Night of the 13," *A Heinous Crime*. She was waiting in the living room with Iris, who wouldn't agree to talk but had made tea for them both. I told her that unless she wanted to go home on all fours and have her kids—if she has any—see their mom a cripple, she'd better get out fast.

At night I dreamt that the children came home. Ben just walked in, and I looked at him, and said, "But you're dead," and he shrugged and went into the living room. He was all beaten up, but I couldn't tell which parts of his body were hurt. I asked him where Beth was, and when he turned to me, I said, "Doesn't all of this have to do with your death?" Later, we went out to the balcony, so I could show Alex to him.

In the evening, Iris collected pairs of shoes and dismantled bicycle handlebars and schoolbooks that belonged to Ben and Beth, and she placed everything in boxes lined with copies of the community newspaper. I asked her what she was doing. She said that, if she couldn't see the children, she didn't want to have to see their stuff either.

"Are you out of your mind?" I asked.

I was standing in the doorway of Ben's room, and I called out to her several times. I told her, "Don't you ever talk to me like that," but it didn't help. She was throwing night-lights and electronic mosquito repellents into the boxes lined with newspapers, and muttering, "Now's the time to start smoking again, right?" I turned and bumped into the metal window frame. Outside, the sidewalk was filled with parked cars. People were walking down the street, clustered in small groups. The scouts handed out maps of the neighborhood and the surrounding area. The small wooded area facing our block had been cordoned off with red tape, but it was only tied to the bushes on one side, the other was dangling in the wind. "Is that the kind of advice you give to people in these situations?"

Iris sniffled behind me and dragged a box down the hall. "I'm not a counselor every moment of my life."

We stood there, Iris and me, the box being the only thing between us.

"It's about time that you open your eyes," she told me, sniffling again. "Open your eyes and do something. Pay attention to the news. Listen to the radio. Children don't come back to this place after they disappear."

That weekend Alex was home on leave again. The police task force had spread out on both sides of the neighborhood. Police representatives, National Security Agency representatives, even one from the Prime Minister's office, had spoken with us. The old lady sat hunched over near her balcony door, then got up to prepare Shabbat dinner in the kitchen. A dark Mazda was parked on the street with its engine running, waiting for Alex. After they had dinner on the balcony, he went out. I stayed up waiting for more than half of the night, and when the Mazda brought him back, stumbling and singing in Russian, I closed the door behind me and got into bed with Iris.

It was late in the afternoon when he came out on the balcony, barefoot, wearing light jeans and without his cigarettes. He sat there wordlessly, his head in his hands.

We drove out of the neighborhood. "Thanks for helping me with this, man," Alex said. We passed the empty guard post that was manned lately with police officers enforcing a checkpoint. Alex took out his cigarettes and lit one for us both.

"Hang on," I said, "let's get out of here first."

He held the two burning cigarettes. "Where do we search now?" he asked once we were on the highway. "Let's get out of here first," I repeated.

I was trying to think what would happen if *everyone* had a home security service, the kind that they recommend you get, and then all of the homes were broken into at the exact same time; what would happen then; how many houses would ten hired security guards in five patrol cars manage to save; and what if *everyone's* children went out after dark at the same time? I slapped myself on the back of my neck. Alex turned on the radio. I turned it off.

"Thanks for helping me with this, man," he said again. "I don't know how I forgot the rifle. I always feel it. I have a hole in my back because of it." He pressed on a point under his back ribs and furrowed his brows. "It's jail, for sure."

We passed a sign that read *Hummus, Falafel, Tahini, Pickles sold by Wait* and had red arrows pointing the way. "How many bullets does your rifle hold?" I asked.

Alex raised his eyebrow and answered. "Thirty. You load twenty-nine."

"And you shot one of your own?"

We drove and drove until we passed Ra'anana Junction, the entrance to Givatayim and its exit, and then Alex said, "Stop there." I pulled up into a gas station. The blue neon lights were blinding. Alex said, "Be back in a sec," he asked for four hundred Shekels, got out of the car, and walked into the convenience store. My heart began to pound. I turned off the air conditioning. Alex disappeared from sight. I thought about the children. Two images were going through my mind: the wind blowing over the sand, and a boy and a girl running into the sea. How come you always run into the sea and never just walk? I pictured Ben, blindfolded in a basement, the smell of urine and iron all around him. I couldn't imagine Beth. I couldn't get a view of Alex from the car.

I nearly honked in order to break the silence as Alex appeared holding a heavy plastic bag that the blue neon lights turned to yellow. He got in the car and pulled two cold, metallic blue cans out of the bag. "Is that what they're drinking at places nowadays?" I asked. Alex smiled and coughed. I saw that he was missing a tooth deep in his mouth.

He poured two shots of vodka into plastic cups. "It helps with the taste." I drank just as he did. I shifted in my seat and had to pass gas. My body was heavy from the past few days, and I laughed coarsely, loudly, how it all hurts, and Alex laughed, too. We drank whatever was left. In the distance, rather close by, we could see the hypnotic lights of the city arranged in geometrical shapes, precise, well-formed like something unbelievable, something that doesn't even exist. I asked whether I should keep driving. Alex hummed a Russian melody, not anything familiar, not something the first settlers sang, but some disgusting, heavy, loud crap that young people dance to. He threw the empty cans on the car mat. We drove through the city's narrow streets. Drops of moisture thickened over the window panes. Where do your friends live? I asked. Alex hummed and tapped his fingers on the window and dashboard. Just tell me already, I said, Where's the weapon, and he laughed again. He had that bitter smell of alcohol again. I kept driving and yelled, Where's your damn weapon? The steering wheel shook in my hands. He said, It's on Mandevoshkes or something street, and burst out laughing. Then he gave me vague directions by memory. We progressed slowly. We reached Mandevoshkes Mocher Sforim Street and stopped before a neglected building. Alex put his hand on my shoulder, then looked at me, narrowing his eyes. He drew closer and said, "You're under a lot of pressure now," and burst out laughing.

His gaze wandered to a small balcony on the second floor. There were four tall guys standing there, talking and drinking. Two of them were peeling the paint off of the banister, and the thick flecks fell into the darkened yard. They looked very much like Alex and seemed shiny, freshly showered. My diaphragm was hurting as if I had just come back from a run. "Is this where your friends live?" I asked. Alex nodded.

"Then get lost." He pushed the door open and got out of the car.

I parked not far from the shrub marked by the dangling tape and walked towards the house. The old lady came out with empty plastic bottles in her hands, heading for the recycling bin. She had left the lights on behind her. She stopped and approached me on the sidewalk. Her eyes were small, blue, and ugly, and she had wrinkles on the sides of her nose. She extended one hand, which remained in the air. "This is not easy," she said, looking me in the eye. Afterwards, we walked up and sat on her balcony. She offered me a chair. I sat and stared at the oil stains on the stone banister, eating her dinner.

That night Iris fell asleep in Ben's bed. I looked at her. Her eyelids were shut, puffy and soft. A few boxes lined with copies of the community newspaper were filled with things. I didn't look inside, but I went into Beth's room, stepping by accident on a pink flip-flop at the entrance. The air smelled of tangerines and coconut, the fabric softener Iris uses. I sat down in the chair facing the small silver computer that we once bought. I leaned over it and blew out air. I had to breathe deeply and keep from looking around. The computer's mouse was covered with sparkles. I rested my palm on it, and the screen turned on with a whir of static electricity. A line ran through in purple. **God damn it. Beth Mautner's blog!! Everything you could possibly want to say!!**

The latest entry date appeared beneath the line running across the screen. It was the day the children had disappeared. After which came the lines: **In those days I talked a lot about weapons. There was Alex, the lone soldier who lived with the old lady across the street. It was unclear whether they were related. On Friday afternoons Alex was always out on the balcony in boxer shorts** and an undershirt, cleaning his short barrel M–16 in the sun, smoking and sweating for an hour or two, and I would watch him from our balcony and say, what a waste of manpower.

The rest was familiar, too. It continued with **Tell them that you wounded one of them, I planned on saying. He'd clean his weapon one last time for my sake and then hand it over along with the ammunition.** And farther down, highlighted in purple:

My dad is in love with the neighbor's soldier...!!!!! OMG!!!!!!!!!!

I sat back down in the chair. It was several sizes too small. Fine hairs of dust moved like long arms from the computer's air vents. The silver table that we bought was there, the same as always. A chill went through my body. I pressed ENTER after **along with the ammunition**. And I began typing. **The night the children disappeared began by someone alerting the neighborhood security watch. The jeeps started circling around, driving at full speed. Their Kojaks blinked like crazy. Police cars joined in and searchlights lit up our dark silence.**

Onen and His Daughter

Dilman Dila

Onen peddled fast over the brown rooftops through the low hanging clouds that swept down from the mountains, bringing a chill to the village, promising a storm that could stop him from seeing his daughter before she died.

He had not seen her in twenty years. He had tried to talk to her, to tell her that he did not kill her lover, but she had refused to answer his calls. Now she wanted to see him.

He used all the strength in his eighty-year-old body to push the bruka, but the ornithopter was too old, too rusty. Its wings had big holes. It could not go fast enough. Tears stung his eyes, clouding his vision, putting him at risk of crashing into the mwiko trees that stood like little mountains above the village. He might crash and end up like his dear little girl, Anena.

The call had come as he sat on a papyrus mat in his living room, drinking beer from a calabash. It interrupted an old movie on the vidisimu, a twenty-one-inch gadget that the government supplied for free. It was illegal not to have one. It combined all the functions of the luxurious gadgets in his pre-teen years—radio, TV, phone, computer—items his peasant parents had never imagined to own. A nurse had appeared on the screen, behind her was a maternity ambulance entangled in a mwiko tree, half of which was burnt.

"It's your daughter," the nurse had said.

Even before she said the name, Onen stiffened, his fingers squeezing the calabash so hard that he felt pain. He did not know that Anena had joined the maternity services. He could not concentrate on the face of the nurse. He kept looking at the background, trying to see if indeed it was Anena in the wreckage.

"She wants to see you," the nurse had added.

"Anena?" he whispered, but the microphone, though over ten feet away, picked it up, and relayed it to the nurse.

"Yes," the nurse said. "There was an accident. She was racing to answer an emergency when strong winds drove her into the tree."

"She wants to see me?"

"Yes," the nurse said. "Please, hurry."

The bruka could not go fast enough. He wished he had a Mosquito, the attack flyers they had used in the military. He would have covered the twenty miles to the grazing fields in under a minute. His bruka was a pioneer model from a time in his childhood when air travel was a reserve for the privileged before the technological revolution delivered ornithopters that were cheaper than bicycles. It was shaped like an egg. It had four wings and two seats. He had bought it with his first salary at the age of eighteen and had flown it every day thereafter until he went to jail. Upon his release, he had fitted it with an engine to comply with new traffic laws, but now he wished he had instead bought a newer model, one that was fully automatic and ran on solar power. It would have been quicker.

Peddling the craft drained his energy, reminding him of his frailty. When he had gone to jail twenty years earlier, although he was already sixty, he still had the vitality of youth. He belonged to the warrior clan, the Abasura, whose role it was to guard the nation. He had served in the military from the age of eighteen. It kept his body youthful. But incarceration had wasted it all away, turning him into just another old man.

He prayed to the ancestors to bless him with his old strength, just one more time, so he could reach Anena before she died. She wanted to see him. That was the only sign of reconciliation he had got from his family. His three wives still ignored him. His eighteen children avoided him. His grandchildren did not know him. But now all that did not matter. Anena was calling for him. She was at the doorsteps of death. She did not call for her mother or her siblings or her husband. He wondered if she had a husband, if she had found another lover and gotten married. He brushed the thought away. She had called for him, her father, who the family had outcasted. It could only mean that she was ready to forgive him.

Upon his release a few weeks before, he had found his homestead in ruins. His children and wives had abandoned it. Weeds chocked the compound. The grass-thatched roof had fallen in. Thieves had stolen everything of value apart from two items. One was his ornithopter, which they probably ignored as junk. The other was a bridal basket, which Anena's fiancé had used to ferry the dowry. It still lay in the front yard under the ruins of the tent her brothers had constructed for the marriage ceremony. It was made of stainless Nyoro iron and was large enough to carry twenty bulls among other gifts. The iron was of high value and could have fetched a handsome price. He could not understand why thieves had ignored it. Was it because of the bloodstains?

Where had that blood come from? Was it her lover's blood?

Onen had rebuilt his home and repaired the bruka, but he left the basket where it had lain for twenty years, overgrown with grass. A creeping plant with yellow flowers had twisted itself around the bars. He was afraid to touch it. The stains of blood. Could it be her lover's? His body had been found at the bottom of a rocky valley, smashed to pulp. Maybe Ajwakas had smeared his blood on it in a ritual to cleanse the home of murder.

I did not kill him, Onen had tried to tell Anena. For twenty years. She had refused to talk to him like everyone else in his family. They thought he did it for he was the only one who objected to her marriage. Her fiancé, Macika, a chubby fellow who crafted chairs for a living, belonged to the Sungura clan, whose traditional role was to clean toilets. Macika had rejected culture and instead became a carpenter. Still, the old customary laws forbade him from marrying a higher clan's daughter.

Being a warrior with a war raging in the Southern Lakelands, Onen had rarely been home. He had already missed two of his children's weddings. When Anena's turn came, she had insisted on his presence. She sent a request to his commanders, and they forced him to go on leave to give away his daughter. On arriving home, Anena and her fiancé, Macika, were waiting in the bruka landing pad to welcome him. She knelt to greet him. Macika bowed his head slightly.

"My son," Onen had said. He had mistaken Macika for one of his children, and as he searched his memory for a name, he remembered that none of his sons kept a beard. The shock of that realization, that he was forgetting his own children, immediately vanished when it struck him that none of his sons had come out to welcome him. They had left that duty to the groom. "Where is—Ocaka?" he asked Anena. Ocaka was his firstborn son and his heir. He should have been there to welcome him. "Where are your mothers? Where is everybody?"

"They are not happy," Anena replied. She did not have to explain why. They did not understand his long absences for other warriors returned frequently to see their loved ones.

At that moment, he decided to retire. He had done the right thing in coming home for his daughter's wedding, and he hoped his announcement would be the first step in asking for his family's forgiveness. Then he saw the tattoo on the groom's neck, the snout of a pig, etched at birth to mark him for life as a Sungura. A toilet cleaner.

"You can't marry him," he told Anena.

She kept quiet for a long time. The smile faded from Macika's face. When she spoke, her voice was so low he almost did not hear it, but it sliced through his skin like the cold winds of the rainy season.

"I thought you were a good man," she said.

She took her lover's hand and dragged him away. Macika kept looking back, maybe to plead, but not once did Anena look back. She climbed into their bruka, and in a few heartbeats they had vanished into the blue sky.

Nobody talked to Onen that night. He visited the huts of each wife and the homes of each son, but they all shut the door in his face. He had been absent in their life for so long, then on his return he spoils a feast they had been planning for months. And all because of a social structure that was imposed by Indian colonialists about three hundred years back. They could not forgive him for that.

The next morning, Onen woke up to find a dozen warriors waiting for him. At first he thought fighting had flared again and his leave was being cancelled until one officer handcuffed him as another showed him a picture of a body smashed to pulp. Macika, Anena's fiancé.

"You are under arrest for murder," the officers told him.

Onen did not get a chance to plead his innocence. The government was trying to stamp out the hate practice of killing interclan lovers. They believed Onen to be the murderer for he was the only one who had objected to his daughter marrying a toilet cleaner. They threw him into jail without a proper investigation, without any trial, though he was a decorated warrior, to send a message to conservatives.

Onen had not seen Anena since then. Now she was stuck on a mwiko tree, two hundred feet above the ground, dying. He had to reach her quick to tell her that he did not kill her fiancé. He did not know why she had summoned him. Maybe she wanted to spit into his face before dying. Maybe she wanted to kill him for what she thought he did to her lover. He could not let her die with hatred in her heart. He had to make her believe in his innocence.

The thought propelled him through the low hanging clouds, through the dangerous airways littered with mwiko trees, over the brown villages that lay far below him happily waiting for the first drops of rain. He wished he could go faster.

He reached the grazing fields just as the rain started to fall. The half-burnt tree stood alone at the top of a hill at the edge of a cliff. The mangled wreck of an ambulance was stuck in the branches, but the place was empty. No police. No medics. No flyers. His heartbeat slowed. When he was close enough to the tree, he saw the nurse. She sat on a branch, holding a large leaf above her head to shield from the rain.

"Where is she?" he said, his voice husky, strained with tears.

She did not hear him above the roar of the wind. She leapt off the tree. A small jetpack propelled her to the bruka. He flipped open a door, and she climbed into the seat behind him. The rain fell hard.

"Where is she?" he said.

"It is dangerous to fly in this storm," she said. "Go down."

The rain blurred his vision. Wipers squeaked as they struggled to clear the windshield of rain. Onen wanted to insist on knowing where they had taken Anena, but a gust of wind hit the bruka, threatening to push it into the tree. He pulled a lever to fold the wings and punched a button to ignite the emergency engine, which could not fly the craft but allowed for safer landing in a crisis. The bruka dropped to the ground. The wind was so strong that, for a moment, Onen feared the engine would fail and they would crash into the tree trunk. The tail of the ornithopter scraped bark off the tree, but the impact did not send the flyer out of control. They landed.

The wind did not give up. It pushed them through the thicket. They had to abandon the craft or risk falling off the cliff in it. A small hut stood a short distance away. They raced to it. They were dripping wet when they entered. Inside were three herdsmen around a fire, eating miraa. The herdsmen welcomed them with goatskin to sit on and khat to chew. Onen declined the miraa, but the nurse shoved a fistful of the leaves into her mouth.

"Is she okay?" he asked.

The nurse shook her head. "I'm sorry," she said.

A long moment passed. Onen stared at the rain pouring outside the hut's door.

The nurse then gave him a black box so small it fit in his palm. He did not know what it was. She pressed a green button on the box to throw up a red light, which then materialized into the head of a woman. It looked like a real head, of flesh, blood, and bones. It was nothing like the blurry holographs he knew. Though she was twenty years older, he recognized her.

"Baba," she said.

Onen dropped the box in terror, and the image went out.

"Don't be afraid," the nurse said. Onen turned to her, but something was wrong with his eyes for he could not see her clearly. She was blurry like the old holographs. That is when he realized that he was crying. "She asked us to record what she wanted to tell you. Please listen."

The nurse picked up the box again and restarted the recording. Onen was afraid of what she would say. Though the recording was done on her deathbed, it captured nothing of the agony or the wounds. Instead, Anena had projected happy images, so her face looked as it would have had they met before the accident.

"I know you didn't kill Macika," Anena said. "I did."

Onen did not know what to feel, how to react to that.

"It was an accident," Anena continued. "We were having an argument because I had not told you about his clan."

Onen hated himself. He should have not loved the warrior's barracks more than he loved his family, then he would not have had to learn about Macika on the wedding day.

"Please, forgive me," Anena said.

Onen looked away from the holograph, out of the door, at the rain that fell upon his old flying bicycle, which the wind was squeezing against a tree trunk. Tears filled the wrinkles on his face with pools of sadness.

The Love Decay Has for the Living

Berit Ellingsen

The shattered windows, blistering paint, and whispering mould drew the Lover to the building in the drowned district. Inattentiveness and bad luck drew him to the nail that protruded from the wall like a curse. The vigor of his bloodstream drew the fungal spores on the sharp metal into his body. There they became progenitors and ancestors. When the Lover woke in his two-room apartment above the small restaurant on the corner the next morning, more than a dozen thin mushrooms peeked out of the wound in his thigh. The fruiting bodies were long and white like the fingers of a ghost, each topped with a tiny, ivory-colored cap. The fungi smelled of ozone and forbidden thoughts.

The Chef had been drawn to the Lover by the ease of his smile and the calm of his eyes, and the two men had lived in each other's orbit for some time. When the Chef saw the white fungal fingers in the Lover's thigh, the Chef's attraction to the Lover was reborn. And just in time.

"Never trust the food of a skinny chef," the Lover used to joke. But lately he had only told the Chef: "You are getting thin."

"Did you know that fungi are neither plants nor animals?" the Chef asked the Lover. "They are so distantly related to animals and plants that they are almost like extraterrestrials, strangers on their own planet."

"I did not know that," the Lover said, "but I can feel it." He had already turned a shade stranger, a hue subtler. His skin smelled like electricity and sparks.

"Shall I fetch the doctor, so he can treat your wound," the Chef said.

"No need," the Lover said. "I will be all right." The gleam of fresh desire in the Chef's eyes had not escaped the Lover, and he would like to keep it more than anything.

Instead of calling the physician, the Chef went to the floating market to find out what type of fungi was growing in the Lover. The Chef thought that the diminutive, leather-skinned women who sold mushrooms and vegetables and flowers and fruits from the bottom of their slim canoes would know more about what was edible in the land than any book or internet site did. The air at the market was swollen with flower fragrance, tobacco smoke, frying oil, and human sweat. The saleswomen's cries cut through the moist air, but the Chef found no mushrooms that matched his Lover's and returned to their two rooms and bed empty-handed.

The ceiling fan moved the humid air in slow circles above the Lover, who was resting on the bed. Raindrops leaked in from the roof and sang their wet song in bowls and buckets on the floor. When the Chef and the Lover wanted to sleep, they must navigate the sea of containers with care. After the monsoon season refused to leave, it kept raining, and few tourists came to their part of the country anymore.

With eyes that shone of curiosity as well as love, the Chef climbed quietly into bed. He cut two of the pale stalks that sat in the Lover's flesh with a broad, curved knife that had been made to decapitate mushrooms. The Lover shuddered and set his jaw but did not open his eyes. The Chef left the damp bedding and padded into the tall and narrow kitchen, rinsed his pale harvest in the tepid water from the tap, put them in his mouth, and chewed. Something in the spectral-looking digits reminded the Chef how decay dissolves every barrier and door, like love, but they brought no pain or regret to him.

The next morning, new fruiting bodies had replaced those the Chef took. They wafted in the air like sea anemones in slow current. The Chef took out the crescent-shaped blade again, leaned across the sticky sheets, and sheared off a handful of the mushroom stalks. The remnants of the ghostly fingers twitched and jerked and filled the air with blue scent.

In his restaurant on the ground floor, the Chef fried the mushrooms in a small round skillet and mixed them with grilled squid and spring onions, toasted red chili, thick dark soy sauce, and a dash of bitter tamarind. The Water Seller who peddled liquid on their street came inside and sniffed the air like a hungry dog.

"What is that?" the Water Seller said.

"Try it," the Chef said and scooped the steaming food onto a fresh lotus leaf on a cracked porcelain plate with faded gold decoration on the rim, then handed the Water Seller a fork.

"Thank you so much," the Water Seller said, while he chewed loudly at the Chef. "I haven't had any breakfast. We can't afford to with the tourists absent and business lagging."

"Yes, the weather has been strange," the Chef said. The years were less moist and warm when he first got together with the Lover.

"This is delicious," the Water Seller said, "there are white truffles in it?"

"Do you know what truffles taste like?" the Chef said.

"A few years ago, my wife and I went to Paris," the Water Seller said. "She always wanted to go to Paris, the most romantic city on Earth. We ate in a real gourmet restaurant to see what it was all about; wild boar, white truffles, red wine, and everything. It was good but not that good. This, though," the Water Seller motioned at the plate, "is different, it reminds me of something good that I have always known but forgot a long time ago and which I ought to remember. What is it?"

"My new course," the Chef said and smiled, quickly and strange, like the ghost lights that flare up in the rice fields at night.

The dish was an instant success, and everyone wanted to know what the ingredients were; but the Chef only said: "It's made with love," and thought about his Lover. The word spread like running lichen, and soon the restaurant was always full despite the lack of tourists in the city. The locals spent their hard-earned currency on the mushroom dish before they bought water or rice.

"You'll never have to work again, you can spend all day taking pictures of dying buildings as you adore doing," the Chef told the Lover. The Lover lifted his head from the pillow and smiled, his teeth ultraviolet bright and his eyes white like the mushroom's ivory buttons.

● ● ●

Every night, the Chef harvested a few of the wafting fingers. Even a quarter of a stalk was enough to remind the eater of the love that decay has for the living. The mushrooms said nothing when he cut them from the colony, they only stiffened a little as if in momentary agony. The Lover did not complain that small pieces of him vanished during the night because he knew what it meant to the Chef. Isn't love also self-sacrifice for the dreams of your beloved?

The Chef sharpened his gently curved mushroom knife at night under the serpentine shadows of the rain that trickled down the windows. The year before he had painted the walls sky blue to give them some sunshine, but the paint couldn't take the moisture and had flaked and peeled like tourist skin. The rivulets of precipitation twisted and turned like the plant fibers that were wound in the ropewalk at the edge of the city.

Every day the crop of ghostly fingers on the Lover's leg became a little smaller and a little thinner while the Chef's smile broadened. The Lover returned to the abandoned building in the drowned district to find the nail with the fungal spores again, but the structure had collapsed from the water's slow consumption and the nails pulled out by scavengers from the steel plant nearby.

Defeated but not lost, the Lover returned home. There, he took the broad-bladed mushroom knife, bit down on a thin scarf printed with blue dragonflies, and cut a deep gash in his other thigh and on his upper arms in the same measured and deliberate way the Chef harvested the fungal stalks. He crushed several ivory buttons between his fingers, smeared them into the wounds, and prayed that they would grow.

The white digits multiplied in their new sites. The Chef saw that the fungi had spread to the Lover's other thigh and both his upper arms but said nothing. When the Lover slept, the Chef harvested what he could.

Journalists and magazines visited the restaurant and wrote about the Chef's delicious dish. He was invited to France to work in a golden restaurant. Paris was bright and warm like the Chef and the Lover remembered their country had been. The Lover hoped the fungi might grow in their new home as well.

But it didn't. The temperature was a little too low, the air a touch too dry. The ghost fingers wilted and dwindled. In despair, the Lover ran the shower in the bathroom and the tap in the kitchen to moisten the air in the tall-ceilinged, many-windowed apartment. He went to the flea market at Porte de Clignancourt and bought an old humidifier. The seller laughed and asked if he was making a sauna in the heat. The Lover kept the humidifier on high, and he and the Chef were constantly wet; but neither of them said anything for the sake of the fungi and for the sake of love.

But the Lover knew the fruiting bodies were dying. They no longer glowed blue at night, and their electrical kisses had ceased. When the Lover woke to the Chef crying above him in bed, he didn't need to ask for the reason.

"We should never have left," the Lover said.

"But you always wanted to live in the most romantic city on the planet," the Chef said. "And the people here are the best and most appreciative eaters in the world."

"This city is too dry," the Lover said. No shadows of running water adorned their walls at night, no raindrops rushed in on the wind's warm breath. Compared with their home country now, Paris was cold and dry.

The Chef relented because isn't that also what love is? His Lover had sacrificed so much for him, now it was his turn. Wrapped in plastic like a dead body, the last of the fungal fingers barely survived the arid air on the plane home. They flew through thunder and lightning, and the electrical discharges enlivened the remaining fungi like defibrillation of a still heart. The Chef and the Lover returned to their apartment above the small restaurant, and its food remained a local delicacy instead of an international sensation.

"They didn't like my other dishes, anyway," the Chef said. "Just the one with the mushrooms."

The Lover only smiled at him, and blue sparks rose from the ends of the white fingers that moved like smooth tentacles on the Lover's arms and legs. The tiny lightning bolts felt like decay's never-ending but always loving thoughts.

First published in Unstuck #2.

Portrait of a Young Zombie in Crisis

Walidah Imarisha

Ralph tore the man's scalp off with his fingernails, bit into the cranium, cracking it with his molars like a walnut. He revealed the gray contents and dove in face first.

"Brains," he drawled contentedly, slurping like a child sucking the gooey center out of a Cadbury egg.

I rolled my eyes and sighed, looking down at the dead woman whose head I cradled in my hands. I used an incisor to pop a hole in her skull, inserted a straw, and sucked gingerly. Most people think brains are a solid mass, but they're actually mostly liquid. They take the shape of any container they're put in. That's why they get everywhere if you're not careful. Most zombies didn't seem to mind being covered in it. In fact, ones like Ralph reveled in it, always making sure to smear some around before finishing. Guess it's like when people take pictures of their dinner and post it on Facebook—everyone wants to remember a good meal.

"Brains," Ralph said again, a little more urgently. Bits of brain matter clung to his lower lip, and his mouth had the same Kool-Aid ring around it I used to get when I was a kid.

Ralph tapped the side of the man's head he was devouring and then pointed toward the one in my hand. He always worried I wasn't eating enough. Gotta keep my strength up to continue terrorizing the world as one of the walking dead. He was right, though—I was far skinnier than any of the other zombies I'd seen since I turned.

"Yeah, yeah, brains," I grimaced, sucking a little bit more of her brain through the straw.

This is the level of discourse that happens amongst zombies. After a time I realized they were like little cannibalistic Pokemon, as they can only say one word, to wit, "brains." That's it. That was what I had to work with. "Good morning." "Brains." "Good afternoon." "Brains." "Oh, that bloodstain on your shirt is just darling." "Brains."

Why, you ask, if I am one of the undead as well, am I able to converse at a higher level? Yeah, I definitely ask myself that question every day. Every day since I woke up to being dead. Or undead. The living dead? I never really understood the difference, but I remember an ex telling me once there was indeed a difference. Since he had seen every zombie film every made and had a tattoo of *Dawn of the Dead* spanning his entire back, I accepted his expertise. However, given that humans either scream and run or start shooting, I haven't found anyone to help me clarify the distinction.

Either way, I woke up a zombie. I remembered I was walking to my car after yoga the night before. Fifteen of us all headed toward the parking lot. Nothing but stretch pants and blue yoga mats as far as the eye could see. Of course, we had all heard the alerts not to go out after dark if you could avoid it and if you did, not to travel in groups, so you were less like a herd of cattle, fat and grazing. But no one really listened to that stuff. After all, there hadn't been a zombie attack in Portland—it was all on the east coast where folks lived more densely populated. There had been no reported outbreaks farther west than Chicago.

Perky Blonde #2 heard them first (I never bothered to learn the names of the other women in my yoga class. They were all white women who fastidiously spent their time ignoring the existence of the one Black woman in their midst. And at this point, I guess it really doesn't matter what her name was). Perky Blonde # 2 shrieked, and I looked in the direction her quivering finger pointed. Shuffling shapes lurched toward us from the darkness. Red eyes glowed. As they got closer, I could hear the zombies moan and growl. It sounded like a mix of a pissed-off Chihuahua and a very tired ghost.

Most of my classmates joined Perky Blonde #2 in screaming. I decided to save my oxygen and turned to sprint in the opposite direction—only to find, while we had been distracted, an even larger group of zombies had snuck up behind us—which is actually pretty impressive when you think about their motor function challenges.

Two of them lunged at me—I tried to beat them off with the yoga mat, but one just bit it, shook, and spit it out.

Zombies move much slower than humans. Painfully slow. Like grandpa with a broken hip, arthritis, and a knee that's acting up because it's about to rain slow. It always seemed asinine to me that people couldn't just run away from a zombie. Hell, all you'd have to do is speed up your walking pace just a little bit. I would watch zombie films with my ex, and I'd think to myself, "Well, if you're that stupid, you deserve to get eaten."

What I learned that night is that it's not zombies' speed that is the threat—it's their numbers. They massed around us like cockroaches in a roach motel. They were everywhere, a swarm of grasping hands and gnashing, dripping teeth. And of course the endless refrain of "Brains, brains, brains!" If I hadn't been so terrified, it would have been highly irritating.

I noticed, however, that the zombies mostly massed around my classmates. The lone zombie who grabbed at me looked put out like I was the leftover kid in Dodge Ball and he's just got stuck with me on his team. He grabbed my arm and began chewing, reluctantly.

You never know what you're going to do in a situation like that. Because of my ex, I had spent hours thinking what I would do if I was attacked by zombies. I always imagined I would fight back, break free. Run away. Hide.

But when faced with the actual imminent danger of a zombie chowing down on my flesh, I did something I would have never imagined—I bit the zombie back. I just clamped down on his shoulder and locked my jaw. I don't know which of us was more surprised. He yelped around my arm in his mouth, tried to shake me off. But I open bottle caps with my teeth all the time, I have a surprisingly strong jaw.

So we just stayed that way until I passed out from blood loss. And when I woke up early in the morning before dawn, I was a zombie.

Except different. I definitely have the living dead limp as I call it, which can be very frustrating. You just have to resign yourself that it takes you five times longer to get anywhere than it did when you were human. But I can still speak (as my white college professors would say with surprise and more than a little condescension, "You are so articulate!"), and I can still reason, whereas I quickly learned my former classmates-now-zombies seemed to have the collective IQ of pudding.

It took me some time of reflecting, but I narrowed down the reason I don't follow the zombie stereotype to two options. The first is the same reason I shocked myself by biting the zombie who turned me.

You see—I'm vegan.

I'm a vegan zombie.

The second is a question of melanin. You see, I'm also Black. I'm a Black vegan zombie in Portland, Oregon. Life is, in a word, rough.

I originally thought my veganness had to be the thing that allows me to still think as a human. It is the only concrete difference between me and my yoga classmates. You'd think there'd have been more vegans in that yuppy yoga studio (that I actually only went to because I got a Groupon), but I'd seen enough fro yo containers in the trash can to know I was probably alone.

My veganness could explain the reaction of the zombies during our attack—they all shied away from me because I smelled different, tasted different.

Or maybe racism persists even after you're (un)dead. All of the zombies I had seen were white. Not surprising given that I live in the whitest major city in the country. But maybe it wasn't just based on demographics. Maybe these white zombies believed some fucked-up Bell Curve eugenicist theories. They could subscribe to turn of the century craniometry, which measures the size of the head to judge intelligence (spoiler alert: Black folks lost that contest). If that's the case, it would make a twisted sort of sense: the zombies wouldn't want to get stuck with a small head. Small head equals small brain. If you're really hungry, what are you going to go for, the appetizer or the main course?

Regardless, if they judge me for my race or my dietary choices, it's clear the other zombies do judge me. Oh sure, they let me mass with them when we are hunting and feeding, but when work is done, they drift off, babbling "brains" back and forth to each other animatedly and leaving me to contemplate my Kafkaesque existence.

All but Ralph. Ralph is the only one who spends time with me. Who seems to like being around me.

Sometimes I envy Ralph and all the others. They have a singularity of purpose, and as long as they get some brains, their lives are fulfilled.

I, on the other hand, have been in the throes of a moral dilemma since I woke up dead. How do you maintain your vegan principles when the only source of food that sates your hunger is flesh?

I have tried to find ways around it. I thought, well, perhaps it's protein we living dead crave. I broke into a health food store and grabbed all the vegan protein bars I could find. When I tried to eat them, though, I was so repulsed I couldn't even swallow.

I even tried to trick myself. I got a head of cauliflower and a can of marinara sauce. Ralph and I went to a 7-Eleven, and while he munched on the clerk, I heated it up in one of their microwaves. When it was piping hot, I pulled it out.

"Hmmm, these brains sure look good," I said as I inhaled deeply, taking in the scent.

Ralph watched me out of the corner of his eye, utterly confused.

"These are gonna be the best damn brains I ever had!" I declared. I grabbed a chunk and shoved it in my mouth. I wanted to retch instantly, but I soldiered on.

"Ugh ... good ... brains," I choked out around the fake-bloody cauliflower.

I chewed as quickly as I could and then swallowed. It took less than ten seconds for my stomach to send my vegan mock brain right back up the way it came.

Ralph looked at me sadly and held out the 7-Eleven clerk's heart to me as a consolation.

No, no vegan substitutes for me; it has to be flesh. Human flesh.

So I feed but just enough to keep me alive—well, not completely dead. And every time I do, I hate myself. Every time I bite into a skull, a little bit more of my soul dies.

"Brains!" Ralph's voice pulled me from my grumpy vegan musings.

He closed his eyes and sniffed the air, turning his head to this side and that. Ralph had a much more developed sense of smell than I did. He could find a human finger in a pile of manure just using his nose. And when he did find it, he would not hesitate to pop it into his mouth. I know this from past experience.

He took off down the street, ambling as quickly as he could. I followed behind him. It had become harder and harder to find food. As the number of the living undead grew, people began to take the recommended precautions.

We lurched through the streets for what seemed like forever, turning left and right like we were in a maze. Sometimes, Ralph would pause to sniff and then set off with renewed vigor—well, as much as you can muster when you don't have a beating heart or blood pumping to help propel you forward.

Finally, I turned a corner and stopped in my limping tracks. There, lit up like the Eiffel Tower at night, was a shining, brand new organic grocery store. People poured in and out—white men with beards and skinny jeans, women in black-rimmed glasses and ironic '50s-style dresses. We had walked into a neighborhood recently taken over by hipsters and yuppies. And they lived in such a protective bubble, they thought they were untouchable; none of them were taking any of the recommended anti-zombie precautions.

Ralph looked like a kid at Christmas. He shambled toward the loading docks in the back, keeping to the shadows. I decided I could use the element of surprise, and I moved to the most isolated poorly lit corner of the parking lot. I crouched down behind one of the countless Priuses.

I didn't have to wait long until I heard movement. I poked my head up and saw a dark-haired white woman in a corduroy skirt and Birkenstocks juggling three cloth bags full of groceries—of course, she had brought her own bags.

I waited until she was within arm's length and then darted forward quickly (for a zombie), grabbing her before she knew what happened.

She froze, stared at me with wide, terrified eyes. Like a baby chick in a factory farm—right before they snap its beak and cut off its legs.

I tried not to look in her eyes. "This might not be much consolation, but I want to assure you I won't enjoy this any more than you will."

Her look of terror mixed now with confusion.

Then I caught a whiff of her scent. I reeled. She smelled like granola and soy milk and rice crisps and organic bananas.

She was the most wonderful thing I had ever smelled in my life.

She smelled vegan. The first vegan I had encountered since I turned. She wasn't compromising her principles. She was doing the right thing for her body, for the animals, for the earth. You know, the most destruction to the ozone layer comes not from pollution but from cow farts? It's true, the flatulence of cattle will destroy us all, but because everyone wants a burger, they just keep breeding more and more livestock.

This woman was above all of that. She was me, back when I had been able to do the right thing.

The closest approximation I could do of a smile split my face. I cracked her head open between my hands and dove in with a gusto that would have made Ralph whistle if he could have. It was sweeter than soy ice cream and tastier than tofu cheesecake.

And for the first time since I became a zombie, my conscience was blessed silent. I'd found a way to enjoy my zombie unlife to the fullest, without the wracking guilt. If I only ate vegans, essentially, I was still a vegan as well. You are what you eat, right?

Ralph shuffled over, fresh brain matter pancaked on his face like makeup. He saw the empty skull, and I could tell he was impressed by my appetite. He gave me a thumbs up—which, since we don't have much joint mobility, was just Ralph lifting his entire hand up sideways.

I burped and patted my stomach contentedly as I stared at the hipsters moving like ants in and out of the light of the store. I sniffed. Three, four—make that five vegans in less than a minute. If Ralph and I kept this a secret, only grabbed one or two at a time, there's no telling how long it would take these people to figure out what's going on.

"Ralph, my friend, this is what Heaven looks like."

Typical

Raquel Castro

● translated by Lawrence Schimel ●

Typical: you wake up in a hospital, connected to a thousand machines, and you don't remember how you got there. Thanks to the wisdom learned from watching more than eight hours of TV a day, you imagine you've suffered an accident. You look for the signal to summon the nurse, who (you imagine: it's what's typical) will be young and pretty, kind and sweet. She will cry just to see you (she'll have fallen in love with you during the long nights of intensive care), and she'll tell you about the accident you don't remember: about the little girl you saved from a terrorist attack or the president who wasn't struck by a Hummer because you pushed him out of the way just in time.

But (typical) the nurse never shows up. It's only when you've grown tired of waiting that you realize that it's too quiet. So you remove the cables you're connected to, and you get up, very slowly.

You leave the room, walking through deserted hallways, and you find a cadaver and then another and another and another, all of them with their skulls destroyed, and *only then* do you realize that something REALLY bad is going on. Typical.

So you search for a pair of pants and some sneakers, you put them on and go out into the street which, typical, is full of the living dead, slow and stiff but implacable, who can't take their eyes off of you and start walking right at you.

You feel fear. As you should: there are cadavers with their faces destroyed, with fractured bones poking through flesh, with loops of dusty entrails. But you recover from your fright, and you get ready to flee from them because you think you can leave them behind. The difficult part can't be now. It will instead be when (typical) you've found a young girl alive and alone in need of love and company.

And you run.

And they pursue you.

And they reach you.

While they destroy your body, you feel pain, but more powerful is your anger, your sadness, and even more, your disappointment.

Typical, only now do you realize: all zombie stories have thousands of extras, and you're just one of them.

Mana Langkah Pelangi Terakhir? (Where is the Rainbow's Last Step?)

Jaymee Goh

I got the text message while waiting to pick my son up at school.

No, I am not one of those goonish parents who insist on creating a traffic jam outside the school gate just so the precious children don't have to walk far to get their ride home. I was sitting on the edge of the drain outside the school fence, doobying on my Samsung, trying to make it show me the time even when it went idle, when I got the text message from an ex-colleague telling me Pelangi Hussein had passed away.

It was upsetting; those superheroes had told me they would personally escort her home. I stood on the shore worrying my prayer beads as they drifted on their raft, promising to reach Malaya on time. She had looked so frail, so thin, but for some reason I placed my confidence in them to take her home, where they had insisted she needed to go.

When I was growing up, my parents used to grouse at me about the rise of the Internet and social media tools. It was an age of wonder for them that information transferred across the globe so quickly.

Today, my nine-year-old son gets to hear me grouse about the rise of heroes, logic-defying feats, and the inevitable great clashes that arise as a result. It is an age of wonder wherein everything I and my peers grew up with in pop culture ephemera came true, if enough people dream of it.

It is also a wonderful time to be a cultural critic. Do you know how satisfying it is to say "the Great White American Suburbs have plunged themselves into a zombie apocalypse as their anxieties of consumerism have clearly overtaken them" and have it taken seriously? I even follow the Black Queens of Detroit on Tumblr (their electronic elite seized its operations in an amazing coup). That a shared imagination would come true—well, there's space to witness all sorts of anxieties and dreams come true, too.

Nothing so exciting happened in Malaysia—Malaya now, I guess, since the indigenous nations of East Malaysia decided they were better off without us, after all. We did get our wish of an information technology multimedia supercorridor. I don't really know what it means; I just know how to use a computer. It does seem to have been a big deal, though, for Che Det and his Vision 2020. Those of us not on the IT highway bandwagon, though? We keep plodding along. The ITMSC does not help me get my child to school and back safely.

The worst of what we feared, however, did not come to pass. Contrary to foreign correspondents' impressions and the haranguing of politicians, racial riots did not tear the country apart. The rate of interracial marriage skyrocketed, though, and my generation waits with bated breath for the new post-racial age that our mixed babies would usher in, a true Malaysian race. Queer marriages also passed into law without a fuss, finding no real barrier in syariah courts or familial arguments. First world countries were surprised at this; none of us in the third world were. (Capitalism still exists, to the gnashing of many activists. Hope springs eternal.)

Hock Heng grinned when he spotted me. He hopped over the drain to the side I was sitting on nimbly and sat down next to me. I put an arm around him and squeezed him tight. "Hey, Double-H, how was school?" (He was currently into spies and code names.) His legs dangled into the drain, but I noticed that soon they would be long enough to touch the other side.

"It was okay." He leaned against me. "What're you reading?"

"Someone I know just died. Did I tell you about her? Pelangi Hussein?"

He frowned. "I dunnoooooo, you tell me so many things."

He was right. Every day, between school and social media, he processed far more information than I ever had to in childhood. The PTA has been talking about instating deadzone times. I think we've been successful. I disagree with the kind of information my peers expose their kids to, but the deadzone times seem to relieve the kids.

"She was a colleague of mine when I used to work for NTV. You remember watching those old cartoons on NTV, right? The Saturday morning ones?"

He laughed. "Yeah! With the monkeys in space!"

Pelangi Hussein's parents had been influenced by the American '70s hippie era, and I'm not sure they ever left that decade. Despite her unfortunate name or perhaps because of it, Pelangi grew up an interminably cheerful person, a pretty woman everyone wanted to be seen with. So when she graduated from Mass Communications, it was natural she would go into the television business and eventually become a TV presenter. The surprising thing was that she became a newscaster rather than stick to her cushy pop veejay gig. I suppose everyone comes to the point where we want something a bit more challenging.

When I first met Pelangi, I thought she would be one of those people stuck in perpetual adolescence: always seeking, always only brimming with potential, manja and mature at turns. When she turned out to be a fairly resilient and astute personality, I was relieved and then impressed. Here was a woman who went into Sarawak's wilds to track the myth of Rajah Brooke's secret treasure (when did we even have one of those?!) and then, barely taking a Raya break, was off reporting on the Penan revolution along the Kalimantan-Sabah border. Then it was back to Peninsular Malaya to cover the General Elections. She was pretty, so everyone paid some attention; she was so articulate she made any complex situation understandable in everyday bahasa. It was slightly unfair, but no one could bring themselves to be jealous, which I personally thought was a feat unto itself. Everybody wanted to date her, men and women. I fell in love with her, too, and hard. We stayed friends somehow.

Then suddenly, she disappeared. Her apartment looked like she had stepped out to buy some groceries. At the NTV station, word was she was off collecting yet another scoop, and I don't know why no one thought to check whether she'd taken a camera crew with her. *I* would have. Her parents, used to not hearing from her for months, asked on Facebook where she was, and that was our first clue that we had no idea. "Mana langkah pelangi terakhir???" Facebook statuses screamed, with jokes about pots of gold at rainbows' ends abounding. Even in the wake of a celebrity's mysterious disappearance, we still had time to make crass jokes about her name.

"I remember this story now!" Hock Heng burst out as we climbed the steps of the pedestrian bridge. "You all went looking, and no one could find her, right? And then you found her in Macau!"

I had been given an assignment to follow scientists who were measuring the presence of some mysterious chemical which apparently accounted for these strange happenings across the world. The chemical had an unnecessarily long name. I called it unobtanium because I am a sloppy journalist.

The trip took me to Macau, which is not exactly one of my favourite cities. I ended up in a fishing village on the coast where a cave had some deposits. This was just one of many locations where they found the substance; there were more sites, particularly concentrated where cultural imaginations turned real ran amok. Then I got into a bar fight through mysterious means still confusing to me and finally, in a prison cell. I haven't told my parents, and I made my wife promise never to mention it.

My fellow cellmates were two martial arts masters. They had been in the drunken bar fight with me. I think we were on the same side. They were called Singing Fist and Whip Blade. The names sounded better in Cantonese, but Singing Fist really wanted to be able to relate to me better and had thus insisted I call them using the English translation.

It was yet another reminder of how the world had changed. Suddenly, there were actualfax heroes, flipping back kicks and flying like in the wuxia movies I grew up with. There were, in fact, people who could fly without benefit of airplanes because they dreamed it so hard. The world was much more dangerous for it. Hock Heng doesn't really understand growing up in a world where these things don't happen. I suppose that's how my parents felt when I brought home my first touchscreen tablet. Hock Heng is about as sympathetic to my bewilderment as I was to my dad's: an attempt is made, but it is never quite successful.

"Those aren't very good names," I commented.

Whip Blade scowled at me. Singing Fist laughed.

When I looked past the bars of the cell, I saw a huddled figure in the corner, shivering under a rag of a quilted blanket. There was a police officer nearby, reading a newspaper behind his table. "Who's that?" I asked him.

He shrugged. "No passport."

"So ... in jail, too?"

"Didn't commit a crime, so why jail?"

"Sick?" I was starting to get really concerned.

The officer shrugged again but this time had a hint of an apology. "No passport."

Some things do not change even in an age of wonder.

When they let me out the next day, I went over to the still-huddled figure and gently shook their shoulders. "Hey, are you okay? Get some water, Singing Fist."

"We've seen her around before," Whip Blade said quietly behind me.

"Oh, yeah? Then why didn't you say anything when I asked?"

"Because she doesn't really belong here" was his eminently unhelpful reply.

When Singing Fist brought a cup of water, I sat the figure up. The quilt fell away from their face, and I almost shrieked.

"Pelangi?"

Her cheeks were sunken in, and her skin, ordinarily a radiant brown, was flushed yellow. Her hair was matted along the sides of her face, unkempt. Her bones felt like dry twigs in my arms. Her eyelids fluttered at the sound of her name. I panicked because she had never felt so fragile in my arms before.

"Oi! Oi, Pelangi Hussein!" I pressed the cup of water to her lips.

She drank and then smiled faintly. "Oi, Ciao Bella." That was her nickname for me.

"Is that your name?" Singing Fist asked, his face way too close.

"Shut up. Pelangi, what happened?"

She'd fallen asleep.

I had some renminbi for an extra bed in my hotel room and nursed Pelangi all night long. Singing Fist and Whip Blade were very interested in hearing about her and gamely sat up with me to listen to my stories about her work. "I've got to get her to a hospital. Can you help?" I asked them.

"Sure," Singing Fist said.

"You've got to get her home," Whip Blade said.

"I can't deal with this right now," I said. "I'm going to bed. You guys come back tomorrow, okay?"

Instead of going to bed, I unwisely Facebooked "I FOUND PELANGI HUSSEIN." My phone beeped incessantly with text messages and Twitter mentions from various people. I had an hour-long conversation with Pelangi's parents who could not seem to understand that I had no idea of where she had been the last five years. I then had another hour-long conversation with my boss who wanted to know whether I was bringing her home and how was my progress on the unobtanium story. I had to turn off my phone but got way less sleep than needed anyway because I periodically got up to check on Pelangi.

It was probably the lack of sleep that pushed me to agree with

Whip Blade and Singing Fist that getting her home immediately was a top priority. Also that they could be trusted with the job of escorting her home. On a raft. Attached to a sampan they punted out to sea.

"This is how we've always traveled," Singing Fist assured me.

"This is how you've always traveled," Whip Blade told me in what sounded like a reminder.

Yes, but, I wanted to say, my family migrated to Malaysia by a much bigger boat, and the rest followed by plane. The problem was that I couldn't afford either at the moment. "How long will you take?" I asked, not very willing to entrust Pelangi to these strangers but not seeing any other practical way.

"However long people think we will."

It made sense to me at the time. If reality was shaped by the force of imagination, a shared desire to see something happen would bring it to fruition, no matter how extreme the notion. I wanted Pelangi to get home safe even though the common sense I grew up with said she wouldn't make it.

When I told Pelangi's parents what I had done, they uttered a "Bismillah" under their breaths and said they would watch for her arrival. I avoided my Facebook feed after that, but my Twitter feed told me that a nationwide candlelight vigil had begun, awaiting her safe return, praying for a quick homecoming. So I believed she would come home safe, too—so many people were fixated on the idea, so there was no reason it wouldn't happen.

That was a few days ago. I returned home to Malaysia and avoided all technology, trying to get back to some semblance of a normal life—helping my son do homework, listen to my wife fuss about her upcoming conference, take long walks with my aging neighbour and her dog—before I sought out Pelangi.

Then came the text. After I put Hock Heng to bed that night, I cried and cried in Ranita's arms. Whether because I never really got over Pelangi or because I was hoping so much for something else, I'm not sure.

The funeral was clean and quick, as all Malay funerals are. I was present for the burial, leaving Ranita and Hock Heng at home to minimize awkwardness. They didn't know Pelangi, anyway. Pelangi's mother was solemn, perhaps meditative, her head bowed most of the time. After the funeral, I plucked up the courage to approach her. "Mak cik, I'm sorry. This is my fault."

Puan Nurazlin's eyes lit up upon seeing me. "Chao Yong, ya? You brought Pelangi home to me!"

"Er, no, I didn't."

She took my hands into hers and pressed them. "Come later to our house. We're having a party for her."

Stories, I discovered, are better when they have a kernel of truth. Moving further away from those kernels, they become fantastic and inexplicable. Then it moves into the realm of science fiction, and so I had trouble following the conversations at hand.

I must have tossed and turned too often that night because Ranita flung an arm over me and held me tight as if she could hold me down.

"Sorry."

"If you have something you need to talk about, you probably should talk about it now because otherwise I won't get any sleep." Her grouchy mumble reverberated from her throat since she was too tired to move her mouth muscles perfectly.

"I just don't get it, Ranita," I began. It took me a moment to find my words. Ranita didn't stir, but I assumed she was still awake and listening to me and plunged on. "I followed Pelangi's career as closely as possible just like everybody else, and I don't know where all these stories are coming from."

"Hrm?" Ranita sounded, which translated best into either "oh?" or "as in?"

"Okay, so you remember the Rajah Brooke story? Pelangi got the lede from it while she was covering a totally different story and interviewing folks in Kajang. Some old man mentioned it, and she asks around and then bam, an actual story."

"So?"

"But people are saying that she was called by some jewel in a cave that sang to her in Arabic."

Ranita took a deep breath like she was going to say something, then changed her mind, and breathed it out instead.

"Yeah, exactly! And that wasn't the only thing! There were so many crazy stories, and I don't even know where they came from! Hazri said that she was in Jurong for the Migration of the Parrots, you remember that? But she wasn't. That time she was in Batu Caves doing an education segment. But somehow Hazri drew a picture of her at the Migration. Made her look glorious, of course, you know lah Hazri how he draws."

Ranita took another deep breath and rolled onto her back. "So. It sounds like people are making up stories about Pelangi that make her sound cooler than she actually was."

"Yes. And not even in the kind of 'repressing all her bad qualities' sort of way. More like completely making up stuff. You know, the kind of stuff you figure takes about five generations of handing down stories that keep getting weirder, like Sejarah Melayu."

"And this bothers you."

"Of course!" I almost shouted, and sat up. "She wasn't like that, okay? She was ... she was *real*. She always wanted to go hunt down the reality behind things. And now this is how people remember her."

I glanced at Ranita, who had rolled over onto her back and took the opportunity of suddenly empty space to sprawl out. "I think there are worse things," she said.

"Yeah, there are! They kept on talking about her like she never died!"

"Oh my God, calm down, Chao Yong."

I took several deep breaths. "That's the worst part. It's like everyone was in denial. They kept on going on about next week's crew assignments and how people were competing to get onto her camera crew. Present tense."

"You sure you weren't mishearing? Bahasa's got no tense, remember? And your Bahasa is kind of ciplak."

"Come on, I'm not that bad."

She sighed again. "You know what, Chao Yong, for someone who makes a big deal about, what is it, ephemera, and social changes, you sure aren't good with accepting when those things happen right in front of your face."

I guiltily lay back down.

She gave me a moment to recover. "People need to remember their heroes the way they want to. And you can remember her the way you want to. It's not hurting anybody, right?"

But what if, I thought, the collective imagination turned against us? I kept that to myself because it was stupid and selfish and maybe I should be happier that Pelangi seemed to be so great in people's minds. If enough people dream it, it becomes real, and that should be a good thing. Except, what if tomorrow people started talking about me and Ranita as if our wedding never happened? What if Ranita and I split, not because of any inherent problem in the relationship but because enough people badmouthed us? Would Hock Heng disappear?

I pulled Ranita close. It was a hot night, and she pulled away from me in annoyance.

● ● ●

I was in the mamak cafe when the next text came.

I should like to say something like, I'm not that kind of hipster who always looks for the nice cafes to hang out at and prefer the down-to-earth environment of the mamak cafe. The fact is that I would rather deal with the humidity of open-air cafes than I would blows to my wallet. Yet at that moment, I rather wished for the air-conditioning of a nice cafe than the heat-induced headache that was coming on because of the text.

got a lede on Rj Kecil's submarine! meet me at jonker st coffeebean next mon 5pm

"But why," I complained to Ranita afterward, "is a dead person texting me?"

"You ask me I ask who," she replied, mouth full of mee siam. "You think you're going to meet a zombie, is it? Did you see that cute cat video Ah Peng posted on FB, by the way?"

I love my wife so much because she always knew how to direct my attention. When I logged onto Facebook for the first time in maybe weeks, I saw Friend Requests from Whip Blade and Singing Fist.

"Found you!!!!" the latter's message seemed to sing at me. "Rainbow told me your FB. How are you?"

"I think I just can't deal with how weird the world's become," I told Ranita.

Ranita shrugged. "Sorry, can't help you. I work in a physics lab."

Pelangi had grown chattier as she approached home, Whip Blade said, in the longest sentence I had ever seen out of him, but she passed into unconsciousness anyway. *Stories take time to recover,* he said. *People take time to remember.*

This is way too much meta for real life, I replied.

Today's age of wonders is an age of meta, he said, as unapologetically cryptic as when we'd first met.

I thought of asking Singing Fist my question, if he ever felt worried about being dreamt out of existence, but it seemed a bit too early in our acquaintance to ask.

How does one explain to a child that people used to just die and they stayed dead? Hock Heng took the news of my latest assignment with the kind of flexible equanimity that only children are capable of. "So you're going to meet the dead person?" he deadpanned.

"I am going to see if she is actually really alive," I said sternly, stuffing the edges of my bag with underwear. "And I want you to listen to your mom while I'm gone, do your chores, yadda yadda." I thought for a moment. Hock Heng had decided that his new career goal was to become a linguist and a secret spy. "Also, I need you to develop a new cipher that can be transmitted through, uh," I glanced around frantically—if he didn't have anything to do, he might get into trouble, "papayas," I finished, reaching for the packet of the dried fruit sitting on the nightstand.

Hock Heng nodded, taking his mission seriously.

I checked into a very expensive hotel room off Jonker Street and SMSed Pelangi that I was in town. As far as I could tell, all the camera crews had been hired on other assignments that day, but that department was fairly cagey about their details.

Pelangi was in my lobby, and I might have slightly hyperventilated. I had seen her grave, I had seen the hospital records, and there had been a funeral. I had never considered that maybe she might come climbing out of the ground. I stared at the woman who once had been the love of my life, and my brain stuttered for explanations.

"How?" was the first thing out of my mouth.

"Hi to you, too," she said, sounding slightly offended.

"No, but seriously."

She gave me a long look. "Do you want to work on the Raja Kecil story or not?" She handed me a folder. As I looked through the notes in it, she continued, "I got an interview with an old uncle who lives on the riverbanks, and he said he got a piece of glass that might have belonged to the box that Raja Kecil used to go underwater. I asked him if he had done any carbon dating yet, and he hadn't, so I was thinking—"

I let her chatter as we walked together down Jonker Street. We visited the old uncle, saw the piece of glass. It looked suitably ancient, and I called up archaeologists in the local universities for help. We recorded the interview and stayed up late into the night transcribing the recording. Pelangi seemed her usual self—we laughed as we worked, and I almost forgot that she had died not too long ago.

"I'm really glad you came out, Chao Yong," she said as we prepared to sleep.

"I'm really glad you're, uh, alive, Pelangi," I answered.

"Yeah, me, too!"

She was still there when we woke up the next day and still there after breakfast. And it seemed every time I tried to reach for a logical explanation for her continued existence, she seemed to fade in and out of reality. At one point, while I was zoning out, she whacked my arm. "Hey! Think less, work more!"

At night, as if to convince me she was real, she curled up next to me, her warm breath even on my neck. "I'm married, Pelangi," I reminded her. Perhaps, it was me who needed the reminder.

Ranita wisely did not bring up my assignment when I got home and allowed me to mull on the subject for the next few days while I tried to make sense of it. Finally, I turned to Whip Blade since he was still conveniently available on Facebook.

She became a story, he said.

Everyone's a story, I said. *Everyone is the protagonist of their own story.*

No. That's not what I meant. He sounded adamant even in expressionless text.

Is it that only some people become stories? I asked. *Are there some people more rooted in reality than others? I'm so torn. In my work philosophy, no one is ever too small to be part of a story, to be written about, to be thought about. Does this age of wonders only pick certain types of people to affect?*

Doesn't your wife work in a lab? Whip Blade wrote back. *Aren't there scientists working on this question?*

Yes, but you seem to know something. Stop holding out.

He didn't deign to answer me after that. I hoped I hadn't offended him.

Pelangi came to my house to work some more on the Raja Kecil story. As she pulled into my driveway, Ranita was watering the plants in our garden, the hose on the mist setting. She handed the hose over to Hock Heng to exchange pleasantries with Pelangi.

"Mummy, look! A rainbow!" Hock Heng gleefully pointed out to me. The sun was high and hit the mist at just the right angle.

"Cool, huh? Check this out, if you stay where you are and just move your head around and move the water around—"

We spent a few moments following the circle of the rainbow over and over.

"Hey," Pelangi said, coming to stand next to us. "Oh, that's cool."

Her smile dimpled her cheeks, and wavering between myth and fact, she had never felt quite so real as she did that moment.

Welcome to Your Authentic Indian Experience™

Rebecca Roanhorse

In the Great American Indian novel, when it is finally written, all of the white people will be Indians and all of the Indians will be ghosts.

—Sherman Alexie, *How to Write the Great American Indian Novel*

You maintain a menu of a half dozen Experiences on your digital blackboard, but Vision Quest is the one the Tourists choose the most. That certainly makes your workday easy. All a Vision Quest requires is a dash of mystical shaman, a spirit animal (wolf usually, but birds of prey are on the upswing this year), and the approximation of a peyote experience. Tourists always come out of the Experience feeling spiritually transformed. (You've never actually tried peyote, but you did smoke your share of weed during that one year at Arizona State, and who's going to call you on the difference?) It's all 101 stuff, really, these Quests. But no other Indian working at Sedona Sweats can do it better. Your sales numbers are tops.

Your wife, Theresa, doesn't approve of the gig. Oh, she likes you working, especially after that dismal stretch of unemployment the year before last when she almost left you, but she thinks the job itself is demeaning.

"Our last name's not Trueblood," she complains when you tell her about your nom de rêve.

"Nobody wants to buy a Vision Quest from a Jesse Turnblatt," you explain. "I need to sound more Indian."

"You are Indian," she says. "Turnblatt's Indian-sounding enough because you're already Indian."

"We're not the right kind of Indian," you counter. "I mean, we're Catholic, for Christ's sake."

What Theresa doesn't understand is that Tourists don't want a real Indian experience. They want what they see in the movies, and who can blame them? Movie Indians are terrific! So you watch the same movies the Tourists do until John Dunbar becomes your spirit animal and Stands with Fists your best girl. You memorize Johnny Depp's lines from *The Lone Ranger* and hang a picture of Iron Eyes Cody in your work locker. For a while you are really into Dustin Hoffman's *Little Big Man*.

It's *Little Big Man* that does you in.

For a week in June, you convince your boss to offer a Custer's Last Stand special, thinking there might be a Tourist or two who want to live out a Crazy Horse Experience. You even memorize some quotes attributed to the venerable Sioux chief that you find on the internet. You plan to make it real authentic.

But you don't get a single taker. Your numbers nosedive.

Management in Phoenix notices, and Boss drops it from the blackboard by Fourth of July weekend. He yells at you to stop screwing around, accuses you of trying to be an artiste or whatnot.

"Tourists don't come to Sedona Sweats to live out a goddamn battle," Boss says in the break room over lunch one day, "especially if the white guy loses. They come here to find themselves." Boss waves his hand in the air in an approximation of something vaguely prayer-like. "It's a spiritual experience we're offering. Top quality. The fucking best."

DarAnne, your Navajo co-worker with the pretty smile and the perfect teeth, snorts loudly. She takes a bite of her sandwich, mutton by the looks of it. Her jaw works, her sharp teeth flash white. She waits until she's finished chewing to say, "Nothing spiritual about Squaw Fantasy."

Squaw Fantasy is Boss's latest idea, his way to get the numbers up and impress Management. DarAnne and a few others have complained about the use of the ugly slur, the inclusion of a sexual fantasy as an Experience at all. But Boss is unmoved, especially when the first week's numbers roll in. Biggest seller yet.

Boss looks over at you. "What do you think?"

Boss is Pima with a bushy mustache and a thick head of still-dark hair. You admire that about him. Virility. Boss makes being a man look easy. Makes everything look easy. Real authentic-like.

DarAnne tilts her head, long beaded earrings swinging, and waits. Her painted nails click impatiently against the Formica lunch table.

You can smell the onion in her sandwich.

Your mouth is dry like the red rock desert you can see outside your window. If you say Squaw Fantasy is demeaning, Boss will mock you, call you a pussy, or worse. If you say you think it's okay, DarAnne and her crew will put you on the guys-who-are-assholes list, and you'll deserve it.

You sip your bottled water, stalling. Decide that in the wake of the Crazy Horse debacle that Boss's approval means more than DarAnne's, and venture, "I mean, if the Tourists like it ..."

Boss slaps the table, triumphant. DarAnne's face twists in disgust. "What does Theresa think of that, eh, Jesse?" she spits at you. "You tell her Boss is thinking of adding Savage Braves to the menu next? He's gonna have you in a loincloth and hair down to your ass, see how you like it."

Your face heats up, embarrassed. You push away from the table too quickly, and the flimsy top teeters. You can hear Boss's shouts of protest as his vending machine lemonade tilts dangerously and DarAnne's mocking laugh, but it all comes to your ears through a shroud of thick cotton. You mumble something about getting back to work. The sound of arguing trails you down the hall.

You change in the locker room and shuffle down to the pod marked with your name. You unlock the hatch and crawl in. Some people find the pods claustrophobic, but you like the cool metal container, the tight fit. It's comforting. The VR helmet fits snugly on your head, the breathing mask over your nose and mouth.

With a shiver of anticipation, you give the pod your Experience setting. Add the other necessary details to flesh things out. The screen prompts you to pick a Tourist connection from a waiting list, but you ignore it, blinking through the option screens until you get to the final confirmation. You brace for the mild nausea that always comes when you Relocate in and out of an Experience.

The first sensation is always smell. Sweetgrass and wood smoke and the rich loam of the northern plains. Even though it's fake, receptors firing under the coaxing of a machine, you relax into the scents. You grew up in the desert, among people who appreciate cedar and pinon and red earth, but there's still something home-like about this prairie place.

Or maybe you watch too much TV. You really aren't sure anymore.

You find yourself on a wide grassy plain, somewhere in the upper Midwest of a bygone era. Bison roam in the distance. A hawk soars overhead.

You are alone, you know this, but it doesn't stop you from looking around to make sure. This thing you are about to do. Well, you would be humiliated if anyone found out. Because you keep thinking about what DarAnne said. Squaw Fantasy and Savage Braves. Because the thing is, being sexy doesn't disgust you the way it does DarAnne. You've never been one of those guys. The star athlete or the cool kid. It's tempting to think of all those Tourist women wanting you like that even if it is just in an Experience.

You are now wearing a knee-length loincloth. A wave of black hair flows down your back. Your middle-aged paunch melts into rock-hard abs worthy of a romance novel cover model. You raise your chin and try out your best stoic look on a passing prairie dog. The little rodent chirps something back at you. You've heard prairie dogs can remember human faces, and you wonder what this one would say about you. Then you remember this is an Experience, so the prairie dog is no more real than the caricature of an Indian you have conjured up.

You wonder what Theresa would think if she saw you like this.

The world shivers. The pod screen blinks on. Someone wants your Experience.

A Tourist, asking for you. Completely normal. Expected. No need for that panicky hot breath rattling through your mask.

You scroll through the Tourist's requirements.

Experience Type: Vision Quest.

Tribe: Plains Indian (nation nonspecific).

Favorite animal: Wolf.

These things are all familiar. Things you are good at faking. Things you get paid to pretend.

You drop the Savage Brave fantasy garb for buckskin pants and beaded leather moccasins. You keep your chest bare and muscled, but you drape a rough wool blanket across your shoulders for dignity. Your impressive abs are still visible.

The sun is setting, and you turn to put the artificial dusk at your back, prepared to meet your Tourist. You run through your list of Indian names to bestow upon your Tourist once the Vision Quest is over. You like to keep the names fresh, never using the same one in case the Tourists ever compare notes. For a while you cheated and used one of those naming things on the internet where you enter your favorite flower and the street you grew up on and it gives you your Indian name; but there were too many Tourists that grew up on Elm or Park, and you found yourself getting repetitive.

You try to base the names on appearances now. Hair color, eye, some distinguishing feature. Tourists really seem to like it.

This Tourist is younger than you expected. Sedona Sweats caters to New Agers, the kind from Los Angeles or Scottsdale with impressive bank accounts. But the man coming up the hill, squinting into the setting sun, is in his late twenties. Medium height and build with pale, spotty skin and brown hair. The guy looks normal enough, but there's something sad about him.

Maybe he's lost.

You imagine a lot of Tourists are lost.

Maybe he's someone who works a day job just like you, saving up money for this once-in-a-lifetime Indian Experience™. Maybe he's desperate, looking for purpose in his own shitty world and thinking Indians have all the answers. Maybe he just wants something that's authentic.

You like that. The idea that Tourists come to you to experience something real. DarAnne has it wrong. The Tourists aren't all bad. They're just needy.

You plant your feet in a wide, welcoming stance and raise one hand. "How," you intone as the man stops a few feet in front of you.

The man flushes, a bright pinkish tone. You can't tell if he's nervous or embarrassed. Maybe both? But he raises his hand, palm forward, and says, "How," right back.

"Have you come seeking wisdom, my son?" you ask in your best broken English accent. "Come. I will show you great wisdom." You sweep your arm across the prairie. "We look to brother wolf—"

The man rolls his eyes.

What?

You stutter to a pause. Are you doing something wrong? Is the accent no good? Too little? Too much?

You visualize the requirements checklist. You are positive he chose wolf. Positive. So you press on. "My brother wolf," you say again, this time sounding much more Indian, you are sure.

"I'm sorry," the man says, interrupting. "This wasn't what I wanted. I've made a mistake."

"But you picked it on the menu!" In the confusion of the moment, you drop your accent. Is it too late to go back and say it right?

The man's lips curl up in a grimace like you have confirmed his worst suspicions. He shakes his head. "I was looking for something more authentic."

Something in your chest seizes up.

"I can fix it," you say.

"No, it's all right. I'll find someone else." He turns to go.

You can't afford another bad mark on your record. No more screw-ups or you're out. Boss made that clear enough. "At least give me a chance," you plead.

"It's okay," he says over his shoulder.

This is bad. Does this man not know what a good Indian you are? "Please!"

The man turns back to you, his face thoughtful.

You feel a surge of hope. This can be fixed, and you know exactly how. "I can give you a name. Something you can call yourself when you need to feel strong. It's authentic," you add enthusiastically. "From a real Indian." That much is true.

The man looks a little more open, and he doesn't say no. That's good enough.

You study the man's dusky hair, his pinkish skin. His long skinny legs. He reminds you a bit of the flamingos at the Albuquerque zoo, but you are pretty sure no one wants to be named after those strange creatures. It must be something good. Something ... spiritual.

"Your name is Pale Crow," you offer. Birds are still on your mind.

At the look on the man's face, you reconsider. "No, no, it is White" —yes, that's better than pale— "Wolf. White Wolf."

"White Wolf?" There's a note of interest in his voice.

You nod sagely. You knew the man had picked wolf. Your eyes meet. Uncomfortably. White Wolf coughs into his hand. "I really should be getting back."

"But you paid for the whole experience. Are you sure?"

White Wolf is already walking away.

"But ..."

You feel the exact moment he Relocates out of the Experience. A sensation like part of your soul is being stretched too thin. Then a sort of whiplash as you let go.

The Hey U.S.A. bar is the only Indian bar in Sedona. The basement level of a driftwood-paneled strip mall across the street from work. It's packed with the after-shift crowd, most of them pod jockeys like you, but also a few roadside jewelry hawkers and restaurant stiffs still smelling like frybread grease. You're lucky to find a spot at the far end next to the server's station. You slip onto the plastic-covered barstool and raise a hand to get the bartender's attention.

"So what do you really think?" asks a voice to your right. DarAnne is staring at you, her eyes accusing and her posture tense.

This is it. A second chance. Your opportunity to stay off the assholes list. You need to get this right. You try to think of something clever to say, something that would impress her but let you save face, too. But you've never been all that clever, so you stick to the truth.

"I think I really need this job," you admit.

DarAnne's shoulders relax.

"Scooch over," she says to the man on the other side of her, and he obligingly shifts off his stool to let her sit. "I knew it," she says. "Why didn't you stick up for me? Why are you so afraid of Boss?"

"I'm not afraid of Boss. I'm afraid of Theresa leaving me. And unemployment."

"You gotta get a backbone, Jesse, is all."

You realize the bartender is waiting, impatient. You drink the same thing every time you come here, a single Coors Light in a cold bottle. But the bartender never remembers you or your order. You turn to offer to buy one for DarAnne, but she's already gone back with her crew.

You drink your beer alone, wait a reasonable amount of time, and leave.

White Wolf is waiting for you under the streetlight at the corner.

The bright neon Indian Chief that squats atop Sedona Sweats hovers behind him in pinks and blues and yellows, his huge hand blinking up and down in greeting. White puffs of smoke signals flicker up, up, and away beyond his far shoulder.

You don't recognize White Wolf at first. Most people change themselves a little within the construct of the Experience. Nothing wrong with being thinner, taller, a little better looking. But White Wolf looks exactly the same. Nondescript brown hair, pale skin, long legs.

"How." White Wolf raises his hand, unconsciously mimicking the big neon Chief. At least he has the decency to look embarrassed when he does it.

"You." You are so surprised that the accusation is the first thing out of your mouth. "How did you find me?"

"Trueblood, right? I asked around."

"And people told you?" This is very against the rules.

"I asked who the best Spirit Guide was. If I was going to buy a Vision Quest, who should I go to. Everyone said you."

You flush, feeling vindicated, but also annoyed that your coworkers had given your name out to a Tourist. "I tried to tell you," you say ungraciously.

"I should have listened." White Wolf smiles, a faint shifting of his mouth into something like contrition. An awkward pause ensues.

"We're really not supposed to fraternize," you finally say.

"I know, I just ... I just wanted to apologize. For ruining the Experience like that."

"It's no big deal," you say, gracious this time. "You paid, right?"

"Yeah."

"It's just ..." You know this is your ego talking, but you need to know. "Did I do something wrong?"

"No, it was me. You were great. It's just, I had a great grandmother who was Cherokee, and I think being there, seeing everything. Well, it really stirred something in me. Like, ancestral memory or something."

You've heard of ancestral memories, but you've also heard of people claiming Cherokee blood where there is none. Theresa calls them "pretendians," but you think that's unkind. Maybe White Wolf really is Cherokee. You don't know any Cherokees, so maybe they really do look like this guy. There's a half-Tlingit in payroll, and he's pale.

"Well, I've got to get home," you say. "My wife, and all."

White Wolf nods. "Sure, sure. I just. Thank you."

"For what?"

But White Wolf's already walking away. "See you around."

A little déjà vu shudders your bones, but you chalk it up to Tourists. Who understands them, anyway?

You go home to Theresa.

As soon as you slide into your pod the next day, your monitor lights up. There's already a Tourist on deck and waiting.

"Shit," you mutter, pulling up the menu and scrolling quickly through the requirements. Everything looks good, good, except ... a sliver of panic when you see that a specific tribe has been requested. Cherokee. You don't know anything about Cherokees. What they wore back then, their ceremonies. The only Cherokee you know is ... White Wolf shimmers into your Experience.

In your haste, you have forgotten to put on your buckskin. Your Experience-self still wears Wranglers and Nikes. Boss would be pissed to see you this sloppy.

"Why are you back?" you ask.

"I thought maybe we could just talk."

"About what?"

White Wolf shrugs. "Doesn't matter. Whatever."

"I can't."

"Why not? This is my time. I'm paying."

You feel a little panicked. A Tourist has never broken protocol like this before. Part of why the Experience works is that everyone knows their role. But White Wolf don't seem to care about the rules.

"I can just keep coming back," he says. "I have money, you know."

"You'll get me in trouble."

"I won't. I just ..." White Wolf hesitates. Something in him slumps. What you read as arrogance now looks like desperation. "I need a friend."

You know that feeling. The truth is, you could use a friend, too. Someone to talk to. What could the harm be? You'll just be two men, talking.

Not here, though. You still need to work. "How about the bar?"

"The place from last night?"

"I get off at 11 p.m."

When you get there around 11:30 p.m., the bar is busy, but you recognize White Wolf immediately. A skinny white guy stands out at the Hey U.S.A. It's funny. Under this light, in this crowd, White Wolf could pass for Native of some kind. One of those 1/64th guys, at least. Maybe he really is a little Cherokee from way back when.

White Wolf waves you over to an empty booth. A Coors Light waits for you. You slide into the booth and wrap a hand around the cool damp skin of the bottle, pleasantly surprised.

"A lucky guess, did I get it right?"

You nod and take a sip. That first sip is always magic. Like how you imagine Golden, Colorado must feel like on a winter morning.

"So," White Wolf says, "tell me about yourself."

You look around the bar for familiar faces. Are you really going to do this? Tell a Tourist about your life? Your real life? A little voice in your head whispers that maybe this isn't so smart. Boss could find out and get mad. DarAnne could make fun of you. Besides, White Wolf will want a cool story, something real authentic, and all you have is an aging three-bedroom ranch and a student loan.

But he's looking at you, friendly interest, and nobody looks at you like that much anymore, not even Theresa. So you talk.

Not everything.

But some. Enough.

Enough that, when the bartender calls last call, you realize you've been talking for two hours.

When you stand up to go, White Wolf stands up, too. You shake hands, Indian-style, which makes you smile. You didn't expect it, but you've got a good, good feeling.

"So same time tomorrow?" White Wolf asks.

You're tempted, but, "No, Theresa will kill me if I stay out this late two nights in a row." And then, "But how about Friday?"

"Friday it is." White Wolf touches your shoulder. "See you then, Jesse."

You feel a warm flutter of anticipation for Friday. "See you."

Friday you are there by 11:05 p.m. White Wolf laughs when he sees your face, and you grin back, only a little embarrassed. This time you pay for the drinks, and the two of you pick up right where you left off. It's so easy. White Wolf never seems to tire of your stories, and it's been so long since you had a new friend to tell them to that you can't seem to quit. It turns out White Wolf loves Kevin Costner, too, and you take turns quoting lines at each other until White Wolf stumps you with a Wind in His Hair quote.

"Are you sure that's in the movie?"

"It's Lakota!"

You won't admit it, but you're impressed with how good White Wolf's Lakota sounds.

White Wolf smiles. "Looks like I know something you don't."

You wave it away good-naturedly but vow to watch the movie again.

Time flies and once again, after last call, you both stand outside under the Big Chief. You happily agree to meet again next Tuesday. And the following Friday. Until it becomes your new routine.

The month passes quickly. The next month, too.

"You seem too happy," Theresa says one night, sounding suspicious.

You grin and wrap your arms around your wife, pulling her close until her rose-scented shampoo fills your nose. "Just made a friend, is all. A guy from work." You decide to keep it vague. Hanging with White Wolf, who you've long stopped thinking of as just a Tourist, would be hard to explain.

"You're not stepping out on me, Jesse Turnblatt? Because I will—"

You cut her off with a kiss. "Are you jealous?"

"Should I be?"

"Never."

She sniffs but lets you kiss her again, her soft body tight against yours.

"I love you," you murmur as your hands dip under her shirt.

"You better."

Tuesday morning and you can't breathe. Your nose is a deluge of snot, and your joints ache. Theresa calls in sick for you and bundles you in bed with a bowl of stew. You're supposed to meet White Wolf for your usual drink, but you're much too sick. You consider sending Theresa with a note but decide against it. It's only one night. White Wolf will understand.

But by Friday the coughing has become a deep, rough bellow that shakes your whole chest. When Theresa calls in sick for you again, you make sure your cough is loud enough for Boss to hear it. Pray he doesn't dock you for the days you're missing. But what you're most worried about is standing up White Wolf again.

"Do you think you could go for me?" you ask Theresa.

"What, down to the bar? I don't drink."

"I'm not asking you to drink. Just to meet him, let him know I'm sick. He's probably thinking I forgot about him."

"Can't you call him?"

"I don't have his number."

"Fine, then. What's his name?"

You hesitate. Realize you don't know. The only name you know is the one you gave him. "White Wolf."

"Okay, then. Get some rest."

Theresa doesn't get back until almost 1 a.m. "Where were you?" you ask, alarmed. Is that a rosy flush in her cheeks, the scent of Cherry Coke on her breath?

"At the bar like you asked me to."

"What took so long?"

She huffs. "Did you want me to go or not?"

"Yes, but ... well, did you see him?"

She nods, smiles a little smile that you've never seen on her before. "What is it?" Something inside you shrinks.

"A nice man. Real nice. You didn't tell me he was Cherokee."

By Monday you're able to drag yourself back to work. There's a note taped to your locker to go see Boss. You find him in his office, looking through the reports that he sends to Management every week.

"I hired a new guy."

You swallow the excuses you've prepared to explain how sick you were, your promises to get your numbers up. They become a hard ball in your throat.

"Sorry, Jesse." Boss actually does look a little sorry. "This guy is good, a real rez guy. Last name's 'Wolf.' I mean, shit, you can't get more Indian than that. The Tourists are going to eat it up."

"The Tourists love me, too." You sound whiny, but you can't help it. There's a sinking feeling in your gut that tells you this is bad, bad, bad.

"You're good, Jesse. But nobody knows anything about Pueblo Indians, so all you've got is that TV shit. This guy, he's ..." Boss snaps his fingers, trying to conjure the word.

"Authentic?" A whisper.

Boss points his finger like a gun. "Bingo. Look, if another pod opens up, I'll call you."

"You gave him my pod?"

Boss's head snaps up, wary. You must have yelled that. He reaches over to tap a button on his phone and call security.

"Wait!" you protest.

But the men in uniforms are already there to escort you out.

You can't go home to Teresa. You just can't. So you head to the Hey U.S.A. It's a different crowd than you're used to. An afternoon crowd. Heavy boozers and people without jobs. You laugh because you fit right in.

The guys next to you are doing shots. Tiny glasses of rheumy dark liquor lined up in a row. You haven't done shots since college, but when one of the men offers you one, you take it. Choke on the cheap whiskey that burns down your throat. Two more and the edges of your panic start to blur soft and tolerable. You can't remember what time it is when you get up to leave, but the Big Chief is bright in the night sky.

You stumble through the door and run smack into DarAnne. She growls at you, and you try to stutter out an apology; but a heavy hand comes down on your shoulder before you get the words out.

"This asshole bothering you?"

You recognize that voice. "White Wolf?" It's him. But he looks different to you. Something you can't quite place. Maybe it's the ribbon shirt he's wearing or the bone choker around his neck. Is his skin a little tanner than it was last week?

"Do you know this guy?" DarAnne asks, and you think she's talking to you, but her head is turned towards White Wolf.

"Never seen him," White Wolf says as he stares you down, and under that confident glare you almost believe him. Almost forget that you've told this man things about you even Theresa doesn't know.

"It's me," you protest, but your voice comes out in a whiskey-slurred squeak that doesn't even sound like you.

"Fucking glonnies," DarAnne mutters as she pushes past you. "Always making a scene."

"I think you better go, buddy," White Wolf says. Not unkindly, if you were in fact strangers, if you weren't actually buddies. But you are, and you clutch at his shirtsleeve, shouting something about friendship and Theresa and then the world melts into a blur until you feel the hard slap of concrete against your shoulder and the taste of blood on your lip where you bit it and a solid kick to your gut until the whiskey comes up the way it went down and then the Big Chief is blinking at you, How, How, How, until the darkness comes to claim you and the lights all flicker out.

You wake up in the gutter. The fucking gutter. With your head aching and your mouth as dry and rotted as month-old roadkill. The sun is up, Arizona fire beating across your skin. Your clothes are filthy and your shoes are missing and there's a smear of blood down your chin and drying flakes in the creases of your neck. Your hands are chapped raw. And you can't remember why.

But then you do.

And the humiliation sits heavy on your bruised-up shoulder, a dark shame that defies the desert sun. Your job. DarAnne ignoring you like that. White Wolf kicking your ass. And you out all night, drunk in a downtown gutter. It all feels like a terrible dream, like the worst kind. The ones you can't wake up from because it's real life.

Your car isn't where you left it, likely towed with the street sweepers, so you trudge your way home on sock feet. Three miles on asphalt streets until you see your highly-mortgaged three-bedroom ranch. And for once the place looks beautiful, like the day you bought it. Tears gather in your eyes as you push open the door.

"Theresa," you call. She's going to be pissed, and you're going to have to talk fast, explain the whole drinking thing (it was one time!) and getting fired (I'll find a new job, I promise), but right now all you want is to wrap her in your arms and let her rose scent fill your nose like good medicine.

"Theresa," you call again, as you limp through the living room. Veer off to look in the bedroom, check behind the closed bathroom door. But what you see in the bathroom makes you pause. Things are missing. Her toothbrush, the pack of birth control, contact lens solution.

"Theresa?!" and this time you are close to panic as you hobble down the hall to the kitchen.

The smell hits you first. The scent of fresh coffee, bright and familiar.

When you see the person sitting calmly at the kitchen table, their back to you, you relax. But that's not Theresa.

He turns slightly, enough so you can catch his profile, and says, "Come on in, Jesse."

"What the fuck are you doing here?"

White Wolf winces as if your words hurt him. "You better have a seat."

"What did you do to my wife?!"

"I didn't do anything to your wife." He picks up a small, folded piece of paper, holds it out. You snatch it from his fingers and move, so you can see his face. The note in your hand feels like wildfire, something with the potential to sear you to the bone. You want to rip it wide open, you want to flee before its revelations scar you. You ache to read it now, now, but you won't give him the satisfaction of your desperation.

"So now you remember me," you huff.

"I apologize for that. But you were making a scene, and I couldn't have you upsetting DarAnne."

You want to ask how he knows DarAnne, how he was there with her in the first place. But you already know. Boss said the new guy's name was Wolf.

"You're a real son of a bitch, you know that?"

White Wolf looks away from you, that same pained look on his face. Like you're embarrassing yourself again. "Why don't you help yourself to some coffee," he says, gesturing to the coffee pot. Your coffee pot.

"I don't need your permission to get coffee in my own house," you shout.

"Okay," he says, leaning back. You can't help but notice how handsome he looks, his dark hair a little longer, the choker on his neck setting off the arch of his high cheekbones.

You take your time getting coffee—sugar, creamer, which you would never usually take—before you drop into the seat across from him. Only then do you open the note, hands trembling, dread twisting hard in your gut.

"She's gone to her mother's," White Wolf explains as you read the same words on the page. "For her own safety. She wants you out by the time she gets back."

"What did you tell her?"

"Only the truth. That you got yourself fired, that you were on a bender, drunk in some alleyway downtown like a bad stereotype." He leans in. "You've been gone for two days."

You blink. It's true, but it's not true, too.

"Theresa wouldn't ..." But she would, wouldn't she? She'd said it a million times, given you a million chances.

"She needs a real man, Jesse. Someone who can take care of her."

"And that's you?" You muster all the scorn you can when you say that, but it comes out more a question than a judgment. You remember how you gave him the benefit of the doubt on that whole Cherokee thing, how you thought "pretendian" was cruel.

He clears his throat. Stands.

"It's time for you to go," he says. "I promised Theresa you'd be gone, and I've got to get to work soon." Something about him seems to expand, to take up the space you once occupied. Until you feel small, superfluous.

"Did you ever think," he says, his voice thoughtful, his head tilted to study you like a strange foreign body, "that maybe this is my experience, and you're the tourist here?"

"This is my house," you protest, but you're not sure you believe it now. Your head hurts. The coffee in your hand is already cold. How long have you been sitting here? Your thoughts blur to histories, your words become nothing more than forgotten facts and half-truths. Your heart, a dusty repository for lost loves and desires, never realized.

"Not anymore," he says.

Nausea rolls over you. That same stretching sensation you get when you Relocate out of an Experience.

Whiplash, and then ...

You let go.

Which Treats of Lázaro's Account of the Friendship He Shared with a Blind Trafficker in Stories and the Misfortunes That Befell Them

Carlos Yushimito

● translated by Elizabeth Bryer ●

"Have you ever seen out in the country at midday an electric bulb aglow? I have seen one. It is one of life's bad memories."
—Juan Emar, *Miltín 1934*

There was a time when I often gazed at the factory chimneys. Each morning they were the same height and their colour resembled zinzolin, a kind of purple that, lacklustre as it is, blended with the red of daybreak. Those details were important to me: they let me know that between night and day nothing had changed. The rain, for example, had not made one chimney grow taller than the other or effaced or discoloured the enamel. It soothed me to note that the black clouds that rose from the chimneys, though unrelenting, would never darken the rest of the sky; the smoke billowed, and it seemed to me that I was watching a giant's fingers as he twirled his hair.

On those occasions I spent hours waiting for the blind man to wake. Between the white eyes of sleep and the white eyes of waking, I learned to distinguish a rift: the sun hastened the contours of the chimneys, and shortly after his hands began to shake as if they were drowning in the light; after this, now with his whole body shaking and his eyes rolled back, he groped his way towards where I was watching him, and with a couple of blows to my head, cried:

"Open your eyes, Lázaro! With no energy there's no voice, and with no voice there's no appetite ..."

And when that happened, the streets were already teeming with the same diligence. The blind man gave the order to go outside and not long after he was crying out, "Have a story told, any story!" He left out nothing that the other traffickers in stories thought to say. People passed by, avoiding his voice; the women, especially, sidestepped him and wrinkled their noses as if they were afraid of getting them wet. But there was always someone who, lured by the words cast by that hoarse and almost violent voice, dropped a coin into our little tin and inclined his or her head to listen more closely. Perhaps owing to his blindness, if the blind man said he remembered, the people believed; and if officials overlooked the fact that he dared spout the lies that came out his mouth, it was because in those times, when stories were forbidden, his were ensconced in the impunity of his useless eyes, which were never taken for anything but harmless and devoid of all authority.

This was how we lived: a little here and a little there. When we amassed enough water, we moved south, never north. There, the factories sprouted; the dogs snarled, and problems piled up. In the south, by contrast, there was still space enough for solitude. But because the blind man migrated often and we had to return regularly, we secured a basement where we could shelter while we took turns to stock up on more ampoules. All I had to do was shake the tin whenever I noted interest on the face of someone who had heard "Forty-millilitre coins; forty-millilitre coins ..." And as I said earlier, if, with a little good fortune, someone dropped us a coin, the blind man rolled his eyes back and remembered the years when there was plenty of water and mankind reproduced; when factories had not been invented and all the things that people say used to happen did indeed come to pass as naturally as nowadays they do not.

Sometimes, however, someone would arrive wanting to buy another kind of story.

Thereupon, the blind man would lower his voice and squeeze my arm.

The man seemed nervous and bit his lip. A longing to be injected with one of our story-filled ampoules had brought him here. I was used to recognising such customers because, since I had been living with the blind man, I had seen that they came in several shapes and sizes. Some, such as this one, peered at us from behind a pair of glasses with transparent frames; these were almost always shy and had sallow skin. Others wore blue tracksuits and dyed their hair white. Their preferences may have often coincided, but they were usually strict in terms of the stories they wanted to experience and the time they had to spare. This was why we went down to the basement. There, next to a small makeshift pallet, the blind man opened the case and exhibited the titles of the ampoules, which were often numerous and came in many sizes. Along the length of the ampoule plastic, you could read the name of the story, and if it was selected, I moistened a little cotton ball with disinfectant and rubbed the nape of the person's neck before guiding the blind man's hand; and he sunk the needle into the flesh and injected the colours.

When we reached the basement alongside the shy young man with the glasses, the blind man said what he always did:

"A one-hour ampoule of story costs half a litre; a two-hour ampoule costs one."

You could see the man had been through this before because his mouth tightened and he replied:

"I'll give you a litre and a half if you get me what I want."

Once more I felt the blind man grab my arm, and the scraping of his shoes on the steps turned protracted and rough.

"Indeed, indeed," the blind man chewed the offer over. "A litre and a half is a fair amount. Tell me what story."

"What I'm after isn't exactly a story," the shy young man lowered his voice so much that for a moment I thought he had begun to swallow his words, "but a name: Felisberto Hernández."

"Felisberto," murmured the blind man while picking at his mole-specked head; "a strange harvest, no doubt about it, but the distiller will know how to get hold of it if we give him some time."

"But it's vital that I experience it today!"

"That makes it tricky." The blind man hastened to feel out the space before him with his crutch until the edge of the wood caught me in the ribs. "You heard, nephew," he let three coins drop into my hand, "be precise with what you stipulate and make sure it's top notch."

He made me repeat the name three times, and then I ran to the distillery. I often went in there with the blind man; beforehand, we had to cross a little room with walls covered in labelled vials that were full of cloudy water; inside them floated objects that I could not always identify. All of it was under the care of a fat woman who picked at her fingernails and had a decisive character. Yet she would get nervous whenever anyone asked after the distiller even though such a thing was not out of the ordinary; she would shake her head and make strange faces as if she were putting up a struggle against words that refused to come out her mouth. If this kept up a long time, she would press a blue button; if a short time, a red one. At that moment the distiller would appear. He was a man with a beautiful moustache who often made apologies, which you could see was because he held the blind man in high esteem. He would take us to a small room where there were two couches, and the pair would sit down to drink a bottle full of the liquid on the walls while they waited for the operator to arrive with a selection of ampoules. The blind man would take a whiff and rejoice; later, sniffing the sample of ampoules, he would say yes to one story, no to another, and one by one the distiller would fill our case, which we would then hide in the basement.

Now I was knocking at the distillery door with both hands; I banged at it until one of the operators stuck his face out the window.

"What do you want?" He was a wide man pitted with smallpox scars and visibly in a hurry.

"The blind man sent me," I replied, "with an emergency."

Clearly, the blind man was important to them because they let me in right away. The fat woman looked me head to toe and, after listening patiently, pressed the red button. I stood there, unsure of what to say. Her jaw wiggled a good while, but finally, words managed to escape her:

"Wait for him in the other room."

I ducked under a curtain; it was the first time I had been in there. Behind the curtain there were several alembics dripping stories, and almost at once it occurred to me that it was like watching a group of obese people sweating in a gymnasium. Every now and then an operator with rubber gloves inspected the alembics; he sniffed the filter and later went out of the room carrying a little tray of vials filled with different colours. I heard his heels pecking at the roof. Several iron pipes descended from the ceiling, and the noise that travelled down them went around in a spiral that was like a sluggish digestion tract.

Soon I sensed that someone brushed against the curtain. The folds of the red fabric softened. I saw the bristles of a moustache.

"This will take some time," said the distiller. "In the first place, it is a tricky item of fermentation. Add to that the whole matter of the tank. We have to search the storehouse, process the dyes, et cetera."

I suspected the fat woman had munched on my thoughts while I was in that room; if not, I was at a loss as to explain how the distiller knew I had come for such a rare ampoule. I lamented thinking unkind things about her and being found out, but above all I was distressed to think our sale would not proceed, and the distiller was saying rushed things as if he wanted me gone. The coins were bulky in my hand and damp; I clenched them, and as if in affinity, my eyes caught their dampness. It was two days since I had eaten, and I had got my hopes up.

"The blind man knows these things take days," said the distiller, convinced he was making a fair statement.

I couldn't contain myself any longer: my hands found my face, and I started to sob.

"Don't cry, boy," he said in pity, "there are always alternatives when you're young."

My tears were salty, and without thinking I licked them from my hands. I realised I was doing something depraved and hurried to tell him:

"I'll end up eating myself."

I immediately dried my eyes with the sleeve of my shirt and realised my words would free me from my predicament, as if in saying them, I had slyly tugged on a small girl's plaits.

"Look," said the distiller, "here's your alternative: you just have to take another story to the blind man. It wouldn't be so hard."

I cleaned my face.

"Might you have a similar story?" I asked, slurping my snot and coming back to my senses.

The distiller stroked his moustache:

"Take another Uruguayan," he said after a while. "I have several."

It was the first time I had heard that word.

Together, we went to the ampoule draw that said "Uruguay." There were many stories there, but I, thinking about the profit I stood to make, turned my gaze to where the remainders were piled and took the first I saw.

The Uruguayan story I chose had a solid sea-green colour. I switched the original label for another that said something very different. Now, along the length of the ampoule, it read, "Unknown." I felt fortunate to have found a way to proceed with the sale and keep, for myself, a couple of coins of such large denomination. I was so elated by my windfall—by my skulduggery, as much as anything— that I started to realise my enthusiasm may have spread to the blind man. Perhaps he had not expected me to return with good news or perhaps he was simply happy for the interruption to the long talk I had left them to.

"If times were different, I would have been a musician, too," the shy young man with the glasses was saying as I went down to the basement.

"And I a spy!" the blind man retorted.

I pulled on the sleeve of his lab coat, and he turned his head, searching me out in the air as if he were following a scent.

"Uncle," I said.

"Ah," the blind man was swift to interrupt, "the ampoule ..."

We lay down a pillow with a clean slip for our customer. I rubbed the nape of his neck with bunched fabric soaked in antiseptic until his skin went red from the heat, and after a while the blind man jabbed him with the syringe. I watched as the level of injectable liquid, which the blind man had drawn from the broken ampoule, lowered until the barrel was dry. Not even a drop was left. Then the shy young man crinkled his forehead and rested the left side of his face against the fabric.

That's how he fell asleep.

"I swore you wouldn't come back with that ampoule," the blind man shook his head. "This Felisberto, you know? ... an odd name ... It's been so many years since I heard it ..."

He told me the story of a Russian spy who was married to a pianist. This woman was only interested in meeting the important men who went to hear him play. She was very obliging to start with: she combed his hair and even knotted his ties. Later, once some time had passed, she only went around with the important men and jotted down everything in a little notebook; she stopped attending his concerts; and the pianist gained weight, and his relationship with the piano deteriorated. The shy young man with the glasses snored softly as I told myself, *In some way, I'm like that Russian spy breaking her promise*. But at the same time I thought, *One cannot escape one's shadow*. And though now you probably don't believe me, I felt all this with an intense guilt that I hid because deep down I would have liked to be a different person from the boy whose two coins weighed so heavily in his pocket.

Several minutes lapsed until the shy young man started making strange noises through his nose. Drops of sweat were clearly discernible above his top lip, and his forehead was furrowed like a muscleman's as he flexes in front of the mirror.

The blind man wasted no time in saying:

"What an uneasy slumber, that of youth ..."

So as not to encourage ruminations since he was a suspicious man, I tried to change the topic; I drew his attention to, among other things, all we could buy with the litre and a half that the young man had promised us and the miles we would save by avoiding another migration south. I added every so often that all this was thanks to him, and I praised the protection he gave me with calculated excess. The blind man celebrated my flattery without any false modesty. Perhaps thinking himself charitable, he added that this would be the first time I would get to eat one of the biscuits produced by the factory, and that, in doing so, I might recognise the taste of my parents. The blind man, so cruel, laughed at his own joke. He knew that before he had taken me in, my parents had been processed by the factory and converted, like other poor people, into biscuits. His laughter tired him out, and his eyes much whiter than usual, he fell asleep.

I was about to do the same. But the shy young man with the glasses made so much noise and jumped and trembled against the pallet so much that the blind man woke up. He banged the floor several times with his crutch until I moved close to him.

"What's going on?" he searched out my hand.

To soothe him I said:

"He's just got a dream moving about inside him."

But the blind man suspected something.

"Go on, be a good boy, bring me that syringe."

I said there was no need, keeping my voice neutral, but underneath, I was panicking to think I might be caught out if he decided to sniff the hollow of the plastic. I was also in torment imagining that for only two coins I had ended up harming the young man, and I was holding in so many tears that my face was puffing up.

Finally, the blind man buried his nose in the syringe, sniffed what residue was left, and licked the tip of the plunger. And he said, deep in thought:

"If I hadn't sent you to the distiller himself, I'd worry you'd been given the wrong dose."

"Rightly said," I responded, "because I'm a boy, and anyone could take advantage of my inexperience."

We had to hold several compresses to the young man's head to calm his fever. At times it raged, and at times it subsided; everything seemed to be infected with that fluctuation except for the pensive mood that had overcome the blind man. After three hours without sleep, I finally heard a sigh escape the young man. I leaned over him to hear what came out: it was a wizened, moustachioed voice that seemed to emanate from deep inside:

> *I return, I want to believe I'm returning,*
> *with my worst and my best story,*
> *I know this path from memory,*
> *but still I'm surprised...*

Perhaps that was the proof the blind man needed to better comprehend my deception. I've never known about stories, but he, simply on hearing those words escape the young man's mouth, frowned and flushed with all the blood in his body.

"You brought me one of the remainders," the blind man said in fury. "Because what he's saying, if my memory doesn't fail me, must be the remainder that's been there longest!"

All of which I denied, swearing on my life, and with each word I took one step closer to the staircase.

Almost at the same time, the shy young man with the glasses jumped up from the pallet and, his eyes alight, started reciting, exalted:

> *So I'm reduced to what I am*
> *Devoid of cultural tools*
> *I close my eyes but*
> *what am I to do*
> *I don't dream of pardons*

Just imagining the blows the enraged blind man would deal me was painful, and I'm sure that if it weren't for the fact that the young man also started running, accidentally obstructing my master, I would not now be sitting beside this rock telling you of these misfortunes. Soon the shy young man with the glasses had unbuttoned his shirt and was naked from the navel up; he wouldn't stop crowing and swung his arms around in circles as if he were about to rise to another dimension where he would be chicken rather than human. That's what inspiration had driven him to. Behind him came the blind man: thanks to all the stories crammed in his head, he was so creative and poetic with his insults that, had they not been directed at me, I would have gladly sat down to listen. At one point, taking advantage of the bewilderment occasioned by the young man's crowing, I hastened to leap onto the steps and ran up them one by one until I was out on the street.

I left behind my master, who was swinging his crutch at thin air while I ran; only the origin of the ampoule, which had been labelled with the name that the blind man managed to remember, seemed to want to escape our basement as if it had turned into feathers floating towards me, the gutted stuffing of a pillow, as if the feathers themselves were saying, "Return ... return ... return ..."

"Benedetti ... Benedetti ... You had to bring me Benedetti ...!"

That night I walked south so as not to come across any of the dogs that the factory people let out at daybreak to hunt down the resources they need to start up factory operations. Along the way there was a forest, and by dragging together branches and leaves, I improvised a shelter, where I barely slept once my legs started to ache. I woke sodden by a fine rain, who knows how many hours or days after my flight. Shortly after circling the river, I sat down beside this rock, intending never to get back up but instead letting myself die here. And I was watching the smoke rising from the chimneys and twirling my hair when a little frog passed by, making agile little jumps that were bold for an animal of her size. It was amusing to watch her jump with such undefeated movements that betrayed no fear of my shadow.

"Frog, my friend," I said sincerely, "might you show me the path I should follow?"

"There," she said.

She pointed northward to the chimneys that never cease their billowing.

"You must be mad," I replied, bewildered. "If I go that way I'll most likely be turned into a biscuit."

"Yes," said the frog.

And she moved her toes while she chuckled as if she were playing the piano.

Tomorrow's Dictator

Rahul Kanakia

The 2029 Northern California Human Resources Conference and Exposition would have long ago gone bankrupt if it had relied solely on the registration fees of the business-suited organization men and women who filled the convention floor. In the current economy there were fewer and fewer conventional HR personnel every year. But ten years ago, the convention had started marketing itself to non-corporate human resources specialists, and the fruits of that effort were scattered across the convention floor: a woman standing in line at the childcare area with seventeen utterly silent children in tow; two men in dapper blue suits whose name tags proclaimed their ties to a large Hindu temple on the outskirts of Milpitas; and a man in a foul-smelling leather jacket who was tapping at a crystal data-earring.

In the midst of such oddities, Sasha barely merited a raised eyebrow when she picked up her name tag from the registration desk outside the North Ballroom. It said:

> *Sasha Boretsky*
> *Community Manager*
> *Walden Three*

"Damn it," said her husband, George Stanschloss. "I told them quite clearly that your title was 'Dictator.'"

"They called to confirm," Sasha said. "I had to correct your idiocy. Our community is looking to attract serious men and women, not more neurotic, drug-addicted fools."

George blanched. He rubbed the needle scars that were covered by his left sleeve.

"Do you really think we can find someone else who's like you?" he said. "How could we trust a stranger with our lives? Our ... our minds?"

"Don't be so dramatic. Running Walden Three is not a feel-good exercise. It is a job, and it is a difficult one. We can *make* an executive love Walden Three, but we can't make a fool into an executive."

"Perhaps you're right." He was picking through the name tags. "I can't seem to find my own tag."

"I cancelled your registration. As my spouse, you can attend for free. There was no need to pay extra. See here, you can make your own name tag using this marker."

"I'll look absurd. Why couldn't you have let them print a tag for me?"

Sasha put a hand on her husband's arm. He twitched and almost shook her off. "Look, are you sure you don't need another adjustment? I'm sensing some resentment from you."

"No ... I just ... no, I'm fine."

"Good," she said. "Now I'm going to get ready for this breakfast meet-and-greet they've scheduled for me."

"But I already ate ..."

"I'm going alone. The whole purpose of this endeavor is to find new managers, isn't it?"

"But—"

"Look at these refugees from the corporate kleptocracy." She gestured at the crowd. "Their souls have been sucked out, and they're practically begging for us to fill them up again; but I can't really examine these prospects if I have to spend all my time looking after you."

He was rendered desperately silent. His love required him to tag along after her, but it also required him to obey her.

She hugged him and kissed his cheek.

"I'm so sorry, George," she said. "Someday soon—after I've found my successor—I'll be able to make myself love you as much as I've made you love me."

She left George by the registration desk. As she walked to the South Ballroom, she sighed. He'd probably stand there all day. She really must get him to accept another adjustment. His last one had rejuvenated his flagging feelings for her, but it had also made him foolish and neurotic. For a moment she remembered that she'd once relied on George; she'd needed his help to get through the day. When had he become just another Waldenite who needed to be taken care of?

The moment she entered the South Ballroom, she knew this breakfast was going to be a bust. The creases in the men's shirts and pants were flattened-out as if they'd hung in a closet for a long time. They shot shy, hungry glances at each person who entered the room. The place reeked of long-term unemployment.

Her first and second handshakes culminated in mumbled elevator pitches from job seekers. The men stumbled over their words and nodded robotically when she replied. She didn't bother telling them about how Walden Three could transform their humdrum lives; they'd already been sapped of the necessary courage. The third man seemed more human, but when he realized where Sasha was from, he told her that he'd accidentally given her an outdated version of his résumé, then he pulled it out of her hand, and bolted from the conversation.

The fourth man gave a start when he read her name tag.

"That's one of those brainwashing cults, isn't it?" he said.

She smiled. Another bust.

But he was still holding onto her hand. He kept shaking it, and she saw the gears clicking in his mind. She sensed his defenses crumbling; he'd just fallen deeper than he'd thought was possible. He was sweating profusely. "Do you take families?" he said.

"Of course," she said. "Most of our members have nonexclusive primary pairings and choose to raise their offspring communally, but we respect all forms of familial organization."

All of the man's reserve dropped away. He babbled to her about his years of looking for work. His wife had gone back to his home country, but his children had stayed here. They were living with a cousin. He had no one. He lived in a one-bedroom with six other unemployed men. If she wanted him, then he was hers.

But when Sasha looked at him, she saw a burden: another person whose complaints would fill her day; another person whose neuroses she'd have to adjust; another person whose life she'd need to manage.

When Sasha returned noncommittal answers to his pleas, the man's shoulders slumped, and his voice lowered. The man had tried to sell himself into slavery and found that his life was worthless.

But the embers of pity flared up inside Sasha. She wondered what everyone had thought of *her* when she'd first come to Walden Three.

"We can help you," she said.

He wiped his eyes with the back of his hand and started babbling his thanks.

She took his hand and turned it upwards as if she were trying to read his palm. "After your first adjustment you'll be able to work sixteen hours without stopping. Your hands are small; I think we can use you in our shoe factory. After only a few more adjustments, you'll *love* the work. You and your family will have to sleep in the barracks for a little while, but you can build a home in your free time. You said you have two sons? The work should go pretty quickly."

His smile congealed. She left him with a business card and a silent prayer. Maybe—if he had enough courage—she'd someday see him standing tall and singing proudly at one of Walden Three's general assemblies. On the other hand, maybe he'd remain mired in fear. These middle-class refugees were rarely able to let go of their pretense at mental integrity and appreciate the real gift that Walden Three was offering them. It was happiness, offered up neat and simple and without stress.

Sasha's next handshake was firm but not a contest of strength. The man's other hand was in his pocket; this was no job seeker.

"Jesus, what line are you laying on these résumé droppers?" the man said. "Most of them are circling the room to avoid you."

His name tag said: *Roger Schultz / VP (Human Resources) / Landon Chemical.* Sasha sucked in her breath. Before she could speak, he flicked his name tag, and said, "Don't worry, I'm not going to explode and poison you."

The bitter joke startled Sasha. Here was the perfect prospect: a dissatisfied senior manager who could come to Walden Three and reform all the tawdry inefficiencies that Sasha didn't have the experience to adjust her way around.

"So you're a cult leader then?" he said.

"A dictator," she murmured.

"What?"

"We're not a cult, and we have no leader. We operate by consensus. We need ninety percent agreement to enact a proposal."

"If there's no leader, then who are you?"

"Nine years ago, they consented to vest much of their decision-making power in me."

"Like the Romans did. You're their dictator."

"That's what they call me. I don't think it's a very funny joke."

"Some of my college friends call me Herr Vice President."

"Oh? Because of the cloud of poison gas that decim—"

"You're offering to adjust people." He smiled as he scanned the room. "I'm surprised that no one here has spit in your face."

His words hung between them. A crowd of job seekers was perambulating restlessly around him; many of them were shooting undisguised stares at the vice president.

"Don't pretend that your firm has never indulged in adjustment," she said. Everyone knew that the top corporations routinely forced their critical employees to undergo adjustment, so they'd work longer and harder."

"We've used it in Asia, but forcing adjustment on employees

is illegal in the U.S.; and so far, public opinion has crushed any company that has tried to pilot an optional adjustment program."

"I doubt that you care about public opinion."

He laughed. "You really don't realize how rare your skill set is, do you?"

"You're pretty rare, too. We could certainly use someone like you. There are a lot of people who are willing to stitch shoes, but there aren't many who are willing to make the sacrifices needed to manage Walden Three."

"Let's discuss it over drinks," he said. "Two-thirty, in the bar."

As he pulled away from her, the swarm of job seekers descended on him. No one else spoke to her for the remainder of the breakfast. She blew off the other morning and afternoon sessions so she could research Roger Schultz. This had to be the man she'd been looking for. He had no loyalty to Landon: he'd only worked there for three years. For two decades he'd skipped across industries and states, but he'd been born right here in the Sacramento area to a working-class family. He'd spent two years in community college before transferring to Chico State. She'd seen for herself how cynical he was about his own business. Sasha knew firsthand exactly how much doubt and self-hatred and insecurity lay behind that sort of cynicism.

This was a highly skilled man who'd been entrapped long ago into using those skills for evil. Sasha needed to make him realize that there was another life waiting for him. Her body vibrated with energy, and she felt the beginnings of a headache. This felt just like the moments before a presentation to a high-profile client. The minibar was right there. She could drink it dry if she wanted. George wouldn't question her. No one would.

She pounded at her forehead with the heel of her hand. She hadn't had those thoughts in a while.

This man had to be it. She needed *some* hope of a successor. Otherwise, what else was there? Another nine years of toil with no chance of relief?

The hotel bar was packed with boisterous HR directors, but Roger was sitting in a semi-private booth toward the back. There were two glasses in front of him.

"Two Manhattans," he said. "The wait for service looked pretty long, so I ordered for you preemptively."

A Manhattan: that had been her drink, fifteen years ago.

"I don't drink," she said.

"Part of your little religion?"

"Not at all," she said. "At Walden Three, you can drink, smoke, eat meat, and inject heroin if you want to. But we can also help you to be better than those things."

"It's hard to believe you've actually practiced employee adjustment. How many people have you done?"

"Oh, I'm one of the most experienced adjusters in California. There's no need to worry about *that*. I've supervised hundreds of initial adjustments and thousands of touch-ups."

Roger's eyes widened. "Hundreds? You have that many folks up there?"

He was leaning forward with his hands on the edge of the table.

What kind of pitch would interest this man? "We have many kinds of operations: factories, stores, schools—we even have two members on the county council. We're small but expanding fast, and we're doing the kinds of things that corporations can never do. We're really getting into the nitty-gritty of how people live. At a company, people go home at the end of the week with a little money and then try to live their real lives. And at the end of all your work, what do you have? Some new fertilizer? Some new pesticide? At Walden Three, you get to build an entire society."

"It's exciting at Landon," he said. "The maneuvering, the strategizing, the planning, and the execution. I even like the disasters. Our decisions affect the whole world."

"Come visit Walden Three," she said. "That's where you'll see real excitement. We're making the kinds of sacrifices that other Americans aren't willing to make, and that's why our revenues have grown three hundred and twenty percent over the last five years. There's nothing as exciting as deciding to build a factory on a plot of land and seeing your people leap to the job, devoting day and night to the task of making your vision come true in the most precise and excellent manner that they can possibly achieve. We're seven hundred people who speak with one voice."

"Your voice," he said.

He scrutinized Sasha, looking her up and down. She felt damp and uncomfortable. She'd spent a whole day in downtown Sacramento trying to find the right suit for this convention, but she still felt poorly dressed.

"Why didn't you try to get back into advertising?" he said.

Sasha slapped the table. The surface of her drink vibrated. "You looked me up online, too?" she said.

"I understand why you left. By the end of your first year, you were coming in late to meetings. In your second year, you started missing work. After a client smelled alcohol on you during a morning—"

Sasha laughed. "Are you headhunting *me*?"

"But after you sobered up, why did you keep doing this cult thing? You still had friends in the industry. You could've come back."

"I'm doing something that's more difficult, more exciting, and more important than trying to brainwash people into buying a different brand of toothpaste."

Sasha felt slightly hysterical. This man wasn't going to come to Walden Three with her. He was trying to get *her* to leave. Dammit, did he know how many times she'd dreamed of leaving? But she knew that Walden Three would fall apart without her.

"They adjusted you, right? That's how you quit drinking."

"No. I always knew that wasn't for me."

"Come off it."

"After drifting around for a few years, I ended up on a farm where some people were operating a then-illegal adjustment clinic. But I never used their skills. I sobered up on my own. I worked sixteen-hour days on my own. I stopped smoking on my own. I lost a hundred pounds on my own."

"Through willpower."

"Some call it that. I think that I just found something better than laziness and hedonism."

"You can't expect me to believe that the apostle of an adjustment cult has never been adjusted herself."

"People feel guilty about adjustment sometimes. They feel weak. They start to idolize those who didn't need to make the compromises they had to make."

"I don't believe it," he said. He tapped his fingers on the table, then stopped. "You were adjusted. When it transformed your life, you saw how powerful the process was. You started working in the adjustment clinic. Afterward, you began adjusting your fellow cult members. You *made* them idolize you. You *made* them respect you."

"Believe what you want. What's your offer?"

"We're opening a plant in the U.S. It'll be our only U.S. factory. We've invented a volatile new product: it doesn't matter what it is. It needs to be manufactured close to the point of sale. We've had three dozen delegations come and beg us to locate our plant in their city. We've had sixty thousand applications on our U.S. jobs portal. But we're still leery of U.S. workers. We've decided that we're going to offer an initial adjustment as an 'option' to all our new hires."

"They won't take it. No matter how much you threaten to fire them, people won't give up their minds. Not to people like you."

"There's no one in the world who has more experience than you at convincing Americans to take adjustments."

"You're wasting your time." Despite herself, Sasha was intrigued. At Walden Three she cajoled and shamed people into taking adjustments. But she'd sometimes pondered other, more impersonal methods.

"If you had to, how would you do it?

She spoke slowly. "People don't want to work harder. They don't even want to make more money. They just want security. They want peace. They don't want to make decisions. They just want to take a pill and feel better."

"And yet they won't take adjustment."

"Oh, they'll take it if it's offered by a doctor," she said. "Offer them free psychiatric treatment. No co-pays. No deductibles. No hassles."

"They don't even offer that kind of benefit to me."

"Have you ever been to a psychiatrist's office nowadays? They're quick places: in and out. They see dozens of patients a day. They listen for fifteen minutes and then prescribe one of the standard adjustments."

"But how do we make sure they get the *right* course of adjustment?"

"The standard initial treatment for stress involves minute changes to a number of neuroreceptors responsible for concentration. By increasing one's focus, they eliminate ancillary concerns and anxieties. This procedure, incidentally, results in increases in productivity for familiar, repetitive tasks—at the expense of a concomitant reduction in productivity for complex tasks like cooking, social interaction, and the like."

She continued: "You would need to make the factory floor into a very stressful place: loud noises, sudden increases in the pace of work, rude and unreasonable demands by foremen ... paired with a campaign to notify workers of their generous mental health benefits."

"So they'll really adjust themselves?" the vice president said.

"People trust their doctors."

"And that's what you do in your little compound?"

"Won't you please come and see it?" Sasha said. "You wouldn't believe how much improved your life can be."

"After you adjust me?"

"No ... we wouldn't adjust you. I think that you're capable of seeing clearly. You would see the importance of what we're doing and the importance of doing it well. To do my job, you can't be satisfied.

You have to change yourself the way I changed myself, and those changes don't make you happier: they make you tougher, hungrier, and angrier."

"Doesn't sound like much of a deal."

"It's exhilarating," she said. "But it's also exhausting. I'm not sure how long I can keep juggling seven hundred lives. They have so many demands."

"You want me to be your 'dictator'?"

"Eventually." Sasha *needed* this to work. She couldn't bear to ride home with George babbling away. She couldn't bear another year of staring down the sheep at the general assembly. She needed someone else. She needed a partner.

"You're the one who needs an escape hatch," he said. "You do something well, and you love doing it. It's all the rest of this personal shit that's dragging you down".

He took out a business card and wrote something on the back of it. "I know that, if I asked for your answer right now, the answer would be no," he said. "But the factory won't be built for another six months. I'll be in touch with you again."

He slid the card across to her. He'd written: *$1.2 mil / year + stock options.*

"There you are!" She whipped her head around. George was bearing down on her. His eyes were glassy. He slid in next to her and put his head on her shoulder as Roger looked on. She was revolted by her husband's childishness.

George was babbling, "I thought about what you said, and I decided to do it. I'll let you adjust me again. I really do need it, don't I? I'm so, so, so sorry about how I acted earlier. Please adjust me again. You have to do it, you really do. I'm, I'm not acting right, the way I am now."

Roger's expression mutated. His smile twisted. He nodded at a waiter and gestured for the check, but as George babbled on, the vice president slowly looked back at them.

Sasha pushed George off her. "This is my husband, George."

"You ... adjust him, too?" Roger said. His voice was soft.

George was looking around with his wide-open, babyish stare.

"Are you married?" she said.

"Three times," Roger said. "But not right now."

"Maybe they would have lasted, if you'd gone in for adju—"

"No," he said. "I don't think I ever would have done that." He looked at his watch.

"It's what *he* wanted," Sasha said. George was happily unaware of

Roger's presence. He was still sitting there, waiting to be petted for having made the right decision.

"If your successor has to be willing to do things like that, then I think she will be very hard to find," Roger said. His hand was moving, perhaps unconsciously, toward the business card he'd left on the table. He looked down and then pulled his hand away.

Roger got up, opened his wallet, threw four twenty dollar bills on the table, and was five feet away before he stopped. "Please call me," he said. "We still need you. Your personal life is ... it will stay your own business."

The vice president hurried out.

George's mouth was hanging open. Sasha smiled weakly at him. This was the man she loved. Not as much as he loved her, of course, but still ... they'd made an agreement to love each other. He'd come to the farm eleven years ago, just as she was finishing her apprenticeship in the adjustment clinic. He'd stopped shooting up by then, but he was still drinking heavily. He'd been so handsome and so intelligent, but he'd broken so many promises to her. He'd sworn he was going to follow in her footsteps. He'd clean himself up using willpower, and then he'd help her with the leadership roles that had, even then, been forced onto her shoulders. But she'd gotten tired of how long he was taking. She'd persuaded him to accept adjustment. And then, while he was going through the first pangs of withdrawal, she'd told him that they should agree to love each other forever. He'd trusted her enough to let her do whatever she wanted. That hadn't been a lie: the person who'd trusted her was the real George, the unadjusted George.

If she had so much willpower, then why had she been unable to resist destroying him?

Sasha pocketed Roger's card. She hoped that George's original personality was still stored somewhere in her files. She'd put him back together before she left.

Geppetto

Carlos Hernandez

"I have aged out of love," Geppetto told the mirror. His wife had left him, and no one falls in love with old men. Mind you, he didn't feel old—he could work as hard as ever and drink just as much, he got in just as many fistfights, and was saluted every morning with a Tower of Piza erection. But he looked old, and for the world that is enough. The skin of his neck draped like an opera house curtain; his face looked like a melted-wax caricature of youth; and he was bald.

Baldness pained him most of all. Once upon a time he sported golden curls that cavorted like a litter of puppies as he walked. Back then they called him "Medusuccio," for his handsome locks petrified anyone he passed with their beauty. It's what first attracted his former wife to him.

She left him the very day his last curl fell like a dead branch from his head.

He was hand-to-mouth poor (the villagers found his marionettes frightening and full of the woes of life, hardly toys at all), but he spent what he could on a wig. His mirror told him it looked not-half-bad. More true to how he felt on the inside. Maybe it would be enough, and someone would love him.

How wrong he was. The villagers started calling him "Polendina," for they said his wig looked like cornmeal mush. He'd beat any child who called him that, fistfight any grown-up, man or woman. But the insult stuck, and pretty soon everyone forgot he'd ever had a Christian name.

No one could love a "Polendina," of course. But how he wanted love. He and his wife had no children, and too late he realized that the only reason to have children was so that someone would love you once you grew ugly.

He did his best to comfort himself. As a young man he had toured Europe's great museums—this was back when he thought he would be a famous sculptor—to study the masters. At night now, in bed, he would recall the women of Ingres and the men of Titian, the nymphs pursued by satyrs, the million Aphrodites with their circular unnatural breasts, and especially, all those chaste Madonnas, expressionless, demurring. Masturbation made his loneliness worse but also better.

But also worse. He needed another option.

And then it came to him. Though his art paid him poorly, it could at least bring him solace. He would make a marionette just for himself.

He got wood from the carpenter, Master Cherry. Master Cherry's Christian name was Maria, but no one remembered that; all anyone saw anymore was her fruit-bright nose. She was just as old and alone as Geppetto, so naturally the two of them hated each other and loved each other. They exchanged insults for a hour and got in two separate fistfights in which each ended up with the other's wig.

But in the end they swore to love each other like family, and Master Cherry gave Geppetto an unusually fine log. Master Cherry thought that particular wood was cursed; it had nearly driving her mad with its jeering. She rubbed the scratches Geppetto had dug into her cheek and said "Enjoy the wood, Polendina!" as Geppetto left.

Back at home, Geppetto sat down, set the log on his lap, and began to carve. As the long, curled shavings piled up around him, he grew increasingly aware he was making the work of a lifetime. Never had the wood grain so aligned with his desire; never had the medium so eagerly acquiesced to his technique. By the time he was halfway done, he was certain he would end up making the most perfect simulacrum of a boy that ever a woodcarver carved.

Perhaps, too perfect. For as soon as he had carved a mouth on the emerging boy's face, it opened. Out of it popped a mocking wooden tongue he had not carved. Then the mouth yelled, with pitch-perfect schoolyard cruelty, "Polendina!"

Geppetto dropped the knife, drew breath. The fever of creation was broken. He looked around.

Now, one doesn't work as a woodcutter for more than half a century without learning to read wood shavings. From the curls of wood on the floor, so like his former hair, he saw his future.

The marionette would come to life! He would have a son!

But the boy would treat him horribly. His antics would get Geppetto arrested. A great fish would swallow them both. Geppetto would grow ill; Death would grip his neck with its skinless hand. Through all these misadventures, the boy would make a fool of him and do him real harm and worst of all, run off again and again. And Geppetto would sacrifice everything to chase after him.

"Because I have aged out of love," thought Geppetto. No one young and new to life could love him. Not for free, anyway. All he could do now is offer adulation and gifts and servitude, all in the vain hope that some scrap of his affection might be requited.

Geppetto spent a long, motionless hour just thinking, the half-finished log-boy giggling like an imp on his lap. For a long time he stared at the hungry, hungry fireplace.

Then unsmiling, he picked up the knife. It took him the rest of the night, but by morning he had transformed the log into a living person, his son, who would be the source of all his future woes and, he prayed hopelessly, some meager joy.

Other Metamorphoses

Fábio Fernandes

As Gregor Samsa awoke one morning from uneasy dreams, he found himself in his bed.

He hadn't been transformed into a gigantic insect.

Disappointed, the small velociraptor started to weep. And braced himself to enter dreamtime again.

Samsa was a member of that elusive caste known as the Oneironauts. Dream travelers—people who, since the dawn of time, were able to master their dreams and bend them at their will.

For them dreamscapes could be the doors to alternate realities. Most of these places could be accessed at will by them; some, not so easily. And even fewer could be tampered with.

Samsa was one of the few who could travel to other realities with his mind and become one with them. He already had done so many times like that series of nightly oneiric escapades that came to be known to his Oneironaut sisters and brothers as his Jurassic Dreams. That was when he woke up as a man-sized beetle.

But that wasn't so easy.

Somewhere along the oneiric corridors, Samsa had lost his original body. Now he was trying to swap it back.

Not an easy task, though.

When weaving through the dreamways, an Oneironaut must be on alert at all times, lest she be swept by the undercurrents and lose herself in memories, dreams, reflections. For it is one thing to change bodies, another (no less frequent and no less dangerous) to swap minds.

Fortunately, this hadn't happened to Samsa. Not that he could totally control it.

He should know better, though; the Oneironauts scanned the dreamways in search of potential criminals, people who used their skills for personal gain and risked destroying the fabric of all realities.

So, as Gregor Samsa awoke one morning from uneasy dreams, he found himself transformed in his bed into a small dinosaur.

This isn't it, he thought.

Again the dreamtime.

It took him half a dozen attempts until he got back his tall, dark-eyed, high-cheekboned, rail-thin, emaciated, and thoroughly comfortable body.

That would really be fine if it wasn't for one small matter.

So, as Josef K. awoke one morning from uneasy dreams, he found himself in the body of another man. He was promptly arrested and put to trial. He never knew why.

Letters Sweet As Honey

Foz Meadows

The Silver City Gazette, 11 Maytober 1510: Social Pages

Dear Miss Manners,

I know my query is outside your usual bailiwick, but as I have nowhere else to turn, I implore your advice, which, as a long-time reader of your column, I have always found to be of the highest quality.

There is no delicate way to put this: I am now and have been for the past few years, a human sentience trapped in a swarm of bees. I shan't bore you with the tedious magical details of how exactly it happened as I don't rightly understand them myself. As to the why, however—of that, I can be quite certain. My brother, Earnest, who dabbles in a great many things but is, I'm sorry to say, rather scatterbrained, decided to try his hand at amateur magecraft and apiary in the same week; and owing to the state of disarray in which he keeps his own apartments, decamped his works to my garden shed without bothering to tell me. Sufficed to say that, when I entered in search of some rose clippings, I experienced a rather nasty shock and woke to find myself reembodied in my current—and, it seems, permanent—format.

Miss Manners, though there are some who consider etiquette to be wholly divorced from political matters, you and I both know that the opposite is more often true: that how we treat our betters, equals, and lessers—and more importantly, how we decide which persons belong to which category—is paramount in discharging social niceties. As such, you cannot be ignorant of the New Truth party's current push to further erode the few rights yet afforded to magical citizens (who are so often now disparagingly referred to as "maggies") and the impact their efforts have on our treatment in wider Amitian society. Before I wore my current bodies, I was, if not a social butterfly, then certainly a social moth: I had many acquaintances, both intimate and casual; maintained, despite Aunt Edna's unfortunate taste in novels, an appropriately cordial yet caring relationship with my extended kin, and in all respects deported myself as a young, unmarried woman ought.

I could therefore be forgiven, could I not, for thinking some of my friends and family might stand by me during my transition—that the plight of one they claimed to love could sway their hearts if not their public votes?

Instead, I am shunned. I find myself no longer welcome at family gatherings, social events, or even on public transport. My bees are the very picture of apian deportment: when out and about, my swarmself adopts an appropriately feminine shape, so as to reduce the alarm my presence might otherwise cause, but even in a city filled with clockworkers, phoenix wives, and lizardines—and whose higher institutes of magical learning count among the most revered in Amitia—my efforts are most often greeted with fright or disgust. And more than this wounds me, it wounds my bees, who go to such lengths to make themselves approachable only to be cruelly rebuffed! Have we no decency nor kindly curiosity? Is human feeling only praised when spared for those deemed human?

I have tried to accommodate within myself the many fears of strangers. I have made my swarm small, gone out adorned with ribbons and unmenacing clover; I have even had my bees bear placards graved with poetry and other soothing words to show I mean no harm. I have tended my patience as once I tended roses. Yet still, still!—I am judged for my bees alone and not the human sentience which guides them.

I am forlorn, Miss Manners. Please, I implore you: what else can I try? Or is the effort hopeless?

Yours sincerely,
Adeline Brooks

PS: Please pardon the messiness of this letter. It takes such effort for my bees to work the typewriter, I lack the heart to beg them fix their errors.

Dear Adeline,

I cannot rightly express how your letter affected me, both in terms of human feeling for you yourself—see, we are not all lost!—and anger at your mistreatment. Though I have never openly expressed my support for the sentient rights movement (certain former, less modern editors having insisted on my silence—not understanding, as you clearly do, the political nature of etiquette), you have moved me to do so now—and for that delay, I can only apologise.

I am appalled by the blindness infesting our society which insists, against all evidence to the contrary, that human flesh is the only true repository for, and source of, human sentience. Did not Saint Elphia of Pharos assume the form of a flock of birds in order to guide Saint Michael home? Did not our Lady imbue the last statue of Kalis Cay with the soul of its dying maker, thereby creating the very first clockworker?

Sadly, I can offer no cure for the foolishness of relatives nor give you palliative against false friends. I can only extend my hand to you and urge the residents of Silver City to do likewise.

(And though it is a lesser outrage, as a lifelong gardener and hobbyist of the natural arts, I am greatly saddened by the ignorance of so many citizens, who instinctively treat bees as threats! From where else, pray, do we find honey? Who pollinates our flowers and crops? Even a disorderly swarm is a thing of beauty; to see one gracefully echo the feminine form of its resident soul—I hope you will not think me impertinent, Adeline, when I say that such a glorious sight is almost beyond my comprehension!)

Yours in etiquette,
Miss Manners

The *Silver City Gazette*, 13 Maytober 1510: Letters to the Editor

Editor's Note: Though I had anticipated a larger than usual response to yesterday's Miss Manners column, the avalanche of opinions which has reached us between then and now has so far exceeded my expectations that, for the first time in my long career, I find myself at a loss as for which to publish. Clearly, this is a topic about which you, our faithful readers and representatives of the general public, feel strongly; and more than that, it is—I think I can safely say—a topic on which you fervently wish to be heard.

As such, thanks to the generosity of Councilman Rudge of the New Truth party and under the auspices of the *Silver City Gazette*, I am proud to announce a public forum—titled "Sentience, Flesh, and Etiquette"—to be held at six o'clock in the evening at the Silver City Chamber of Commerce this coming Friday, 15 Maytober 1510. The forum will be jointly moderated by Councilman Rudge and our very own Evelyn Carmichael, otherwise known as Miss Manners, and shall no doubt foster a lively and informative debate.

I look forward to seeing you there and to hearing your fine opinions in person. —Cornelius Drake, Editor in Chief

The Silver Tongue, 16 Maytober 1510

GAZETTE GUTTED BY GHASTLY GAFFE: THE MISS MANNERS ETIQUETTE FORUM FIASCO

By Ashley Max: *the silver-tongued sentinel of Silver City's secrets*

A public forum held at the Chamber of Commerce last night became the cause of a riot when representatives of the "sentient rights movement" (a term this reporter cannot help but find deeply ironic) interrupted a stirring oration by Councilman Rudge by bullrushing the stage and screaming obscenities, causing mass panic and hundreds of dollars of damage to city property. Among the offenders were many so-called magical "citizens"—and lest my detractors accuse me of poor fact-checking as they have often done in the past, let me assure you that I report nothing less than the testimony of my own two, human eyes.

The trouble started five days ago, when Cornelius Drake, the Editor in Chief of the *Silver City Gazette*, allowed the publication, not only of a rambling, hysterical letter in support of magical "citizens," but of a wholly biased and unduly favourable response from the *Gazette*'s current Miss Manners, Evelyn Carmichael (a decision which provoked more controversy than the *Gazette* felt able to handle without outside assistance; hence the excuse of a public forum).

The original letter writer, one Adeline Brooks, is a maggie who— if you can credit it—is composed entirely of bees; and that, too, dear readers, you have straight from the unicorn's mouth as such an unlikely creature bearing such an incongruously pretty name— bearing literally, on a piece of card within her swarm—did, indeed, make an appearance at last night's meeting, stinging several innocent bystanders out of pure carelessness as she pushed her way to the stage. It was this selfish act which ultimately precipitated the forum's collapse.

Though Councilman Rudge did his best to keep order despite the untimely interruption of Miss Brooks, the ineffectual dithering of Miss Carmichael (who is, perhaps, better suited to dispensing advice about handkerchief fashions than meddling in politics) soon led to chaos. When a mob of individuals loudly professing support of the "sentient rights movement" charged the stage, the "security" provided by the *Silver City Gazette* proved inadequate to the task of quelling so many maggie protesters, with the predictable result that many regular citizens, feeling justifiably threatened, fled the scene in disarray.

As of this writing, city officials are still in the process of restoring the Chamber of Commerce to its rightful state while this reporter has been reliably informed that the Silver City police are in hot pursuit of several violent maggies and maggie sympathisers known to have participated in the affray, including two phoenix wives, a calumny, several Rei University students, and of course, Miss Brooks herself (or should I say itselves?) who vanished during the proceedings.

If such "persons" cannot behave in a civilised fashion at such an informal event, then how can they be trusted at all levels of Amitian society? As Councilman Rudge himself said, *"The bestowal of human rights is dependent upon an acceptance of human responsibilities— but how can such an acceptance take place when the pivotal quality of humanity itself is so clearly absent? It is not prejudice to enforce such distinctions but commonsense; else what is to stop us from conferring citizenship on every passing wasp or treating dolls as people? Every dog has sentience, but only we have humanity."*

True words, Councilman. Let's hope the *Gazette* has learned its lesson. This is Ashley Max, your silver-tongued sentinel, signing off for now.

From the desk of Evelyn Carmichael, 31st Maytober 1510

Dear Evie,

Please forgive my leaving this way; and forgive me, too, this illegible beescrawl, which is already leaving marks on your lovely table. You have been so patient with me, wasting good ink and paper on my fumbling efforts at speech, that I hate to seem ungrateful; but oh! How I miss my typewriter! Do you think the mob even realised that they were smashing, not just iron and ink, but my very voice? It was so much more than a mere machine, and yet they lack even the courtesy to notice what their destruction means. They are brutes, these Truth Now zealots, and thanks to my foolishness, Councilman Rudge is empowered to give them a freer rein than ever.

And that, dear Evie, is why I must leave you. I have felt more at home—more at peace—in your beautiful gardens with their strawberries and persimmons than I can rightly recall; and I could not bear the guilt and grief if so much as a single stem were broken on my account. You have taken in me in and trusted me with the gift of touch—it has been so long since anyone let me touch them; yet I have walked through your hair and across skin no less soft than rose petals, and never have you flinched.

You have given me something I wanted but never knew I needed; and so, in turn, I gift you a thing you do not want but surely know you need: my absence. I will follow the wind to Valencei as perhaps I should have done long ago, the better not to have caused all this trouble in the first place—but then I would never have met you, and that is a loss too grievous for me to contemplate.

How strange life is. How varied, and cruel, and—ultimately—beautiful.

I remain, as always, your loving friend,
Ada

From the desk of Evelyn Carmichael, 3 Junember 1510

Dear Corny,

I can call you that now, Cornelius, on account of the fact I'm quitting. Don't make that face—you know the one, where you go all squinty and blue like you've forgotten how to breathe—we both know I'm doing you a favour, jumping before you're forced to give the final push. And don't insult me either by trying to chase me down with talk of *compromise* this and *apology* that—I stand by every line of every editorial I've written since Rudge started slapping wrists, and I'll no more retract a word of it than you'll give up your lovely phoenix wife. (Oh yes, I know *all* about Vhairi—or did you think I was fool enough to stand my ground on principle alone? Please give her my best, and if either of you can't bear the truth of your scandalous liaison to be written down, she has my permission to burn this note as a feather-gift at her next undying. There's so much more to me than etiquette, isn't there?)

Which is the other reason why I'm writing this. Two days ago, I lost something more precious to me than I realised until it was gone, and though I hate to leave you with such a fight on your hands, I'll be cutting out a piece of myself if I let this slip away. (Of course, you were right about her, you smug, old fox—and me, too. But as I'll be gone before you can say I-told-you-so, I see no harm in admitting it.)

Should you be so inclined, you may write to me care of Leitalia Second Post Office, Leitalia, Heuven Province, Valencei. I hear their lemon trees are superb; in response, I might even deign to send you some lemon butter, given your fondness for it.

All my best,
Evelyn

From the desk of Adeline Brooks, 13 Jovian 1510

Dear Earnest,
Please don't discard this letter unread. I know you feel guilty about my accident and have made it abundantly clear in the past how hearing from me pains you, but on this one occasion, I beg your indulgence.

I don't know how up to date you are with news from Silver City, but even with your customary avoidance of both newspapers and the political scene—I say so with love, dear brother; I have always adored your quirks—you must surely have heard by now of what are, to my sorrow, being called the Maggie Riots and the sweeping legal changes instituted in their wake by Councilman Rudge and the New Truth party. Perhaps, you have even heard of my involvement: that your baby sister took the stage at the Chamber of Commerce and buzzed so angrily, like an alien thing, that several society ladies collapsed in a faint. (They did not; or at least, if they did, it was not my doing. The true events of that night have by now been so thoroughly distorted, if not replaced by outright lies, that I no longer have the strength to combat them. Nonetheless, I assure you that we were not to blame!)

As such, it is my sorrowful duty to tell you that, in the aftermath of the Maggie Riots, my beautiful cottage at Kilber Lane was burned to the ground and all my possessions, including the Memeworth typewriter you gave me, destroyed. I know how you once loved that cottage, dear Earnest, but though I mourn its loss, I cannot say I am wholly upset. Against all odds, I have found happiness in tragedy, and it is for this reason, and not to relate my woes, that I write to you now.

I have resettled in Valencei, in a ramshackle house overlooking an orchard I pledge will not be derelict for long; and I am not alone! For with me is the dearest, kindest woman in all the world. Her name is Evelyn, and though our acquaintance has been brief, it has yet unfolded with such a certainty, a sweetness, and a depth of human feeling that I can scarcely credit my fortune. She has sun-kissed hair and freckles from spending so much time in the garden and a wicked sense of humour; and, Earnest, she has bought me a voice! Not a typewriter, as you did, but an honest, sound-making voice, such as I used to have, and whose utterances can even be said to resemble my former tones. She had it made on commission by a Valenceian clockworker: a little golden heart my swarm now bears within itself and will forever more.

It was an engagement gift, she said, and I accepted it readily. My bees have made it the basis for a new honeycomb, and it is my dearest wish, Earnest, that you should see it for yourself at our wedding, the details of which are enclosed. I cannot imagine such an event without you there if only in order to show you the depths of my current joy.

You did not kill me that day in the garden as once you feared. Instead, you set me free.

All my love,
Ada

The Leitalia Herald, 22 Nova 1511:
Births, Deaths and Marriages

We are pleased to announce the union of MS. EVELYN CARMICHAEL (human) and MS. ADELINE BROOKS (apian heartswarm), which took place in the Old Gardens, Leitalia, this past weekend. The brides were resplendent in white silk and sunflowers; MS. CARMICHAEL was given away by MR. CORNELIUS DRAKE, and MS. BROOKS by her brother, MR. EARNEST BROOKS.

Having exchanged their vows, the new wives shared a ceremonial meal of tears and honeycomb before proceeding to the reception. (The flowers were homegrown.)

Consciousness

Zig Zag Claybourne

Internally: *Tuesday*

The Jackalope drank slowly; flavor was never a thing to hurry along. The blend of dried berries and ginger reminded it of a walk it had taken some ancient or recent summer ago. Across the room the young man spoke. Too loudly for the human ears in the room; definitely too loudly for the Jackalope's, whose ear tips twitched with each word.

"As the Buddha," said the slender fellow, "I do not believe in the Jackalope. He is a fancy, a piece of fluff—" the left ear twitched extra at the low insult directed at its round tail.

"That you," said an even younger monk, "in your wisdom deny."

"That I, in my wisdom, deny," said the Buddha, pointedly catching the Jackalope's eye. "And," said the Buddha loudly, having had several drinks more potent than tea not long before entering the home of Wei Yu Hei, "I find this tea weak, uninspired, and reflecting badly on character."

Please not again, thought the Jackalope.

"I shall find spirits," said Buddha.

The Jackalope closed its eyes, drew curlicues of fragrant steam deep into its wet nostrils, and allowed the exhalation to be soothing as Buddha's chair scraped outward.

The Buddha stood without seeing anyone else in the room. He walked stiffly toward the door.

The Jackalope, ignoring all in the room but the steam, finished its tea. It made a habit of noting the nearest drinking establishments wherever they traveled. It would take the Buddha a fair amount of time on foot to reach the one near the village's entrance. The Jackalope, being much faster, had all the time in the world.

• • •

Externally: *Night*

"As the Buddha," the Buddha said, "I find your wife's ass divine and worthy of introspection." By then the young man had already offended enough people to be circled outside the tavern. One man lay on the ground with a broken clavicle for which the Buddha would cry later. Violence was abhorrent.

The Jackalope was thoroughly tired of the Buddha's tears.

The circle closed a few steps. Weapons had been drawn. Focused as they were on the Buddha, the Jackalope's huge paw, appearing as out of nowhere when really it was merely a matter of practice and silence, slammed into the back of one of the offended, knocking the man several feet forward and frightening the man beside him. Two frightened men, driven the opposite extreme by fear, jumped on the Jackalope's back and pounded but only managed to rain ineffective blows against a weathered leather vest. It shook them off easily, picked the largest man in the circle, lifted him, then shook the body like a rag doll until the man screamed for help. The other men accepted this lesson. The Jackalope dropped the man, and the circle scattered. The Jackalope turned to the Buddha, who was about to fling an ill-advised curse at the furry giant. The Jackalope raised a paw to its mouth for silence, knelt, felt the Buddha climb its haunches, felt the Buddha swing his way to its back to hold onto the great beast's antlers, then flexed its huge furry feet and bounded off.

Interior: *Night*

"You know nothing of love!" railed the Buddha. "The ass was sweet." He patted the folds of his tunic for his flasks even though he knew the Jackalope would have already removed them. "They are the wines of life and knowledge!" he said of the precious flasks. "Not meant to be handled by the dirty feet of beasts! Where did you put them?"

The Jackalope, busy staring at wood to create a fire, ignored him.

Buddha stood to swing at him.

The Jackalope stared at the slight man.

The Buddha sat down. "Where are we?" he asked.

"Dao-Xi," said the beast. Very slowly. Speech, human speech, no matter the language, was laborious for it.

"I should have stayed in Cush. Look how pale I've become. They're sucking me dry."

"Have," said the huge furry guardian, "tea."

The Buddha ignored him. "I am done telling others their stories. Those men wanted to harm me. There was violence in their hearts."

"I think they see now."

"They see nothing! Umbrage. What is umbrage but self folly? They see a huge beast pounding them, never themselves. Never. Thus, you do not exist."

The Jackalope had no problem with that. The teacup in its thick paws was a delicate yet supremely protected thing holding hot, lightly sweetened bliss. "How many times shall we do this?" it asked around a sip.

"Until we get home."

The beast shook its head. Despite all else about it, the clothing, the speech, its handling of their daily affairs, the Buddha found that one small motion to be the most human thing about it. "No," said the beast. "I am done rescuing you to tell your story as well. I am done dreaming you. I am done explaining your life over tea."

Buddha adjusted his clothing; stood a bit straighter. "I have never believed in you."

"Nor I you."

Without another word the Buddha left the dining room of their dimensional ship.

The Jackalope drank its tea.

"Captain's log," said the human broadcasting, because she had always wanted to say that. One could tell from her intonation and facial expressions. The mental connection missed nothing. "We've been on this ship for twenty years internally. Externally, I've seen Ramses, Shaka, a dinosaur, and Tina Turner's last dance, in that order."

The Jackalope came up behind the Buddha. "This is her fortieth from the beginning again?"

"I'm experiencing all of them," said the Buddha.

"Again."

The Buddha flicked a hand of annoyance at him.

The Jackalope left him to his waste of time.

Both it and the Buddha had experienced the recordings of several crews on this ship. None of the crews were around anymore. Scooped at random, deposited at random. That was the prevailing theory. The builders of the ship had left instructions on the best way to experience this synaptically-driven gift to the dimensional universe, but they had been beings of vapor.

Which meant too that the ship was vapor, the crews just hadn't thought so.

The ship was large and empty. Organic. Even the quiet footfalls of the Jackalope's pads registered as unnecessary noise within a large silent system.

Exterior: *Sunday*

The field it came from was as purple as a burst grape, especially under high sun. The sudden scoop of the ship that didn't exist had confused it a moment; had it always known it had a scar on the pad of its right paw? Did it know that loving Penny Pinwiddie hurt so much? Such a bright child whom the Jackalope would have done anything to protect. Being aware of a world in which a child actually needed protection drove it inward. Downward. Love was untenable. Fortunately, it had been alone for fifty years for all love to have drained off. Then the great random scoop again, and he came. The Jackalope had been around the world seeing myths and religions made real. It recognized the Buddha even if the Buddha played at being a young fool.

One hundred thirty-five internal years with him. Tens of thousands by the outside world.

No purple fields of flowers as far as the eye could see.

Internally: *Tuesday*

He consumed the logs again and again between sweeps, never making a single one. Only watching. He hated that he was now so unsure, and if there were clues or directions in these recordings, then receiving the neurogram is where he would be. A small ignorant village might believe he was the Buddha if he told them and spouted undeniably trenchant words until the alcohol kicked in; but *he* had to believe it, and he no longer did. A mind that had expanded to the edges of time and space was now trapped in a foolish young body, this body itself constrained by the limits of its neural capabilities.

He hated being a fool.

He was practiced enough in medicine that he could bandage the Jackalope's paw while still mentally viewing the ship's engrammatic recordings. An idiot wanted for multiple murders in very smelly London had slashed the beast's left paw. In return the Jackalope had hit the man so hard one of his fragile human ribs made a quick tent of his breast pocket. The rescued woman, rescued only because the Buddha had been taken with the flow of her hair for the two steps it took to glance at her in the alley directly off the pub and see the man quickly pull his knife for an immediate stab and run, this woman was aware of her station in the world: a man of fine clothing had been injured. The law already looked unfavorably on her. No point hoping it would tender a change of heart.

The Buddha watched Jack the Ripper take a few labored breaths, then there was nothing in the alley but the Buddha, the Jackalope, and death, which left them with no reason not to return to the ship. The Buddha tied off the Jackalope's bandage, patted the fur of his only friend, and re-diverted his attention to the tales of Captain Fiona Carel. "Please be more careful," he said before his eyes unfocused.

The Jackalope left.

Internally: *Wednesday*

The Buddha had found James Brown. James Brown was not the best thing for an obsessive compulsive to find.

"Bobby! Can I take 'em to the bridge?" bellowed through the corridors one more time. Someone named Regina Nevills had a recording of it when the ship scooped her up. The Buddha was deep in her logs now, enthralled at such a find. Intricate, syncopated beats that merged, rose, dipped, and bounced off Mr. Brown's stirring vocals.

Marvelous.

Utterly marvelous. He began his own log.

"There's a scream out there what will solve everything. A pitch, a tone ... a vibrato ..."

And he was pleased with the sound of this.

Exterior: *Friday*

The Buddha was fat. "My life has been meaningless," said the Buddha at their usual table outside Cafe Diem.

"What of nonattachment?'

"I can do without it."

The Jackalope's ears no longer twitched. What did this man know of the lingering ache in a stomach from longing for a field of purple flowers from a child's storybook? It shrugged. "This is not a world where things happen for a reason. It's a world where things happen."

Its stomach no longer worried it; it just was.

The Buddha looked at the newspaper that wasn't paper. It was thin and interactive. A man in a long blue jacket spoke to a large crowd. The Buddha adjusted the volume. "There is a new world about to open up," the very rich man said. "A new way of thinking. The computer, many have said, is bored with the way we are using it." A young couple still in love with their hands took seats at an adjacent table. The Buddha smiled at them and muted the volume to text-only. The Blue Jacketed Man called his new software approach "Revolve." It was time, he said, the computer decided the world revolved around it.

Fat Buddha tapped the paper. "Friday," the Buddha said. "Twenty thirty-one." Zero one two three. How appropriate. Basic. The lovers spoiled his contemplation with laughter. The Buddha forgave them. He sighed and stretched an ache from his shoulders. "Is your tea good?"

"It is good," said the Jackalope, ducking its head just a bit at the tip of the table's umbrella to shield its eyes from the noonday sun.

Twenty thirty-one was loud and full of concrete and plastic. Screens of information everywhere. Data overflowing but no one knowing what river it returned to. What an odd future. "This could be where it started," the Buddha said, tapping the paper. "With thinking machines."

Far out in the San Francisco Bay a plesiosaur raised its beautifully strong neck out of the water. The Jackalope saw it. Dinosaurs fascinated the Buddha. He caught the beast's powerful strokes and undulating head before it submerged again; he set the paper on their table. It was nice here in San Francisco. The weather was agreeable, and even here, in twenty thirty-one, robed monks walked the streets, hoping to bless or be blessed with random bliss.

It was a good day.

It was the only day left to them. The ship had not returned in twenty years.

The Buddha got the attention of their young waiter. He was a lovely young man with an excellent smile. "I shall have tea, too," the Buddha said, hoping he would smile at him.

He did.

Younis in the Belly of the Whale

Yasser Abdel-Latif

● translated by Robin Moger ●

Younis in the belly of the whale.
Oh belly like a casket:
Younis lives, he does not die.

— Naguib Surour

I entered the mall through one of its sixty-nine gates. It is the biggest mall in North America, sprawling out over eight residential blocks: an entire commercial district in a town that lacks the very concept. Though situated on the west side of town, it is the central district for a city without a centre.

I entered through the gate that leads into the food court: a spacious area more like a little plaza than anything else ringed by a line of counters dispensing multinational fare and in the centre tables and chairs belonging to no one restaurant in particular. You just help yourself: buy food from a counter, carry it over on a plastic tray, then sit, and eat at one of the tables. Four fountains were positioned in the middle of the tabled area, shooting out water in beautiful formations, lightly speckling those seated with their spray and giving off a burbling sound that initially seemed romantic until bit-by-bit your awareness of it grew and it took over your mind, impairing your ability to speak and listen simultaneously—that's if you had anything to say.

Japanese sushi, Teriyaki chicken with white rice, beef à la

Szechuan with green onion and ginger and carrot and cabbage-stuffed spring rolls, Thai-style prawn soup with celery and sliced bamboo, vegetable masala for vegetarians and for dessert rice pudding with cardamom, mutton tagine cooked with red plum from Marrakesh, Russian kielbasa served with a yoghurt and cabbage garnished borscht, Swedish meatballs with gravy and chips, Mexican red beans and mincemeat with guacamole wrapped in tacos, sheets of Ethiopian bread with red paprika sauce for dipping and strips of cured beef, Italian dishes from lasagne to cannelloni through to pizza plus every other kind of pasta and sauce, Greek souvlaki with a salad of tomatoes, onion, lettuce and feta, doner kebabs with Lebanese hummus and olive oil and even Egyptian falafel and tahina wrapped in shami bread ... plus, of course, the presiding monarchs of American fast food, Kentucky Fried Chicken, McDonalds, Burger King: genuine culinary globalization. Indian immigrants eating Chinese, Arab women in hijab chewing Turkish shwarma, Chinese teens wolfing burritos. I was left dizzy by the sheer variety of dishes and by the water splashing and burbling ceaselessly inside my head and the choices on offer exhausted me.

I went to the Italian outlet and bought a slice of pizza like someone taking refuge with a half-known relative amidst a crowd of strangers. (You can't trust falafel made in North America by white hands: any ball of taamiya that hasn't been fried in motor oil is not to be relied on). I took the slice and sat down at one of the tables to eat it with cola.

When I'd finished, I left the court and like a sleepwalker made my way over to a passageway signposted, PlayLand. Down the passageway I went, surrounded by dozens of children, unaccompanied or with their guardians. The passage was long, and I walked it with my mind fuddled from the irritating burbling that was even now going round my head. As soon as that sound started to die away, the din of games and rides rose up to blend with it. The farther my slow, child-dogged steps took me, the more the water's burbling faded, ceding its place to the roar of entertainment. I didn't notice that the passageway I trod had suddenly turned into something like a suspension bridge. The walls on either side and the roof above vanished and vast contraptions filled the space around it. Serpentine tracks for four different grades of roller coaster coiled through the air: one for children, its rails set just off the ground and moving gently, a second with a line of teenagers at the gate, which made an initial circuit around the hall, then plunged into the shadows of the Tunnel of

Love to drop still farther beneath the ground where, at some point, it became a kind of boat meandering across an artificial lake through a darkness brushed by dreamlike lights, a darkness that allowed the young lovers to steal feverish embraces and kisses ... then the one with sharp climbs and drops for the grown-ups and finally, the lunatic coaster that rose and fell at terrifying angles, made sudden swerves, whose passengers had to possess strong nerves and sound hearts.

On either side of this passage/bridge were gates, stations for the roller coasters' passengers, and at each one children and adults stood in line for their chance at the pleasure of the thrilled scream. The space around me with its gigantic fairground rides, its roller coasters and the rattle of wheels on rails snapping through the air, its carnival throng of kids and teens, was the embodiment of a mysterious spirit the meaning of which escaped me however much I recalled previous experiences at the amusement parks I'd visited back home as a young man. In fact, my alienation extended to swallow the very idea itself: In what "spirit" did they build these dancing monuments to steel and technology, to an imagination devoted to the pursuit of pleasure, in our wretched cities?

The suspension bridge came to an end, and the passageway became a passageway once more, proclaiming the end of the huge machines and heralding the start of the smaller games that lined both sides of the corridor. Wandering past them, my attention was caught by something that looked like an astronaut's outfit beneath a sign reading: Scuba Diving Simulator. A machine that replicates the experience of diving then, like those computer games that let you fly or drive. Then a second phrase in cheerful font: Dive into the depths without getting your clothes wet! That's my game, I told myself. Diving dry's perfect for a wanderer from the East like me: a Melancholic, a detached Apollonian observer.

I stood for some moments inspecting the apparatus: a spacesuit, or a virtual diving suit to be precise: a huge helmet, clearly constructed to accommodate a screen in front of the eyes, a trunk of some lead-like metal, arms and legs of flexible silicon terminating in a pair of gloves and perfunctory flippers, and on the back of the metal trunk, an oxygen tank just like the real thing, if slightly smaller. The instructions stated that it was equipped with hi-fidelity speakers that played sound effects from the ocean's depths and sensor pads at the palms and neck to give the user the impression of being underwater via his sense of touch. First, removing shoes and coat, you put on—or get into—the suit, feed it four dollars' worth of coins, and once closed, it swivels you from an upright stance to the horizontal, and all you have to do is move your arms and legs in a swimming motion to power yourself through the depths ... Enjoy.

I fed the coins into the machine, donned the silicon arms and legs, and shut myself into the helmet and metal trunk. For a brief moment, the darkness inside was absolute. Then I heard a whine and felt the whole apparatus tilt me over. An axle was fixed to the waist of the metal casing, which allowed it to tilt down a recumbent position and up straight again while my arms and legs moved freely inside their rubbery sleeves.

At first, through the speakers, I heard a faint whispering and muffled sounds recorded underwater, then the screen lit up. The screen curved around my face at a fixed distance from my eyes to give one-hundred-and-eighty-degree vision. It was just like peering out through a diving mask. I found myself in turquoise water, not too far down: ten meters, say. The graphical fidelity of the underwater scenery was not what I'd expected: it was incredibly realistic, and from its velvety quality, I could tell that it had been shot with a high-definition camera and converted into cinematic footage using 3-D technology. Thanks to the sensors against my skin, I really did feel as though I was underwater and in my ears the same pressure that comes from depth. I watched shoals of fine silver fish swirl around me, and as per instructions, I paddled my arms and legs and found myself moving forward ... What astonished me was that the little fish broke apart when I moved among them, the shoal scattering chaotically, then regrouping at a distance. The machine's software must be incredibly advanced for the footage to respond to the movements of a person in PlayLand inside some Canadian mall. It even occurred to me that these scenes might be a live feed from a camera set up beneath the sea somewhere, but I decided to stop thinking about the technicalities and enjoy the experience. With pure delight I started swimming through the shallow turquoise waters, and then I got the idea of going to the surface to see what I could see. I spread my arms, lifted my head, and began kicking my feet vigorously until I saw that I was approaching the surface; and when I got there, a sentence flashed across the bottom of the screen in red: It is not permitted to break surface ... Please make your way to the surface simulator ... This unexpected division of labour alarmed me, but I decided to see the game through to the end and swum on underwater.

I saw a huge ray, its flat black body like a triangular carpet and its two flippers beating like the wings of a Roc cruising with measured speed over the seabed. Its electric tail stirred storms in the white sand each time it touched the bottom, and in its wake, the clear water clouded. I saw great hordes of jellyfish swaying back and forth and clouds of blue-tinged sardines glistening in the rays of sunlight that pierced the water. Suddenly, I found myself face to face with a deep blue, a vast abyss. I saw that I'd been swimming over a platform of coral covered with a layer of white sand, which is what was lending the water its turquoise clarity, and now here I was, confronting the true depths. Darkest blue. The coral platform came to an end like a cliff, beneath which the deep stretched away for miles. I stopped where I was for a moment, uncertain, as though I were in a real sea, then went forward into the unknown.

Sinking down the face of the coral cliff, I saw dazzling fish the likes of which no eye has seen before, all shapes and sizes, singly and in shoals, in orange and every shade of blue and green. Even a medium-sized grey shark. It approached me: came closer with his terrifying jaws and dead eyes to confront me, then peacefully withdrew. I'd read somewhere that fish gather in large numbers next to reefs because of the plentiful supply of food and thus—following the famous law by which all fish abide—the plentiful supply of food for those that feed on the feeders.

I began to swim over the coral, watching or diving down in search of a change of scene, and when a shoal of yellow fish scattered, I found myself facing a gaping hole in the coral that led into a featureless darkness. Cautiously, I approached, knowing full well that this was a coral cave, favoured haunt of deadly sea serpents. To my surprise there was a ray of light cutting through the gloom, some opening in the cave's roof through which the sunlight crept down to these terrifying depths. This opening, I reasoned, must lead to the shallow turquoise waters above the coral platform. Protected by my metal suit and virtual state, I took heart and decided to enter the cave and pass through the opening in the roof to the other side. In my mind was a neglected spot on the Alexandrian shoreline known as Masoud's Well. Masoud's Well was a hole in the rocks near Miami connected to the sea by a tunnel. In the 1970s, kids would compete by jumping into the well, passing along the tunnel, then bobbing up in the sea. I started swimming forward into the cave, heading towards the light. It wasn't a negligible distance, but the light shining out into the blackness made such measurements somehow hard to judge. Minutes passed, swimming along, bumping from time to time against the reef, hearing the echoes of these collisions rebounding redoubled through the speakers. Once again the software's sophistication stunned me. When I reached the opening, I discovered it was too narrow to let me through, and each time I tried, I heard a siren wail off and on like a warning, so I decided to alter the plan and turned back towards the cave's entrance. The darkness was absolute on the return journey. You could barely make out a thing, and I was colliding against the coral with increasing frequency, the muffled squeak of metal on rock amplified by the echo chamber of the deep and rendered tangible by the speakers that picked up each and every movement left or right. Inside the lined silicone tubes, my hands and feet began sweating heavily. Has the game turned real? I wondered, and felt a dizzying disorientation in the darkness. A real dizzy spell, perhaps. I paused to catch my breath and gather my thoughts, and as I did, the warning sirens went off, louder this time, and at the bottom of the screen a phrase stood out in red: Oxygen about to run out ... Please exit the diving simulator as quickly as possible ... and it seemed I had forgotten how to open this metal suit from inside.

The Churile
of Sugarcane Valley

Vashti Bowlah

Her long jet-black hair, unbound and disheveled, streams over her face as she wails sorrowfully, while her child cries for milk like a kitten's meow. Ever since she died during childbirth, she has been seen dressed in a white gown covering her ankles as she seeks revenge on those who wronged her.

Not that anyone believed in such things anymore, but a few elders in the village swore that they have seen her; sometimes standing at the side of the road, or under a tree. "A churile always gets revenge on those who hurt her," everyone agreed.

Miss Neela first moved into Sugarcane Valley two years ago to care for her ailing grandmother. She was a seamstress and filled the void left by old Mrs. Dass, who retired a few years earlier. But the villagers had their reservations about the new arrival. It was suspected that she never spoke much because of a lisp and had a birthmark across her right shoulder in the shape of the devil's head. But Miss Neela was never bothered by the rumors or the strange behavior of the villagers. At the ripe old age of thirty-three, she was the subject of old maid jokes wherever she went. She was also the topic of choice when housewives met at the vegetable stalls or while they waited near the gate to collect their children after school.

"Poor girl, she never find a decent man to marry she," commented one woman.

"Must be karma," said another. "Maybe she do something bad in she previous life, so she paying for it now. Why else she go have a birthmark like that."

"Well, I still feel sorry for she, for letting a good-for-nothing man like Raj fool she up like that," added the third woman. "If she did only ask somebody they woulda tell she about the other girls he fool up and then drop them like ah old shoe."

Miss Neela rarely went out except with her grandmother to keep her appointment at the District Health Facility or to purchase sewing accessories at the haberdashery store. She walked the two miles to the main road to catch the train to San Fernando, clutching a small handmade tote bag on her shoulder. Raj would be sitting at Jaikaran's Bar near the train station after completing his early morning task in the cane field.

"I bet I could get she to go out with me," he boasted to Jaikaran one morning.

"She only living here about five months now, so leave the girl alone and don't even think about doing anything stupid," warned Jaikaran.

"Nah boy, if I don't get a piece of that, then my name is not Raj."

Raj wasted no time visiting her to hem his pants or sew on a shirt button he often ripped off himself. He was soon accompanying her to the haberdashery store and even hired a car at one time to take her and her grandmother to the District Health Facility. His quest took longer than anticipated, but there was a visible glow on Miss Neela's face and a bounce in her step that could not be misconstrued for anything but love.

Some months later and much to everyone's surprise, she suddenly refused new jobs and finished sewing all the clothes that were in her possession. She was never seen or heard from again until the news spread that Miss Neela had given birth with the help of her grandmother. Neither the mother nor the child survived. Her grandmother died heartbroken days later.

The villagers were convinced that Miss Neela's grieving spirit would not move on until she had her revenge on Raj. Her vengeful spirit was announced at night by the continuous howling of the neighborhood dogs. Villagers carried garlic and lime in their pockets for protection and threw salt in their doorways and windows to keep away any evil spirit that might have followed them home. Some even wore their clothes on the wrong side if they were returning home at midnight.

It wasn't long before Raj's body was pulled out of the rice lagoon by a farmer. It was rumored that the last thing he did was scream out Miss Neela's name in the dead of the night under the huge mango tree. The churile was never sighted again.

Come Tomorrow

Jayaprakash Satyamurthy

It was a summer of superstition. It was also the summer I fell away from my life.

I was 16 and in college when I first heard of the Come Tomorrow ghost. My mother's fortunes had just taken a downward turn. She had left my father and with no husband and two children, shifted to a house on the very edge of a lower middle-class neighbourhood fading into slum. Ours was the very last street that could still make some claim to respectability with narrow two-storey houses, scooters and occasional cars, menfolk working in offices and shops, womenfolk who were housewives and had at least one part-time servant working for them, children who went to the English medium school on the main road instead of the government school down the lane.

Across the street were the tiny, mud-and-plaster homes of the slum dwellers. Ragged men and pinched women worked as rickshaw drivers, mechanics, cooks, sweepers, and waiters. Scrawny young men in tight trousers and colourful shirts combed oily hair on street corners, humming film songs or listening to cricket commentary on small radios with tinny speakers. Runny-nosed, filth-encrusted children sniveled and crawled in the street unattended until they were old enough to be put into service as apprentice dish washers, mechanics, or maidservants.

That same summer, rumours of an outbreak of plague did the rounds, inspired and fuelled by reports of an actual case in Surat in the north. The fears spread at the speed of ignorance and superstition, making their way even to my college, where there were dark whispers of rats in the kitchen, a student who'd collapsed in the canteen. The nearby temples rang with the bells and chants of special prayers, many of my neighbours and even classmates sported protective amulets and talismans. It was like I'd stepped back into the dark ages.

I learned a lot that summer. I learned about fear. I learned about hate. I learned about the slum.

A slum, I discovered, is not made by the people in it—instead, it makes them, shaping and moulding them until they fit its mould. It is a container that lends its shape to the sad human fluid poured within.

The shape is like this:

Every night the men get drunk and beat their wives and children. Every morning the wives spend hours screeching their grievances at their hungover husbands or their frightened children, sometimes also beating the children or the more hungover and fuddled husbands. As the boys become older, they sometimes join their fathers in beating up their mothers or siblings. Small children shout at and beat up smaller children. The only creatures who are immune from this ecosystem of abuse are the mongrel dogs, who are given a share of everyone's scant food and affection and served as guards for the slum in the absence of a police force with any interest in protecting those who are too poor to pay either taxes or bribes.

Living so close to the slum, we began to be shaped by it, too.

I started to stay out late, smoking furtive beedis with the son of a rickshaw driver. My sister played and squalled in the dirt in our tiny, untended garden. My mother sat weeping and raging inside the house, only emerging from her depression when her lover, a traveling salesman for a pharmaceutical company, came to visit us. I watched her change from a smart, self-reliant woman who read French existentialists and smoked Navy Cut cigarettes into a ragged-haired hysteric, hollow-eyed and increasingly akin to the starved creatures who lived across the street. She lost weight, her face became permanently caught in a resentful frown, she started lighting incense sticks, ringing bells, and praying loudly at odd hours of the day. Even her eyes had somehow changed, shifting shape and size to become more like the small, hard eyes of the women across the street.

We started fighting each night; long, acrimonious no-holds-barred slum fights. It didn't happen overnight—perhaps one night my mother lost her temper and called me a name when I came home late or was surly at dinnertime. A few nights later, when the epithet was repeated, I would respond in kind. The next time this happened, my mother would slap me and say I was like my father. I would slap her back, telling her that she wasn't good enough for my father. My sister, who still missed her father, would cry, and my mother would backhand her across the face. I would shove my mother and tell her to leave my sister alone.

And so on, night after night, until we were just as unabashedly, vocally, physically dysfunctional as any of the slum dwellers. In this way, I learned to fear and to hate and to hate and fear myself.

Sometimes afterwards, I would sit on my bed, staring out of the window through tears, and the slum would take on the aspect of an old woman—squat, crouching, emptiness in her eyes, clutching her sides as she laughed to herself, cackling and hissing in glee, watching us slide away from our middle-class certainties. At times like that, I partially identified the slum with the Plague Mother, the ambiguous she-deity who was said to hold the power of a cure from the plague everyone was speaking about but who also spread its seeds in the first place. Something from the slum had blown in our window and infected us. I had no idea where a cure could come from.

Meanwhile, in the long, sultry summer, superstitions combined and grew.

I saw a new variant on the "Come Tomorrow" formula, "Plague Mother Come Tomorrow" chalked on more and more of our neighbours' houses. I asked Chandru, the auto-rickshaw driver's son, what they meant. He laughed knowingly and told me the old story of the ghost who comes to visit in the nights, updated to accommodate the recent plague scare and the merciful, cruel figure of the Plague Mother. I laughed, too, despite the unease the story made me feel and turned my head to spit out some juice from the betel leaf I'd been chewing.

Just then, my mother appeared. She'd been shopping, and I hadn't realized I was loitering about and chewing paan on the street that led from our house to the market. She grabbed me by the ear and asked me what I thought I was doing. She made me spit out all of the paan and then dragged me home. It seemed as if all the defiance and all the blows that I offered her in the nights disappeared in the daylight, out in the open, away from the hag-ridden slum squatting across from our house. I was expecting a fight to erupt once we got back, however. In a weird way, I was looking forward to it.

Instead, when we got home, my mother pushed me in, locked the door behind herself, and then collapsed onto the cot that served as a living room sofa and began to weep.

"What's the matter, ma?" I asked, suddenly alarmed by how lost and scared she looked. In some sweet, sick way I still loved my mother even then. "What's the matter?" she asked, looking up at me, still sobbing. "Everything is the matter. I hate this place, I hate these people. There's black magic in these places, black magic and bad spirits. How can I keep you both safe from all that?"

My little sister, who had come out of the bedroom she shared with my mother, went and sat next to my mother, hugged her, and started to cry, too. I was close to tears, too. Instead of crying, though, I laughed.

"Is that all? You're scared of the Come Tomorrow Ghost? Ma, that's a stupid slum superstition, you know it's nonsense."

"No, it's not. I've heard about this in our native place. The ghosts there are virtuous, and they protect the way of the law. There are special dances to worship them and ask them to look after us. Here in this city, nobody does the dances, and the ghosts are angry. That's why the people are scared of a ghost. That's why they want the ghost to stay away."

I could not believe what I was hearing. My freethinking, independent mother was gone. She had crossed over entirely. We may as well have taken up a hut across the street. I told her all this, and she began to wail incoherently, her cries joining with my terrified sister's. Fed up, I stormed into my room, pulled on my headphones, and lay down in bed, listening to Guns N' Roses cranked up loud to drown their crying and wailing out.

I never spoke to my mother again.

Each night, coming back from school, I'd see the words "Come Tomorrow" scrawled on our door, and I'd rub them out. Then I'd go to my room, change into my torn jeans and Metallica T-shirt, and lock the world out with heavy metal tapes played on my Walkman until I fell asleep. I even stopped meeting Chandru—I wanted to have nothing to do with the slum dwellers, whom I came to think of as an amorphous mass of subhuman life that had somehow subsumed my mother. Meanwhile, the Come Tomorrow ghost or the Plague Mother, whoever she or it was, did its rounds from door to door, waiting for a sign that it was welcome. Fever mists shimmered in the summer haze, and various ailments spread from household to household; but none of them, yet, were the plague. Footsteps were heard at night, knocking at many doors, but fewer and fewer living people were seen walking abroad at nights. A rank smell compounded of sweat, drains, oily food, and misery rose up from the slum, becoming denser and more palpable as the summer approached its peak. Amidst all this, in its shadow, we crawled along, the ruined remnant of what was once a functioning family unit.

● ● ●

Then as I lay in bed one night listening to music, the air of fear and filth seemed to intensify, and I sensed a presence in my room. Thinking that the latch had slipped—which it sometimes did—and either my mother or sister had entered my room, I looked up, tense, ready to snap, when I realized that the figure that had entered my room bore the general outlines of a squat old woman in a ragged sari and my door was still firmly shut.

"What the fuck—" I blustered, pulling off my headphones.

"You didn't say to come tomorrow ..." I heard the woman say. Her voice was soft, it sounded old and weak.

"What do you mean? Who are you? Why come tomorrow ..." Suddenly, I stopped. I knew. And for all my show of contempt for the superstition, I believed. You always believe in the nightmare when it is right there in your room, staring you in the face.

"You're the Come Tomorrow Ghost, aren't you? You must be!'" I was not scared; instead, I felt more excited than I'd been in a long while. More alive. Thinking back, I realize how strange it was, my lack of fear, given how much I had learned of fear that summer. How strange and ill-advised. The only conclusion I can come to is that I had not yet learned all that I had to learn about fear at that moment. Or about hate. Soon I would.

"I am not a mortal creature, not anymore, and I only enter homes where I am not unwelcome. So yes, I must be your Come Tomorrow Ghost."

"Well, why have you come tonight, and what do you want?"

"Because no one else would have me. I want is to talk, to pass the time. It is good to be inside away from the silence. And the darkness." The Come Tomorrow ghost omitted to mention that there are more things that can be achieved just by talking than just the passing of time. At the time, I didn't notice the omission. Or perhaps, I ignored it, glad for a change, for something new to deal with, anything other than my broken life and my hate.

"Talk about what?" I asked.

"You tell me. I've been here for a long time and can talk about nearly any subject you'd care to bring up."

"Tell me, do you know of any other ghosts? Not like you, ghosts that haunt places, I mean."

"Do I know of haunters? Why yes, I do." Her voice seemed to gain in volume and strength as the conversation progressed. "What sort of ghost shall I tell you about?" She looked around my room at the discarded T-shirts and jeans, the pile of comics and music magazines, the pin-ups and rock band posters on the walls. "I shall tell you of another young man, much the same age as you at the time, and the ghost he met in this very city when you were only an infant."

This was the story she told me:

"Jaichand was the son of the moneylender, Jairam, and he had all the time in the world to loaf and dream and idle. He had many fine clothes and his own servant. But in the evenings, he would slip away and wander restlessly at the edges of town, singing songs from the movies and thinking of fame and adventure and women. He wanted to be a doer of great deeds, a lover of many women, a man of action and romance, not just a smug, oily lender of money like his father. But there were no great deeds to do, no women to love, no action, and no romance to be had, it seemed.

Then early one night after the first rains, when the sky was aglow with that eerie orange moonlight that comes once a year, Jaichand wandered a little farther than before, and from a mansion in the midst of a lush garden, he heard a woman's cry.

Daring to hope that the adventure he longed for was at hand, he jumped the compound wall and ran up to the mansion. There, he found a young girl just a year or two younger than him, dressed in the finery of a merchant's daughter, and clutching her hand to her mouth. Before her was a cobra, rearing its hooded head at her. In a moment, Jaichand had picked up a stick and was upon the cobra, beating it to death and smashing its skull. Once it was over, he threw the stick away and shuddered. The girl was beside him at once, thanking him, vowing gratitude, asking who he was. She took him into her home, where jeweled servants brought him spirits to drink and sweets to eat. The servants were fleet-footed and discreet. The girl's eyes gleamed as she gazed adoringly at Jaichand. He was charming and gallant, paying her many little compliments he had learned from the matinees, and by and by, she led him to her chamber where they passed the night.

From then on, Jaichand's life was bliss. All day he lay in bed dreaming of his wealthy, beauteous paramour, and each night, he made his way to her mansion, where they passed the nights in song, laughter, and love.

But Jairam was not happy. He worried about his son, who seemed weaker and more distant every day, sleeping through most of the day, then wandering out late at night, only to return even more tired and drained out, just past dawn. He refused food and only looked away silently when Jairam tried to speak to him. Finally, Jairam sent for Lokesh. Lokesh was the Gorkha watchman who had guarded Jairam's house for more than two decades. Short but fair and strong-limbed like all the men of his tribe, Lokesh seemed to become tougher and more formidable with age.

"Something is wrong with Jaichand. Someone has led him astray, and he spends his nights away from home. It is a terrible misfortune to have a disobedient, wayward son."

"Tell me how I can help, sahib."

"First, we must find out what the matter is. I want you to follow him tonight. Just follow him, see where he goes, what he does, whom he meets. Come back and tell me what you have learned. Then we can decide what to do next."

Lokesh nodded. That night he followed Jaichand, secretly determined to take matters in his own hand and thrash whoever had led the young man astray.

He followed Jaichand to a barren field outside town, where the young man entered a broken-down old shack with no roof and a dirt floor. Lokesh peered in, ready to spring into action. He saw the young man laughing and singing and writhing about on the floor and talking. He must have been talking to himself for he was alone.

Lokesh's courage fled as did he. He knew no fear of mortal creature, but the supernatural was more than he was willing to handle. He made his was back to Jairam's home where he let himself in by a side entrance and made for Jairam's office room, where the anxious moneylender sat telling beads, waiting for news about his son.

"It is worse than I thought, Sahib." More than the words that Lokesh spoke, it was the way he said them that frightened Jairam. Normally, a steady, calm drawl, Lokesh's voice was now a breathless, quavery rush.

"What do you mean?"

It was hard to make sense of Lokesh's semi-hysterical report, but eventually Jairam extracted the whole story from him. Once he realized what had happened, he whispered the single word "yakshini" to himself. After an uneasy silence in which he seemed on the verge of either tears or madness, he sent Lokesh to call a priest from a temple to one of the darker Goddesses.

When Jaichand returned that morning, Jairam was waiting for him. He greeted him as if it was the most normal thing in the world to welcome one's son home at the crack of dawn. He had the cook make breakfast for Jaichand and sat and chatted with the young man, making small talk about business, upcoming festivals, and news from the provinces. When a bemused Jaichand retired to his room, Jairam locked his son in, only unbolting the door to let a wild-eyed priest in a few hours later.

After several days of starvation, whipping, and listening to the priest's eerie chanting, the young man's will was broken, and he swore never to return to the shack in the field. Today, he is a moneylender like his father before him, and he never speaks of the nights of love and glamour he knew as a young man."

"That's just a story," I blurted out. "It isn't true."

"It is true," she replied, "and that shack still stands. No one dares tear it down for fear of a curse. It is surrounded by buildings and streets now, but you can find it if you search."

"Then tell me where it is!"

She told me. And then she held her sides and laughed, cackling and muttering to herself. I could hear the cackling and muttering long after the rest of her had faded away. The heavy sense of decay and fear still hung around me, too. It has never left me since, and sometimes I still hear echoes of the old woman's laughter.

Of course, I had to find the shack for myself. Her story was just bait, and I had swallowed the hook, eager for my own undoing. I was anxious to fall away from my life as it then was, somehow. I would have been happy to fall upwards to glory but was willing to plunge into other realms as well as long as I could escape where I was.

She'd told me that the shack was in a run-down commercial area, not too far from where I lived, and I set out to find it that very night. It was soon after the first rains, when the sky was aglow with that eerie orange moonlight that comes once a year. I walked for a long time through streets that were emptier than usual because of the plague and ghost scares. I wandered among the smells of dung and filth washed away by the recent rains, occasionally evading sleepy, drunk guards or alert, vigilant packs of stray dogs. I was often lost, wandering blindly, before I found the shack from the story. It was a decrepit ruin, surrounded by the backs of shabby office buildings on three sides and a garbage dump on the fourth. I walked through the dump and entered the shack through a ruined door. Inside, there was a decayed, old cot on which I lay down, waiting for the girl ghost to appear.

I dozed intermittently, drifting in and out of troubled, indistinct dreams. It was damp, and I felt cold and sleepy. After what seemed a very long time, a bat flew in through the ruined roof and hung upside down from a beam. I started and stared at it.

"Get out of here," it cried at me in Tamil, in a cracked, wheezy old woman's voice. "You get out of here! You don't belong here, get out!" I should have run, but I was too terrified to move. I lay there, shivering and afraid, my jeans wet with urine as the bat cackled and flew away. After some time, I felt something moving over me. It was a mass of rats—a dark, heavy, writhing, wriggling, blanket of rats. I screamed and leaped up, beating them off me, throwing them against walls, crushing them underfoot, sobbing, yelling, running, running, running away.

I ran for the longest time, lost and scared. The sun rose and set and rose again many times over, but the rats still covered me, a foul cloak that adhered to me no matter what I did; and I could not make out where the streets I was running through were. They were all dilapidated and deserted, and the few shadowy figures I occasionally saw paid me no attention. I ran for ages through places more and more obscure. Very rarely I would catch a glimpse of a fellow sufferer—running, running, covered in a seething blanket of vermin. Once, I thought I saw my sister among the shadowy figures who passed by quietly, but what she was doing with them I could not tell. Another time, in the shadowy streets, I thought I saw my mother and her lover walking from door to door, holding lanterns and calling my sister's name. All this while, my sister was just a few paces behind them, but they did not turn to see her. I tried calling out to them, but the rats had gnawed away my tongue.

Finally, there was nothing left of my flesh for the vermin to devour, and they fell away from me one by one.

There followed a long period of silence and darkness. Time had passed me by as I ran, and I was beyond the world I'd known. It took many years of crawling in a space where there is no space before I found my way back to the world I had fallen away from.

By this time, my mother's fortunes have shifted again, sideways rather than downward. She lives with a new husband but no children on the edge where a town is beginning to fade into a city. My sister is very far away from them, farther even than I, in a place beyond all worlds. I cannot find her at all. She is beyond love, hate, and fear now. I do not know who the creature was crueler to—her or me. I do not even really know who the creature was—ghost, plague mother, the slum itself, or some other nightmare from the empty heart of the cities and towns we have built across the land.

I want to visit my mother, to talk to her one more time. Every time I try, I realise that I am not welcome, and I go away, resolving to try again some other day—maybe tomorrow. In the meantime, I crouch here, emptiness in my eyes. I watch the people hurrying about their lives. I think of how a slum is just a sort of layer of scum that settles on the surface of any city, and I laugh to myself.

The Soulless

Walter Dinjos

The *Mona Lisa* flashed in my mind. I wasn't thinking of it, yet it appeared again and hovered there like a disquieting memory from an unknown past—the word "Sentient" carved into the woman's ambiguous expression in a glowing blue font. I found myself shivering, not only because I'd expected a ringimage wouldn't have the same disturbing effect on me as a mental ringtone (I was wrong), but because they said that, when one received a call from Sentient, bad news usually followed.

I pulled away from the interrogation room's door and considered the boy's stoical calmness via the viewing glass as Detective Ifeyinwa Uche questioned him. There was something strange about him—apart from the fact that he had been muttering for over thirty minutes now. His eyes and skin didn't look right. Then I took a slow, deep breath and tapped the tiny neurophone attached to my temple.

"Hello, Detective Okoli."

It still felt strange hearing a voice in my head. The human race ... we had lost our minds.

"Detective?" The voice was feminine. Almost seductive.

I sighed. "I'm listening."

"Detective, a torch just went out in the city, and sadly, it's your wife's."

The hair on my skin prickled at the news. I felt the urge to reach through my neurophone and throttle the unsympathetic idiot on the other end of the call. A wave of sadness immediately subdued that fiery feeling, suffusing my heart with such gloom that my vision blurred with tears.

After a moment, I growled, "You people really need to work on your marketing."

"Detective, I realise your shock at the news, and I can assure you of our deepest sympathies. I hope you don't mind one of our agents coming over to your office to discuss the price of her soul?"

My teeth bit at one another. The words pushing at the roof of my mouth were curses, so I desisted from replying.

"Detective? Are you there? Due to the limited time between death and dissipation, I am compelled to remind you that the earlier we come to terms, the higher the price. Death doesn't have to be all losses. So please—"

Without following the safety procedure, I ripped the neurophone off my temple and wincing, felt a sharp pain behind my right eyeball. I didn't care about any possible neurological ramifications or the fact that I felt the room reeling around me. I could see blood clinging to the tiny copper wires that had just been under my skin before I threw the thing to the ground and crushed it under my shoe.

With my hand I scrubbed my eyes clean of tears before opening the door to the interrogation room. Ifeyinwa looked askance at me, and her eyes homed in on my bleeding temple. "What happened to your neurophone?"

"Just get me a cell phone, will you?"

She hesitated, and I saw a frown brewing on her black face.

"Just get me a cell phone!" I snapped.

She rose and left.

The boy paid me no mind at all. His lightclothes, a straight-cut gown and trousers, were dull with no wallpapers, and his brown skin had a grey tint. His eyes were blank and, oddly, didn't reflect the fluorescent light hanging from the ceiling. He wore the image of a beaten man—a man whose hope had been ripped away. He looked ... dead.

Yes, that was the word. *Dead*.

Ifeyinwa walked in slowly and placed a soft hand on my shoulder. "I've placed the order. Should be here in an hour. Ndu, the Chief wants you off the case. Said you should go home."

"What?"

"The news is all over the station. A Sentient agent is waiting outside."

"I don't want to see her."

"Her? It's a man."

I contemplated the boy. "There is something off about him." Something I had seen before.

"Apart from the fact that he murdered his father in cold blood?"

"Look at him. How old is he? Twelve? Thirteen?"

"Ten," she replied.

"He's just a boy."

"A tough one. Hasn't said a word since, save for the unintelligible stuff he's been mumbling."

"Maybe because we have been asking the wrong questions."

Ignoring Ifeyinwa's attempts to stop me, I went and slouched in the chair across from him as if my shoulders were saddled with the grief in my heart. "Why?" I asked him. "Why did you kill him?"

He gazed deep into my eyes, unblinking, and said, "He sold my soul."

I fought the bitterness that threatened to betray my attempts at being strong as I stared at my wife's dead face and the rope print around her neck. "Isn't her skin grey?"

"She's dead, Ndu," Ifeyinwa said.

"I mean, too grey." I turned to the lanky morgue attendant of the Bishop Ilonze Hospital. "How long has she been dead?"

"Nearly two hours," he replied.

I started toward the corridor, Ifeyinwa in my wake. "It takes six hours for the soul to dissipate after the death of its host. Hers shouldn't be totally gone."

"You can't be sure that it is totally gone—we know it has been dissipating for two hours now. Maybe the grey you saw is a sign of that."

The tint was too obvious for anyone to miss. Nkiru wouldn't have missed it.

"No. She is soulless."

I still couldn't shake away what the boy had said. Of course, people sold the souls of their deceased for many good reasons, mostly financial, but what could make a man sell the soul of his own son—a living human? It was diabolical—a Class A felony.

"I should have known. That Sentient bitch."

"Ndu—"

"This isn't the first time I've seen this."

"What?"

"The girls the kidnappers dumped at Agu Awka. By the time we arrived at the scene, they were only dead for about an hour. Yet their skin was grey just like Nkiru's."

"Ndu, I know you blame yourself, but—"

"Yes, I blame myself! I blame us!" I stopped in the hallway outside the morgue. "We are the reason she did it. I know it in my heart."

"Oh God, Ndu. I'm so sorry." She hugged me, the vanilla scent emanating from her skin filling my nose. This reminded me of our time together, and I was ashamed to admit that I almost entertained the thought of how perfect she was under her gleaming lightclothes—tight trousers and a long, body-hugging gown with a side parting from the waist down. The thought both saddened and consoled me. "I'm so, so sorry," she whispered. "You should be with her people."

I pulled away. "No, Ify, they know. There is no absolution for me now. There is—"

"You killed her!" a voice barked, shocking me into lifting my face toward the extremity of the corridor. Nkiru's mother angrily approached us. "You both have killed her! My daughter! Are you happy now?" Mrs. Ogba tore at my lightshirt, ripping the neck and damaging its power circuit. The shirt's light blue wallpaper faded, exposing a blurred image of my bare chest.

Mr. Ogba was with her and, giving Ifeyinwa a glare that made her rethink saving me from Mrs. Ogba's claws, he pulled his crying wife away from me and brought her into his embrace. Then from the top of his old-fashioned glasses, he gave me that disapproving, scrutinising look he had given me the first time Nkiru introduced us.

"One look at you and I knew you were an abomination," he spat at me. "I don't want you anywhere near my daughter's corpse again. You have done enough."

People in the hospital were gathering, and I was contemplating how to escape the scene when a voice from Ifeyinwa's radio alerted us to a situation at Unizik Junction. As the Ogbas held each other and cried, I hurried off toward the exit. Ifeyinwa scurried to keep up.

"Ndu!" she called after me. "You need to go home."

I stopped cold by the glass door and turned to face her, every muscle in my face twitching with irritation. Her company suddenly didn't feel right to me—my wife was dead because she had caught Ifeyinwa and me together.

"Go home?" I said, spittle darting out of my mouth. "Are you nuts?"

She pulled back, a brief frown on her face. "The chief's orders, not mine. Besides, you are unsightly right now."

I just glared at her and then barged through the door and toward our glider in the vehicle-crowded parking lot, her pesky motherly voice following me to our glider.

"Take the time off. Put on something decent. Rest ..." she pleaded as we got in.

The traffic beyond the parking lot was clamorous, but it was in the dreary thoughts of my wife's death that I drowned Ifeyinwa's words.

● ● ●

By the time we arrived at Unizik Junction, the place was already surrounded by police cars, gliders, and choppers. We docked our glider inside Tracas Park and hurried over to the neighbouring Samkos Plaza to meet the Chief of Police's frown.

"What are you doing here? And like that?" the albino man asked over the siren in the air, gesturing at my damaged lightshirt.

"We heard the radio call, and ... I don't really want to be alone right now. If that's okay with you, Chief?" I replied.

After Chief nodded, I asked, "What's her story?" while tipping my head toward the woman standing beside the fountain in the middle of the plaza. She was wearing a red textile gown and had a blue explosive belted to her waist.

The Chief hesitated. "She isn't talking."

"Doesn't she seem too calm?" Ifeyinwa asked. "She should at least be a little rattled by our presence."

The woman calmly shifted toward the fountain as if to give way for the dozens of people running out of the towering plaza.

Her expression, eyes, and skin ... "That's familiar," I said before I realised that nobody would believe I could see the tint on her skin from this distance. This made me wonder if my wife's death was truly getting to me as Ifeyinwa had insinuated.

"Familiar?" asked the Chief.

"She's broadcasting." I touched a finger to my temple. "You see the camera there?"

"Good," said the Chief. "She wants something then."

It suddenly hit me. "It's an execution!"

Ifeyinwa winced. "An execution?"

"What are you talking about?" the Chief asked.

"Her own execution. See how she avoids the people from the building. Instead of taking hostages, she lets them escape. And the explosive is a nanoburst. I have some at home; the one in her possession can only consume anything within a four-meter radius."

"Wait! You have nanobursts?" Ifeyinwa was alarmed.

"For turning trees and grasses into mulch," I replied.

"You have a farm? Who still does that?" the Chief distractedly asked while keeping an eye on the woman.

"Her skin ..." I started toward the woman. "It's just like the boy's."

"Oh, God," I heard Ifeyinwa moan. "Not again."

"Get back here, Detective! If you have a death wish, it's not going to happen on my watch. Okoli!" The Chief's voice failed as the woman began to recoil toward the fountain on seeing my approach.

"Stay back," she said while pulling further backwards. The mist from the fountain now sprayed on her, but her voice and manner still seemed relaxed. "Don't come any closer."

"Couldn't you have thought of a less dramatic way to do this? Why do this?"

She was now inside the pool of the fountain, her gown drenched in the water, and I was just about five meters away from her. "I had no choice," she said. There was no emotion in her voice. "I have to feed my children. They need to go to school." Then her face hardened. "I sold my soul."

"I see," I said as I stepped into the fountain. I could only feel the coolness on my face and neck. Even though my lightshirt was damaged, its material still resisted the water. "But you can't take anyone with you, can you? It's not their fault. Neither is it mine. Give it to me." I pointed at the detonator in her hand. "I will take you to a place where you can do this without hurting anyone. And we will broadcast it."

She gazed into my eyes as if searching for the truth there. Then her shoulders drooped, and she slouched forward, letting me snatch the detonator from her hand.

I stood there, staring unseeing at the elephant from whose trunk the water of the fountain sprayed while two officers handcuffed the woman and escorted her away. Then I turned around to find the Chief behind me. His face was red from rage, his right hand extended toward me.

"Give me the detonator and your sidearm. You are relieved of duty. Go home. Now."

"You can't continue like this," Ifeyinwa said as we docked at the parking space beside the Zenith Bank's skyscraper at Ukwu Ogi Roundabout and stepped out of our glider. "Look at your chest. You are almost naked, Ndu."

I contemplated the towering buildings surrounding the roundabout. They all glowed with adverts. One, the First Bank Tower, in fact, played a feed that said, *Kill your power bill: Buy a soul today*. What was the world turning into? The frame shifted, and another replaced it. *A single soul can power a five-bedroom flat for at least a hundred years.*

However, on the foot of the tallest and most magnificent tower, the Sentient Building, a group of activists protesting against soul energy bore video banners that called the CEO of Sentient "the

Antichrist." Much as that resonated with my present investigation, it still felt funny. Who talked about Christ, much less the Antichrist, these days? The discovery that the soul was a viable energy source had pretty much crushed the Bible.

Irritated that I had ignored her, Ifeyinwa continued, "We can't go demanding an audience with the owner of a multinational corporation just like that. This could cost us our jobs, especially after what happened at Samkos Plaza. Please, let me take you home!"

"Can't you see? Everything is connected. The kidnappings, the boy, the suicide bomber, my wife. There is only one corporation in the world able to harness soul energy, and it had no right to take my wife's soul without my consent." I walked toward the protesters blocking the entrance. Ifeyinwa's footsteps weren't following. I halted and turned.

"I can't do this, Ndu," she said, her eyes gleaming with welling tears. "I just can't. I'm sorry." She spun around and headed for our glider's parking spot.

I watched her until the glider took off. I could not see her face behind the mirrored canopy. Turning, I shoved my way through the protesters, past the doors, and into the vast ground floor of Sentient Tower, only to be immediately grabbed by building security.

"It's all right, let him go," said the smooth voice of Dr. Chudi Iloibe, the CEO of Sentient, as he approached. With nods the guardsmen released me and resumed their stations. It was almost as if he had been waiting for me.

"Detective Okoli! How very gracious of you to come to us." The beige-skinned man extended a greeting hand to me, but I didn't take it.

There was a glowing blue octagonal crest about the size of an old naira coin attached to each of his wrists. I didn't recall him having those when, as a child, he went on the legendary twenty-year space expedition to Alpha Centauri that killed his father. A closer look suggested the crests were actually part of his body—one with his skin.

"How were you the first to know of my wife's death?"

Without hesitation, he replied, "I am always the first to know."

I frowned. "I've heard of the tech, but I want to see."

"I thought you might—let me show you." He gave out a smile that accentuated his gray eyes, which complemented his gray hair and gray fingernails, and ushered me to the elevators. All the gray made him look old for a thirty-five-year-old man.

We exited the elevator on the one hundred and fiftieth floor—

there were guards everywhere. We strode across two perpendicular corridors whose walls glowed blue like the crests on Dr. Iloibe's wrists and into a hall with walls made of black screens dotted with thousands of tiny yellow labelled lights. Walking on my left, he guided us a short way down the hall, then stopped, and had me face one of the screen-walls on our right.

The lights on the screen directly in front of us existed within a map of Awka. Farther to my right, dozens of similar lights fit into what looked like a building plan. After a moment, I realized that each light appeared to be moving.

"Lightscanners," Dr. Iloibe said. "With these, every soul in the city is accounted for. The ones you are looking at right now," he said while gesturing to my right, "are the souls in the building right now."

"Those are souls?" I asked while stepping away from him. The one labelled with my name moved, too. There was no light for Dr. Iloibe on the map. "That's how you knew she had died so quickly."

He nodded. "When a host dies, her torch dims here as the soul begins to dissipate."

His statement forced me to shake off my awe. "You took her soul!"

"I did ask nicely," he said, smiling that disarming smile of his as if that absolved him of any wrongdoing.

But I had seen dead bodies before, bodies dead for days; there was never a grey tint to them.

I turned to face him, fists clenched. "No! You killed her!" I shouted. "You took her soul, and you killed her. Or you took her soul, and she committed suicide. Either way, you are responsible for her death! I'll have you arrested, your company bankrupted!"

His smile vanished. "The soul is the most powerful energy source in the world. The ones harvested from the dead last for at least a hundred years but eventually die; the ones from living humans are self-sustaining—or so my scientists believe."

I had never wished I had my sidearm with me the way I wished for it then. "To hell with you!" I cursed, barrelling toward him.

I think he smiled before he quickly lifted his hands, so that his crests faced each other right before his chest. When I crashed into him, I didn't feel his body. Instead, what I met was a wall shaped like a man, and it repelled me—throwing me backwards. I fell to the floor. My head and neck seared with pain, and I don't know if it was the clash or the fall that caused it. As he lowered his hands and paced the corridor, I thought I glimpsed a flimsy blue light dissolve away.

"Now that we've got that out of the way," he said, "what was it I was talking about before this mess? Ahem, my scientists believe souls harvested from living humans are self-sustaining. From a living human experiencing a particularly strong emotion? The power becomes amplified as well."

I gingerly stood, rubbing my nape, staring at him with such rancour I wished I could melt him right there.

"Your wife loved you. You betrayed her," he continued. "Imagine what, how, she felt and how that affected her soul. What do you feel now, Detective?"

I didn't have to answer, but I needed him to know. "I feel like throttling you."

He chuckled. "Grief. Anger. One would think that happiness would have more impact on the soul, but it's actually the negative emotions that we feel more consciously. You grieve, and it feels as if that feeling overrides everything."

Again, I was losing patience with him. "What's your point?"

He gestured at the screen to my left, and the city appeared. A giant round tower, which I had never seen before, reached for the sky right in the middle of it. Numerous glowing blue lines descended from the heavens and funnelled into the tower. They reappeared from the base of the tower, looking slim and refined, and evenly distributed themselves across the whole city.

"Do you believe in teleportation, Detective?"

I didn't answer.

"Imagine a world where we no longer have the need for cars, airbuses, planes, or gliders. Imagine a world where you could enter a lightbooth, punch in your destination, and get transported there in a flash. Your souls will make not only the use of these transit rays possible but also the creation of other technologies beyond your imagination.

"Imagine a city with lightwalls and lightbeacons. Imagine a city where everyone has a biocrest and soulcrest—like these." He showed me his wrists. "Via the biocrest, the lightwalls can access each person's biological makeup and store that information. We can know where everybody is at any given time. It would eliminate crime.

"The lightbeacons, on the other hand, draw power from the souls of anybody within a fifty-meter radius of them via the soulcrest and distribute the power across the city. Mind you, the soul is self-sustaining when still inside its host. This would solve the world's energy problems.

"Look at your lightshirt—dead and dull. Let us assume it ran out of power—it happens every day and you see folk walking about almost naked. With the soulcrest that wouldn't happen as lightclothes— just like lightbeacons—would also be drawing power from the souls of their wearers."

"You want my soul," I whispered. I wasn't going to walk out of there alive. I felt I deserved it.

"How very perceptive of you, Detective. Your soul, and that of your wife, harvested from your live bodies will help us lay the foundation for this vision. And I assure you, you will be remembered." He flung a hand at the screen; and the video of the city vanished, and a transparent vault door appeared and then opened.

Beyond it was a sterile chamber that contained an oddly-shaped horizontal glass tube large enough to fit a man inside. From inside the tube came a strange blue glow. Every other equipment in the lab was equally unnerving, and my eyes hadn't the appetite to digest their alien features.

Standing next to the tube was a middle-aged bald Caucasian man wearing a pristine white lab coat and holding a clip board. His skin had a grey tinge to it, and he peered at me with lifeless eyes from behind plain black, military-issue glasses.

As I started to back away, ready to turn and run back toward the elevators, Dr. Iloibe said, "I didn't give you all this information to solicit your cooperation," as a pair of security guards marched into the hall, one from either end, and grabbed me. I tried to struggle as they carried me into the lab, but it was no use. "I just want you to understand the value of your sacrifice. Everything here today was bought with my father's life—and those of his crew members. This was his dream."

He clapped his hands in excitement. "With your wife's and your souls as its energy sources, we can begin the initial powering up of the lightbeacons!" Dr. Iloibe then nodded at the bald man.

"Strip him," the bald man said, and the guards did, careful to avoid damaging what was left of my lightclothes. Once I was naked, the bald scientist added, "Put him in the extractor." The tube had networks of giant cables attached to its roof and sides and seemed made of material that resembled a combination of a strange metal and glass. It glowed with a deep blue light.

"No! Please!" I began to scream and tussle as the guards dragged me toward the pentagonal cylinder. With the way my heart was beating, I was sure it was going to betray me and extricate itself from the rest of my body to escape the danger in which I had landed myself.

Watching my struggles, Dr. Iloibe sighed, and said, "I was hoping we wouldn't have to do this," before nodding at the bald man. The bald man, then approached me as I was being held fast by the guards, pulled a black device out of one of his pockets, and touched it to my chest. My body immediately went numb, and I lost all motor control. I hung limply in my captors' grips.

"Before I ventured into space, Africa was the least developed continent," Dr. Iloibe's voice sounded behind me as they dragged me toward the tube. "Now the Western World is in chaos; Asia is in ruins; the whole of Europe depends on Nigeria for soul energy. We, my friend, are the centre of the world. And we are about to change the world yet again."

As we reached the tube, the top of it dissipated—tormenting me with the sight of glowing blue wisps floating inside it. They shoved me inside the tube, and it shut me in.

Suddenly, the tube started vibrating, and the wisps began to settle onto my skin, my face, my eyes. I tried to scream, but the one on my mouth had a firm grip on my lips. Weakness assailed my body, and dizziness did the same to my mind. My eyes failed, but I could see my wife. She was smiling, and we were on the Bar Beach celebrating our honeymoon. We carried a calabash of cowries into the waves to ask the mythical water mamas to bless our marriage. I didn't believe in those magical creatures, but she did. I saw us argue about it, and her smile faded. Her face followed, and the rest of her dispersed.

Next, I saw Ifeyinwa. We were cuddling in bed. She looked so happy, but her smile belied a feeling—the guilt of our affair. I knew it because I felt it, too. She pulled away and climbed out of bed, shaking her head. Then her image shrank further away like one being zoomed out until I could no longer see her.

My mother appeared. Then it was my father. The happy moments in my life took the same course, one after the other. It was like reaching into the very core of my soul and pulling out my joy, my good memories, my everything, and letting me see them for one more time before ripping them away from me.

I lay there in the tube, helpless, until everything was gone. Then I too was gone.

I opened my eyes. I was no longer inside the tube. Instead, I found myself belted to the driver's seat of my wife's glider, and the vehicle was spinning uncontrollably in the air.

He stole my soul.

That thought drummed in my head like the clangour of a busy city trapped inside a tin can. It raged like a giant wave, overriding the fact that I was going to crash.

Smoke filled the glider, blinding me and making me cough, but somehow my heartbeat remained steady. It wasn't that I didn't care. I cared but only about the fact that he had stolen my soul. I knew what I had to do.

I unbelted myself, grabbed the steering, took control of the glider, and pulled up. I somehow managed to veer right to avoid the spire of the Saint Patrick's Cathedral. The Love City Recreational Park appeared at Regina Junction in the distance. I set course for the park, then let go of the steering, and shoved the door open. The vehicle now descended rapidly, and as it flew over the park, I leaped out of it and hit the grassy field hard. I barely had time to tuck into a ball before I tumbled across the ground and came to a rest, facedown.

Although my head, left shoulder, and right leg ached, I managed to stand and began to stagger homeward. Ignoring the people screaming, I didn't care to check where my wife's glider had crashed even as I heard its explosion. Sirens were approaching. I managed to limp away from the park and hide in a nearby backyard before making my way slowly home.

With a backpack slung over one shoulder, I limped through the protesters and into the Sentient Building through the rotating front door, and as four security men approached me, I stooped and pulled out a few chains of the nanobursts from my backpack so that they drooped over the mouth of the bag.

The guards hesitated but then went for their sidearms while numerous people in the atrium began to scream and flood toward the doors at the other end of the hall.

"Don't even think of it," I said to the security guards while bringing out the detonator from my leather jacket's breast pocket and raising it up for everyone to see. "And don't come closer." Alarms began to go off.

I moved away from the door and toward the elevators. The guards just stood there, unsure of what to do. As people, reacting to the alarms, exited the stairwells, they ran away from me, flowing out of the building in terror. If they all ran outside, I could blow up the tower with Dr. Iloibe in it. I hoped I had enough nanobursts.

Several minutes later, police vehicles gathered outside. A steady stream of people was still exiting the stairwells. Clearing the building was going to take longer than I thought.

Then I heard panicked screaming as the revolving doors ceased rotating, preventing people from leaving the building. One of the elevators opened, and Dr. Iloibe stepped out, flanked by guards.

"Nobody leaves," he said calmly while his guards rushed to further secure the doors. "Everyone stay where you are. It is me, only me, he wants. He wouldn't blow up the building as long as we are all here. Isn't that right, Detective? Now give me the detonator," he ordered as he stepped toward me, extending a hand.

I stood there, silent. *That's right. Keep coming,* I thought.

"The detonator," he commanded again and, to my dismay, halted some meters away.

"You took my soul," I replied. "You sabotaged my wife's glider and tried to kill me and make it look like an accident."

He smiled. "The detonator."

"When you took my soul, you made three mistakes: you told me your plans; you stripped away my fear of you; and you made me invisible to your lightscanners."

If my words made him uncomfortable, it didn't show. His smile lingered, and he stepped closer again, now standing a meter or so from me. "Look at these innocent people. You don't want to hurt them, do you? Let's settle this somewhere only you and I will be affected."

I glanced outside beyond the people stuck in the atrium and saw Ifeyinwa staring at me in a way I didn't understand. The look was somehow familiar, but I could no longer interpret it. I felt nothing for her. She was just another police officer standing outside.

The only person in the world that mattered at that moment was Dr. Iloibe, and I didn't dawdle to return my gaze to him.

"You are right," I said as I slid my backpack far away from us across the polished marble floor. I then tossed the detonator to the nearest guard who, with wide eyes, barely caught it.

The doctor's eyes tracked my actions and darted back to me again in bewilderment.

"But don't worry, it's a small bomb." I ripped the zipper of my jacket down—exposing a very small nanoburst taped to my chest and another detonator belted to my waist—and tackled him so that he couldn't bring his wrists together.

"No!" he shouted, struggling to push me away. "Shoot him! Shoot him now!" he screamed at his guards.

They raised their weapons. People screamed. I pushed down on the red button at my waist.

Simulacrum

Ken Liu

"[A] photograph is not only an image (as a painting is an image), an interpretation of the real; it is also a trace, something directly stenciled off the real, like a footprint or a death mask."
—Susan Sontag

Paul Larimore:

You are already recording? I should start? Okay.

Anna was an accident. Both Erin and I were traveling a lot for work, and we didn't want to be tied down. But you can't plan for everything, and we were genuinely happy when we found out. We'll make it work somehow, we said. And we did.

When Anna was a baby, she wasn't a very good sleeper. She had to be carried and rocked as she gradually drifted to sleep, fighting against it the whole time. You couldn't be still. Erin had a bad back for months after the birth, and so it was me who walked around at night with the little girl's head against my shoulder after feedings. Although I know I must have been very tired and impatient, all I remember now is how close I felt to her as we moved back and forth for hours across the living room, lit only by moonlight, while I sang to her.

I wanted to feel that close to her, always.

I have no simulacra of her from back then. The prototype machines were very bulky, and the subject had to sit still for hours. That wasn't going to happen with a baby.

This is the first simulacrum I do have of her. She's about seven.

—Hello, sweetheart.
—*Dad!*
—Don't be shy. These men are here to make a documentary movie about us. You don't have to talk to them. Just pretend they're not here.

—*Can we go to the beach?*
—You know we can't. We can't leave the house. Besides, it's too cold outside.
—*Will you play dolls with me?*
—Yes, of course. We'll play dolls as long as you want.

Anna Larimore:

My father is a hard person for the world to dislike. He has made a great deal of money in a way that seems like an American fairy tale: Lone inventor comes up with an idea that brings joy to the world, and the world rewards him deservedly. On top of it all, he donates generously to worthy causes. The Larimore Foundation has cultivated my father's name and image as carefully as the studios airbrush the celebrity sex simulacra that they sell.

But I know the real Paul Larimore.

One day, when I was thirteen, I had to be sent home because of an upset stomach. I came in the front door, and I heard noises from my parents' bedroom upstairs. They weren't supposed to be home. No one was.

A robber? I thought. In the fearless and stupid way of teenagers, I went up the stairs, and I opened the door.

My father was naked in bed, and there were four naked women with him. He didn't hear me, and so they continued what they were doing, there in the bed that my mother shared with him.

After a while, he turned around, and we looked into each other's eyes. He stopped, sat up, and reached out to turn off the projector on the nightstand. The women disappeared.

I threw up.

When my mother came home later that night, she explained to me that it had been going on for years. My father had a weakness for a certain kind of woman, she said. Throughout their marriage, he had trouble being faithful. She had suspected this was the case; but my father was very intelligent and careful, and she had no evidence.

When she finally caught him in the act, she was furious, and wanted to leave him. But he begged and pleaded. He said that there was something in his makeup that made real monogamy impossible for him. But, he said, he had a solution.

He had taken many simulacra of his conquests over the years, more and more lifelike as he improved the technology. If my mother would let him keep them and tolerate his use of them in private, he would try very hard to not stray again.

So this was the bargain that my mother made. He was a good father, she thought. She knew that he loved me. She did not want to make me an additional casualty of a broken promise that was only made to her.

And my father's proposal did seem like a reasonable solution. In her mind, his time with the simulacra was no different from the way other men used pornography. No touching was involved. They were not real. No marriage could survive if it did not contain some room for harmless fantasies.

But my mother did not look into my father's eyes the way I did when I walked in on him. It was more than a fantasy. It was a continuing betrayal that could not be forgiven.

Paul Larimore:

The key to the simulacrum camera is not the physical imaging process, which, while not trivial, is ultimately not much more than the culmination of incremental improvements on technologies known since the days of the daguerreotype.

My contribution to the eternal quest of capturing reality is the oneiropagida, through which a snapshot of the subject's mental patterns—a representation of her personality—can be captured, digitized, and then used to reanimate the image during projection. The oneiropagida is at the heart of all simulacrum cameras, including those made by my competitors.

The earliest cameras were essentially modified medical devices similar to those legacy tomography machines you still see at old hospitals. The subject had to have certain chemicals injected into her body and then lie still for a long time in the device's imaging tunnel until an adequate set of scans of her mental processes could be taken. These were then used to seed AI neural models, which then animated the projections constructed from detailed photographs of her body.

These early attempts were very crude, and the results were described variously as robotic, inhuman, or even comically insane. But even these earliest simulacra preserved something that could not be captured by mere videos or holography. Instead of replaying verbatim what was captured, the animated projection could interact with the viewer in the way that the subject would have.

The oldest simulacrum that still exists is one of myself, now preserved at the Smithsonian. In the first news reports, friends and acquaintances who interacted with it said that, although they knew that the image was controlled by a computer, they elicited responses from it that seemed somehow "Paul": "That's something only Paul would say" or "That's a very Paul facial expression." It was then that I knew I had succeeded.

Anna Larimore:

People find it strange that I, the daughter of the inventor of simulacra, write books about how the world would be better off without them, more authentic. Some have engaged in tiresome pop psychology, suggesting that I am jealous of my "sibling," the invention of my father that turned out to be his favorite child.

If only it were so simple.

My father proclaims that he works in the business of capturing reality, of stopping time and preserving memory. But the real attraction of such technology has never been about capturing reality. Photography, videography, holography ... the progression of such "reality-capturing" technology has been a proliferation of ways to lie about reality, to shape and distort it, to manipulate and fantasize.

People shape and stage the experiences of their lives for the camera, go on vacations with one eye glued to the video camera. The desire to freeze reality is about avoiding reality.

The simulacra are the latest incarnation of this trend and the worst.

Paul Larimore:

Ever since that day, when she ... well, I expect that you have already heard about it from her. I will not dispute her version of events.

We have never spoken about that day to each other. What she does not know is that after that afternoon, I destroyed all the simulacra of my old affairs. I kept no backups. I expect that knowing this will not make any difference to her. But I would be grateful if you can pass this knowledge on to her.

Conversations between us after that day were civil, careful

performances that avoided straying anywhere near intimacy. We spoke about permission slips, the logistics of having her come to my office to solicit sponsors for walkathons, factors to consider in picking a college. We did not speak about her easy friendships, her difficult loves, her hopes for and disappointments with the world.

Anna stopped speaking to me completely when she went off to college. When I called, she would not pick up the phone. When she needed a disbursement from her trust to pay tuition, she would call my lawyer. She spent her vacations and summers with friends or working overseas. Some weekends she would invite Erin up to visit her in Palo Alto. We all understood that I was not invited.

—*Dad, why is the grass green?*
—It's because the green from the leaves on the trees drips down with the spring rain.
—*That's ridiculous.*
—All right, it's because you are looking at it from this side of the fence. If you go over to the other side, it won't be so green.
—*You are not funny.*
—Okay. It's because of chlorophyll in the grass. The chlorophyll has rings in it that absorb all colors of light except green.
—*You're not making this up, are you?*
—Would I ever make anything up, sweetheart?
—*It's very hard to tell with you sometimes.*

I began to play this simulacrum of her often when she was in high school, and over time it became a bit of a habit. Now I keep her on all the time, every day.

There were later simulacra when she was older, many of them with far better resolution. But this one is my favorite. It reminded me of better times, before the world changed irrevocably.

The day I took this, we finally managed to make an oneiropagida that was small enough to fit within a chassis that could be carried on your shoulder. That later became the prototype for the Carousel Mark I, our first successful home simulacrum camera. I brought it home and asked Anna to pose for it. She stood still next to the sun porch for two minutes while we chatted about her day.

She was perfect in the way that little daughters are always perfect in the eyes of their fathers. Her eyes lit up when she saw that I was home. She had just come back from day camp, and she was full of stories she wanted to tell me and questions she wanted to ask me. She wanted me to take her to the beach to fly her new kite, and I promised to help her with her sunprint kit. I was glad to have captured her at that moment.

That was a good day.

Anna Larimore:

The last time my father and I saw each other was after my mother's accident. His lawyer called, knowing that I would not have answered my father.

My mother was conscious, but barely. The other driver was already dead, and she was going to follow soon after.

"Why can't you forgive him?" she said. "I have. A man's life is not defined by one thing. He loves me. And he loves you."

I said nothing. I only held her hand and squeezed it. He came in, and we both spoke to her but not to each other; and after half an hour she went to sleep and did not wake up.

The truth was, I was ready to forgive him. He looked old—a quality that children are among the last to notice about their parents—and there was a kind of frailty about him that made me question myself. We walked silently out of the hospital together. He asked if I had a place to stay in the city, and I said no. He opened the passenger side door, and after hesitating for only a second, I slipped into his car.

We got home, and it was exactly the way I remembered it even though I hadn't been home in years. I sat at the dinner table while he prepared frozen dinners. We spoke carefully to each other, the way we used to when I was in high school.

I asked him for a simulacrum of my mother. I don't take simulacra or keep them as a rule. I don't have the same rosy view of them as the general public. But at that moment, I thought I understood their appeal. I wanted a piece of my mother to be always with me, an aspect of her presence.

He handed me a disc, and I thanked him. He offered me the use of his projector, but I declined. I wanted to keep the memory of my mother by myself for a while before letting the computer's extrapolations confuse real memories with made-up ones.

(And as things turned out, I've never used that simulacrum. Here, you can take a look at it later if you want to see what she looked like. Whatever I remember of my mother, it's all real.)

It was late by the time we finished dinner, and I excused myself.

I walked up to my room.

And I saw the seven-year-old me sitting on my bed. She had on this hideous dress that I must have blocked out of my memory—pink, flowery, and there was a bow in her hair.

—*Hello, I'm Anna. Pleased to meet you.*

So he had kept this thing around for years, this naïve, helpless caricature of me. During the time I did not speak to him, did he turn to this frozen trace of me and contemplate this shadow of my lost faith and affection? Did he use this model of my childhood to fantasize about the conversations that he could not have with me? Did he even edit it, perhaps, to remove my petulance, to add in more saccharine devotion?

I felt violated. The little girl was undeniably me. She acted like me, spoke like me, laughed and moved and reacted like me. But she was not me.

I had grown and changed, and I'd come to face my father as an adult. But now I found a piece of myself had been taken and locked into this thing, a piece that allowed him to maintain a sense of connection with me that I did not want, that was not real.

The image of those naked women in his bed from years ago came rushing back. I finally understood why for so long they had haunted my dreams.

It is the way a simulacrum replicates the essence of the subject that makes it so compelling. When my father kept those simulacra of his women around, he maintained a connection to them, to the man he was when he had been with them, and thus committed a continuing emotional betrayal that was far worse than a momentary physical indiscretion. A pornographic image is a pure visual fantasy, but a simulacrum captures a state of mind, a dream. But whose dream? What I saw in his eyes that day was not sordid. It was too intimate.

By keeping and replaying this old simulacrum of my childhood, he was dreaming himself into reclaiming my respect and love instead of facing the reality of what he had done and the real me.

Perhaps, it is the dream of every parent to keep his or her child in that brief period between helpless dependence and separate selfhood when the parent is seen as perfect, faultless. It is a dream of control and mastery disguised as love, the dream that Lear had about Cordelia.

I walked down the stairs and out of the house, and I have not spoken to him since.

● ● ●

Paul Larimore:

A simulacrum lives in the eternal now. It remembers, but only hazily, since the oneiropagida does not have the resolution to discern and capture the subject's every specific memory. It learns up to a fashion, but the further you stray from the moment the subject's mental life was captured, the less accurate the computer's extrapolations. Even the best cameras we offer can't project beyond a couple of hours.

But the oneiropagida is exquisite at capturing her mood, the emotional flavor of her thoughts, the quirky triggers for her smiles, the lilt of her speech, the precise, inarticulable quality of her turns of phrase.

And so, every two hours or so, Anna resets. She's again coming home from day camp, and again she's full of questions and stories for me. We talk, we have fun. We let our chat wander wherever it will. No conversation is ever the same. But she's forever the curious seven-year-old who worshipped her father and who thought he could do no wrong.

—*Dad, will you tell me a story?*

—Yes, of course. What story would you like?

—*I want to hear your cyberpunk version of Pinocchio again.*

—I'm not sure if I can remember everything I said last time.

—*It's okay. Just start. I'll help you.*

I love her so much.

Erin Larimore:

My baby, I don't know when you'll get this. Maybe it will only be after I'm gone. You can't skip over the next part. It's a recording. I want you to hear what I have to say.

Your father misses you.

He is not perfect, and he has committed his share of sins, the same

● *288* ●

as any man. But you have let that one moment, when he was at his weakest, overwhelm the entirety of your life together. You have compressed him, the whole of his life, into that one frozen afternoon, that sliver of him that was most flawed. In your mind, you traced that captured image again and again until the person was erased by the stencil.

During all these years when you have locked him out, your father played an old simulacrum of you over and over, laughing, joking, pouring his heart out to you in a way that a seven-year-old would understand. I would ask you on the phone if you'd speak to him, and then I couldn't bear to watch as I hung up while he went back to play the simulacrum again.

See him for who he really is.

—Hello, there. Have you seen my daughter, Anna?

The Human I Never Was

Jeremy Szal

I gaze down at the new body they've slotted me into. It's a hulking one this time, all slick black and gunmetal gray with a hint of red. The limbs meticulously designed, the metal folded over each other like overlapping scales. I'm strapped in a mechanical cradle, watching greasy engineers scrambling to piece my body together like some sort of puzzle. A coil of guts spills out from my kneecaps, twisting cables and jet-black rivets. Tubes loop down from the ceiling, anchoring me. I try to move, try to get up, but my joints refuse to budge. It's like being set in concrete.

One of them glances up from a flexi-glass monitor. "Hey, he's awake!"

Took them long enough. One of the scientists strides up to me. She's got greying hair and wrinkly skin—way past her expiration date. Heels click on the polished marble floor. Voices flash through my mind. Faces, names. A woman's face, someone I'd known. Handing me a figure swaddled in quilts that can only be a baby. Their names are swimming somewhere in the back of my mind. I struggle to reach out and grab it, but it slips away

"It's a marvellous body this time." This new woman's voice cuts the memory to shreds. "You'll see."

She's probably told me that before. Slowly, slowly, I swerve my eyes around and spot my last iteration lumped on a desk. It's a smaller model, all charred and twisted from battle. I can even see the ravaged chest plate peppered with bullet holes, the metal eaten away by cerulean-coloured acid. I remember how much it hurt getting shot. Back when I was still human.

"Won't be long." She rests a frail hand on my arm, offers a semi-sincere smile. Seriously, the old hag should have kicked the bucket years ago—how the hell is she still alive?

A holoscreen flickers in a corner. Words scroll across images of smoking buildings and ravaged city streets. A frantic voice booms out of the speakers. Tetrahedron-shaped objects hover in the sky, a horde of objects spilling out of its belly. I want to ask someone to explain it to me, but suddenly I don't know how to form the words. I've forgotten the sound of my own voice.

In the corner of my eye, I see more parts coming in on conveyor belts. Hands. Arms. Legs. Torsos. Rifles. Railguns. All being split into various segments. They slide out of my peripheral vision.

Someone's coming over. Suddenly, my entire world is rattling, my head filled with the sound of a massive drill boring into my thigh. Numbness shoots up my body, spreads across my chest. The white-clad engineer offers me an apologetic smile, like it means anything. He switches to my shoulder, and the rattling grows. Another smile, bigger this time. My spine creaks, the metal across the nape of my neck tightens, and my vision goes out of focus.

Finally, he finishes and steps away. Wipes away beads of sweat. White-clad engineer number two paws at his datapad with fat sausage fingers. I feel a jolt as my pieces slide into place. My vision sharpens back, gears whirling inside my head. "Calibration complete. We're good to go."

"Excellent. Zone him out."

Don't you dare! Blackness crawls at the edge of my vision. I make one last effort to move, to object, to do anything at all, but the shadows swallow me whole.

A moment later I'm staring out into space. I can finally move again. I'm stuffed into some sort of pod, a million lights flashing in my face. I strain against my anti-grav harness and gaze outside the portal window. I'm falling down to a dark green planet, orange licking the sides. Dozens, no, hundreds of ovoid-shaped objects are falling with me, burning through the atmosphere like crimson hail. Shavings of blood-red light slip over the horizon, and beyond that are stars, a shifting blanket of colour. Any other time and it just might have been beautiful.

I'm slammed backwards; gel-padding protecting me from the impact as the pod crashes, splitting the ground open. My vision's blurry, a high-pitched whine ripping through my head. I tear free, ram my shoulder into the pod door. It bursts open, light pouring in. I stumble out onto mushy soil, my sight still hazy. Gunfire rattles from a billion miles away

Get moving. I scoop up an autorifle from the ground, the weapon glowing as I hug it to my chest.

The scream of twisted metal fills the air, mechanic grunts and weapons being discharged. Bodies dash past, vehicles roaring and billowing ribbons of smoke. I stumble over fallen bodies as I charge towards the enemy. My HUD detects a grenade thrown my way. I dive for cover, but I'm too late; and it blows a chunk of my chestplate away. I'll make sure to bill them.

Suddenly, a red beam spits out, and I'm spinning through air like a flipped coin. Heads or tails? I wonder as I crash to the ground with a crunch, pieces of my body raining down.

Then it all comes rushing back like blood to the head. I remember it all. Deep in my mind, memory fragments of myself running towards the enemy. Young, stupid, and green as grass. I see myself being torn apart by the railguns, bullets punching through my stomach, shattering bones, and shredding my body. I lay there for hours, my mind intact as I waited and waited and waited for someone, saying my wife's name over and over and over.

I see a shadow and manage to roll my eyes upwards. MedBots stream through the air, coming to retrieve my old body and collect the scraps.

Darkness looms. Not again, I think, the sound of battle fading around me. Not aga—

The Song of the Sky

Sanem Ozdural

The Sky seems empty only to those who cannot fly ...

We are many
We are One.
We are unseen under the Sun
But under the Dark One, we sparkle as if touched by the golden hand of the Sun.
In the deepest ocean where the Sun never ventures, and only the Dark One adventures ... Our cousins glimmer and flicker like tiny morsels of the Golden One.
Under the stars we dance with a blue green fire in the darkest forests, and we glow in earthly corners under the black mantle of the Dark One.
Indeed we do. Under the Sky at night, each and every One.
And the Sun?
She is asleep in the River; she cannot see us, not one, not Anyone.
Unseen by the Sun
But not unseen by Everyone.
Have we borrowed the light of the Sun?
No, indeed. Light is not the sole domain of the Golden One. Light can indeed be worn by Anyone from the deepest ocean to the darkest forest
Anywhere, anywhen ...

There is a pond in a forest. The surface of the pond is unbroken, disturbed only by concentric ripples caused by various insects, flying, hovering, dipping, and diving but never quite breaking the surface skin of the pond. For those that fly and hover on the surface, the pond is the World.

There are trees in the forest that surround the pond. Each tree is a World, and the forest, too, is a World.

There are also two worlds that exist both within and without the world of the forest. These two worlds are defined, not by the physical domain of wood, trees, earth, and water, but by light. While there are significant overlaps, the world of the forest by day is startlingly different from the world of the forest by night. For instance, fireflies do not dance in the world of the day. This is simply the way of things, and it will never change.

The bluest sky is reflected in the deepest ocean, and the moods of the ocean change with the motions of the Sky: from the wildest to the mildest.

The ocean is one world, and it consists of many worlds. There are also worlds in the ocean, like the forest, that are defined by light, or more particularly sunlight: its presence and absence. There are creatures of all sizes that exist within these two worlds. There are overlaps, to be sure, but the differences sparkle! Literally. Like fireflies dancing in the forests in the night, so do creatures in the sea sparkle and glitter like starlight. This is the way of things, and it will never change.

One day, a small bird swooped down from the Sky. She swooped in an arc across the Sun's bright golden eye.

By all accounts, it was a blue bird with a sharp black beak and ruffles of white in its tail feathers. These accounts, of which I speak, are to be found lapping gently upon the shore, for it is there, they said, that the small bird first found its place. It was cousin to the seagulls, said eyewitnesses that sparkled in waves at night. So many eyewitnesses are hard to discount.

The time of day is important, say our analysts, and who are we to argue? As previously mentioned, the bird was arcing across the golden Sun, but what was not mentioned was that it was at the time when the Sun was but a few steps from her rest, sinking, red-gold, into the horizon. It was the between-time for the worlds of night and day.

The bird grew hungry, and indeed, this was the reason for its soaring approach in the first place, we are given to understand. Our eyewitnesses tell us that the bird was a swooper of some note, and the small fish that had caught its sharp eye hadn't the shadow of a chance. Now this small fish was not part of the bird's regular diet, for it (the bird) belonged to the world of day, and the other (the fish) was a dark dweller. But the bird was hungry, as we have ascertained, and in that state, was not particular about its palate, and swallowed the fish in haste.

Our eyewitnesses once again recount that this fish was a sparkler like them. Due to the nature of light in water (it does not go as far as light on water), creatures that belong to the world of the Dark One do not necessarily appear at the same time as nighttime dwellers on land. Some, particularly those that inhabit the deeper reaches of the ocean, are forever locked in a world of utter darkness, broken only by such light as might be produced by them. The small fish that the bird espied was not a creature that dwelt in the nether portions of the sea, but nevertheless, its life revolved around a lightscale different to that of the bird that flew above the sea.

Is the timing so important? we asked. And we were assured by our analysts that this was the cause of all that came to be in the thereafter, and who, in the world, are we to argue with such authority?

But one fish? One single fish? we retorted, could hardly be the cause of all that followed. Not *all* that followed, some of it perhaps, we conceded.

It was not one fish, replied the analysts reasonably; it could not be one single solitary sparkler in the sea that caused an event of such magnitude. But it was the beginning. Not the beginning of the end, but the beginning of the beginning ...

The forest is close to the sea in this place. These worlds—that of the forest and of the sea—coexist comfortably within a short geographical distance. The forest was a convenient distance for one blue bird of distant seagull extraction, and it grew accustomed to exploring this new space where it found plenty to forage for in the pond.

We have already stated that the bird belonged to the world of day but with that one fish, had started to find its alimentary niche in the between time when the Sun wanes but before the Dark One completely reigns. The bird was a stickler for things that worked, and it had found that hunting at twilight gave it a competitive advantage over its brethren. Good for the bird! we applaud.

In any event, the little bird took its newfound advantage to the world of the forest and started to hunt and forage in the twilight hour. Now remember that these are two different worlds that the little bird had started to inhabit, and when doing so, even the most careful and assiduous traveller is apt to make a mistake, a misstep, a miscalculation ...

● ● ●

We will leave the narration of the next part of this tale to our key eyewitness, our one and only Shadow:

Now the small bird flew around the pond, for water was the place she best knew
And she flew ...
Longer and longer she flew, looking for a morsel or two
All through the day the little blue bird flew ...
And as the light grew dim, brothers, what did the bird do?
She could not see as well as before, for her eyes belonged not to the world of the other, the one they call the Sun's brother.
No, indeed, the little bird's eyesight was not accustomed to the half light.
And as she flew, keeping her eyes trained on the surface of the pond for a morsel or two ...
She caught sight of a flicker, a glimmer, a tiny flash of bluish light, similar to the sparkler she'd first caught in the water. With her eyesight none too keen, the little bird assumed it was the same thing and swooped low.
Reaching for the bluish glow ...

... The blue-white flicker danced a complicated step in the waning light. It was quite a sight, said our keen eyewitness. A tiny star-like mite dancing to an unheard strain in the Night. This dancing light turned out to be, not a fish as the myopic bird surmised, but a winged denizen of the night, out to snare himself a mate, and perhaps a bite. As our keen eyewitness would say: these are things that happen in the Night. It is the way of things, and it is right.

This tiny sparkling dancer has been called a firefly by those who do not inhabit the world of the forest. But in the forest they are known as star dancers. Names can be confusing, especially when they refer to the same thing.

In any event our blue bird turned out to be a philosopher in this instance, and when it had gulped down the unsuspecting mote, it might have blinked a few times on account of the unfamiliar flavor but went ahead, undeterred, on her route.

And the little bird decided that, since this sparkler in the night was easier by far to catch than the little fishies, she would do best to stick to the pond rather than the sea. Besides, the wind tended to be less wicked on account of the trees.

This went on day after day, and many moons waxed and waned as the residents of the forest watched the little bird's progress ...

And all the while, the little bird lived amidst the flowering trees, all through summer's greenery and stayed on in the forest as the air got colder.

In time, it is said, the blue bird found a mate, who had found his way from the beach in the same way as the first bird. This, too, is the way of things: it only takes one to make a path.

My kin, this is the way of things. This is how it all begins.

Over time, the birds grew in number, now living under the shade of trees instead of flying across the sea.

And like the first blue bird, they foraged for winged creatures instead of sparklers of the sea ...

And one day, one small bird, descendant of the original blue bird, picked up the fallen fruit of a tree ...

As the little bird ate the fruit, the seed of the tree was transformed by its alimentary canal, report our researchers. Our analysts confirmed that this is a reasonable, and moreover *probable* explanation for the events that unfolded in the thereafter. Our analysts remind us that the blue bird and its descendants had grown accustomed to consuming the star dancers in the forest as part of their regular diet. To put it succinctly: they ate insects that glowed with an inner light. These birds ate light.

And so, when this unassuming descendant of the original blue bird ate the seed of a tree ... What tree was it, you ask? After careful research our analysts have placed it in the same family as one solid, stocky character with large, flat, dark green leaves and a soft sweet fruit with a velvety purplish brown skin—known by certain non-forest dwellers as a *fig*. Names *can* be confusing, as we established, and in the forest this tree is known as much for its girth and its shade as for its fruit. By those who shelter beneath the expansive welcome of its leaves or nibble upon its honey-sweet fruit, it is known as the sweet shelterer.

Can you guess what came to be? Of the seed of the tree that the bird that ate light swallowed?

● ● ●

luminescent

blue   white   bright light

blue white   sparkling glittering star-like

bejeweled diamond bright   in

darkest Night blackest

sky

branches black and bright with star-like glittering

flickering marble-like

sweet shelter   shelter bright in darkest Night

velvet black

under moonlight   sit under sky-dark leaves

studded with starlight

Come, sit

Under me

I   am
Light   Tree
We are many
We are One
We provide shelter under the Sun
But when the day is done
We glitter like stars under the Dark One
And we are seen
By Everyone
Who can say
We are None?

● ● ●

That, at least, is the account of our eyewitnesses, including none other than our star and one and only Shadow who happened to inhabit the very pond next to which this remarkable (might we say *miraculous*?) event occurred, and we do have it on the best authority (our analysts) that this is the most *probable* explanation for the birth of the first Light Tree. THE FIRST LIGHT TREE!

Shadow also related that it, too, occasionally found shelter from the Sun under the dark, velvety leaves of the first Light Tree. Our Sun is a good sort in many ways, but there are times when she—quite unintentionally—is apt to get ahead of herself in the heat and brightness departments. She can get just a tad overzealous; a bit of a workaholic, say some of our analysts (we know they mean it in the best possible way), who does not always know when enough is enough ... and that is exactly when large, dark, velvety leaves provide the most welcome relief. Until the Sun comes to her senses, of course, and either gives way to her brother or at least pulls some cloudy curtains to cover up some of her blasting brightness! What a sizzler!

And the fruit of the Light Tree? The original Light Tree, that is ... We wonder how different it might have tasted from the kind one gets nowadays, which has such a distinctive flavor, and of course, the aroma, well, can only be said to smell of light! Our researchers, as always, seek to enlighten us on this point, but it has proved elusive thus far. Our analysts, on the other hand, who have spent countless days poring over what data the researchers have been able to glean, suggest—they stress there is no certainty—that the fruit is likely to have been lighter in texture and translucent, illuminated like a beacon by the cold bluish light of the seed of the lightberry. As everyone knows, the flesh of the lightberry nowadays—a most distant incarnation of the original—is dense and dark, almost black, unwilling to let the light of the seed shine through, and the only time that the Light Tree is able to appear in full lightful splendor is during the awakening season when it flowers. Oh, the flower of the Light Tree! That transcendent translucence shining like liquid stars decked out in glorious hues of pink, purple, and blue. What a sight to behold in the Night!

Yes, yes, I hear you say, we all know the beauty of the flower of the Light Tree, but do get on with the story.

And who better to recount the next chapter than our star, the inimitable, the one and only Shadow, our key eyewitness:

• • •

So the tree grew
And the birds flew
>*until they grew tired and rested upon*
the bough of the tree ...
>*and flew*
>>*until they became hungry and nibbled*
upon the berry of a tree
>*that ate light ...*
>>*and still they flew*
>*Through the air the birds flew*
>*Beating their wings, gently at times,*
gliding, fluttering at times
>*Upon the blue canvas of the sky*
>>*They flew.*
>*And the Sun shone*
>>*all day long*
>*Upon the blue canvas of the sky through*
which
>*the birds flew*
Did the birds fly at night too?
Yes, so they did. They flew all along the
black mantle that the Dark One
>*had flung across the sky*
In darkness they flew ...
Even when the dark was complete, my kin
When the sky was blacker than his dark eyes
Blacker even than the starling's wing ...

How? You are right to ask. How could these birds, relatives (distant) of a certain blue bird with uncertain eyesight, manage to fly through the night sky without encountering some serious mishap?

They were aided by the Light Tree. Guided is a better word, perhaps. They were *guided* by the Light Tree, let us say. We saw how the light of a sparkling fish (inadvertently) guided the little blue bird to a new life in the forest, and then it was the bird who in turn helped guide the birth of the Light Tree, so the guidance appears to have come full circle as a steady diet of the berries of the Light Tree transformed those distant descendants of the original blue bird into something altogether different ... I *could* tell you, but I would not do it justice. For the end of our story let's listen to the Song of the Light Tree:

Fly! Soar!

In the
swelling sky, fly
As high as you wish,
Bird
As long as you must,
Bird, fly...
There is nothing to stop you
Nothing can stop you,
Bird, fly!
High!

So fly!
Are lit like stars, Bird
Your wings, Bird
High!
So you can fly!
Even in the night, Bird
There is light, Bird
Fly!
Higher, Bird

This is the way of things. As it was then, so it is now ...

(From the Book of Shadow)

Tree of the Forest Seven Bells Turns the World Round Midnight

Sheree Renée Thomas

Thistle stepped over an upturned root that twisted from the dark, wet earth.

"Your mama live near the river?"

"Naw."

"Your mama live in a tree?"

"Nope."

"Then what we doing?"

"Mama the river and the tree." She moved with deliberate grace, each footfall a code that unlocked another hidden key. Wilder should have known. Every other word out of her mouth was some strange, cryptic poetry. She was more siren than sage, more whistle than song. In the few months they'd been hanging, he had gotten used to her "magic woman" guise. Bohemian bruja, wide-hipped hoodoo. Unlike the other women Wilder tried to lay with, Thistle felt sincere. At least she was original. Most other relationships Wilder had had all ended the way he felt now, lost. With the others he would soon lose interest—or they would, tossing him back on the street, the fascination over before it had begun. Then he'd be off, duffel bag in hand, looking for cover. To Wilder, everyone worked so hard to be just like the next. What was the challenge in that?

Thistle stood with her back to him, all curve and joy, a plum-skinned promise of delight. He tried to follow her, but his feet wouldn't move. With each step forward he kept stumbling backward as if his body wanted, *needed* to withdraw every footstep to retrace their path under that lone glimmering star. His car was locked and parked way down the road that flanked high above the river. If he hadn't been with Thistle, he never would have seen the trail.

"What I'm trying to understand is why we got to come see her in the pitch damn night?" He held himself steady, grabbed hold of a tender birch tree. All he saw was branches and limbs and more wobbly trees. Bark fell away from his hands in flakes, fluttered to the damp ground like layers of skin. "I'm cool with meeting your family, but why can't we go to Piccadilly or the China Inn? Don't your mama like buffet? That's what *normal* folks do."

Thistle turned her head, hesitated. Even in the deepening darkness, Wilder could see her eyes narrow into slits, her full lips poked out like she might offer a kiss. "When have you known me to be normal?"

Laughter shook the leaves of a mayhaw. Fireflies flitted a warning message in the faded light. Wilder didn't see. His eyes were in the future, back to the cool, thin sheets in the rented room. The air was hot and humid, thick enough to slash a knife through. The sky was full, twilight now turning away from dusk. A super moon and that strange, twinkling star Thistle swore was a planet. Which one did she say? *Venus.* Or was it Jupiter? Wilder used to know stuff like that back when he thought it was important. Astronomy, astrology, tarot cards, and divination, none of it foretold anything close to what Wilder had come to know, his hard truth. Ghostly light shone through the waist-high grass, and the blossoming weeds cast shadows across Thistle's face, her arm outstretched to him like a luscious vine. This he believed in, this he could follow—the curved finger of flesh. An open palm, his favorite invitation.

"It's just a little farther."

"I hope she got something to drink."

Thistle giggled, moved through the path, a silent wind. Wilder had made her a jacket with spikes on the shoulders and bright, colorful Ankara print for a lining. He hadn't sewn anything new until she'd tumbled into his life like a weed. In the black, weathered upcycled leather and the scraps from an old African caftan, she looked like the punk queen he imagined her to be. He had woven the jacket for her, his first gift, when she initially refused to go out with him. "I'm not fit for human consumption," is what she'd said. "Try harder," is what he heard. Wilder was persistent. He'd followed her, held signs at every protest, passed flyers out with other activists at the Riverwalk, harangued downtown hipsters who would bulldoze century trees for their new LEED condos. Finally, at a Mid-South

Peace & Justice Center ice cream social, she relented. The jacket she donned like a crown. And she had worn it every day, her second skin she called it, even in the 105° heat.

But Thistle never sweated. A fact that startled Wilder, made him lie awake some nights and wonder, that and her spooky, stony sleep. Gulping it down every chance she could get, Thistle drank water like a catfish, slept like an old dead log. But each time he saw her, a wildfire in his arms, remarkably awake, or asleep, corpse-like by his side, he grew more fascinated.

Wilder had met her at a friend's lecture at Rhodes on the music of John Coltrane, sacred geometry, and physics. Melvin discussed how Coltrane had composed "A Love Supreme" using African fractals and indigenous design, the same design found in ancient West African compounds, in passed-down rites of passage and patterns of braided hair, in the wooden sculptures of the Mende, in pine cones, and even in drops of water. Melvin was a philosopher, the baddest bassist in the world—*Time Out New York* had declared it, and Wilder knew from personal experience that to be true. Only one other bassist gave him a run, and she wasn't a bassist at all. She was a goddess; she was music itself, not even a fair comparison. Wilder had been planning to give Melvin the full Memphis roots midnight tour when he spied Thistle, fluttering in the periphery of the concert hall. Her back was pressed against the yellow papered wall, arms folded as if she were too good to squeeze her hips into the plush student seating. Her eyes were closed, head nodding as if she were hearing some other music beneath Melvin's words.

Later, Wilder would learn she was rarely still—except frighteningly so in her sleep. Awake, she flitted through the world, an emerald-throated hummingbird. Even now she stooped to caress a crooked row of foxgloves. Her bangles stacked high up her arm like brass armor, glinted in the night. "Look how they bow their heads." She stroked the purple blossoms as if they were pets. "They're always the first ones asleep." She rose and darted ahead, a bejeweled black dragonfly.

Barefoot, Thistle used to collect ferns and moss and polished river stones, dark mushrooms, and wild weeds for the birdcages and terrariums she hung throughout the city. She said her found art was a public indictment, a statement from the elders. Wilder never asked who the elders were. He simply chalked it off as more of Thistle's spirit speak.

So when she grabbed fistfuls of earth and held them before her nose as if to breathe a prayer, Wilder only shrugged. "You should take off your shoes," she said and kicked off her boots, the tongues lolling as if they were hot and tired, full of thirst.

"Here? I'm not doing that." Thistle tied her shoestrings together and flung the pair over her left shoulder. The strings got caught in the patch of spikes. She shrugged, the leather jacket arched across her back like a pair of wings. "The earth is cool and damp here," she said and held out her hand. "Come on, every step is like a kiss." Wilder shook his head, no. She threw her head back and danced, her toes sinking into the moist grass. "Best massage ever."

Wilder paused. "I can think of better."

A sudden burst of wind carried Thistle's laughter through the air, lifted it above his head, lingered in his ear. The breeze felt cool, inviting. He sighed and unlaced one shoe.

"Got me messed up," he muttered and kicked off the other. He stuffed his socks in his back pocket, strung his shoes over his shoulder, and dug his toes in. The grass smelled sweet and wet, felt like heaven on his soles and heels. Within the circle of trees, he went beyond thought, beyond feeling. As his feet sank into the earth, he felt himself yielding to a soft green breath, a sensation he hadn't felt since childhood. He stood there, eyes closed, remembered what it felt like to run barefoot without worry, without fear. A deep presence filled the space around him, within him. Wilder glanced up, saw in moonlight the silvery threads of a webbed work of art, dangling from an elm. And like his lover, the spider was nowhere to be seen.

"Thistle?"

Only the familiar whoosh of the river replied. All he heard was the waves of the water, sloshing somewhere ahead, down below, and the sound of his own voice whispering in the waist-high grass and weeds. Slowly, his eyes adjusted to the dark and the silver. The light was strange as if waking inside a dream. Wilder followed the crush of green where Thistle's hips had slashed through the ferny veil. Her footprints led him inward, deeper into the night where he didn't want to go. He walked in slow, plodding steps at first, searching for Thistle's trail, but each time he moved, he felt the air move behind him, only to turn and find no one there. Uneasy, Wilder moved faster, twisting through the rambling path, fighting the woods. He ducked beneath branches, cursing as he worked to untangle them from his hair. Instead of thinning out, the trees grew thicker all around. Wilder didn't like it here, the way the ground sucked at his feet, gentle at first, but more insistent with each step as if the land were hungry.

He stopped. *That* was how she looked—hungry. Those nights

when he would wake, the room suddenly filled with the weight of a presence that made him turn over only to find Thistle lying flat on her back, hands at her side, still and cold, eyes flung wide open, mouth parted ...

"How does it feel?" he had asked once when the sun had risen and she moved, thankfully, once again part of the living.

"Like I woke up dead." Wilder remembered frowning until she kissed him. "It's like my mind is awake, but this body is not ..." Thistle often spoke of herself as if she were not part of herself, as if every day were an out-of-body experience and Wilder were her witness.

"Like you're trapped?" he'd asked.

"No, like I'm finally free." Her arms were wrapped around his throat, his head resting in her hands. She was curled beneath him, their legs entwined, her breath like peppermint and lemongrass, sweet herbal spice.

"But your eyes are wide open and you look ... you look ..."

"What?" She stared as if to dare him.

Wilder had searched for another word to describe what he could not say. *Dangerous* is how she looked, *feral,* but what he whispered then was "terrified."

Thistle raised one brow, rubbed her knee. "Sleep paralysis, common enough. I've had it all my life. It's like the body is paralyzed and your mind is still awake. REM atonia, when your brain awakens and your eyes start to open. You become alert, conscious." Sitting cross-legged on the rumpled sheets, she gulped noisily from a glass of water, then pressed a cool fingertip at Wilder's temple. "But then you realize you can't move, you can't speak, and you feel a weight pressing down on you, on your chest, and you feel like you can't breathe, you can't ..."

"That's fucked up."

Her tongue darted out, licked the tip of his nose. "It's merely a question of transitions. The brain and the body, the spirit and the mind, move all the time, between state to state. Sometimes, you are just caught in between."

"If I had to sleep like you, I think I'd just skip sleep."

"I don't sleep. I wait."

But she didn't wait. She'd left him, creeped out alone in the damned woods. And she didn't sleep. She didn't sweat. And when she did sleep, she looked wide awake. Dead. Thirsty. Hungry. The last few weeks she had given up her normal diet of vegetables, fresh fruit, and nuts. "What happened to the kale?" She had only shrugged. Wilder was relieved. It was as if his whole body was starving and all he needed was to nibble on one bit of bacon for release. He hated pretending, acting as if he was into all that vegan stuff. He had done worse for less. Hunger was something he'd gotten used to, a dull ache until he did some odd jobs or found a steady gig or another cool-sheeted bed to lie in. With Thistle's new appetite, Wilder ate heartily, satisfied. He collected every meat recipe he could remember and watched as Thistle sat eating strip after strip of barely cooked meat, mostly seafood, from the river that she caught herself and piles of freshwater mussels with garlic and butter and white wine sauce.

Thistle was in a good mood these days, almost giddy, and she slept, if you could call it that, less and less. Wilder had started to think that this was one time it would be all right until she had insisted it was time for her mother to meet him.

Wilder stooped to scrape a pebble from between his toes and rose, wiping a streak of mud against his thigh. When he brushed his hair out of his eyes, he saw a circle of stones. Wilder frowned. It was as if the trees had hidden them. One minute there was a wall of green, the next, a circle of stone. They rested upon each other like giant children holding hands in a ring. The wind picked up here, the air cooler. It carried the rustle of leaves and the rush of waters, the sound of the reeds clattering in the breeze as if each were an open throat, rising to speak. Wilder wrinkled his nose. The wind carried a strange scent, something that made him wipe his face with his sleeve. Wilder had lost Thistle's trail. Instead, he felt as if he'd stumbled upon an ancient conversation, the rocks and the grass, the river and the moss arguing about shadow and light. Wilder didn't like the sound, the sounds. They buzzed in his ears like static, a cloud of gnats. The hair on his arms felt prickly. He wanted to put his shoes back on, drive as fast as he could all the way home, but he realized he had dropped them somewhere back in the thickening bush. *Out here wrassling weeds.* And where had she brought him? Wilder felt as if someone had told him to drive to the end of the world, to drive and drive and when he got there, keep driving on.

Ferns and foliage had sprung up where he didn't recall seeing them before. The great stones seemed to rise higher, pressed all around him like a great crushing wall. The air felt old, godless. Why did Thistle leave him alone in the dark in the middle of night, and who would choose to live in such a place?

He felt the slow shifting of eyes he could not see, then a sound like a bell, Thistle laughing, her voice high and clear. She was waiting for him beside a tree just beyond the tallest rock, the one shaped like a raised elbow and a fist. A large web, the shape of a shield, sparkled in the moonlight inches from his face. Wilder recoiled, waved his hand.

"It's bad luck to kill a spider," Thistle said, and she ducked beneath the web and pulled him close. Her voice was a murmured apology in his ear as her nails scraped his jaw, razed the skin. Her ringed fingers ripped away at his collar, exposed his throat. Thistle tore off his shirt, kicked it into the ground that was covered in a thin layer of rising mist. She rolled up his tank, scraped at his back and neck, her tongue deep in his throat, stumbling through the tangled branches and moss-covered stones until he fell limp into a bed of leaves, shoulders stooped, arms hanging at his sides. Tiny, hot scratches scraped along the softness of his belly down the length of his arms; a cut stung on his chin. Thistle nipped, nibbled at his nose.

As odd as she was, Wilder loved being with Thistle. He felt himself expand in her presence. Her strangeness and stories awakened in him a vague awareness of his own. It wasn't that he didn't care about the land or "her sisters," the damn weeds and the river, or whatever Thistle was always so amped up about. It's just that he saw the state of the world as out of his hands—something decided by others more predatory, more resourced than he. For Wilder, fighting was a losing proposition. Someday the meek would inherit the earth but not in real time, so why spend what little time you've got, stressed? Wilder didn't want to make a difference; he wanted fucking change. When that didn't happen when he thought it should, he gave up.

A long time ago Wilder had had skin in the game. He'd put his neck out there like Thistle, believing, marching, singing, guitar playing, airbrushing, phone banking, door knocking, and leafleting, only to have it crushed by the world again and again. There had been some successes, but the failures were more than he could bear. The night Thistle finally came to him, he had marched with her and the others against the Stiles Water Treatment plant. Stiles was vile. It dumped partially treated sewage wastewater into the river, claiming rapid dilution by the Mississippi's vast flow and hiding under the cover that the river was used mostly for industry and commercial traffic. Thistle and the other activists knew that state law required all Tennessee waters to be fishable and swimmable. The only folks who fished and swam in the river bottoms were too dumb to know better or desperate or both. Or Thistle. Thistle painted a beautiful, huge canvas mural that had to be carried by twenty hands, calling for disinfection and respect for her "mother," the river. Wilder joined the protest only because he wanted to be near her. He wanted to show that he was willing to go wherever she was, that he was down with the cause, her cause, even if it didn't make much sense.

When he dropped out of school, Wilder had spent years on the streets, lonely and hungry and denying both while searching for truth in flesh. He couldn't find his tribe, but wherever he wandered, music was his solace. Wilder never stayed in one place long, never loved one heart long. He had learned to survive, to protect the soft parts of himself. But the world had eaten his spirit up and spat him out, left him pulp and gristle at Thistle's feet.

"It's not enough that I'm barefoot and getting eaten up by bugs, but now we've got to play hide and seek in the dark?" Thistle bowed her head, smiled. Wilder held her close, lifted her chin. Damp pine needles pricked his back. "You know we could have done that back at the house."

"Mama's not back at your house."

"Where the hell is Mama?"

Thistle pulled away and rose, turning her back to him. He stood up, wiping matted leaves off his legs. "What's wrong?" She didn't answer but offered her hand, her palm cool and damp. Wordless, she led him through an opening in the stone door he had not seen, her hand still clasped in his. As they walked, waves of coolness trickled between his toes, tickled Wilder's soles. He looked down, stared at the flat surface of the water. It stared back up at him, a dark mirror. A dense, blue fog clung to the trunks of the trees. Behind him, the old stones groaned. Up above, the stars revealed themselves one by one in the veil of night.

"This way. She's here."

Together, they waded through the river mud and muck. Thistle held his hand in a tight, possessive grip, squeezing his fingers with her silver rings as if he might flee. She walked with her back to the darkness, her eyes willing him forward toward a tunnel of trees ahead. Her feet moved expertly, as if she had walked the unseen path a hundred times before.

"Slow down, Thistle, you're going too fast. You're going to fall."

"Hasn't happened yet." The hair bristled on the nape of his neck. How many times had she walked this path before?

Thistle's steps through the stream had become quick and light, silkfire dancing through the night. She moved as if possessed, as if each step were a key she played in a song for the earth. Wilder's footsteps were heavy and unsure. His breath grew ragged. Sweat trickled down his chest and back, made his skin stick to his tank top, made him wipe his shoulder with his chin.

They passed a stand of young saplings. Thistle paused to stroke their stalks tenderly, whispered as if telling them secrets. The wind rustled in a red maple's leaves. She tilted her head as if to listen. Wilder sighed, swatted a mosquito that looked big as his hand. "Please, can we go now? I don't want to be out here all night, Thistle. I'm getting eaten alive here."

She stopped. He could hear distant voices, perhaps from a barge floating by. A muffled grumbling sound rumbled through the air like the echo of trucks speeding across the I-55 bridge. Wilder frowned. The old bridge was too far away for that. "Let's hurry then. You're more than ready," Thistle said.

"Look, we could be home by now, eating. I know you're hungry. You're always hungry these days. I mean, why are we here? Is this even necessary right—"

"I wanted to show you where I came from," Thistle interrupted. "Who I came from, why I am."

Wilder shuddered. His feet were cold. The drying sweat had chilled on his skin, but despite his discomfort, he accepted her answer. It was what he'd wanted to hear. For months she had been secretive, silent. If he hadn't seen her student ID, he never would have known that she had been working on her Master's in bryology. Her thesis was on the role of moss in rejuvenating, human-scarred land, healing poisoned waters. "Ecological succession" is what she'd called it. "Every hour the Mississippi River Delta is disappearing; one football field of wetlands vanishes at a time. Your levees have strangled it, your channels and canals have allowed saltwater and waste to poison it. Whole ecosystems are drowning in muck."

"You think moss and algae and shit can save it?" he'd asked.

She'd nodded. "I do." Wilder had snorted. Thistle had sat back, watched him in silence. Maybe that was when it had changed. Her sleeping patterns, her eating, everything, even the way she looked at him, held him when they made love, before she drifted off into her open-eyed sleep.

Thistle claimed she already had a lifetime of degrees in environmental forestry and the science of trees, but moss was a new interest for her. The change in scale, she'd said, the smaller focus, enriched her life, changed her view.

"You have to expand your vision and make your spirit very small. I'm so used to being—"

"Being what?" he'd asked. She'd slipped the photo card back into her satchel. Her face was ashen, her lips a thin, grim line.

"Being rooted in everything."

Now she looked amused, almost giddy. She moved in an intoxicated sway as if she were dancing to a furious music.

"Remember when you asked me about the others, the ones before you?"

"Yeah, and you said to leave the past the past." She smiled. "Don't you want to know?"

"No, I don't." Wilder's eyes darted like the fireflies that fluttered past them. He was starting to imagine movement in the dark. A rustle by that tree, a whispered hiss underneath a bush. He grew more unsettled the longer she stared at him, humming and swaying. "I know everything I need to know about you— don't need to know anymore—and besides, I've already met your mother. See," he said and stomped his feet in the rising water that grew colder, "the river. And here—" He leaned against a gnarled, narrow black gum so twisted it almost looked bent. "The tree. Pleased to meet you, Mama. Now can we go?"

Thistle shook her head. "If you core these trees, you'll find that some of them are over 150 years old. Or older, like that one there. So now you've met Loridant. He was one of my favorites."

Wilder frowned. "Favorite what?"

"They say he disappeared after he led an expedition here when the Chickasaw tended this land, but I see you have found him."

Wilder jerked away from the alligator bark, sucked in air, steadied his voice. "Come on, where is she? I see you're not going to end this game until I meet her, so let's go."

He marched ahead of Thistle, snatching at branches that leaned in his face, swatting at the high grass, cursing the weeds that created a wall around him. *Why did he let her toss his good shirt?* His white tank top wasn't much defense against the scratches and the bug bites. It glowed in the dark, making him look like a ghost slipping through the trees. The air was more fragrant here, dark and sweet, cloying. He could hear Thistle giggling behind him. She was practically singing now.

"There better be some Fireball when I get there."

Wilder would have kept marching and cussing if he hadn't fallen into the marsh.

"What the—Thistle? Thistle!"

It was as if the land had given up and the river had taken over. Wilder found himself knee-high in a black bowl of muddy, sludge-like water, but it wasn't the water that worried him. The moonlight reflected an image so uncanny that it made the inside of Wilder's scalp itch. Straight ahead in the center of the circle was a huge cypress tree. Its great dark, tall plumes stabbed against the sky. Its trunk, or trunks, rose from the water in a huge entwined knot covered in green fungus. It appeared to combine at least two other trees. Huge tangled roots rose in and out of the water like knobby knees, a great serpent's nest. The limbs were massive and coiled in the air like mighty arms. The bark around its base was smooth, save for a series of fire scars as if someone had tried to burn it many times over. Standing in the shadow of this giant, Wilder felt as close to God or the Devil as he had ever felt.

Thistle stopped just short of the water. Her face calm, her eyes shining in the light.

"Mama."

The ground shook, rippled beneath them, and the triple tree seemed to bow in answer. *This shouldn't be here.* Wilder knew nothing like that grew in the area. Maybe a couple hours away in Mississippi where the cypress trees in Humphreys County were some of the largest in the world, 97 feet around, 118 feet tall, the South's own sequoias, or maybe down in Texas and Louisiana but not down in the delta in the mouth of the river in West Tennessee.

As if hearing his thoughts, the tree's great limbs bent forward, but Wilder did not feel any wind or breeze. Instead, the water around him began to warm and bubble. Water lilies with huge poppies bobbed and floated in the bubbling water. Wilder tried to back out, his voice lost in the rumbling of the strange tree, but something twisted around his ankles, held him in place. He screamed, fearing it was a snake, and reached into the water. Instead of scales, his fingers felt wet vines and scale-like leaves. He tried to rip the heavy vines off, his fingers digging into them. He yanked one and tossed it. It landed in the muddy pool with a splash, heavy as a walking stick. Wilder felt the air whirling behind him. He turned to see the triple tree's branches twisting like angry snakes. Wilder turned to run, but his legs were caught again in a nest of vines. They dug into his flesh, stung, and burned him like fire ants. "Thistle, help me. Why are you just standing there?"

She stared past him, at the great knotted tree, at the swirling waters; then her eyes rested on him.

"You could say," she said, "in my way, I *am* helping you. This is one of the oldest, most sacred spots. Right now, you are in the intersection of the river and the tree. You are in the delta of civilizations, a place most dear to me, the place where I was born. Where I am seen."

Wilder flailed his arms in the water, legs rooted. "Listen, baby, I see you, and you are so beautiful to me—I just need you to help me right now. See if you can help pull me up. I'm tangled in these weird vines. Some kind of bad storm is coming, and I think that old tree is about to fall down."

Wilder didn't like how she was looking. She was facing him, but her water-eddy eyes seemed to peer through him, focusing on something else. Wilder felt more wind at his back. The air filled with the rustling of leaves and needles, the sound of a hundred cicadas, a humming, buzzing sound that rattled his ears, jarred his teeth.

Thistle closed her eyes and nodded her head. She opened them, a peaceful smile on her face as she crouched before him. "I like to believe in balance, in the natural order of things. I take from life, and I like to think that I'm giving life as well." She reached above him. Wilder gripped her arm.

"Thistle, please," he hissed. He leaned forward and stroked her cheek, his muddy fingers caressing her hair. "I don't know what's happening, but I need you—"

"You don't see me," she said. "Even now. You never did." Thistle jerked out of his grip. A clump of black hair fell away in Wilder's hand. He stared, his breath shallow. "Thistle, what's wrong?" he whispered. He held the hair for a moment, then let it drop into the water. It floated like a feather. "Are you sick? Why didn't you tell me? Is that why you wanted me to meet your mother? How long have you known?"

His mind was racing, panic spreading. If she had cancer, he thought he could deal. *Maybe.* He wanted to hold her, but he couldn't get out of the water. He was pulling with all his strength, and the vines that held him barely budged. *Why did he have to find out like this?*

"You're going to have to try, baby, to pull me or go for help. I can't stay out here, not like this."

Thistle's eyes were on the hair that still floated on the skin of water. Her hands flew to her scalp.

"Damn," she said. She held her hands up. Her nails were gone. She slipped her silver rings off and tossed them into the water next to Wilder. They sank with tiny, little bubbles. The nail on her index finger dangled by a thread of cuticle. No blood, just dry, flaking skin. The air hummed again, a whispering sound like many rushing waters. "I know, Mama," she whispered. "I know."

"Thistle, stop it." Sickness and anger rose to his throat. "Your nails are falling off. You're falling apart, and you're talking crazy!" He swallowed, covered his mouth with a muddy fist, lowered his voice. "What kind of cancer do you have?" She frowned at him, stared. Wilder shook his head, tried to make sense of Thistle's decay. *How could she hurt like that and not bleed?* "You wouldn't accept chemo, no matter what the doctors said, so that means you've been trying to fight it naturally this whole time?" He closed his eyes. "That's why you've been eating all that weird shit?" *But her hair, her hair fell out in his hand.* He shook his head, confused. "Baby, I'm so sorry. Why didn't you tell me?"

Wilder jerked and strained in the mud, trying to walk. He clawed at the sediment and silt, his legs struggling underwater. For a moment, he felt the vines loosen from his knees, then creep up his legs again, holding him still. The vines pricked and stung him more, held him tighter. Everywhere they touched him, his skin felt itchy and scaly as if sunburned. His legs began to feel heavy, leaden. He tried to reach for Thistle, but her eyes looked different. They caught the silver light, giving her face an eerie amber glow. Her skin was ashen, her cheeks hollow. Thistle stared in the space above his head as if she hadn't heard anything he'd said. Wilder looked up to see one of the knotted tree's long thick branches hovering above him. He froze. Thistle picked seven bell-like yellow blossoms from the limb and held them in her open palms. An invitation.

Wilder shook his head no, but Thistle kissed him, her mouth filled with tiny, razor-like teeth. He tried to pull back, but he felt sleepy. Her tongue was sweet like honey and mead, and she held him as she always did and whispered to him, the songs that only she could sing with words that only she remembered the meaning to. His eyes grew bleary, and he heard more than he ever had—the croak of the plump, brown toad beneath an unfurled leaf, the jewel beetle scuttling across algae-covered bark, and the wind in the leaves, the many hundred leaves rustling above his head and a chorus of crickets.

Thistle smelled of maple syrup and buttermilk, of wet grass and rain-soaked walking sticks, of a wet stone covered by moss and babbling brook. Her eyes were too round, too full of silver and purple-golden light. Her skin was riven by deep whorls and lines as if it had been carved with a knife.

When Thistle fed him the seven bells, Wilder's mouth was still full with the taste of sweet nectar; but then the blossoms stung the inside of his jaw, and the tip of his tongue went numb. He stared at her, struggled to keep his thoughts clear, to make his lips and teeth form words. Only shallow gasps escaped, a jaw harp deflated, out of tune. Recognition clouded his eyes. Wilder's heart was brittle, ready to break.

As the poison flowed through him, he felt the hum of a strange touch; fallen roots blossomed in electric earth. He was being lifted, carried backward through the waters. "Don't struggle," Thistle called to him. "Mama just wants to meet you."

As the vines covered him, the limbs pulling him closer to the great tree's bosom, Wilder felt pieces of himself, like pieces of dusk, fall apart and be gathered in the bark and dirt. Thistle was naked. Now he could see her—a body no longer woman but willowy tree. Her bright, round forehead shone in the moonlight. Her skin was tattooed with the whorls and swirling textures found on old-growth trees. Snails and mussels clung to her legs. Flowering vines and green moss wrapped around her thighs. Wilder thought he saw blue mountains, perhaps galaxies flowing in her ancient hair that now fell away in clumps like riverweed and algae at her feet. If he could move, he would have reached for her. He would have tasted her with his fingertips and tongue, but she was out of reach. He wanted to cringe, to creep away. He wanted to lean into his lover's palms. He couldn't do either, so Wilder no longer tried to move.

His eyes asked the question his lips could not. "People are the cancer," she said as she flicked an emerald beetle from her shoulder and followed him into the muddy pit. "Not all of them, of course, but enough of the wrong ones to wreck the balance. The movement needs people with heart," she said. "Spirits committed to systemic solutions, long-game change," she said. "But that's not you, is it, Wilder? At least, not yet."

Wilder felt his breath grow short. Where each began, a tickling fire flowed through his blood. Seven thousand songs surged from stones as Thistle walked over to him. In the ghostly light, she still looked almost human, beautiful. Wilder's ears hummed. Alarm, desire, and fear echoed in his temples, a competing heartbeat.

She embraced him, smelled like the strange, yellow blossoms.

Thistle caressed his throat with a sandpaper tongue; the skin peeled off in gentle flakes like wet, dark bark. "I told you Mama would love, love you ..." Her voice was airy, a solemn fractal, whispery as the wind. Wilder craned his neck to reach for her. The fragrant pheromones released from the tree dulled his pain, mixed it with his hunger. Even in the face of his dwindling energy, the memory of life fading fast, desire welled inside him; however, Thistle had completely transformed. She was no longer recognizable, and he was no longer sure how he could love her; but he did.

He remained still as a rock in a river of sound as Thistle and her Mama pulled apart the disparate shreds of who he used to be. In their presence, his thoughts felt noisy, cluttered. He tried to clear his throat to speak, but he could not feel it or his mouth. A gurgle and a rush of air escaped the hole where his throat and esophagus used to be. If he were a pipe, she could have played him. Wilder the bone harp, the baddest instrument in the world.

Thistle gently ran her fingers across his chest, then ripped his tank off. His eyes widened. "Don't worry, Wilder," she said, her lips and sawteeth stained blood red, his back sinking into the smooth base of the knotted tree. Mama licked him, and he sensed another part of himself slide away. A spine of bones exposed to the night's air, he thought he could hear pieces of the old flesh drop into the waters, remnants of his former selves sink into the muck, but he was no longer certain if he still had ears.

"The Tupelo, black gum tree has a strong heartwood," Thistle said. "It's one of the oldest native trees here, like the oaks and the poplars, but of course, not as old as Mama. And you've probably guessed, Mama is not from around here. She came with the river. But Wilder, you'll have plenty of time to contemplate the true meaning of change. Mama will keep you company. She'll sing you the old songs and tell you her stories. She'll keep you safe with the others until—"

Brambles curved around his chin. Thorns pierced his flesh while he tasted her final honeysuckled kiss. His thoughts disappeared in the rising mist. Wilder's mind rang with a new truth. He would die here. Perhaps he would be reborn. To spring from the earth, a fresh green shoot, dark roots twisting deep beneath the river's belly. A sapling tree, straining for the scent of rain, reaching for change. Wilder felt as if he had traveled through a dream, as if he woke beneath a river and there were no way back through the forest except to become clear water, a spring to fill and heal himself. His eyes wide awake, his body unable to move, his fear vanished into the dark center of things. As Wilder watched over Thistle's shoulder, her tiny teeth sinking into his cheek, he saw where she had dropped the first gift he had made for her into the bubbling earth. Muddy, watery fingers reached in languid waves to snatch the jacket up. The world afar, *the last spike floated in dark womb-water, shimmered a sinking star.*

Rooting

Isha Karki

Branches jut towards us, splinters scrape our skin, and sap leaks from bark split open, coating the curves of our shoulders, pooling in the dips of our clavicle. The forest anoints us.

We can't see through the curtain of leaves; we part our way with batons. A decade ago, we would have used RazorSticks, sliced through the wood in nanoseconds, the laser whip-whip-whipping. Areas like these are under Earth Conservation laws now: the first global initiative in seventy years. The West, a construction of metal and glass and impossible heights, leeched of everything green, pays no heed. But out here in the wild, the laws are words tumbling from the mouth of gods.

This country, partitioned into isolated chunks like the rest of the world, is heavily guarded. The border gates only relented when we pricked our thumb, smeared DNA on the scanner as an offering, Eklavya giving guru dakshina; no other Rep could have gained entry. Yet inside, we see no signs of surveillance, only the violent shiver of leaves in the wind. We don't expect anything more than CCTV; even before it collapsed, this country was still using nanobytes and power stations. The last known British expedition into this region— Rep-funded, illegal—brought back relics for the World Museum in Bloomsbury. We went to stare at the exhibits imported from our homeland: mosquito rackets powered by batteries, dismantled parts of a rickshaw cycle, wide blades of a ceiling fan—how the blunt edges must have sludged through air.

We yearned to see in these bits of metal a reflection of ourselves. But all we saw was rust. Restless, we rushed to the Hospital. The explorers had also brought with them dated petri dishes. We stood untouched, but the Saps suffered, their immunity to local disease not including foreign bacteria. We pressed our noses against glass, breath fogging our vision. Raised spots on Sap skin, heat rippling from their bodies, feces dribbling. Eleven dead: we had never seen such mortality. We marvelled; fear licked us clean. Perhaps this was our true reflection.

The air is swollen here. It clings to our nose: waterlogged mud, fruit ready to burst at seams. We hear the distant roar of water. *Jharna*—the word floats into our thoughts. Ever since we stepped foot on this land, words and images have been leaking into our minds: a buried language resurfacing.

Mosquitoes swarm us. They are harmless against the immunisation code we spent months developing in secret. The Rep Council warned us against chasing illusions. How could we explain the dream lodged into our brain stem like a virus? A lone figure sitting cross-legged under a peepal tree, whispering to us in our language: *We don't die, but we bleed.* How could we explain that no word of our mother tongue ever passed anyone's lips; that we thirsted to see others like us, touch their skin, and know it wasn't an aberration?

For months, after lights out, we hooked ourselves onto BlackNet, poured our dream into the system, waited for Globe to locate the phantom figure. Globe is off-limits to us; yet we stood with bated breath, tried to stifle our clicking hearts as pixelated images formed in front of us. We saw a chalky spire crumbling before our eyes; dark hands and machines rebuilding the tower, aiming for the sky, and that, too, turning to dust. Dharahara, Nepal. No recent footage from the region, nothing to show how the open space, the cemented roads, turned into a jungle thick with the smell of damp earth and old bones. We plotted our route on outdated GPS. We left under the blanket of night; the Council wouldn't notice if one of us was missing.

If we bring back a mind-cache full of geographical data, our subterfuge will be overlooked: another victory for the Reps. The Council talk of expanding borders, claiming uninhabited territory, eyes turned towards Asia—speaking as if we're not there. Against their warnings, two Saps travelled to the region six months ago and disappeared. As the Council says: Sap research is impractical, their bodies, ill-designed for collecting data, not like ours. If we succeed, the Council will ignore the fact our success shoots from our Nepali genes; perhaps they will finally own us as their own.

Our difference pulses from us. Ever since we remember, we have had our own pods, our own work stations, our own toilets, security so tight you'd think they were afraid of us. Years we tried to become them, the throng of slick, light-skinned bodies. We developed lightening codes for skin, hair, eyes. They took the codes, patted our backs, turned them into wholesale capsules, *forbid* us from using them.

Something is different under this canopy: the air sings to our skin.

Snakes, thin as earthworms, slither over our feet. Humidity makes salt water trickle down our chest and curl our hair. We reach a scheduled stop, tongue sticking to the roof of our mouth, feet throbbing. Our thermostat picks up a spike in heat. We shudder with relief, tears seep from our eyes. Weeks we have been travelling, walking, crawling.

The leaves part ahead of us. We stumble forward, wounded moths, and through blurred vision, we see that same vermillion-robed back. A figure who, from a distance, looks like a mutated laliguras, bloated and human-shaped.

Hope weights our whisper, "Hajurba?"

We feel his eyes open. We pause, surprise muddles our thoughts. We can only sense movements and thoughts of our sisters through the Hive, a live data stream in our mind. No one can infiltrate; no one can escape. Yet we hear, as if it were happening to our own body, the way his breath creaks his ribs, the faint whistling at the back of his nose.

After the global data shutdown, no one knows anything for certain—there are only swirling rumours, snatched words from illegally tuned transmitters, half-lived dreams. But on BlackNet we discovered coded reports speaking of a sadhu living deep in the woods equidistant from what once bordered India and China. They say he was one of the first to spring to life. That he lives, tucking centuries of history into gossamer folds of his brain, one of the richest independent mind-caches in the world.

We don't believe in myths. We know what happens when flesh is made god. We worship facts. Fact 1: We were born of need, hope, and love. Fact 2: Saps can't survive without us. Fact 3: We were migrated to the West in miniature glass cases. Our home ripped through by quakes that came in revolutions of eighty years, then twenty, then five, till the earth rolled under your feet as you walked. Fact 4: We don't know who we are or who we used to be. Fact 5: Hajurba might be able to tell us.

Batons elongate into canes as we hike up, clothes chafing our skin. We round the hill, come to face him and stop. Hajurba doesn't move. Though he has a beard wisping into his chest, the breasts lumping his—her—body are unmistakable. We filter the information, add it to the Hive.

"Hajur," we revert to a gender neutral term. All eyes turn towards us. The third eye, grooved centre of forehead, vertical instead of horizontal, lids lash-less, opening from the middle out, screams alien. They say third eyes look into your soul—if you have one, that is. "You called us here?"

Yes, chhori. Hajur nods, voice a pool of ice in our minds. *Come, receive aashirvaad.*

We don't move, caution stilling our limbs. "How did you find us? What *happened* here?"

Hajur stares, third eye unblinking. We look at its ridged corners and wait, the click-click-clicking of our hearts echoing with the shriek of birds. *Let me tell you a tale first, and you decide what happened—who was right, who was wrong, who was human, and who was not.*

o.

You are sitting on the chhatt, chin tilted up, the sun a field of orange behind closed lids. Phulmaya, massaging oil into your head, sighs, "If only we had a few sets of hands! Durga Mata was a bit kanjus, no? Made ordinary folk too limited."

You smile, imagining Phulmaya floating on a lotus, hands in eternal mudras. "What would you do with the extra pairs?"

You expect her to say *swing scythes and draw talwaars,* but her voice drops, "Cook, clean, knit. I could knead the pittho and roll rotis together. It would save time ..."

She tapers off. You don't ask what she would like time for. Head buried in newspapers and books, following blogs and YouTube channels, bouncing from lectures to talks, you are too busy to ever ask.

Your mother must have overheard because she shouts, "Eh, Phulmaya, don't take Mata's name with your dirty mouth."

Your shoulders stiffen. Phulmaya continues pressing your scalp.

A cry floats from the road below: "Sunnu hos, aaja ko Dinay rate, aunnu hos."

The chowk pedlar at it again. A few months ago, this was something only whispered about in hospitals and research centres, perhaps debated in the secrecy of government circles. Journalists and newsrooms were banned from speculating, and internet posts written by college students taken down. But now the city jostles with Nepali pedlars, bought out by Indian and Chinese corporations.

Your mother forbids you from conversing with them; these sellers of bodies and souls who will be punished in their next lives. She always speaks of karma and dharma. She believes Phulmaya—who fed you her own milk, fanned you tirelessly in monsoon heat, who slaves day and night in your tiny kitchen, pumping the kal, dragging metal cylinders of gas, eating baasi bhaat, washing your mother's period rags—is atoning for sins in her past life. She thinks the bhikari who calls from the street—dark skin creased with dust, baby with bloated belly and slack mouth slung across her body—is also responsible for her own fate. Your mother doesn't believe in accident of birth; she gives them a handful of rice, her own dharma done.

You find yourself paying attention to the discussions around this DNA project: social change, dismantle the caste hierarchy, revolutionise Nepal. You're not naïve: you know it's a way for multi-nationals to win over the militant left. There must be another line they're spinning for the rich. The religious sects, sadhus and gurujis, pockets lined with rupees and yuans, trumpet it as the blessing of gods, who have spilled into the human mind the secret of being one and many all at once.

And yet there is a seed of hope stuck in your throat, a bald supari you have swallowed whole. That night you dream of it flowering out of your mouth and decide: you will donate your DNA. You will not cheapen it by accepting payment.

1.

You will be forty when you see the first one.

She appears in your living room as you click through channels. You stop when you catch sight of the hologram, sharper than the flickering images surrounding you. She cooks—steam billows from rice cookers, pressure cookers whistle, she wraps momo like a machine; she cleans—gone are jharus and mops; she blitzes dirt and purifies rooms in seconds; she plays with children—two babies at her teat, others gurgling as she sings. She is the face of the new domestic. One-time fee for a lifetime investment.

Goosebumps scatter on your skin. You clutch at facts: her eyes are glassy, she doesn't smile. But as the hologram changes, she looks straight at you, and you see it. A flicker in those eyes. An emotion. She looks exactly like you did when you were twenty years old.

Though it is mild autumnal sun bleeding through the jaali, you blast the heating and wrap yourself in blankets, clinging to the hope that the Phulmayas in the world will soon have time to do whatever their hearts desire.

● ● ●

2.

The second time, you see two of them, sitting side by side as if they are friends or sisters.

You are at the CTC mall, dropping on a bench; your feet ache—you have inherited your mother's bad knees and your father's bad back. Someone sits behind, back against yours; their hair brushes your neck.

Something about the moment feels so intimate, you almost weep. Too fraught to relax, you struggle up, grab your bag, and swing around to face the mirror opposite.

You see yourself three times. A woman in a wilting cotton dhoti, hair loose, cheap plastic at her ears, bright potay around her neck, kajal dots on her chin, an Om tattooed on her wrist: she is you when you were twenty.

The woman sitting next to her is also you, though her hair is shorn and she has smeared on candy pink lipstick, a colour ill-suited to your complexion. She has a wriggling baby at her left breast, hums quietly, while her companion rustles around in bags and boxes. Where did they learn it? This taste for cheap jewelry and religion; this predilection for short hair, pink lipstick, and an instinct to mother. Could they naturally be so different to you?

You step back. Hearing, they look up, eyes catching yours. You are suspended for a few moments in this unholy trinity, longing to see in their gaze a deep-seated recognition, repulsed by the very thought of it.

Before either can move or say anything, you turn away, rush out into the sticky heat. From the left, you hear thunderous rumbling. People in tattered shirts, patched trousers, threadbare saris, once cooks, drivers, maids, nannies, helping hands integral to all homes—real people, you remind yourself—are blockading New Road, a people-led Nepal band. Two years and nearly all of them are out of a job and home. Their demand: abolish the new domestics.

You blink back tears, shove aside the knowledge that you helped make this happen.

3.

Five years later the Court agrees to hear the first case.

The defence's argument centres on the nonhuman aspect of the victim. Every time he stands to hammer the point—his client isn't breaking any laws because there are no laws protecting domestics from battery, assault, murder, rape, only guidelines tacked onto property laws which don't account for their very tangible aliveness—there are jeers from the public. The first time, you glanced back in surprise, eyes widening as dozens of you looked out, skin glistening with sweat, rage twisting their mouth. Gone was the glassiness; gone were the docile limbs.

Years you worked to improve the social condition of women. You volunteered at rape shelters for the abused and vulnerable. You ploughed your own money into maintaining schools for the underprivileged. You trained in victim counselling. How can you then ignore the whispers in the streets, the chants you hear on the cusp of sleep: *We don't live, but we breathe. We don't tire, but we hurt. We don't die, but we bleed.*

You think of Phulmaya, her arthritic flesh sullied by male hands, unwanted and unrelenting; your mother cast her out of your home. Her corpse could be lying in some naali, and you will be here, breathing easily. Though the realisation has been creeping on you, it is in this moment you admit that you were wrong. There has been no social revolution. People have transferred their cruelty onto a new social rung, deemed barely human.

The judge rules in favour of the offender. You shouldn't feel shock; you have watched scores of women, young and old, cheated out of justice in this very room—why should this be any different?

He leaves, smug mouth under a brill-creamed moustache, hair oiled to his scalp, paunch jiggling, a cloud of aftershave around him as he shakes hands with his lawyers, the police, the judge. A seething silence from the seats.

It will be ten years before you witness a landmark ruling in favour of the domestics, acknowledging them as living beings. In between, there will be hundreds of cases: rape the forerunner. How easy it is for men to rape without consequence, to plough their dicks into a lifeless hole. They will go unpunished; no one will predict the revolution that will flood the streets, the quakes that will come in succession—the gods collecting penance.

Now in the courtroom, there are only hands damp with sweat, cholos stuck to backs, hair frizzing into fearsome halos.

In two days, they will find the offender hanging from a creaking ceiling fan, remnant of a brutish past.

We don't anger, but we raze.

● ● ●

We gasp as the images stop. It is as if Hajur has pressed a switch in our brain and flicked it off again.

Faint sensations come to us: the burst of oranges on our tongue; the stickiness of mangoes on our fingers; tart berries staining our mouth red. Are these our memories?

There is something, some emotion, clawing up our throat. "What happened to her?"

That is not my place to say—you must discover for yourself.

"She looked like us."

Yes.

So this is the history that has been hidden from us. Our origin. Money and labour. An experiment gone wrong. Replicas of a Sap who thought she had a social conscience, who palpitated with useless guilt. The facts pillaring our existence start to crumble.

"And what you showed us, that is the truth?"

Hajur stirs. *The truth is that there is never one truth.*

"Why were we taken from here?" We imagine ourselves as dormant cells, pulsing with identical DNA, carried across oceans.

To be studied. Foreigners wanted to examine what in your genetic makeup made you prone to dissent.

We hold our breath, half-predicting, half-fearing what Hajur would say.

They wanted to find it and eliminate it. Replicate the genetic pattern, produce, and subdue factories of their own fair-skinned domestics, workers, machines ... but I hear Replica is the ruling force in Britain, that the humans live under their thumb.

The mosaic of our history is slotting into place, excruciating tile by tile.

"Replica hate the Homo-Saps, *and* they hate us."

So they aren't immune to social hierarchies or racial prejudice. They allowed you to mature untampered, and the seed of dissent flowers. Will they praise it or punish it?

New images surge through our mind: masses of bodies heaving, gunshots, fire, buildings disappearing. The acid stink of vomit and blood. Charred bodies on countless pyres. A country in ashes. We don't need a switch; the land speaks to us. Memory or dream? Past or future? Questions are forming on our lips when the sound of screams, raw and bleeding, overwhelm us.

A resounding click and everything fades.

• • •

We wake up to the earth under our body, flies buzzing around our head, ants crawling over our stomach, and a glimpse of the blue-veined moon.

Though the forest is dense with the screech of monkeys and the flap of wings, there is a yawning silence within us. Our mind-cache has been rinsed, data recoded. We—*I?*—have been cut off from the Hive. We scramble for facts, anything to shove the terror aside.

New facts structure us. Fact 1: Saps existed before us. Fact 2: Our home is being rebuilt; we must help. Fact 3: Our sisters are waiting for us. Fact 4: We must get back to them; we must fight.

We heave up, swallowing bile, vision sharpening. A figure swathed in vermillion robes advances towards us. Certainty builds within us; we know what we must do. We move towards Hajur and the fleet-footed crowd following behind.

We are ready. Leaves caress us as we pass; flowering trees drip nectar onto our skin. The forest anoints us.

These Constellations Will Be Yours

Elaine Cuyegkeng

I see you the moment your pale white slipper touches my floor. Silk on white marble, roses at your feet, a sweep of golden bees falling from throat to hip on your white dress—the oraculo's sign.

What compels me? I have ferried a hundred thousand passengers and will ferry a hundred thousand more: each of them a tapestry of past and present, a constellation of possible futures. For all of your finery, you are just another Buyin girl travelling to the Homeworld. But I draw up your name, I see your profile: seventeen years old, destined for the Conservatorio. I shift my oraculo's eye and look into your present, your past, the starlight threads of all your possible futures. Dancing ancient Balanchine in the Glass Cathedrals with white roses at your feet; bargaining down the price of nephila silk in the Buyin Merchants Association. Suddenly, inexplicably, there are infant spiders in your brown-black hair.

(I see the infant spiders again in the dark of your prison. Your cheeks starved to sharpness, lungs wracked with fever, your back flayed open. They have chained your hands behind your back, and I can hear you weeping.)

In the present, you turn your head. I know you see me as I see you. Two oraculos will always recognize each other, mirrors reflecting each other in an endless loop. I saw your future, you see my past. Me, at sixteen, undressed for my assignation and my back laid bare for the engineer's art.

In an enclosed chamber in the heart of the galleon ship, I lay on my belly, my arms outstretched as if I were at worship. I remember Madre Eglantine speaking from the Book of the Rose. I remember the bioengineers painting cool antiseptic gel against my back, the growing sense of weightlessness as they drugged me to open up my oraculo's eye. I remember floating high, watching with an archangel's serenity as they exposed my spinal cord, the flower of my brain stem. Watched as they attached hundreds of bioluminescent tendrils to brain and nervous system, connecting me to the galleon ship's systems, opening my oraculo's eyes to the great expanse of the celestial sea. To the stars' present, their past, all slivers of their possible futures.

What Katalinan scientist, what bioengineer first thought to take their knife to a Buyin oraculo's back? To the delicate webs of an oraculo's nervous system and connect them to the navigation systems of the great galleon ships? Their names are legion. All of them are Blessed, their names and genetic lines canonized in the Book of the Rose.

But I, like all my peers, am destined to remain unnamed. I will only be known by the name across my hull: *Empress of Our Stars*.

But you, you are an oraculo unmade. You only see my back. You only see what should have been you.

In the present, you turn as if to run. Sweep yourself out of the ship like a child running from ghosts. But your mother clasps your arm. "It's for the best, sweetheart."

She thinks you're afraid of leaving home, but it's *me* you're running from.

I shut the doors. I lock you in before you can cause an unpleasant scene. I shut the gates to past and possible futures, both yours and mine, and prepare trajectories from Buyin to the Homeworld.

They call Buyin the Pearl of the Katalinan Empire.

By rights, in the great expanse of the celestial sea, it should have remained an insignificant backwater. A little moon of no great interest. But then the Katalinans found it, found us: a population of clairvoyants and telepaths; empaths and mediums and most importantly, oraculos. The scientists among the First Expedition wept to find us. They had spent untold years toiling to find an alternative to the generation ships, a cumbersome and uneconomical way of creating Empire. But with Buyin, they had a wealth of acceptable raw material to which they could put their theoretical science to use. They founded the Orders of the various disciplines, built the Torres de Oraculos, where little ones are typed and measured, then raised and trained. Service in the Torres de Oraculos is mandatory for a Buyin subject of precognitive talent. It cannot be refused unless a family is wealthy enough to pay the tribute price, like yours.

Imagine me then, imagine us. While your hand rested lightly, lightly on a barre, your silhouette golden in the afternoon light, I was one of a dozen children with bracelets on their right wrist, a long light chain of starlight silver running to our ankles. Purpose was symbolic only, but Madre Eglantine rapped our hands for blubbering.

"You should be grateful," she said and pointed to the portrait of the Rose Infanta above with her long, thin hand.

The portrait was a universe unto itself, the Rose Infanta in a glittering black dress that looked like the celestial sea. Looped around her neck were necklaces of black Aphroditian pearls, butterfly gold, and obsidian from Itzpapalotl.

Each bead symbolized a colonial possession of the Katalina, Madre Eglantine explained. And look, on the Infanta's finger, held out to us as a treasure: a single ring with a white pearl as pure as an infant's soul.

"That pearl is Buyin," Madre Eglantine said, sweeping her hand across the dusty room. "That pearl is *you*."

She told us of the First Expedition's struggles: the pioneering experiments in bioengineering and on oraculo bodies, the multitude of failures before they found success. She told us how they established the breeding programs that tracked and combined the best bloodlines until they produced us, the now-famed oraculos of Buyin. Voyages that once took centuries now take months or years, and even rival empires court the Katalinan for the sake of this product. The oraculos of Buyin are our greatest gift to humanity, far more than Buyin's indigo moths, our spider silk, our starlit pearls, and black sugar.

"None of you are children," Madre Eglantine said, touching my cheek with one long, thin hand. "So stop crying."

In the Torres de Oraculos, they fed us bowls of marrow and cream and taught us the difficult art of celestial navigation. We learned to marry doctrine and precognitive science. We learned that all futures are possible, that nothing is inevitable. It is, in fact, simply a matter of discipline to turn from one future to another as delicately as a dancer might arrange herself: the composition of her arms, the position of her feet. It is possible to step back from the abyss.

In my first few days in the Torres, I prayed for the death of Madre Eglantine. I prayed for my family to come tearing at the walls in the night. For my mother to find me and carry me out with her hands.

But one night I dreamed of the Torres in flames, our baby hands scrabbling bloody at the brick.

The Madres hauled me screaming out of the dormitories as the others wept in their beds. I was taken to the chapel where Madre Eglantine waited in a confession box and yawned as I babbled about fire and blood.

"Everyone dreams of the fall of the Torres de Oraculos," said Madre Eglantine. "Everyone wants it destroyed. Everyone dreams of a knife in my back."

Out of the confession box, she showed me a scar: a constellation of knotted flesh at her back. She told me: "Once, there was a husband and wife who infiltrated the Torres de Oraculos and tried to butcher me in my sleep." She shrugged. She had them buried alive in the Torres de Dolor. Their child still roams the stars, a galleon ship obedient to the Empire and the Rose Infanta, and thankful for Madre Eglantine's intercession. For she had seen in her oraculo's eye the consequences of disobedience.

"So I know what you saw," Madre Eglantine said and put her hand around my throat. "Shut up that future. Brick it up alive. There have always been threats of rebellion, and they have always been stillborn. There is only one future that ensures peace, and that is the one where you take your place among the galleon ships."

In our grey, bare classroom, she showed us a map of the celestial sea. She showed us the constellations as they were from the Homeworld: Calypso, Isabella of Castile, Aphrodite, Inang Maria. The Katalinans conquered them, system by system, star by star, linking the constellations in fact: geopolitical boundaries and economic trade. Until the Empire could say with all seriousness that they owned all their mapped constellations in full.

"One day," said Madre Eglantine, "these constellations will be yours."

We would link them, system by system, star by star. We were the future galleons of our Empire, and ours was the fate of starlight.

So you see, I have no patience for your pity or your horror. I am more. I have always been more than your bleak reflection.

For two days and two nights, I let you disappear into the background of a hundred thousand passengers: births and deaths, future loves and betrayals, and a thousand sunderings of the heart. I foresee a few deaths by drowning, one in the heights of the Nieve mountains, a few bloodied bones wracked by the Inquisition. You are nothing more than a moment of inconvenience, nothing more than background noise.

"Hello," you say, out of the blue.

Inside the dancing rooms, you are bending delicately over an outstretched leg as if your bones are made of quicksilver. In hyperspace the galleon ship picks up slightly more speed than is strictly recommended. In the hold a medic frowns at my elevated heart rate.

I see you: a constellation of freckles over skin the color of sunlight on water, your brown black hair tightly pinned back. I see your starlit futures. Under the mellowed lights of a stage, you are surrounded by dancers the color of knives and—

("Did you imagine you were above the law?" Madre Eglantine asked coldly as they strap you down on the cross: your flayed back to be displayed like a banner in the city. You wept—later, historians will say you were serene as a saint despite your suffering. That you turned your face towards the brightness of the stars.)

"I know you can hear me," you say softly. You move now to the other leg. Your clothing slowly contracts, responding to your cooling skin. "The Kapitan said you could."

Inside his quarters, my Kapitan frowns at his coffee, served at a temperature slightly higher than normal, slightly more bitter than to which he is accustomed.

"What is your name?" you say. "What *was* your name? How old were you when you were made? Did it hurt?

"Are you angry with me?"

What could I say? What would it be like to have your future—all of your possible futures? What would it be like to drink chocolate with my mother at breakfast, bitter-dark in white mugs the size of my palm? To argue art and politics with her over a supper of pheasant and kale and dance with the light of an alien star on your skin? And here you are, hurtling towards a future I cannot turn away for you. When you could have a future under the light and under the snow.

I say nothing. I leave you in silence. But I compose a note to be sent to you and opened when you next sit down at the breakfast table with your slate.

Madre Eglantine always said girls like you were a waste.

Never ask a question when you don't wish to hear the answer.

I didn't say it to be cruel. I said it because it was true. So what if your merchant mother could pay the tribute in exchange for your galleon service? So what if mine could not? You are an oraculo unmade and inside you, a thousand fortunes and possibilities that will never be born. I am the pearl on the Rose Infanta's finger. I am the ship that cuts through the fabric of space and time. The constellations are *mine*. And you, what are you?

In her quarters, Madre Eglantine sighs over her books and fondly pats my walls.

She is old now and treats me as if I were a favored child. She confides to me serious matters: "Allowing monetary tribute in exchange for galleon service was shortsighted," she says. Powers higher than her had made that decision years ago, and now the shape of Empire is paying for it. She tells me that the year's harvest is poor and grows poorer every year.

More and more people pay tribute rather than give up their sons and daughters or send them to the Homeworld or elsewhere. Through apprenticeships and indentures, they earn education in the arts, the sciences. They compose treatises on the shared divinity of humanity with their dancing; they paint images of the brutality of the stars. A few are moved to write bad novels with evil Madres and tragic romances of young oraculo men and women. The kindest of the Katalinans are moved to outrage: how could the people who moved them so, who danced for them, be subject to such barbaric practices?

Their anger has been slow, collective. But it has built to the point where Madre Eglantine has been summoned to the Homeworld to answer charges of cruelty on behalf of her order.

To soothe herself, Madre Eglantine requests our passenger list. She counts the number of unmade men and women, the fortunes and possibilities lost from their service. It calms her, this choreography of numbers and lost futures, the potential. Her finger rests against your name.

"I saw her, too," she tells me. "If she had been taken to Torres de Oraculos, we would never have stood so close to the unraveling of the order of things." She sweeps her thumb, if by doing so, she could sweep you all into the Torres de Oraculos and teach you your duty.

When we reach the Homeworld, crowds have gathered to greet us at the ports. Madre Eglantine and I watch you and your mother leave in a sweep of white lace and spider silk. Your white slipper steps away, and I catch another glimpse of you in the dancing rooms of the Conservatorio, golden with the light of an alien star.

I don't see the dark future with spiders in your hair, your back flayed open. I don't see you being raised up like a martyr for revolutionaries and malcontents to see. We are in the Homeworld, far away from the brutality of Buyin. In this moment in time, there is nothing in your eyes but the future with roses at your feet.

You are both going to the capital. Madre Eglantine, to answer the Rose Infanta's summons, to defend her Order. You, to attend the Conservatorio.

For the love of God, keep out of her way.

I don't see you for years.

But I think of you. I think of you and the future that might still be yours. At my breakfast tables gentlemen and women open their slates, watch recorded images of you in the corps and become your devoted following. You graduate to soloist and finally *principal*, dancing ancient Balanchine in the Glass Cathedrals. It is a feat unheard of for someone so young. My passengers bend over the white tablecloth and debate your aesthetic, your measurements, your merits against other dancers.

And occasionally: *Is it true that she's some half-Indio girl from the colonies?*

Her mother is from the Lorraine Empire, I think.

It's the other half that offends me. What did she do to climb so high and so fast? A scatter of scandalized laughter.

I can't burn their meals—my poor staff will be blamed. Instead, I mark their names. I lower the temperatures of their rooms. I disturb their sleep with ghostly noises, the sounds of hollowed breath. They complain to the Kapitan about hauntings, and I tell the poor man his salary is for dealing with the complaints of spoiled merchant princes.

I follow the Inquiry as my passengers do. For most, their interest is distracted, casual. I look at the news footage: I watch Madre Eglantine's hair grow white. They say the case is not going well though the Rose Infanta favors it. It is not going well though the fashionable continue to debate its progress. Surely, the tribute is not unreasonable or cruel, given the benefits Buyin has enjoyed? Is Buyin not under the Light of the Rose? Do its natives not enjoy prosperity and trade?

My Buyin passengers tread carefully on the topic—this is not a pleasant discussion for them. Too many remember a time when their family could not pay the tribute and too many bear a loved one's absence like a scar. They would rather forget Buyin's grief, their grief, in the marble of my rooms. They would rather watch you dance. But the arguments in my drawing rooms grow vigorous, even crass.

"There's only one place where the Indio belongs," a Katalinan merchant says. "On her back or in the fields."

"Is that what you tell your little girls?" her breakfast companion says. For the Katalinan merchant had three, pretty little mestiza daughters, too young to understand Indio applied to them.

I have my staff drench them both in ice water. It is, I have found, the only cure for a brawl.

Then one morning, my breakfast rooms chatter and clink and hush-whisper with your scandal.

What were you thinking, performing such a piece in the Grand Cathedral? In front of the Rose Queen, the aristocrats and merchant princes, the Heads of the Various Disciplines? *Andromeda and the Stars*. I've seen footage of the choreography, and it is beautiful; that cannot be denied. You unfolding like a rose in the centre, wearing a dress with golden bees. Your fellow dancers arrayed around you, their skin painted starlit silver and wearing dresses the color of knives. Slowly, they draw out slivers of red ribbon from you as you dance. You fold slowly into a rosebud of a dead girl, succumbing to their demands.

It is incendiary, and your profession has never admired incendiary. Dancers are meant to serve as vessels for human yearning, for the divine. They are not supposed to have political opinions, it demeans their art. You are relieved of your position despite the outrage of city balletomanes and students, your fellow mestizos and Buyin-born and their allies.

My Katalinan passengers are offended by your gaucherie, but my Buyin passengers are dismayed. *How could she do it?* they ask each other. It will reflect poorly on them, they think. Aspersions will be placed on their loyalty. Everyone gossips over your disgrace, your mental stability, the poor example you set. How this will affect the little ones still studying in the Torres de Oraculos and learning their duty.

But still, they all watch footage of *Andromeda and the Stars* over and over again. They cannot look away. Mothers of oraculos find themselves with tears in their eyes even if they insist they have no revolutionary sympathies (and threaten to disown their children if they show even a glimmer of a sign). And when the Katalinans call you *That Mestiza*, flapping your arms, dancing in the square like some madwoman who should be in the sanatorium, they are surprised to find themselves met with antagonism. Brawls break out in my hallways, in my antechambers and drawing rooms.

You are nowhere near me, you have caused me no end of inconvenience, and given us a small fortune in fines for uncivilized behavior. I hope you are satisfied.

And now here you are again on my marble floors.

You do not look like a dancer disgraced. You wear dove grey instead of your white: the sweep of golden bees is gone. Your brown black hair is gathered in a net. You look like a serious young woman, returning home to embark on a merchant's career and take up your mother's work.

"Hello," you say softly.

I brace myself for the onslaught of your future. I see nothing of infant spiders or your flayed back. Instead, I see you and your mother assessing the quality of spider silk, the pale fabric frail and beautiful in your hands. Sweeping into the Buyin Merchants Association to register the child in your arms, someone to pass on your mother's work. You will probably have to pay tribute for her to keep her by your side. Perhaps one day, she will dance like you.

It is a good future, a good life. I suggest you take it.

"I remember you, you know," you say. "*Empress of Our Stars*. But what was your name? Your real name?"

(They haul you up, they haul you at the top of the church, at the top of the Torres de Oraculos your flayed back bare, your face hidden, the crowd weeping below, smashing themselves against the fortifications to force their way in, anything to save you. Madre Eglantine—)

I send you a message: *It is not important, and it is none of your concern.* I ignore you for the rest of the voyage. I hope now you'll understand.

But at the end, you stand in my reception hall, waiting with other passengers for the ship to dock. You let them leave one by one. You wait until it is mostly empty. Until it is only me and you.

"I can't forget you had a name," you say softly. "I can't forget you." Inside the hold, my lungs draw a sudden, sharp intake of breath. A junior medic fusses over my vitals until my pulse and breathing rates have slowed back to their steady, glacial calm.

"There is a future that you deserve," you say, "and it isn't this."

You touch my honey-colored walls and turn to go.

Madre Eglantine returns a year after you.

In the courts the Madres have won a temporary victory. It was expected, of course it was expected, say my passengers. So many of the Katalinan aristocracy and merchant princes benefit from the trade.

But the damage is done. They listen to the arguments. They dream of you bleeding out red ribbons to the indifferent stars. They cannot unsee it. They cannot stop seeing *you*.

Neither can I.

Madre Eglantine is old, older than I have ever remembered her, and sadder. My passengers doff their hats, bow to her out of habit; but it is impossible not to sense the reserve in their deference, and my poor staff suffers her temper. Her coffee and chocolate are served to perfection; she is served breakfasts of crystalline fruits. But still I have to comfort the staff who serve her, reassure them her comfort is out of their hands. She reprimands them for the impending end of the galleon trade, the mandatory harvests. The unending clamor from reformists, for Buyin's equal rights as a Katalinan state.

"The Indio would like nothing better. Your people are lazy, and your people are ungrateful. You do not possess the long view," she laments. She tells them: they cannot see the beauty of the whole, the beauty in the part they play. I usher them out before they say something they might regret, and I let her rail at me in solitude.

"They should bend their knees," Madre Eglantine said in the privacy of her rooms. She talks to me as if I were still a child in her schoolroom and not the ship ferrying her from one star to the other. "They should be grateful for our work, civilizing and educating the population, bringing them into the Light of the Rose."

But they are not grateful. We are not grateful.

On the streets of Buyin, dancers don masks and perform Andromeda, shocking the Madres and respectable Katalinans. In my drawing rooms Buyin artists and dancers debate and dream of a new world where the tribute and the harvests exist no longer. They barely hush themselves when Madre Eglantine steps into the rooms. When they speak your name, Madre Eglantine grips her hand tight,

tight. As if she were digging her fingers into my arm. As if she were closing her hand around your wrist like a vice, snapping it close to breaking.

There is nothing I can do.

I perform my function as a galleon ship should. My obedience buys peace, Madre Eglantine has taught me. And so, obedient I remain.

I travel to the Homeworld and back. To the Stars of the Lorraine Empire, to the Stars of the Tsin and the Benedice. I carry narwhal horn, sea horses, spider silk, the quicksilver of Indigo Moths, robotics expensively and lavishly made. From the exiled world of Mari Sheli, I carry genetic blueprints for cats that chirp like birds and songbirds that chime like little bells—in addition to the occasional live specimens with the added cost of feeding and care. I carry passengers with a hundred thousand fortunes, an infinite number of fates and fortunes tied to Buyin.

We are at dock in the Homeworld when we hear of the inevitable: the outbreak of war and a mob assailing the Torres de Oraculo.

The news is scattered and thin. The Madres and Sentinela had barricaded themselves in the Torres de Oraculo, Katalinan civilians in the Interred City. What compelled our Birthworld finally? What served as the igniting point?

"The Madres have taken hostages," my Kapitan explains. His hair has turned grey-black in the intervening decade. "We have been given orders to evacuate them as well as the Katalinan population."

I should have felt betrayed. I remained obedient. I brooked no revolution, no dissent in my oraculo's heart. I turned my oraculo's eyes away from any future that ended in this: anarchy and the cacophony of rage.

But my kindred have not, they could not. How long do you tolerate the harvests, the trade? How long do you tolerate the empty place at your table, the scars on your heart? The problem is that people are reasonable. They are very reasonable until they cannot be reasonable anymore.

I was not asked about my loyalties. Neither were my Buyin crew: it was never in question. We made the journey to Buyin with eleven other galleons, empty save for staff and medical personnel. We docked at the ports where evacuees waited, terrified of revolutionaries and the furious crowd.

I did not bother to listen in on the radio recordings. If I had, I would have known. I should have known.

It has happened. It has already happened, and now neither of us can turn that reality away. Two Madres carry you in: you hang between them as a dead weight. They have flayed your back, and the Madres have not bothered to dress you, cover your salted back with spider silk, synthetic skin, or bandages. You are still wearing what you wore when they hauled you up as a warning to the Insurrectionists: nothing but a grey penitent's skirt. And now I know why our kindred have turned to war.

"Their discontent demanded a lesson," Madre Eglantine says, sweeping through my reception hall. "So I gave them a martyr. A reminder for the need for *obedience*." It is all the explanation she will give to the Kapitan, to my appalled, silent crew. She sniffs as a medic rushes forward without her go-ahead. She is disappointed that the Indios are taking the wrong lesson to heart, but it is not her fault. Her students have always been flawed.

I know her so well.

"Keep her alive," Madre Eglantine snaps as the medic unravels a wad of spider silk. "But don't mend her back."

In my heart is a roar.

I wrench controls from the pilots. I shut them down.

"What are you doing?" my Kapitan says.

Madre Eglantine turns slowly. She had not expected this. That once interred, once made, we could turn from our designated purpose. *She made us for this.* How could we refuse?

I say to her: *You had us. You should have let her go.*

"An Indio unmade is a mistake," she says as if her doctrine truth might turn me back. "I gave you the *stars*. Why would you throw that away?"

I wrench myself down into the earth below.

I hear the scattered signals of our kindred calling your name, unwilling to let you go. Unwilling to let the Madres seize control of one more daughter, one more young woman who should have been left as she was. As it is, they watch us fall and over the radio, they calculate our projected landfall, ordering medics and troops to that location. Our kindred will carry you out. They will carry you out and heal your back, give you water, dress your wounds, and give you comfort. You will never drink the light of stars in the celestial sea.

I see myself, my hair growing back, my face upturned towards the sun of our birthworld.

"I knew you had a name," you say, your future self to mine. "You have always had a name. Do you remember? Will you give it to me now?" And you hold out your hand.

You are unbroken. I am unmade, and the light of our sun is on my back. You reach out to touch my face. You say—

Read Before Use

Chinelo Onwualu

The basement of Satellite City's main library was made up of several levels dug deep into the earth. Even this early, several hours before dawn, each level was filled with scholars poring over old documents, students fetching and carrying, and stewards and handmaids scurrying about. Alia flashed her cartouche at the attendant on duty and wound her way down the wide stairs to the level where one of the most extensive collections of pre-Catastrophe literature in the land was housed.

The staircase was crowded with people coming up to the main levels or heading deeper into the underground caverns. At the topmost levels of the basement, the walls were lined with brick, and the floors covered in plush carpets; but as one descended, the brick gave way to raw stone, and the ground became uneven, littered with rock and debris. The air grew colder as well, and Alia shivered as she continued down.

At the bottom of the stairs, the rock walls were damp, and the high cavernous ceiling was lost in gloom. Everlights hung in sconces along the walls feebly lighting what they could. They were the latest victims of the city's energy crisis. The vast generators that powered the city were slowly failing. No one knew why—let alone how to fix it. There were fears that the weather machines that made life beneath the dome possible would eventually shut down. But Alia was convinced that somewhere among the vast records in this underground cavern was the answer; she just needed to know where to look.

She slipped her pen and notebook out of the carry-all slung across her back and rolled up her sleeves. She looked about, making sure she was alone. In the four years that she'd been coming down here, she'd never seen another soul this deep in the library's vaults. The texts housed here were written in an ancient dialect of her homeland, Zahabad, and none of the city's academics had ever bothered to learn it. Clenching her left fist, she flexed a mental muscle. Her hand burst into flames, but she did not burn. With a swirling motion, she turned the flame into a small ball of fire and launched it into the air. It hung above her head high enough to avoid the risk of burning any of the ancient manuscripts but still bright enough to illuminate the space around her. Hitching her bag more firmly over her shoulder, she moved deeper into the cavern.

By the time Alia emerged from the library's basement, the sun was setting on the horizon. She was tired, hungry, and in dire need of a bath. But there would be no time for any of that. A ping on her AI told her that Shiloh Kestrel wanted to see her immediately. She sighed.

The family homes of the Great Houses were located in the part of the city known as the Scions' Quarters. Here, modest but immaculately constructed homes were surrounded by manicured hedges planted in intricate arabesque designs. Gravel-lined pathways were flanked by shrubs of lavender, rose, hibiscus, and violet. Even the benches, nestled underneath shady flame trees, were padded and comfortable. The lack of walls or fences suggested a pleasant communitarian spirit, but anyone who knew about Satellite City's politics knew that the Houses were locked in fierce competition with each other. Those who fell afoul of this carefully camouflaged rivalry could be counted on to never repeat the mistake.

As Alia hurried along the garden paths, her heart leapt when she spied a familiar figure. Gilead Two Rivers was a solid man of middle height, but he gave the impression of being taller. He smiled when he saw her, his grey eyes sparkling with good humour, and she fought to tamp down the heat that began to smoulder somewhere in middle of her belly.

"Good morning, professor," he said. She returned the greeting coolly, careful not to meet his gaze. Like her, he was a professor of antiquities. But unlike her, he did not teach at the prestigious City University. Once a brilliant scholar, Gilead had dropped out of the Academy following a scandal with another professor's wife. Now he specialised in procuring hard-to-find objects for collectors. It would not do for a full member of the Academy to seem overly familiar with a rogue scholar—at least in public.

And he certainly had the look of a rogue about him. His jet-black hair was in sore need of a trimming. It hung past his shoulders in fat, shaggy curls, giving him the look of a savage from the Forest Tribes. His tunic was of the finest linen but wrinkled and open at the collar, revealing a hint of the muscled chest beneath. His black scholars' vest was dusty, and he wore a pair of loose trousers over old leather sandals.

"We missed you at the last evaluations," he said, blocking her path. "I heard you were ill?"

"I was," she said tightly. The annual intelligence evaluation was a test only non-Scions were required to take. She had pretended to be sick to avoid the humiliating ordeal even though she knew it would cost her lecturing privileges. What did it matter? She was barely allowed any classes anyway.

"I trust you are recovering well?"

"As well as can be expected," she replied as she moved to go around him.

"I should think so." As she passed, he leaned in close to whisper, his breath hot against her neck, "Given I was your carer."

The smoulder flamed to a sudden heat that tore up from the pit of her stomach, and she nearly dropped her carry-all. It was times like these that she was grateful for her Zahabadi heritage. Her brown skin was dark enough to conceal her blushing.

Gilead laughed. "Good day, professor," he called as he moved off. But Alia was too flustered to respond. She was grateful, too, for the gathering gloom. In the twilight, no one would be able to see the steam that rose from her clothes as her body warmed up.

By all the gods, she thought, that man ...

When she got to Kestrel House, she took a moment to compose herself. Calming thoughts of water worked best. Few knew of her true nature or the powers that accompanied it, and she meant to keep it that way. Besides, it did not pay to show weakness when among the Scions. With this one least of all.

Finally, she climbed up the front steps and rang the bell above the door. A serving girl answered the door and led her through the house. Shiloh Kestrel was standing on the veranda overlooking the inner courtyard. He was tall, even for his people, and his silk kimono did little to hide his powerful physique. Like all pure-blood Scions, he was bald, his silver hair shaved close to his scalp. Pale, colourless skin that seemed to glow in the gloom had given rise to the rumours that the Scions were not human. But Alia knew that was not true.

"Have you found it?" Shiloh asked without turning.

"No," Alia said flatly. "If I had, you would know." If Shiloh was irked by the sharpness of her tone, he did not show it.

"I have word that some of the other Houses have joined the search," he said. Alia groaned inwardly. It was no secret that all the

Great Houses were scrambling to find the city's next new source of power.

"Perhaps if I still had my team—" she began, but Shiloh silenced her with an imperious gesture. He turned and fixed her with a hard stare.

"My mother may have had the wherewithal to indulge your academic fantasies, but I do not. The only reason I haven't cut off your funding and sent you back to your homeland is out of respect for her poor health. But my patience is wearing thin. If this book of yours truly does exist, you will need to find it soon."

Alia fought to contain her anger. In Zahabad, she had been the Ivory Tower's leading scholar in pre-Catastrophe texts. It was why Shiloh's mother, Ramah Kestrel, had personally recruited her to come to Satellite City. However, few in the city shared Ramah's vision. Alia still remembered the scowls of disapproval from the Scribes at the university during her intelligence evaluation last year. Despite her credentials and consistently stellar performance on those tests, many of her colleagues were still unconvinced that a woman born outside the dome could be worthy enough for their ranks. If Alia lost the support of House Kestrel, she would have to return home in disgrace. She shuddered to think what would happen to her should she be so shamed.

"If the other Houses are getting involved, that must tell you something," Alia said.

"A delusion shared does not make it reality, professor."

"The Mechanichron is real, Shiloh. The Ancients had a source of unlimited energy that powered all their artefacts. The specifics of it were written down in a text accessible only to Master Builders—all their records reference it," Alia said irritably. She had to explain this each time they met. "This text must have been hidden away to protect it from the destruction of the Catastrophe. It would have been far too valuable to leave unprotected."

"Then find it," he snapped. "You have one week."

As she was led out to the front door, Alia fumed. He hadn't even given her a chance to tell him what she'd found that day: A reference in a pre-Catastrophe text that mentioned a Master Builder facility nearby. However, it lay beyond the protective dome of the City in the area now known as Raven's Crag. Without a security team, venturing off-grid would be suicidal, but what choice did she have?

It was well after midnight before Gilead came home. Alia had fallen asleep on his foldout couch when she heard the authorisation beep from his key code. Leaping up, she ran to the front door just as the apartment's automatic lights brightened. She was waiting for him as he entered.

"By the sword!" he swore in surprise when he saw her. "What are you doing here?"

"Where have you been?" Zahabadis always answered a question with one of their own. The lights quickly dimmed, but they were bright enough for her to see his bruised features and the way he cradled his left arm. "What happened to you?"

"Ran into an old client of mine," he said wearily as he brushed past her and lowered himself painfully onto the couch. "I'd rather not talk about it."

Alia went to fetch the first aid kit. It was not the first time she had tended unexplained injuries on Gilead. His was a dangerous world, and Alia had learned not to ask questions.

He was sitting on the floor—the couch had obviously been too much for him—and was taking off his shirt when she returned. She could see his body was in no better shape than his face. Three angry gashes stretched across his right shoulder. Slipping onto the couch behind him, she ran a UV wand across the wounds to disinfect them. Then she sprayed an aerosol dressing which would harden into a flesh-like graft and help stitch the lesions together. The rest of his bruises would heal in time.

When she was finished, Alia leaned back and studied him. He lay splayed out against her legs with his eyes closed, his chest gently rising and falling. Tenderly, she ran a finger along his cheek tracing the rough stubble of his beard. Despite his mystery, he was the man she loved. Could she really involve him in the misadventure that finding Mechanichron might become?

She slipped out from behind him and rose to put away the first aid kit, but he grabbed her hand and pulled her down on top of him.

"Thank you," he murmured as he wrapped his arms around her. "Let me repay your kindness."

He kissed her deeply, and her body warmed to him. He often teased her that she was like ice—because it had taken months of relentless pursuit on his part before she had showed him any affection—but the truth was that she had burned for him from the moment they'd met. Her hesitation had been born out the struggle to control that fire. Even now when she was with him, she had to be careful. Detachment worked best. She observed his caresses with an artists' eye, noting the contrast of their skins—his cured leather to her rich earth. The way his square hands were crisscrossed with scars as they explored the hidden depths of her body. She listened to her moans of pleasure commingled with his and dissected them for pitch and volume as they climbed to climax. But her control always left her, and in the end she would be forced to withdraw lest the flames of her desire set them both alight. Only in the aftermath of their union, as the conflagration inside her banked down to its embers, did she recall her purpose.

"Take me to Raven's Crag."

"What?" His eyes snapped open. "Absolutely not, it's too dangerous!"

"I must get to Raven's Crag, and you are the only one who can take me there."

"Why in the seven hells do you want to go there?"

"I can't tell you that. Suffice it to say, it's important." She squared her shoulders. "You will be well-compensated," she added.

"You have no money, unless the Academy is suddenly paying in more than sweet titles." But something in her face must have told him she was serious.

He sighed and leaned back.

"As you wish. Only pray that the gods lay us both a straight path."

It had taken two days to arrange everything: false cartouches, travel supplies, and—most importantly—for Alia to smuggle out the ancient text that had referenced Raven's Crag from the city library. It was a slim volume that had been slipped in between the covers of another tome, both of which were old even before her people had settled in the Land. If she was caught with it, she would likely be exiled on the spot. But it was their only clue to the location of the *Mechanichron*.

Getting out of the city had been easier than she'd expected. A quick scan to make sure they had no contraband technology and they'd been able to board a caravan going to one of the northern kingdoms. Everyone joked that leaving Satellite City was easy; it was getting back in that was the problem.

"Where are we?" Alia asked when they disembarked in a shallow valley several hours later.

"Just east of the Plains," he said. "Raven's Crag is about half a day away." She nodded at that. Half a day of walking would not be too taxing.

It was still a few hours before dawn, and the air held a hint of frost. Out here in the world beyond the weather controllers, it would be winter soon. She could see the white wisp of the city's near-transparent dome on the horizon. She turned her back on it and walked on.

"You seem very familiar with the wilderness for a scholar," she joked. "Do you sneak out of the city often?"

"Often enough," he said, shrugging. "I suppose not having any students gives one a lot of free time. And it helps to not have the Council of Scribes breathing down my neck."

"Yes, they are good at that ..." Alia trailed off. "Is that why you left the Academy?"

"I'm sure you've heard the rumours."

"I'd like to hear it from you."

Gilead snorted at that. "If you must know, she wasn't married when we first met. We'd known each other since we were children, and we'd made a pledge that should I become a full professor of the Academy, we would marry. I kept my word, but when we went before her family, they opposed our union. She was a daughter of a Great House and I, a nameless bastard of the Forest Tribes. She married another, and for my impertinence, I was stripped of my position."

A silence hung heavy between them, and for a time all that could be heard was the crunch of their boots on the gravel.

"That was a grave injustice," Alia spoke finally. "What does it matter that your mother was not city-born? You gained a full professorship with one of the finest institutions in the Land. You are more than their equal."

"I don't need you to tell me that," he said, roughly. He glanced back at her and blushed when he caught the look on her face. "But it does help to hear it once in a while," he said with a wink.

Alia laughed and looked up to the cloudless blue sky ahead of them. What she saw made her mind go blank.

"What's that?" Alia fought to keep the fear out of her voice. She'd never seen dragons in life, but she'd seen plenty of pictures of the mangled remains of their victims—eaten, it was said, while they still lived. A flock of them was cresting over the horizon. Gilead cursed softly.

"Do you know how to use a bow?"

Without waiting for her answer, he produced a crossbow and a quiver full of metal-tipped arrows from his large rucksack of supplies and thrust them into her hands. She notched an arrow into the dock and lifted the bow to her shoulder. Gilead squinted into the oncoming flock and suddenly looked ill; they were heading straight towards them. From the belt around his waist, he pulled out a hunting knife.

"Run."

He sprinted toward the nearest range of boulders scattered across the valley floor. Alia gripped the pommel of the crossbow and took off after him. Years of city jogging and a long, lithe frame allowed her to easily keep pace. She prayed to all the gods old and new that they'd make it to safe ground in time.

They didn't.

The air was suddenly filled with the sound of beating wings and the shrill cries of the creatures. From the sky above, an ink-black creature bore down on her, and she caught the gleam of a claw seconds before it gouged long furrows along her right shoulder. She threw herself onto her back, twisting her body away from it, and managed to point the crossbow up and fire. The bolt connected with a satisfying thud. The creature screamed in pain—a sound that was oddly human—before it veered away, leaving her sprawled in the dust. The contact hardly slowed the others, and they zipped past, skimming the air just above her. Finally, when the last of them fluttered over her, she sat up and looked around. She saw no sign of Gilead.

"Gilead!" she called out, but all she heard was the chirping of strange birds in response. "Gilead!" she called again, fighting the rising sense of panic within her. If anything happened to him, she would never forgive herself. Before she could call again, she heard a groan behind her. She almost cried with relief when she saw him emerge from behind a boulder.

"Are you all right?" she asked as he reached her.

"Are you?" he asked. She nodded, not trusting herself to speak just yet.

"Good," he said softly. Then she saw him catch sight of her right shoulder and frown. His eyes slid over the blood and torn cloth, and he turned away. The act stung her in a way she could not name.

"Let's go," he said curtly. And he walked off.

They got to Raven's Crag just as the sun began to dip in the sky. The crag was a single tower of red rock jutting high into the sky like a finger accusing the gods. It was a monolith so vast it took a full hour to circle it. Unlike the surrounding hills, its sides were smooth as glass, broken only by a few ledges of rock that jutted out from its face. Local legend said that the crag had once been a home of the Ancients and that deep in its bowels secrets from before the Great Catastrophe still lay. Alia believed it was more than legend.

On the way, they had fought off more wild creatures and had to flee a band of marauders. Wracked with exhaustion, they fell into a tired heap at the crag's sandy base and stared up at the rock with the sun setting behind it. The air was cooling quickly, and Alia could feel the chill seeping into her bones. Her wounded shoulder ached, and she clenched her jaw to keep from shivering. She willed her body to heat up, warming her. As usual, she had to be careful not to get hot enough to burn.

"We need to build a fire," she said when she felt strong enough to talk. Gilead nodded wearily. He hadn't quite recovered from his beating earlier that week, and she could see the walk had taken its toll on him. He was pale and shivering, his eyes like hollow bruises. He struggled to his feet and went to search for firewood.

She reached into her robe to make sure the slim volume she'd smuggled out of the library was still strapped to her waist and then took the opportunity to tend her injuries. She slipped her shirt off her wounded shoulder and shone a light on the long gashes. They looked oddly familiar. She nearly dropped her torch when she realised why. She had seen wounds exactly like them not more than a few days ago. On Gilead.

She waited until full nightfall, after they'd built a roaring bonfire, before she spoke. She had been careful lighting the kindling, but she couldn't resist playing with the fire. As Gilead drowsed opposite her, she surreptitiously manipulated the flames into creatures that had only previously existed in her nightmares.

"How long have you known about the *Mechanichron*?" she asked finally. It was not quite a question, and Gilead did not seem surprised to hear it. He sat up and stretched with a sigh. The warmth seemed to have strengthened him as his face had lost its pallid hue.

"For the last year or so."

"So who are you really working for?"

"The House of Crow," he said simply, almost sadly. "My mother was a warrior from the tribes of the Forest Omin, and my father is Obed Crow."

She nodded curtly, taking deep breaths to fight the shock. She'd been sleeping with the son of House Kestrel's foremost rival. "Then why are you helping me?"

He shrugged. "Because you are a brilliant scholar whom I can never hope to equal. And because, unlike Shiloh Kestrel, I know you're right."

Unbidden, she recalled the first time they'd met in the gardens of the Scion's Quarters. She had just arrived in the city and had been so lost in the scenery that she hadn't seen him walking up the path. They had collided in that comic way only seen in stage plays. How he had smiled when he apologised ... She felt a stab of pain that was almost physical, and she fought to keep her tears in check. She would not cry in front of him. She would not.

"So it was all a lie," she said flatly. "Did you ever love me?" She hated the note of pleading that had crept into her voice. He set his jaw stubbornly and looked off. He glanced back at her and let out a long breath.

"We are both pawns in this never-ending game between the houses, Alia," he said softly. "You of all people should know that."

The next morning they made their way into the crag. The entrance was a crumbling archway that could be easily missed if one did not know where to look. Beyond it was a flight of steps carved out of raw stone that climbed upwards into darkness. Clenching both her fists, she set her hands to a controlled burn and turned the flames into a massive ball of fire that hung above them.

"You're a firestarter," Gilead gasped.

"And you are a midnight man."

His face darkened at that. "How did you know?"

"Oh come now, did you think I wouldn't notice how good your eyesight is at night? Or how dim the lights in your quarters are? The genetically-modified always know each other."

"Do you think this changes anything?"

Alia shrugged. He was right, revealing her powers had been a foolish move. But for some reason she had wanted him to know. She had wanted him to see her as she truly was. Perhaps there was a part of her that hoped it would make a difference.

"You're not the only one with secrets," she told him coldly. She moved into the tunnel, not caring if he followed or not.

The steps continued relentlessly upwards, occasionally branching left or right or dead ending at a stone entrance. This far from the grid, they had to rely on their own knowledge of the language of the Ancients to decipher the security technologies that guarded each entrance and work their way deeper into the facility.

They found the chamber almost by accident. A right when they should have gone left, and there it was beyond an open doorway: A library.

Inside the chamber, Alia shrank the ball of flame to keep it from setting anything alight at the same time brightening it until it shone like a small sun as she did whenever she was in the basement of the city library. In the sharp light they saw that the room was actually several levels of balconies whose walls were lined with books. Each level was linked by a winding flight of stone steps at the centre of the room which led down into darkness. Alia moved to the nearest shelf of books and read the titles printed on their spines. She was shocked to find she recognised the language they were written in. It had been one of the most popular dialects among the Ancients just before the Catastrophe. She had been right: Raven's Crag was a Master Builder facility and likely a repository of much of the Ancients' knowledge. Further investigation revealed that the library's filing system was similar to what was still in use in Zahabad's Ivory Tower.

The *Mechanichron* itself was nestled in between other tomes discussing the philosophy of engineering. She felt an involuntary surge of joy as she cradled the book in her hands. At long last, it was real. It was heavy, its covers made of a wood-like material that had probably perished with the civilisation that invented it. Gingerly, she opened it and began to read the first page, but she barely had time to turn the page before she felt the cold of a blade at her throat.

"Hand it over," Gilead whispered in her ear. She closed the book and passed it over her shoulder to him. Something white-hot, though, blazed to life within her, and for a moment she was tempted to set both him and the book on fire. As if reading her thoughts, he sheathed the hunting knife and came to stand in front of her.

"By all the gods, I wish it hadn't come to this." He spoke with such sadness she almost believed him.

"You don't have to do this, Gilead. You said yourself, we're just pawns. They don't care about us. We could leave the city and disappear."

"And where do you think we'll go, hmm? To my mother's hut among the Forest Tribes? Or to the backwaters of your homeland? If I bring back the *Mechanichron*, I'll be granted a full reinstatement to the Academy; my father might even recognise me as his rightful heir."

"You really think they'll accept you? You're just like me—"

"I am city-born with the blood of scions running through me. I am nothing like you!" Gilead snarled, cutting her off.

The savagery of his response took her aback, for in it she caught the same contempt she saw on the faces of Scions whenever they thought she wasn't paying attention. It dawned on her that this was why Gilead had never spoken about his parentage. It wasn't an attempt at mystery, it was shame. For the first time, Alia realised she was seeing the true man behind the smiles and the jokes. She felt as if a bucket of ice water had been dumped over her head, and all thoughts of fire fled from her.

"No. You're right," she said. "You are nothing like me."

With that, he hit her with the book.

When she opened her eyes, she was outdoors, and the ground beneath her was hard and rocky. She looked up, and the sun was blazing with noonday strength. She had a headache, and touching the side of her head, she could feel the bruise that had formed when Gilead had knocked her unconscious. Gingerly, she got to her feet and studied her surroundings. She had to clap a hand to her mouth to keep from screaming.

Just beyond her—no more than an arm's length away—the ground ended in a dizzying expanse of sky. She was standing on one of the granite slabs that jutted out from the smooth sides of the vast rocky crag. Above her, the cliff continued straight up, its top lost somewhere in the clouds. She was gripped by a sudden feeling of vertigo, and for a moment she thought she might faint. Alia backed away from the edge until she felt the cool touch of a stone entrance behind her and took several deep breaths till the feeling passed. Her mouth was still too dry, and she desperately needed to urinate.

She turned and scanned the rock door behind her, but there were no buttons or pads, no way to open the door. She was on the wrong side of the entrance. Slumping against the rock, she slid to the ground in despair. Gilead Crow had lied to her, stolen her life's work, and abandoned her to die. He was gone; she was sure of it. She thought of the feel of his lips on hers and waited for the familiar heat to flare up in her. It did not. Instead, she felt cold like something had died inside her, like she would never know warmth again.

She wrapped her arms around her knees and heard the crinkle of paper. Reaching into her robe, she brought out the slim booklet that had led her out here in the first place. She hadn't told Gilead what she'd noticed in reading that first page of his book. She had made a mistake. The *Mechanichron* was actually two volumes which described a single mechanism. The book Gilead had taken away only contained illustrations of the mechanism in various states of assembly. The slip of papers she held was the machine's instruction manual.

She reflected on the few years she'd spent in Satellite City. Built by the last remnants of the Ancients to protect themselves from the effects of the Catastrophe, the city had become an oasis of technology in a world that still lived by sword and stone. But perhaps it was time for their machines to die. Perhaps if the dome were to come down, the proud scions would finally be forced to open up their city. Maybe, in time, they would come to appreciate the richness of the worlds beyond their own and understand that they were no better than those they scorned.

The thought warmed her. Smiling, Alia began to heat up her body. Soon she would be on fire—and so would the book. This time, she would let herself burn.

Soul Case

Nalo Hopkinson

Moments after the sun's bottom lip cleared the horizon, the brigade charged down the hill. Kima stood with the rest of the Garfun, ready to give back blow for blow.

The pistoleers descended towards the waiting village compong. Their silence unnerved. Only the paddy thump of the camels' wide feet made any sound. Compong people murmured, stepped back. But Mother Letty gestured to the Garfuns, defending them to stand still. So they did. Kima felt her palm slippery on her sharpened hoe. The pistoleers advanced upon them in five rows; some tens of impeccably uniformed men and women posting up and down in unison on their camels. Each row but the last comprised seven gangly camels, each camel ridden by a soldier, each soldier kitted out à la zouave in identical and pristine red-and-navy with clean white shirts. Near on four muskets for each of them and powder carried by a small boy running beside each camel. There were only twelve muskets in the compong.

Now the first rows of camels stepped onto the pitch road that led into the village. The road was easily wide enough for seven camels across. The cool morning sun had not yet made the surface of the pitch sticky. The camels didn't even break stride. Kima made a noise of dismay. Where was the strong science that the three witches had promised them? Weeks and weeks they'd had them carting reeking black pitch from the deep sink of it that lay in the gully, rewarming it on fires, mixing it with stones, and spreading it onto this road that led from nowhere to the entrance of the compong and stopped abruptly there. Had they done nothing but create a smooth paved surface by which the army could enter and destroy them?

From her position at the head of the Garfuns, the black witch, the Obe Acotiren, showed no doubt. She only pursed her lips and grunted once. Standing beside her, white Mother Letty and the Taino witch, Maridowa, did not even that. The three should have been behind the Garfuns where they could be protected. If the villagers lost their Knowledgeables, they would be at the mercy of the whites' fish magic. Yet there the three stood and watched. Acotiren even had her baby grandson cotched on her hip. So the Garfuns took their cue from the three women. Like them, they kept their ground, ready but still.

"Twice five," whispered Mother Letty. "Twice six." She was counting the soldiers as they stepped onto the black road. Kima thought it little comfort to know exactly how many soldiers had come to kill them, but she found herself counting silently along with Mother Letty.

The leading edge of the army was almost upon them, scant yards from the entrance to the compong. Camels covered almost the full length of the road. A few of the Garfuns made ready to charge. "Hold," said Mother Letty. Her voice cut through the pounding of the camels. They held.

Maridowa turned her wide, brown face to the Garfuns and grinned. "Just a little more," she said. She was merry at strange times, the young Taino witch was.

The soldiers had their muskets at the ready. The barrels gleamed in the sun. The Garfuns' muskets were dull and scorched. "So many of them," whispered Kima. She raised her hoe, cocked it ready to strike. Beside her, the white boy, Carter, whimpered but clutched his cutlass at the ready, a grim look on his face. He'd said he would rather die than be press-ganged onto the ships once more as a sailor. He had fourteen years. If he survived this, the village would let him join the boys to be circumcised; let him become a man.

Thrice six ...

The thrice seventh haughty camel stepped smartly onto the battlefield, a little ahead of its fellows. "That will do it," pronounced the Obe Acotiren. It wasn't quite a question.

The pitch went liquid. It was that quick. Camels began to flounder, then to sink. The villagers gasped, talked excitedly to each other. They had laid the pitch only four fingers deep! How then was it swallowing entire camels and riders?

The pitch swamp had not a care for what was possible and what not. It sucked the brigade into its greedy gullet like a pig gobbling slops. Camels mawed in dismay, the pitch snapping their narrow ankles as they tried to clamber out. They sank more quickly than their lighter riders. Soldier men and women clawed at each other, stepped on each others' heads and shoulders to fight free of the melted pitch. To no avail. The last hoarse scream was swallowed by the pitch in scarce the time it took the Obe Acotiren's fifth grandchild—the fat brown boy just past his toddling age, his older sisters and brothers having long since joined the Garfun fighters—to slip from her arms and go running for his favourite mango tree.

The black face of the road of tar was smooth and flat again as though the army had never been.

One meager row of uniformed soldiers stared back at the Garfuns from the other side of the pitch. Their weapons hung unused from their hands. Then together, they slapped their camels into a turn and galloped hard for the foot of the hill.

All but one, who remained a-camelback at the bank of the river of pitch.

The pistoleer slid off her beast. She stood on the edge of where her fellows, suffocated, were slowly hardening. She bent her knees slightly, curling her upper body around her belly. Fists held out in front of her, she screamed full throat at the villagers; a raw howl of grief that used all the air in her lungs, and that went on long after she should have had none remaining. She seemed like to spit those very lungs up. Her camel watched her disinterestedly for a while, then began to wander up the hill. It stopped to crop yellow hog plums from a scraggly tree.

On the hill above, the general sounded the retreat. In vain; most of his army had already dispersed. (Over the next few weeks, many of them would straggle into Garfun compongs—some with their camels—begging asylum. This they would be granted. It was a good land but mostly harsh scrub. It needed many to tend it.)

Some few of the Garfuns probed the pitch with their weapons. They did not penetrate. Cautiously, the Garfuns stepped onto the pitch. It was hard once more and held them easily. They began to dance and laugh, to call for their children and their families to join them. Soon there was a celebration on the flat pitch road. An old matron tried to show Carter the steps of her dance. He did his best to follow her, laughing at his own clumsiness.

The Obe Acotiren watched the soldier woman, who had collapsed onto her knees now, her scream hiccoughing into sobs. While the army was becoming tar beneath the feet of the villagers, Acotiren had pushed through the crowd and fetched her fearless grandchild from the first branch of the mango tree. He'd fallen out of it thrice before but every day returned to try again. She hitched him up onto her hip. He clamped his legs at her waist and fisted up a handful of her garment at the shoulder. He brought the fist happily to his mouth.

Acotiren's face bore a calm, stern sadness. "Never you mind," Kima heard her mutter in the direction of the grieving woman. "What we do today going to come back on us, and more besides." Maridowa glanced at the Obe but said nothing.

Then Acotiren produced her obi bag from wherever she had had it hidden on her person and tossed it onto the pitch. Mother Letty started forward. "Tiren, no!" cried Mother Letty, her face anguished. She was too late to intercept the obi bag. It landed on the road. It was a small thing, no bigger than a guinea fowl's egg. It should have simply bounced and rolled. Instead, it sank instantly as though it weighed as much in itself as the whole tarred army together.

Maridowa was dancing on the road and hadn't noticed what was happening. It was Kima who saw it all. Acotiren pressed her lips together, then smiled a bright smile at her grandchild. "Come," she said. "Make I show you how to climb a mango tree."

Tranquil, as though she hadn't just tossed her soul case away to be embalmed forever in tar, she turned her back to go and play with the boy, leaving Mother Letty kneeling there, tears coursing through the lines on her ancient face as she watched her friend go.

In less than a year, Acotiren was frail and bent. There was no more climbing trees for her. Her eyes had grown crystalline with cataracts, her hands tremulous, her body sere and unmuscled. One morning she walked into the bush to die and never came out again. But by then her daughter's child, Acotiren's fifth grandchild, was so sure-footed from skinning up gru-gru bef palms and mamapom trees with his nana, that he never, ever fell. Wherever he could plant his feet, he could go. His friends called him Goat.

Big Thrull and the Askin' Man

Max Gladstone

Everybody knows about Thrull. Thrull like legend among us folk—biggest, greenest, meanest, nastiest, and dirtiest of all—with one big difference: legends false, Thrull true. We tell the story of Thrull and the reindeer feast, and the story of Thrull and the Mountain Witches, and the story of how Thrull wrestled Winter and wed Summer on Grandmother Rock, and the story of how Thrull broke Stone Peak making love, but the best story I know, that the story of Thrull and the Askin' Man. Now pour some hard stuff for yourself and pour a glass for me. Set your tape deck down and listen. This tells the day Thrull got smart.

Thrull not so slow as a box of rocks but not so fast as a snail neither. This story tells Thrull after she had two eyes again, one big and green as usual, the other small and sharp and red—but this not the story of how Thrull lost her eye and took another in its place. Those two stories got joy to offer, and someday I'll show you the graves that mark them true. But now I tell a better story.

Back then Thrull live in that grove upslope, the stone lean-to you see when you come over the mountain shoulder. To this day, you part the moss that hangs from the big lintel stone, and you see Thrull's old bed made from thornhollow with sharp bits facing up. You know thornhollow? Sometimes an old oak takes sick, and what's left over looks like oak outside, but inside all hollow and hard, covered in spikes long as your finger and sharp as a hair. Thrull made her bed from a thornhollow oak split open, and she slept on the spikes. When old folk ask Thrull why, she answer, my hide itch, and none so good as to scratch it.

Nobody mind a good brace of nails on their hide every then and now but to sleep on thornhollow, that some hardness. Thrull hardness and hard. Normal folk carve raw meat off the bone before they eat. Thrull eat bones and all. Normal folk draw a hot bath. Thrull bathe in a stew pot she stole from giants back before the grass was grass. She heat it up to boil and jump in. Watch out! Don't get splashed.

But hardness not always hard enough.

So: the tale.

Askin' Man come to town one day, just over that mountain shoulder.

Askin' Man small and slick, don't come up to the young folks' ribs, when he walks, the ground don't shake. Askin' Man step sharp, polite as never, say please and thank you. Askin' Man wear leather shoes and bring a briefcase with a catch. With Askin' Man everything got its catch: his smile and his eye, his voice and his shake. Even his hunger got a hook in it.

If this were a false tale, I'd say Askin' Man came at dawn, but Askin' Man people got their own way of making time, don't look to sun or moon. They got ticks for telling. They listen to gears in their belly, and sometimes when they think no one watches they pull their gears out and dangle them on a chain. Askin' Man people wound by springs. So Askin' Man show up not at dawn but when his gears tell him to show.

Askin' Man ponder us from the mountain shoulder. The young folk all out minding mammoth, and the old folk slow waking. Thrull herself asleep: she spent the last three days and three nights chasing a wandering calf, and when she came back at dusk, she drank six glasses of the hard stuff and punched and fought and cursed till her skin smoked from the fire in her. It took all the young folk together to hold her down and douse her with rainwater from a barrel. When they did, she steamed and slept. They dragged her up to her house and laid her on her bed and left her snoring to shake the moss.

Askin' Man does not go to the village first, not even to drink from the well, kiss the stone, bleed himself for the forest Hungries. Askin' Man turns onto the narrow trail to Thrull–house and stands before the moss curtain. He waits outside and watches the moss blow back and forth with breath and snore. Thrull sleeping still, you see.

Askin' Man not brave, but Askin' Man not dumb neither. Steps through the curtain, soft. Waits. Thrull can see in the dark better than most folk; Askin' Man people cannot see in the dark at all. Askin' Man barely sees or smells or hears. To him, I guess, Thrull–house pitch and black and worrying soft underfoot. Leather shoes make wet sounds in muck. And as Askin' Man eyes open to the dark, he sees mountain Thrull atop her spike bed, her piles of muscle and flesh, the points of her tusks and the glint of her red eye and the big blunt moons of her nails.

Thrull sleeps deeper than the deep mines, but she also got the knack of the trapper's dream, and wakes up quick. Up she rolls and off her spike bed, stands head almost ascrape the roofstone, stares down at this little man.

The Askin' Man starts small.

"Can I have a glass of water?" he says.

He got golden hair, not a line of it out of place. He got smooth skin so thin you could cut it with a knife. He got a voice that roll like honey from the comb. He got thin weak legs and a cold steady brain, but he knows how to ask and what and he listens when people tell him.

This what Thrull sees when she look at Askin' Man: he wears no trophies, no clan mark on his face, Askin' Man alone in the world, cast out, most like, and needing help. All us folk out here in the wildlands got a way: help a cast-out who asks because you never know when you cast-out in their place. Maybe you kill folk on accident while hunting. Maybe you bed with the wrong folk at the wrong time. Maybe Summer plague or Winter cold or Mountain Witches or Great Gaum swallows your town whole and leaves you to weep. Maybe you just fight too much. Thrull herself cast-out twice, taken back three times, she knows the way. If the cast-out don't want your help, you can't make them take it. But they ask, you aid.

Thrull knuckles boulders from her eyes and wanders out into steam-breath cold to get the Askin' Man water. She punches the pond out back until the ice breaks, she fills her waterskin, rumbles back into Thrull-house, and gives Askin' Man what he ask for. Askin' Man arms barely strong enough to hold Thrull's water-skin when full, but he drinks anyway. Water so cold his lips turn blue.

"I'm cold," Askin' Man says. Though his lips blue, he don't shiver. "Can you please build a fire?"

Thrull not the slightest cold, but Thrull traveled far and wide, over the mountains and back again, far enough to know Askin' Man people don't deal so well as folk with winter. She wanders out to the woodpile, bears a few big split logs on each shoulder back home, makes a tinder twigpile in her firepit, and lights it with a mean glare. Askin' Man draws close to the flame. "I'm still cold. Can you build it higher?"

Thrull adds logs until the fire taller than Askin' Man sitting down. Thrull-house too warm for Thrull to sit in comfort now. Askin' Man draws closer, still not shivering, but asks again, "Can you build it even higher?"

Thrull lurches out into the snow to get more logs, and more still after those, until the fire taller than Askin' Man standing up. The smoke makes Thrull sneeze, the flame makes Thrull so warm she sweats and shifts and breathes heavy. Askin' Man never sweats. "Thank you," he says, and smiles a thin smile, and fire dances in the black at the core of his eyes.

Thrull don't ask where he come from. We never ask a cast–off that. Sometimes they say it of themselves, but Askin' Man don't. "You stay with us," Thrull says, "you got to go down to the village and drink the water and kiss the stone and give blood to the Hungries."

"Then I will," Askin' Man says. "Where can I live?"

"You can build yourself a house."

Askin' Man holds out his hands, which are thin as spring branches and break as easy as the rest of him. "It will take me a long time to build a house. Can I stay with you meanwhile?"

Thrull says, "Yes," and thinks, "What harm?"

She brings Askin' Man down the mountain, but Askin' Man walks slow. "Can I ride on your shoulders?"

She hoists him up and takes him to the village, where she shows him the way: to dip his own hand into the well–bucket and drink from his palm, to kneel before the stone, to dig a shallow pit with his hands and shed his own blood there. His thin smooth skin parts easy.

The old folk gather round to watch and wonder. None of them ever traveled so far as Thrull, and back then they don't know much of Askin' Man people. They bare their teeth and jut their tusks and ask Thrull if she brought supper.

"My guest," Thrull says, and the folk draw back. "A cast–off from far away. I seen his people before."

They let Thrull be.

Thrull hoists the Askin' Man on her shoulder and returns uphill, and Askin' Man keep askin'. Where the village stone come from, that glittery rock he kneel to? Up Grandmother Rock, like all that's holy. Anyone herd up that way? No. Water from Grandmother Rock has a foul taste. The grass that grows on her flank gives mammoth shivers and shakes. You won't be around all the time, will you? No, I got herding to do, says Thrull. (Thrull never herd well, she fights with other herdsfolk and lets her mammoth wander loose.) Will the old folk come here and eat me when you're gone? No. You drank the water, knelt to the stone, shed your blood. Good as folk now. And you my guest, long as it takes to build your house. I stand for you. Anybody eat you, they got me to reckon with, and nobody reckons with Thrull. I beat 'em all before, together and separately.

"Good," Askin' Man says.

Now, the way I figure, Askin' Man must have known the answers to all these questions before he came. He chose too well for one who didn't know already: who to approach, how to ask, what to do, and in what order. But some ask questions, questions they already know, so the one who answers has to hear herself say the answers back.

Thrull goes herding. Six big wolves worry at a calf; she busts two of 'em and sends the others running. The hurt calf she hoists on her shoulder and takes to Old Selk who lives in the cave. "Hear you got a small pink guest," Old Selk says as she sews up the calf nice and neat with gut thread. "From a small pink place."

"He asks a lot of questions," Thrull says, "but he don't know the ways. I can help."

"Maybe he expects that."

Old Selk sews the calf whole, and Thrull hoists it back home.

When Thrull comes back that night, the old folk say, "Your guest walking around by Grandmother Rock. We roared at him, but he didn't leave."

Thrull climbs the hill, and says to Askin' Man: "You be careful. Old folk don't like pushing around Grandmother Rock."

"Would they try to hurt me because of it?"

"No. They know my guest and fear my arm."

"If you went to Grandmother Rock and they wanted to stop you, would you let them?"

"No." But Thrull can't see the question's point. "But I don't go to Grandmother Rock."

"I think some things on Grandmother Rock will help me build my house. Can you ask the others to leave me alone when I go there?"

"I can," Thrull says.

"Can you build the fire higher?"

She does. Sweating in the heat, Thrull makes herself dinner.

"Can I have some meat?"

She passes it to him, and he tries to sear it in the fire but burns his hands. Thrull goes to bed. Askin' Man tosses and turns on the ground beside her, cold in his dirty gray suit.

The second day Thrull tells the old folk to give Askin' Man room to go about his way even if he go to Grandmother Rock. They growl, but she growls back—and then she marches off to herd. One big cow takes sick, and she leads it to Old Selk in the cave. "Hear the old folk grumbling about you, Thrull."

"They grumble," Thrull says. "But my Askin' Man don't ask for anything but a little help. And anyways he sleeps under my roof."

Old Selk scratches the tip of her tusk. "'Ware,' she says, "that little helps don't turn large." She draws the cow's sick with a poultice of death's-eye root and vinegar, and Thrull leads the cow away.

When Thrull comes home that night, the old folk catch her on the path and say, "Your guest showed other pink ones the way to Grandmother Rock. We chased 'em off, but we didn't eat 'em."

Thrull climbs the hill, and says to Askin' Man: "You bring friends?"

"Should I not?" Askin' Man replies.

"You under my roof," Thrull says. "Your friends, not so."

"They will not stay here," the Askin' Man says. "Can they merely pass through tomorrow and leave, carrying whatever they may carry on their backs?"

"I'll tell the old folk," Thrull says.

Again the Askin' Man asks for meat, and again Thrull gives him some, and again he burns his fingers trying to sear it for himself. He goes down hungry and sleeps uneasy on cold hard ground.

The third day Thrull tells the old folk to let Askin' Man's friends through with whatever they carry on their backs, and the old folk roar. But Thrull asks again and roars louder, and they don't roar back.

After that fight, Thrull reaches her herd late, too late: while she's gone a great old bull stumbles into a Slitherking nest, gets coiled up and crushed. Thrull follows the screams. Slitherking tries to catch Thrull in his coils, but Thrull waits until his mouth draws near, rips a Slitherking tooth out his jaw, and pierces that tooth through Slitherking's eye. She burns the bull mammoth and drags Slitherking through the forest to Old Selk's cave.

Old Selk charms the poison from Slitherking fangs one gland at a time like drawing moth-silk. "You got to watch when answering questions," she says. "Some folk have a question behind their question, a need behind their need. They don't tell you why they ask."

Thrull frowns and shifts where she sits. "Simple answers always best."

About that time, Grandmother Rock blows up.

Thrull and Old Selk see it, hear it, miles away: that big dark peak just snaps in half, and there's a bright light and a brighter noise after the light. The whole slope slides off, and Grandmother Rock no more.

Thrull runs back through the woods. She jumps gorges and gullies, crashes through briars, and busts down tree trunks until she reaches the wreck of Grandmother. And when Thrull crashes from the woods, what does she see but a whole pile of Askin' Man people picking through the rubble, finding stones with shine to 'em, tossing 'em in packs, carting 'em away on their backs. Thrull wrestled Winter and wed Summer on the slopes that were those stones, but now they just pieces, some in bags, some tossed away.

Thrull roars, and Askin' Man people scatter and scramble; but Askin' Man himself comes up and says, "What you on about, Thrull? We got a deal, right? You said my friends could come through and away, carrying only what they got on their backs. Didn't you say that?"

"I did. But you didn't say you would break Grandmother Rock."

"I'm sorry," he says, though he doesn't sound sorry. "I didn't know it was important to you. I'm new here. Did you say I shouldn't?"

Thrull shakes her head, amazed by now. Grandmother Rock has hung over her head every dawn for all her years, and now she lies in pieces. "Why would I say something like that? Why would you think to do this?"

"These rocks will help me build my house," Askin' Man says. "They like rocks like these down on the other side of the mountain, and they trade well for them. You said you'd help me build my house, didn't you?" She doesn't answer. "Didn't you?" That time his question don't have much question to it.

"Yes," she says.

"I want to build such a house," he says, "as no one's ever seen before. I can sell these rocks for such a sum and build a tower so high angels will come rest on the balcony."

Thrull sits down, amazed. She never thought like this before. She wants to hit Askin' Man and kill him and eat him, but Askin' Man still her guest.

The earth rumbles, and the old folk come. They roar and howl and swing their clubs.

Foam-mouthed and red-eyed, Thrull rises up. She swings her club and screams them off, and they fall back.

Askin' Man, you see, still Thrull's guest. He lacks a house of his own. And what a guest asks, Thrull have to give. That's the way.

Three times the old folk rush the hill, and three times Thrull throws them back, roaring to shake the mountainside, while the Askin' Man watches and smiles.

After the old folk's third rush fails, Thrull falls into the snow and does not weep.

She thinks first: kill the Askin' Man.

But no—can't break the guest way, and Askin' Man a guest.

She thinks second: stop him from doing what he wants.

But no—Askin' Man knows how to ask and what he ask, so long as it's not killing or word–breaking, Thrull can't refuse because Askin' Man a guest.

She thinks third: *You got to watch when answering questions. Some folk have a question behind their question, a need behind their need.*

Thrull waits in her house for Askin' Man that night.

Soon as Askin' Man steps through the moss curtain, Thrull says: "Askin' Man, I fix you some dinner. You want it?"

And she holds out a platter to Askin' Man: a match to hers, a slab of Slitherking, scale and bones and all.

Now Askin' Man, he got to take it and eat it because if he don't, he not Thrull's guest anymore. So he eat, bones and all.

Slitherking flesh pretty vile even for Thrull, rancidish meat and sharpish scales, but Askin' Man brave. He tenses his stomach, and he bites in; and he thinks, unless I miss my guess, about the piles of gold to come his way when he get back to Askin' Man people. Scales cut his mouth, but he swallows them. Meat gags him, but he swallows it, too. Bones, he crushes between his teeth, bite by bite.

Thrull watches.

"I see you sleep rough on the ground," Thrull says. "Why don't you sleep in my bed tonight? Comfiest in the village."

Comfiest for Thrull, you know.

Askin' Man goes paler than he is, but he says "yes," in the end because if he don't, he not Thrull's guest anymore.

But Askin' Man smart. "I'm cold," he says, and, "can I have furs to wrap myself in?"

And Thrull got no way for it but to give him furs. He wraps himself head to toe, then asks for more and more after until he got a mattress of fur to lay atop Thrull's thornhollow bed. Even so, the spikes jut through the furs until they rest right against his skin. Askin' Man sleeps fitful that night and bleeds. Thrull sleep on soft ground between Askin' Man and the door.

Thrull wakes up early next morning to get ready.

"Askin' Man," she says when Askin' Man just waking, "I been far and wide, over the mountains and back again, and I know your people like to stay clean."

Oh, I see you maybe heard this part before.

Well, let me tell the rest anyway.

"I made you a bath," Thrull says, "in my very own tub." Which as anyfolk knows is the highest honor one of us can give a guest. Any fool can get a pile of furs, but a drawn bath's a thing of work and art. Askin' Man follows Thrull through the moss curtain. The giants' stew-pot has a full roil on, and a fire blazes beneath. Thrull already added carrots and turnips and parsnips and mallowroot and witchgrass and salt. She tests the boiling stock with her finger, just like this, and licks it clean, like that. "The water's fine."

Askin' Man looks to the stew-pot and looks to the tree line.

"Won't you have a bath?" Thrull asks Askin' Man.

Askin' Man tries. Won't nobody not give him that much. Askin' Man reaches his pink hand out; and it trembles over the stewpot bath, and at last, at last, he forces it into the water.

But he pulls his hand out as soon as it goes in and screams.

Then he meets Thrull's eyes, the big ol' green one, and the smaller red.

He runs for the tree line.

He don't make it far.

Thrull had much answerin' to do that day, and for a long time after the folk shunned her well; but the story of how Small Gram Got Thrull Talking ain't this story.

Now, friend. You came here to ask about Thrull. And when I asked you why, you talked some about the folk and how we've lasted so long while so much changes all 'round. I don't know as this story has any whats and whys inside, but if you want them, maybe they're there to find. Maybe we mind our ways well, but we mind 'em deep. Maybe we learn from our mistakes.

Not always. But I'll tell those stories later.

Now: did you want to ask another question?

The Language of Knives

Haralambi Markov

A long, silent day awaits you and your daughter as you prepare to cut your husband's body. You remove organs from flesh, flesh from bones, bones from tendons—all ingredients for the cake you're making, the heavy price of admission for an afterlife you pay your gods; a proper send-off for the greatest of all warriors to walk the lands.

The Baking Chamber feels small with two people inside even though you've spent a month with your daughter as part of her apprenticeship. You feel irritated at having to share this moment, but this is a big day for your daughter. You steal a glance at her. See how imposing she looks in her ramie garments the color of a blood moon, how well the leather apron made from changeling hide sits on her.

You work in silence, as the ritual demands, and your breath hisses as you both twist off the aquamarine top of the purification vat. Your husband floats to the top of the thick, translucent waters, peaceful and tender. You hold your breath, aching to lean over and kiss him one more time—but that is forbidden. His body is now sacred, and you are not. You've seen him sleep, his powerful chest rising and falling, his breath a harbinger of summer storms. The purification bath makes it easy to pull him up and slide him onto the table where the budding dawn seeping from the skylight above illuminates his transmogrification, his ascent. His skin has taken a rich pomegranate hue. His hair is a stark mountaintop white.

You raise your head to study your daughter's reaction at seeing her father since his wake. You study her face, suspicious of any muscle that might twitch and break the fine mask made of fermented butcher broom berries and dried water mint grown in marshes where men have drowned. It's a paste worn out of respect and a protection from those you serve. You scrutinize her eyes for tears, her hair and eyebrows waxed slick for any sign of dishevelment.

The purity of the body matters most. A single tear can sour the offering. A single hair can spoil the soul being presented to the gods ... what a refined palate they have. But your daughter wears a stone face. Her eyes are opaque; her body is poised as if this were the easiest thing in the world to do. The ceramic knife you've shaped and baked yourself sits like a natural extension of her arm.

You remember what it took you to bake your own mother into a cake. No matter how many times you performed the ritual under her guidance, nothing prepared you for the moment when you saw her body on the table. Perhaps you can teach your daughter to love your art. Perhaps she belongs by your side as a Cake Maker even though you pride yourself on not needing any help. Perhaps she hasn't agreed to this apprenticeship only out of grief. Perhaps, perhaps ...

Your heart prickles at seeing her this accomplished after a single lunar cycle. A part of you, a part you take no pride in, wants her to struggle through her examination, struggle to the point where her eyes beg you to help her. You would like to forgive her for her incapability, the way you did back when she was a child. You want her to need you—the way she needed your husband for so many years.

No. Treat him like any other. Let your skill guide you. You take your knife and shave the hair on your husband's left arm with the softest touch.

You remove every single hair on his body to use for kindling for the fire you will build to dry his bones, separating a small handful of the longest hairs for the decoration, then incise the tip of his little finger to separate skin from muscle.

Your daughter mirrors your movements. She, too, is fluent in the language of knives.

The palms and feet are the hardest to skin, as if the body fights to stay intact and keep its grip on this realm. You struggle at first but then work the knife without effort. As you lift the softly stretching tissue, you see the countless scars that punctuated his life—the numerous cuts that crisscross his hands and shoulders from when he challenged the sword dancers in Aeno; the coin-shaped scars where arrowheads pierced his chest during their voyage through the Sear of Spires in the misty North; the burn marks across his left hip from the leg hairs of the fire titan, Hragurie. You have collected your own scars on your journeys through the forgotten places of this world, and those scars ache now, the pain kindled by your loss.

After you place your husband's skin in a special aventurine bowl, you take to the muscle—that glorious muscle you've seen shift and contract in great swings of his dancing axe while you sing your curses and charms alongside him in battle. Even the exposed redness of him is rich with memories, and you do everything in your power not to choke as you strip him of his strength. This was the same strength your daughter prized above all else and sought for herself many years ago after your spells and teachings grew insufficient for her. This was the same strength she accused you of lacking when you chose your mother's calling, retired your staff from battle, and chose to live preparing the dead for their passing.

Weak. The word still tastes bitter with her accusation. How can you leave him? How can you leave us? You're a selfish little man.

You watch her as you work until there is nothing left but bones stripped clean, all the organs in their respective jars and bowls. Does she regret the words now as she works by your side? Has she seen your burden yet? Has she understood your choice? Will she be the one to handle your body once you pass away?

You try to guess the answer from her face, but you find no solace and no answer. Not when you extract the fat from your husband's skin, not when you mince his flesh and muscle, not when you puree his organs and cut his intestines into tiny strips you leave to dry. Your daughter excels in this preparatory work—her blade is swift, precise, and gentle.

How can she not? After all, she is a gift from the gods. A gift given to two lovers who thought they could never have a child on their own. A miracle. The completion you sought after in your youth; a honey-tinged bliss that filled you with warmth. But as with all good things, your bliss waxed and waned as you realized: all children have favorites.

You learned how miracles can hurt.

You align his bones on the metal tray that goes into the hungry oven. You hold his skull in your hands and rub the sides where his ears once were. You look deep into the sockets where once eyes of dark brown would stare back into you.

His clavicle passes your fingers. You remember the kisses you planted on his shoulder when it used to be flesh. You position his rib cage, and you can still hear his heartbeat—a rumble in his chest the first time you lay together after barely surviving an onslaught of skinwalkers, a celebration of life. You remember that heart racing as it did in your years as young men when vitality kept you both up until dawn. You remember it beating quietly in his later years when you were content and your bodies fit perfectly together—the alchemy of flesh you have now lost.

You deposit every shared memory in his bones and then load the tray in the oven and slam shut the metal door.

Behind you, your daughter stands like a shadow, perfect in her apprentice robes. Not a single crease disfigures the contours of her pants and jacket. Not a single stain mars her apron.

She stares at you. She judges you.

She is perfection.

You wish you could leave her and crawl in the oven with your husband.

Flesh, blood, and gristle do not make a cake easily, yet the Cake Maker has to wield these basic ingredients. Any misstep leads to failure, so you watch closely during your daughter's examination, but she completes each task with effortless grace.

She crushes your husband's bones to flour with conviction.

Your daughter mixes the dough of blood, fat, and bone flour, and you assist her. You hear your knuckles and fingers pop as you knead the hard dough, but hers move without a sound—fast and agile as they shape the round cakes.

Your daughter works over the flesh and organs until all you can see is a pale scarlet cream with the faint scent of iron while you crush the honey crystals that will allow for the spirit to be digested by the gods. You wonder if she is doing this to prove how superior she is to you—to demonstrate how easy it is to lock yourself into a bakery with the dead. You wonder how to explain that you never burnt as brightly as your husband, that you don't need to chase legends and charge into battle.

You wonder how to tell her that she is your greatest adventure, that you gave her most of the magic you had left.

Layer by layer, your husband is transformed into a cake. Not a single bit of him is lost. You pull away the skin on top and connect the pieces with threads from his hair. The sun turns the rich shade of lavender and calendula.

You cover the translucent skin with the dried blood drops you extracted before you placed the body in the purification vat and glazed it with the plasma. Now all that remains is to tell your husband's story in the language every Cake Maker knows—the language you've now taught your daughter.

You wonder whether she will blame you for the death of your husband in writing, the way she did when you told her of his death.

Your stillness killed him. You had to force him to stay, to give up his axe. Now he's dead in his sleep. Is this what you wanted? Have him all to yourself? You couldn't let him die out on the road.

Oh, how she screamed that day—her voice as unforgiving as

thunder. Her screaming still reverberates through you. You're afraid of what she's going to tell the gods.

You both write. You cut and bend the dried strips of intestines into runes, and you gently push them so they sink into the glazed skin and hold.

You write his early story. His childhood, his early feats, the mythology of your love. How you got your daughter. She tells the other half of your husband's myth—how he trained her in every single weapon known to man, how they journeyed the world over to honor the gods.

Her work doesn't mention you at all.

You rest your fingers, throbbing with pain from your manipulations. You have completed the last of your husband's tale. You have written in the language of meat and bones and satisfied the gods' hunger. You hope they will nod with approval as their tongues roll around the cooked flesh and swallow your sentences and your tether to life.

Your daughter swims into focus as she takes her position across the table, your husband between you, and joins you for the spell. He remains the barrier you can't overcome even in death. As you begin to speak, you're startled to hear her voice rise with yours. You mutter the incantation, and her lips are your reflection; but while you caress the words, coaxing their magic into being, she cuts them into existence so the veil you will place around the cake spills like silk on your end and crusts on hers. The two halves shimmer in blue feylight, entwine into each other, and the deed is done.

You have said your farewell better than you did when you first saw him dead. Some dam inside you breaks. Exhaustion wipes away your strength, and you feel your age, first in the trembling in your hands, then in the creaking in your knees as you turn your back and measure your steps, so you don't disturb the air—a retreat as slow as young winter frost.

Outside the Bakery, your breath catches. Your scream is a living thing that squirms inside your throat and digs into the hidden recesses of your lungs. Your tears wash the dry mask from your cheeks.

Your daughter takes your hand gently with the unspoken understanding only shared loss births, and you search for her gaze. You search for the flat, dull realization that weighs down the soul. You search for yourself in her eyes, but all you see is your husband—his flame now a wildfire that has swallowed every part of you. She looks at you as a person who has lost the only life she had ever known, pained and furious, and you pat her hand and kiss her forehead, her skin stinging against your lips. When confusion pulls her face together, her features lined with fissures in her protective mask, you shake your head.

"The gods praise your skill and technique. They praise your steady hand and precision, but they have no use of your hands in the Bakery." The words roll out with difficulty—a thorn vine you lacerate your whole being with as you force yourself to reject your daughter. Yes, she can follow your path, but what good would that do?

"You honor me greatly." Anger tinges her response, but fights in these holy places father only misfortune, so her voice is low and even. You are relieved to hear sincerity in her fury, desire in her voice to dedicate herself to your calling.

You want to keep her here where she won't leave. Your tongue itches with every lie you can bind her with, spells you've learned from gods that are not your own, hollow her out, and hold onto her even if such acts could end your life. You reconsider and instead hold onto her earnest reaction. You have grown to an age where even intent will suffice.

"It's not an honor to answer your child's yearning." You maintain respectability, keep with the tradition, but still you lean in with all the weight of death tied to you like stones; and you whisper. "I have told the story of your father in blood and gristle as I have with many others. As I will continue to tell every story as best as I can until I myself end in the hands of a Cake Maker. But you can continue writing your father's story outside the temple where your knife strokes have a meaning.

"Run. Run toward the mountains and rivers, sword in your hand and bow on your back. Run toward life. That is where you will find your father."

Now it is she who is crying. You embrace her, the memory of doing so in her childhood alive inside your bones, and she hugs you back as a babe full of needing and vulnerable. But she is no longer a child—the muscles underneath her robes roll with the might of a river—so you usher her out to a life you have long since traded away.

Her steps still echo in the room outside the Baking Chamber as you reapply the coating to your face from the tiny, crystal jars. You see yourself: a grey, tired man who touched death more times than he ever touched his husband.

Your last task is to bring the cake to where the Mouth awaits, its vines and branches shaking, aglow with iridescence. There, the gods will entwine their appendages around your offering, suck it in, close, and digest. Relief overcomes you, and you sigh.

Yes, it's been a long day since you and your daughter cut your husband's body open. You reenter the Baking Chamber and push the cake onto the cart.

The Good Matter

Nene Ormes

"You see," Gustav said to the woman in the armchair, "relics are hard to come by these days, so many turn out to be forgeries or distortions rather than the real thing. And it's not as if there are that many new saints to collect from." He poured the tea for himself and his guest, the thin bone china making discreet tinkling noises as he set each cup and saucer down on the table. "You might say that goodness has fallen out of fashion."

They sat in armchairs angled towards each other with a small table filling the space between them. The room was illuminated by candles on side tables and the soft backlight from the wall-mounted glass display cases containing his prized possessions.

The woman in the other armchair—she had only given her first name, Eve—reached for her cup with a gloved hand and sipped her tea. "I wouldn't say that goodness has ever been in fashion," she said, "but that does make it even more unique when it appears, wouldn't you say?"

She briefly looked Gustav straight in the eye before turning her attention to the room itself.

It was a room worthy of study, if he said so himself, hidden at the back of the antique store and filled with things of great variation, but at this moment the one feature of the room that interested him was his guest and what she'd brought.

Eve was impeccably dressed, her shoes beautifully uncomfortable and the stockings opaque. She had let him take her coat but had kept her gloves and scarf on, and they complimented her suit nicely. A single strand of pearls lay on her collarbones and moved when she swallowed. It was a serious mode of dress for a serious transaction.

Keeping her gloves and scarf on could be a display of her ability, or it could be a courtesy, to keep him from accidentally touching her.

No matter her attire or the intriguing question of her abilities, Gustav felt his eyes return to the briefcase at her feet, and he trembled. The mere thought of the contents of that case and the possibility inside made his mouth dry and sucked at his attention.

But this moment had to be savoured. The possible end of a quest, the treasure hunter's excitement before opening the vault and catching the first glitter of treasure.

Or of dust.

There really was no telling which it would be until he had his ungloved hands on it.

Her legs, next to the case, uncrossed, stretched, and crossed again, the movement pulling him out of his reverie. With effort he lifted his eyes to hers again. She was watching him, one well-painted eyebrow cocked.

Eve did not tremble. A smile formed on her lips, the first since entering the antique shop, and he was sure she had watched him as he gazed at the case.

He couldn't help but blush and hope against hope that she hadn't noticed. Like a young, eager lover, he thought, amused and embarrassed at himself.

"You could have a closer look at my collection, if you want to." Gustav nodded towards the glass displays set into the walls. "I think I may have a couple of artefacts that could be of interest to you or your client, even if most of them are of a more personal value."

She rose in one fluid movement, her poise pure elegance, like a ballet dancer. Her bearing made Gustav straighten in his chair.

She made a circuit of the room. Each case got a fair glance, and some made her tilt her head a bit; but she didn't ask about any of them. Not about the broken fan open to show its fractured ribs, not the child-sized dinner set in pale blue, not the bell on its stand even though that case was open. No, it was obvious after a moment that she gravitated towards the last glass case, her face turned so that she missed seeing the glass orb and the verdigrised bronze belt buckle. She stopped in front of the obsidian dagger.

"I assume it's authentic." It wasn't a question, but Gustav nodded anyway, not that she looked at him. "May I open it?" she asked.

He murmured a consent and held his breath when she moved the door to one side. The knife was displayed on a pink silk cushion, and the greenish-black glass had an inviting shine in stark contrast to the jagged saw teeth punched into the blade.

The hair on his arms stood on end. Gustav had only touched the thing once to verify its age and value and would never do so again.

She placed her gloved hand on the blade, exhaled, and withdrew it. With languid movements she took off her glove one finger at a time. Very slowly, she touched the edge of the blade with her index finger.

From the armchair Gustav could see waves of shivers run through her body, her cheeks flushed and her back arched slightly. She pulled away reluctantly, he thought, and turned her back to him. A few moments passed. Gustav tried to not show any reaction to her heavy breathing and the struggle to regain control over it and pretended not to notice how she twisted the glove between her hands over and over again. He knew something of how it felt and would've liked privacy himself.

"I dare say that you have at least one item that my client might be interested in." Eve's voice, less calm than before, reminded him of a smoky whisky, rough but still warm.

He cleared his throat. "Would you like some more tea?"

"Please. Or if you have something stronger."

Gustav opened a bottle of cognac and poured the amber liquid into two perfect nineteenth-century crystal glasses. He handed her one of them.

"Now I can't promise that this is the very cognac that they drank at court in the day, but it is possible. The glasses come from the very table of Emperor Napoleon. They came to Sweden by way of his steward and ended up with me as part of a gambling debt. Together, they make for the most delightful experience."

He watched her expectantly. Would he be right? Was she like him? Would she feel the passing of the decades back to the engraver who had patiently and proudly worked each glass by hand? Or would she feel something else?

After what seemed like an eternity, she reached towards the glass and grabbed it by its foot. She held it in three fingertips, her hand unsteady as she lifted the glass to her lips.

Gustav felt a knot in his gut and could not take his eyes off her. The cognac passed the rim of the glass, and she swallowed, looking beyond the confines of his room.

If he had been less focused on her, he would never have noticed her body going limp, her arm losing strength and almost dropping the glass. He quickly stretched over the table, grabbed her by the elbow, and placed his other hand under the glass. Without touching her skin.

"You didn't get these thanks to a gambling debt," Eve said. "The financial dilemma was caused by other vices."

"But ..."

"Trust me, knowing people's darkest secrets is my ... specialty."

"Oh, I am so sorry!" Gustav felt rather slow. He really should've guessed, after the knife. "I didn't mean for you to go through something like that without due warning ..."

She smiled at him again, warmly. "Don't worry. My 'gift' doesn't trouble me. I just thought that you ought to know."

Without withdrawing her arm from Gustav's firm grip, she twisted her wrist to move the glass to her lips again and touched the rim with her tongue. It was soft, pink, and moist from the cognac. He swallowed hard.

"He was quite a character, your nobleman." Her voice had a dreamy quality. "Deviant, depraved, and ruthless. Most delightful."

As she set down the glass, she let her hand travel along his sleeve to the cuff where she rested it and looked at him.

"Would you be willing to negotiate the knife for what I have brought? Or should we leave it for another time?"

"Ah ... yes. I mean, let's have a look at the item before we discuss that, shall we?"

Gustav cursed his trembling voice and the dryness of his throat as she placed the briefcase on the table and opened it. Set into the middle of the padding was a small box. She took it out, closed the briefcase, and placed the box on the table before taking a small key from her jacket pocket and unlocking it.

"Now I would like to see the payment before proceeding."

Gustav retrieved a large carton box from the sideboard and opened the lid. With two sets of tweezers, he peeled back the tissue paper inside to reveal a faded, embroidered waistcoat.

"One piece of clothing worn by Marquis de Sade." He couldn't control the wave of shivers going up his arm.

"Excellent." Eve opened the box. "Mother Teresa's headcloth. Guaranteed authenticity."

Gustav could barely think straight. His ears were buzzing, and his fingertips itched. Would he finally experience true goodness? Unaware of his movements, he reached for the box and was surprised when she grabbed him by the arm.

"I would prefer that we finalised this transaction first. We don't want to risk damaging any future dealings between us, do we?"

He, reluctantly and with some difficulty, tore his attention from the tempting glimpse of white. It was no more than a piece of fabric, but it had been part of something bigger. A wholeness. A life.

"Of course."

"You contacted my client through an agent and made an agreement regarding Mother Teresa's headcloth, in part or whole, in exchange for clothing worn by Marquis de Sade, of which you have given previous proof of authenticity." She placed a small stack of documents on the table. "As per the agreement, these documents give a detailed account of all locations that the headcloth has passed through since Mother Teresa last took it off. The people who have handled it have been kept anonymous for ... business purposes. That, too, is in accordance with the agreement."

Gustav scanned the documents, not really caring, and nodded, looking up at her. "Everything seems to be in order."

"Good." She slid the box over to him, and for a brief moment, her fingers touched the back of his hand. Gustav caught a short glimpse of an obsidian blade caressing a woman's leg, over a stocking and naked skin before cutting a garter in one swift motion.

When the vision had faded, he found her sitting with her legs primly crossed and her gaze fixed on the knife display.

"Ah, yes, about the knife ... Perhaps we could reach an agreement?"

"Perhaps." She smiled warmly at him as she pulled her glove back on, wrapped up the large box, and stood up. "But I can see that your mind is elsewhere, and that knife deserves complete attention, wouldn't you say?"

Since Gustav could not let the glimpse of white out of his mind, he had nothing to say, but her comment still made his mouth go dry. As she stood, Gustav rose immediately, got her coat, and held it out for her.

"It has been a pleasure doing business with you. I do hope to see you again soon."

That was a weak version of what he would've liked to say, but he stumbled over even that.

He knew that she had seen his desire at the same time as he had seen the vision of hers. So he made an effort to quiet his mind and think of nothing but the woman in front of him. Of her ability, of the knife, of everything that two people with such similar, but still opposite, gifts could have to offer one another. She stood very still as he put the coat over her shoulders, and with her subtle scent in his nostrils, he caressed the skin right above her pearls with the tips of his fingers. She gasped and stepped away.

"I believe we will meet again," her voice rough around the edges, "soon."

Without a second glance she took the large parcel and walked out of his sanctuary. He heard the chiming doorbell over the front door as she left the shop.

Gustav sat down again, reached for the box, and set it on his lap.

The wood was cool and smooth. He made himself sit with it just so, closed, for a little while. If this was to be the end of his quest, he wanted to treasure this moment of anticipation. And if not?

Well, there was only one way to know.

With trembling fingers he opened the lid, gripped the delicate fabric, and lost himself. The world fell away and turned into minute details: vegetable fibres, processing, weaving, sewing, then the daily use, the gentle touch of hands shrivelled with age. Snapshots of prayers, wishes, and pleas for mercy flickered by. Desperation, rapture, deep love. Worship. Kindness. Mild and tired. It filled him to the brim, and he flowed over.

But it was not what he had been looking for.

Not a pure, unadulterated feeling of goodness.

Gustav wiped his cheeks with the backs of his hands, stroking away the tears that kept rolling, before he carefully put the fabric back in its box and locked it.

Better luck next time, he thought, draining the last drops of cognac from her glass.

No Other City

Ng Yi-Sheng

Listen: next Monday at four-thirty p.m. Singapore will disappear. The entire island, its earth and its earthworks, its rivers and reservoirs, its megamalls and museums will vanish, poof, like so much gun smoke. Its flora and fauna, too: its orchards and orioles, its rain trees and roaches, its mosquitoes and monkeys. Its people also: citizens of all creeds and races, permanent residents, guest workers, tourists, illegal aliens. Gone in the twinkling of that old proverbial eye.

You, of course, will be spared. You'll have accepted a job then, in Beijing or Baltimore or Bengaluru, so you'll be only halfway puzzled when you start to notice the silence of half your Facebook friends. You'll double-click on their profiles, see that none of them have updates beyond that specific timestamp, click around to the Singapore-hosted sites, the *Straits Times* and the *Temasek Review*, and discover that most of them are down, down, down.

What the hell, you'll think. You'll try e-mailing your missing compadres. No reply. You'll try Facebook messages and phone calls and Twitter. Nothing. You'll start to worry, especially when the few of them seconded to faraway franchises or on holiday in the Gold Coast tweet you back, saying they're hitting the same silent wall.

Then finally, you'll get through to an ex-girlfriend who moved across the straits to Johor Bahru for the cheaper rent and commuted every day, and she'll send you the pics: the Causeways, once financial lifelines to the heart of the Malayan peninsula, now ending on cliffhanging stubs.

Water beneath. Bridges to nowhere.

Why isn't this on CNN? You'll turn on the TV, click, panicked. But the same placid faces on BBC, Fox, Al-Jazeera, will stare back, reciting the old schtick about crises in the Middle East and DC and Brussels. You'll pick up a shoe as if to hurl it angrily at the screen, but then you'll stop yourself, remembering how much the TV cost. You're still rational. You're still a Singaporean at heart, after all.

In the evening, you'll ask your friends. The cool black Frenchman in IT, the quiet Korean lady in marketing. They'll stare at you, confused. Singapore? Never heard of it. Then where am I from? you'll ask, furious. And they'll blink back, chewing their udon, and say, Somewhere in China? You ought to splash the hot green tea in their faces, storm out of the ramen shop, never to return. But you don't. You go back to your noodles. You can't afford to lose any more friends. Not now.

You'll go quiet. You'll return to work as per normal, keep your head down, keep your nose clean, think as little as possible. Whenever the worm of panic creeps along your skin, you'll recall the words they taught you in school during National Education sessions. No one owes us a living. At all costs, you must survive.

The world forgets. Now and then you'll still scan the headlines at the newsstands, but you'll know it's no use: you've been wiped clear from the collective conscious, not even an ink smear left to tell the tale.

It's ridiculous, really. All those billionaire magnates on the island, the maybe trillions of dollars in the federal reserves, the stock exchange, the regional business hubs, the hospitals where Burmese generals and Zimbabwean dictators went for medical treatment. You'll understand how the common man was forgotten, even your half-assed hybrid patchwork culture, your overpriced casino-driven tourist industry. But what about all the genuine bling the country stood for, huh? The international economic thingumajigs? Didn't you matter, at least only for that?

One night, when you really can't help yourself, you'll log into a Reddit forum and compare notes with other survivors. They won't all be Singaporeans, not in the strictest sense. They'll be left behind wives of expatriates, mothers and fathers of lost backpackers, Malaysians and Indonesians and Bruneians who're used to being lied to by the press, all grieving together, all struggling to understand, why, why, why, and also how. A flood à la Atlantis? A rain of fire and brimstone from heaven? Extraterrestrials with tractor beams? The Illuminati? The orang bunian?

There'll still be documents, weirdly enough. Online photos and blogs, books of geography and economics and history. A miniature Merlion in Suzhou, an ersatz HDB town centre in Surabaya. You'll discover a *Cracked* article joking about this, describing it all as the wildest inside joke ever perpetrated in human history—like the extensive Hollywood filmography of Alan Smithee. You'll check Wikipedia. Most entries about the country will be gone. Those that remain will have been edited to fit the genre of mythos like the geography of the DiscWorld, the economy of Westeros.

Months will pass. Facebook and LinkedIn will start to get rid of what it calls dead accounts. You'll save what photos of your friends you can. You're grateful for that digital print of your mum and dad you developed at Beach Road Market just to make them happy. You'll wonder if you should hold funeral rites for them, but then everyone you used to know deserves something. Maybe you should donate to a house of worship in their name.

One day, your Reddit group will suggest meet-ups in meatspace. None of them will be happening nearby: they'll be in places like London, Hong Kong, NYC. You'll chew on this a while. You'll have tons of unused vacation time, and hell knows you won't be flying back home anytime soon, given that home isn't there anymore. You'll cave in. You'll book a ticket.

You'll pack your bags. Amazingly enough, your passport will work. Thuggish immigration officers will sometimes lock countrymen up and question them for hours, but mostly border controls will have decided it's the sign of some special diplomatic club. They'll usher you through the airport's speediest lanes.

Then you'll arrive at the hotel. A three-star affair: not exactly shabby, but the cabbie wouldn't have known where to take you without an address. You'll check in. You'll check out the conference room. You'll realise to your delight that there's a table piled high with catered Malaysian food. You'll go over and immediately stuff your face with satay, ketupat, sayur lodeh, laksa, beehoon, Hainanese chicken rice, teh tarik, red bean soup. You'll admit to yourself, grudgingly, that the Malaysians always made it better.

Into your third helping, you'll realise there are other people in the room, sipping rose syrup drink. They'll be speaking Singlish: the kind of singsong broken tones with mixed-in Hokkien vocab that you won't have heard since maybe the Jurassic. They'll be reminiscing about public transport, 4-D, the New Paper, Jack Neo films, the army, all the terrible things you never thought you'd miss. You'll start to tear up. They'll see you. They'll make room for you. You'll introduce yourself awkwardly. And you'll sit down in the circle, find yourself slipping into that half-forgotten patois yourself.

One of the guys at the table will be different. He'll be white, really white. Blond hair, blue eyes, skin so pale you'll be able to see the pink and violet veins in it. When the conversation moves his way, he'll tell everyone he's never actually been to Singapore. He'd thought about doing a semester abroad there in college but went to Osaka instead.

Backpacked around the Philippines once, transited through Kuala Lumpur.

He's a journalist now, he'll say, and he's hot on the trail of this story, trying to understand what happened. You and the others will exchange glances. You'd thought you'd feel weird about this, like your inner sanctum's been invaded, but instead it's a relief. He's outside confirmation. You're not the crazy ones. He's the proof.

Over Saturday and Sunday there'll be presentations by ancient professors, heritage hobbyists, wild-eyed activists screaming conspiracy. There'll even be an experimental dancer who was stranded in Copenhagen on tour. She'll show off her latest creation: an agglomeration of tai chi, silat, bharatanantyam, hip-hop, and the Great Singapore Workout, which you'll personally think is in bad taste. Now and then there'll be movie screenings by filmmakers you've never heard of. BS Rajhans, Tan Pin Pin, Anthony Chen. You'll note down their names.

The cleaners and waitstaff will sometimes stand by the doors, watching. You'll notice they're avoiding your gaze even when you're sipping brandy and scotch alone in the hotel bar. You'll realise you must appear to them like a peculiar species of nutjob: Young-Earth Creationists, 9/11 Truthers, millenarians. You'll feel sick at their sight. You'll decide to go up and order room service instead.

Then the white guy will come over, the blond guy you met on your first day, and ask if the next barstool is taken. He'll be charming and comforting, and he'll tell you he has a private stash of Tiger beers in his suitcase. You don't normally do this kind of thing, but you'll end up spending the night with him. After all, no one's there to set the rules anymore.

When you get home, or what you might as well call home now, you'll see he's dropped you an e-mail. It'll be him, saying he'll be in your city next month. You'll go ahead and share your number since it's the polite thing to do and because he was tender and considerate and passionate in a way it's been hard to find lately.

You'll see him again, a few times. Over Christmas he'll invite you to meet his family. They'll be lovely. You'll be lovely. You'll cook them fried rice, and they gasp at it, impressed, even though it's burnt at the edges and not salty enough and completely devoid of sambal and green chillies. On his advice, you'll tell them you're from China. His little sister, the irritating grad student who speaks ten languages, will ask, Oh, what part of China? You'll bite your tongue and say she wouldn't have heard of it. He'll squeeze your hand.

● ● ●

Now it's years later. Geopolitically, it'll have become apparent that the world is coping. The role of Southeast Asian financial hub will now be a contest between Bangkok, Jakarta, and, to everyone's surprise, Yangon. Private banking will center itself again in Zurich. The world's biggest port will be Shanghai, followed by good old Rotterdam. When the topic of 21st-century city-states comes up, they'll talk about Dubai and Monaco.

You'll be married to him. It'll have been tricky finding a registry that'd do it, given that you didn't technically have a nationality anymore. But he'll pull a few strings and hire a lawyer he knows. Now you're both Canadian citizens, which was something he'd been wanting for a while. You'll be a handsome couple. Everyone'll say so at the wedding reception.

He'll have kept his promise, by the way. Publishing that story: his exposé on the disappearance of Singapore. He'll even have put out a book about it, *The New Atlantis,* which will hover around the *New York Times* nonfiction best-seller lists for a year. It'll be translated into Mandarin, Japanese, Korean, Arabic, French, Russian, Italian, Spanish, Dutch, Thai, and, for some reason, Finnish. You'll have travelled the world with him on a few book tours, sat in on a few public lectures in Ubud, Busan, and Hay-on-Wye. You'll often appear together in the press, him joking that you're good for his street cred. Sometimes you'll even be wearing something pan-Asian, approximating a national dress.

The Singapore Conferences will be bigger than ever. They're not for survivors anymore, of course: they're for fanboys and fangirls, all clustering together, united by the dream of this fabled utopia that somehow slipped out of existence. A few of the other survivors will have printed autobiographies, memoirs of their hellish experiences—one of them will claim to have been held in a Saudi refugee camp—and when they appear at these events, they'll be immediate stars, signing autographs till their knuckles ache, so luminous with glamour that they could choose any eager young thing in the hotel to be their sex bunny for the night.

At first, you'll be tolerant. But then the cosplay trends will begin. You'll rationalize to yourself that these are mere children: most of them not even born by the day of the vanishing, and yet there'll be something in you that wants to scream every time you see a ginger-haired teenager in an SIA stewardess kebaya or a scrawny

Rasta man in all-whites and orchid garlands sporting a Lee Kuan Yew-style squint.

Then one day, you'll log onto the Internet and discover that they've been writing fan fiction. You spend hours in front of the monitor, unable to stop scrolling through these mad vicarious fantasies of tantric sex on the Singapore Flyer and battles against fire-breathing vampires at Marina Bay Sands. Some of the stories will even have Singlish in them. It's pretty convincing. When your husband gets home and asks what's wrong, you'll start weeping uncontrollably. He'll see the site, look all solemn for a moment, then proceed to dictate an immediate edict to his followers, condemning their actions, alerting them to the distress they've caused you and your fellows, the disrespect to the unmourned victims of one of the 21st century's greatest secret massacres.

But suddenly you can't even bear to be in the same room as him. You'll run into the bathroom and refuse to come out, not even to eat and drink. He'll ask you why, and you'll yell something stupid along the lines of, You don't get it. It's all because of you.

After that, you won't attend the conferences anymore. You won't write that memoir he's always bugged you to work on. You won't help maintain his web page and electronic newsletter. You'll stop posing for cute interracial couple photos. You'll stop cooking your fucking fried rice. You'll stop speaking to him. You'll put in more hours at the office. You'll sleep on opposite sides of the bed.

One night, you'll go through your drawers and find that photo of your parents. They'll look younger than they did before, yet more old-fashioned in their silly turn-of-the-millennium clothes. You'll try and remember what they sounded like and what they would have made of you right now, freezing your ass off in this unholy Canadian winter. You'll light up the fireplace and throw the photo in.

It's rather beautiful how it burns. How the canvas curls and melts and spindles, a cross between wax and paper. The faces of your father and mother will glow bright, then turn sepia and coal-black, crumbling their way once more into brightness.

You'll undress for bed. Tomorrow, you'll think, you will try going native. You'll enroll in a French course even though you don't live in Quebec. You'll stock up on back bacon and maple syrup. You'll even have a go at making your own poutine.

But listen: that morning, at four-thirty a.m., Singapore will reappear. At daybreak you'll find your husband in the kitchen, munching coffee and cornflakes and grumpy over hate mail from your countrymen, who just don't get the parodic genius of his mockumentary novels. You'll find your inbox is full of birthday greetings from long-vanished friends, much older of course, who are annoyed that you haven't written back for so long.

You'll surf the Net, looking for info. Everything and nothing will be there: footage of the island over the last few decades will have magically materialized, representing the changes in politics, society, economy, and architecture. You'll pull up an image, bending your mind around how everything looks different and yet is unmistakably the same.

Then the phone will ring. It's your parents, who're calling to say hello to their grown-up baby. Your husband will put them on speaker and start chattering away with them like an old friend, which he must be, you suppose. You'll brew your own coffee and pour your own cereal, then collapse into your chair, trying to digest it all.

We're booking our tickets to come and see you again, your mother will say. How is Canada, my love?

And your husband will reply, Same old, same old. It's like you never left.

Señora Suerte

Tananarive Due

I hate this place.

Someone got the idea—brilliant or inane, depending on how the meds are tickling my brain that day—to dress up this place with games. Someone thought the general air of Death might smell better with a whiff of Fortune. General collection of losers that we are, it would be nice if someone could win something once in a while. That's the idea.

Brilliant or inane, it truly does not matter. You'd have to live here to see the boldness of the notion. You'd have to be breathing in the urine-soaked air. Picture Fidel's worst prisons with festive shooting galleries—not with real bullets, mind you, but pellets knocking over rows of smiling duckies—and maybe you would get the picture.

Have I mentioned yet that I don't like it here?

I hate this place.

A few years ago, I could have sat you down over a few rounds of mojitos and sifted through other facts that could have been called pertinent, at least at the time: Born in La Habana province outside of Mariel, Cuba. Second of five children. Bank manager in Hialeah, Florida, for thirty years. Married twice, once happily. Widower twice, once unhappily.

Brace yourself: Only child, a son, died in a car crash at seventeen. That was once the defining fact of my existence. A whisper of my son's death, and I got hisses, moans, blinking eyes, tears. I got laid, even. It was a powerful fact. That's Gilberto. His son died. His *only* son. His namesake. (Gilberto. Not Gil. Not Bert, for God's sake. Gilberto.) Gilberto lost two wives and a son, they clucked. What an unlucky man. *Come to me, pobrecito.*

But before I came here, I was a virgin. I thought bad luck was a myth and had vastly underestimated the phrase's meaning in either Spanish (mala suerte) or the English I worked so hard to learn as a young man in my twenties, when I had to begin my life anew. Mala suerte. Now, I live in bad luck's bosom. It suckles me to sleep—that, and the meds. Thank goodness for sleep. My only goal in life is more sleep. I'm so far behind. Raul, in the bed next to mine, sleeps all day, the lucky bastardo. All day, and no one bothers him.

No sleeping for me. When I first arrived, I got trotted around like a poster boy for recovery. *Look at Gilberto, Mrs. Sanchez. He had a stroke only three months ago, and he can stand on his own two feet. Look at Gilberto, Mr. Ortiz. He's already feeding himself with both hands. Look at Gilberto, Mr. Benton. Look at Gilberto.*

The day of the stroke, I had a beautiful dream. No pain, just visions. One minute I'm munching on pastelitos at my favorite Cuban bakery on Flagler, and the next minute I'm at the emergency room. In my dream, I see my first wife, Maritza. The woman had a beautiful face, but I called her El Diablo. She was a horror. When I saw her again, I thought I must be on my way to Hell. So I asked her: "Why were you so unkind?" And she shrugged her shoulders in her awkward, unrefined manner. "I didn't know how to be another way," she said softly. Of course, no? It made sense at the time, so I forgave her. Deep in my heart, I forgave her. I told her I was sorry for the way I danced when her headache turned out to be a brain aneurysm, my problems gone like that. And she smiled. Such a weight was lifted from me!

Then her face became Camilla's. Mi reina. Mi vida. Not as beautiful as Maritza—in her younger years, judged by her face, Camilla had been lonely—but I saw her clean, pure spirit. All kindness. And I understood: As in life, I had to pass my first test, Maritza, to see Camilla again. Perhaps it was Heaven calling for me. She touched my face, and an indescribable feeling bathed me. Better than sex, better than rum, better than music. A feeling we don't find in this world.

The next thing I knew, no Camilla. I was in a hospital room. I could not speak, I could not move the right side of my body. After an eternity, in answer to my prayers for a cessation of misery, I was brought here. So either God has a grudge against me or has no better way to amuse himself. Either way, we don't speak anymore.

Was it not enough I was an exile? Exiled first from my homeland and next from my loved ones? Did I ever complain? When others would have cursed God, I never did. But for this place, God has some answering to do.

There is no excuse.

I hate this place.

Here we are not exiles, engineers, postal workers, grocers, bankers, grandparents, or deserted lovers. No—here we are beds. Sixty beds. This is a place where people come to die when there is no one to take them in, like unwanted mongrels. Most of us are helpless to carry out even the most basic dignities of life, worse than babies. And someone of authority—the new administrator or someone trying to impress him—looked out at this collection of sad human debris and said, "Ah! Let the games begin." So now there is Bingo. B-I-N-G-O, like the gringo children's song.

I can hear you laughing, so you must get the joke. Bingo in Hell's parlor.

"You have a very bad attitude, Gilberto," a young nurse, Antoinette, chides me. No one has taught her not to call her elders by their Christian names, but I tolerate this because she understands the words from my ruined mouth. My translator.

"¿Que? Did I say anything?"

"You don't have to say it. I see it in your face. They like the Bingo. Why come watch others play every day just to make fun? You should play, too."

But she is wrong. I don't come to watch the others play. Only a sadist would be entertained watching scarecrows listing in their wheelchairs, raising trembling fingers when they win, hardly realizing when they are wetting themselves. Does this sound like a sane person's amusement? Yet, it is true. I come every Friday. I wheel myself to the lounge by two p.m. without fail. I am the first one inside, the last one to leave.

But I never win. Remember? Mala suerte. Playing to win would be a waste of my time.

I come for Her. My angel.

Unlike me, she doesn't come every week. Angels cannot be summoned like pizza delivery, and I accept this. But the entire room changes when she walks inside. The light shifts to a bright golden hue, the exact color of twilight. The walls, which are usually growling at us with the promise of suffering, begin to sing.

The first day I saw her, I admit it, I believed it was only the meds at work. At first glance, she seemed to be a typical nurse, invisible in a powder blue uniform that would make any woman seem boyish, white shoes squeaking across the floor, and a name tag that read ROSARIA. Her skin was browned with the echoes of an abuela negra whose African genes kinked her hair into tight brown ringlets she wore like a crown atop her head.

Then I noticed her eyes.

Dios mío, such eyes! Beneath her luxuriant lashes, her eyes are black coffee beans shining like the night itself. I saw her eyes from across the room, and they stole my concentration from the droning call of the Bingo numbers, my hand frozen above my cards. Her eyes held none of the dull dispassion or thinly masked contempt of the other nurses who occasionally gazed upon our pathetic game. Her eyes darted and dashed the way my little Gilberto chased our house cat to and fro when he was small, soaking up every detail about us. Instead of seeing only our tubes and wheelchairs, she lingered on our faces, memorizing our existence, blessing us with personhood.

You can believe me or not, but I swear to what happened next on my dear Camilla's soul: As soon as I noticed her eyes, I gained new eyes myself. Her image changed. I was no longer staring at a nurse in a uniform but a visage who glided across the floor in a sheen of pale light. *Floating*, you see. Her hair was suddenly an impossibly long mane behind her, following her on the floor like a wedding train spun of dark lamb's wool.

She met my eyes and smiled at me. I have seen dying men resuscitated with electric shock, and that sensation can be no more jarring than her eyes. Her gaze shocked me back to life.

No one else at the Bingo game seemed to notice her. Not Pedro, who breathed through oxygen tubes and coughed blood into his handkerchief, making such a racket that it was hard to hear the numbers—not Dixon Washington (or Washington Dixon, I forget which), who always sat with his hand shielding his Bingo cards as if his neighbors could somehow cheat if they saw what Fate had dealt him—not Mrs. Martinez, who dressed up for Bingo games in her fading white lace dress and spring hat as if Bingo days were Easter Sunday—not Stella Rothman, a World War II widow who always cupped her ear to try to hear the numbers, complaining that her hearing aid was made in Japan and therefore wasn't worth a damn— and not Crazy Joe, who called Bingo! every other number even though he was the only one with worse luck than mine.

No one else glanced in the direction of this magnificent creature. Only me. To them, she was a nurse named Rosaria making an obligatory tour to see to it that no one dropped dead at a table. Such a death, after all, might ruin the game.

But she is much more than a nurse. I know that now. Perhaps she is Oyá herself. I have reasons for speaking so. I alone see her. I alone know what she does.

Our game is the perfect place for her to visit undetected. Bingo, you see, is not a game of skill nor of will. There are no true choices— only luck. Each player is issued six cards, so in our game anyone can expect to win at least once even in a fellowship as cursed as ours. During the three hours we play, there are three or four winners. Sometimes more. Not me, of course—winning is not in my makeup—but *usually*. From time to time, even Crazy Joe is right when he claims he has his Bingo numbers lined up. A broken clock tells the time twice a day, after all.

So I do not blame the others for not seeing it as I do. They would have to see *her*.

The first day Rosaria arrived in the Bingo room—the first time her eyes gave me access to the truer vision of her—I watched her glide from table to table, pausing like a honeybee collecting nectar. She lingered over one wheelchair for a time, then moved to the next. And the next. With each person she passed, she seemed to be *listening* for something only her ears could discern. I watched her so closely that I lost my concentration, forgetting the administrator's bored drone as he called the Bingo numbers. How I longed for her!

Not as a woman, mind you. I will confess she is beautiful—with a face that is fine-featured and yet ever-changing, with cheeks as hollow as an Indian princess in one moment and then as full as my Camilla's in the next—but it was not her beauty that commanded my eyes. I have not known hunger in my loins since Camilla left this Earth, and my body no longer craves a woman's touch. But as I watched her, even the first time, all of my heart cried out: Choose me.

Bless me. Save me. Choose me.

But she did not.

Several minutes passed before she made her decision. My eyes had never left her, so I saw the exact moment: She took her hand and rested it across Pedro's shoulder, her lithe fingers weightless. He was so intent on smothering his constant cough in his handkerchief that he never noticed the rare gesture of kindness. But I did. All at once, Pedro's cough went silent.

The visage was gone. And the nurse Rosaria, unnoticed, slipped away to her duties.

But the change that came over Pedro! Without his cough to bedevil him, Pedro sat straighter in his chair with a young man's posture. He marked his cards with fervor, his ears virtually twitching every time a number was called. His pencil flew. I heard him laugh to himself, a sound of boyish joy. On that day, as I witnessed the transformation, I believed the Bingo games were a brilliant stroke and felt my faith in our caretakers renewed. I shared Pedro's sudden belief that he *could* win, and that winning a simple game could matter to creatures such as we.

As I had anticipated, it was only moments before Pedro's voice rose, silencing the room: *"Bingo!"* he called through phlegm. Like a conqueror. He waved his card above his head.

The prizes in our Bingo game are nothing to speak of. What is money to us? The staff gives the winners little tokens—brightly wrapped sugarless candies, postcards of beaches and mountain ranges, photo frames in which to display the evidences of younger days on our nightstands—but winning the game meant everything to Pedro that day. His skin flushed pink. His eyes danced. I never heard him cough again the entire game. When he won the second time, he nearly leaped from his wheelchair.

Pedro was not the only winner that day. But he was the only one *chosen*.

That very night, you see, Pedro died in his sleep. His monitors made no sound to alert the nurses, and later it was discovered that his oxygen machine had been unplugged. His roommate,

Ben Wallenbech, said he slept so soundly that he never heard his neighbor's machine stop.

There was no outraged family to answer to, so the "investigation" amounted mostly to shrugged shoulders and shaking heads. Many speculated that Pedro himself had unplugged his oxygen. Those who had seen him at Bingo recalled his last moment of triumph, saying he chose death on that night because he wanted to leave this world on a winning streak.

After that, I kept a special eye for the nurse, Rosaria. She frequently visited the Bingo games, but I never saw the amazing metamorphosis I saw the day she chose Pedro. I came to believe I had hallucinated or perhaps that I'd simply had a flash of premonition like my Tía Maria, the way I knew in my bones that my little Gilberto would not come home from football practice the night he died.

A week after Pedro's death, I suffered another stroke, one so minor that I did not notice it while it happened. But one morning I realized I could no longer stand and walk even the few steps I had mastered a short time before, the model of recovery. To this day, whenever I try to stand, my legs tremble as if I have no bones.

I can still mark the Bingo cards. But most days for a time after that, I only watched. Even the sight of Rosaria could not cheer me because she never again appeared as she had that day, and I stopped believing in magic.

I lost my spirit of play.

Until a month passed. And everything changed.

The Bingo game was flourishing. A male nurse named Jackson volunteered to be the new caller, and he was so animated that he might have been a preacher at a Baptist church. Jackson made all the difference. The sound of laughter regularly filled our tiny Bingo hall now, ringing through the hallways to the ears of those who were not well enough to participate. But I could not share their laughter.

"Gilberto, your face is gonna be in a permanent frown if you don't practice smiling again," Antoinette told me as she wheeled me into the hall as she always does. "Don't worry, papi. Your legs will grow stronger." Such a sweet, young face to already be such a liar! The truth is plain to me now. I believed their lies even when I fought not to. No one here grows stronger. No one here gets better.

And on that day, when I felt most mired in my helplessness, I saw her again.

This time, I did not even see her as plain-dressed Rosaria, the nurse who came and went without notice. I saw a shadow emerge in the doorway, impossibly long for the lighting from the hall, and at its tip was a large, winding spiral shape I could hardly make sense of.

She followed her shadow into the doorway. This time, she wore her dark hair in thick, ropy shapes splaying from all sides of her head. The largest was an oversized, upright whorl the size of a python that looked as if it weighed several pounds. Her face was obscured behind the light that floated around her like a swampland mist, but how could I mistake her?

This time, I knew. My veins raced with adrenaline.

"We got lucky number O-72, ya'll. That's the year the Dolphins went undefeated, so you know that's lucky. You got O-72, you're a winner," Jackson called on, unaware.

She floated serenely down the rows of tables toward mine. Something blocked my ears suddenly; perhaps my heart itself, silencing everything except its own excited thrashing. If my legs had obeyed me, I would have stood up and fallen to my knees in her path. When she passed only a foot from me, I nearly pissed myself. I smelled Camilla's favorite perfume in her wake, and tears came to my eyes. I opened my mouth to speak, but I had forgotten all language.

"What's that? N-32?" Stella Rothman said, cupping her ear.

"O-72," someone yelled. "Jesus, will you get that thing fixed?"

Stella tugged at her hearing aid. "It's my fault it's made in Japan? Not worth a damn."

The entity did not dally this time as she had the first time I saw her. She went straight to Stella. She glided behind her and laid her hand gently on Stella's shoulder, her fingers like twigs.

"Seventy-two?" Stella said. "Wait a second. Just a second." As she stared at her cards, light brightened her face, erasing her furrowed brow. She had told me once that her life ended the day the telegram from the War Department came; I couldn't remember the last time I had seen her smile. "Seventy-two? I can't believe ... I got it! Bingo!"

Need I tell you? It was only Rosaria who stood behind Stella then, stripped of her magnificent visage. Amidst the groans of disappointment from players who had not been as lucky as Stella, no one saw Rosaria lower her face, hiding her inscrutable eyes. I was the only one who watched the nurse leave, back to her mundane duties.

I was in a state that night, as you can guess. I had less appetite than even this food deserves. I could not sleep. Had I more control of my limbs, I might have taken myself to Stella's room to watch her doorway. To see the outcome for myself.

But in the end, of course, I already knew.

Stella died in her sleep. There were no machines unplugged this time and fewer questions. She was eighty-six, after all. When an eighty-six-year-old dies, it isn't a mystery.

I wrestled with myself in the days to come, as anyone would. Should I report the girl, Rosaria? And tell the administrators what, exactly? That she touched the dying? That she gave them one last smile? That I suspected she was sneaking into their rooms at night?

Or that she was Oyá herself coming to call, shepherding her chosen from one realm to the next?

No one listens to our kind, those who are cloistered away from the raging world outside. That is why living here is worse than death, you see. Bingo for the damned? The idea seems brilliant or inane to me, depending on how the meds are tickling my brain that day.

I hate this place.

"I'll never understand you, Gilberto," my young Antoinette says. "You complain about the Bingo game, but you're always first at the door."

Of course I am, and now you see why. I no longer simply watch—I play. I listen closely, and I mark my cards when my numbers are called. I feel my heart leap as the rows fill.

Because she is here today. Rosaria is here. She has not yet shed her human form, but I see the light glowing in embers from her skin. Her dainty nest of hair will grow. Her white nurse's shoes are mewling against the floor now, but soon her feet will glide on the air itself.

She passes from one table to the next, closer to me. Studying me.

And I am a believer again. Perhaps my mala suerte is banished at last. Will my number come up this time? Just this once, Rosaria—this one time—will you give me luck? Will I win?

Bless me. Save me. Choose me.

The Bois

R.S.A. Garcia

I rest Mags down on the lavender grass and kneel beside she. My hands cover with blood, dark and hot. She breathing with a whistle, chest rising and falling in fits. When her lips part, I see teeth that stain red. A fist squeeze my heart, and I run my wired hand over she cold cheeks. I avoid the little clump of plants lying next to her arm; try not to see the pulsing fluorescent trails that make a sick light under she skin from the tips of she fingers to she elbow. The lavender grass almost shadowed in the glow. I can feel the azure tendrils of the trees above me waving like extended fingers.

"Girl, why you do that? Why?"

I don't expect she to speak, but she surprise me with a whisper. I lean down to hear.

"... wasn't ... wasn't suppose to be like this."

"What wasn't?" I ask. Mags sit on the barstool next to me, big smile on she face, black hair held back by the rag tied 'round she forehead. She dark brown eyes too pretty, and I hide the flutter in my stomach behind a sip of my beer.

"We first date." She motion to Chester behind the bar, and a mug appear in front she like magic. She hold it with long, slender fingers; her skin light brown and prettier than mine.

"You smoke or what? This ain't no date." My wired hand steady, but my left side tremors as she pulls her stool nearer, forcing me to look at her.

"No, is not," she agree softly. "Next time, we go be more private."

For the first time in my life, I don't know what to say. I am Tantie. I know the Law, and I know the History. I don't know this. The accident take my hair, so I bald. Is only synthskin cover my wired parts. I'm a good few years older than Mags, too. Men don't chase me, far less girls.

"Mags, be serious. I not for you. Besides, your father go kill you."
She smile slow like molasses from a bottle. "He could go to hell."
She pause. "I'm grown. I know what I want."

Panic rise in me like the tide. I stand up so fast, the stool slam into the wooden floor. Chester glance up, frowning. Mags continue to smile, she gaze taking in all of me, resting finally on the gun at my hip. I can't speak, so I just walk away, heart thumping and skin fevered.

I walk till I reach the only place they come near me at all. Trees stand around a purple clearing, reaching scaly blue tendrils toward the pale sky. Their shade don't hide the thing standing in the centre of the patch. It must have heard the commotion. Terror sweep over me like the day I lose my arm and face; but I think of Mags lying alone in the forest behind me, dying, and I fall to my knees and bend my forehead to the ground.

"Good day to you, Papa Bois."

It don't speak. The Bois don't have language. But impressions and emotions push against my mind, and the metallic taste of them fill my mouth. It's angry, disgusted, but curious, too. I grab hold of that feeling like a lifeline.

"We didn't intend disrespect, Papa. She didn't know you was here. I never tell nobody. She didn't know the forest is yours."

That every piece of it is separate and the Bois at the same time. That she can't harvest plants because when she hurt one part, she hurt all. I only hear a rustle as it moves; the thick grass muffle the sound. It over me now, but I don't look up. Somehow, I know Papa Bois would take that as disrespect. Its beard touches my shoulder, slippery vines cold like Mags' skin. It still mad, but it ask the question.

"Help," I say, tears welling without warning. "Please. She innocent and good, and she go die."

It's dismissive; all things die.

"If she die, is my fault. I can't take that."

It pause, considering.

"Please," I whisper.

Long seconds go by. I feel every one as blood dripping from Mags' mouth.

My emotions amaze and confuse it. But it have new understanding. Beneath its resolve, cruelty prick at me. It want something.

"A sacrifice?" I confused. But it determined—it want something

I can't afford to lose. Something I value. My heart thumping, but I don't hesitate.

I look up.

Mags smile down at me. "I tell you I soon come."

My heart skip a beat. Is months now Mags coming to my hut near the forest. I try to discourage her, but she wear me down like water on stone. She sits down beside me as I calibrate my gun on the bench outside my home. It's quiet here with nothing but the blue trees of the Bois forest in front us. The wind too light to move the tocsin hanging above my head. Not that it need to ring. It quiet for weeks now with no trouble in the colony.

She nod toward the forest. "What you does see in there so? You always staring at it."

I shrug, looking up at the waving branches to avoid she face. "It pretty," I lie. "Peaceful. Is just me and the forest. Anybody come here either looking to leave or to get me to leave. The forest just let me be."

It accept me because I don't belong, I think but don't say. I keep my secret from Mags because no one can know. It too dangerous still. The colony young and foolish, and the forest can't be fucked with. But to tell people "no" is to tell people "go." I glance at the deepening indigo twilight of the trees to make sure nothing watching us together. So is a shock when she take the gun from me and fold my wired fingers into hers.

I am an Outcast. A freak. Everybody always avoid me. Nobody ever touch my synthskin so before. It tingle and jump, and I try to pull back; but she lips cover mine, and just like that, I lost. When the sun go down, it was a long time before I light my lamp. But maybe something see. Maybe something mark we. This planet cruel—hard and dry with a sea that eat flesh.

I should have guess the forest would devour we sooner or later.

The Bois face not human. It have no features I could name. Just twisting fronds. They fold and turn and bend over each other. Thousands and thousands of them. Some thin as threads, some thick as fingers. A few trail toward the seething mass of the lower body, which is just a column of vibrating tentacles. It should be disturbing, but it not; and that's because of the colours. Shifting and changing all the time, colours run through the tentacles and tissues, blending and tumbling into each other like waves in the ocean. Is a terrible, beautiful sight.

I could only see it out of my wired eye.

Is the only reason people don't know 'bout the Bois. They blind to them. Everyone just know to avoid the forest. Sometimes is as if they could sense them. It make everybody uncomfortable to come by my house on Law matters. They always grumble about why I live so far outside the colony.

But since I first catch a glimpse of them as a child, I drawn to the Bois. I know better than to approach them or try to talk to them.

But I see them—and they know it. Is like a truce for a war that never happen. I stay out they way, and they let me see them as they flit through the trees. Keep me company where no one else willing to come.

Until Mags.

Poor, sweet Mags, who don't 'fraid nothing and decide to go exploring today despite the fact that every fool in Diego know the forest is no place to go and it have nothing in it but darkness and bad juju.

I don't know how I know what happen or where she was. I just know I wake up from a deep sleep, she voice in my ears, and the bed cold on she side. I never dress so fast. I never run so quick. Every human part of me was trembling with panic.

The wired part was cold and calm as ever.

When I find her, she have some fading orange growths next to her. The forest version of flowers. Only they not pretty, harmless things. I can see the twisting trail of poison running through the veins of she arm, a flame of orange under she cappuccino skin. The wired part of me jolt like I get an electric shock because I know what she was trying to do and I know why and is my fault.

I never tell nobody my birthday before.

I also never tell nobody what I see the Bois do. How sometimes a tree would be turning dark like a bruise, bending its head to the ground, weary with life. And then one special Bois would come. Bigger than the others. Brighter. It would pass it rainbow tentacles over the tree—caress it for hours—and days later, the tree standing tall again. Pale blue and full of life.

Mags need life now. This creature I call Papa Bois, after the protector of the forest Tantie Pearl tell me about as a child—it could help. It could save Mags like it save the trees.

If it want to.

If the sacrifice big enough and given willingly.

So I don't flinch as it bend over me, tentacles sliding down my shoulders like ice water. I look straight into the rainbow face as cold amusement scorch my mind.

Hurry, I think, blood beating in my ears.

And it does. Papa Bois beard whip toward my face and pluck both my eyes out of my skull before the scream could swell my throat.

Weeks later I sit on the bench outside my home and listen to the wind in the trees. I alone and these days only Lucretia from the clinic does check me to see if I healing okay. She don't make no talk, really. Just check the bandages and help me bathe and so on. Today before she leave, she tell me the doctor go come and take off the bandages tomorrow. Is the only good news in a long time.

Everybody avoid me because I kill Mags. They don't know how, but they know she dead because of me. It don't matter that the flowers poison her; what kill she was the stupid idea to go in the forest in the first place. Despite the fact that it have nothing in there. Despite the fact that the first generation off the ship tell stories about how when the *Diego Martin* crash-landed, the Captain himself went in there with some of the crew, and nobody ever come back.

I bewitch she. I make she throw away good sense. I take her in the forest, then bring she body out. Blind and bleeding, I ring the tocsin for help, and I wouldn't say what happen to we. You don't see I guilty?

I hear from Lucretia when they tell Mags father, he lock himself in he house and drink. That he still drinking.

I think that good, though. A drunk man in a house can't make no trouble. And the less trouble the better because I can't carry out the Law for a while. Not until my new eyes ready. It go be hard. I treasured my one human eye. I treasure all the normal parts. I see things different, but that was good for a Tantie.

Papa Bois take that from me. He take the sunsets and the emotions on people face. The tears I cry for Mags. He leave calibrations and scrolling menus. X-Ray and night vision. A wired eye is a complex thing—accurate and full of features like a flight deck on a starship. But it can't see humanity. It can't see ordinary.

Tonight, I sit on my bench, and I sense them. Hear the whisper of emotions in my head. The Bois here, watching—waiting. They curious. Surprised. Something new happen.

A solitary emotion detach itself from the Bois and drift toward me, a tendril on the wind. It settles on me, a loose thread around my thoughts and heart just before something touch me. Chilly threads slide under and between my fingers, but warmth explodes inside me—I can almost taste secret kisses and feel tight arms around me.

Papa Bois keep he promise. It was too late for Mags' body. But she energy—she soul—it was still there. And Papa take it, along with my sacrifice.

The Bois don't die, you see. They is energy, and energy don't really end. It does just change form. And that change take a long time. Almost as long as a wired woman like me have to live. I will never kiss Mags on she soft lips again. But I will never lose her either. I have the feel of tendrils between my fingers and the presence of a spirit that nothing like the alien Bois to keep me company in my home at the forest's edge.

I can't cry anymore, so I smile instead and tilt my face into the evening breeze. I let the fronds move against my hand while a new world flood my mind with colours and impressions and emotions I never dream 'bout.

Tomorrow my bandages come off.

Tomorrow, I will see.

Issue 4, June 2017 of Truancy

The Spook School

Nick Mamatas

It was the twenty-hour journey on which neither Gordon nor Melissa slept a wink and the strong Greek coffee at the Athena Tavern they both chugged down at Melissa's request and the long-seeming walk in the plish across Kelvingrove Park at Gordon's insistence that took them to the museum. A wayward cinder got into Melissa's contact lenses, and she was exhausted and jittery from the caffeine and excited to finally be meeting her lover's parents; and it was her first trip to Scotland, and if we're being entirely honest, Melissa was a bit of a fanciful creature and always hoping for some transcendent experience, so she got one. Really, truly, the sacred rose in Charles Rennie Mackintosh's famed gesso panel, *The Wassail,* did not wink at her as she and Gordon stood before it. She imagined the whole thing in the back of her mind, which made the front of her mind startle, then shut down, and so she swooned, falling to the floor like a pair of empty trousers after the belt was whipped out of its loops.

"I love it here," Melissa said later. "I do wish people would stop calling the bathroom 'the toilet,' though. That makes me think of the commode." Melissa had spent a while bent over the tiny European toilet in the "toilet" of Gordon's parents after she woke up. "I could live here, otherwise," she said. She drank the tea Gordon had prepared for her.

"Live here on the couch, being waited on hand and foot?" Gordon asked. "I'm sure you're meant to, my faerie queen." Gordon was like that.

"It just seems ... quaint."

Gordon snorted. "Don't call anything 'quaint' in earshot of my mum and dad, honey bee. In the United Kingdom, 'quaint' means 'fucking terrible.'"

"Lovely?" Melissa tried.

"Aye, that's much better," Gordon said.

"When I showed Customs my passport, the officer called my pic 'lovely.' I didn't know whether to feel complimented or offended until they called your passport lovely, too."

"Am I not?" Gordon struck a pose: pursed lips, knuckles under chin, shoulders jauntily angled.

"You are."

Gordon's parents burst into the kitchen, bringing rain and wind with them. Gordon stood to greet them, and Melissa waved from the living room couch. They were a matched pair, almost spherical in their rain gear, and chattering in thick Glaswegian accents.

"Are you feeling a wee bit better?" Gordon's father called out to Melissa.

"Mostly, yes. Thank you," Melissa said. She had come to their home semi-conscious and muttering about roses. Now she tottered into the kitchen and accepted more tea while politely refusing a little something stronger offered by Gordon's father. "Suit your own self," he said, then after a swig added with a wink, "So, got ... spooked, did ya?"

Mackintosh and his wife, Margaret MacDonald, her sister, Frances, and Herbert MacNair were called "The Four in Scotland," and they were acclaimed for infusing their art with Celtic, Asian, and outright occult imagery. Over in London, where the entire political and cultural apparatus was then as now bent toward the diminishment and marginalization of all things Scots—to hear Gordon talk about it, anyway—they were christened "The Spook School." That's what got Melissa so keen to visit Glasgow in the first place. To see the art up close and in person.

"I guess I did, Mr. Paterson," Melissa said. Gordon reached over and squeezed her shoulder. "But I'll be back at it tomorrow."

"Bring a pillow in case you try for another kip," Mr. Paterson said to Gordon, winking. Everyone chuckled but his wife.

"I never could ken all the fuss about The Four," Mrs. Paterson said. "We had to study them in school—class trips and such. It all just looked to me like they made some lovely drawings and paintings and then stretched them all out and bleached half the color away. But you're Greek, no? Much more interesting art among the Hellenes, I think."

"Greek-*American*, yes," Melissa said. "But ..." But when you're raised among cheap plaster miniatures of bone-white statuary; when tin reliefs of the Acropolis feature on every wall; when even your flatulent theias are named Aphrodite and Artemis; when all your relatives smell of the deep fryer and shout at the television news because they personally were the ones who invented democracy, you just get tired, you see, ever so tired of ...

"I guess I've always liked Celtic things." She shot Gordon a smile. Mr. Paterson took the opportunity to wax poetic about his perverse support for Rangers—Gordon rolled his eyes and sharply warned him "Dad!"—and the stupidity of anti-sectarian regulation that made singing songs a criminal offense, though with the caveat that "Billy Boys," with the line "We're up to our knees in Fenian blood" (which he sang quite well in a steady tenor) should likely remain out of bounds. By the time Mr. Paterson had exhausted himself, his wife had finished preparing the traditional Scots meal of reheated take-away curry served on her own plates. Gordon drank Irn-Bru with his, like a child.

If this were a story, after dinner Melissa and Gordon would beg off pudding and report to Gordon's childhood room—untouched since he went off to America—and try to catch up on sleep. And the excitement of the day with its embarrassing medical emergency and attendant barking of the Polish nurse to just "Pick yourself up and get on with your holiday!" would combine with the curry and Mr. Paterson's terpsichorean endeavors to entrap Melissa Poulos in a portentous nightmarish dreamscape of Spook School art come to life, seeking to devour her. And perhaps this was indeed the dream she dreamed, but from Gordon's point of view, all the evening consisted of was her elbow in his nose, her knees jammed up against his chest when he tried to throw an arm around her, some snoring, a mouthful of her curls as she turned away and presented her back and arse for spooning. Then she managed to bark his shin. There was likely more abuse than that, but sleep finally took Gordon as well. Neither remembered their dreams, which is indeed the most common result of the human subconscious attempting to process proximity to genuine occult phenomena. It's the nightmares you don't recall even having that get you in the end.

In the morning Melissa impressed the Patersons with her ability to roll her Rs. She had a light breakfast in the manner of an American while the Patersons ate full Scottish, inexplicably including haggis. Melissa tried a bite and decided that it wasn't so bad after all. "Haggis has a poor reputation thanks solely to propaganda," Mr. Paterson explained. "English propaganda swallowed and then regurgitated by their fellows in America."

"If you dislike the English so much, Dad, why do you support Rangers?" Gordon asked, his question both petulant and well-rehearsed.

"I never cared for haggis myself," Mrs. Paterson stage-whispered to Melissa conspiratorially. "It shows from the taste!" Mr. Patterson said. And with that, Gordon and Melissa whisked themselves out of the flat and headed to the city centre and its museums. Glasgow's venerable yet primitive subway loop served to bring them over to Kelvingrove from Ibrox. Melissa was less keen to walk in the dreach today.

"Are you concerned?" Gordon asked.

"About the rain?"

"No, about the ...?" Gordon said. Melissa had told him about the winking Mackintosh rose, and they had silently agreed to tell neither the medic nor the Patersons about it. The end result was that they hadn't the chance to discuss it privately either.

"I just feel really good about today," Melissa said. "*The Wassail* really is beautiful. I need to study it closely. Did you notice that the figures in the center formed the outline of a scarab?"

"You tossed and turned all night."

"No, that was you," Melissa said. "I hardly slept a wink. It was like sharing a twin bed with an excitable circus seal."

"Likewise, I'm sure, madam."

Melissa said, "I want to see the panel again. There's a lot of hidden meanings in it. Do you know that wassailing was originally a type of Yuletide home invasion scenario? Madness of crowds and all that."

"And if the rose winks?"

"We passed any number of roses in that gallery. It's a motif. I think I saw a billboard with one when we got our tickets."

"Not the original, though."

There were many things Melissa could say to that, quoting Benjamin and the age of mechanical reproduction, the fallacy of the notion of the original, and especially how that fallacy related to art nouveau in general with its emphasis on using modern technique and "craft" over traditional visions of originality and artistic creation, but the argument required significant nuance; and clearly Gordon wasn't in the mood.

Nor was Melissa. "Why are you ignoring everything I say?"

Gordon huffed as the subway stopped at Kelvingrove. "I know all about it. I'm a Weegie; I know all about getting drunk and rowdy, and I've not had a drink in two years, three months, and eighteen days. I've been marched through Kelvingrove as often as you were brought to see that big whale hanging in the Natural History Museum back in New York; I've heard all the mystical bugger. It's just that, you know? Bugger and bullshite. Plenty of Americans come to Scotland looking for fairy circles or highlanders cutting a path through heathery moors with their huge cocks or their great-grandma's chamber pot. You fainted, all right? That's all. And I don't want you fainting again, you ken? I worry for you, pet." And with his rant over, they were through the gate and through the turnstile and past the frowning faces of the teachers bringing children on a field trip to the museum and standing before *The Wassail* again. Melissa was pleased that somewhere in his juvenile belligerence Gordon used the word *ken* with her, as that sort of thing usually embarrassed him back in the States. *Pet* too was nice but not nice enough.

The Mackintosh rose winked at her again. This time, Melissa steadied herself and winked back. The women, elongated limbs as diaphanous as the gowns they wore, shimmered as if a breeze were moving through the plane of gesso. The scarab formed by the outline of their figures seemed to scuttle. *Right then*, thought Melissa, and she excused herself to go to the ladies' and told Gordon not to worry; she was feeling rosy, haha, get it?

In the woman's restroom—Melissa still balked at the word *Toilet* on the sign—she dug into her purse for the fingernail clipper, as the TSA had seized her full-size nail file back at Newark International. She decided to start with the upper lip frenulum, and with the help of her reflection in the mirror, she clipped right through it. There was a lot of blood, but the other woman using the long row of sinks just stared down at her hands and started scrubbing roughly, refusing eye contact. By the time Melissa had pulled her lip past her nose and up to her prominent eyebrows, the toilet door slammed resoundingly shut.

Her mouth gaping open like the loose hood of an oversized sweatshirt, Melissa popped her skull off her C1 vertebra and placed it in the sink before her. Then she righted her face and reached in to her throat with both hands and with a decisive yank, got the rest of her spine out. That went in the sink as well. It was getting quite messy, both inside and out, but Melissa had withdrawn plenty of Scottish £100 notes in her purse to make it worth the while of the clean-up crew. (Gordon had objected to getting Scottish notes, which many English shops south of the border won't accept, but Melissa was just the sort of annoying romantic that insists upon them.)

Melissa withdrew her pelvis via what method she couldn't help but think of as "the hard way," and the ribs, which had collected in the cavity of the structure, spilled out after and clattered about her ankles. The long bones of her limbs were the hardest to remove—it was a bit like trying to nail one's own lonely self to a cross—but she managed it, legs first through the anus, and then arms out her mouth. She was looking quite good, Melissa was. A foot taller, easily, and floating several inches above the ground. Her clothes were a bloody puddle of cotton and denim at her feet, and her metacarpals and metatarsals littered the floor like so much windshield glass after a fatal car accident, but Melissa knew that she'd receive a gown just as soon as she joined the festivities. She'd hardly be the only nude in the Kelvingrove Art Gallery and Museum, and surely the field trip of school kids had broken for lunch by now, no?

She sauntered back to *The Wassail* to the sound of screams and the thumps of matrons and patrons falling faint to the floor, but it was Gordon's unearthly howl of rage and fear after she caressed his shoulder to say both hello and goodbye that finally caught Melissa up as if in a gale and sent her flitting into the paint to join the eternal parade.

The Little Dog Ohori

Anatoly Belilovsky

The young soldier jumps to his feet, snaps to attention.

"At ease, Comrade Corporal," the officer says. "And please sit down." A white coat hangs off the officer's shoulders; it hides her shoulder tabs, leaving visible only the caduceus in her lapel.

The soldier hesitates. The officer leans against the wall; her coat falls off one shoulder, revealing three small stars. The soldier's eyes widen.

"Begging Comrade Colonel's pardon," he says and sits down. The movement is slow and uncertain, as if his body fights the very thought of sitting while an officer stands.

"Sit," the officer says, more firmly now. "This is an order."

"Thank you, Comrade Colonel," the soldier says, sees a small frown crease the officer's face, and adds: "I mean, Doctor."

The officer smiles and nods. A strand of graying hair escapes her knot and falls to her face; she sweeps it back with an impatient gesture.

"Carry on," she says.

The soldier hesitates again.

"That's an order, too," she says and points to the caduceus in her lapel. "A medical order."

"Thank you, Doctor," the soldier says. "I only came to visit; I'm not here as a patient."

"She is," the doctor says and tilts her head at the hospital bed.

The soldier turns to face the dying woman in the bed, leans toward her, takes her hand, and whispers to her in a language the doctor does not understand.

Cold.

Lying on the riverbank in a puddle of blood and melting snow, she listens for the sounds of gunfire, the roar of engines, the clatter of tank tracks, anything to say she is not alone. She no longer feels her hands though she can see her right hand on the trigger of her

Tokarev-40, the index finger frozen into a hook. She no longer feels pain where the shell splinter tore into her belly, only cold. Cold comfort, too, in the bodies scattered on the ice beyond the riverbank, eleven black specks against relentless white, eleven fewer Waffen SS, eleven plus two hundred and three already in the killbook makes two hundred and three fewer who could threaten—

Her mind's eye projects a glimpse of Selim's face against the night, then all is dark again.

She listens and hears a friendly sound.

The little dog Ohori is barking.

"*Help ...*" From a throat parched raw through desiccated lips, one of the last small drops of strength drains into the word.

The barking stops, but silence does not return. There is a noise like leaves fluttering in the wind.

No, wait. It's winter; a white cloak for camouflage in the snow. No grass to hide, no leaves to whisper.

Whisper.

"Is she ...?"

A woman's whisper, in Russian.

"I don't know."

Another voice, a woman, too, or a goddess.

"*Please ...*" Another drop of strength gone, but now she can see Selim again, him with his great happy crooked smile. She tries to touch it, but it is out of reach. Could this be Ogushin, the taker of souls, or the nine-tailed werefox, Kumiho? She can no longer tell what is real and what is not. There is only strength enough to hope:

— *Please, little dog Ohori, who brings lost loves together* —

— The darkness deepens —

— *please, angel Oneuli, who watches over orphans, please, Sister Sun and Brother Moon* —

— *please. If only for a moment* —

— *please let me see my family again* —

"Were you close, the two of you?" the doctor asks.

The soldier opens his mouth, closes it again. His eyes grow distant, focus far away.

"Sorry," the doctor says. "Stupid of me to ask."

The soldier nods. The doctor takes it as "Yes, we were close," not "Yes, stupid of you to ask."

The woman's breathing is becoming ragged: a burst of rapid gasps, then slow breaths, then rapid again.

"I'm sorry," the doctor says. "It won't be long now."

The soldier reaches into his tunic pocket, brings out a tattered notepad.

The doctor bends forward to look at it. "Her diary?"

"Her killbook," the soldier answers.

"Ah," the doctor says. "I see."

The captain's name, Kryviy, is Ukrainian.

"Age?" he says.

"Nineteen," she answers, a pang of guilt for lying.

"Ethnicity?"

"Uzbek," she says. A smaller pang.

"Why do you want to enlist?"

This is a question she does not expect. This question wouldn't ever be asked of a man. Or a Great Russian.

She rifles through a list of plausible lies and settles on a partial truth: "I want to be a sniper."

The captain looks up from his notes. His ice blue eyes aim at her face. "Sniper?" he says. "Can you see well enough with those ..." He squints in imitation of her features.

She looks out at the sun-baked desert beyond the open window. Some distance away, a truck approaches, raising a plume of dust behind it. She points in its direction.

"Truck number 43-11," she says and looks at the captain again.

The captain stands up, approaches the window. He watches the truck approach, squints, this time in concentration, and leans out the window.

"I see the 11," he says slowly, then after a pause: "Yes. 43-11." He returns to his chair, crosses a line off his notes, and writes another. "You'll do," he says, and shouts: "Next!"

The woman's hand tightens, just enough to see the tiny twitch. The soldier puts the killbook in her hand. Another twitch.

The doctor leans against the doorjamb. The wood plank creaks. The soldier looks up.

"It took an hour to pry her from that riverbank," the soldier says. "Two nurses from the Medical Sanitary Battalion. In the dark. Under enemy fire." He shakes his head. "And then they dragged her back to the Division hospital three kilometers away." He touches his chest; two of his medals ring together. "No matter what I do, I'll never be their equal."

The doctor's hands are in the pockets of her tunic. Her fingers itch for something—a cigarette, a scalpel—she worries at the knots in the pocket's seam, rolls specks of lint into a ball. *Surgery is easy*, she thinks. *Listening is hard.*

She looks at the kill book. "I'll remember her name. Heroes should never be forgotten."

The soldier raises his head, looks straight at her. She sees the hesitation in his eyes and the crystallization at a decision.

"That's not her real name," he says slowly and looks at the dying woman again.

The doctor does, too. She compares the dying woman's features with the soldier's, her trained mind catalogs the differences.

She reaches for the killbook, turns its pages with reverence. Places: Stalingrad, Kursk, Smolensk. Dates: last in December, 1943. Ranks: Scharfuhrer SS, Feldwebel, Hauptmann. And on the last page, a stick figure of a dog and writing in neither Cyrillic nor Arabic nor Latin. She looks up for a moment, then turns to the soldier sharply.

"Korean?" she says.

The soldier nods.

"Passing for ..." she hesitates. "Kazakh?"

"Uzbek," the soldier says quietly.

"Nineteen thirty-seven?" the doctor asks. Matching the soldier's tone comes naturally; suppressing the urge to look behind her does not.

The soldier looks up. "Not many people know about that."

The doctor says nothing.

"My grandfather was selling lamb samsa at a train station," the soldier says. "A train carrying deportees stopped there one day. It had been traveling from Vladivostok for a month."

The doctor's fingers scramble in her pocket. She bites her lip.

"They stopped to bury the dead in the desert. Her mother was one of them. She was thirteen and an orphan. Grandfather brought her back to our qishlaq. She became one of the family."

Selim comes out of the recruiting office, a happy grin on his face.

"I did it!" he says. "They are sending me to sniper school. And I have you to thank."

She draws a breath. "Did you tell them—"

He shakes his head. "I'm not that stupid. Can you imagine? 'Oh yes, Comrade Captain, a little girl taught me everything I know about hunting.' They would call a neuropathologist next to have my head examined."

"I am not little, Selim," she says firmly. "I'll be eighteen come spring, and I'll enlist, too. I'll ask to join your unit, and we'll be together again."

His face grows somber. "They won't take you. I'm sorry."

"What are you talking about?" She puts her hand on her hips. "They take girls!"

"They don't take Koreans," he whispers. "They have a list of undesirables only assigned to labor battalions: Tatars, Volga Germans, Chechens." He looks down, spurns a clod of dirt with the toe of his boot, then looks at her again. "Koreans, too. I'm sorry."

She does not answer except for a glint in her eyes: exactly, he thinks, like a reflection off the barrel of Grandfather's old Mosin-Nagant .300.

Exactly like the glint she had on the first anniversary of her joining the clan when, returning to the qishlaq with an antelope and two hares in the back of their donkey-drawn arba, she turned to him and said in too-precise Karakalpak Uzbek:

"When I am old enough, Selim, we will be married."

The doctor is used to silences; the soldier is not.

"You might not believe this, but she taught me to shoot," the soldier says.

The doctor says nothing. She reaches for the kill book, turns its pages with reverence.

"What am I saying?" the soldier says. "Of course, you believe it, Colonel. Most people—"

"Most people don't command a military hospital," the doctor says. "Most people haven't seen what soldiers are made of."

"You must have as a surgeon," the soldier says.

"That, too," she whispers.

The train approaches, the smoke from its engine thinning, the chuffing slowing down.

"This makes no sense," says Uncle Tsoi. "First of all, there is no war now; the Japanese were beaten at Halhin-Gol, and they are not coming back. Secondly, even if they were, why would we help them? We left Korea to get away from the Japanese. And thirdly, why resettle all of us? They could just arrest the richer peasants, like the Pak family." He sighs. "No, I think it's a mistake. I think someone misunderstood what Comrade Stalin said, and when that becomes clear, the train will turn around and bring us back here. I just hope it won't be too late for the apple harvest."

He looks up to find that his niece isn't looking at him. She is staring at the train in the distance.

"This isn't polite," Uncle Tsoi says. "You should pay attention when your elders are talking."

She nods absentmindedly.

"Haven't you ever seen a train before?" Uncle Tsoi says and follows her gaze.

His face drops. "This isn't a passenger train," he whispers. "We are going to travel ten thousand kilometers in cattle cars."

They wait for the train in silence.

A man approaches, a Great Russian by his appearance.

"Comrade Tsoi?" he calls. "Which of you is Comrade Tsoi?"

Uncle Tsoi stands up straighter. "See," he says. "Someone realized it's a mistake." He turns to the man and raises his hand. "I'm Tsoi," he says loudly.

"Please come with us," the man says softly.

Uncle Tsoi turns to her. "Go get your mother."

"Just you," the man says.

The train stops. The gates slide open with a clatter.

"All aboard!" a man shouts from the locomotive.

She watches Uncle Tsoi escorted away from the train, past a line of armed soldiers, until she feels her mother tug at her hand.

She turns. There are tears in her mother's coal-black eyes rolling down her face that is the palest she had ever seen.

"Come. Have to go," her mother says. A cough escapes before she can cover her mouth.

They board the train in silence, find a spot to sit. More people come until there is no more room. Then some more. Then more.

Then finally, there is a whistle, the gates clang shut, and the train departs.

"My brother," her mother whispers.

She leans closer to her mother. They are both too old to believe in Little Dog Ohori, but she decides she'll never be too old to hope.

● ● ●

"Do you see your target?" Uncle Tsoi says.

Her head tilted over the stock of Uncle Tsoi's Berdan rifle, she gives a tiny nod.

"What are you aiming at?" Uncle Tsoi asks.

"The big pine cone," she says.

"That is wrong," says Uncle Tsoi. "Pick a scale. One scale on the whole pine cone. Aim at that. Have you got that?"

She nods again.

"Now breathe in, then out, and on the *out*, close your whole hand on the trigger."

She presses on the trigger, flinching just a bit before the rifle bucks and the shot explodes. The pine cone dances but does not fall.

"Two more things," says Uncle Tsoi. "First, squeeze the trigger slowly enough that the shot comes as a surprise to you. Understand?"

She nods. "And the second?" she says.

"Connect with your target," says Uncle Tsoi. "Some people imagine reaching out and touching it; some talk to the target in their minds. Some apologize in advance for hitting it. You have to care, in some way, about the target to shoot true."

She aims again, breathes in and out, imagines the little dog Ohori running to the pine tree, leaping to sniff the pine cone, leave a wet print of its nose on one particular scale.

The shot rings out, startling her. The pine cone disintegrates into a cloud of chaff.

"She talked about her uncle so much, I felt like I knew him," the soldier says. "Sometimes I could almost hear his voice come out of her mouth. 'When Brother Moon and Sister Sun lived together on Mount Baekdu, they had a little dog named Ohori who loved them both. And when the supreme god Cheonjiwang sent each of them to a different part of the sky, Ohori ran from one to the other until he brought them together; but when they met, they shone light only on each other, leaving the Earth in pitch darkness, so Queen Baji petitioned Cheonjiwang to allow them only one meeting a month. So each night of the new Moon, Ohori is free to roam the Earth, and when you hear barking on a moonless night, it just might be Ohori searching for you to bring you back to someone you miss very much.'"

The soldier's voice wavers on the last words. The doctor reaches to touch the soldier's shoulder. Her hand trembles an inch above his shoulder board, then pulls back to wipe her tears. She blinks and hopes her eyes have time to dry before he sees them.

Colonels don't cry. Not with a corporal present.

Is it a star shell or dawn already? It is light: light enough to see green grass, birch trees in leaf—it can't be spring—or does it matter? The rhythmic footfalls she hears—pulsing blood or boots measuring time? And—faces, smiling faces she never thought she'd see again and voices she never hoped to hear cry once more, just one more time:

"Hurrah! Hurrah! Hurrah!"

And nipping at their feet, the little dog Ohori, his barking mixing with laughter and with the shouts of welcome.

The hand gives one more twitch; the chest rises, falls, never to rise again. The soldier frees his hand from her grasp, smooths her hair, stands up face to face with the doctor.

"Thank you," he says.

"For what?" the doctor says.

"We got to see each other," the soldier says.

"It's worth so much to you?" the doctor says.

"To me?" The soldier raises his eyebrows. "It does not matter what it's worth to me. It's what *she* wanted. She had been worth a million of me, you know." He pats his pockets, takes out his cap, places it on his head, draws to attention, and salutes. "Goodbye ..." he begins, but then his voice gives out.

The doctor reaches for a carafe on a bedside table, looks for a glass, finds none, and hands the carafe to the soldier.

"Here. Drink from that. Go ahead, drink."

The soldier brings the carafe to his mouth, takes a long swallow.

"Thank you," he says. "And thank you for bringing her here. I know you bent the rules—"

"We take care of our own," the doctor interrupts. "Which includes you. Go get some sleep. Stop by my office in the morning, I'll have my clerk process a leave extension."

The soldier shakes his head. He steps past the doctor through the door, takes another step in the corridor, stops, turns around, and faces the dead woman again.

"Goodbye, Grandmother," he says. "Give my regards to Grandpa

Selim. And to all of your old comrades." He takes a breath. "And a few of mine."

He turns to the doctor. "Please, Comrade Colonel, don't order me to stay. We, too, take care of our own. My unit is short a man till I come back, and ..." he checks his watch "... an Antonov-24 scheduled to lift off for Kandahar in an hour." He draws to attention and salutes again. "I beg the Colonel's permission to be dismissed," he says in crisp militarese.

"Granted," the doctor says and watches him march away. It isn't lost on her that his cadence is the same as for the change-of-watch before the Monument to the Unknown Soldier.

The doctor waits until she hears his footfalls no more before she covers the old woman's face.

Sunset

Hiroko Minagawa

● translated by Karen Sandness ●

It happened again. When I unfolded the newspaper to read, the printed characters slid off the pages, leaving them blank. The characters advanced across the floor in a line and headed up into the aquarium, which was in the recess of a bay window.

It had been several days since I had picked up the two mollusks on the tidal flats. They were a pale pink, but they were as big as the palm of my hand and therefore more substantial than the pink clams that one finds on the beaches of southern Japan. They were so unusual that I took them home and placed them in the aquarium where I keep my tropical fish and fingers. The shells opened slightly as if settling in, but what emerged from between the two halves were not tongue-like pseudopods but fingers.

If I had forced them all the way open, I might have injured them or at worst, killed them, so I had no way of seeing whether the shells contained only fingers or a whole arm or even an entire body. Since they were so fond of printed characters, I thought they might have eyes. Or maybe they just enjoyed the sensation of touching the print.

I was already keeping three fingers in the aquarium, but none of them was so fond of printed characters.

I wonder when it was that maxims such as "Life is precious" and "Thou shalt try to stay alive" or "Thou shalt not kill" came to be bandied about as ironclad principles. Every once in a while, some incident comes up in which the criterion is the degree to which one should or should not consider life to be precious.

All my life, not only throughout my schooling but also in every form of mass media, this has been continually pounded into our heads. Perhaps for that reason, we have a fanatical belief that it is the right of and proper for all creatures, whether they have a brain or just four legs, to keep on living. At least, I think that's what happened.

No pundit mentioned the contradiction between "Thou shalt try to stay alive" and "Thou shalt not kill." Researchers announced results that showed that, if you raised a severed finger in an appropriate environment, it would be so obsessed with staying alive that it would change form. Raising them in water seemed to yield the highest success rate. Supposedly, this was because they could easily model themselves on fish. Once these results were released, raising fingers in aquariums became wildly popular.

If there's a demand, the supply increases, as in former days when impoverished students used to sell their blood to make ends meet. When it comes to fingers, fresh ones are the most desirable. Observing the process by which the fingers change in imitation of fish is what owners find most pleasurable, so owning one that has already gone through the process is boring, and old fingers that have not changed are unlikely to do so in the future. If a finger in a retailer's aquarium just lies there and decays, everyone assumes that the owner had an insufficient desire to live.

It is possible that people would have grown tired of these fingers and stopped paying attention to them, but rumors began flying that the government would ban them, so the retail price rose sharply.

When the ban was issued, a single finger became worth its weight in gold, and with the possibility of being subjected to severe punishment if found out, raising fingers became a secret hobby of the bourgeoisie. Human rights and citizens' groups had already taken the hobbyists to task on the grounds that they were fiends who violated human dignity. However, since this position had originated in respect for human life, those who were opposed to it embraced the inherent contradiction. Since their mission in life was to oppose the government no matter what it did, they started holding demonstrations as soon as the ban was issued on the grounds that the government was not respecting the principle of free will.

Of the three fingers that I was raising, one had completed the transformation. It was swimming around, outwardly indistinguishable from the tropical fish that I had put into the aquarium with it.

The doorbell rang. My visitors were Arteria and Vena, who lived in the lowlands on the other side of the mountain. Their real name was Ayako, but at some point, Ayako's body had split in two. It's a phenomenon that often happens to people who suffer a severe emotional shock or are in a distracted state. It's happened to me several times. If the two halves remain in close contact with each other, nothing serious happens. They reintegrate, and the person is his old self. But occasionally this fails to happen for some people. Most of them die if they take too long to reintegrate, but some people hold such deep convictions about the value of staying alive that they come back to life. If both halves revive, the body exists in duplicate. That's what happened to Ayako. The halves share the same name, but I distinguish them by calling them Arteria and Vena.

It wasn't as if one of them outranked the other. Arteria was yang and Vena was yin; and they gave the impression that Arteria was the leader and Vena the follower. They were like inbound and outbound trains. The reason that I dubbed the right half "Arteria" (the Latin word for "artery") when they split was that it seemed like a natural concept for a right-handed person like me. Actually, Arteria appeared to take the lead in their actions, if only a little. Yet Ayako's heart was on the left side when she split in two, so perhaps I should have ranked the left half higher and called it "Arteria." Even so, the right half created a heart on its own, so it's fair to say that its desire to live overwhelmed that of the left half. I suppose then that it was appropriate to think of the right half as predominant.

"We heard that your brother passed away," they said in unison. Behind their polite words lay an implied criticism of me for not notifying them right away. "May we take him as you promised?"

"He's all ready. Please come in."

When I asked whether they could transport him, they said that they had brought a cart. "It's the one we used for our touring act."

As they passed through the living room, they glanced at the aquarium. "You have more new ones," they said. "Those characters are diving down to those mollusks, aren't they?"

The mollusks had evidently finished sucking in the print from the newspaper, but the black shapes of printed characters extended from under the books on my shelf and were advancing toward the aquarium.

I showed Arteria and Vena into my brother's bedroom.

"Will he be of any use to you?"

"He's fantastic! Thank you!"

"The internal organs are what causes decomposition, so I've removed all of them, and I've embalmed the rest," I said smugly. "I've done a perfect job even if I do say so myself. I planned to let you know as soon as I was finished. I'm sorry about not telling you sooner."

Their dissatisfied faces showed that my sarcasm had gone completely over their heads.

"Your brother's beautiful!" Arteria and Vena said, their faces flushing with excitement.

His opened and preserved innards were wax-colored with a slight reddish cast like the inside of an Akoya pearl oyster. In fact, the coloration of his entire body made him look like a wax sculpture.

As I helped Arteria and Vena carry my brother through the living room, they hesitantly looked up at me, and said, "It's really out of line of us to ask after you've given us your brother and everything, but we wanted to buy a finger; but before we could get around to it, they issued the ban and so on, and they're so expensive now ..."

"Do you want some?" I asked, anticipating their request. They squirmed as if embarrassed.

I filled an empty jar with water, scooped the mollusks out of the aquarium, and dropped them in. The mollusks snapped shut as if flustered by this turn of events. "Here, take them."

Although they clearly wanted the mollusks, Arteria and Vena made a show of hesitating. "Oh, do you really mean it?"

"Please take them. I picked them up on the shore, so they're free."

"It's really weird that someone threw these away when they sell for such high prices. This is the first time I've seen fingers inside a mollusk. I wonder if they went in on their own or whether the person who threw them away put them there."

"I have no idea."

I was fed up with having the print stolen from my newspaper every day. I was so fed up that I no longer cared about the slogans "Thou shalt try to stay alive" and "Thou shalt not kill," but I felt that just discarding the mollusks by the side of the road would be as painful as abandoning newborn kittens whose eyes were not yet open. What I was doing was getting rid of a nuisance.

I placed the jar containing the finger mollusks in my brother's open belly, and the three of us carried his body out to the cart.

On the floor of the cart lay a thin quilt with an overall pattern of tiny flowers.

"How shall we lay him out?"

"On his right side."

We laid him on his side like a statue of a sleeping Buddha.

The two of them reached under the quilt, took out light blue banners with diagonal red stripes, and affixed them to the edge of the cart. "Grand Puppet Theater" was emblazoned on the banners in black characters.

My brother had been a good friend of Ayako's before his death, but that didn't mean that he had been in love with her. She was just a neighbor girl whom he had known since childhood. Ayako, on the other hand, seems to have been infatuated with him. In fact, she had gone into hysterics and split in two upon finding out that he was fatally ill. Dazed, she had momentarily forgotten to keep the two halves close together. The result was Arteria and Vena.

Ayako's father had earned his living pulling a stage mounted on a cart from alley to alley, putting on puppet shows and selling candy. His shows were more popular than those of the storytellers who accompanied their stories with illustrated cards; but there were a lot of traveling puppeteers, and competition was fierce. Ayako had taken over the show after her father's death, but things were not going well. My brother had promised that Ayako, now split in two, could have his body to use as a stage after he died. According to his plan, there would be far more buzz about Ayako's shows than those of her competitors if she had an unusual stage. It's something he thought up because my graduate work involved researching ways of preventing protein decomposition. It was an unsavory idea from an emotional point of view, but I agreed. My brother had not been affected by the slogans "Thou shalt not die," "Thou shalt not kill," and "Thou shalt try to stay alive," and he died quickly and easily.

Arteria and Vena left, bowing slightly as they pulled the cart along. I caught glimpses of blue sky in the gaps between their banners.

The next morning, I was finally able to read my newspaper in peace.

I think it was a few days later that I spotted an article reporting the deaths of Arteria and Vena. It was a short article amid four-panel comic strips in a corner of a local news page. All it said was that they had died in a freakish way since major newspapers shy away from sensational articles. But the evening edition of a tabloid paper gave the story extensive coverage. It reported that the corpse that they had been using as a stage had suddenly closed its hollowed-out belly, acting like a giant mollusk as it engulfed their heads and snapped them off.

My bookshelf held a lot of medical books. I first noticed that the pages of several volumes were blank after giving the finger mollusks to Arteria and Vena. Without my noticing it, the mollusks had stolen the print from the medical books and become deviously clever.

I wondered whose hand the fingers had originally grown on.

I could imagine all sorts of possibilities, but it was a futile effort, so I stopped thinking about it and went to the aquarium to feed my tropical fish. One of the fingers had completed its transformation and was imitating the fish by moving what looked like its mouth. The other two had not yet reached the point where they were able to eat. I tentatively held a razor blade to my little finger. I wondered how my wrist would change if I cut my hand off above the wrist and dropped it into the aquarium. I was like my brother in that I was not affected by the slogans, so it would probably not change into anything and would just rot away.

I stuck my hand into the aquarium. The finger-fish nibbled at it as the setting sun streamed through the window filling the aquarium with a golden light.

Ghostalker

T.L. Huchu

Bindura sucks! The whole town's essentially one main road, a few side streets, and not a whole lot else. I spend half my pocket money jamming Space Invaders on the retro at the Total Service Station. I probably get high off the petrol fumes as I whoop every boy's ass on the game, and so they let me jam with no wahala. Well, there used to be hustle until someone tried to touch up my tits.

They found his balls dangling from a msasa tree half a mile away. Let's just say, the boys keep a respectful distance now.

I'm not really supposed to use my powers for my own benefit. To be fair, most of the time I'm more Peter Parker than Tony Stark, still I Bruce Banner out sometimes. My dad went all Sauron and left us, so I live with my mum and little sis in Chiwaridzo Township.

Sis and I go to work every day, Sunday to Sunday. All mum does is veg out on the couch and watch Mexican soaps and Nollywood dramas. No wonder dad left. I don't care anyway. Not really, I've got too much stuff to do. Knapf! I'm dead. I have to stop thinking about all this kak in the middle of the game.

I buy a freezit and am walking away from the petrol station when my first client of the day flashes in the corner of my eye. It's 2 p.m., the sun's blazing and this ghost is out in the shade of the acacia outside Spar. Must be really desperate. Deados avoid coming out in the day if they can help it. They're all white and stuff, so I reckon they don't have sunscreen in the great beyond. My client beckons with her pale hand. People walk past her without seeing anything.

"All right, all right, I'm coming already!" I shout out, waiting for a car to pass before I cross the road. She looks impatient, but I'm not getting run over just to join her sorry ass.

She's naked, of course. Ghosts are like the ultimate naturalists. Used to freak me out when I was younger, but you get used to it. I hop onto the pavement and say hello.

She replies with something like, "Booga-wooga-wooga," or some such jazz. It's all right, they get a bit looney in the afterlife—the ones that get left behind, that is. You would, too, if you had to wander about the earth butt naked like that.

I say, "Is there anything I can help you with?"

"Wooga-wooga-wooga."

Lord, give me strength. I inhale, hold my breath for a few seconds, and blow on her face. She goes fuzzy for a bit, then comes back in focus.

"Okay, I can deliver a message from you to anyone you want within the town limits," I say. Rules and regulations. "There is a three-tier charge for this service banded in a low flat fee, a middle flat fee, and a high flat fee plus twenty percent VAT. The band you fall into depends on the length, complexity, and content of the message. If you cannot pay the bill, the fee will be reverse-charged to the recipient with a ten-dollar surplus. Please note: this service does not allow vulgar, obscene, criminal, or otherwise objectionable messages, but a fee may still be incurred if we decide to pass on a redacted version of the message. Do you understand?"

"Booga."

"I'll take that as a yes."

Okay, now the kauderwelsch's out of the way, I can go about helping this goon. I fish out my 22-key mini-mbira from my handbag. My sekuru made it; that was his thing, making instruments, right up until he died. That's what my dad does, too, the douchebag. My mbira's small, but the mubvamaropa wood used to make the soundboard is pretty heavy; and then you add on the metal keys, and you have quite a bit of heft. I try to stand out of the stream of people walking past before I jam. I'm hoping this doesn't take too long because I hate crowds gathering around when I'm in the middle of working. It's so knapf. Like, you think I'm a fucking street musician? Get a radio.

I pull a riff from Chiwoniso's melody, "Mai." She's, without a doubt, my favourite mbira player ever. I play it soft, soothing like the leaves swaying in the tree above us. I can feel Chiwoniso in my thumbs as they dance from key to key, callus striking the hard iron underneath. Ka-ra-ka-kata, ka-ra-ka-kata, ka-ra-ka-kata. And I sing:

> *Zita renyu,*
> *Zita rake,*
> *Shoko renyu,*
> *Zviri mumoyo menyu,*
> *Taurirai mwana wenyu,*
> *Taurai zvenyu.*

Over and over, until at last her face lights up, and she understands my voice. Tell me your name. Tell me his name. Your will. The deepest part of your heart. I am your child.

And she tells me she is Cecilia Mukanya. She died six months ago. I have to be very careful and ask her today's date. That's because ghosts travel through time as well, so sometimes you get future ghosts coming back all confused, and the stuff they tell you doesn't make any sense because it hasn't happened yet or the people concerned haven't been born yet. Worst blunder I ever made was telling a guy a message from his future ghost, like, I told him how and when he was going to die, stuff like that. Major, major violation. If he'd reported me, I'd have had my licence revoked. Most important thing when dealing with future ghosts is to tell them to return to their own time line right away. Don't get sucked in, don't give them the time of day, otherwise it gets real messy.

Cecilia tells me her husband remarried pronto-quick, like, the month after her funeral. (If you've been in this game as long as I have, you'll know men are bastards like that). The new wife is abusing the kids. Cecilia wants it to stop. Or else.

I play my mbira around her sweet voice, each note I strike catches a tear on her face which I can't dry. And I find I'm crying with her like a fool in the street. I promise to deliver the message right away. She thanks me by blowing away with the summer breeze. Shhh.

My mum used to be in this business. She was the best ghostalker in all of Mashonaland Central. Even got a certificate from the governor's office in '96. But after a while, she just burnt out and never got her spark back. Apparently, the same thing that happens to shrinks. One day, she just didn't have any light in her eyes.

You gotta be careful when you deal with the dead. They've got a lot of crazy kak going on, so it's important to be firm, set boundaries for them. Like, I have this one stalker ghost that won't go away. He/she/it is like always following me around. I don't get paid enough for that kind of weirdness. That's why I started doing deliveries during the day, makes it harder for he/she/it to follow me.

I go to the phone box opposite the POSB. There's a long line stretching out onto the pavement, people trying to withdraw their cash. The receiver on the phone in the booth's been broken and stolen. Smells of pee or something in here. I'm not Clark Kenting, though; I just come in to use the phone book, so I can get addresses for my deliveries.

My cell rings retro-Crazy Frog style. I check the number, and it's Kush again. Full name's Kushinga, he's, no, was my boyffff, call him my ex, my, well, it's complicated. I wanna answer it, but I don't—I let it ring out. Twenty-seven missed calls. It's kinda psychocute in a strange way. I've got way too much to do. Call me career woman. I give a thaza to the crazy beggar woman walking past in rags. At least she can get something to eat. What goes around comes around.

I catch the kombi to Trojan. There's a few deliveries I have there. You can smell Trojan before you even get to it. The chemical smell from the smelter. Then it appears sprawled out on a hill, small matchbox houses climbing up the terraces. And the whole town is black from slag dumped everywhere. Huge Caterpillars and earth-moving equipment caked in dirt drive around.

The men in Trojan all either wear blue overalls or khaki outfits if they're the bosses. I got my lucky steel-toe cap boots from a miner here. They're really good for kicking people's shins if they try to fuck with me. But I don't Bruce Lee that often, not really, anyway.

The tallest things here are the two chimney pipes striped red and white like a barber's pole. Women line the streets selling forest fruit and maheu. I climb up the hill and find the right house, then I brace myself, and wear my serious grown-up face.

People react differently to ghostalkers. Some are welcoming, others are harsh. They are a bit suspicious because there are so many charlatans out there; but I have an official government ID, and that usually makes it kosher. A woman answers the door.

"I have a reverse charge message for Melody Makunike from her grandfather Sixpence Molaicho," I say.

"What is this about?"

"The sharing of the goats, but you have to pay me first if you want to hear the rest." I dangle part of the message to show I'm authentic, then I wait to get paid. I can read Melody thinking, trying to decide whether or not to take the message. Rule number zero: never, ever, ever, relay the message before you've been paid.

"Okay, how much?"

They always bite. Too curious or fearing to incur the wrath of the dead. Though sometimes ...

I was eleven when I got sick, like really, really sick. I had a fever, my sweat could have formed a river thick and fast like the Mazowe. Doctors thought I had malaria, and they put me on norolon or something like that. Didn't help one bit. And I was seeing all sorts of fantastic kak swimming around me, sort of like a blurry picture taken from far, far away. They called in my Grandpa, Garaba; and he said that I had the gift, but first I must be cleansed. On and off, I remember three days in a mud hut in Madziwa, smoky as hell, good thing I don't have asthma. The old man did some chanting to the ancestors, waved stuff about, and made me drink vile potions (yuk). Three days later, I was right as rain. Except I saw dead people everywhere. Didn't have a choice in the matter. You kinda get drafted into this gig. There are worse ways to earn a living, I suppose.

Missed call alert. Go away, Kush, it's over. Twilight; the sun's getting low. I'm walking to Chipindura, but I have to take the long way round, avoid the cemetery. Most ghosts are all right one on one, but they go insane when you meet them in a group. Sort of the same herd mentality that soccer fans have. So you gotta avoid that cemetery or risk getting your ass booga-woogaed.

I have a home visit—happens sometimes. A ghost has taken up residency in Rudo Chisano's house, and it's spooking the kids out. Hasn't paid any rent either, so the Chisanos want it out. Kak, stalker ghost appears out of the corner of my eye. I speed up, jog a little, and hurry towards the two-bedroom bungalow in front of me. I hop over the low fence and knock on the door. Stalker ghost is drawing closer and closer. I give him/her/it the finger just as I jump inside. He/She/It won't follow. Most ghosts don't like being indoors unless you build over their graves, then you're pretty much stuck with them.

I make sure the Chisanos pay me first before I whip out my mbira. Their living room is spare, blackened walls, and I can smell the primus stove burning in the kitchen. There's a photo of an old granny on the wall alongside some wedding pics.

Mbuya Stella Chiweshe has the best jams for this sort of situation, so I riff off "Paite Rima." Everyone knows that song, so the family sings along with me. Their little girl, maybe seven or eight, has a beautiful voice. I've just started when the ghost pops up from between the floorboards.

"What do you want?" he says, all gruffy.

"You spooking people out," I reply. "I wanna know what you're doing here."

"Who the hell do you think you are?"

"I'm the diplomat. If you don't play nice, I'll bring in a Mapostori air strike."

His toothless face cracks up, and he laughs, long, loud, and rattily. He's got balls, I'll give him that. Then he looks at the little girl and points. Stupid me, I should have noticed that from the start.

"There's a mhondoro in the making here, and the ancestors have sent me to protect her."

Bummer. No one can dislodge an emissary from the ancestors.

"You know if you had wings and a halo, people might be okay with you," I say. Resolution: "How about you fix up your face, stop popping up unannounced, and stay in the background like a good bodyguard? That way everyone will be copacetic."

The family aren't exactly happy that they've paid me to tell them they're stuck with the ghost. I try to convince them he's there to protect their daughter and won't bother them too much from now on. They'll probably try someone else and lose a lot of money doing it, but hey, that's life. Just because you pay to see the doctor doesn't mean she can cure you, right? I should know.

Withheld number calling. Nice one, Kush, but I won't fall for that. Ignore. Sooo annoying, just can't take a hint. But that's why I fell for him in the first place. Dorky comic book reading kid, thick glasses, of course he was my type. Okay, I made the first move. We swapped my *Spawn* for his *Beano*, and it was magic. The two of us sitting at the athletics grounds, reading or just holding hands. Kush. But that was another life. Should have seen his tears when I broke it off. The whole thing was wimp-adorable. But it was for his own good. Too much on my plate with my condition.

I love moonlight pouring through my window. The silver light has a cool purity to it. I feel it cleansing my pores and washing everything away. Power's gone off again, so I can see millions of stars in the sky, ghosts wandering the streets, smoke rising from chimneys and open fires in the township.

My little sis, Chris, walks in. She's come back from Bindura Musika, where she sells kachasu moonshine to the folks getting on and off buses to Glendale and Mt. Darwin. It's a good little business she's got, but I make sure she goes to school. Won't be much without an education. I make sure her fees are paid and her uniform is clean and pressed for her first thing in the morning.

From the canned laughter on TV, I know mum's watching ZBC reruns of *Sanford and Son* on her battery-powered mini. She's not just watching it, she's in it, deep inside a part of that fake reality in ways I could never understand. Dad said she saw her future ghost, and it fried her brain, inducing permanent vegeosis. I squash a big, fat mosquito, smearing blood on the white walls of my bedroom.

I spent two months' wages visiting the doctor's surgery. No use going to the government hospital where I was born—they have long queues and not much else there. I don't like doctors anyway, the way they touch you like you're a disease, not a person. And the smell. Knapf.

She sat all prim and proper behind the desk in her office, posters on the walls for malaria, HIV, and cholera, and read my test results. It was two weeks before my sixteenth birthday when I was told I was going to die.

"Without treatment, you have six months, maybe up to a year."

It felt more like she was talking about someone else's sickness. I knew death. Hell, I saw dead people all the time. But it was something that happened to other people, not to me. I was sick to my stomach.

"We don't have the right type of specialists in this country for your condition. You'll need to go abroad for treatment," Doc said, keeping a straight face as if that was a possibility.

Did she see Bruce Wayne sitting in the chair opposite? Abroad— I'd never been to Harare, let alone left the fucking country. Who was gonna pay for that?

So I left her office with a death penalty and prescription painkillers.

I suppose in many ways, GTs are just like the old telegram service, only we link up two worlds. I hold my surgery at the shopping centre between 7 p.m. and 10 p.m. There's still a lot of people at the centre, especially the bottle store, so the deados are well-behaved.

I sit down on the pavement with my mbira on one side and a notepad on the other. I've seen all types of ghosts out there, needy ghosts, spooky, pervy, aggressive, manipulative, you name it. The key thing is to let them know who's in charge. But I sometimes wonder why anyone would want to stay on this little rock if they were free to fly to all corners of the universe. If I was a ghost, I'd be busy exploring outer space. I wouldn't waste my time on this planet. I suppose the ones that get left behind are sort of like those losers who hang around school after they've finished because they can't let go.

A grotesque appears in front of me. Head swollen up to the size of a pudzi, face smashed into a pulp. Doesn't scare me one bit. I play my mbira, jamming Sekuru Gora's hit tune, "Kana Ndafa," and let the grotesque tell his story as drunks walk by carrying scuds and empty bottles. Litter blows across the dusty forecourt, and a firefly blinks along.

The ghost wants me to help his family find his body. It's hidden somewhere, a dam or a reservoir of water. The water fills his lungs, he can't breathe. It's everywhere around him and inside of him. Fish have eaten his eyeballs. He refuses to name his killers. He doesn't want revenge. It's pointless, he says. All he wants is a decent burial in the family plot and for his mother to gain some closure.

I let him weep to the mbira, playing the chords gently, very lightly, almost inaudibly, especially with the bar radio nearby blasting pop songs.

I leave the shops as I always do, notepad full of leads, clients I have to find tomorrow. If I steal the directory, I can save myself quite a bit of time, getting my addresses at home instead. Seems kinda low, though, stealing a directory, WTF?

Knapf, stalker ghost appears out of the corner of my eye. I pick up the pace, break into a slow trot. Truth: I'm kicking up dust, Barry Allening it. Stalker ghost is booga-wooga-ing and tearing down towards me. All I can see is one gigantic mouth, dangling uvula dancing like a Zulu.

Dogs bark behind fences as I bolt along the dirt track. Stalker ghost is gaining on me. I hit a pothole, feel my ankle twist slow-mo, then I'm watching my feet swing over my head before I hit the ground. I don't even have half a second to cry ouch before stalker ghost is there, proper mupogonyonyo style, all tall, head in the clouds.

The ground underneath me trembles.

My elbows and the palms of my hands bleed. I pick up my mbira and sing.

"Tortured Soul" is the quintessential Zimbabwean song of all time, and in quintessential Zimbabwean fashion, it was composed by a

Mozambican, Matias Xavier. It's always on rotation on ZBC during the Heroes, Independence, and Defence Forces holidays.

As I strum my mbira, replacing Matias's acoustic guitar, I let the lament escape my throat, "Yeeeyi, yeeeyi, yeyelele". This song contains all time within it, every grief spoken and unspoken, every fear, lost love and lost time, all of human history beyond word. Truth. It contains truth you can't run from. And as the stalker ghost shrinks back down to normal size, I see her face, I see my naked face in hers, she's my future ghost.

I take a day off, pick up the phone, and call Kush. It's break time at Chipindura High, and the yard is full of maroon-and-white uniforms walking about. He comes out of somewhere in the crowd with his A-Level swag. I used to learn here, once upon a distant past.

"You wanna go somewhere with me?" I say.

He doesn't ask where I've been or why I haven't answered his calls. Just throws his satchel over the diamond wire fence, climbs up it, and lands next to me. His face shines from too much Vaseline. It makes me smile.

"I have the latest *Civil War* if you want it," he says.

"I'm sorry I've been AWOL. Had a lot of crazy kak going on," I reply.

"I missed you."

We hold hands under the hot sun and head out past the town into the forest to find a ruware where we can sit down, carve our names into the stone, and watch the clouds drift across the sky.

I don't tell him I'm the walking dead, that at any moment my heart could explode. I picture it, a giant spray of blood from my chest. I don't tell him that I'm trying to make sure mum and Chris are okay for when I'm gone, that I haven't told anyone I'll be going away soon. I don't tell him that I'm here because after I'm gone, I ain't coming back. Never. Ever. But before that happens, I'm going to wear my suit of armour, make memories that last forever, and wipe away every molecule of regret.

I Tell Thee All,
I Can No More

Sunny Moraine

Here's what you're going to do. It's almost like a script you can follow. You don't have to think too much about it.

Just let it in. Let it watch you at night. Tell it everything it wants to know. These are the things it wants, and you'll let it have those things to keep it around. Hovering over your bed, all sleek chrome and black angles that defer the gaze of radar. It's a cultural amalgamation of one hundred years of surveillance. There's safety in its vagueness. It resists definition. This is a huge part of its power. This is a huge part of its appeal.

Fucking a drone isn't like what you'd think. It's warm. It probes gently. It knows where to touch me. I can lie back and let it do its thing. It's only been one date, but a drone isn't going to worry about whether I'm an easy lay. A drone isn't tied to the conventions of gendered sexual norms. A drone has no gender and, if it comes down to it, no sex. Just because it can *do* it doesn't mean it's a thing that it *has*.

We made a kind of conversation, before, at dinner. I did most of the talking, which I expected.

The drone hums as it fucks me. We—the *dronesexual,* the recently defined, though we only call ourselves this name to ourselves and only ever with the deepest irony—we're never sure whether the humming is pleasure or whether it's a form of transmission, but we also don't really care. We gave up caring what other people, people we probably won't ever meet, think of us. We talk about this on message boards, in the comments sections of blogs, in all the other places we congregate, though we don't usually meet face to face. There are no dronesexual support groups. We don't have conferences. There is no established discourse around who we are and what we do. No one writes about us but us, not yet.

The drones probably don't do any writing. But we know they talk. Drones don't come, not as far as we can tell, but they must get satisfaction out of it. They must get something. I have a couple of orgasms in the laziest kind of fashion, and the vibration of the maybe-transmission humming tugs me through them. I rub my hands all over that smooth conceptual hardware and croon.

There was no singular point in time at which the drones started fucking us. We didn't plan it, and maybe it wasn't even a thing we consciously wanted until it started happening. Sometimes a supply creates a demand.

But when something is around that much, when it knows that much, it's hard to keep your mind from wandering in that direction. *I wonder what that would feel like inside me.* One kind of intimacy bleeds into another. Maybe the drones made the first move. Maybe we did. Either way, we were certainly receptive. *Receptive,* because no one penetrates drones. They fuck men and women with equal willingness, and the split between men and women in our little collectivity is, as far as anyone has ever been able to tell, roughly fifty-fifty. Some trans people, some genderfluid, and all permutations of sexual preference represented by at least one or two members. The desire to fuck a drone seems to cross boundaries with wild abandon. Drones themselves are incredibly mobile and have never respected borders.

Here's what you're going to do. You're not going to get too attached. This isn't something you'll have to work to keep from doing because it's hard to attach to a drone. But on some level there is a kind of attachment because the kind of closeness you experience with a drone isn't like anything else. It's not like a person. They come into you; they know you. You couldn't fight them off even if you wanted to. Which you never do. Not really.

We fight, not because we have anything in particular to fight over, but because it sort of seems like the thing to do.

No one has ever come out and admitted to trying to have a relationship with the drone that's fucking them, but of course everyone knows it's happened. There are no success stories, which should say something in itself; and people who aren't in our circle will make faces and say things like *you can't have a relationship with a machine no matter how many times it makes you come,* but a drone isn't a dildo. It's more than that.

So of course, people have tried. How could you not?

This isn't a relationship; but the drone stayed the night after fucking me, humming in the air right over my bed as I slept, and it was there when I woke up. I asked it what it wanted, and it drifted toward the kitchen, so I made us some eggs which of course only I could eat.

It was something about the way it was looking at me. I just started yelling, throwing things.

Fighting with a drone is like fucking a drone in reverse. It's all me. The drone just dodges, occasionally catches projectiles at an angle that bounces them back at me, and this might amount to throwing. All drones carry two AGM-114 Hellfire missiles neatly resized as needed because all drones are collections of every assumption we've ever made about them, but a drone has never fired a missile at anyone they were fucking.

This is no-stakes fighting. I'm not even sure what I'm yelling about. After a while the drone drifts out the window. I cry and scream for it to call me. I order a pizza and spend the rest of the day in bed.

Here's what you're going to do. You're not going to ask too many questions. You're just going to let it happen. You'll never know whose eyes are behind the blank no-eyes that see everything. There might not be any anymore; drones regularly display what we perceive as autonomy. In all our concepts of *droneness,* there is hardly ever a human being on the other end. So there's really no one to direct the questions to.

Anyway, what the hell would you ask? *What are we doing, why are we this way?* Since when have those ever been answers you could get about this kind of thing?

This is really sort of a problem. In that I'm focusing too much on a serial number and a specific heat signature that only my skin can know. In that I asked the thing to call me at all. I knew people tried things like this, but it never occurred to me that it might happen without trying.

It does call me. I talk for a while. I say things I've never told anyone else. It's hard to hang up. That night while I'm trying to sleep I stare up at the ceiling, and the dark space between me and it feels so empty.

I pass them out on the street, humming through the air. They avoid me with characteristic deftness, but after a while it occurs to me that I'm steering myself into them, hoping to make contact. They all look the same, but I know they aren't the same at all. I'm looking for that heat signature. I want to turn them over, so I can find that serial number nestled in between the twin missiles over the drone dick that I've never actually seen.

Everyone around me might be a normal person who doesn't fuck a drone and doesn't want to and doesn't talk to them on the phone and usually doesn't take them to dinner. Or every one of them could be like that.

At some point we all stopped talking to each other.

Here's what you're going to do. Here's what you're not going to do. Here's a list to make it easy for you.

You're not going to spend the evening staring out the window. You're not going to toy endlessly with your phone. You're not going to masturbate furiously and not be able to come. You're not going to throw the things you threw at nothing at all. You're not going to stay up all night looking at images and video that you can only find on a few niche paysites. You're not going to wonder if you need to go back into therapy because you don't need therapy. You're not going to wonder if maybe you and people like you might be the most natural people in the entire world, given the way the world is now. You're not going to wonder if there was ever such a thing as *natural*.

Sometimes I wonder what it might be like to be a drone. This feels like a kind of blasphemy and also pointless, but I do it anyway. So simple, so connected. So in tune. Needed instead of the one doing the needing. Possessing all the power. Subtly running more and more things until I run everything. The subjects of total organic surrender.

Bored, maybe, with all that everything. Playing some games.

It comes over. We fuck again, and it's amazing. I'm almost crying by the end. It nestles against me and hums softer, and I wonder how screwed I actually am in how many different ways.

Anyway, it stays the night again, and we don't fight in the morning.

A drone wedding. I want to punch myself in the mouth twenty or thirty times for even thinking that even for a second.

It starts coming every night. This is something I know I shouldn't get used to, but I know that I am. As I talk to it—before sex, during, after—I start to remember things that I'd totally forgotten. Things from my early childhood, things from high school that I didn't want to remember. I tell with tears running down my face, and at the end of it, I feel cleaned out and raw.

I don't want this to be over, I say. I have no idea what the drone wants, and it doesn't tell me; but I want to believe that the fact that it keeps coming back means something.

I read the message boards, and I wish I could tell someone else about this because I feel like I'm losing every shred of perspective. I want to talk about how maybe we've been coming at this from all the wrong angles. Maybe we should all start coming out. Maybe we should form political action groups and start demanding recognition and rights. I know these would all be met with utterly blank-screen silence, but I want to say them anyway. I write a bunch of things that I never actually post, but I don't delete them either.

We're all like this. I'm absolutely sure that we're all like this, and no one is talking about it; but in all of our closets is a thing hovering, humming, sleek and black and chrome with its missiles aimed at nothing.

We have one more huge fight. Later, I recognize this as a kind of self-defense. I'm screaming and beating at it with my fists, something about commitment that I'm not even sure that I believe, and it's just taking it except for the moments when it butts me in the head to push me back. I'm shrieking about its missiles, demanding that it go ahead and vaporize my entire fucking apartment, put me out of my misery, because I can't take this anymore, because I don't know what to do. We have angry sex, and it leaves. It doesn't call me again. I stay in bed for two days and call a therapist.

Here's what you're going to do.

You're going to do what you told yourself you had the courage to do and say everything. You're going to let it all out to someone flesh and blood, and you're going to hear what they say back to you. For once you're not going to be the one doing all the talking. You're going to be honest. You're going to be the one to start the whole wheel spinning back in the other direction. You're going to fix everything because you have the power to fix everything. You're going to give this all a name and say it like you're proud. You're going to bust open a whole new paradigm. You're going to be missile-proof and bold and amazing, and you're not going to depend on the penetrative orgasmic power of something that never loved you, anyway.

I stop at the door. I don't even make it into the waiting room.

I fiddle with the buttons on my coat. I check my phone for texts, voice mail. I look down the street at all those beautiful humming, flying things. I feel a tug in the core of me where everything melts down into a hot lump and spins like a dynamo. I feel like I can't deny everything. I feel like I don't want to. I feel that the flesh is treacherous and doomed.

I made this promise to myself, and it takes me half an hour on a bus and five minutes of staring at a name plaque and a glass door to realize that I don't want to keep it.

I look back out at everyone, and I consider what it could be like to step through those doors, sit in a softly lit room with tissues and a lot of pastel and unthreatening paintings on the wall and spill it all and look up and see the therapist nodding, nodding knowingly, mouthing the words *me, too*.

I don't really think anyone can help any of us.

Here's what you're going to do. You're going to stop worrying. You're going to stop asking questions. You're going to stop planning for tomorrow. You're going to go out and get laid and stop wondering what might have been. You're going to stop trying to fix anything. You're going to stop assuming there's anything to be fixed.

You're going to look out at all those drones and not wonder. You're going to look out at all those people, and you're going to *know*. Even though no one is talking.

Me, too. Me, too. Me, too.

Increasing Police Visibility

Bogi Takács

Manned detector gates will be installed at border crossings, including Ferihegy Airport, and at major pedestrian thoroughfares in Budapest. No illegally present extraterrestrial will evade detection, government spokesperson Júlia Berenyi claimed at today's press conference ...

Kari scribbles wildly in a pocket notebook. How to explain? It's impossible to explain anything to government bureaucrats, let alone science.

Kari writes:

To describe a measurement—

Sensitivity: True positives / Positives = True positives / (True positives + False negatives)
Specificity: True negatives / Negatives = True negatives / (False positives + True negatives)

Kari decides even this is too complicated, tears out the page, starts over.

To describe a measurement—

Janó grits his teeth, fingers the pistol in its holster. The man in front of him is on the verge of tears, but who knows when suffering will turn into assault without another outlet?

"I have to charge you with the use of forged documents," Janó says.

"How many times do I have to say? I'm—not—an—alien," the man yells and raises his hands, more in desperation than in preparation to attack.

"Assault on police officers in the line of duty carries an additional penalty," Janó says.

The man breaks down crying.

Kari paces the small office, practices the presentation. *They will not understand because they don't want to understand,* e thinks. Out loud, e says:

"To describe any kind of measurement, statisticians have devised two metrics we're going to use. Sensitivity shows us how good the measurement is at finding true positives. In this situation a person identified as an ET who is genuinely an ET."

The term *ET* still makes em think of the Spielberg movie from eir childhood. E sighs and goes on. "Whereas specificity shows us how good the measurement is at finding true negatives." How much repetition is too much? "Here, a person identified as an Earth human who's really an Earth human."

The whole thing is just about keeping the police busy and visible. Elections are coming next year, Kari thinks. *Right-wing voters eat up this authoritarian nonsense.*

"So if we know the values of sensitivity and specificity and know how frequent are ETs in our population, we can calculate a lot. We can determine how likely it is for a person who was detected at a gate to be a real extraterrestrial."

Alien is a slur, e reminds emself.

Eir officemate comes in, banging the door open. He glances at eir slide, and yells, "Are they still nagging you with that alien crap?"

The young, curly-haired woman is wearing an ankle-length skirt and glaring down at Janó—she must be at least twenty centimeters taller than him, he estimates. She is the seventh person that day who objects to a full-body scan.

"This goes against my religious observance," she says, nodding and grimacing. "I request a pat-down by a female officer." She sounds practiced at this.

Janó sighs. "A pat-down cannot detect whether you are truly an extraterrestrial."

"I will sue you!"

"Sue the state, you're welcome," he groans and pushes her through, disgusted with himself all the while.

• • •

Kari is giving the presentation to a roomful of government bureaucrats. E's trying to put on a magician's airs. *Pull the rabbit out of the hat with a flourish.*

"So let's see! No measurement is perfect. How good do you think your gates are at detecting ETs? Ninety percent? Ninety-five percent? You know what, let's make it ninety-nine percent just for the sake of our argument." *They would probably be happy with eighty,* e thinks.

E scribbles on the whiteboard—they couldn't get the office smartboard working nor the projector. Eir marker squeaks.

$$SENSITIVITY = 99\%$$
$$SPECIFICITY = 99\%$$

"And now, how many people are actually ETs in disguise? Let's say a half percent." *That's probably a huge overestimate still,* e thinks.

"So for a person who tests as an ET, the probability that they truly are an ET can be calculated with Bayes' theorem ..." E fills the whiteboard with eir energetic scrawl.

E pauses once finished. The calculations are relatively easy to follow, but e hopes even those who did not pay attention can interpret the result.

Someone in the back hisses, bites back a curse. Some people whisper.

"Yes, it's around 33 percent," Kari says. "In this scenario two-thirds of people who test as ETs will be Earth humans. And this gets even worse the rarer the ETs are." *And the worse your sensitivity and specificity,* e thinks but doesn't add. E isn't here to slam the detection gate technology. "This, by the way, is why general-population terrorist screenings after 9/11 were such abysmal failures." Americans are a safe target here; the current crop of apparatchiks is pro-Russian.

This is math. There is nothing to argue with here. Some of the men still try.

Kari spends over an hour in discussion, eir perkiness already worn off by the half-hour mark.

"We can't just stop the program," a middle-aged man finally says. "It increases police visibility in the community."

Kari wishes e could just walk out on them, but what would that accomplish?

● ● ●

"I had a horrible day," Kari/Janó say simultaneously, staring at each other: their rumpled, red-eyed, rattled selves.

"I hate myself," Janó says.

"I'm useless," Kari says.

Then they hug. Then they kiss.

Below their second-story window on Klauzál Square, an extraterrestrial materializes out of thin air, dodging the gates.

Endnotes:

For those interested in the actual calculations, the Bayes' Theorem page on Wikipedia demonstrates them with the numbers used in the story, in the context of drug testing.

I first heard the terrorism comparison from Prof. Floyd Webster Rudmin at the University of Tromsø, Norway.

The House at the End of the World

Carmen Maria Machado

After our parents disappeared, the house was ours. We wrestled in the garden, writhing in the ivy and creeping jenny; we dropped rocks into the ocean and listened to them *glug* in the glassy deep; and when the late-afternoon wall of milky fog rolled in off the water, we stood at the edge of the cliff and lifted our arms to welcome it. Mary said that we were destined to become savages, so when we found the first dead bird we laughed and strung the sun-bleached bones over the doorway to ward off intruders. It was only when the second one was found, wingless—and then another, and then the horse—that we began to worry.

The Unvanished

Subodhana Wijeyeratne

The world ends in silence.

I'm sitting by my window. The east of the city is burning crimson and yellow against the night sky. The silhouettes of buildings are like giants gathered to watch the conflagration. There is a hint of char in the air.

There's no one on the streets below, or at least, I don't think there is anyone. It's hard to tell in the darkness. The streetlights are all long dead, and it is as if my building rises from a black sea. In any case, it is silent. No sound of footsteps, no swish of cars, no susurrus of a thousand wandering voices. Nothing but the inaudible settling of feather-soft ash drifting down from the sky as slowly as a body sinking to the bottom of the sea.

I don't know who I'm writing this for.

I don't remember how it started. I only remember when I noticed it, when Salim went missing. We gathered every Saturday as usual, a pack of foreigners basking in the glitter of the city. The dazzling storey-high kanji and the pineapple haircuts. To laugh and be laughed at. He had said he was coming, but he was not there. We did not wait long, for he was prone to such disappearing acts and none of us knew where he lived.

Then a week later, Preethi calls me.

"Hey, do you know where Salim lives?"

"No. Why?"

"No one's seen him in a week."

"And?"

"No one's seen him in a week. No one."

"He hasn't been into work?"

"No. They asked me today."

"Hold on."

He lives in a tiny building, pre-earthquake ordinance, three stops out of town. Where the countryside creeps up to the city as furtive as a fox. Old people squatting on their haunches and smoking in thick inhalations and watching us with eyes barely visible beneath rolls of velvet-soft skin. We clamber up the stairs linked by an inexplicable urgency, sweltering and assaulted by a cacophony of cicadas. We bang on his door a while, the thin metal shuddering under our palms.

"Where the Hell is he?"

"Should we call the police?"

Preethi chews on her nails.

"Let's give it another day. You have his FB, right?"

"Yeah."

"Let's message his friends."

I don't remember much of what happens next, but I remember her getting off the train. The little dark patches under her armpits. The fluorescent light on her mahogany skin. That last glance she gives me as the train pulls away, over her shoulder, half-sad. As if she knows what's coming.

When revelation came, it came hard and fast and with no warning. A pilot disappearing on a plane caught on camera. One moment he is there, the next moment he is gone. No body in his clothes. His sunglasses laying on the chair. The camera veers away, and all you can hear is screams. Then thuds and jolts and someone crying. Then the newsreader, brow furrowed, a little white flower on his lapel. I don't remember why he is wearing a flower. Some memorial day, maybe. Irrelevant now. There is no one left to remember but me.

I thought there would be anarchy. That's the way it is in stories. Perhaps on some level we wish that this is the way the world would end, with one last chance for heroism. A world that brings out the best of us before it ends. But this is not how it happens. There is panic for a few days. Planes are grounded. Subways begin to flood. Looting, of course. Before the electricity goes out, when I still had the Internet, there were people ranting about aliens and conspiracies. People who swore that those who disappeared did so in a flash of light to the sound of an angelic choir. People desperate to make a story out of what was happening.

But there is no story.

The first mass disappearance is a prison. No bodies; just rotting food and empty clothes. People scour the building for details, and they disappear, too. Lovers wake up alone, and women wail by empty cribs.

I watch it all, and I think, I need some bourbon.

I get to my favourite bar, but it is closed. There is a porcelain dog outside, a waist-high St. Bernard, wide-muzzled and happy. It knows nothing of what is happening, and it is happy; and it is nice, I think, to see something smiling after so long. I pet it on the head and sit down. A warm rain descends, and there is nothing refreshing or cleansing about it. A guy rushes past, still in his suit, dripping wet. He stops and stares at me for a moment, and says, "Why are you sitting there?"

I shrug.

"Why are you running in the rain?"

He points down the street. "The supermarket down the road. It's open. I want to grab some stuff before it all goes missing." He peers at me. "Come with me."

There is nothing else to do so I get up, and we trot along the wet tarmac, our feet slap-slapping on the ground, moisture and fragments getting into my flip-flops and between my toes. We finally make it to the supermarket; and I am soaked in sweat-mingled rain, and the front door is slightly ajar. It is dimly lit, and inside is an old woman who freezes when she sees us and watches us with big eyes and clutches a little bag of tomatoes and radishes to her chest.

I turn to speak to the man, but he is gone.

I stay in bed awhile, and I am miserable. I tell myself that this too will pass; but this is the problem with such truths: they are truths that too often feel like lies.

Sometimes, I cry.

Eventually, I make it out to the balcony with my binoculars. There used to be a few people left around. A woman who kept flowers on her balcony two or three buildings down. But her door has been open wide for two weeks now; and the plants are beginning to wilt, and there is paper flapping out of her room like escaping pigeons. There was also the man with the white flag, but I will tell you of him later. There is no one else these days.

After a while I go back inside, and I eat something. Cold from a can. Sometimes, I find a box of dry pasta. On days like that, I make the effort to take out the gas burner and sit on the balcony and enjoy the wet bite of the stuff between my teeth. I think of how much I hated it back before. Then I think of how my worries from back then were so trivial. Those times when loneliness was as heavy as the fog on me. When all I could foresee was myself growing old and more alone until I was decrepit and pitiful and all chance for love had faded like the last shimmer of a sun long sunk beyond the horizon.

I read for the rest of the day. Here is something you may not know—when the end of the world comes, no one will ransack the bookshops. At first that made me sad, but now I have unlimited Dostoyevsky and Kafka and McCarthy and Asimov. On good days, when the temperature is just right and I have something to munch on, I am away for a few hours until the sun begins to set and I have to light candles.

I lie in the dark for a long time. I feel sorry for myself a lot.

There is one other thing I do: I go downstairs to see Setsuko every other day. Her door is never locked. I think even before, when there were things to be afraid of—people—she never locked it. She is never surprised to see me, even on those occasions when she is asleep when I arrive and wakes to find me by her bed or emptying her chamber pot or depositing a couple of cans of whatever in her cupboard. She always picks up her conversation right where she left off the last time.

"He wasn't cruel to me," she says this time.

I have to think for a moment to remember what she is talking about, and she waits until I nod and pull up a stool and take her wrinkled, old hand in mine.

"You never left him, though," I venture.

"Oh, I did. I was too good for that. I was beautiful. Men wanted me. I married someone else."

She grins, and her teeth are yellow rimmed with black. She wears lipstick all the time and pearls, and when it is hot, they are glossy with her aged sweat. She shakes her head and snuggles deeper into her bed and sighs.

"You still miss her," she says.

I nod. "I do."

"You'll always miss her."

"Until I disappear, anyway."

"Maybe you'll miss her after that, too."

"Maybe I won't be able to think or feel anything after that."

She shakes her head and doesn't say anything.

It wasn't long after the sixth wave of vanishings that I stumbled across the last desperate partiers who became my universe. Back then it was almost fun having the run of the world. To be able to smash windows—after the power went out there were no more alarms—and take what you pleased. To transgress without consequence. Piss on police cars and feed stray dogs. By the time I find the bar, I haven't seen so many people in one place for weeks. I feel the tap-tap-tap of bass through the walls. It is packed with people, and they turn and cheer. For a few moments I think I am hallucinating, but then I smell the sweat and the smoke and know it must be real.

"I've never seen you before!" says the man behind the bar. He is too large for the waistcoat he is wearing, and he speaks in bursts like machine gun fire. He points the shelf behind him, still crammed with colourful bottles. "Take whatever you want."

"I don't have any cash right now."

He laughs.

"Haven't you heard? It's the end of the world, man. No one uses cash anymore."

There are others in those smoky depths, that world of shadow and neon. A man alone at a table. He smokes and stares at his ashtray and then at the tip of his cigarette. He is crying. In the next cubicle, a clutch of bros in hats, sweat glistening on their naked arms, their hair spiked and glossy.

In the cubicle beyond that is the most beautiful woman I've ever seen.

She is sitting with two men and another woman, laughing. Her head tilted back, hair the colour of golden syrup, hoop earrings and green lipstick. She looks as if she is meant to be there and is there absolutely. I cannot remember what the men look like or who they were. So diminished are they in her presence that, in my memory, they are as gauzy as ghosts and empty as silhouettes.

I do not remember when she comes up to me to talk, but she does. She sits next to me and looks at me as if we were old friends who had agreed to meet there and then and that we both knew what the other knew and there was no need to talk of anything else.

"What's it like outside?" she asks.

"Outside? Shadows and dust and the end of the world."

She smiles at this. "Nice."

"Is it?"

"Your turn of phrase. It's very nice."

I pour some more booze into a shot glass—tequila, or vodka maybe, it doesn't matter, they're all out of bourbon—and down it. She takes the bottle and chugs directly from it and hands it back to me. A little smear of lipstick on the rim. A little rivulet of the stuff trickling over her lip and onto her chin. I realise she is drunk.

"I'm not that drunk," she says and pats her face gently with a tissue. "It's the end of the world, right?"

"I guess."

"So what're you doing about it?"

"Not much."

She isn't looking at me. She is looking everywhere in the room but at me. I do not know this then, but later I learn that that is how you knew she was listening: when she was looking at everything in the room but you.

She takes the bottle out of my hands and takes another solid chug and shudders. Then she smacks it down on the counter, and the bartender looks up at her for a moment; and a crystal spurt of the stuff splashes onto the wood and shatters into little glistening blobs. She reaches into her pocket and tosses some keys to the barkeep, and says, "Lock up afterwards, I'm not coming back." Then she launches herself off the barstool. The swish swish of her hair on her bomber jacket. She disappears into the back, and for a moment the bar is completely silent. When she returns she comes straight to me holding a backpack and a pistol and hands the pistol to me.

"Can you shoot?"

"Yes."

"Come on then."

"Where're we going?"

"To find reinforcements."

She winks and walks out. Of course, I follow. I still have the pistol. I keep it next to my bed. I have two bullets left.

Setsuko is up and about when I arrive and acknowledges my arrival with a rickety bow. I bow back and step around her and start doing the dishes in her sink. She sits down at the table by the window and stares out over the city.

"Cigarette?" she says after a while.

I put one in her mouth, and it fidgets like a twig in the breeze. I light it and put an empty can on the table in front of her and return to the dishes.

"You never got married, did you?" she says.

"No."

"Why?"

"I'm not sure."

"You never wanted to?"

"I did. Very much."

"So why didn't you have a, whatsit, arranged marriage?"

I don't know the answer to this so I swipe a sudsy hand across the porcelain and listen to the squeaking and the patter of the water and say nothing. Nor does Setsuko. She has done this before, wait out my reticence with reptilian patience. Eventually, I am down to the last plate, and say, "I think I always wanted to find someone who liked me back."

"Liked you back?"

"Wanted to be with me the same way I wanted to be with them."

"Yes, but if it was an arranged marriage, wouldn't it have been the same to you both?"

"But what does that even mean? What're we married for?"

"What's anyone married for?"

"Love."

She laughs at this, and the laugh becomes a coughing fit. Then an aerosol spray of blood on the table. Her chest cracks with every heave. I give her a glass of water and wipe the tabletop and pluck the cigarette from her hand.

"You shouldn't be smoking."

She wheezes for a bit and grabs the rag off me and wipes the blood off the corner of her mouth.

"I suppose not. Don't want to die before I disappear."

"Really?"

"Of course not. What if I miss out?"

"Miss out on what?"

She waves one hand in the air. "On whatever's afterwards. Heaven. Where everyone else went."

"What if it's not Heaven?'

She is very still for a while and keeps facing the window, and I cannot tell if she has drifted off to sleep or maybe died. But I can still hear her clattering breath, and after a few moments I realise she is crying.

"Heaven is other people," she says after a while.

"I thought Hell was other people."

"Other people are everything," she says. And then, after a few moments: "I was married once."

"Just once?"

"Just once. He was a nice guy. A good friend."

"What happened?"

"I didn't love him."

"So why did you marry him?"

"Because he was a good man."

"But you didn't love him."

"No. So I left."

"If you didn't love him, it was probably the best thing for both of you."

"It wasn't. For either of us. He hated me after that. Couldn't even look me in the eye. And then he died. I think he killed himself, but none of his family would speak to me. I always thought it was because I kept his grandmother's jewelry; but sometimes I think he killed himself, and they blamed me."

"I'm sorry, Setsuko."

"No point in being sorry."

"But if you didn't love him."

"It doesn't matter if I didn't love him. He was good for me. He made me happy. There's no such thing as love, only evidence of love, and what better proof of love is there than a happy life together?"

"But could you have had one without loving him?"

"I did." And then she sighs and wraps her arms around her shoulders, and says, "Ah, me. To be left here after everyone's gone with nothing but regrets."

I don't know what to say to that so I put my hands on her shoulders, and together we watch the city burn.

Her name was Althea, but I never called her that. And she never called me by my name. We always had something else to call each other. Stupid things, like Pistorella and Butthunter.

We wander the city, just the two of us. She is always overdressed, and by the end of the day, her clothes are usually destroyed. The bomber jacket scarred by the jagged edge of chain-link fence and mud stains on her shoes. But the next day she always has something new. Sometimes I think it is her and her alone who has smashed the windows of every clothes shop I see. When I ask her, she denies this, and says, "I just like clothes."

Of course, I fall in love with her. This one incandescent bud of life in a city haunted by lives unfinished. She does not seem to question what has happened or regret it at all. She sees opportunity where I see only the past. She is always armed and determined, and I am dragged along in her wake and cannot stand to be elsewhere.

Actually, that is not true. She weeps when we see corpses. At first

I think it is all bodies, but it is always the bodies of women that set her going. She will not let me touch her when she is sobbing and walks away and crouches and spends some time wiping the tears from her eyes and looking up and down the facades of the buildings opposite. Then she pulls her makeup set out of her bag and does her face and her hair, and finally she turns to me in a great reveal, grinning fondly as if it were all a test and I had failed but she was going to pass me nonetheless. We never talk about these moments, and they never seem to last long. Always she thumps me on the shoulder afterwards as if I were the one upset, and says, "Come on, Loser, let's go adventuring."

One day we are in my flat standing on the balcony, and I show her my binoculars. She chuckles and immediately begins to scan the surroundings.

"There's so many people left!"

"What? I only ever see four or five."

"That's four or five people we don't know."

"Not that many, though."

"That's a lot of Unvanished."

"Of what?"

She turns to me, and the sun is on the left side of her face and twinkling between her hair and her cheek is a long earring like a wind chime, a fantasy of lapis and gossamer metalwork whipped into insectoid poetry.

"Unvanished," she says, and pokes me in the chest. "You." She pokes herself. "And me."

"I didn't realise there was a word for it."

"There's a word for everything. People just haven't found them all yet."

I smoke and watch her scanning our surroundings, and suddenly she turns to me, and goes, "Somebody needs our help."

"What?"

"There."

I look through the binoculars, and there is a man in a building four or five blocks away. He is standing on the balcony holding his stomach and waving a white flag. He knows we are looking at him, it seems, because he waves more furiously and then drops the flag and leans over his balcony and retches. The vomit and the flag spiral down to ground level in unison, and the instant they hit it, they become one with the detritus now migrating in herds over the asphalt.

"Come on," she says, and heads for the door.

She is wearing bright red canvas shoes and a little tennis outfit and a black cardigan and is faster than me. We find the building and ascend the stairs. There is someone dead at the bottom of the stairwell in the basement. I catch a glimpse of black trousers and a congealed mass of blackening blood. Althea goes on ahead.

When I catch up with her, she is already in the apartment, and the man is lying on the floor clutching his stomach and sobbing. His hands are bloody. He is clutching her ankle, and she is staring down at him and silhouetted against the vista of the city beyond, the pistol in her hands, a brief vision of true apocalypse.

"Oh, God," says the man. "Thank God."

"Let me see," she says.

He takes his hands away, and there is a horrific wound in his belly. The mess of glossy and tangled reds and blacks. It smells rotten and glistens and leaks. She sniffs and crouches down beside him and takes a good hard look and then looks at me. I do not want to, but I get close too and feel the thick stench of it in my nostrils; and I know that this man is going to die.

"That's bad," I say.

"No shit," hisses the man.

"What happened?"

"Dog." He gasps and retches again. "Kill me."

"What?"

"Kill me. Kill me."

She and I look at each other, and in an instant I know she has decided that she will.

"Outside," I say.

"Don't leave, you bastards," the man says.

"We're coming back," she says, closing the apartment door behind her.

In the stairwell it is pitch dark; and I can hear her and smell her, but she could just have been a voice in my head. And then suddenly I feel her hand on mine, and she interlaces our fingers; and her lips are so close to my ear that I can feel them brushing against my skin.

"We've got no choice," she whispers.

"I know," I say.

"We can't leave him like that."

"I'm not sure I can kill a man in cold blood."

"I can."

We go back inside; and the man sees us, and he begins to cry again. She crouches down beside him, and says, "What's your name?"

"What does it matter?"

"Don't you want anyone to remember you when you're gone?"

"You'll all be gone. Soon enough."

"You sure? You don't want to wait to vanish?"

"To hell with that. I'm not going to no Limbo. If I'm going to Hell, I want to go and get it over with."

"Limbo?"

"Well, it isn't Heaven, for sure. If it's Heaven, how come all the bad people get to go, too?"

She stands up, and says, "All right, but I'm not doing it here."

We help him into bed; and I offer him a cigarette, and he smokes it and asks for another one. When he is done with that, he leans back and closes his eyes, and says, "I'm ready." A skinny man in a dirty bed. His face smeared with grime and sporadic stubble ringing his balding pate. He is shaking gently.

She looks at me, and says, "You don't have to be here."

"I don't mind."

She stands up and points the gun straight at the man's forehead. The muzzle matte-black and vicious. She releases the safety with a click, and the man spasms and opens his eyes.

"My name's Tatsuo," says the man. "Nakajima Tatsuo."

She nods.

"Good luck, Nakajima Tatsuo."

Afterwards, we go back to her bar, and it is locked. I am crying, but she is not. She opens it and goes inside and takes a bottle of something down from the shelf, and we both drink until we can no longer stand. We lie on the floor, and she curls up in front of me and takes my arm and puts it around her. In the instant before I sleep, all I want from her is for her to love me as she has never loved anyone before, and it does not seem to be so much to ask.

Setsuko is dead.

This morning I wake up earlier than usual. Or maybe I just think so because of this pall in the sky. An undulating sheet of seething grey cloud rippling with wind—cutting wind from high above. The fire across town has raged for a week now. It shows no sign of coming close but blankets my neighbourhood instead in ash, dank and soft to the touch. Like snow somehow gone rotten.

I go down to see Setsuko. Perhaps I feel sorrier for her than usual after our last conversation. No, this is not true. I am feeling sorrier for myself than usual. I dreamt of Althea last night. I dreamt of a moment that never was and a feeling that was never felt. I woke up, and for a few moments I thought perhaps it was all real. But soon I realised it wasn't and needed human company.

Setsuko is lying on the floor in the kitchen when I walk in. Her loose-skinned legs with their varicose veins like rivers seen from space, akimbo.

I empty her flat out bit by bit. I take anything of use, and then I carry her over to her bed. It is filthy, so I clean it out. I think of dressing her in something nice, but I do not want to take her clothes off. She is heavy in death, and my back hurts. She still smells of herself, of lavender and tobacco and the sickly sweetness of age. I cover her up to her armpits in a duvet and put her hands on top and take her diary with its little metal clasp and its pictures of swallows chasing one another in creamy blue silhouettes on the cover. I put it on her chest and put her hands over it and take one last look at her face.

I don't feel anything for her. My thoughts are ceaselessly of myself. Of the silence that I will now have to endure. Of how I am the last person I know. That is when I start crying, and I do not stop for a long time. Not until the day has already begun to darken and I am forced back up to my room and into my bed with nothing but the flickering light of the distant inferno on my ceiling for company.

I do not see Althea again for a long while. That is not true. When I do, she is with someone else. Another man. The first time they are sitting on a wall and sharing a cigarette. The man is wearing cargo pants and has cropped hair and big black rings inserted in his earlobes. She touches his chest and laughs, and she plays with her hair.

I go to the bar alone that night, and there are only three people there. One of them is the woman with Althea that first night I met her. I go over and take a shot from the bottle of whiskey she is nursing.

"So she dumped you, huh?" she says.

"Who?"

"Althea." She points at my cigarettes. "Can I have one?"

She lights, and she inhales and coughs up a spray of smoke and spit that billows over the table and onto my face.

"You don't smoke."

"Good a time as any to start."

"What's your name?"

"Candy."

"Really?"

"No, not really."

We get drunk, and she comes back to my flat with me and inside casts her eyes around my living room as if she is not familiar with the kind of thing she is looking at. I go to the windows and draw the curtains. When I turn around, her tights are laying on the floor next to her a bag, and she is watching me.

"Why did you do that?" she asks.

"People might see."

"What people?"

I open the curtains again. Now she is in her underwear. Little sheer black panties. A corset top, wrinkled, one of the hooks bent out of shape.

"Gimme a dollar," she says.

"A dollar?"

"Yeah."

She just stands there, diminutive and wide-eyed, naked feet pale against the wood of my floor. It is not cold, but she wraps her arms around herself. I reach for my wallet.

"Why do you do this?" I ask.

"This?"

"Yeah."

I don't have a dollar, but I have ten. I give it to her, and she flicks it onto the floor by her bag.

"What else is there to do?" she asks.

Her movements are gentle and methodical and her skinny legs smooth and cool against mine. When we are near finished, she leans in, sighs, and grazes my nipple with her lips. It is only afterwards that I notice the scar on her belly. I want to reach out and touch it, to say I'm sorry, but I don't. I lie there and have a cigarette and listen to the listless wind meandering through the streets.

Afterwards, we stand in the living room, staring at each other. She looks as if she is about to say something, but she doesn't. When I walk her to the door, she looks at me, and says, "So, if you wanted to again, later ..."

"Sure."

When I close the door, she is still standing there, those mournful eyes in that overthin face, clutching her bag as if it were a baby.

I never see her again.

I finally meet Althea's new man a few days later. He eyes me with disinterest and pumps my hand twice, viciously, when I offer to shake his. His other arm is around Althea's waist, and she is pressed close to him. The curve of her breasts against his chest. Her hair spilling over his shoulder like luxurious fabric.

"Bet you wish you'd done something else now, right, Professor?" he says to me.

"Sorry?"

"Philosophy. What the fuck good is it now, right?"

I shrug. "Helps me cope."

She laughs at this and thumps him on the chest, and says, "See? I told you he was funny."

They head off without telling me where they are going. I wander the streets a while. Two little dogs follow me, yapping and whining, and I smash the window of a shop and grab two cans of dog food and start smacking them with a concrete block. I smack them for a long time and so hard that the stewy meat splatters against the paving stones and over my trousers like roadkill.

Late in the evening, in the glimmering infernal night, Althea bangs on my door. I open it and cannot see what she looks like, but she rushes past me wordlessly and out onto the balcony and stays there smoking. I light a few candles and step outside, and she is crying. I reach out to wrap my arms around her, and then I hesitate and stand there beside her instead, watching her spent butts spiralling down to the darkened street like glowing orange buds falling off a tree.

"He didn't hurt you, did he?" I ask.

"No." Her face is wet with tears. "I'd've ripped his balls off."

I wait a moment, but before I can ask, she says, "I didn't kill him."

"Do you want something to eat?"

She nods. I go inside and use the gas burner to warm up some soup and put it steaming into a mug and take it out to her. She leans against the railings and watches the city as she sips.

"Do you think there's anyone else out there?"

"I don't think so."

"Where the fuck did they all go?"

"I don't know."

"At least, you're here. Don't know how I'd cope without you."

When she has finished, she comes over to me and hugs me and rests her head against my shoulder, and we stand like that a while, watching the empty city and the hollow buildings and the wind harassing shreds of cloth and paper and ash over the rooftops. The fire seems to be burning itself out slowly, but it is still spectacular. I realise that between us and it and obscured by the flames is the river and that as long as it does not jump, my part of town will be safe.

She kisses me gently on the cheek, and says, "I love you."

I kiss her back on the corner of her mouth, and she sighs. I kiss her on the lips, and she wraps her arms around me and works her fingers into my hair and pushes against me as if she were trying to melt into me and make us the last person on earth together. I can taste the soup and booze and tobacco in her mouth; but it does not matter because it is her, and she could taste of anything and still be wondrous to me. We stumble in through the door, and clumsy and fervid, we collapse into the bed; and it is only then we slow down enough to look at each other, long enough for me to say, "I love you, too," and kiss her again.

That is not how it happened. I'm lying again.

This is how it happened.

She kisses me gently on the cheek and wraps her arms around me sideways, and says, "I love you. You're like the brother I never had."

I hug her back and swallow, and I say, "I love you, too." But I do not mean it the way she does. After a few moments she moves away from me and shakes her head and opens her mouth to say something. The next instant, she is gone. Her clothes tumbling empty to the ground, her mug shattering.

I am alone on the balcony with my own half-finished cup of soup and the starless sky.

Like I said. The world ends in silence.

Our Talons Can Crush Galaxies

Brooke Bolander

This is not the story of how he killed me, thank fuck.

You want that kind of horseshit, you don't have to look far; half of modern human media revolves around it, lovingly detailed descriptions of sobbing women violated, victimized, left for the loam to cradle. Rippers, rapists, stalkers, serial killers. Real or imagined, their names get printed ten feet high on movie marquees and subway ads, the dead convenient narrative rungs for villains to climb. Heroes get names; killers get names; victims get close–ups of their opened rib cages mid–autopsy, the bloodied stumps where their wings once attached, baffled coroners making baffled phone calls to even more baffled curators at local museums. They get dissected, they get discussed, but they don't get names or stories the audience remembers.

So no. You don't get a description of how he surprised me, where he did it, who may have fucked him up when he was a boy to lead to such horrors (no one), or the increasingly unhinged behavior the cops had previously filed away as the mostly harmless eccentricities of a nice, young man from a good family. No fighting in the woods, no blood under the fingernails, no rivers or locked trunks or calling cards in the throat. It was dark, and it was bad; and I called for my sisters in a language dead when the lion–brides of Babylon still padded outside the city gates. There. That's all you get, and that's me being generous. You're fuckin' welcome.

However, here is what I *will* tell you. I'll be quick.

• • •

He did not know what I was until after. He felt no regret or curiosity because he should have been drowned at birth. I was nothing but a commodity to him before and nothing but an anomaly to him after. My copper feathers cut his fingertips and palms as he pared my wings away.

I was playing at being mortal this century because I love cigarettes and shawarma and it's easier to order shawarma if your piercing shriek doesn't drive the delivery boy mad. Mortality is fun in small doses. It's very authentic, very down-in-the-dirt nitty-gritty. There are lullabies and lily pads and summer rainstorms, and hardly anyone ever tries to cut your head off out of some moronic heroic obligation to the gods. If you want to sit on your ass and read a book, nobody judges you. Also, shawarma.

My spirit was already fled before the deed was done, back to the Nest, back to the Egg. My sisters clucked and cooed and gently scolded. They incubated me with their great feathery bottoms as they had many times before, as I had done many times before for them. Sisters have to look out for one another. We're all we've got, and forever is a long, slow slog without love.

I hatched anew. I flapped my wings, and hurricanes flattened cities in six different realities. I was a tee-ninsy bit motherfuckin' pissed, maybe.

I may have cried. You don't get to know that either, though.

We swept back onto the mortal plane with a sound of a 1967 Mercury Cougar roaring to life on an empty country road, one sister in the front seat and three in the back and me at the wheel with a cigarette clenched between my pointed teeth. You can fit a lot of wingspan in those old cars, provided you know how to fold reality the right way.

It's easy to get lost on those back roads, but my old wings called to us from his attic. We did not get lost.

He was alone when we pulled into his driveway, gravel crunching beneath our wheels like bone. He had a gun. He bolted his doors. The tumblers turned for us; we took his gun.

Did *he* cry? Oh, yeah. Like a fuckin' baby.

I didn't know what you were, he said. I didn't know. I just wanted to get your attention, and you wouldn't even look at me. I tried everything.

Well, kid, I says, putting my cigarette out on his family's floral carpet, you've sure as hell got it now.

Our talons can crush galaxies. Our songs give black holes nightmares. The edges of our feathers fracture moonlight into silver spiderwebs and universes into parallels. Did we take him apart? *C'mon.* Don't ask stupid questions.

Did we kill him? Ehh. In a manner of speaking. In another manner of speaking, his matter is speaking across a large swathe of space and time, begging for an ending to his smeared roadkill existence that never quite reaches the rest stop. Semantics, right? I don't care to quibble or think about it anymore than I have to.

Anyway. Like I said way back at the start, this is not the story of how he killed me. It's the story of how a freak tornado wrecked a single solitary home and disappeared a promising young man from a good family, leaving a mystery for the locals to scratch their heads over for the next twenty years. It's the story of how a Jane Doe showed up in the nearby morgue with what looked like wing stubs sticking out of her back, never to be claimed or named. It's the story of how my sisters and I acquired a 1967 Mercury Cougar we still go cruising in occasionally when we're on the mortal side of the pike.

You may not remember my name, seeing as how I don't have one you could pronounce or comprehend. The important thing is always the stories—which ones get told, which ones get co-opted, which ones get left in a ditch, overlooked and neglected. This is *my* story, not his. It belongs to me and is mine alone. I will sing it from the last withered tree on the last star-blasted planet when entropy has wound down all the worlds and all the wheres, and nothing is left but faded candy wrappers. My sisters and I will sing it—all at once, all together, a sound like a righteous scream from all the forgotten, talked-over throats in Eternity's halls—and it will be the last story in all of Creation before the lights finally blink out and the shutters go *bang*.

The Memcordist

Lavie Tidhar

Polyphemus Port, Titan, Year Forty-Three

Beyond the dome the ice storms of Titan rage; inside it is warm, damp, with the smell of sewage seeping through and creepers growing through the walls of the aboveground dwellings. He tries to find her scent in the streets of Polyport and fails.

Hers was the scent of basil and the night. When cooking, he would sometimes crush basil leaves between his fingers. It would bring her back for just a moment, bring her back just as she was the first time they'd met.

Polyphemus Port is full of old memories. Whenever he wants, he can recall them, but he never does. Instead, he tries to find them in old buildings, in half-familiar signs. There, the old Baha'i temple where they'd sheltered one rainy afternoon and watched a weather hacker dance in the storm, wreathed in raindrops. There, what had once been a smokes bar, now a shop selling surface crawlers. There, a doll house for the sailors off the ships. It had been called Madame Sing's, now it's called Florian's. Dolls peek out of the windows, small naked figures in the semblance of teenage boys and girls, soft and warm and disposable with their serial numbers etched delicately into the curve of a neck or thigh. His feet know the old way, and he walks past the shops, away from the docks and into a row of box-like apartments, the co-op building where they'd first met, creepers overgrowing the walls and peeking into windows—where they'd met, a party in the Year Seventeen of the Narrative of Pym.

He looks up, and as he does, he automatically checks the figures that rise up, always, in the air before him. The number of followers hovers around twenty-three million, having risen slightly on this, his second voyage to Titan in so many years. A compilation feed of Year Seventeen is running concurrently, and there are messages from his followers, flashing in the lower right corner, which he ignores.

Looking up at her window, a flower pot outside—there used to be a single red flower growing there, a carnivorous Titan Rose with hungry, teeth-ringed suckers—her vice at the time. She'd buy the plant choice goat meat in the market every day. Now the flower pot is absent; and the window is dark, and she, too, is long gone.

Is she watching, too, somewhere, he wonders—does she see me looking up and searching for her, for traces of her in a place so laid and overlaid with memories until it was impossible to tell which ones were original and which the memory of a memory?

He thinks it's unlikely. Like the entire sum of his life, this journey is for his benefit, is ultimately about him. We are what we are—and he turns away from her window, and the ice storm howls above his head beyond the protective layer of the dome. There had been a storm that night, too; but then this was Titan, and there was always a storm.

Onboard the *Gel Blong Mota*, Earth-to-Mars Voyage, Year Five

There are over twenty million followers on this day of the Narrative of Pym, and Mother is happy; and Pym is happy, too, because he'd snuck out when Mother was asleep, and now he stands before the vast porthole of the ship—in actuality, a wall-sized screen—and watches space and the slowly moving stars beyond.

The *Gel Blong Mota* is an old ship, generations of *Man Spes* living and dying inside as it cruises the solar system from Earth, across the inner and outer system, all the way to Jettisoned and Dragon's World before turning back, doing the same route again and again. Pym is half in love with Joy, who is the same age as him and will one day, she confides in him, be captain of this ship. She teaches him asteroid pidgin, the near-universal language of Mars and the belt, and he tells her about Earth, about volcanoes and storms and the continental cities. He was not born on Earth, but he has lived there four of his five years; and he is nervous to be away, but also happy and excited, and it's all very confusing. Nearly fifty million watched him leave Earth, and they didn't go in the elevator; they went in an old passenger RLV, and he floated in the air when the gravity stopped, and he wasn't sick or *anything*. Then they came to an orbital station where they had a very nice room and there was gravity again, and the next day they climbed aboard the *Gel Blong Mota*, which was at the same time very very big but also small, and it smelled funny. He'd seen the aquatic tanks with their eels and prawns and lobster and squid, and he'd been to the hydroponics gardens and spoken to the head gardener there, and Joy even showed him a secret door and took him inside the maintenance corridors beyond the walls of the ship, where it was very dry and smelled of dust and old paint.

Now he watches space and wonders what Mars is like. At that moment, staring out into space, it is as if he is staring out at his own future spreading out before him, unwritten terabytes and petabytes of the Narrative of Pym waiting to be written over in any way he wants. It makes him feel strange—he's glad when Joy arrives and they go off together to the aquatic tanks—she said she'd teach him how to fish.

Tong Yun City, Mars, Year Seven

Mother is out again with her latest boyfriend, Jonquil Sing, a memcordist syndication agent. "He is very good for us," she tells Pym one night, giving him a wet kiss on the cheek, and her breath smells of smoke. She hopes Jonquil will increase subscriptions across Mars, Pym knows—the numbers of his followers have been dropping since they came to Tong Yun. "A dull, provincial *town*," Mother says, which is the Earth-born's most stinging insult.

But Pym likes Tong Yun. He loves going down in the giant elevators into the lower levels of the city, and he particularly loves the Arcade with its battle droid arenas and games-worlds shops and particularly the enormous Multifaith Bazaar. Whenever he can, he sneaks out of the house—they are living on the surface, under the dome of Tong Yun, in a house belonging to a friend of a friend of Mother's—and goes down to Arcade and to the Bazaar.

The Church of Robot is down there and an enormous Elronite temple and mosques and synagogues and Buddhist and Baha'i temples and even a Gorean place; and he watches the almost-naked slave girls with strange fascination, and they smile at him and reach out and tousle his hair. There are Re-Born Martian warriors with reddish skin and four arms—they believe Mars was once habituated by an ancient empire and that they are its descendants and they serve the Emperor of Time. He thinks he wants to become a Re-Born warrior when he grows up and have four arms and tint his skin red, but when he mentions it to Mother, once she throws a fit and says Mars never had an atmosphere and there is no emperor and that the Re-Born are—and she uses a very rude word, and there are the usual complaints from some of the followers of the Narrative of Pym.

He's a little scared of the Elronites—they're all very confident and smile a lot and have very white teeth. Pym isn't very confident.

He prefers quiet roads and places with few people in them, and he doesn't want anyone to know who he is.

Sometimes he wonders who he is or what he will become. One of Mother's friends asked him, "What do you want to be when you grow up?" and he said, "A spaceship captain—" thinking of Joy— and Mother gave her false laugh and ruffled his hair, and said, "Pym already *is* what he is. Isn't that right, sweetheart?" and she gathered him in her arms, and said, "He's *Pym*."

But who is Pym? Pym doesn't know. When he's down at the Multifaith Bazaar, he thinks that perhaps he wants to be a priest or a monk—but which religion? They're all neat.

Fifteen million follow him as he passes through temples, churches, and shrines, searching for answers to a question he is not yet ready to ask himself and might never be.

Jettisoned, Charon, Year Fifty-Six

So at last he's come to Jettisoned, the farthest one can get without quite leaving completely, and he hires a small dark room in a small dark co-op deep in the bowels of the moon, a place that suits his mood.

Twenty-three million watch, less because of him and more because he'd chosen Jettisoned, the home of black warez and wild technology and outlaws—the city of the Jettisoned, all those ejected at the last moment from the vast majestic starships as they depart the solar system, leaving forever on a one-way journey into galactic space. Would some of them find new planets, new moons, new suns to settle around? Are there aliens out there, or God? No one knows, least of all Pym. He'd once asked his mother why they couldn't go with one of the ships. "Don't be silly," she'd said, "think of all your followers and how disappointed they'd be."

"Bugger my followers," he says now aloud, knowing some would complain and others would drop out and follow other narratives. He'd never been all that popular, but the truth was he'd never wanted to be. Everything I've ever done in my life, he thinks, is on record. Everything I've seen, everything I've touched, everything I smelled or said. And yet, had he said or done anything worth saying, anything worth doing?

I once loved with all my heart, he thinks. Is that enough?

He knows she'd been to Jettisoned in the past year. But she'd left before he arrived. Where is she now? He could check but doesn't. On her way back through the outer system—perhaps in the Galilean Moons, where he knows she's popular. He decides to get drunk.

Hours later, he is staggering along a dark alley, home to smokes bars, doll houses, battle arcades, body modification clinics, a lone Church of Robot mission, and several old-fashioned drinking establishments. Anything that can be grown on Jettisoned gets fermented into alcohol sooner or later. Either that or smoked. His head hurts, and his heart is beating too fast. Too old, he thinks. Perhaps he says it out loud. Two insectoid figures materialise in the darkness, descend on him. "What are you—?" he says, slurring the words as the two machines expertly rifle through his pockets and run an intrusion package over his node—even now, when all he can do is blink blearily, he notices the followers numbers rising and realises he's being mugged.

"Give them a show," he says, and begins to giggle. He tries to hit one of the insectoid figures, and a thin, slender metal arm reaches down and touches him—a needle bite against his throat—

Numb, but still conscious—he can't shout for help, but what's the point, anyway? This is Jettisoned, and if you end up there, you have only yourself to blame.

What are they doing? Why have they not gone yet? They're trying to take apart his memcorder, but it's impossible—don't they know it's impossible?—he is wired through and through, half-human and half-machine, recording everything, forgetting nothing. And yet suddenly, he is very afraid, and the panic acts like a cold dose of water; and he manages to move, slightly, and he shouts for help, though his voice is reedy and weak and anyway there is no one to hear him ...

They're tearing apart chunks of memory, terabytes of life, days and months and years disappearing in a black cloud—"Stop, please," he mumbles, "please, don't—"

Who is he? What is he doing here?

A name. He has a name ...

Somewhere far away, a shout. The two insectoid creatures raise elongated faces, feelers shaking—

There is the sound of an explosion, and one of the creatures disappears—hot shards of metal sting Pym, burning, burning—

The second creature rears, four arms rising like guns—

There is the sound of gunshots, to and from; and then there's a massive hole in the creature's chest, and it runs off into the darkness—

A face above his, dark hair, pale skin, two eyes like waning moons
—"Pym? Pym? Can you hear me?"

"Pym," he whispers, the name strangely familiar. He closes his
eyes; and then nothing hurts any more, and he is floating in a cool,
calm darkness.

Spider's Hold, Luna, Year One

Not a memory as much as the recollection, like film, of something
seen—emerging from darkness into a light, alien faces hovering
above him, as large as moons—"Pym! My darling little Pym—"

Hands clapping, and he is clutched close to a warm, soft breast,
and he begins to cry; but then the warmth settles him and he
snuggles close and he is happy.

"Fifty-three million at peak," someone says.

"Day One," someone says. "Year One. And may all of your days be
as happy as this one. You are born, Pym. Your narrative's began."

He finds a nipple, drinks. The milk is warm. "Hush now, my little
baby. Hush now."

"See, already he is looking around. He wants to see the world."

But it isn't true. He only wants to sleep, in that warm, safe place.

"Happy birthday, Pym."

He sleeps.

Polyphemus Port, Titan, Year Seventeen

The party is crammed with people, the house node broadcasts out
particularly loud Nuevo Kwasa-Kwasa tunes, there is a lot of Zion
Special Strength passing around, the strong, sweet smell latching on
to hair and clothes, and Pym is slightly drunk.

Polyport, on his own: Mother left behind in the Galilean Republic,
Pym escaping—jumping onto an ancient transport ship, the *Ibn-al-
Farid*, a Jupiter-to-Saturn one-way trip.

Feeling free for the first time. His numbers going up, but he isn't
paying any attention for once. Pym, not following the narrative but
simply living his life.

Port bums hanging out at Polyport, kids looking for ships for the
next trip to nowhere, coming from Mars and the Jovean moons and
the ring-cities of Saturn, heading everywhere—

The party: a couple of weather hackers complaining about

outdated protocols; a ship rat from the *Ibn-al-Farid*—Pym knows him slightly from the journey—doing a Louis Wu in the corner, a blissful smile on his face, wired-in, the low current tickling his pleasure centres; five big, blonde Australian girls from Earth on a round-the-system trip—conversations going over Pym's head— "Where do you come from? Where do you go? Where do you come from?"

Titan surface crawlers with that faraway look in their eyes; a viral artist, two painters, a Martian Re-Born talking quietly to a Jovean robot—Pym knows people are looking at him, pretending not to— and his numbers are going up, everybody loves a party.

She is taller than him, with long black hair gathered into moving dreadlocks—some sort of mechanism making them writhe about her head like snakes—long slender fingers, obsidian eyes—

People turning as she comes through, a hush of sort—she walks straight up to him, ignoring the other guests—stands before him, studying him with a bemused expression. He knows she sees what he sees—number of followers, storage space reports, feed statistics— he says, "Can I get you a drink?" with a confidence he doesn't quite feel, and she smiles. She has a gold tooth, and when she smiles, it makes her appear strangely younger.

"I don't drink," she says, still studying him. The gold tooth is an Other, but in her case it isn't truly Joined—the digital intelligence embedded within is part of her memcorder structure. "Eighty-seven million," she says.

"Thirty-two," he says. She smiles again. "Let's get out of here," she says.

Jettisoned, Charon, Year Fifty-Six

Memory returning in chunks—long-unused backup spooling back into his mind. When he opens his eyes, he thinks for a moment it is her, that somehow she had rescued him from the creatures; but no— the face that hovers above his is unfamiliar, and he is suddenly afraid.

"Hush," she says. "You're hurt."

"Who are you?" he croaks. Numbers flashing—viewing figures near a hundred million all across the system being updated at the speed of light. His birth didn't draw nearly that many ...

"My name's Zul," she says—which tells him nothing. He sees she has a pendant hanging between her breasts. He squints and sees his own face.

The woman shrugs, smiles, a little embarrassed. Crow's-feet at the corners of her dark eyes. A gun hanging on her belt, black leather trousers the only other thing she wears. "You were attacked by wild foragers," she says and shrugs again. "We've had an infestation of them in the past couple of years."

Foragers: multi-surface machines designed for existing outside the human bubbles, converting rock into energy, slow lunar surface transforms—rogue, like everything else on Jettisoned. He says, "Thank you," and to his surprise, she blushes.

"I've been watching you," she said.

Pym understands—and feels a little sad.

She makes love to him on the narrow bed in the small, hot, dark room. They are somewhere deep underground. From down here it is impossible to imagine Charon, that icy moon, or the tiny cold disc of the sun far away or the enormous field of galactic stars or the shadows of Exodus ships as they pass forever out of human space—hard to imagine anything but primal human existence of naked bodies and salty skin and fevered heartbeats, and he sighs, still inexplicably sad within his excitement for the smell of basil he seeks is missing.

Kuala Lumpur, Earth, Year Thirty-Two

At thirty-two there's the annoyance of hair growing in the wrong places and not growing in others, a mole or two which shouldn't be there, hangovers get worse, take longer to dissipate, eyes strain, and death is closer—

Pym, the city a spider's web of silver and light all around him, the towers of Kuala Lumpur rise like rockets into the skies—the streets alive with laughter, music, frying mutton—

On the hundred and second floor of the hospital, in a room as white as a painting of absence, as large and as small as a world—

Mother reaches out, holds his hand in hers. Her fingers are thin, bony. "My little Pym. My baby. Pym."

She sees what he sees. She shares access to the viewing stats, knows how many millions are watching this, the death of Mother, supporting character number one in the Narrative of Pym. Pym feels afraid and guilty and scared—Mother is dying, no one knows why exactly, and for Pym it's—what?

Pain, yes, but—

Is that relief? The freedom of Pym, a real one this time, not as illusory as it had been when he was seventeen?

"Mother," he says, and she squeezes his hand. Below, the world is spiderwebs and fairylights. "Fifty-six million," she says, and tries to smile. "And the best doctors money could buy—"

But they are not enough. She made him come back to her by dying, and Pym isn't sure how he feels about it; and so he stands there and holds her weakened hand and stares out beyond the windows into the night.

Polyphemus Port, Titan, Year Seventeen

They need no words between them. They haven't said a word since they left the party. They are walking hand in hand through the narrow streets of Polyport, and the storm rages overhead. When she draws him into a darkened corner, he is aware of the beating of his heart and then her own, his hand on her warm dark skin cupping a breast as the numbers roll and roll, the millions rising—a second feed showing him her own figures. Her lips on his, full, and she has the taste of basil and the night; and when they hold each other, the numbers fade, and there is only her.

Jettisoned, Charon, Year Fifty-Six

When they make love a second time, he calls out her name, and later, the woman lies beside him, and says, her hand stroking his chest slowly, "You really love her," and her voice is a little sad. Her eyes are round, pupils large. She sighs, a soft sound on the edge of the solar system. "I thought, maybe ..."

The numbers dropping again, the story of his life—the Narrative of Pym charted by the stats of followers at any given moment. The Narrative of Pym goes out all over space—and do they follow it, too, in the Exodus ships or on alien planets with unknown names?

He doesn't know. He doesn't care. He rises in the dark and dresses and goes out into the night of Jettisoned as the woman sleeps behind him.

At that moment he decides to find her.

● ● ●

Dragon's Home, Hydra, Year Seventy-Eight

It feels strange to be back in the Pluto system. And Hydra is the strangest of the worlds ... Jettisoned lies like a sore on Charon, but Hydra is even farther out, and cold, so cold ... Dragon's World, and Pym is a guest of the dragon.

When he thinks back to his time on Jettisoned in the Year Fifty-Six—or was it Fifty-Seven?—of the Narrative of Pym, it is all very confused. It had been a low point in his life. He left Jettisoned shortly after the attack, determined to find her—but then he had done that several times and never ...

Dragon's World is an entire moon populated by millions of bodies and a single mind. Vietnamese dolls, mass-produced in the distant factories of Earth, transported here by the same *Gel Blong Mota* he had once travelled on as a child, thousands and tens of thousands and finally millions of dolls operating with a single mind, the mind of the dragon—worker ants crawling all over the lunar surface, burrowing into its hide, transforming it into—what?

No one quite knows.

The dragon is an Other, one of the countless intelligences evolved in the digital Breeding Grounds, lines of code multiplying and mutating, merging and splitting in billions upon billions of cycles. It is said the dragon had been on one of the Exodus ships and been Jettisoned, but why that may be so no one knows. This is its world—a habitat? A work of strange, conceptual art? Nobody knows, and the dragon isn't telling.

Yet Pym is a guest, and the dragon is hospitable.

Pym's body is in good shape, but the dragon promises to make it better. Pym lies in one of the warrens in a cocoon-like harness, and tiny insects are crawling all over his body, biting and tearing, sewing and rearranging. Sometimes Pym gets the impression the dragon is lonely. Or perhaps it wants others to see its world and for that purpose invited Pym, whose numbers rise dramatically when he lands on Hydra.

The *Gel Blong Mota* had carried him here from the Galilean Republic on a slow, leisurely journey, and its captain was Joy; and she and Pym shared wine and stories and stared out into space, and sometimes made love with the slow, unhurried pace of old friends.

Why did you never go to her?

Her question is in his mind as he lies there in the warm confines of Dragon's cocoon. It is very quiet on Hydra, the dolls that are the dragon's body making almost no sound as they pass on their errands—whatever those may be. He thinks of Joy's question but realises he has no answer for her and never had. There had been other women, other places, but never—

Polyphemus Port, Titan, Year Seventeen

It is the most *intimate* moment of his life: it is as if the two of them are the centre of the entire universe and nothing else matters but the two of them, and as they kiss, as they undress, as they touch each other with clumsy, impatient fingers, the whole universe is watching, watching something amazing, this joining of two bodies, two souls. Their combined numbers have reached one billion and are still climbing. It will never be like this again, he thinks he hears her say, her lips against his neck, and he knows she is right, it will never—

Kuala Lumpur, Earth, Year Two

Taking baby steps across the vast expanse of recreated prime park land in the heart of the town, cocooned within the great needle towers of the mining companies, Pym laughs, delighted, as adult hands pick him up and twirl him around. "My baby," Mother says, and holds him close and kisses him (those strange figures at the corner of his eyes always shifting, changing—he'd got used to them by now, does not pay them any mind)—"You have time for everything twice over. The future waits for you—"

And as he puts his arms around her neck, he's happy, and the future is a shining road in Pym's mind, a long endless road of white light with Pym marching at its centre with no end in sight; and he laughs again and wriggles down and runs towards the ponds where there are great big lizards sunning themselves in the sun.

Dragon's Home, Hydra, Year One Hundred Fifteen

Back on Dragon's Home, that ant's nest whose opening rises from the surface of Hydra like a volcanic mouth, back in the cocoons of his old friend the dragon—"I don't think you could fix me again, old friend," he says, and closes his eyes—the cocoon against his naked skin like soft Vietnamese silk.

The dragon murmurs all around him, its thousands of bodies marching through their complex woven-together tunnels. Number of followers hovering around fifty million, and Pym thinks, They want to see me die.

He turns in his cocoon, and the dragon murmurs soothing words; but they lose their meaning. Pym tries to recall Mother's face, the taste of blackberries on a Martian farm, the feel of machine-generated rain on Ganymede or the embrace of a Jettisoned woman, but nothing holds, nothing is retained in his mind anymore. Somewhere it all exists, even now his failing senses are being broadcast and stored—but this, he knows suddenly with a frightening clarity, is the approaching termination of the Narrative of Pym, and the thought terrifies him. "Dragon!" he cries, and then there is something cool against his neck and relief floods in.

Pym drifts in a dream half-sleep, lulled by the rhythmic motion of his cocoon. There is a smell, a fragrance he misses, something sweet and fresh like ba—an herb of some sort? He grabs for a memory, his eyes opening with the effort, but it's no use, there is nothing there but a faint, uneasy sense of regret; and at last he lets it go. There had been a girl—

Hadn't there?

He never—

He closes his eyes again at last, and gradually true darkness forms, a strange and unfamiliar vista: even the constant numbers at the corner of his vision, always previously there, are fading—it is so strange, he would have laughed if he could.

Polyphemus Port, Titan, Year Forty-Three

He walks down the old familiar streets on this, this forty-third year of the Narrative of Pym, searching for her in the scent of old memories. She is not there, but suddenly, as he walks under the dome and the ever-present storm, he's hopeful: there will be other places, other times, and somewhere in the solar system, sometime in the Narrative of Pym, he will find her again.

The Mighty Slinger

Karen Lord and Tobias S. Buckell

Earth hung over the lunar hills as The Mighty Slinger and The Rovers readied the Tycho stage for their performance. Tapping his microphone, Euclid noticed that Kumi barely glanced at the sight as he set up his djembe and pan assembly, but Jeni froze and stared up at the blue disk, her bass still limp between her hands.

"It's not going anywhere," Kumi muttered. His long, graying dreadlocks swayed gently in the heavy gravity of the moon and tapped the side of a pan with a muted "ting." "It'll be there after the concert ... and after our trip *and* after we revive from our next long-sleep."

"Let her look," Vega admonished. "You should always stop for beauty. It vanishes too soon."

"She taking too long to set up," Kumi said. "You-all call her Zippy, but she ain't zippy at all."

Euclid chuckled as Jeni shot a stink look at her elder and mentor. She whipped the bass out stiff like she meant business. Her fingers gripped and danced on the narrow surface in a quick, defiant riff.

Raising his mic-wand at the back, Vega captured the sound as it bounced back from the lunar dome performance area. He fed the echo through the house speakers, ending it with a punctuating note of Kumi's locks hitting the pan with a ting and Euclid's laughter rumbling quietly in the background. Dhaka, the last of the Rovers, came in live with a cheerful fanfare on her patented Delirium, an instrument that looked like a harmonium had had a painful collision with a large quantity of alloy piping.

An asteroid-thin man in a black suit slipped past the velvet ropes marking off the VIP section and nodded at Euclid. "Yes, sir. Your pay's been deposited, the spa is booked, and your places in the long-sleep pool are reserved."

"Did you add the depreciation protection insurance this time?" Euclid answered, his voice cold with bitter memory. "If your grandfather had sense I could be retired by now."

Kumi looked sharply over. The man in the suit shifted about. "Of course, I'll add the insurance," he mumbled.

"Thank you, Mr. Jones," Euclid said in a tone that was not at all thankful.

"There's, ah, someone else who would like to talk to you," the event coordinator said.

"Not now, Jones." Euclid turned away to face his band. "Only forty minutes to curtain time and we need to focus."

"It's about Earth," Jones said.

Euclid turned back. "That rumour?"

Jones shook his head. "Not a rumour. Not even a joke. The Rt Hon. Patience Bouscholte got notification this morning. She wants to talk to you."

The Rt Hon. Patience Bouscholte awaited him in one of the skyboxes poised high over the rim of the crater. Before it: the stands that would soon be filling up, slanting along the slope that created a natural amphitheatre to the stage. Behind it: the gray hills and rocky wasteland of the moon.

"Mr. Slinger!" she said. Her tightly wound hair and brown spider silk head scarf bobbed in a slightly delayed reaction to the lunar gravity. "A pleasure to finally meet you. I'm a huge admirer of your sound."

He sat down, propped his snakeskin magnet-boots up against the chairback in front of him, and gave her a cautious look. "Madame Minister. To what do I owe the pleasure?"

All of the band were members of the Rock Devils Cohort and Consociate Fusion, almost a million strong, all contract workers in the asteroid belt. They were all synced up on the same long-sleep schedule as their cohort, whether working the rock or touring as a band. And here was a Minister from the RDCCF's Assembly asking to speak with him.

The RDCCF wasn't a country. It was just one of many organisations for the people who worked in space because there was nothing left for them on Earth. But to Euclid, meeting the Rt Hon. Patience Bouscholte felt like meeting a Member of Parliament from the old days. Euclid was slightly intimidated, but he wasn't going to show it. He put an arm casually over the empty seat beside him.

"They said you were far quieter in person than on stage. They were right." Bouscholte held up a single finger before he could reply and pointed to two women in all-black bulletproof suits who were busy scanning the room with small wands. They gave a thumbs-up as Bouscholte cocked her head in their direction and retreated to stand on either side of the entrance.

She turned back to Euclid. "Tell me, Mr. Slinger, how much have you heard about The Solar Development Charter and their plans for Earth?"

So it was true? He leaned toward her. "Why would they have any plans for Earth? I've heard they're stretched thin enough building the Glitter Ring."

"They are. They're stretched more than thin. They're functionally bankrupt. So the SDC is taking up a new tranche of preferred shares for a secondary redevelopment scheme. They want to 'redevelop' Earth, and that will *not* be to our benefit."

"Well, then." Euclid folded his arms and leaned back. "And you thought you'd tell an old calypso singer that because ...?"

"Because I need your lyrics, Mr. Slinger."

Euclid had done that before, in the days before his last long-sleep, when fame was high and money had not yet evaporated. Dishing out juicy new gossip to help Assembly contract negotiations. Leaking information to warn the workers all across the asteroid belt. Hard-working miners on contract struggling to survive the long nights and longer sleeps. Sing them a song about how the SDC was planning to screw them over again. He knew that gig well.

He had thought that was why he'd been brought to see her, to get a little something to add extempo to a song tonight. Get the belt all riled up. But if this was about Earth ...? Earth was a garbage dump. Humanity had sucked it dry like a vampire and left its husk to spiral toward death as people moved outward to bigger and better things.

"I don't sing about Earth anymore. The cohorts don't pay attention to the old stuff. Why should they care? It's not going anywhere."

Then she told him. Explained that the SDC was going to beautify Earth. Re-terraform it. Make it into a new garden of Eden for the rich and idle of Mars and Venus.

"How?" he asked, sceptical.

"Scorched Earth. They're going to bomb the mother planet with comets. Full demolition. The last of us shipped into the Ring to form new cohorts of workers, new generations of indentured servitude. A clean slate to redesign their brave new world. That is what I mean when I say *not to our benefit.*"

He exhaled slowly. "You think a few little lyrics can change any of that?" The wealth of Venus, Mars, and Jupiter dwarfed the cohorts in their hollowed-out, empty old asteroids.

"One small course adjustment at the start can change an entire orbit by the end of a journey," she said.

"So you want me to harass the big people up in power for you, now?"

Bouscholte shook her head. "We need you to be our emissary. We, the Assembly, the last representatives of the drowned lands and the dying islands, are calling upon you. Are you with us or not?"

Euclid thought back to the days of breezes and mango trees. "And if they don't listen to us?"

Bouscholte leaned in close and touched his arm. "The majority of our cohort are indentured to the Solar Development Charter until the Glitter Ring, the greatest project humanity has ever attempted, is complete. But, Mr. Slinger, answer me this: where do you think that leaves us after we finish the Ring?"

Euclid knew. After the asteroid belt had been transformed into its new incarnation, a sun-girdling, sun-powered device for humanity's next great leap, it would no longer be home.

There were few resources left in the belt; the big planets had got there first and mined it all. Euclid had always known the hollow shells. The work on the Glitter Ring. The long-sleep so that they didn't exhaust resources as they waited for pieces of the puzzle to slowly float from place to appointed place.

Bouscholte continued, "If we can't go back to Earth, they'll send us farther out. Our cohorts will end up scattered to the cold, distant areas of the system, out to the Oort Cloud. And we'll live long enough to see that."

"You think you can stop that?"

"Maybe, Mr. Slinger. There is almost nothing we can broadcast that the big planets can't listen to. When we go into the long-sleep as we wait for our payloads to shift around the belt, they can hack our communications to read and study us. But they can't keep us from talking, and they'll never stop our songs."

"It's a good dream," Euclid said softly, for the first time in the conversation looking up at the view over the skybox. He'd avoided looking at it. To Jeni it was a beautiful blue dot, but for Euclid all it did was remind him of what he'd lost. "But they won't listen."

"You must understand, you are just one piece in a much bigger game. Our people are in place, not just in the cohorts, but everywhere, all throughout the system. They'll listen to your music and make the right moves at the right time. The SDC can't move to destroy and rebuild Earth until the Glitter Ring is finished, but when it's finished, they'll find they have underestimated us—as long as we coordinate in a way that no one suspects."

"Using songs? Nah. Impossible," he declared bluntly.

She shook her head, remarkably confident. "All you have to do is be the messenger. We'll handle the tactics. You forget who you're speaking to. The Bouscholte family tradition has always been about the long game. Who was my father? What positions do my sons hold, my granddaughters? Euclid Slinger ... Babatunde ... listen to me. How do you think an aging calypso star gets booked to do an expensive, multiplanetary tour to the capitals of the Solar System, the seats of power? By chance?"

She called him that name as if she were his friend, his inner circle intimate. Kumi named him that years ... decades ago. *Too wise for your years. You were here before*, he'd said. *The Father returns, sent back for a reason.* Was this the reason?

"I accept the mission," he said.

Day. Me say Day-Oh. Earthrise come and me want go ...

Euclid looked up, smiled. Let the chord go. He wouldn't be so blatant as to wink at the VIP section, but he knew that there was a fellow Rock Devil out there, listening out for certain songs and recording Vega's carefully assembled samples to strip for data and instructions in a safe location. Vega knew, of course. Had to, in order to put together the info packets. Dhaka knew a little but had begged not to know more, afraid she might say the wrong thing to the wrong person. Jeni was still, after her first long-sleep, nineteen in body and mind, so no, she did not know, and anyway how could he tell her when he was still dragging his feet on telling Kumi?

And there was Kumi frowning at him after the end of the concert as they sprawled in the green room, taking a quick drink before the final packing up. "Baba, you on this nostalgia kick for real."

"You don't like it?" Euclid teased him. "All that sweet, sweet soca you grew up studying, all those kaiso legends you try to emulate?"

"That ain't your sound, man."

Euclid shrugged. "We can talk about that next time we're in the studio. Now we got a party to be at!"

After twenty-five years of long-sleep, Euclid thought Mars looked much the same except maybe a little greener, a little wetter. Perhaps that was why the Directors of the SDC-MME had chosen to host their bash in a gleaming biodome that overlooked a charming little lake. Indoor foliage matched to outer landscape in a lush canopy, and artificial lights hovered in competition with the stars and satellites beyond.

"Damn show-offs," Dhaka muttered. "Am I supposed to be impressed?"

"*I* am," Jeni said shamelessly, selecting a stimulant cocktail from an offered tray. Kumi smoothly took it from her and replaced it with another, milder option. She looked outraged.

"Keep a clear head, Zippy," Vega said quietly. "We're not among friends."

That startled her out of her anger. Kumi looked a little puzzled himself, but he accepted Vega's support without challenge.

Euclid listened with half his attention. He had just noticed an opportunity. "Kumi, all of you, come with me. Let's greet the CEO and offer our thanks for this lovely party."

Kumi came to his side. "What's going on?"

Euclid lowered his voice. "Come, listen and find out."

The CEO acknowledged them as they approached, but Euclid could sense from the body language that the busy executive would give them as much time as dictated by courtesy and not a bit more. No matter that Euclid was a credentialled ambassador for the RDCCF, authorised by the Assembly. He could already tell how this meeting would go.

"Thank you for hosting us, Mx. Ashe," Euclid said, donning a pleasant, grinning mask. "It's always a pleasure to kick off a tour at the Mars Mining and Energy Megaplex."

"Thank *you*," the executive replied. "Your music is very popular with our hands."

"Pardon?" Kumi enquired, looking in confusion at the executive's fingers wrapped around an ornate cocktail glass.

"Our employees in the asteroid belt."

Kumi looked unamused. Euclid moved on quickly. "Yes. You merged with the SDC ... pardon me, we are still trying to catch up on twenty-five years of news ... about ten years ago?"

A little pride leaked past the politeness. "Buyout, not merger. Only the name has survived to maintain continuity and branding."

Euclid saw Dhaka smirk and glance at Vega, who looked a little sour. He was still slightly bitter that his ex-husband had taken everything in the divorce except for the de la Vega surname, the name under which he had become famous and which Vega was forced to keep for the sake of convenience.

"But don't worry," the CEO continued. "The Glitter Ring was always conceptualised as a project that would be measured in generations.

Corporations may rise and fall, but the work will go on. Everything remains on schedule, and all the hands ... all the—how do you say— *cohorts* are in no danger of losing their jobs."

"So the cohorts can return to Earth after the Ring is completed?" Euclid asked directly.

Mx. Ashe took a careful sip of bright purple liquid before replying. "I did not say that."

"But I thought the Earth development project was set up to get the SDC a secondary round of financing to solve their financial situation," Dhaka demanded, her brow creasing. "You've bought them out, so is that still necessary?"

Mx. Ashe nodded calmly. "True, but we have a more complex vision for the Glitter Ring than the SDC envisioned, and so funding must be vastly increased. Besides, taking money for a planned redevelopment of Earth and then not doing it would technically be fraud. The SDC-MME will follow through. I won't bore you with the details, but our expertise on geo-engineering is unparalleled."

"You've been dropping comets on vast, uninhabited surfaces," Dhaka said. "I understand the theory, but Earth isn't Venus or Mars. There's thousands of years of history and archeology. And there are still people living there. How are you going to move a billion people?"

Mx. Ashe looked coldly at Dhaka. "We're still in the middle of building a Ring around the sun, Mx. Miriam. I'm sure my successors on the Board will have it all figured out by the next time we wake you up. We understand the concerns raised, but after all, people have invested trillions in this project. Our lawyers are in the process of responding to all requests and lawsuits, and we will stand by the final ruling of the courts."

Euclid spoke quickly, blunt in his desperation. "Can't you reconsider, find another project to invest in? Earth's a mess, we all know it, but we always thought we'd have something to come back to."

"I'm sure a man of your means could afford a plot on New Earth—" Mx. Ashe began.

"I've seen the pricing," Vega cut in dryly. "Musicians don't make as much as you think."

"What about the cohorts?" Jeni said sadly. "No one in the cohorts will be able to afford to go back."

Mx. Ashe stepped back from the verbal bombardment. "This is all speculation. The cohorts are still under contract to work on the Glitter Ring. Once they have finished, negotiations about their relocation can begin. Now if you will excuse me, have a good night and enjoy the party!"

Euclid watched despondently as the CEO walked away briskly. The Rovers stood silently around him, their faces sombre. Kumi was the first to speak. "*Now* I understand the nostalgia kick."

The SDC, now with the MME
You and I both know
They don't stand for you and me

There was still a tour to play. The band moved from Elysium City to Electris Station, then Achillis Fons, where they played in front of the Viking Museum.

The long-sleep on the way to Mars from the Moon had been twenty-five years, as usual. Twenty-five years off, one year on. That was the shift the Rock Devils Cohort and Consociation Fusion had agreed to, the key clause in the contract Euclid had signed way-back-when in an office built into the old New York City sea wall.

That gave them a whole year on Mars. Mx. Ashe may have shut them down, but Euclid wasn't done yet. Not by a long shot.

Kumi started fretting barely a month in.

"Jeni stepping out with one of the VIPs," he told Euclid.

"She's nineteen. What you expecting? A celibate band member? I don't see you ignoring anyone coming around when we breaking down."

Kumi shook his head. "No Baba, that's one thing. This is the same one she's seeing. Over and over. Since we arrived here. She's sticky sweet on him."

"Kumi, we got bigger things to worry about."

"Earth, I know. Man, look, I see why you're upset." Kumi grabbed his hand. "I miss it, too. But we getting old, Baba. I just pass sixty. How much longer I could do this? Maybe we focus on the tour and invest the money so that we can afford to go back some day."

"I can't give it up that easy," Euclid said to his oldest friend. "We going to have troubles?"

Back when Euclid was working the rocks, Kumi had taken him under his wing. Taught him how to sing the old songs while they moved their one-person pods into position to drill them out. Then they'd started singing at the start of shifts and soon that took off into a full career. They'd traveled all through the belt from big old Ceres to the tiniest cramped mining camps.

Kumi sucked his teeth. "That first time you went extempo back on Pallas, you went after that foreman who'd been skimping on air lock maintenance? You remember?"

Euclid laughed. "I was angry. The air lock blew out, and I wet myself waiting for someone to come pick me up."

"When you started singing different lyrics, making them up on the spot, I didn't follow you at first. But you got the SDC to fire him when the video went viral. That's why I called you Baba. So no, you sing, and I'll find my way around your words. Always. But let me ask you—think about what Ashe said. You really believe this fight's worth it?"

Euclid bit his lip.

"We have concerts to give in the belt and Venus yet," he told Kumi. "We're not done yet."

Five months in, the Martians began to turn. The concerts had been billed as cross-cultural events paid for by the Pan-Human Solar Division of Cultural Affairs and the Martian University's division of Inter-Human Musicology Studies school.

Euclid, on stage, hadn't noticed at first. He'd been trying to find another way to match up MME with "screw me" and some lyrics in between. Then a comparison to Mars and its power and the people left behind on Earth.

But he noticed when *this* crowd turned.

Euclid had grown used to the people of the big planets just sitting and listening to his music. No one was moving about. No hands in the air. Even if you begged them, they weren't throwing their hands out. No working, no grinding, no nothing. They sat in seats and *appreciated*.

He didn't remember when they turned. He would see it on video later. Maybe it was when he called out the "rape" of Earth with the "red tape" of the SDC-MME and made a visual of "red" Mars that tied to the "red" tape, but suddenly those chair-sitting intercultural appreciators stood up.

And it wasn't to jump.

The crowd started shouting back. The sound cut out. Security and the venue operators swept in and moved them off the stage.

Back in the green room, Jeni rounded on Euclid. "What the hell was that?" she shouted.

"Ex tempo," Euclid said simply.

Kumi tried to step between them. "Zippy—"

"No!" She pushed him aside. Dhaka, in the corner of the room, started disassembling the Delirium, carefully putting the pieces away in a g-force protected aerogel case, carefully staying out of the brewing fight. Vega folded his arms and stood to a side, watching. "I damn well know what extempo is. I'm young, not ignorant."

Everyone was tired. The heavy gravity, the months of touring already behind them. "This always happens. A fight always come halfway through," Euclid said. "Talk to me."

"You're doing extempo like you're in a small free concert in the belt on a small rock. But this isn't going after some corrupt contractor," Jeni snapped. "You're calling out a whole planet now? All Martians? You crazy?"

"One person or many, you think I shouldn't?"

Euclid understood. Jeni had been working pods like he had at the same age. Long, grueling shifts spent in a tiny bubble of plastic where you rebreathed your own stench so often you forgot what clean air tasted like. Getting into the band had been her way "off the rock." This was her big gamble out of tedium. His, too, back in the day.

"You're not entertaining people. You're pissing them off," she said.

Euclid sucked his teeth. "Calypso been vexing people since all the way back. And never mind calypso, Zippy, entertainment isn't just escape. Artists always talking back, always insolent."

"They paid us and flew us across the solar system to sing the song they wanted. Sing the fucking song for them the way they want. Even just the 'Banana Boat Song' you're messing with and going extempo. That shit's carved in stone, Euclid. Sing the damn lyrics."

Euclid looked at her like she'd lost her mind. "That song was *never* for them. Problem is it get sung too much; and you abstract it, and then everyone forget that song is a blasted lament. Well, let me educate you, Ms. Baptiste. The 'Banana Boat Song' is a mournful song about people getting their backs broken hard in labor and still using call and response to help the community sync up, dig deep, and find the power to work harder 'cause *dem ain't had no choice.*"

He stopped. A hush fell in the green room.

Euclid continued. "It's not a 'smile and dance for them' song. The big planets don't own that song. It was never theirs. It was never carved in stone. I'll make it ours for *here*, for *now*, and I'll go extempo. I'm not done. Zippy, I'm just getting started."

She nodded. "Then I'm gone."

Just like that, she spun around and grabbed her bass.

Kumi glared at Euclid. "I promised her father I'd keep an eye on her—"

"Go," Euclid said calmly, but he was suddenly scared that his oldest friend, the pillar of his little band, would walk out the green room door with the newest member and never come back.

Kumi came back an hour later. He looked suddenly old ... those raw-sun wrinkles around his eyes, the stooped back. But it wasn't just gravity pulling him down. "She's staying on Mars."

Euclid turned to the door. "Let me go speak to her. I'm the one she angry with."

"No." Kumi put a hand on his shoulder. "That wasn't just about you. She staying with someone. She's not just leaving the band, she leaving the cohort. Got a VIP, a future, someone she thinks she'll build a life with."

She was gone. Like that.

Vega still had her riffs, though. He grumbled about the extra work, but he could weave the recorded samples in and out of the live music.

Kumi got an invitation to the wedding. It took place the week before the Rovers left Mars for the big tour of the asteroid belt.

Euclid wasn't invited.

He did a small, open concert for the Rock Devils working on Deimos. It was just him and Vega and fifty miners in one of the teardown areas of the tiny moon. Euclid sang for them just as pointedly as ever.

> So it's up to us, you and me
> to put an end to this catastrophe.
> Them ain't got neither conscience nor heart.
> We got to pitch in and do our part
> 'Cause if this Earth demolition begin
> we won't even have a part/pot to pitch/piss in.

Touring in the belt always gave him a strange feeling of mingled nostalgia and dissonance. There were face to face reunions and continued correspondence with friends and relatives of their cohort, who shared the same times of waking and long-sleep, spoke the same language, and remembered the same things. But there were also administrators and officials, who kept their own schedule, and workers from cohorts on a different frequency—all strangers from a forgotten distant past or an unknown near-present. Only the most social types kept up to date on everything, acting as temporal diplomats, translating jokes and explaining new tech and jargon to smooth communication between groups.

Ziamara Bouscholte was social. Very social. Euclid had seen plenty of that frivolous-idle behaviour from political families and nouveau-nobility like the family Jeni had married into, but given *that* surname and the fact that she had been assigned as their tour liaison, he recognised very quickly that she was a spy.

"Big tours in the belt are boredom and chaos," he warned her, thinking about the argument with Jeni. "Lots of downtime slinging from asteroid to asteroid punctuated by concert mayhem when we arrive."

She grinned. "Don't worry about me. I know exactly how to deal with boredom and chaos."

She didn't lie. She was all business on board, briefing Vega on the latest cryptography and answering Dhaka's questions about the technological advances that were being implemented in Glitter Ring construction. Then the butterfly emerged for the concerts and parties as she wrangled fans and dignitaries with a smiling enthusiasm that never flagged.

The Vesta concert was their first major stop. The Mighty Slinger and his Rovers peeked out from the wings of the stage and watched the local opening act finishing up their last set.

Kumi brought up something that had been nagging Euclid for a while. "Baba, you notice how small the crowds are? *This* is our territory, not Mars. Last big tour we had to broadcast over Vesta because everything was sold out."

Vega agreed. "Look at this audience. Thin. I could excuse the other venues for size but not this one."

"I know why," Dhaka said. "I can't reach half my friends who agreed to meet up. All I'm getting from them are long-sleep off-shift notices."

"I thought it was just me," Kumi said. "Did SDC-MME leave cohorts in long-sleep? Cutting back on labour?"

Dhaka nodded. "Zia mentioned some changes in the project schedule. You know the Charter's not going to waste money feeding us if we're not working."

Euclid felt a surge of anger. "We'll be out of sync when they wake up again. That messes up the whole cohort. You sure they're doing this to cut labour costs or to weaken us as a collective?"

Dhaka shrugged. "I don't like it one bit, but I don't know if it's out of incompetence or malice."

"Time to go," said Vega, his eyes on the openers as they exited stage left.

The Rovers drifted on stage and started freestyling, layering sound on sound. Euclid waited until they were all settled in and jamming hard before running out and snagging his mic. He was still angry, and the adrenaline amped up his performance as he commandeered the stage to rant about friends and lovers lost for a whole year to long-sleep.

Then he heard something impossible: Kumi stumbled on the beat. Euclid looked back at the Rovers to see Vega frozen. A variation of one of Jeni's famous riffs was playing, but Vega shook his head *not me* to Dhaka's confused sideways glance.

Zia's voice came on the sound system, booming over the music. "Rock Devils cohort, we have a treat for you! On stage for the first time in twenty-five years, please welcome Rover bassist Jeni 'Zippy' Baptiste!"

Jeni swooped in from the wings with another stylish riff, bounced off one of the decorated pylons, then flew straight to Kumi, and wrapped him in a tumbling hug, bass and all. Prolonged cheering from the crowd drowned out the music. Euclid didn't know whether to be furious or overjoyed at Zia for springing the surprise on them in public. Vega smoothly covered for the absent percussion and silent bass while Dhaka went wild on the Delirium. It was a horrible place for a reunion, but they'd take it. Stage lighting made it hard to tell, but Jeni did look older and ... stronger? More sure of herself?

Euclid floated over to her at the end of the song as the applause continued to crash over them all. "Welcome back, Zippy," he said. "You're still good—better, even."

Her laugh was full and sincere. "I've been listening to our recordings for twenty-five years, playing along with you every day while you were in long-sleep. Of course, I'm better."

"You missed us," he stated proudly.

"I did." She swatted a tear out of the air between them with the back of her hand. "I missed *this*. Touring for our cohort. Riling up the powers that be."

He raised his eyebrows. "*Now* you want to shake things up? What changed?"

She shook her head sadly. "Twenty-five years, Baba. I have a daughter now. She's twenty, training as an engineer on Mars. She's going to join the cohort when she's finished, and I want more for her. I want a future for her."

He hugged her tight while the crowd roared in approval. "Get back on that bass," he whispered. "We got a show to finish!"

He didn't bother to ask if the nouveau nobility husband had approved of the rebel Rover Jeni. He suspected not.

In the green room Jeni wrapped her legs around a chair and hung a glass of beer in the air next to her.

"Used to be it would fall slowly down to the floor," Jeni said, pointing at her drink. "They stripped most of Vesta's mass for the Ring. It's barely a shell here."

Dhaka shoved a foot in a wall strap and settled in perpendicular to Jeni in the air. She swirled the whiskey glass around in the air. Despite the glass being designed for zero gravity, her practiced flip of the wrist tossed several globules free that very slowly wobbled their way through the air toward her. "We're passing into final stage preparations for the Ring. SDC-MME is panicking a bit because the projections for energy and the initial test results don't match. And the computers are having trouble managing stable orbits."

The Glitter Ring was a Dyson Ring, a necklace of solar power stations and sails built around the sun to capture a vast percentage of its energy. The power needs of the big planets had begun to outstrip the large planetary solar and mirror arrays a hundred years ago. Overflight and shadow rights for solar gathering stations had started turning into a series of low-grade orbital economic wars. The Charter had been created to handle the problem system-wide.

Build a ring of solar power catchments in orbit around the sun at a slight angle to the plane of the solar system. No current solar rights would be abridged, but it could catapult humanity into a new industrial era. A great leap forward. Unlimited, unabridged power.

But if it didn't work ...

Dhaka nodded at all the serious faces. "Don't look so glum. The cohort programmers are working on flocking algorithms to try and simplify how the solar stations keep in orbit. Follow some simple rules about what's around you and let complex emergent orbits develop."

"I'm more worried about the differences in output," Jeni muttered. "While you've been in long-sleep, they've been developing orbital stations out past Jupiter with the assumption that there would be beamed power to follow. They're building mega-orbitals throughout the system on the assumption that the Ring's going to work. They've even started moving people off Earth into temporary housing in orbit."

"Temporary?" Euclid asked from across the room, interrupting before Dhaka and Jeni got deep into numbers and words like exajoules, quantum efficiency, price per watt and all the other boring crap. He'd cared intimately about that when he first joined the cohort. Now not so much.

"We're talking bubble habitats with thinner shells than Vesta right now. They use a layer of water for radiation shielding; but they lack resources, and they're not well balanced. These orbitals have about a couple hundred thousand people each, and they're rated to last fifty to sixty years." Jeni shook her head, and Euclid was forced to stop seeing the nineteen-year-old Zippy and recognise the concerned forty-four year old she'd become. "They're risking a lot."

"Why would anyone agree?" Vega asked. "It sounds like suicide."

"It's gotten worse on Earth. Far worse. Everyone is just expecting to hit the reset button after the Glitter Ring goes online. Everyone's holding their breath."

Dhaka spoke up. "Okay, enough cohort bullshit. Let's talk about you. The band's heading back to long-sleep soon—and then what, Zippy? You heading back to Mars and your daughter?"

Jeni looked around the room hesitantly. "Lara's never been to Venus, and I promised her she could visit me ... if you'll have me?"

"If?" Vega laughed. "I hated playing those recordings of you. Rather hear it live."

"I'm not as zippy up and down the chords as I used to be, you know," Jeni warned. Everyone was turning to look at Euclid.

"It's a more confident sound," he said with a smile. Dhaka whipped globules of whiskey at them and laughed.

Kumi beamed, no doubt already dreaming about meeting his "granddaughter."

"Hey, Zippy," Euclid said. "Here's to change. *Good* change."

"Maybe," she smiled and slapped his raised hand in agreement and approval. "Let's dream on that."

The first few days after long-sleep were never pleasant, but this awakening was the worst of Euclid's experience. He slowly remembered who he was and how to speak and the names of the people who sat quietly with him in the lounge after their sessions with the medics. For a while they silently watched the high cities of

Venus glinting in the clouds below their orbit from viewports near the long-sleep pools.

Later they began to ask questions, later they realised that something was very wrong. They'd been asleep for fifty years. Two long-sleeps, not the usual single sleep.

"Everyone gone silent back on Vesta," Dhaka said.

"Did we get idled?" Euclid demanded. They were a band, not workers. They shouldn't have been idled.

The medics didn't answer their questions. They continued to deflect everything until one morning an officer turned up, dressed in black sub-uniform with empty holster belt as if he had left his weapons and armour just outside the door. He looked barely twenty, far too young for the captain's insignia on his shoulders.

He spoke with slow, stilted formality. "Mr. Slinger, Mr. Djansi, Mr. de la Vega, Ms. Miriam, and Ms. Baptiste—thank you for your patience. I'm Captain Abrams. We're sorry for the delay, but your recovery was complicated."

"Complicated!" Kumi looked disgusted. "Can you explain why we had two long-sleeps instead of one? Fifty years? We had a contract!"

"And *we* had a war." The reply was unexpectedly sharp. "Be glad you missed it."

"Our first interplanetary war? That's not the change I wanted," Euclid muttered to Vega.

"What happened?" Jeni asked, her voice barely a whisper. "My daughter, she's on Mars, is she safe?"

The officer glanced away in a momentary flash of vulnerability and guilt. "You have two weeks for news and correspondence with your cohort and others. We can provide political summaries and psychological care for your readjustment. After that, your tour begins. Transport down to the cities has been arranged. I just ... I have to say ... we still need you now more than ever."

"The *rass*?" Kumi stared at the soldier, spreading his arms.

Again that touch of vulnerability as the young soldier replied with a slight stammer. "Please. We need you. You're legends to the entire system now, not just the cohorts."

"The hell does that mean?" Vega asked as the boy-captain left.

Jeni's daughter had managed one long-sleep but woke on schedule while they stayed in storage. The war was over by then; but Martian infrastructure had been badly damaged, and skilled workers were needed for longer than the standard year or two. Lara had died after six years of "extra time," a casualty of a radiation exposure accident on Deimos.

They gathered around Jeni when she collapsed to her knees and wept, grieving for the child they had never known.

Their correspondence was scattered across the years, their cohort truly broken as it been forced to take cover, retreat, or fight. The war had started in Earth orbit after a temporary habitat split apart, disgorging water, air, and people into vacuum. Driven by desperation and fury, several other orbital inhabitants had launched an attack on SDC-MME-owned stations, seeking a secure environment to live and revenge for their dead.

Conflict became widespread and complicated. The orbital habitats were either negotiating for refugees, building new orbitals, or fighting for the SDC-MME. Mars got involved when the government sent its military to protect the Martian investment in the SDC-MME. Jupiter, which was now its own functioning technodemarchy, had struck directly at the belt, taking over a large portion of the Glitter Ring.

Millions had died as rocks were flung between the worlds and ships danced around each other in the vacuum. People fought hand to hand in civil wars inside hollowed-out asteroids, gleaming metal orbitals, and in the cold silence of space.

Humanity had carried war out of Earth and into the great beyond. Despite the grim history lesson, as the band shared notes and checked their financial records, one thing became clear. They *were* legends. The music of the Mighty Slinger and the Rovers had become the sound of the war generation and beyond: a common bond that the cohorts could still claim, and battle hymns for the Earth emigrants who had launched out from their decayed temporary orbitals. Anti-SDC-MME songs became treasured anthems. The Rovers songs sold billions, the *covers* of their songs sold billions. There were tribute bands and spin-off bands and a fleet of touring bands. They had spawned an entire subgenre of music.

"We're rich at last," Kumi said ruefully. "I thought I'd enjoy it more."

Earth was still there, still a mess, but Vega found hope in news from his kin. For decades Pacific Islanders had stubbornly roved over their drowned states in vast fleets, refusing resettlement to the crowded cities and tainted badlands of the continents. In the last fifty years, their floating harbours had evolved from experimental platforms to self-sustaining cities. For them, the war had been nothing but a few nights filled with shooting stars and the occasional planetfall of debris.

The Moon and Venus had fared better in the war than Mars, but the real shock was the Ring. According to Dhaka, the leap in progress was marked even for fifty years. Large sections were now fully functional and had been used during the war for refuelling, surveillance, barracks, and prisons.

"Unfortunately, that means that the purpose of the Ring has drifted once again," she warned. "The military adapted it to their purposes, and returning it to civilian use will take some time."

"But what about the Assembly?" Euclid asked her one day when they were in the studio, shielded from surveillance by noise and interference of Vega's crafting. "Do they still care about the purpose of the Ring? Do you think we still have a mission?"

The war had ended without a clear victor. The SDC-MME had collapsed, and the board had been tried, convicted, and exiled to long-sleep until a clear treaty could be hammered out. Jupiter, Mars, Venus, and some of the richer orbitals had assumed the shares and responsibility of the original solar charter. A tenuous peace existed.

Dhaka nodded. "I was wondering that, too, but look, here's the name of the company that's organising our tour."

Euclid leaned in to read her screen. *Bouscholte, Bouscholte & Abrams.*

Captain Abrams revealed nothing until they were all cramped into the tiny cockpit of a descent craft for Venus's upper atmosphere.

He checked for listening devices with a tiny wand and then satisfied, faced them all. "The Bouscholte family would like to thank you for your service. We want you to understand that you are in an even better position to help us, and we need that help now more than ever."

They'd come this far. Euclid looked around at the Rovers. They all leaned in closer.

"The Director of Consolidated Ring Operations and Planetary Reconstruction will be at your concert tonight." Abrams handed Euclid a small chip. "You will give this to him—personally. It's a quantum-encrypted key that only Director Cutler can access."

"What's in it?" Dhaka asked.

Abrams looked out the window. They were about to fall into the yellow and green clouds. The green was something to do with floating algae engineered for the planet, step one of the eventual greening of Venus. "Something Cutler won't like. Or maybe a bribe. I don't know. But it's an encouragement for the director to consider a proposal."

"Can you tell us what the proposal is?"

"Yes." Abrams looked at the band. "Either stop the redevelopment of Earth and further cement the peace by returning the orbitals inhabitants to the surface or ..."

Everyone waited as Abrams paused dramatically.

"... approve a cargo transit across Mercury's inner orbit to the far side of the Glitter Ring and give us the contracts for rebuilding the orbital habitats."

Dhaka frowned. "I wasn't expecting something so boring after the big 'or' there, Captain."

Abrams smiled. "One small course adjustment at the start can change an entire orbit by the end of a journey," he said to Euclid.

That sounded familiar.

"Either one of those is important?" Euclid asked. "But you won't say why."

"Not even in this little cabin. I'm sure I got the bugs, but in case I didn't." Abrams shrugged. "Here we are. Ready to change the solar system, Mr. Slinger?"

Venusian cities were more impressive when viewed from the outside. Vast, silvery spheres clustered thickly in the upper atmosphere trailing tethers and tubes to the surface like a dense herd of giant cephalopods. Inside, the decor was sober, spare, and disappointing, hinting at a slow post-war recovery.

The band played their first concert in a half century to a frighteningly respectful and very exclusive audience of the rich and powerful. Then it was off to a reception where they awkwardly sipped imported wine and smiled as their assigned liaison, a woman called Halford, briskly introduced and dismissed awestruck fans for seconds of small talk and a quick snap.

"And this is Petyr Cutler," Halford announced. "Director of Consolidated Ring Operations and Planetary Reconstruction."

Bodyguards quickly made a wall, shepherding the Director in for his moment.

Cutler was a short man with loose, sandy hair and bit of orbital sunburn. "So pleased to meet you," he said. "Call me Petyr."

He came in for the vigorous handshake, and Euclid had already palmed the small chip. He saw Abrams on the periphery of the crowd, watching. Nodded.

Cutler's already reddened cheeks flushed as he looked down at the chip. "Is that—"

"Yes." Euclid locked eyes with him. The Director. One of the most powerful people in the entire solar system.

Cutler broke the gaze and looked down at his feet. "You can't blackmail me, not even with this. I can't change policy."

"So you still redeveloping Earth?" Euclid asked, his tone already dull with resignation.

"I've been around before you were born, Mr. Slinger. I know how generational projects go. They build their own momentum. No one wants to become the executive who shut down two hundred years of progress, who couldn't see it through to the end. Besides, wars aren't cheap. We have to repay our citizens who invested in war bonds, the corporations that gave us tech on credit. The Earth Reconstruction project is the only thing that can give us the funds to stay afloat."

Somehow, his words eased the growing tightness in Euclid's chest. "I'm supposed to ask you something else then."

Cutler looked suspicious. He also looked around at his bodyguards, wanting to leave. "Your people have big asks, Mr. Slinger."

"This is smaller. We need your permission to move parts across Mercury's orbit, close to the sun, but your company has been denying that request. The Rock Devils cohort also wants to rebuild the surviving temporary Earth orbitals."

"Post-war security measures are still in place—"

"Security measures, my ass." Jeni spoke so loudly, so intensely that the whole room went quiet to hear her.

"Jeni—" Kumi started.

"No. We've sacrificed our lives and our children's lives for your damn Ring. We've made it our entire reason for existence, and we're tired. One last section to finish that could finish in less than three decades if you let us take that shortcut to get the last damn parts in place and let us go work on something worthwhile. We're tired. Finish the blasted project and let us live."

Kumi stood beside her and put his arm around her shoulders. She leaned into him, but she did not falter. Her gaze stayed hard and steady on the embarrassed Director who was now the centre of a room of shocked, sympathetic, judging looks.

"We need clearance from Venus," Director Cutler mumbled.

Euclid started humming a quick backbeat. Cutler looked startled. "*Director*," Euclid sang, voice low. He reached for the next word the sentence needed to bridge. *Dictator.* How to string that in with ... something to do with the project finishing *later.*

He'd been on the stage singing the old lyrics people wanted to hear. His songs that had once been extempo, but now were carved in stone now by a new generation.

But right here with the bodyguards all around them, Euclid wove a quick song damning him for preventing progress in the solar system and making trouble for the cohorts. That's right, Euclid thought. That's where the power came from, singing truth right to power's face.

Power reddened. Cutler clenched his jaw.

"I can sing that louder," Euclid said. "Loud enough for the whole system to hear it and sing it back to you."

"We'll see what we can do," Cutler hissed at him, and signalled for the bodyguards to surround him and move him away.

Halford the liaison congratulated the band afterwards. "You did it. We're cleared to use interior transits to the other side of the Ring and to move equipment into Earth orbit."

"Anything else you need us to do?" Dhaka asked.

"Not now, not yet. Enjoy your tour. Broadcasting planetwide and recording for rebroadcast throughout the system—you'll have the largest audience in history."

"That's nice," Euclid said vaguely. He was still feeling some discomfort with his new status as legend.

"I can't wait for the Earth concert," Captain Abrams said happily. "That one will really break the records."

"Earth?" Kumi said sharply.

Halford looked at him. "After your next long-sleep, for the official celebration of the completion of the Ring. That can't happen without the Mighty Slinger and his Rovers. One last concert for the cohorts."

"And maybe something more," Abrams added.

"What do you mean, 'more,'" Euclid demanded, weary of surprises.

Halford and Captain Abrams shared a look—delight, anticipation, and caution.

"When we're sure, we'll let you know," the captain promised.

Euclid sighed and glared at the door. He nervously twirled a pair of virtual-vision goggles between his fingers.

Returning to Earth had been bittersweet. He could have asked to fly over the Caribbean Sea, but nothing would be the same—coral reef islands reclaimed by water, new land pushed up by earthquake and vomited out from volcanoes. It would pollute the memories he had of a place that had once existed.

He put the past out of his mind and concentrated on the present. The Rovers were already at the venue working hard with the manager and crew in technical rehearsals for the biggest concert of their lives. Estádio Nacional de Brasília had become ENB de Abrams-Bouscholte, twice reconstructed in the last three decades to double the seating and update the technology, and now requiring a small army to run it.

Fortunately, Captain Abrams (retired) knew a bit about armies and logistics, which was why Euclid was not at technical rehearsal with his friends but on the other side of the city, waiting impatiently outside a large simulation room while Abrams took care of what he blithely called "the boring prep."

After ten minutes or so, the door finally opened, and Captain Abrams peeked around the edge, goggles pushed up over his eyebrows and onto his balding head. "We're ready! Come in, Mr. Slinger. We think you'll like what we've set up for you." His voice hadn't lost that boyish, excited bounce.

Still holding his goggles, Euclid stepped into the room and nodded a distracted greeting to the small group of technicians. His gaze was quickly caught by an alloy-plated soprano pan set up at the end of the room.

"Mr. Djansi says you were a decent pannist," Captain Abrams said, still brightly enthusiastic.

"Was?"

Captain Abrams smiled. "Think you can handle this one?"

"I can manage," Euclid answered, reaching for the sticks.

"Goggles first," the captain reminded him, closing the door to the room.

Euclid put them on, picked up the sticks, and raised his head to take in his audience. He froze and dropped the sticks with a clang.

"Go on, Mr. Slinger. I think you'll enjoy this," Abrams said. "I think we all will."

On the night of the concert, Euclid stood on the massive stage with his entire body buzzing with terror. The audience packed into stadium tiers all around him was a faceless mass that rose up several stories; but they were his family, and he knew them like he knew his own heart. The seats were filled with Rock Devils, Gladhandlers, Sunsiders, and more, all of them from the cohorts, workers representing every section of the Ring and every year and stage of its development. Many of them had come down from Earth orbit and their work on the decaying habitats to see the show.

Euclid started to sing for them, but they sang for him first, calling out every lyric so powerful and sure that all he could do was fall silent and raise his hands to them in homage and embrace. He shook his head in wonder as tears gathered in his eyes.

Kumi, Vega, Dhaka, and Jeni kept jamming, transported by the energy, playing the best set of their careers, giving him a nod or a sweet smile in the midst of their collective trance as he stood silently crying and listening to the people sing.

Then it was time.

Euclid walked slowly, almost reverently, to the soprano pan at the centre of the stage. Picked up the sticks just as he had in the simulation room. Looked up at his audience. This time he did not freeze. He played a simple arpeggio, and the audience responded: lighting a wedge of stadium seating, a key for each note of the chord, hammered to life when he hammered the pan. He lengthened the phrase and added a trill. The cohorts followed him flawlessly, perfected in teamwork and technology. A roar came from overhead as the hovering skyboxes cheered on the Mighty Slinger playing the entire stadium like it was his own personal keyboard.

Euclid laughed loud. "Ain't seen nothing yet!"

He swept his arm out to the night sky, made it a good, slow arc, so he was sure they were paying attention. Then the other arm. Showmanship. Raise the sticks with drama. Flourish them like a conductor. Are you ready? *Are you ready?!*

Play it again. This time the sky joined them. The arc of the Ring blazed section by section in sync with each note and in step with each cadence. The Mighty Slinger and his cohorts, playing the largest instrument in the galaxy.

Euclid grinned as the skyboxes went wild. The main audience was far quieter, waiting, watching for one final command.

He raised his arms again, stretched them out in victory, dropped the sticks on the thump of the Rovers' last chord, and closed his eyes.

His vision went red. He was already sweating with adrenaline and humid heat, but for a moment he felt a stronger burn, the kiss of a sun where no sun could be. He slowly opened his eyes, and there it was as Abrams had promised. The *real* last section of the Ring, smuggled into Earth's orbit during the interior transits permitted by Venus, now set up in the mother planet's orbit with magnifiers and intensifiers and God knows what else, all shining down like full noon on nighttime Brasília.

The skyboxes no longer cheered. There were screams, there was silence. Euclid knew why. If they hadn't figured it out for themselves, their earpieces and comms were alerting them now. Abrams-Bouscholte, just hours ago, had become the largest shareholder in the Ring through a generation-long programme of buying out rights and bonds from governments bankrupted by war. It was a careful, slow-burning plan that only a cohort could shepherd through to the end.

The cohorts had always been in charge of the Ring's day to day operations, but the concert had demonstrated beyond question that only one crew truly ran the Ring.

The Ring section in Earth orbit, with its power of shade and sun, could be a tool for geoengineering to stabilise Earth's climate to a more clement range ... or a solar weapon capable of running off any developers. Either way, the entire Ring was under the control of the cohorts, and so was Earth.

The stadium audience roared at last, task accomplished, joy unleashed. Dhaka, Jeni, Kumi, and Vega left their instruments and gathered around Euclid in a huddle of hugs and tears like soldiers on the last day of a long war.

Euclid held onto his friends and exhaled slowly. "Look like massa day done."

Euclid sat peacefully, a mug of bush tea in his hands, gazing at the cold metal walls of the long-sleep hospice. Although the technology had steadily improved, delayed reawakenings still had costs and consequences. But it had been worth the risk. He had lived to see the work of generations, the achievements of one thousand years.

"Good morning, Baba." One of Zippy's great great grandchildren approached, his dashiki flashing a three dimensional pattern with brown and green images of some offworld swamp. This Baptiste, the head of his own cohort, was continuing the tradition of having at least one descendant of the Rovers in attendance at Euclid's awakening. "Are you ready now, Baba? The shuttle is waiting for you."

"I am ready," Euclid said, setting down his mug, anticipation rising. Every hundred years he emerged from the long-sleep pool.

Are you sure you want this? Kumi had asked. *You'll be all alone.* The rest of the band wanted to stay and build on Earth. Curiosity had drawn him to another path, fate had confirmed him as legend and griot to the peoples and Assemblies of the post-Ring era. *Work hard. Do well. Baba will be awake in a few more years. Make him proud.*

They *had* done well, so well that this would be his last awakening. The Caribbean awaited him, restored and resettled. He was finally going home to live out the rest of his life.

Baptiste opened the double doors. Euclid paused, breathed deeply, and walked outside onto the large deck. The hospice was perched on the edge of a hill. Euclid went to the railing to survey thousands of miles of the Sahara.

Bright-feathered birds filled the air with cheerful song. The wind brought a cool kiss to his cheek, promising rain later in the day. Dawn filtered slowly over what had once been desert, tinting the lush green hills with an aura of dusty gold as far as the eye could see. *Come, Baba. Let's go home.*

Acknowledgment is Made for Permission to Reprint the Following Materials:

About the Editor

Bill Campbell is the author of *Sunshine Patriots, My Booty Novel, Pop Culture: Politics, Puns, "Poohbutt" from a Liberal Stay-at-Home Dad, Koontown Killing Kaper*, and the spaceploitation comic, *Baaaad Muthaz*, with David Brame and Damian Duffy. Along with Edward Austin Hall, he co-edited the groundbreaking anthology, *Mothership: Tales from Afrofuturism and Beyond*. He also co-edited the Glyph Award-winning comics anthology, *APB: Artists against Police Brutality*, with Jason Rodriguez and John Jennings, the Locus Award-nominated anthology, *Stories for Chip: A Tribute to Samuel R. Delany*, with Nisi Shawl, and *Future Fiction: New Dimensions in International Science Fiction and Fantasy* with Italian publisher, Francesco Verso. Campbell founded Rosarium Publishing in 2013.

About the Authors

Yasser Abdel Latif was born in Cairo in 1969. He graduated from Cairo University in Philosophy in 1994. He has one collection of poetry (*Naas wa Ahjar*, 1995). He wrote several scripts for TV documentaries. In 2005 he was awarded the Sawiris Prize for his debut novel, *Qanoon al-Wiratha*, excerpted in *Banipal No. 26*.

Anatoly Belilovsky was born in a city that went through six or seven owners in the last century, all of whom used it to do a lot more than drive to church on Sundays; he is old enough to remember tanks rolling through it on their way to Czechoslovakia in 1968. After being traded to the US for a shipload of grain and a defector to be named later (courtesy of the Jackson-Vanik amendment), he learned English from *Star Trek* reruns and went on to become a pediatrician in an area of New York where English is only the fourth most commonly used language. He has neither cats nor dogs but was admitted into SFWA in spite of this deficiency, having published original and translated stories in *Nature, F&SF, Daily SF, Kasma, UFO, Stupefying Stories, Cast of Wonders*, and other markets. He blogs about writing at loldoc.net.

Brooke Bolander writes weird things of indeterminate genre, most of them leaning rather heavily towards fantasy or general all-around weirdness. She attended the University of Leicester studying History and Archaeology and is an alum of the 2011 Clarion Writers' Workshop at UCSD. Her stories have been featured in *Lightspeed, Tor.com, Strange Horizons, Uncanny*, and various other fine purveyors of the fantastic. She has been a repeat finalist for the Nebula, Hugo, Locus, and Theodore Sturgeon awards, much to her unending bafflement. Follow her at brookebolander.com or on Twitter at @BBolander.

Vashti Bowlah is a writer from Trinidad and Tobago. Her stories have appeared in various international publications such as *The Caribbean Writer, St. Petersburg Review, Poui, WomanSpeak Journal*, Akashic's *Duppy Thursday, Signifyin' Guyana, Tongues of the Ocean, Jewels of the Caribbean, Susumba*, and *St. Somewhere Journal*. Her stories center on the humble lifestyle, culture, and traditions of East Indians in Trinidad & Tobago. Bowlah is an advocate for reading and literacy, and enjoys sharing her life experiences and journey as an author through visits to schools and public libraries. She is the author of *Under the Peepal Tree*.

Tobias S. Buckell is a *New York Times* Bestselling author born in the Caribbean. He grew up in Grenada and spent time in the British and US Virgin Islands, which influence much of his work. His novels and over 50 stories have been translated into 18 different languages. His work has been nominated for awards like the Hugo, Nebula, Prometheus, and the John W. Campbell Award for Best New Science Fiction Author. He currently lives in Bluffton, Ohio, with his wife, twin daughters, and a pair of dogs. He can be found online at www.TobiasBuckell.com.

Raquel Castro is an award-winning Mexican author for both children and adults. She won the Premio Aguilar in 2012 for her YA horror novel, *Ojos Llenos de Sombras* (*Eyes Full of Shadows*), and recently co-edited an anthology of Mexican zombie stories with Rafael Villegas, *Festín de Muertos* (*Feast of the Dead*). She lives in Mexico City.

Phenderson Djéli Clark's short stories have appeared in *Daily Science Fiction, Heroic Fantasy Quarterly, Tor.com,* and several print anthologies, including *Griots I & II, Steamfunk,* and *Myriad Lands*. His story "The Mouser of Peter the Great" was first published in the anthology, *Hidden Youth: Speculative Fiction from the Margins of History,* in October 2016. He blogs on SFF, diversity, and more at his blog *The Disgruntled Haradrim* (pdjeliclark.com). He also tweets stuff: @pdjeliclark.

Zig Zag Claybourne has appeared in *Strange Horizons, Vex Mosaic, Alt History 101, FlashShot, The Reverie Journal, Stupefying Stories, The City: A Cyberfunk Anthology, UnCommon Origins, Rococoa: The Sword & Soul/ Steamfunk Anthology, Extraordinary Rendition,* and others. His latest novel is *The Brothers Jetstream: Leviathan*. Visit him at www.WriteonRighton. com.

Elaine Cuyegkeng was born in Manila, Philippines, where there are many, many creaky old houses with ghosts inside them. She loves eusocial creatures both real and imaginary, '80s pop stars, and caffeinated drinks with too much sugar. She now lives in Melbourne with her partner and a rose named Blue. She has been published in *Strange Horizons, Lackington's, The Dark,* and *Rocket Kapre*. You can find her on @layangabi on Twitter and on Facebook.

Indrapramit Das (aka Indra Das) is a writer and artist from Kolkata, India. His fiction has appeared in several publications including *Clarkesworld*

Magazine, Asimov's, Lightspeed Magazine, Strange Horizons, and Tor. com, and has also been widely anthologized. He is an Octavia E. Butler scholar and a grateful graduate of Clarion West 2012. He completed his M.F.A. at the University of British Columbia (class of '11) in Vancouver, where he wore many hats, including dog hotel night shift attendant, TV background performer, minor film critic, occasional illustrator, environmental news writer, pretend-patient for med school students, and video game tester. He never wore any actual hats, except a toque during winter. He divides his time between India (where he has worked as a consulting editor for publisher, Juggernaut Books) and North America, when possible. Indra has written about books, comics, TV, and film for publications including *Slant Magazine*, *VOGUE India*, *Elle India*, *Strange Horizons*, and *Vancouver Weekly*. Indra's debut novel, *The Devourers*, is available in South Asia and North America from Penguin India and Del Rey (Penguin Random House), respectively.

Teresa P. Mira de Echeverría, born in Buenos Aires, holds a doctorate in philosophy. She has published articles and stories in *Axxón*, *Super Sonic*, *Cuásar*, *Ficción Científica*, *miNatura*, *Próxima*, and *NM*, as well as the anthologies, *Terra Nova*, *Alucinadas*, *Antología Steampunk*, *Buenos Aires Próxima*, and *Psychopomp II*. She has also published books including *Memory*, translated by Lawrence Schimel, *Diez variaciones sobre el amor*, a collection of stories, and *Lusus Naturae*. (Her blogs: teresamira.blogspot. com.ar and diezvariaciones.blogspot.com.ar)

Dilman Dila is the author of a critically acclaimed collection of short stories, *A Killing in the Sun*. He has been listed in several prestigious prizes, including the BBC International Radio Playwriting Competition (2014), the Commonwealth Short Story Prize (2013), and the Short Story Day Africa prize (2013, 2014). His short fiction has been featured in several magazines and anthologies. His films include *What Happened in Room 13* (2007), which has attracted over six million views on Youtube, and *The Felistas Fable* (2013), which was nominated for Best First Feature at Africa Movie Academy Awards (2014) and won four major awards at the Uganda Film Festival (2014). In 2016, he released his second feature film, *Her Broken Shadow*, a sci-fi story set in a futuristic Africa. It is now on the festival run and has screened in places like Durban International Film Festival. More of his life and works are online at www.dilmandila.com, and you can watch his films on www.youtube.com/dilstories.

Walter Dinjos is Nigerian, a Writers of the Future winner, and a runner-up in the Writers Bureau's Writer of the Year 2017 Award. His short stories have appeared (or are upcoming) in *Writers of the Future Volume #33, Beneath Ceaseless Skies, Deep Magic, Galaxy's Edge, Lamplight Magazine, Abyss & Apex*, and elsewhere. His poems have appeared in three *The Literary Hatchet* issues, and he hopes to portray the peculiar beauty of Nigerian cultures through his writing. When he is not writing, he travels across Nigeria, visiting the country's many historic sites and communities to experience their diverse cultures and traditions first-hand, and when he writes, this rich cultural heritage becomes the heart of his prose.

Tananarive Due is a former Cosby Chair in the Humanities at Spelman College (2012-2014), where she taught screenwriting, creative writing, and journalism. She also teaches in the creative writing MFA program at Antioch University Los Angeles. The American Book Award winner and NAACP Image Award recipient is the author of twelve novels and a civil rights memoir. In 2010, she was inducted into the Medill School of Journalism's Hall of Achievement at Northwestern University.

Berit Ellingsen is the author of three novels, *Now We Can See The Moon* (Snuggly Books 2018), *Not Dark Yet* (Two Dollar Radio), and *Une ville vide* (PublieMonde), a collection of short stories, *Beneath the Liquid Skin* (Queen's Ferry Press), and a mini-collection of dark fairy-tales, *Vessel and Solsvart* (Snuggly Books). Her work has been published in *W.W. Norton's Flash Fiction International, SmokeLong Quarterly, Unstuck, Litro*, and other places and has been nominated for the Pushcart Prize, Best of the Net, and the British Science Fiction Association Award. Berit is a member of the Norwegian Authors' Union. http://beritellingsen.com.

Fábio Fernandes lives in São Paulo, Brazil. He has published two books so far, an essay on William Gibson's fiction, *A Construção do Imaginário Cyber*, and a cyberpunk novel, *Os Dias da Peste* (both in Portuguese). Also a translator, he is responsible for the translation to Brazilian Portuguese of several SF novels, including *Neuromancer, Snow Crash*, and *A Clockwork Orange*. His short stories have been published online in Brazil, Portugal, Romania, the UK, New Zealand, and USA, and also in *Steampunk II: Steampunk Reloaded, Southern Fried Weirdness: Reconstruction, The Apex Book of World SF, Vol 2*, and *Stories for Chip*. He also co-edited (with Djibril al-Ayad) the postcolonialist anthology, *We See a Different Frontier*. He's a graduate of Clarion West, class of 2013 and a slush reader for *Clarkesworld Magazine*.

R.S.A. Garcia's debut science fiction mystery novel, *Lex Talionis*, was published by Dragonwell Publishing in May, 2014. It received a starred review from *Publishers Weekly* and the Silver Medal for Best Scifi/Fantasy/ Horror Ebook from the Independent Publishers Awards (IPPY 2015). She lives in Trinidad and Tobago with her extended family and far too many dogs. You can find out more about her work at rsagarcia.com.

Max Gladstone is the author of the Hugo-nominated *Craft Sequence*. The sixth *Craft* book, *Ruin of Angels*, was released in September 2017. Max's interactive mobile game, *Choice of the Deathless*, was nominated for the XYZZY Award, and his critically acclaimed short fiction has appeared on *Tor.com* and *Uncanny Magazine* and in anthologies such as *XO Orpheus: Fifty New Myths* and *The Starlit Wood: New Fairy Tales*. Max has sung in Carnegie Hall and was once thrown from a horse in Mongolia.

Jaymee Goh writes fiction, poetry, and academese. A graduate of the 2016 Clarion Science Fiction and Fantasy Workshop, she has been published in *Science Fiction Studies, Strange Horizons,* and *Lightspeed Magazine*. She recently edited *The WisCon Chronicles Vol. 11: Trials by Whiteness* (Aqueduct Press).

Nick Harkaway is the author of *Gnomon* (William Heinemann, October 2017), as well as *The Gone-Away World, Angelmaker,* and *Tigerman*. He lives in London with his wife and their two children and once shared his breafast quite accidentally with a tiger. He loves reading Borges, Gibson, Proulx, and Winterson. Other important influences include Benjamin Zidarch and Susana Balbo.

Carlos Hernandez is the author of the short story collection, *The Assimilated Cuban's Guide to Quantum Santeria* (Rosarium 2016), and over 30 works of SFF, including stories, poetry, and drama. By day, he is a CUNY Associate Professor of English with a passion for game design and game-based learning.

Nalo Hopkinson was born in Jamaica and grew up in Guyana, Trinidad, and Canada. Her debut novel, *Brown Girl in the Ring,* was the winning entry in the Warner Aspect First Novel contest and led to her winning the Campbell Award for Best New Writer. She has since published many acclaimed novels and short stories as well as numerous essays. She currently teaches writing at the University of California, Riverside. Her latest novel is *Sister Mine*.

T.L. Huchu's fiction has appeared in I*nterzone, Space and Time Magazine, Ellery Queen Mystery Magazine, One Throne Magazine,Shattered Prism, Electric Spec, Kasma Magazine, Shotgun Honey, Thuglit, Mysterical-E,* and the anthologies, *AfroSF, African Monsters,* and *The Year's Best Crime and Mystery Stories 2016.* Between projects, he translates fiction between the Shona and English languages. He is not to be confused with his evil twin @ TendaiHuchu or on www.tendaihuchu.com.

Walidah Imarisha is an educator, writer, public scholar, and spoken word artist. She edited two anthologies, including *Octavia's Brood: Science Fiction Stories From Social Justice Movements.* Imarisha's nonfiction book, *Angels with Dirty Faces: Three Stories of Crime, Prison, and Redemption,* recently won a 2017 Oregon Book Award. She is also the author of the poetry collection, *Scars/Stars.* She is currently working on an Oregon Black history book.

Emmi Itäranta was born in Tampere, Finland, where she also grew up. She holds one MA in Drama and Theatre Studies from the University of Tampere, and another from the University of Kent, UK, where she began writing her debut novel, *Memory of Water,* as a part of her Creative Writing masters degree. She later completed the full manuscript in both Finnish and English. The novel won the Fantasy and Sci-fi Literary Contest organised by the Finnish publishing house, Teos. It was published to enthusiastic reviews in Finland in 2012 under the title, *Teemestarin kirja.* In 2015 the English language version was nominated for the Philip K. Dick award in the US and the Arthur C. Clarke award in the UK. Translation rights to the award-winning novel have been sold in 21 territories to date. Itäranta's second novel, *Kudottujen kujien kaupunki,* was published in 2015, and it won her the Tampere City Literary Award. In the UK the novel is known as *The City of Woven Streets* and in the US as *The Weaver.* Itäranta's professional background is an eclectic blend of writing-related activities, including stints as a columnist, theatre critic, dramaturge, scriptwriter, and press officer. She lives in Canterbury, UK.

Rahul Kanakia's first book, *Enter Title Here* (Disney-Hyperion), is a contemporary young adult novel. Additionally, his stories have appeared or are forthcoming in *Apex, Clarkesworld, Lightspeed, The Indiana Review,* and *Nature.* He holds an M.F.A. in Creative Writing from Johns Hopkins. Originally from Washington, D.C., Rahul now lives in San Francisco. If you want to know more you can visit his blog at http://www.blotter-paper.com or follow him on Twitter at http://www.twitter.com/rahkan.

Isha Karki is a research student at Newcastle University, UK, and an editor of *Mithila Review.* She worked in publishing for a few years before opting for some good-for-the-soul solo travel, and now she writes essays about feminist theory, women, and violence in South Asian literature and film. She grew up on a healthy dose of Bollywood, fanfiction, and dystopian literature. She is deeply invested in post-colonial narratives, feminist perspectives, and SFF that isn't white-washed. Her work has appeared in *Lightspeed, Mithila Review,* and *Mslexia.* @IshaKarkin

Ken Liu (http://kenliu.name) is an author of speculative fiction, as well as a translatgor, lawyer, and programmer. A winner of the Nebula, Hugo, and World Fantasy awards, he is the author of *The Dandelion Dynasty,* a silkpunk epic fantasy series (*The Grace of Kings* [2015], *The Wall of Storms* [2016], and a forthcoming third volume), and *The Paper Menagerie and Other Stories* (2016), a collection. He also wrote the *Star Wars* novel, *The Legends of Luke Skywalker* (2017). In addition to his original fiction, Ken also translated numerous works from Chinese to English, including *The Three-Body Problem* (2014) by Liu Cixin, and "Folding Beijing" by Hao Jingfang, both Hugo winners.

Barbadian, born in 1968. Writer and research consultant, BSc, MSc, MPhil, PhD, **Karen Lord** builds worlds, one word at a time. She was nominated for the John W Campbell Award for Best New Writer in 2012. Her first novel, *Redemption in Indigo,* won the Frank Collymore Literary Award for 2008. It won the 2011 William L. Crawford Award, the 2011 Mythopoeic Fantasy Award for Adult Literature, the 2010 Carl Brandon Parallax Award, and the 2012 Golden Tentacle (The Kitschies, Best Debut Novel) and was nominated for a World Fantasy Award in 2011. Her second novel, *The Best of All Possible Worlds,* won the Frank Collymore Literary Award for 2009. It also won the 2013 RT Book Reviews Reviewers' Choice Award for Best Science Fiction Novel and was nominated for Book of the Year, and was a finalist for the 2014 Locus Awards Best Science Fiction Novel. *The Galaxy Game* was published in January 2015 as a sequel to *The Best of All Possible Worlds.* She also edited the anthology, *New Worlds, Old Ways: Speculative Tales from the Caribbean* published by Peekash Press in 2016 through the kind collaboration of Peepal Tree Press and Akashic Books. She is @drkarenlord on Twitter and drkarenlord on Tumblr.

Carmen Maria Machado's debut short story collection, *Her Body and Other Parties,* was a finalist for the National Book Award and the Kirkus Prize and the winner of the Bard Fiction Prize. She is a fiction writer, critic, and essayist whose work has appeared in the *New Yorker, Granta, Tin House, Guernica, Electric Literature, Best American Science Fiction & Fantasy,* and elsewhere. She is the Artist in Residence at the University of Pennsylvania, and lives in Philadelphia with her wife.

Nick Mamatas is the author of several novels, including *I Am Provi-*

dence and *Hexen Sabbath*. His short fiction has appeared in *Best American Mystery Stories, Year's Best Science Fiction and Fantasy, Tor.com*, and many other venues. Nick is also an anthologist: his work includes the Locus Award nominees, *The Future Is Japanese* and *Hanzai Japan*, both co-edited with Masumi Washington; and the hybrid cocktail recipe/fiction anthology *Mixed Up*, co-edited with Molly Tanzer.

Haralambi Markov is a Bulgarian critic, editor, and writer of things weird and fantastic. A Clarion 2014 graduate, Markov enjoys fairy tales, obscure folkloric monsters, and inventing death rituals (for his stories, not his neighbors...usually). Markov runs the *Innumerable Voices* column over *TOR.com*, profiling short fiction writers. He works as a freelance copywriter tweets at @HaralambiMarkov. His stories have appeared in *The Weird Fiction Review, Electric Velocipede, TOR.com, Stories for Chip, The Apex Book of World SF, Uncanny*, and are slated to appear in *Genius Loci* and *Upside Down: Inverted Tropes in Storytelling*. He's currently working on a novel.

Foz Meadows is a genderqueer fantasy author, essayist, reviewer, blogger and poet. She has most recently published *An Accident of Stars* and *A Tyranny of Queens* with Angry Robot and *Coral Bones* with Rebellion. Foz is also a reviewer for *Strange Horizons*, a contributing writer for *The Huffington Post* and *Black Gate* and a repeat contributor to the podcast, *Geek Girl Riot*. Her essays have appeared in various venues online, including *The Mary Sue, A Dribble Of Ink*, and *The Book Smugglers*. She is a two-time Hugo Award nominee for Best Fan Writer in 2014 and 2017 and won the 2017 Ditmar Award for Best Fan Writer, for which she was also nominated in 2014 and 2016. In 2017, *An Accident of Stars* was a finalist for the Bisexual Book Awards. Foz currently lives in Brisbane with not enough books, her very own philosopher, and their voluble spawn. Surprisingly, this is a good thing.

Born in Gyeongseong, Korea, in 1930, **Hiroko Minagawa** is a Japanese writer of mystery, fantasy, horror, and historical fiction. Her debut work was a children's book called *The Sea and the Cross* (1972), and she won the Shosetsu Gendai New Writers Prize the following year with Arcadian Summer. She has won numerous literary awards including the Mystery Writers of Japan Award (1985), the Naoki Prize (1986), the Shibata Renzaburo Prize (1990), Yoshikawa Eiji Prize for Literature (1998), and the Honkaku Mystery Award (2012). In 2013 she received the Japan Mystery Literature Award for Lifetime Achievement.

Sunny Moraine is a humanoid creature of average height, luminosity, and inertial mass. They're also a doctoral student in sociology and a writer-like object who focuses primarily on various flavors of speculative fiction, usually with a decidedly queer bent. They spend most of their days using writing to distract from academics, except for the occasions when the two collide. They live just outside Washington DC with a husband and two cats, which is a poor replacement for their home dimension, which is positively full of cats and also chocolate and very bad TV.

Ng Yi Sheng is a Singaporean gay writer. He has published a collection of his poems entitled, *last boy*, which won the Singapore Literature Prize, and a documentary book on gay, lesbian and bisexual Singaporeans called *SQ21: Singapore Queers in the 21st Century* in 2006.

Chinelo Onwualu is editor and co-founder of *Omenana*, a magazine of African speculative fiction. Her writing has appeared in several places, including *Strange Horizons, The Kalahari Review, Brittle Paper,* and *Ideomancer.* She has been longlisted for the British Science Fiction Awards, the Nommo Awards, and the Short Story Day Africa Award. Find her on her website at: www.chineloonwualu.me or follow her on Twitter @chineloonwualu.

Nene Ormes was born and lives in the southern part of Sweden where she writes about her hometown, Malmö, in all manner of ways. She spends her days in a genre bookshop and specialises in pairing the right reader with the right sf/f book. She also works for Statens Kulturråd, reading books for children and teenagers. It's two really good jobs if you can get them. Before submerging herself in books, she was an archaeologist and a tour guide in Egypt, and in her spare time she swims synchro and hangs out with her puppy, Eevee.

Sanem Ozdural was born in Turkey and spent her childhood in England. In 1989 she made her way to the US, where she studied economics at Princeton University. She moved to New Orleans after graduating from Boston University law school, where she practiced as a prosecutor and civil litigator and spent seven wonderful years living in the French Quarter. In 2004 she migrated from New Orleans to New York, where she practiced law, and from thence to Istanbul, Turkey in 2013 to teach international business law at Koc University. She moved back to New Orleans 2016, where she practices law and loves living in the French Quarter.

Pavel Renčín entered the Czech literary scene as an original, disruptive influence. He debuted with his short story, "The Creator," in 1999 and then won several literary contests. Since then, his name comes up regularly in the best speculative fiction anthologies. Most of his work is in the genres of urban fantasy, magical realism, and horror. His first novel, *Nepohádka* (*No Fairy Tale*), was published in 2004. His second, *Jméno korábu* (*The Name of* *the Vessel*), in 2007. A year later, he finished *Labyrint* (*The Labyrinth*), one of the first online novels in the Czech Republic written alongside the readers (published in print in 2010) and published the first part of his *Městské války* (*Clash of the Cities*) trilogy, which was nominated for the Academy of Science Fiction, Fantasy, and Horror award and won the Aeronautilus award for the best book of the year. Parts two and three were published in 2009 and 2011, respectively. A collection of Renčín's best short fiction, *Beton, kosti a sny* (*Concrete, Bones and Dreams*) was published in 2009. His most recent and most successful book is a horror novel set in Böhmerwald, *Vězněná* (*Imprisoned*). It was published in 2015 and received the Academy of Science Fiction, Fantasy and Horror award for the best Czech or Slovak spekulative fiction book.

Rebecca Roanhorse is an Ohkay Owingeh Pueblo/African-American writer and a VONA workshop alum. She is also a lawyer and Yale grad. She lives in northern New Mexico with her daughter, husband, and pug. Her debut novel, *Trail of Lightning*, is slated for publication with Saga Press (Simon & Schuster) summer 2018. Her recent nonfiction work can be found in the upcoming *Invisible 3*, and her article, "Decolonizing Science Fiction and Imagining Futures: An Indigenous Futurisms Roundtable," can be found in *Strange Horizons*. Find her on Twitter @roanhorseBex.

Yoav Rosen is the editor of the Classics section and Audio Stories section in *The Short Story Project*. He is a literary critic in Haaretz's literary supplement, *Sfarim*, and held creative writing workshops for exceptional youth in Matan-Arts, among others. His translations into Hebrew include Toni Morrison's "The Dancing Mind" and James Baldwin's "The Rockpile." His short stories have been published in various anthologies and literary magazines, including *Mita'am, Alaxon, Keshet Hahadasha, Masmerim*, and in Haaretz's annual short story contest. *Copy and Paste* (*Afik*), his first collection of short stories, won the Ministry of Culture Prize for New Authors in 2014. In 2016, *Copy and Paste* was chosen by The National Library in Israel as one of ten outstanding debuts published in the past year.

Jayaprakash Satyamurthy is the author of two chapbooks of weird fiction from Dunhams Manor Press—*Weird Tales of a Bangalorean* (2015) and the upcoming, *A Volume of Sleep*. He is also the bass guitarist and primary composer of the doom metal band, Djinn and Miskatonic. He lives in Bangalore, India, with his wife and an ever-growing horde of cats and dogs.

Nisi Shawl wrote the 2016 Nebula finalist and Tiptree Honor novel, *Everfair*, and the 2008 Tiptree Award-winning collection, *Filter House*. In 2005 she co-wrote *Writing the Other: A Practical Approach*, the standard text on inclusive representation in the imaginative genres. Her stories have appeared in *Analog* and *Asimov's* magazines and many others. With Bill Campbell she co-edited *Stories for Chip: A Tribute to Samuel R. Delany*. Shawl is a Clarion West board member and a founder of the Carl Brandon Society.

Naru Dames Sundar writes speculative fiction and poetry. His fiction and poetry have appeared in *Strange Horizons, Lightspeed, PodCastle*, and *Nature Magazine*. He was a recipient of the 2016 Prix Aurora for his poem "Origami Crane/Light-Defying Spaceship." You can find him online at www.shardofstar.info and on twitter as @naru_sundar.

Jeremy Szal was born in 1995 in the outback of Australia and was raised by wild dingoes. His speculative fiction has appeared in *Nature, Abyss & Apex, Lightspeed, Strange Horizons, Tor.com*, and *The Drabblecast* and has been translated into multiple languages. He is the fiction editor for Hugo-winning podcast *StarShipSofa* and holds a rather useless BA in Creative Writing and Film Studies. He carves out a living in Sydney, Australia, where he drinks too much craft beer and watches too many films. Find him at http://jeremyszal.com/ or @JeremySzal

Bogi Takács (e/em/eir/emself or they pronouns) is a Hungarian Jewish agender trans person and a resident alien in the United States. E writes, edits, and reviews speculative fiction, nonfiction, and poetry. You can find eir work in *Clarkesworld, Lightspeed, Strange Horizons*, and *Uncanny*, among other places. Bogi lives in Kansas with eir cheerful neuroatypical family. You can find Bogi online at http://www.prezzey.net or read eir book reviews at http://www.bogireadstheworld.com, or eir QUILTBAG space opera webserial at http://www.iwunen.net. Bogi is @bogiperson on Twitter, Instagram, and Patreon.

K. A. Teryna is an award-winning author and illustrator. A number of her stories have been published in the Russian SF magazines, *Esli, Mir Fantastiki*, and others since 2008. An English translation of her story "Black Hole Heart" appeared at *Apex Magazine*. She lives in Moscow.

Natalia Theodoridou is a media & cultural studies scholar and a writer of strange stories. Her work has appeared in *Clarkesworld, Shimmer, Strange Horizons, Beneath Ceaseless Skies*, and elsewhere. She is also the dramaturge of Adrift Performance Makers (@AdriftPM), with whom she experiments with interactive fiction and immersive, digital performance. Originally from Greece, she now lives in Devon, UK. For more, see her website, www.natalia-theodoridou.com, or follow @natalia_theodor on Twitter.

Sheree Renée Thomas is the author of *Sleeping Under the Tree of Life* (Aqueduct Press, August 2016), named on the 2016 James Tiptree, Jr. Award Longlist, *Shotgun Lullabies* (Aqueduct Press, January 2011), and the editor of the World Fantasy Award-winning *Dark Matter* anthologies. Read her new essay in the collection, *Luminescent Threads: Connections to Octavia E. Butler* (Twelfth Planet Press, September 2017) and her short stories and poems in *Sycorax's Daughters* (March 2017), *Apex Magazine Issue 95* (April 2017), *Stories for Chip, Revise the Psalm, The Moment of Change, Mojo: Conjure Stories, An Alphabet of Embers, Strange Horizons, Mythic Delirium, Jalada, So Long Been Dreaming, Memphis Noir*, Harvard's *Transition*, and *Mojo Rising: Contemporary Writers* (September 2017). Find her @blackpotmojo or visit her publisher's website.

Lavie Tidhar is the author of the Jerwood Fiction Uncovered Prize winning and Premio Roma nominee, *A Man Lies Dreaming* (2014), the World Fantasy Award winning *Osama* (2011), and of the critically-acclaimed and Seiun Award nominated *The Violent Century* (2013). His latest novel is the Campbell Award winning and Locus and Clarke Award nominated *Central Station* (2016). He is the author of many other novels, novellas, and short stories.

Sabrina Vourvoulias is the author of *Ink*, a novel that draws on her memories of Guatemala's armed internal conflict and of the Latinx experience in the United States. It was named to Latinidad's Best Books of 2012. Her short stories have appeared at *Uncanny Magazine, Tor.com, Strange Horizons, Crossed Genres*, and in a number of anthologies, including Long *Hidden: Speculative Fiction from the Margins of History* (Fox and Older, eds.), *The Year's Best Young Adult Speculative Fiction 2015* (Twelfth Planet Press; Krasnostein and Rios, eds.), and *Latino/a Rising* (Wings Press; Goodwin, ed.) in 2017. She is also freelance op-ed columnist whose commentaries have appeared at *Philly.com, Philadelphia Weekly, Philadelphia Magazine, City and State Pennsylvania*, and *The Guardian US*, among others. Follow her on Twitter @followthelede. She lives in Pennsylvania with her husband, daughter and a dog who rules the household.

Subodhana Wijeyeratne was born in London, UK, and has lived in the Soviet Union/Russia, Sri Lanka, Japan, and the United States. When he's not researching the history of rocketry in Japan at Harvard University, he's reading good literature, or trying to make it to the few countries within the reach of a poor graduate student. He has been writing science fiction for over ten years and had work appear in *LampLight, The Colored Lens, Expanded Horizons*, and *Liquid Imagination*. You can find his blog at sub-oworld.net

Carlos Yushimito has published the story collections, *El mago* (*The Wizard*, 2004), *Las islas* (*The Islands*, 2006), *Lecciones para un niño que llega tarde* (*Lessons for a Child Who Arrives Late*, 2011) and *Los bosques tienen sus propias puertas* (*Forests Have Their Own Doors*, 2013). In 2008, he was chosen as one of the best young writers in Latin America by Casa de las Americas and Centro Onelio Cardoso from Cuba; and in 2010 by *Granta* as one of the best Spanish language authors under the age of 35. He earned his PhD in Hispanic Studies at Brown University and is currently a visiting professor at the University of California, Riverside.